CONQUERORS OF THE SKY

By Thomas Fleming from Tom Doherty Associates

Praise for *Conquerors of the Sky*

"Fleming knows how to turn history into captivating fiction."
—*Publishers Weekly*

"Superbly told. . . . Historian Fleming comes up with another winner."
—*Abilene Reporter-News*

"*Conquerors of the Sky* is a fascinating novel from a first rate historian who is also an outstanding storyteller. Thomas Fleming makes the past vividly alive."
—WEB Griffin, author of the bestselling series *Brotherhood of War*, *The Corps*, *Honor Bound* and *Badge of Honor*

"*Conquerors of the Sky* just may be the finest novel master craftsman Thomas Fleming has ever offered us. Superbly researched and handsomely written, this epic tale is as rich in character as it is in drama. First-rate."
—Ralph Peters, bestselling author of *Flames of heaven* and *Twilight of Heroes*

"A masterful story of a century of flight, the air is truly conquered in Thomas Fleming's amazing new book, which tells the story of aviation from Bleriot to B-2, with all the thrills, fame and heartache that the conquerors of the air experienced."
—Walter Boyne, bestselling author of *The Wild Blue*

Praise for *When This Cruel War is Over*

"Gripping."
—*Militray Images*

"Fleming recreates, in precise detail, not only history, but atmosphere. The story he tells is one that will come as a surprise to many Civil War buffs. His research is so thorough, however, that they can believe what they read. Fascinating, high, drama, breath-holding suspense, and memorable characters make this an extraordinary novel I would not hesitate to give to anyone."
—Morgan Llywelyn, International bestselling author of *1916*

"Intriguing."
—*Kirkus Reviews*

CONQUERORS OF THE SKY

Thomas Fleming

TOR®

A TOM DOHERTY ASSOCIATES BOOK
NEW YORK

To Ted Chichak, colleague and friend

This is a work of fiction. All the characters and events portrayed in this book are fictitious or are used fictitiously.

CONQUERORS OF THE SKY

Copyright © 2003 by Thomas Fleming

A Tor Book
Published by Tom Doherty Associates, LLC
175 Fifth Avenue
New York, NY 10010

www.tor.com

Tor® is a registered trademark of Tom Doherty Associates, LLC.

ISBN 0-765-34217-0
EAN 978-0765-34217-1

First edition: January 2003
First mass market edition: June 2004

Printed in the United States of America

0 9 8 7 6 5 4 3 2 1

MY PLANE WAS MY WORLD TO ME.

—*Charles Lindbergh*

BOOK ONE

CHIEF EXECUTIVE OFFICER

The dark brown whiskey splashed sullenly over the ice in the bottom of Cliff Morris's glass. He raised the cold rim to his parched lips. The sharp musty odor of the single-malt Scotch flung him back, back in time like a plane trapped in jet stream winds, an airborne Flying Dutchman spiraling down out of tomorrow into yesterday. So many memories thickened, clotted in his big throbbing body, coalescing with that old companion, fear, for a moment he thought of death as simplicity, a cleansing.

No. He let the living liquid slide down his hollow throat to burn beneath his breastbone. It was a foul taste, harsh, almost brackish, like water sucked from a crankcase. Was that why he liked it? Was this whiskey borne out of memory and misery telling him something about himself? Life still beat stubbornly in his middle-aged body, mocking the withered crybaby who clawed at the soft inner flesh of his belly like a pilot in a doomed plane. Maybe his bravery was not a fake.

Why? shrilled the crybaby. Why? Give me one reason why you deserve anything but oblivion? Cliff drowned the wail in another gulp of Scotch. The ice slid against his teeth. He sucked a cube into his mouth and crunched it slowly, bitterly, on the right side of his John Wayne jaw.

Clunk went the glass on the teak desk. Cliff loosened his 150-dollar Gucci tie and struggled for altitude: a deep relaxing breath. He was sitting in the tenth-floor boardroom of the Buchanan Aircraft Corporation. The floor-to-ceiling windows looked out on Los Angeles International Airport, known to the air traveling world as LAX. The runways were dark and silent; it was close to midnight. Beyond the airport tens of thousands of car headlights streamed along the city's freeways and boulevards. Millions of house windows glowed against the night all the way to the guardian mountains. Cliff liked to contemplate Los Angeles. He liked everything about it—its immensity, its variety, its incomprehensibility.

Cliff Morris had helped create this opulent planetary metropolis with its endless eccentric moons of towns and subcities and villages sprawling from the sea to the desert. It was no longer the city of his birth, a laughingstock full of loony cults and glitzy movie moguls and their sycophants and stars, with endless miles of orange groves on its borders. He and his fellow plane makers had made it a megacity, a megaregion that rivaled Pittsburgh and Chicago as an industrial giant, New York as a financial powerhouse.

For thirteen years Cliff had enjoyed being one of the leaders of this phenomenal place. Heads turned, smiles of recognition blossomed when he entered the Polo Lounge or the California Club. From surf-swept Malibu to sunbaked Palm Springs, from the jutting headlands of Palos Verdes to the teetering mansions of Holmby Hills, Cliff Morris was recognized, flattered, favored, sought.

Now there was an undercurrent of mockery, disdain, even contempt in that recognition. If a career can be imagined as a plane and the man inside the career as the pilot, Cliff's aircraft had recently taken a terrific beating in the all-or-nothing war American executives fought in their heads and hearts and boardrooms. He was struggling to stay in the air in spite of shredded ailerons and ravaged tail surfaces and wings that were starting to flap like feathers. Cliff was in danger of vanishing into the realm of the crashed, the cremated, the forgotten. The thought filled him with sullen rage—and that old companion, the secret crybaby in his belly—anxiety.

The boardroom was splendidly decorated in California style. The walls were white. A series of abstract paintings in red, white, and blue added color and a hint of patriotism. The gleaming oval table, the high-backed, gull-winged armchairs, were teak, adding a Hawaiian or South Seas effect. At the far end of the room a solid silver shield emblazoned with the Buchanan Corporation's seal, a plane soaring above a rainbow, glistened in the subdued lighting.

Dick Stone was sitting a few feet away from Cliff Morris, who was in the CEO's chair at the head of the table. Burly, short-armed, thick-necked, Dick was Buchanan's executive vice president for finance. His hunched aggressive posture emanated a tense urgent energy, part physical, part mental. If an audience were watching them, Cliff was sure his six-foot-four physique and laid-back California style would win most of the applause.

But there was no audience at this movie. For the previous hour, on a screen that had just returned to its recess in the ceiling, Dick Stone had displayed an array of flow charts and summaries, depicting the current and future profits of the company's divisions. The bottom line was a shortfall of 240 million dollars for fiscal 1979. Unless they got a government bailout or persuaded several banks to loan them serious money, they were broke.

"Our corporate budget this year is six billion dollars. How in Christ can you go bankrupt on six billion dollars?"

"You know the answer to that, Cliff. Almost every cent is locked into total-performance contracts with the Pentagon that don't give us room to breathe," Dick Stone said.

First the right cross, then the left hook, Cliff Morris thought. He tried to weave, duck, clinch.

"What does Shannon say about our chances of getting more money on the Article?"

"Zero minus, unless Reagan wins next year."

"And then?"

"Five, maybe seven on a scale of ten."

The Article—a secret plane that was costing them millions of dollars—drew Cliff's eyes to the two paintings on the boardroom wall facing the windows. Cliff Morris had supplied old photographs that helped the artist capture their founder and chief designer, Frank Buchanan, in his prime. His bear-like physique, his shock of uncombed red hair, the lined hawk-nosed face vivid with visionary force all but leaped from the wall. From one angle he seemed to be glaring at the nearby portrait of the man who considered himself

Buchanan's real founder—Adrian Van Ness. Adrian's response was an enigmatic smile. His domed forehead, his hooded eyes, seemed to deepen the enigma, stirring new anxiety deep in Cliff Morris's body and mind.

"What about Adrian's trip to England? If he can get a hundred million from their banks it could loosen things up over here."

Adrian Van Ness had gone to England with the head of the Armed Services Committee of the House of Representatives and the chairman of the Senate Finance Committee to bolster his plea for a major loan. He was probably over the Atlantic at this moment in his Argusair business jet, bringing home the good—or bad—news.

"I don't think he's going to get a damn thing out of them," Dick Stone said. "Unless we do something dramatic."

Cliff Morris had begun to suspect Dick Stone knew exactly what *something dramatic* meant. Sitting on Cliff's desk in his house on the Palos Verdes peninsula was a letter that told him in Adrian Van Ness's oblique, soothing way that he should consider resigning as president. It was the only way they could persuade bankers and congressmen that the Buchanan Corporation deserved to be forgiven for its recent financial and political sins.

Cliff lit a cigarette and put his voice, his face, into his chief executive officer mode. "How much did we make in the last quarter playing the exchange rates, Shylock?"

It was dirty, using the Jewish thing. He knew it disrupted Dick Stone's concentration. But Dick's invitation to this midnight movie was pretty dirty too. His old friend had not spent thirty years in the plane business without learning how to fight dirty. Especially in the last ten years, when Adrian Van Ness had coldly, consciously pitted them against each other, like two gladiators competing for Caesar's approval.

"About fifty million," Dick Stone said.

"That's more than the goddamn aircraft division made last year. Maybe we ought to sell everything and turn the joint into a bank."

"What fun would that be?" Dick Stone said. He looked up at the portraits on the wall, his eyes lingering wistfully on

Frank Buchanan's visionary face. "They'd both come back and lead a stockholder revolt. It would be the first time they agreed on anything."

Cliff Morris nodded. "It's always meant more than money. That's been the best part of it. Imagine coming to work every day and figuring out how to sell refrigerators or aspirin? How do those guys stand it?"

Suddenly they were together, not in the boardroom but in a B-17 called the *Rainbow Express*. They were hurtling above burning German cities, with Captain Cliff Morris telling his skeptical navigator they were flying into a future as conquerors of the sky. For reasons only Cliff Morris understood, Dick Stone's intensity faltered. Cliff had time to breathe, to think.

The telephone rang. Both Cliff Morris and Dick Stone froze. The big clock on the wall, showing the time zones of the world, told them it was 10 A.M. in Tel Aviv and 8 A.M. in London and 2 A.M. the next day in Tokyo. Cliff thought of the other times the phone had rung in the middle of the night.

Whenever a Buchanan plane went down anywhere in the world, the tentacles of the long distance lines reached out on undersea cables or on whirling satellites to clutch the maker by the throat with the gruesome statistics—and the threat of ruinous lawsuits.

"Christ," Cliff Morris said, and picked up the white receiver.

The hollow voice belonged to Mike Shannon, head of Buchanan's Washington office, former tailgunner of the *Rainbow Express*. "The Charlottesville police—Adrian—dead." Cliff could not tell whether Shannon was gasping for breath or the stunning impact of the news disconnected the sentences in his own mind.

"Are you still in Washington?"

"Yes."

"Get the hell down to Charlottesville. Make sure no one but you gets into his safe. Bring someone from the National Security Agency with you to handle the local cops. There's stuff in that safe that could put us out of business!"

Cliff Morris dropped the white earpiece into its cradle and stared numbly at Dick Stone. "Adrian's dead."

Dick shook his head, like a boxer who had just been hit with a Sunday punch. He could not believe it either. "A crash?" he said.

"A heart attack. In Charlottesville. The housekeeper called the police. They contacted Shannon."

Dick shook his head again. His incredulity summed up both their relationships to Adrian Van Ness. Neither could imagine life without this man. The absurdity—and the reality—of that thought momentarily appalled Cliff. Fifty-six years old and he could not imagine life without the son of a bitch?

Cliff took a deep slow breath. He could imagine it. He could handle it. Sudden death was part of the plane business. For thirty-five years Cliff had trained himself not to think about death as anything more than a fact.

Except for certain deaths. One was a death Cliff still found unbearable to contemplate, a death that had left him falling free for a long time, like a jumper whose parachute had failed to open. Another was a death he and Adrian had shared, as mourners, accomplices, betrayers. A death that stirred his buried hatred of the man who had made him chief executive officer of this six-billion dollar corporation.

Nothing could heal the free-fall death. Part of him would spin through space into eternity regretting it. But Cliff was suddenly able to believe Adrian's death was connected by a shadowy cosmic justice to the betrayal death. Maybe that made Adrian's death a large, breathtaking fact that led to an even larger possibility. For the first time Cliff Morris might become the real chief executive officer of the Buchanan Corporation.

Cliff pondered Dick Stone's stunned face. He sensed a state of mind or soul radically different from his own. Dick was bereft. He was almost—perhaps actually—mourning Adrian Van Ness. Cliff did not understand why. He did not even try.

Other possibilities churned through Cliff's mind. Perhaps it was not too late to reach an understanding with a woman in a Malibu mansion where he had once been welcomed with extravagant love. For a moment she was naked in his arms, teasing, laughing, resisting, finally surrendering with a rueful cry. For another moment their son was in his arms, almost repealing the eternal gravity of the free-fall death.

Where did that leave another woman who was living in the desert near Palm Springs—his wife of thirty-six years? Cliff's response to that question was a mixture of animosity and regret almost as complex as the one Adrian's death had evoked. He had reasons—good reasons—for hating Sarah Chapman Morris and she had equally good reasons for hating him. Maybe they should leave it that way.

Fleeing this cruel thought, Cliff lurched to his feet. The important thing now was to concentrate on a return from the limbo of defeat and humiliation. "Where are you going?" Dick Stone asked.

"Never mind. I'll see you in the morning. We'll talk. We've got a lot to talk about," Cliff said.

The misgiving in Stone's eyes was almost an accusation. Did he know about Adrian's letter? That made it all the more important for Cliff to see Frank Buchanan as soon as possible. But the woman in the house on the beach at Malibu was almost as crucial in Cliff's new scheme of things.

He groped for his original exultance and regained it. Love, power, happiness—all the meanings of a California life were still possible. Cliff Morris strode out of the boardroom, his big confident body alive with hope.

NIGHT FLIGHT

For another ten minutes Dick Stone sat in the empty boardroom staring at the portraits of Adrian Van Ness and Frank Buchanan. For thirty years his feelings, his ideas, his life had been interwoven with these opposites. He had alternated between admiration and dislike from decade to decade.

For a while Dick had given his allegiance to Frank Buchanan, to his vision of the plane as a spiritual symbol, carrying man's hope toward a better world. But the vision had not been enough to enable the Buchanan Corporation to survive. That had required Adrian Van Ness's guile. He was proof that guile transcended vision in the second half of the American century.

Or did it? Dick Stone wondered. Did the man of guile need vision to justify playing the game by survival rules? Was that why Dick Stone was telling Cliff Morris it was time to pay the price guile finally exacts? What's your answer, Adrian? Dick asked the man who had won his grudging allegiance.

Back in his office, Stone regained his executive instincts. He had been running the day-to-day operations of the Buchanan Corporation for almost a decade while Cliff sold their planes around the world. He decided Mike Shannon was not the man to put in charge of safeguarding Adrian's papers. Grabbing the telephone, he told the night operator to get him Daniel Hanrahan.

In sixty seconds, the sleep-heavy voice of Buchanan's security chief was on the line. Dick told him what had happened. "Mrs. Van Ness. Is she all right?" Hanrahan asked, instantly wide-awake.

"As far as we know," Dick said.

"Can you spare me a plane to get to Virginia?" Hanrahan said.

"I'll spare you a SkyDemon. You'll be there before you've started."

The SkyDemon was a jet fighter-bomber that could hit 1,600 miles an hour. "Roll it out," Hanrahan said. "I'll be there in a half hour."

Dick punched the phone again and told the operator to get medical director Kirk Willoughby. In a moment, Buchanan's chief physician was on the line. Stone told him what had happened. Willoughby groaned. "I knew that goddamn anticoagulant wasn't working. I wanted him to have open heart surgery."

"Why the hell didn't you insist on it?" Dick snarled.

"You know Adrian. He always had the final say. He decided the unknowns were about the same in both routes."

"You should have decided that for him!"

"Calm down, Dick. Adrian wasn't your father."

The words froze the telephone in Dick Stone's hand. Willoughby had nailed him. He was feeling *filial*, he was grieving for Adrian Van Ness. While his real father babbled passages from the Torah in a nursing home in New York.

Was it a reaction to Cliff Morris's barely disguised delight? Stone knew Cliff had several reasons to hate Adrian Van Ness. Cliff had almost as many reasons to mourn him. But hatred was a more powerful emotion. That was why Cliff had to be stopped.

"He wasn't your father either," Dick said. "But we all owe him enough loyalty not to bad-mouth him. It won't do the company any good, for one thing. That's what we have to worry about now. The company."

"Has Cliff heard the news?"

"That's why I'm calling you. I'm the new CEO. Cliff's resigning. But he may not go quietly. Get your ass out of bed and into a helicopter. I want you to talk to Frank Buchanan before dawn. Make sure he's on my side."

Dick Stone punched the phone again to rouse the night operator. "Get me a Hydra and a pilot. I'll be leaving in five minutes."

"Mr. Morris just asked for one too. There's only one pilot on duty."

"I'll fly my own."

Dick slammed down the phone and sat there, appalled by his recklessness. He had a pilot's license but that did not mean he was qualified to handle a Hydra. He had received a thorough checkout from Buchanan's chief pilot only a week ago. But going solo was still close to insanity.

The plane was out on the runway. Buchanan's chief mechanic, an ex–Navy aviation machinist named Kline, was giving it a final checkoff with another mechanic. "Where you headed, Mr. Stone?" Kline asked. "I got to file a flight plan."

"Dreamland. Notify the usual characters so they don't blow me away."

"I got you, Mr. Stone."

Dick buckled himself into the pilot's seat and studied the controls for a moment. Okay. Ready to go on a wing and a prayer, even if no one was interested in prayers from Dick Stone. No one named God, anyway.

He applied the power to the rotors and rose vertically into the night sky. In two minutes he was roaring north above the coast highway at fifteen hundred feet. Flight! It always aroused fierce exultance in Stone's throat.

Behind him he left a half dozen Dick Stones. The fugitive from Jewish New York enjoying a different shiksa each night at the Villa Hermosa with the Pacific's surf rumbling in the distance. The lover prowling the lobby of the Bel Air Hotel in search of a woman who did not exist beyond her ability to torment him. The husband whose embittered wife drunkenly accused him of loving planes more than people.

Past, gone, obliterated, Stone told himself. The future was the only thing that mattered. The past was a junkyard of false hopes and naive dreams. He was flying above it, beyond it into a new dimension.

It almost worked. He almost stopped hearing Amalie Borne whispering his name.

A dozen miles further up the coast Dick shoved the Hydra's throttle to full and in less than five minutes he was whizzing over the San Gabriel Mountains into the empty immensity of the Mojave Desert. He roared over Edwards Air Force Base where Billy McCall and Buchanan's other test pilots had risked their necks in new planes. For a moment all of them—the planes—flew in Dick Stone's mind. He marveled at the way they made men delirious with pride and pleasure and snuffed out their lives as inexplicably and as unpredictably as a woman broke a man's heart.

In an hour Dick was far up the Mojave, where the California desert met Nevada. Ahead of him was Dreamland, a base whose exact location was known only to a few hundred Air Force officers and aircraft executives. From the air it was an innocuous setup, a scattering of hangars with no planes visible. It looked like an abandoned airport, a place old pilots and plane lovers visited in their nightmares. Dreamland was where the Black Programs, the planes that would protect America in the twenty-first century, were tested.

The desert was turning from gloomy night to graying dawn. In a few minutes the first glow of the rising sun crept over the Sierras. Runway lights clicked on and an air controller in an invisible tower said: "Good morning, Mr. Stone. You are cleared for landing on runway two. Wind from the east at twelve knots."

The sensible thing to do was switch to the tilt rotors and make a helicopter descent. But Dick Stone had found out a long time ago that in the aircraft business the sensible thing was often the wrong thing. There were people watching him land and most of them—99 percent of them—would not land the Hydra that way when there was 4,000 feet of runway waiting for it. Unlike its competitor, the Osprey, the Hydra's propellers were not too big for a conventional landing. Why not show off—and demonstrate the aircraft's flexibility? It was an unbeatable argument.

Dick could hear Billy McCall telling him thirty-seven years ago: *Any asshole can get a plane in the air. Getting it back on the ground is the real trick.* Sweat oozed down Stone's chest as he cut his airspeed and lined up the Hydra for a propeller landing. Down, down, flaps lowered, altimeter reading—the tilt rotors on the wings made it a very unforgiving plane to handle. *Whump.* It was a heavy-footed performance. But he was on the ground, taxiing toward the nearest hangar.

Major General Anthony Sirocca, the burly commander of Dreamland, was waiting in front of the operations building. They were old friends. "We got a flash from Washington about Adrian," Sirocca said, as they shook hands. "Is it true?"

"I'm afraid it is."

"Anything suspicious about it?" asked Tom Guilford, the gaunt six-foot-six Buchanan vice president who had spent most of the last three years at Dreamland. His wife had di-

vorced him a month ago, adding two more emotional casualties to the history of the aircraft business.

"We don't know yet," Dick Stone said. "We don't know
a goddamn thing except he's dead."

They walked to the operations building, where Dick grate-
fully accepted a cup of coffee. Sleeplessness was beginning
to suck life out of his brain. "We'll be having a special board
meeting soon. I thought it might be a good idea to give the
bankers a firsthand report on how things are going up here."

Tony Sirocca's bushy brows rose a fraction of an inch. He
knew that was not the real reason Dick Stone was here. Tony
heard things over the military grapevine. He knew a lot about
Buchanan's financial problems. "Things couldn't be better,"
Sirocca said. "We've got ourselves a hell of a plane."

"You're just in time for a demonstration," Guilford said.
"She's coming in from the Canadian border in about fifteen
minutes."

In the checklist on Buchanan's executives Dick Stone carried in his head, Tom Guilford acquired a bundle of white
points. He had understood the purpose of the visit the moment he heard about it.

They walked down the concrete walled corridor, freshly
painted Air Force blue, to the communications center. At
least thirty men and women sat before consoles. The officer
in command of the room, a brisk blond major named Wallis
Thompson, gave Stone a cheerful hello.

"How's it going?" he said.

"We've got every kind of radar in the book out there looking for him, including a whole fighter wing. Not a trace,"
she said in a throaty voice that made Dick consider inquiring
about her next leave. But the business at hand swiftly side-
tracked this erotic impulse.

Roaring toward them across the desert was an immense
black plane made not of steel or aluminum but of carbon
fiber and epoxy, materials created in the laboratory. Her radical design and the complex counter-radar devices in her
belly made the latest version of the BX bomber invisible to
the most sophisticated air defenses the minds of men in Moscow or Beijing or Washington could devise.

Tony Sirocca looked at his watch. "She'll be overhead in about two minutes."

They strolled out a side door and walked to the runway. The rising sun was almost visible over the peaks of the Sierras. The upper horizon was fringed with red. But everyone's eyes were on the empty desert that stretched for a hundred miles between them and the mountains. Suddenly it was there, a black blur against the brown slopes of the Sierras.

On she came, a bare fifty feet off the ground, traveling just below the speed of sound. Over their heads she whizzed in a roar that was almost instantly consumed by distance. An incredible sight as she banked far out on the desert and began a landing approach. The minuscule tail, the fusion of wing and fuselage, the beaked nose made her look like a creature from a science fiction movie. A true denizen of dreamland.

For a moment Dick Stone could only think of the heartbreak this plane had caused so many people in Buchanan Aircraft over the last twenty years. Denounced, junked, revived, reviled. Yet here she was, Frank Buchanan's last and perhaps greatest gift to the country he no longer loved. Adrian Van Ness's final triumph. And Dick Stone? Was it his consolation? Or his nemesis?

The plane lived. But she threatened the life of the company that had created her. Dick Stone was here to see if he had the courage—or the cowardice—to kill her. Take your pick of motives and alternatives. The world into which this plane was flying had become so complex, words lost their meanings, motives wavered and shimmered like air in the desert at high noon.

Down, down came the black bomber, exhaust pouring from her four turbofan engines. Without a trace of a bump, her tires kissed the runway and she rolled past them. In the cockpit window, the pilot gave them a thumbs up. General Sirocca and Tom Guilford raised their thumbs in response. Dick Stone found his hand high in an involuntary wave.

Dick took a deep slow breath. He was part of it again, the brotherhood he had joined when he climbed aboard the *Rainbow Express* in 1942. He had come out here hoping to find a reason to kill this plane. To tell Tony Sirocca and Tom Guilford that the numbers no longer made sense. A company that was running out of money could not keep spending a hundred million dollars a year on a plane that the U.S. government might not buy.

"There's only one thing wrong, Tony," Dick said. "You could paint two hundred of the goddamn things with the red ink she's generating."

"We'll get some real money for you next year. I guarantee it."

"You've been guaranteeing that for a long time, Tony."

"I'll get it or I'm out of this uniform," Tony said.

"The things we're learning will change the history of aviation, I swear it," Tom Guilford said.

For a moment exhaustion and the emotional side of Dick Stone's Jewish-American nature overwhelmed him. Guilford was frowning at him like a son who could not believe his father would betray him. He was a sort of son. Dick had picked him for this difficult job. He knew what it had already cost him.

"It'll guarantee the survival of the fucking country. That's what I care about," Tony Sirocca said.

Stone sighed. He had heard similar things said about other planes. But this one, with its freight of history and heartbreak, might be the one that deserved the rhetoric.

"You know me. I like to take a look at things close up," Dick said.

"Sure. Sure," Sirocca said. "I wish you came out more often."

"Tom keeps me up on everything. He writes a good report."

They walked toward the Hydra that Stone had flown to their impromptu demonstration as the sun slanted tentative red rays across the desert. "Don't you think it'd be a good idea to let a pilot fly you back?" Guilford said.

Again, the pain of fatherhood stirred in Dick Stone's chest. He could not get used to it. He had played a son's part to Adrian Van Ness and Frank Buchanan for so long. A difficult, combative son. Once—a memory that still filled him with twisting regret—a treacherous son.

"What do you mean 'good idea'?" Tony Sirocca said. "It's an absolute necessity. It's a miracle this asshole got here without killing himself in that screwy machine."

"Go to hell," Dick said. "I survived three and a half years in the U.S. Army Air Force with generals like you trying to kill me every day."

"After seeing you land tonight, I'm ready to believe you're indestructible. But why ruin a perfectly good aircraft, even if it's more or less useless?" Sirocca said.

General Sirocca was letting Stone know that the Air Force was not happy with the way the Marines, the Coast Guard, and the Navy were salivating over the Hydra. Tony wanted Buchanan to work exclusively for the boys in blue. Dick Stone had no intention of going broke to keep Sirocca happy. He could hear Adrian Van Ness telling him that governments and their departments and branches did not know the existence—much less the meaning—of the word *gratitude*.

Did that mean second thoughts about the BX bomber? Maybe.

Another cup of coffee and ten minutes with the ebullient young major who had flown the BX and Dick Stone was on his way. He dozed in his seat beside the baby-faced twenty-six-year-old Air Force captain who was flying the Hydra after a ten-minute conference with Tom Guilford. The captain was ecstatic at the chance to get his hands on the controls of such a top-secret item. It was making his day, his week, his month, his year.

Stone nodded and in his mind walked across miles of desert to a woman waiting in the silence. For years now he had found a strange monkish satisfaction in thinking of her there in the arid wastes. She was a kind of sentry, guarding a border that he some day hoped to cross. Now he began to think—to fear—it was going to become another failed dream, another hope that would never fly. Mournfully, while the boyish captain chortled, Dick talked to Sarah Morris.

If Cliff refuses to leave quietly I can deal with it one of two ways. I can cancel the BX, and stand tall as Buchanan's rescuer, the man who can make the hard decisions. If I keep the plane, that exposes me to Cliff coming forward as the BX's executioner, the man with the titanium backbone. He'll never convince a majority of the board but he may confuse enough people to make us a setup for a corporate raider, someone who'll carve us up and sell off the pieces. To stop Cliff I'll need your help. That means I can never ask you for anything else.

Could he do it? Could he dismiss happiness so finally, so irretrievably? Was this Adrian Van Ness's last demand, the final requirement of sonship? As he drifted down into sleep, Dick wondered if it was the only way he could reach out to Adrian now, the only way he could say: *I'm sorry.*

THE MEDICINE MAN

In his shack on the slopes of the San Jacinto Mountains, eighty-three-year-old Frank Buchanan lay awake. In his head he was soaring through the desert's blue sky, while in the front seat of his gull-winged fiberglass sailplane Sarah Chapman Morris uttered cries that could only be described as erotic. He had begun flying these engineless creatures about a year ago, at her suggestion. It was a uniquely spiritual sensation, riding the winds blowing off the mountains for an hour or two before gravity made its ultimate claim on the body and the airship. Frank always came home feeling renewed, able to endure his creaking physique and the nauseating American world of the 1970s for a while longer.

What an interesting woman Sarah had become. Frank realized he had rated her much too low because she was Cliff Morris's wife. He was amused by her insatiable curiosity about Buchanan Aircraft. She wanted to know everything, back to the dawn of time. She said she hoped understanding would lead to forgiveness, a lovely idea. It had not worked for him. Frank thought he understood almost everything about Adrian Van Ness but he still hated him.

Dozing off, Frank dreamt he was flying a Bleriot Experimental Model 2 biplane over southwestern England. The cranky sixty-horsepower engine pulled him along in the stiff headwind at a satisfying forty miles an hour. Below him in the darkening sky was another BE2 piloted by a man whom he had begun to regard as an older brother. Edward "Teddy" Busk was an ebullient Cambridge University mathematician who had devoted his first-class mind to the new science of aerodynamics. His insights had prompted Geoffrey de Havilland to reposition the wing, redesign the lateral tail and create the first truly stable plane. Not only had Busk shared his ideas with Frank Buchanan and other eager pupils—he had learned to fly as an act of faith in his computations.

As Frank looked down on Busk's plane, he saw a twenty-foot ribbon of flame streaming behind him. In sixty seconds, the fabric-covered wings and fuselage were engulfed by livid tongues of fire. As Frank watched, horrified, Busk made a perfect landing on a wide swath of downs called Laffan Plain. It was an ironic tribute to the stability of the BE2— but it did nothing to extinguish the flames.

Awake, his body twisting in anguish, Frank remembered the rest of the story. He had landed at nearby Farnborough, the home of the Royal Flying Corps, and raced back to Laffan Plain in a fire truck. They were much too late. Teddy Busk's blackened corpse sat in the charred skeleton of the plane, his grimaced teeth gleaming in the truck's headlights. They took the body and the remnants of the plane back to Farnborough and found that the fire had been caused by the motor's vibration breaking a pipe joint. The motor had run out of fuel and backfired, igniting the gasoline tank. Mournfully, they redesigned the fuel system to make sure it did not happen again.

Tears streamed down Frank Buchanan's face. The sacrifices men had made to create planes! His mind leaped from this lost brother to other brothers and sons. One above all, whose name he still could not pronounce without tears. Part of the reason he was living in this shack was a desperate wish to reach Billy McCall, wherever he was, beyond the sky.

Frank lay on his back on the boards that served for his bed, hearing his mother hiss: *death machine.* Slowly, carefully, he sat up and waited for the blood to circulate in his numbed feet and hands. Seizing his cane, he hoisted himself erect and waited again to make sure he had located his center of gravity. His body had become as fragile, as unpredictable as the planes of 1910, with their translucent fabric wings and fuselages, their jungle of guy wires and primitive controls.

Carefully, creakily, Frank heaved himself from his narrow bed and hobbled to a table. Switching on a battery-powered lamp, he sat before a blank sheet of white paper in a looseleaf folder, pen in hand. For an hour, the paper remained pristine. The gnarled hand, with the blotchy skin where it had been burned off in the crash of a long vanished plane, remained motionless.

Finally, the hand began to move. *Father. Father,* it wrote. It was Billy, still calling for help. Frank had heard from him a dozen times since he retreated here. Once more Frank struggled to send a message to his mother. *Find him and rescue him. Even if you never loved him. Even if you hated him in my name.*

As usual, Althea Buchanan replied: *I can't find him in the spirit world. He has no soul. It often happens when a child is born of fierce opposites.* She had told him this when Billy was eleven. Frank had struggled to prove she was wrong. But history, another word for mystery, had been like a gigantic windshear, undercutting his hopes and prayers.

Frank stumbled out on the porch and sat down in a canebottomed rocking chair. The wind rushed up the mountain to tear at his loose shirt and pants. He looked down on the darkened desert and beyond it, a glare against the overcast, the lights of the city of Los Angeles behind her barrier mountains.

Two hundred years ago, the great Indian medicine man, Tahquitz, had withdrawn to this mountain to brood in lonely despair about the decline of his people. Frank Buchanan had followed him here, also a man in mourning for his people.

The Americans of the seventies seemed to have lost their way. Sexual, political, religious extremists hurled insults and slogans. A president betrayed his office and senators and congressmen revealed themselves as hypocrites worshipping the newest goddess, Publicity. Night after night, Buchanan sat at his desk opening his mind to the guardian spirits, hoping for wisdom—an old man's consolation for his losses. But Tahquitz remained silent.

Frank could almost hear Adrian Van Ness laughing. For a moment he had to struggle against a demoralizing surge of hatred.

Thinking again of Edward Busk in his burning plane, Frank wondered if there was another meaning in the memory. Somewhere a compatriot had died in the long upward struggle men called flight. He was still linked to the great enterprise, so crucial in the conflict between darkness and light, above all to the company he had founded, now an immense family of machinists and designers and analysts and salesmen and executives, working beneath his name. Scarcely a day passed without a letter or a postcard from one of them, recalling the rollout of a famous plane, the triumph of a controversial design, the pathos of an old failure.

They were all linked, the living and the dead, in the cosmic sea of the worldsoul. Frank Buchanan still retained that primary faith, imparted to him by his mother. Within that cosmic soul, each individual soul was part of an eternal struggle between good and evil, between the guardians and the destroyers.

Adrian Van Ness had mocked that childhood faith. Adrian had mocked many things. His soul was an abyss of hatred or loss that Frank Buchanan had never been able to penetrate. That was another reason for his sojourn in the desert—he wanted to eradicate the last vestige of hatred for Adrian from his spirit. All he had to show for it was another failure.

A clattering, poppering roar in the sky above him. Searchlights blazing, a Buchanan helicopter was descending to the small landing strip a few hundred yards from the shack. In a few minutes Bruce Simons, Buchanan's tall flashy director of public relations, and a young stranger approached the porch. Behind them came Kirk Willoughby, the company's pink-cheeked, balding chief physician.

"Frank, how the hell are you?" Bruce said in his breeziest style, pumping his hand. "I hope you don't mind us dropping in this way at five A.M. We tried to call you but your phone doesn't seem to be working."

"I disconnected it a month ago."

"This is Mark Casey of the *L.A. Times*. Their aviation reporter."

"I told you I was through giving interviews, Bruce."

"This isn't just another interview, Frank. Adrian Van Ness died last night. Mark would like to talk to you about your memories of him—the early days of the company—where you see it going now that his influence—"

"Adrian! You're sure? How—what was the cause?"

"A heart attack, apparently. The doc here was treating him for heart disease—"

"Amanda—Mrs. Van Ness—how is she—where is she?"

"She's still in Virginia. But I presume she'll return to California. We're going to have a memorial service for Adrian at the company next week," Simons said.

Suddenly Frank Buchanan's world was no longer a gray meaningless place. He no longer belonged in the desert. But he could not possibly explain that to Simons or to this earnest young reporter, who looked as if he was born the day before yesterday.

Kirk Willoughby understood, of course. He knew more about Adrian and Frank and Amanda than anyone in the company, except inquisitive Sarah Chapman Morris. He was here to make sure the news did not abort Frank's laboring heart. A superfluous worry.

They sat down on the porch and Mark Casey began asking him the standard questions. What was the secret of his long, successful collaboration with Adrian Van Ness? What was their most important plane? What was Adrian Van Ness's contribution to Buchanan's success? Was he involved in the company's recent difficulties with the government? How did Frank see Buchanan's future now?

Frank's answers were not lies. He said the secret of his

collaboration with Adrian was mutual respect. Of course they argued now and then, ho ho ho. But they realized each had a part to play. As for their most important plane—each one was important while they were building it. Frequently important enough to be the margin between bankruptcy and solvency, ho ho ho.

Adrian's greatest contribution was forethought. He was always thinking ahead to the next generation airliner or fighter plane. Of course he wasn't always right but neither were Douglas or Lockheed or Boeing right all the time, ho ho ho. As for Adrian's involvement with the company in recent years—he had retired to the cheering section, like him. The company's future? It was bright. The Buchanan rainbow—Adrian's idea, by the way—still reached over the horizon—and the plane soaring above it might soon be flying at hypersonic speed.

Almost all of it was true. But it was only one percent of the truth. Watching the boyish reporter take it down, Frank remembered so many things he could never tell him, so many things a thirty-five-year-old would find it hard—perhaps impossible—to understand.

Mark Casey said he was delighted with the interview. Bruce Simons said they had to get back to Los Angeles as soon as possible. "I think I'll stay with this old curmudgeon for a while. Check out a few things like his blood pressure and his heartbeat," Kirk Willoughby said. "You can send the chopper back for me in an hour or two."

The helicopter clattered into the sky. Frank Buchanan gazed at Willoughby. "It's impossible to explain," he said.

"I know," Willoughby said.

"You'd have to go back to the beginning."

"I know," Willoughby said.

He pulled a flask of Scotch out of his pocket and poured a drink for himself and Frank. "Dick Stone's going to be the new CEO. Cliff's out. Does that bother you?"

"It's a pretty raw deal in some ways. Cliff isn't really responsible for our sins. Adrian's the culprit."

Frank sipped the Scotch. Bitter memories flowed into his mind with the taste. "The culprit—in so many ways."

"I think you've got Adrian wrong. You've always had him wrong."

"You're saying you never know the whole truth about a man—even when you work with him for forty-seven years?"

"I'm afraid not."

Maybe he was right. Maybe none of them, including himself, were as innocent as they wished they were—or as guilty as they feared they were. "Amanda—do you think it's possible—?"

"I don't know. I hope so."

"If I can hold her in my arms for a year—or even a month—I'll forgive the universe."

The two men sipped their Scotch in silence, while from the empty desert welled the faces and the voices, the illusions and the heartbreak of the living and the dead. Above them flew the planes—from the wobbling fabric creatures of the first decade to the titanium projectiles of today. Seventy-six years of flight through Frank Buchanan's life and Adrian Van Ness's life and so many other lives.

This was their journey, Frank thought. Only someone who flew the route across memory and time and history could decide who should be forgiven, who should be condemned. For himself, he relied on two lines from his favorite poet.

> Let the gods forgive what I
>   have made.
> Let those I love try to forgive
>   what I have made.

EXILE

As usual, Sarah Chapman Morris awoke an hour before dawn. She lay in bed, watching the windowpane grow gray. Around the house stretched the southern California desert, arid mile after mile to the Salton Sea and Death Valley. It was a landscape as different from the green flowering England of her youth as nature—or the imagination—could devise. The aridity, the emptiness corresponded exactly with her state of mind and soul.

Thirty-six years. Thirty-six years since Sarah Chapman walked down the aisle of the country church outside Rackreath Air Base arm in arm with Captain Clifford Morris, the handsome American bomber pilot, whose indifference to religion dismayed her devout Catholic mother. Her brother Derek, flying fighters for the RAF, had asked in his brutal way how she could marry anyone from the "Bloody 103rd" bombardment group. Did she have some peculiar desire to become a widow?

Sarah put on a dressing gown and padded through the silent house to the room that had been her husband's study. She pressed a button on the desk. Along the wall to the right of the terrace doors, concealed lights illuminated an immense painting of a B-17 plowing through flak-infested skies, spewing bullets from its turret and tail and waist guns at German fighters. Beneath the cockpit window was a crescent rainbow with a plane soaring above it. At least once a day, Sarah stared at the painting as if she needed to convince herself that her life was not a dream.

On the empty desk was a letter from Adrian Van Ness.

Dear Cliff:

We have weathered the worst of the scandal without losing a single contract. This is a tribute to your reputation within the aircraft industry and in Congress. Alas, the same thing cannot be said for the Buchanan Corporation. Over the years we have acquired enemies in the press and in Washington, D.C. who are still pursuing us. The other day I heard from one of our closest Pentagon friends that our chief tormentor in the Senate was threatening to start a new round of hearings to explore our "continuing culpability" because we have, he claims, displayed not a single sign of repentance for our sins. I am sure you realize more negative publicity would make it impossible for us to obtain the financing we so badly need.

For thirty years you have demonstrated a readiness to work,

to serve, to sacrifice for Buchanan. Can I ask you to consider
an ultimate sacrifice, your resignation?

I have told Dick Stone you might want to discuss the terms
of your retirement. He has orders from me to be even more
generous than he would be under ordinary circumstances.

Regretfully,
Adrian

The bastard, Sarah Chapman Morris thought. The corrupt
ruthless brilliant bastard. She should have known it was coming. She should have known Adrian Van Ness would send
her a copy of this letter. It was exactly what a master of
forethought would do. He was trying to stir pity in her forlorn heart.

A crash. The wind was blowing a shutter or a door somewhere in the house. Sarah padded through the rooms full of
sleek chrome-and-glass furniture. The noise was coming
from one of the patio doors. She stepped outside and let the
cold desert wind cut into her flesh for a long minute. A plane
was coming over the Funeral Mountains, beginning its descent to Los Angeles. The way she and Cliff had arrived
thirty-four years ago.

The passengers would soon be looking down on the awesome sea of lights, the forty-six square miles of a city that
was not a city, a vast collection of canyons and arroyos and
flats and seacoast in search of an identity, with Hollywood
in the center of it, infecting everything with its amoral he-
donism.

No. That was the old Sarah talking, the once proper English girl with her devotion to spiritual ideals. That woman
was dead. As obliterated as the test pilots who smashed their
experimental jets into the desert floor at 2,500 miles an hour.
Miss Sarah Chapman was gone into some region where souls
occasionally communicated with the living. Now she was a
semi-divorced American wife named Ms. Sarah Morris shivering in the desert wind beneath a starry California sky with
the blank black bulk of the mountains looming in the night
a few dozen miles away.

They had all come so far.

Was the distance the human equivalent of losing your soul—or finding it? Sarah pondered that question for another thirty seconds as the jetliner descended, wingtip lights blinking. In a few more minutes the landing headlights would come on and it would resemble a prehistoric creature, a pterodactyl or some other monster plunging out of time into man's exhausted mind.

She hated planes.

Was that true? She had always loved the idea of planes. Maybe she just hated what men did to make and sell them. That thought led to eighty-three year-old Frank Buchanan in his shack above Tahquitz Canyon. To memories of yesterday's soaring session in his sailplane, *Rainbow's End*. My God, how she loved those motorless hours in the sky with him! Almost as much as she loved the hours of reminiscence she had mined from his shy, reclusive soul.

Sleep was out of the question now. In the bathroom, Sarah washed her face and studied herself in the mirror by the dim glow of the night light. She looked ghostly as well as ghastly. Maybe she had become Miss Sarah Chapman again. Maybe she had died and was starting to relive her life, backwards. But Adrian's letter to Cliff mocked that silly idea. The letter was like a gaff in her flesh, flinging her forward into time again.

Sarah padded into the sunken living room and pulled a video at random from a rack beside the television set. She shoved it into the VCR and sat down. A stubby-winged, thick-bodied plane hurtled toward her on the television screen. She almost cried out.

"The Wild Aces," growled a gravel-voiced narrator. "They take the fight to the enemy. They hit him where it hurts."

It was a video of a film Buchanan had made to help sell their ground-support plane, the Thunderer. The narrator told why it was the best plane the U.S. Marines had ever bought for the money, his voice rasping against the rising beat of a frenzied orchestra. The Thunderer could carry more bombs, more hardware than anything the enemy could put in the sky. It could carry two-hundred-and-fifty-, five-hundred-, thousand-pound bombs. It had a twenty-millimeter cannon that fired 600 rounds a minute. It had Shrike missiles that could demolish the enemy's surface-to-air missile sites. That was the Thunderer's job. To come in low and get those SAM sites to make things safe for the bombers following them.

Sarah sat and watched the pilots getting into their G suits. She prayed she would not see her son. She no longer thought God was listening but she prayed anyway. It did no good. They all looked like Charlie. They were all young and cheerful and had short hair and strong jaws and firm, proud American mouths.

Sarah watched them climb into their cockpits and put on their shiny plastic helmets and clamp the oxygen masks on their faces. She watched them taxi down the runway, shove the throttles forward and vault into the sky, flame spewing from their afterburners.

"Taking it to the enemy," roared the narrator. Sarah watched the bombs explode on bridges, rail yards, factories, on what the narrator called troop concentrations but looked like trees and farms. The bombs burst and burst, sometimes leaping up in great orange gushes of flame, usually mushrooming into serrated puffs of earth and exploding dust.

Click. The screen went dark. Susan Hardy stood beside it, a blur against the gray desert dawn. "Are you crazy?" she said. "Are you trying to drive yourself crazy?"

"Maybe," Sarah said.

Her fellow pilgrim, with the burning passion for peace in her eyes. Sarah had traded her life as the wife of the chief executive officer of the Buchanan Corporation for exile with this woman. Susan was her oldest American friend. She had divorced her unfaithful husband years ago. She had led Sarah into the exhilarating bewildering worlds of the women's movement and the peace movement.

Without turning on a light, Susan sat down on the couch beside Sarah and kissed her on the cheek. "You're trying to accept it, aren't you? The whole thing. But that's the wrong way to go. Acceptance is just another word for surrendering to the bastards."

"Yes," Sarah said automatically. She no longer agreed with Susan but it was too exhausting to argue with her.

"Once and for all you have to ask yourself—what, who do you love," Susan said.

"I'll do that," Sarah said.

"The right answer is you love yourself. You are the most important person in your world."

Susan retreated to her bed. Sarah sat on the couch and watched the sun tip the Sierra's peaks with fire. Was I ever in love with anyone? she wondered. Was I really in love with a dream of glory, a destiny in the sky? Was I as drunk with the beauty, the terror, the mystery of planes as all the rest of them?

The telephone rang. Who in the world could be calling at this time of day? She walked into the hall to answer it. "Sarah?" Dick Stone said. "Adrian Van Ness died of a heart attack about four hours ago. I think it's time you came home. Cliff needs you."

Trailing the extension cord, Sarah stumbled back into the living room and sat down on the couch again with the phone in her numb hand. The fiery light was spilling over the Funeral Mountains. In the nearer distance, it created an aureole around a Joshua tree. The giant cactus seemed to be thrusting its prickly stumps into the glowing air in a silent hallelujah. Or was it a desperate plea?

And you don't? You don't need me? cried the ghost of Miss Sarah Chapman somewhere in her married mind. The ghost wanted to shout those words into the phone's white mouthpiece. But Sarah only sat there staring at the Joshua tree, deciding to let the ghost write the whole story. She would tell it objectively, with the crystalline clarity of the stratosphere, tell it without so much as a whimper of an I, an echo of an ego. She would tell everything she had learned in England and America, in Los Angeles and in the Mojave and on the ridge above Tahquitz Canyon.

"Sarah?" Dick Stone said. "Sarah?"

She would begin with Adrian Van Ness and Frank Buchanan, the original spinners of the web of profit and loss, betrayal and commitment, exaltation and compulsion that became the years of their lives. She would go back to the moment when men first discovered the omnipotence, the wonder, of the sky and began to explore the meaning, the power, of wings. Only by regaining the illusion of innocence could she hope to explain the stunning inevitability of it all.

She would *control* her *rage* at the *obscenities* they *committed* in the *name* of their *planes*. She would not *lament* the *women* they *mutilated*, the *lives* they *twisted* and *tormented* like the metal they *bent* and *hammered* into *shapes* they *loved* more than their *children*. She would *write* of *love* and *hate* and *despair* with the debonair *courtesy* of the *damned*, the irony of the *unforgiven*, the blank-eyed *calm* of the angel of *death*.

The ghost would live in all the tormented hearts and anguished heads with a phantasm's duplicity, telling the truth the truth the truth about everyone, even about that riven ruin of reproach and regret known as Sarah Chapman Morris.

"Sarah?" Dick Stone said. "Sarah?"

BOOK TWO

BROTHERLY LOVE

In 1912 Americans were dancing the Crab Step, the Kangaroo Dip, the Chicken Scratch, and the Bunny Hug. The slang expressions of the year were *flossy, beat it!, peeved,* and *it's a cinch.* Movies were attracting five million people a day. An eastern Democrat named Woodrow Wilson was running for president. The U.S. Marines landed in Cuba to restore order. Frank Buchanan did not pay much attention to any of these things. He was too busy being the happiest sixteen-year-old in California, working as mechanic and factotum for his brother Craig, the pilot of a bright green biplane called *Rag Time.*

Craig had thundered up to Frank's door in his Harley-Davidson motorcar two years before to take his younger brother to the Dominguez Hills air meet outside Los Angeles. His mother had begged Frank not to go. She did not want him to have anything to do with her swarthy swaggering older son, who had defied her exhortations and admonitions practically from birth. In 1905, at the age of eighteen, Craig had gone off to race motor cars, becoming as famous as Cal Rodgers and Eddie Rickenbacker in that daredevil sport.

Frank had found the invitation to Dominguez Hills irresistible. Craig had said it would be the first air show in the United States. Airmen from France and America were going to fly balloons, dirigibles, and planes. It was going to make California famous for something besides orange groves and sunshine.

On the green mesa between Compton and Long Beach, a crowd of 20,000 swarmed off the big red Pacific Electric Railway cars to see the most miraculous sight in history—men flying through the air. The planes were the main attraction. Balloons were old stuff and dirigibles had been wob-

bling through the California sky for several years. One had
raced an automobile from Los Angeles to Pasadena in 1905
and won.

Frank watched easterner Glenn Curtiss begin the festivities
with a flight in his gleaming yellow biplane, the *Golden
Flyer*, which had won the world's first air meet in Rheims,
France in 1909 with a top speed of 46.5 miles an hour. The
Flyer had a tricycle landing gear and a sixty-horsepower
"pusher" motor that purred away behind the pilot's back. The
crowd roared with excitement as Curtiss circled the field at
a height of fifty feet, flying over a half mile and making a
smooth landing in front of the grandstand.

Other pilots took to the air in similar machines. They soon
demonstrated that flying was not only marvelous—it was
dangerous. For reasons no one seemed to understand, planes
suddenly slipped sideways out of the air or plunged to the
ground nose first. The organizers of the meet did not let these
accidents stop the show. Ambulances rushed to haul the fliers
from the wreckage of their planes, the mangled struts and
wires and fabric were towed out of sight into a nearby ra-
vine—and another plane was in the air, dazzling the spectators again. Only the next day did they learn in the
newspapers that the crashed flier was badly injured—or dead.

The star of the meet turned out to be a Frenchman, Louis
Paulhan. He performed sharp banks and dives that made Curtiss and other fliers look timid. In eleven days of flying before crowds that totalled 176,000, Paulhan won 14,000
dollars in prize money.

"That does it, kid," Craig said. "From now on we're in
the plane business." With his usual magnificent self-
confidence, Craig introduced himself to Paulhan and soon
learned the secret of his acrobatic skills. "It's those hinged
sections on the wings. He calls them ailerons," Craig said.
"They keep the ship steady in a turn."

Craig paid Paulhan five hundred dollars for a week's flying
lessons. This gave him a chance to inspect Paulhan's plane
and discreetly sketch the design. At night Craig gave lessons
of another kind to the Baroness von Sonnenschein, a statu-
esque blond Viennese who had traveled to America with

Paulhan's party. She liked Craig's lessons so much, she rented a cottage in the Malibu Hills and let Paulhan go back to France without her.

Craig and Frank went to work on building an imitation of Paulhan's plane. Frank took a course at the Los Angeles YMCA to improve his woodworking skills and did so well he personally carved the laminated walnut propeller the day before they rolled the plane out of Craig's Santa Monica garage. *Rag Time* had a wingspan of thirty-three feet. The hickory and ash struts were covered with green pegamoid, a fabric made of calico treated with celluloid. Craig had improved the rudder controls and widened the ailerons to give the ship added stability. They put a sixty-horsepower motor developed by a San Francisco automaker behind the pilot's seat and *Rag Time* was ready to fly.

The Baroness was naturally the first passenger. She cried out in French and German as Craig zoomed over the ocean and dipped and banked and dove to within inches of the whitecaps. Later Craig told Frank the exclamations were identical to those he heard at midnight in the cottage in Malibu.

Frank found Craig's attitude toward women confusing. He often came back from a visit to the Baroness and described in vivid detail what they had done, while Frank worked on *Rag Time*. Then Craig would drink a cup of coffee to sober up, take off his coat and say: "That's all they're good for, kid. The rest is yak-yak."

Craig completed *Rag Time*'s maiden flight with a perfect three-point landing. Frank helped the ecstatic Baroness descend from the passenger seat. Craig winked and said: "Get aboard, kid."

Down the grassy meadow they raced to soar above the horizon as Craig pulled back on the control stick. Up up they mounted against a strong headwind until the entire coast—the great headlands of Palos Verdes, the flat undulating shore of Long Beach and San Pedro, the wooded crests of the Santa Monica Mountains and the scattering of houses and business buildings called Los Angeles were visible in one magnificent sweep.

It was not simply the vista, it was the sensation of riding the wind that made Frank Buchanan an instant convert to the air age. Flight created a lightness, a happiness in his body and mind that seemed exactly like his mother's description of the soul's journey to the realm of peace and light after death. It was heaven on earth, divinity within the grasp of living men!

Craig was soon flying *Rag Time* all over California, winning prizes at other air meets, including a second show at Dominquez Hills in 1911, where he picked up 450 dollars as the best novice flyer. At that show, the organizers had added something new to the excitement. They staged a mock bombing raid. A detachment of national guardsman hunkered down behind some earthworks and Craig and another pilot dropped smoke bombs on them. The soldiers ran out and surrendered.

The extra seat they had added to the plane was a moneymaker. After William Randolph Hearst took a ride with Louis Paulhan and reported it in his newspapers like the Angel Gabriel announcing the second coming, hundreds of people were eager to fly at five dollars a head. Few pilots were more popular than Craig. With his racing car driver's peaked hat perched sideways on his head, a big cigar clamped in his mouth, he was the essence of heroism on the ground and in the air.

So here it was, 1912. They were on the way to an air show in San Diego. As they climbed aboard *Rag Time*, Frank said: "Can we stop in Santa Ana and see Mother?"

"How many times do I have to tell you to put that crazy woman out of your mind once and for all?" Craig said.

That was not easy for Frank to do. He had spent his boyhood defending Althea Buchanan from the ridicule of her neighbors and his friends. She never sought the messages that came to her in the night, voices of guardian spirits who told her of forgotten wars and evil conspiracies in the blank centuries before history began in books. The English-born pastor of the Church of the Questing Spirit said she was one of the rare few who could communicate directly with the world beyond the grave. But outside the tiny circle of true believers in the church, her gift had brought Althea Buchanan little but scorn and heartbreak.

Craig flew *Rag Time* above the coast highway, telling Frank to get over his "momma's boyitis." They were going straight to San Diego. But Frank knew they had to land for gas somewhere. When the village of Santa Ana appeared on the left, he grabbed Craig's sleeve and pointed to it. Cursing, Craig banked over the town and circled the Buchanan ceramics factory, with its beds of blooming flowers between the office and kiln. He landed in a grassy field just beyond it.

Althea Buchanan manufactured plates and pitchers and platters portraying Spanish days in old California. She had no training as a painter. Her designs were primitive but the colors were vivid and the expressions on the faces of her Mexicans and Indians emanated an innocence that Anglos found irresistible. There was scarcely a house in the Southwest that did not have at least one of her creations.

She had come to the sleepy town in Orange County just after Frank was born in freezing Kansas. One of her guardian spirits had told her to seek warmth and sunshine for the infant or he was doomed. Her husband, delighted (according to Craig) to find an excuse to split up, declined to accompany her. She had taken ten thousand dollars from him and headed for California with her two sons, confident that her guardian spirits would guide her when she arrived. They had told her to found the ceramics factory and she had done so with astonishing success.

Althea hurtled toward Frank and Craig, her cheeks streaked with dirt, her red hair cascading in all directions beneath an immense sun hat. Behind her trooped the twenty Mexicans who did the hard labor at the furnaces. Althea was only four feet eleven and at fifty still had the complexion of a sixteen-year-old. Her perpetual youth sharpened the aura of unreality that always surrounded her.

"What is it? Where did you get it?" she cried.

"It's a plane, Madam," Craig said. He always treated her with mocking courtesy, no matter how much she abused him.

"It's beautiful," she said, making a wide circle around *Rag Time*. "Does it have a soul?"

"It's a machine, Madam. Machines don't have souls."

"I've seen a creature like it in a dream," she said. "Galdur, the tyrant who ruled Palestine a thousand years before the Jews came there, used it to conquer Atlantis." She glared at Craig. "You were born under the same dark sign. You'll turn this into a death machine!"

She whirled on Frank. "Have you given up your great ambition—to worship this evil thing?"

Frank blanched. She was talking about the project to which he had vowed to dedicate his life until Craig took him to the Dominguez Hills air meet—to prove scientifically the survival of the soul after death.

"I'll never give it up entirely, Mother. But flying is so marvelous. You can't believe how wonderful it is until you try it. Why don't you let Craig take you for a ride?"

"If we crash, you can nag me for all eternity," Craig said.

"Your pride will be your undoing, Craig. You'll meet the same fate as your ur-soul, Gath."

According to the Church of the Questing Spirit, every person in the world was an emanation of a handful of primary ur-souls, some of them evil, others good. The world was in perpetual conflict between these agents of light and darkness. If, as in Craig's case, his ur-soul was evil, it required extra effort to achieve the light. Effort he of course declined to make.

"In the meantime, Madam, I hope to enjoy myself," Craig said. "You should see how excited this death machine makes the girls in Long Beach. Frank is finding that out too, right?"

"Just—by observation," Frank said, blushing the color of his mother's hair.

"Abominable!" Althea cried. "He's a child of light, an emanation of Mana, the noblest of the ur-souls. That's why I brought him to California. So he would thrive in sunlight. If you corrupt him, you'll wander among the galaxies for ten thousand years, I warn you. Not even Gath will consider you worthy of rebirth."

Craig laughed. He picked up Althea and announced he was going to give her one of his "Long Beach kisses." Althea punched at him furiously. "I won't accept your affection. I no longer consider you my son."

Craig kissed her anyway and set her down with a jolt. Frank saw he was angry. "I knew this was going to be a waste of time," he said. He climbed back aboard *Rag Time*. "Let's get on to San Diego, kid."

"Frank, I beg you. Don't let him seduce you with this evil creature," Althea said. "The spirit should soar without man-made wings! This will only swell men's pride and folly."

Craig was in the pilot's seat, adjusting his goggles. Frank hesitated, in torment. On one side was adventure, heroism, on the other side, the life of the spirit, the exploration of its mysteries.

"Let's *go*, kid," Craig said.

Suddenly Frank was almost as angry at his mother as Craig was. Couldn't she see he was a *man*? Craig was right. She was trying to make him a momma's boy for the rest of his life. Women were dangerous.

He spun the prop and leaped into the passenger seat. In a moment they were in the air, climbing to five hundred feet. Frank watched his mother dwindle to a speck in the green field where for a moment she had seemed so formidable.

The air meet in San Diego was a big success. Craig won four thousand dollars in prizes. His bombing routine was the hit of the show. He used giant firecrackers that went off with a big bang. That night Craig urged Frank to join him and Muriel Halsey, an actress who followed him everywhere in her white Dusenberg touring car, for a night on the town. (The Baroness had returned to Vienna "*haxausted*," according to Craig.) Muriel said she would find him a girl.

Frank shook his head. He was feeling guilty about making his mother unhappy. She had warned him against drinking liquor. She said it was dangerous for a child of light. She also warned him against women who did not match his em-anations. They could destroy his spiritual gifts.

Craig returned to the hotel room around 1 A.M. with two Mexicans. Half asleep, Frank heard only snatches of the con-versation. It had something to do with bombing and revolution and a town named Los Banyos. There was laughter, the clinking of glasses.

Craig shook Frank awake at dawn. This was unusual. The day after a meet, they usually slept until noon. At the air field, they gassed up *Rag Time* and took off into a splendid sunrise. "We're heading south!" Frank shouted, pointing to the Pacific, which was on their right.

Craig nodded. "Mexico!" he shouted. "We're going to war!"

A civil war had been raging in Mexico for several years. In a half hour they were over the border, flying across a barren, rocky landscape. In another hour they landed in a field not far from a camp with a half-dozen tents and hundreds of horses tethered in rows on wires stretched between posts. Soldiers rushed up to them firing rifles and pistols in the air. The two Mexicans who had visited the hotel room appeared, smiling broadly. With them was a big-nosed sweaty man wearing a white sun helmet.

"I have six bombs for you," he said in a thick German accent. "The fuses are set to explode on contact. Do you understand?"

"*Jawohl*," Craig said.

The German examined *Rag Time* with great interest. "We have better in Germany," he said.

"Yeah, but we're in Mexico," Craig said. "Where's the money?"

The Mexicans gave him a thick roll of bills. They loaded the six bombs, snub-nosed artillery shells, into the bomb basket along with one or two smoke bombs. Someone blew a bugle and the soldiers rushed to their horses. Craig studied a map supplied by the German, Frank spun the prop and they took off.

At least, they tried to take off. *Rag Time* bounced down the field and Craig hauled back on the stick. They wobbled into the air and came back down with a shuddering crash. Cursing, Craig gave her full power and this time they got off the ground. But they were not climbing. They were heading straight for the face of a nearby ridge.

"Throw out two of those goddamn bombs!" Craig shouted.

The bombs created awesome explosions. Lighter by a hundred pounds, *Rag Time* cleared the ridge and zoomed down a road that wound behind it. The Mexican army galloped after them, shouting and firing their rifles in the air. Beyond another ridge lay a small valley with a town full of white-walled buildings at the end of it. Craig flew back and forth until the horsemen caught up to them. They formed up in a long line under the directions of the German. He waved a red flag and they charged. *Rag Time* roared ahead of them until they reached the outskirts of the town.

"Smoke bombs!" Craig yelled.

Frank hurled two bombs over the side, creating a billow of white smoke that drifted across the fronts of the houses. Below them, on the roofs of the houses, dozens of men were lying down aiming rifles at the charging horsemen. In one place three men crouched around a machine gun.

Craig roared over the rooftops at two hundred feet. Some of the riflemen rolled onto their backs and began shooting at *Rag Time*. A bullet whined by Frank's head. Another one snapped a wing strut. "Give 'em the first one, kid!" Craig bellowed.

Frank hauled one of the shells out of the basket and held it over the edge of his seat. It had small fins wired to the side to guide it down. He let it go and it hit only a few feet from the men on one of the roofs. It exploded with a tremendous crash and the roof, the men, vanished. Through a swirl of smoke Frank saw nothing but a dark hole between shattered walls. A man crawled out of the house into the street. Frank realized he was crawling because one of his legs had been blown off below the knee. After a few feet he stopped and lay facedown while a stream of blood trickled from the stump into the gutter.

"Nice going, kid!" Craig shouted. "Get ready for another run."

Frank looked over his shoulder and saw the Mexican army was charging through the smoke, firing their rifles from horseback. The machine gun chattered, emptying a dozen saddles. Craig came in even lower this time. "Get the machine gun," he shouted, pointing below them.

Frank shook his head. All he could hear was his mother hissing *death machine*. He clutched the bomb to his chest. "We're killing them!" he screamed.

"That's the idea!" Craig yelled. "They're paying us a thousand bucks to do it."

"Why are we killing them? What have they done to us?"

"It's a goddamn war!" Craig bellowed.

"I won't do it. It's wrong!" Frank cried.

"Jesus Christ, you're still a momma's boy!" Craig snarled.

He grabbed the bomb out of Frank's hands, banked and came in even lower, no more than fifty feet above the roofs. More enemy soldiers were shooting at them. But others were jumping off the roofs into the streets in panic. Craig planted the bomb about twenty feet from the machine gun. It blew the men firing the gun off the roof into the field in front of the town. The gun lay on its side like a dead insect.

The charging horsemen hurtled into the town. Some of the defenders tried to make a stand in the streets but the horsemen rode into them, swinging sabers, firing pistols. Those who were still alive fled out the other end of the town. Craig followed them and demanded another bomb.

"They're beaten! Let them go!" Frank said. He grabbed the last two bombs and threw them over the side. They blew big holes in the ground and probably made the fleeing defenders run a little faster. Craig banked back over the town. The victors were dragging people out of houses and shooting them in the streets.

"Jesus," Craig said. "Let's go home."

Back in California, Frank made Craig promise he would not fly *Rag Time* as a bomber again. Frank even wanted Craig to give up the bombing part of the act at air shows but Craig refused. "We've got to keep eating, kid," he said.

A month later, on August 23, 1912, Craig was flying low over the ocean before a huge crowd at Long Beach. The concessionaires along the Long Beach Pike, a big amusement park, had hired him to attract customers. On the beach beside Frank, in a swimsuit that displayed a lot of her knockout figure, Muriel Halsey wiggled her bottom excitedly in the sand and said: "He promised to show me something special."

A moment later, Craig took his hands off the stick and spread his arms wide. *"That's how safe flying is, ladies and gentlemen,"* boomed the Pike's master of ceremonies through a big megaphone.

"Gosh, he's got nerve," cried Muriel. She had just finished a movie in Hollywood and was sure she could get Craig a part in one. They were shooting five and six pictures a week and were desperate for brawny leading men. She had already urged a director to write a script about a pilot who rescued a blond American girl from Mexican bandits.

Suddenly *Rag Time* yawed to the right, her nose dipped and she dove straight down. *A trick. He'll pull it out,* Frank thought. This was the stunt Craig was going to show Muriel. He must have learned it in secret so not even Frank knew about it.

But *Rag Time* did not pull out. The plane plunged into a flock of gulls riding just beyond the surf. It happened so fast, no one in the crowd made a sound for a full minute. Then a kind of wail swept the beach. The fuselage and the right wing crumpled around Craig, trapping him in the wreckage.

Frank rowed frantically out with some lifeguards to pull Craig from the hulk minutes before *Rag Time* sank. But there was nothing more they could do for Craig. His neck was broken. He died in the hospital about an hour later, trying to say something to Frank.

"Care—care—"

Take care of Mother? Be careful? It did not matter. As he closed Craig's eyes, Frank Buchanan vowed to build a better, safer plane, one that was not a death machine. He would learn the science of flight, instead of merely tinkering with ailerons and controls like a clever mechanic, which was all Craig had been. He would care about planes in Craig's memory. He would abandon his mother's dream of proving the survival of the soul after death. That was a job for a momma's boy. Building planes was a job for a man.

Craig's spirit entered Frank with that word, care. He did not know whether it partook of darkness or of light. It did not matter. Part of Frank became the swaggering older brother who loved and left women as casually as he risked

death in the air. Part of shy, studious Frank Buchanan was
abandoned that day in 1912 so life could triumph over death.

Muriel Halsey had sobbed beside the hospital bed as Craig
died. She took Frank home to her villa in the Hollywood
hills overlooking Los Angeles and fixed him something powerful to drink. Frank gulped it in Craig's memory, as part of
his determination to keep him alive in his mind and body.

They had several drinks in Craig's memory. Pretty soon
Muriel was telling him how much he looked like Craig. His
hair was redder but he had the same build. The same big
heart. Muriel joined him on the couch and began kissing him.
She said she wanted to give him something to remember
Craig by, something Craig liked even more than flying.
Frank did not object. He did not worry about Muriel's em-
anations. It was another way of becoming Craig.

In the bedroom, Frank marveled at the design of a
woman's body. All those fascinating curves and cunning
concavities and fragile bones. It made him wonder if his
mother was right when she contended that Eve, the Creator's
second attempt, was an improvement on the first clumsy
model, Adam. As Muriel slithered up his chest to slide her
tongue into his mouth, Frank decided the answer was yes yes
yes. Women and planes—two aspects of beauty in space and
time—two ascents to bliss.

THE FUTURE IN THE SKY

"Here he comes!"

"We're in the perfect spot!"

Nine-year-old Adrian Van Ness stood beside his mother
and her English friends on Shakespeare Cliff at Dover, where
King Lear once raved against malignant fate. They were
watching an incredible sight—a man flying an airplane from
France to England. Hundreds of people had flocked to the

white chalk bluffs to witness this sensation of the new century.

"By jove, it makes my blood boil to think a frog's doing it first," said a husky English voice above Adrian's head. Geoffrey Tillotson had broad shoulders and hooded eyes. His black bowler seemed to blot out the sky.

"It's glorious nonetheless, Geoffrey."

That silken American voice belonged to Adrian's mother, Clarissa Ames Van Ness. She was almost as tall as Geoffrey Tillotson. She wore a wide-brimmed black straw hat with a spume of white aigrettes. The hat was tilted on her beautiful head like a Jules Verne spaceship.

"You're right about that. Keep your eye on him, young fellows. You're seeing the future overhead. Everyone's future!" Geoffrey Tillotson said.

The white monoplane sailed over their heads, its motor clattering. At first it looked more like an insect than a bird, with the whirring propeller in its snout. But the outspread wings, the wheels jutting below the fuselage, recaptured a resemblance to the gulls that glided overhead, shrilling excitedly at this intruder in their sky.

"What keeps him up?" Adrian's mother asked.

"Aerodynamics," Geoffrey said.

The plane was so low you could see the pilot at the controls, wearing a helmet and goggles. "I say, Father, I'm going to learn to fly one of those things straightaway," said Peter Tillotson, Geoffrey's fourteen-year-old son. He was thick-bodied and muscular like his father.

Adrian did not like Peter very much. At the Tillotson house in Kent, not far from Dover, he had insisted on teaching Adrian how to play rugby, knocking him down repeatedly in the process. Adrian hated sports. Books were what he loved. He was reading Edward Gibbon's *Decline and Fall of the Roman Empire*. He had found it in the Tillotson library. He was enthralled by the descriptions of Rome's armies and emperors.

Peter had called *Decline and Fall* "eighteenth-century rubbish." Geoffrey Tillotson had defended Adrian's fascination with it. He said it was a great book. Then he told a funny story about it. When the author completed the second volume, he presented it to his patron, the Duke of Gloucester, who said, "Another damn thick square book. Always scribble scribble scribble. Eh, Gibbon?"

Everyone laughed and Adrian felt his face, his whole body grow hot. He thought they were laughing at him. He did not know exactly why he was often afraid people were laughing at him. It had something to do with his father. At St. Edmund's School in New York several boys had told him his father should be in jail. When Adrian asked his mother about it, she had gotten very angry. "That's a filthy lie!" she said.

Adrian thought she was angry at him and began to cry. His mother had cried too. Then she wrote the headmaster a letter. He had preached a sermon in chapel about the sin of slander. The next day at lunch, one of the boys had said, "My father still says your father belongs in jail, Van Ness." Everyone at the table had laughed.

The airplane tilted to the left after it passed over their heads and soared over Dover Castle. It tilted again and dropped lower and lower. He was going to land! They rushed to a big open touring car that Geoffrey Tillotson owned. The chauffeur cranked the motor and they beeped through the crowd pouring down the narrow street into town.

The plane was sitting in the center of the North Fall Meadow behind the eastern cliffs. The pilot, a stocky Frenchman named Louis Bleriot, was standing beside it, pleading with the hundreds of people swirling around him. "*Non, non, s'il vous plaît*, do not touch," he begged as they pressed closer. "It is easily damaged."

The thing looked very fragile. You could almost see through the fabric on the body and wings. Above them loomed Dover Castle, with its scarred octagonal Pharos, a relic of an original Roman fort. It was the oldest standing building in England. Geoffrey Tillotson pointed to it and said: "Forts, armies, ships, this thing will make them obsolete, mark my words."

Back in New York, Adrian's mother transferred him to the Trinity School. No one taunted or laughed at him there but Adrian often thought he saw hints of it in some boys' eyes.

He made no friends. He spent most of his free time reading or talking to his mother or the maids. The following summer when they returned to England, Adrian's mother enrolled him in the Anson School. She told him he would be happier there than he was at Trinity or St. Edmund's in New York. She was wrong.

The school was in a gloomy set of buildings on a hill in Sussex. Adrian did not like any of the boys in his form any more than he liked Peter Tillotson. They all seemed to take special pleasure in flattening him in the compulsory rugby games. Night after night Adrian lay in bed, his body an aching bruise.

He spent most of his free time in the library, reading history books like *Decline and Fall*, which seemed to infuriate the boys in his form. They called him the American wog and massacred him relentlessly on the rugby field. He became a prime target of sixth formers who selected lower formers to be initiated into a tradition of the Anson School known as The Deflowering.

Adrian declined to cooperate. This soon led to a midnight summons. A rough hand shook him awake in his darkened dormitory. "Get up, wog. The council is meeting," hissed a commanding voice. In his bare feet, Adrian hurried along the icy floor and up the equally icy stone stairs to the top floor of the three-hundred-year-old dormitory.

Candles flickered in teacups. The council sat in an awesome row, their faces obscured by silk stockings they had stolen from their mothers. "Who's this?" asked the chairman.

"The American wog."

"What's the charge?"

"For the fifth consecutive night, he was told to get a pound of butter from dinner for the usual purpose and he refused. He also failed to save the correct portion of his dessert. We suspect he's trying to start a bloody revolution."

"We've been checking on you, wog. We think your real name's Von Ness. We think you're a bloody German," the chairman said.

"I'm not. Van Ness is a Dutch name. My father is descended from some of the first settlers in America."

"What does your father do for a living, wog?"

"Nothing."

Laughter. "Why doesn't he do anything, wog?"

"None of your business."

"We're making it our business, wog. Explain."

"My mother has money. He doesn't have to work."

"Very suspicious. He's either a spy or a layabout. Tell us more about your mother."

"Her maiden name was Ames. She's from Boston."

"Why is she living in England while your father stays in New York?"

"I don't know."

"Is she a spy, wog?"

"No. She hates the Germans like everyone else."

Adrian did not pretend to understand the antagonism for Germany seething through England in 1911. Even schoolboys talked confidently, eagerly, of fighting a war to teach the Kaiser and his generals a lesson in humility.

"You know what the butter is used for, wog?"

"It's for the Rammer," Adrian said.

"What does the Rammer do, wog?"

"He—he breaks in virgins."

"Why didn't you bring the butter, wog?"

"I don't want to be broken in."

"Wog, how many times do you have to be told what you want doesn't matter? We're the rulers, you're the slave. Tomorrow night you will visit the Rammer with the pound of butter or your life will cease. You will become one of the living dead. Do you understand that, wog?"

"Yes."

No one spoke to the living dead. They were treated as if they were invisible. Everyone walked straight at them in the corridors. They stepped on their feet in class. They refused to pass them food in the dining hall.

"For the present you are sentenced to double the usual punishment. Bend over."

Adrian pulled down his pants and bent double, his hands gripping the back of a chair.

"My god, that's a fat one. I can practically hear the Rammer salivating," one of the council said.

"Apply the punishment."

Again and again the paddle smashed against Adrian's buttocks. Waves of pain flooded his body. He thought for a while he was going to suffocate. Tears poured down his face. The council counted each stroke in chorus. "Twenty-one, twenty-two, twenty-three." They stopped at twenty-five.

Curled into a sobbing fetal ball in his icy bed, Adrian vowed not to tell anyone why his father lived in such a peculiar way. Last spring, before they left for England, Adrian had found the courage to ask his mother to explain it. His mother had taken him into her bedroom, which smelled of lilacs. They sat in two barrel chairs by the bay window overlooking Central Park. She told him how his father had been ruined in 1893, seven years before he was born.

The word *ruined* had tolled on her lips like a funeral bell. The stock market on Wall Street had crashed and some people who had given his father money to invest blamed him for losing it. She said the crash had not been his fault and no one really thought he should go to jail. When people lost money they said mean things.

His mother had seized Adrian by his shoulders and said: "Your father is a good man. We live on my money. You must never mention any of this to your father or anyone else."

It was enormously confusing. *Ruined* meant your wife seldom used your first name. In England his mother called many people by their first names. In New York his mother called his father *you*. Will you be home for dinner tonight? Do you plan to go to Bar Harbor this summer? Are you going to Long Island this weekend?

Ruined acquired spiritual as well as financial reverberations for Adrian Van Ness. As far as he could see, his father had almost ceased to exist. He was an adult version of a living dead man, haunting the house, the city. At dinner he seldom spoke about anything important. He talked about the weather—he could discourse on a late frost or an early snowfall for a full half hour—on who was marrying whom, or on who had just been admitted to the Union League Club or the Century. He seldom talked to Adrian; he seemed to think there was no hope of winning his respect or friendship.

Ruined became another reason why Adrian liked to read history books. The past made the dismal present easier to accept, if not to understand. History often made people unhappy. He imagined himself as the son of a baron who had supported King Richard II, or of a general who had fought for Napoleon. They too had been ruined by different kinds of catastrophes. What happened to their sons? The history books never mentioned the sons.

His mother pretended she was staying in England for his sake but Adrian suspected she was enjoying herself. She was much more cheerful in London than she was in New York. There she was always solemn. Her eyes had a dull, pained expression. It had to have something to do with his father. She was glad to stay away from him. Why?

Adrian lay in his icy bed thinking about these mysteries until the pain in his buttocks subsided. Should he get the butter and let the Rammer have him tomorrow? The boy in the bed next to him, Carlo Pontecorvo, whom everyone called Ponty, had obeyed the summons last week. He was the son of an Italian nobleman who was a passionate admirer of England. Ponty had cried all night and told Adrian there was blood in the toilet bowl when he shit. Maybe it was better to be one of the living dead. He would be like his father. *Ruined.*

The next night, Adrian came back from the dining hall without the butter. He was consigned to the living dead. On the way to dinner the following day, Ponty whispered he had done the right thing. Someone ratted and Ponty got fifty strokes of the paddle for speaking to a living dead man.

Day after day, Adrian went to class and ate in the dining hall and studied in study hall and went to bed without speaking to anyone. At first he did not mind. He felt close to his father. It was almost as good as getting a letter from him. His father never wrote to him. His mother wrote almost every day, telling him about the war between Turkey and Bulgaria and the wild protests of the suffragettes, women who wanted the right to vote and threatened to blow up Parliament if they did not get it. She kept him up to date on what their friends were doing. Peter Tillotson had graduated from Sandhurst, the British West Point, and joined the newly formed Royal Flying Corps to become a pilot.

One day in the spring of 1912 Adrian was walking across the school's inner quadrangle. Ponty strode toward him. Suddenly Adrian wanted to say hello to him. He wanted Ponty to answer him. Both lonely outsiders, they had naturally gravitated to each other. Ponty used to make Adrian laugh. He did funny imitations of their fat headmaster, Mr. Deakwell. When Ponty passed him without even letting his eyes flicker toward Adrian, it hurt in a new way deep inside. It was a pain worse than the paddle.

Even stranger things began happening inside Adrian as he continued walking across the quadrangle. Something almost as big as Louis Bleriot's monoplane began doing loops inside him. He felt hot and cold at the same time. His heart pounded and he thought he was going to faint. When it did not stop he thought he was going to die.

When the looping finally stopped Adrian felt so tired he went to bed. He did not go to supper and he did not get up for class the next day. He lay in bed and listened to the rain falling outside. *Ruined ruined ruined* it said with every drop. It was so sad. He wept for himself and his father. *Ruined* filled the whole world with fog and drizzle and mist.

After a while Adrian lost track of time. He vaguely remembered being hot and thirsty and hungry and being carried from the dormitory through the rain to another part of the school. The next comprehensible thing he heard was a man's hoarse voice.

"A living dead man? I don't understand. Is it some sort of American expression?"

Adrian was in the infirmary. The headmaster, Augustine Deakwell, was standing on the right side of his bed. He was very fat and wore sideburns, big white puffs of hair on both cheeks.

"It's a form of coventry, Mr. Deakwell. The senior boys invoke it for various reasons."

That was Mr. Goggins, the young master who was in charge of the third form. He was on the left side of Adrian's bed. He had big teeth and a stiff brush mustache. He had brought Adrian to the infirmary when he found him lying in his dormitory bed, sobbing.

"Hah? What's he done? Ratted on someone?" the headmaster asked.

"I think it's a good deal more malicious, Mr. Deakwell."

"If what Goggins tells me is true, Deakwell, you've got a first-class scandal on your hands."

It was his mother's friend, Geoffrey Tillotson. He loomed at the foot of Adrian's bed, scowling at the headmaster. His cheeks seemed pinker than usual, his jowls more formidable. He was wearing a black suit and a gray vest and gray tie with a large pearl stickpin in the center of it. His black derby was perfectly straight on his large head.

"If my son Peter wasn't a graduate, I'd have your head on a platter by next Monday, Deakwell. I leave it to you to straighten things swiftly—and mercilessly. In the meantime, I'll take this lad to his mother."

On the train, Tillotson bought Adrian a roast beef sandwich and a mug of cocoa. He told him he was proud of him for defying the sixth formers and becoming a living dead man. He said he was very sorry for what had happened and he hoped it would not make him dislike England. It was the fault of a few boys who misused their power as sixth formers. They forgot it was their responsibility to teach second and third formers the traditions of Anson, to make them proud of the famous men who had graduated from it.

"Every so often in all sorts of places, from schools to Parliament, rotters get into power," Tillotson said. "Eventually some brave fellows stand up to them and put things right."

"Like the Reform Acts," Adrian said. He had read about this great struggle for democracy in Macaulay's *History of England.*

"Exactly."

For the rest of the trip Tillotson talked about airplanes. He said his son Peter was becoming a very good pilot. An Englishman named de Havilland was building planes that were better than the ones the French made. Even better than the ones made by the Wrights, the Americans who had invented the machine. He gave Adrian a book full of photographs of planes at an air show outside Paris.

After a week with his mother, Adrian returned to Anson with Geoffrey Tillotson. On the train Tillotson assured him matters had been "put right." Remembering St. Edmund's, Adrian was not so sure. He still felt very sad.

In the quadrangle, Adrian encountered Ponty, who gave him a broad smile and said: " 'Allo, Van Ness. Glad you've come back."

That night Mr. Goggins had Adrian and Ponty and a half-dozen other third formers to dinner in his rooms. He talked about things having "gone wrong" but would be "ripping" now, he was sure of it. He said he hoped they would all try to be more friendly to their American guest, who had proved himself a "brave fellow."

"Bravissimo!" Ponty said. The other boys rapped their tea mugs on the table and said, "Hear, hear."

The next day, something even more remarkable happened. A biplane zoomed low over the school and climbed high into the sky to do a series of spectacular dives and banks. The pilot landed on the north playing field and the entire student body rushed there for a close look at the machine. The pilot climbed out and everyone gasped. It was Peter Tillotson, who had graduated two years ago.

"Where's my friend Van Ness?" Peter asked.

Adrian was shoved forward by wide-eyed third formers. "Get in," Peter said in his rough way.

Adrian climbed into the front seat and Peter buckled a thick belt around his waist. He asked Mr. Goggins to spin the propeller. In a moment they were bouncing down the playing field toward a line of trees in the distance. "Hang on!" Peter shouted, and they cleared the trees by a foot.

Aloft, Adrian looked down on the school and marveled at the way it was dwindling, exactly the way Shakespeare had described the men and boats below the cliffs at Dover in the scene where Lear went mad. Everyone was mouse-size and

the buildings looked more and more like toys. The sadness
started to fall away from him. He began to feel proud and
free and happy.

"How do you like it?" Peter shouted above the roaring
motor.

"Ripping!" Adrian shouted.

"This is only the third time I've been up alone. Soloing,
they call it. You can get killed with no warning but it's worth
it. Hang on, we'll try a loop."

He pointed the nose of the plane toward the sky and
climbed straight up. Instead of flipping over, they hung there
for a second, then fell off to the right in a screaming dive.
"Afraid I've got to practice that," Peter said, after they pulled
out.

They made a rather bumpy landing. The entire student
body swarmed around them again. "I've only got time for
one more ride. Who will it be, Adrian?"

"Ponty," Adrian said.

Peter took him up and this time completed a loop. Ponty
said it was the most remarkable sensation of his life. He
vowed to learn to fly as soon as possible.

From living dead man, Adrian soared to leader of the third
form. No more was heard of Von Ness, son of the German
spy. The next two months were the happiest of his life.

One afternoon in mid-May, as Adrian sat in the library
reading about the Battle of Waterloo, Ponty tapped him on
the shoulder. "The head wants you, Van." He puffed his
cheeks and stuck out his stomach and waddled away in a
perfect imitation of Mr. Deakwell.

In the headmaster's office, his mother sat alone. She
looked unusually beautiful in a jet-black suit. Adrian often
thought she resembled one of those tall, proud Gibson girls
in magazine illustrations. "Oh, darling," she said. "I've got
some bad news. We have to go home."

"Why?"

"Your father's dead. He was killed in an accident. Fox-
hunting. He ran into a low-hanging limb and broke his neck."

Adrian waited for her to weep, to let him weep. But she
did nothing of the sort. She told him to go to his room and

pack. They were catching the fastest ship home, the SS *Lusitania*. It was sailing from Southampton the next day.

Adrian trudged across the quadrangle, suddenly remembering everything. Von Ness the spy, the months as a living dead man, the sadness. He felt angry at his mother for having exposed him to these ordeals. Beneath that anger was a deeper, colder enmity for her refusal to weep for his ruined father. He found himself wishing he could get in a plane and fly thousands of miles away from his mother and never see her again.

HISTORY'S LASH

"You—you there, young fellow—is that an American accent I hear?"

Frank Buchanan paused in his effort to tune the motor of a de Havilland Scout, wiped grease from his hands and nodded. The man had the lean face, the spaded beard, the fiery eyes of Mephistopheles in his youth, when his hair was bright red. A flowing gray coat enveloped him almost to his shoetops. He gestured at Frank with an ebony cane. He was surrounded by a half dozen of the most elegant women Frank had ever seen.

"It sounds like I'm hearing one too," Frank shouted as his helper got the motor to stop choking and sputtering and emit a racketing roar.

"Hailey, Idaho," the man shouted, holding out his hand. "The name's Pound. Ezra Pound."

"The author of *Canzoni*?" Frank said.

"A mechanic who reads poetry!" Pound cried. "You see what I've been saying? Americans aren't a lost cause. There's hope—if we can get more of them to Europe."

They were standing on the grassy airfield at Hendon, a suburb of London, on a sunny Saturday afternoon in May

1914. Every week some two hundred thousand people came out to see the latest planes race around the pyloned course. Britons of all classes had become fascinated by flight. A pilgrimage to Hendon was a must to those who hoped to have any claim to sophistication.

"Do you understand how these things work?" Pound said, leading Frank away from the snarling Rhone rotary engine. "Why one crashes, another stays in the air? The principle behind it?"

"I've learned a few things from Geoffrey de Havilland," Frank said modestly. He could have said much more. He had spent a year in France working for Louis Paulhan, the pilot he had met at the Dominquez Hills air show. Paulhan and other designers were churning out planes in a dozen factories around Paris. He had even accompanied Paulhan to the wind tunnel constructed by Louis Eiffel, builder of the famous tower. In the tunnel French designers studied the effect of airflow on models of the planes they were building.

In England, a photograph of *Rag Time* had won him a job in de Havilland's design department. The big blond Englishman had built one of Britain's first flyable planes in 1910. He was now working for the Aircraft Manufacturing Company, which operated from an old bus garage in Hendon. Frank had come to England to learn more about the changes the British were making in the airplane's basic design. De Havilland was working with scientists who had been studying aerodynamic problems in their laboratories. They recommended moving the wings of a plane back to the middle of the fuselage, closer to the center of gravity, enlarging the tail and the ailerons—all aimed at giving the aircraft as much stability in the air as a boat on the water.

A few minutes' conversation convinced Pound that his American discovery was the perfect man to introduce his circle of poets and poetry lovers to the mysteries of flight. Pound saw the plane as a prime example of his artistic theories. Since he arrived in England in 1908, he had become a one-man cultural crusade, churning out poetry and critical essays proclaiming that the new century required an entirely new art. He called his theory Vorticism and he publicized it in the pages of a magazine called *Blast*.

Vorticists believed art could and should represent reality with the same precision as an equation in fluid dynamics or solid geometry. They wanted to make a poem or story work as precisely as a machine. At the heart of every work of art there was a vortex, a pulsing fist of forces that gave it energy and meaning. It was the critic or the editor's task to find that vortex and help the writer exploit it to the utmost.

Within a week, Frank Buchanan found himself the center of attention in Pound's small dark apartment in Kensington. A dozen guests, most of them women, listened wide-eyed as he proposed to demonstrate the central idea of flight. He took a piece of paper and curled one end of it over a pencil. Raising it to the level of his lips, he blew on it. The paper rose. "I have just produced lift," he said. "You are now in the world of aerodynamics."

Why does air traveling over a wing create lift? "The air on top of the wing moves faster than the air under the bottom. In the eighteenth century, a Swiss mathematician named Bernoulli experimented with water flowing through a pipe. He proved that the faster it flowed, the lower the pressure in the pipe. Later, an Italian scientist named Venturi proved the same thing was true for air. That's why the higher pressure of the slower air under the wing creates lift."

"Exactly how emotion works in a poem or story!" Pound cried.

"The other components of a plane are weight, drag, and thrust," Frank continued. "These are easier to understand. Drag is created by the resistance the surface of the plane meets as it moves through the air. Weight is the force of gravity and thrust is the forward motion we get from the engine."

"In a poem or story," Pound said, "Drag corresponds to the writer's ability, weight to the reader's stupidity, and thrust to the publisher's greed."

So it went for the length of the lecture, Pound finding literary analogies for all Frank's aeronautical terms. Pound was particularly fascinated by the way air flowing over the wings and down the fuselage of a plane formed negative vortexes that created a phenomenon known as *flutter*, which could tear a wing or a tail apart.

"Precisely the way the wrong metaphor can wreck a stanza, the wrong rhythm can ruin a poem, the wrong character can mangle a story!" Pound said.

A blond young woman in the center of the semicircle asked: "What is the future of this marvelous machine?" She had the face of a Pre-Raphaelite angel—the pale cheeks, the wide blue eyes, seemingly vacant, waiting to be charged with emotion.

"Its future is as unlimited as the sky above our heads," Frank said. "The plane can abolish distance, annihilate frontiers, unite peoples in Tennyson's wonderful vision of a Parliament of Man!"

"Tennyson!" Pound exclaimed. "My dear fellow—that's a name we don't allow in this house. He's a has-been."

"He never will be, to me," Frank said. His mother had read the great English poet aloud to him almost every night in his boyhood. *"The Idylls of the King"* was his favorite poem.

"The danger of teaching mechanics to read has now become visible," Pound said. "They form their own opinions."

"But Ezra," said the blond young woman. "He also likes your *Canzoni*."

"That only demonstrates, to use an aeronautical term, his instability," Pound said.

The highlight of the evening was a midnight supper cooked by Pound, a delicious oyster stew, complemented by an Italian white wine that he served with an inimitable toast. "Come let us pity those who are better off than we are. Remember that the rich have butlers and no friends and we have friends and no butlers."

The conversation swirled over art and politics, with the blond girl quizzically probing Frank's opinions. Her name was Penelope Foster and she was unquestionably attracted to him. "Do you think we shall have peace or war, Mr. Buchanan?" she said in a liquid voice that sent shimmers of desire through Frank's flesh.

"Oh, peace," Frank said. "War would be a ridiculous waste of time and energy."

"The British upper class can hardly wait to go to war with Germany. Proving, among other things, their imbecility," Pound said.

"You're quite wrong, Ezra. The Huns need to be taught a lesson," Penelope Foster said.

The rising power of Germany obsessed almost everyone in England. Their fleet and army were challenging Britain's supremacy everywhere, in Africa, China, the south Pacific. Their corporations were invading markets such as America, where English goods had once been supreme.

"If we have a war, do you think your planes will be in it?" Penelope asked.

"As scouts," Frank said. "They'll be the eyes of the army. In fact, their mere presence may make war impossible. How can a general maneuver a great army when a plane can swoop down and discover it miles before he can reach his objective? Planes can produce a stalemate, where neither side can gain an advantage."

"I think you badly underestimate the brutality of generals," Pound said. "What about planes as bombers? In the *Arabian Nights*, Sinbad the Sailor describes how two ships were destroyed by Rocs, giant birds carrying huge stones."

"We don't have motors powerful enough to lift a serious amount of bombs," Frank said, guiltily omitting his experience bombing Mexicans from *Rag Time*. He did not want to believe that anyone who experienced the exaltation of flight could use it to rain death on human beings. Even Craig had been dismayed by the effect of their bombs on Los Banyos.

Frank escorted Penelope Foster home to a nearby flat. The daughter of a colonial office civil servant, she was a poet who tried to create small, exact word portraits of nature and humanity in a style Pound had dubbed *imagism*. Pound told her she had talent and the samples she showed Frank in her rooms proved it. She called them *London Lives*. In ten lines or less, each depicted a London type, a burly bus driver, a screeching fishmonger, a banker flourishing his umbrella "like a scepter," a scrawny messenger on his bike, risking his life in the traffic "like a sparrow in a gale."

"All lift, no drag," Frank said. "I hope I can create planes like these some day."

"You will. I can sense it in you. A pulsing thing Ezra calls the gold thread in the pattern. Some people possess it instinctively."

"How does it work?" Frank asked.

"I'm not sure. It's part spirit, part technical mastery. A desire to grasp the essence of things—in art, in machines."

A plaintive sadness throbbed in Penelope's voice. Her lovely head drooped in a kind of mourning. "I sense the gift has passed to you Americans. You're the guardians of it now. We English nurtured it for a century—"

"Can I—may I—kiss you?" Frank said.

He wanted to possess this Sibyl, to explore her body as well as her soul. "No," she said. "It's much too soon."

"I want to make you part of my golden thread, my essence," Frank whispered. "In California, we believe it's never too soon."

The first part of that plea was Frank Buchanan, the second part was Craig. Frank was still an unstable blend of the two personalities. But Penelope proved she was worthy of her classic name when it came to evading suitors.

"This isn't California," she said.

In love for the first time, Frank became a regular visitor to Pound's Kensington circle. He listened to the poet read his magical translations from the Provençal and the Chinese and discourse with casual brilliance on Dante, Shakespeare, Homer. Frank took Penelope Foster up for a ride in a de Havilland Scout, the sturdy two-seat reconnaissance plane they were building for the Royal Flying Corps. She adored it but unlike the Baroness Sonnenschein and Muriel Halsey, she still declined Frank's offer of a similar ascent in her bedroom. Instead, she gave him a poem.

Crouched on the grass
The plane is a clumsy cicada
Who could believe
It devours clouds

Consumes cities and rivers
Challenges the sun
With its growling shadow?

Frank called Penelope his priestess and accepted the celibacy she imposed on him. Although they saw themselves as citizens of the new century it was a very Victorian love. Pound was their high priest, weaving a spell of beauty, a promise of triumphant art, around their lives. For three months Frank Buchanan, soaring in planes and poetry, was a happy young man.

But history was rumbling toward them on the continent. The Great Powers, as the newspapers called them, had devoted millions to building huge armies while their frantic diplomats devoted hundreds of hours to weaving intricate alliances to maintain a balance of power that was supposed to make war impossible. When a Serbian anarchist assassinated the crown prince of Austria, the illusion of peace evaporated. Austria threatened Serbia, Russia warned Austria, Germany threatened Russia. France warned Germany.

On August 4, 1914, Frank Buchanan awoke in his Hendon rooming house. Guy Chapman, his fellow junior designer, was pounding on his door. "Frank, Frank!" he was shouting. "It's the bloody war. It's started!"

Frank stumbled out of bed and found Chapman clutching a copy of the *London Times*. GERMANS INVADE BELGIUM roared the headline. England had warned Germany that if they violated Belgium's neutrality to attack France, Britain would declare war. At the Aircraft Manufacturing Company, chaos reigned. Geoffrey de Havilland and several other key people had been drafted by the Royal Flying Corps. Frank and Guy Chapman were the only designers still on the job.

Over the next year, Frank watched the airplane turn into a weapon of war. From the scout the generals had envisioned it became a fighter plane, when a Dutch designer named Anthony Fokker taught the Germans how to synchronize a machine gun to fire through the propeller. Then it became a bomber as more and more powerful motors created larger and larger planes capable of carrying as much as a thousand pounds of high explosives.

Penelope Foster's first reaction to the war was exultation. She was sure Germany would be smashed in a matter of weeks. As dozens of her friends and relatives, including her older brother, were killed by German machine guns and artillery in France, rage became her dominant emotion. She changed from a cool, detached imagist poet to a ranting, chanting writer of patriotic verse in the Kipling tradition. She shouted her poems from platforms to intimidate men into enlisting in the British army.

At night, in her Kensington flat, Penelope wrote more bad poetry to the heroic dead, and abused Frank Buchanan. She still refused to let him touch her. "Where are your heroic countrymen?" she hissed. "Why aren't they here, fighting for civilization? The barbarians are at the gates!"

Frank tried to defend President Woodrow Wilson's neutrality. He portrayed America as the one nation that could negotiate a just peace between the warring powers before they destroyed each other. Penelope called him a coward and a fool.

One terrible night at Pound's flat, after one of the best imagist poets, T. H. Hulme, was killed in Flanders, Penelope reviled Pound for not fighting beside him. Her diatribe was a paradigm of the way the war annihilated Pound's dream of a civilization redeemed by art. He began to sneer at the idea of patriotism, to see literature and art, not as a vortex transforming the world, but as a refuge from a world gone mad.

When German zeppelins and Gotha bombers appeared over London, smashing churches and homes, killing hundreds of people, Pound mocked Frank's vision of the plane annihilating frontiers. Its new goal was the annihilation of the countries behind the frontiers.

"I can hardly wait for them to bomb you American cowards," Penelope raged. She glared at Frank, her Pre-Raphaelite face livid with loathing.

The dreamer-designer Frank Buchanan shuddered under these blows. He wandered the streets of London consoling himself with streetwalkers while Craig whispered in his soul. *They're only good for one thing, kid. When you listen to their yak-yak they drive you nuts.*

One night, after a particularly unsatisfying encounter with a prostitute, Frank found himself on Brompton Road, standing before a building with a small sign crudely lettered over the doorway: *Church of the Questing Spirit.* Inside about two dozen people listened to a gray-haired minister talk about a world beyond their tormented visible one. The rectangular room, with a dome of stars painted on the ceiling, was the London headquarters of the sect Althea Buchanan had joined in California.

At the end of the sermon, the minister gestured to Frank, in the first row, and said: "Young man, are you as troubled as you look?"

Frank poured out his growing despair and confusion over the war. The woman he loved called him a coward for defending his own and his country's refusal to fight. What should he do?

The minister stepped into an anteroom and emerged with a shirt that had somehow been ripped almost to shreds. "Put this on," he said.

Frank shrugged off his jacket and thrust his arms into the shirt. Instantly he felt an incredible lash of pain across his back. Again again again, a fiery agony unlike anything he had ever experienced seared his flesh. He ripped off the shirt and flung it at the minister.

"What is it? What are you trying to do?" Frank gasped.

"That shirt belonged to a seaman in Nelson's navy who was lashed to death," the minister said. "You're one of us. Everyone in this room has felt that pain when they wore this shirt. Most people feel nothing."

"What does it mean?"

"Each of us has to find his own interpretation of that pain."

Outside the church, Frank found the night sky full of searchlights and flares. The Gothas were raiding London again. Huge explosions made the sidewalk tremble. The bombs were falling only a few blocks away, around Marble Arch. A man grabbed his arm. "Where's the nearest subway

station, pal?" he asked. His accent was as American as his
vocabulary. People were using London's underground for
air-raid shelters.

"I don't know this neighborhood."

"Ah, what the hell. Let's have a drink."

They pounded on the door of a nearby pub. Behind the
blacked-out windows a dozen fatalists were savoring what
could be their last pints. The American ordered double
Scotches for himself and Frank and held out his hand.

"Buzz McCall's the name, flying's my game."

"Likewise," Frank said.

Buzz was a chunk of a man, with black hair and a complexion as swarthy as an Italian's. He had a square fighter's
jaw and a swagger to his walk and talk. Except for his stock-
ier physique, the resemblance to Craig was uncanny.

Buzz began telling Frank he was on his way to France. A
group of Americans had volunteered to form a squadron in
the French air force. They were going to call it the Lafayette
Escadrille. "We're gonna teach these German fuckers a couple of lessons for bombin' women and children," he said.

"Have you got room for another pilot?" Frank said.

Death machine, his mother whispered. But Frank dismissed her once and for all. Buzz and Craig and this war-
maddened world were suddenly connected to the fiery shirt
he had just torn from his back in the Church of the Questing
Spirit. If he hoped to live as a man and not a momma's boy,
he would have to wear that ancient shirt, no matter how
much pain it cost him. He would have to endure history's
lash.

THE GIRL FROM THE GLORIOUS WEST

"America stands for peace and nothing but peace!"

Auburn hair streaming to her waist, Amanda Cadwallader trembled in the icy January wind cutting through Harvard Square. The barbaric weather was not the only reason for her tremors. It was her first public speech, her first attempt to bring California's message of peace to war-infatuated eastern America.

As a crowd gathered, two of her fellow sophomores at Wellesley handed out leaflets quoting poets and philosophers, including Harvard's own William James, on the folly of war as the solution to settling quarrels between nations. A big bulky young man in a well-tailored dark suit snatched one of the leaflets, glanced at it and crumpled it into a contemptuous ball. He planted himself directly in front of Amanda and shouted: "Are you German?"

"I'm from California," Amanda said.

"That explains the nonsense you're preaching. You've got an orange for a brain!" the young man bellowed. His thick-lipped wide-boned face had an adult cast. He looked like a faculty member.

"Yeah, yeah," jeered a half-dozen grinning young men in the crowd. "An orange for a brain."

"I've got a perfectly good brain," Amanda said. "I had a straight-A average at Stanford. I'm getting the same grades at Wellesley. Why can't you discuss the subject like—like gentlemen?"

"Because there's nothing gentle about a German. A German is a Hun," her chief antagonist said. "If we had any guts, we'd be over there fighting them now."

"Right. Absolutely right," rumbled from the crowd.

"We don't agree with you in California," Amanda said.

"America should be a voice of peace in the councils of the nations."

"Tell it to the Kaiser," sneered her antagonist.

Amanda glanced at her two followers, one of whom was her Wellesley roommate. Both easterners, they had been dubious about this venture. She had persuaded them to try it with the sheer force of her western enthusiasm.

"My friends told me this would happen. I had to see for myself. You're nothing but—barbarians."

She began to weep. Abominable! Amanda hated the way she wept whenever she was extremely angry—or extremely happy. Her mother had opposed the idea of letting Amanda go east. Her half-brother had been almost gleeful, he was so sure she would make a fool of herself. Her father had encouraged her. He said it would be a good way for her to find out just how confused and spiritually sick America was on the Atlantic seaboard.

The crowd began to disperse. But Amanda's chief antagonist remained behind—and was strangely contrite. "We're not barbarians," he said. "We're perfect gentlemen on every topic but the one you've chosen. To prove it—let me buy you all lunch."

Amanda turned to her two followers. The idea unquestionably appealed to them. The young man was remarkably self-possessed. His tailoring was expensive and foreign. There was something mysterious, intriguing, about his tufted brows and hooded eyes.

Twenty minutes later, Amanda and her friends were gorging on lobster salad, caramel cake, and ice cream sodas in the Crimson Cafe off Harvard Square. Adrian Van Ness talked to them earnestly and honestly about the war in Europe as he saw it in January 1916.

"I spent a year at the Anson School in England," he said. "Ten of my friends from the upper forms have died in Flanders, at Ypres, on the Somme. I've had letters from some of them. There was no doubt in their minds—or in mine—that they were fighting civilization's battle against the German hordes. Almost every faculty member and every student at Harvard believes this by now. We're all in favor of American intervention. There are over two hundred graduates already serving with the French and British armies as volunteers. Over a dozen have been killed—"

"Doesn't all this prove the madness, the stupidity of war?" Amanda said.

"It proves the courage, the heroism of ordinary men," Adrian said. "The war is a great testament to our civilization's capacity for self-sacrifice—and courage. Especially in the air. I have a number of friends in the Royal Flying Corps. One of them, Peter Tillotson, is the leading British ace at the moment with forty victories. Another friend, Carlo Pontecorvo, is flying for Italy. He thinks single combat in the plane is reviving some of the ancient ideals of chivalry. It may create a whole new race of men, with a code of honor like the knights of the Crusades."

Amanda was fascinated by the glow of idealism on Adrian's face as he talked about planes. Her followers, both from the east, began to change their minds about the war. Adrian was a remarkably persuasive young man. Amanda was losing the argument, but to her surprise she did not care. She sensed Adrian was genuinely distressed that he had hurt her feelings. Almost everything he said was for her. He barely glanced at her followers.

Outwardly, Amanda remained unconverted. She quoted Stanford's pacifist president, David Starr Jordan, at length. He had inspired her and a half-dozen other "peace missionaries" to transfer to Wellesley and Smith and Mount Holyoke to convert the warmongering easterners. She could hardly surrender to a spokesman for the evil East in her first encounter. But she secretly hoped she would see Adrian Van Ness again.

Within the week Adrian telephoned Amanda and invited her to another lunch at the Crimson Cafe—alone. Over more lobster salad he apologized for his slurs on California. "Actually, I know nothing about the place. What's it like?" he said.

A delighted Amanda talked about southern California— she dismissed the northern half of the state as a foggy, chilly wasteland—with an eloquence even she found surprising.

She described the lush beauty of the mountain-ringed San Fernando Valley, the majesty of the coast above Los Angeles, the vistas of the desert.

"Southern California is the last paradise in the Western world," Amanda said. "A place where art and poetry and philosophy will flower in a new renaissance."

"Who said that?" Adrian asked.

Amanda blushed and cast her eyes down: "My father."

"What does he do for a living?"

"He grows oranges. Cadwallader Groves is the largest producer in Orange County. He serves in the state legislature too. In 1910 he was one of the leaders in the fight to reform the constitution. He helped break the power of the railroad barons and other vested interests."

Amanda sipped the last of her ice cream soda. "What does your father do?" she asked.

"Nothing. He's dead."

Adrian's voice was so cold and curt, Amanda wondered if she had somehow offended him. "I—was never close to him. He was an—introvert," Adrian said.

Even in 1916, psychology had become an instant explanation for everything. Amanda murmured sympathetically. "My father hates crowds, cities," she said.

"Maybe I'll pay you a visit," Adrian said. "See if southern California improves my poetry."

Amanda asked to see some of this poetry. Surprise, surprise, Adrian had a half-dozen poems in his pocket. She made him read them to her. Many were about the nobility, the glory of flight.

"They're very good," Amanda said.

Adrian glowed. "When I showed them to my mother, she said 'most poets die poor.' "

"What's wrong with being poor? All the Mexican pickers at our grove are poor. But they're happy."

As Adrian opened the door of the taxi that would take Amanda back to Wellesley, she kissed him on the lips. "I like you," she said.

When Amanda told her roommate about the kiss, she was horrified. "You can't be that *forward*. It just isn't *done* in this part of the country. He'll never call you again."

Adrian called the next night to arrange another Saturday lunch at the Crimson Cafe—and a trip to the movies after it. That soon became a Saturday routine. At lunch Adrian read her other poems full of sadness and anger at life's cruelty. Amanda sensed some wound deep in his soul and longed to heal it. She also discerned how lonely he was at Harvard. He seemed to have made almost no friends.

Adrian said he did not get along with New Yorkers even though he had been born there. They were only interested in making money. He disdained Bostonians—although he had numerous cousins there—because they thought making money was vulgar. At other times he claimed most of his fellow students were childish. "They haven't found out what life is all about," he said. "You have to read history—and experience it—to do that."

As Amanda puzzled over his melancholy, Adrian invited her for dinner with his mother at her Beacon Hill town house on a rainy night in late March 1916. Amanda wore a loose blue lace dress and a soft blue velvet hat she had rushed into Boston to buy the previous day. Clarissa was regal in black silk and a pearl choker. She sat with her back as straight as a West Point cadet's, barely smiling as Amanda said hello.

She was awed by Clarissa's hauteur. Amanda was sure there were no women like her in California. Her own mother, so indifferent to clothes and style, so moody and impulsive, gave her no preparation for dealing with such glacial self-control. Clarissa was a block of dark New England ice. Trembling, Amanda understood Adrian's melancholy. This woman did not know how to love anyone—even a son.

"Adrian tells me you're from California," Clarissa said. She made it sound as if it were a communicable disease.

"Yes," Amanda said. She talked nervously, defensively, about her birthplace. "I had a letter from my mother yesterday. The temperature hasn't gone below seventy since January. I told her here it hasn't gone above twenty-five."

"No question, the entire state is a gigantic playground," Clarissa said. "But doesn't that get rather boring? You can't play all the time."

Floundering, Amanda pictured herself as the heroine of her favorite novel, *Ramona*. She too had been despised by arrogant easterners. But she had found pride and love in her California heritage. "We don't play all the time," she said. "We've produced some important literature."

"Oh?"

"Frank Norris's *The Octopus*, Mary Austin's *The Land of Little Rain*."

By this time they had sat down to dinner. Clarissa carefully carved another small slice from her lamb chop. "Personally, I prefer Richard Henry Dana's view of California."

Amanda replied with equal care: "He was one of those New Englanders who hated California."

"He loved it on his first visit. It was his second visit that disillusioned him. It had changed so utterly—for the worse."

"He hated it," Amanda said. "The second visit was his way of satisfying his puritan conscience for falling in love with it the first time."

"You think poorly of a puritan conscience?"

"My father says California makes puritanism superfluous."

Amanda glanced at Adrian. He was watching them with disbelieving eyes. He apparently never imagined anyone could challenge his formidable mother this way. In spite of his adult physique, he looked like a bewildered boy.

Love, the emotion that Amanda's father had taught her was life's noblest experience, stirred in her soul. With it came a wish to share with Adrian the richest memory of her childhood, the gift her father had told her she could only offer to the Precious One.

In the silence at dawn her mother and father and Amanda and her brother Gordon drank cool orange juice on the porch of their turreted white mansion, which her father had named Casa Felicidad, the house of happiness. They stepped out of their night clothes and walked naked among the blossoming trees. "There is no shame," her father said. "California is a new beginning. We can stop believing in ridiculous things like God. We're free to be noble and good without God."

He let Amanda touch the dangling part of his body. She put her hand into the russet hair beneath her mother's belly and felt her cleft. Her brother Gordon did the same things. Then in the dawn stillness on the dewy grass with orange blossoms drifting around them her father and mother showed Amanda and Gordon how men and women loved each other.

Amanda gazed at Adrian and spoke the meaning of this memory carefully, softly, intending the words only for him, indifferent to what Clarissa thought. "For those who believe in it, California is Eden," she said.

WAR HERO

A week after he brought Amanda Cadwallader to dinner, Adrian Van Ness visited his mother's Beacon Hill town house for tea. She was wearing the pearl choker that Geoffrey Tillotson had given her for her fortieth birthday. The Tiffany lamp beside the tea table cast a golden glow on the silvery jewels.

"Your little girl from the golden West is charming," Clarissa said. "So unspoiled. It's hard to believe they even have schools out there."

"I think I'm in love with her," Adrian said.

"Darling, never confuse love and sympathy. You feel sorry for someone who's such a lost lamb. Can you imagine her as hostess at a New York dinner party?"

"She's very intelligent. She has excellent taste in poetry."

"You mean she likes yours."

Clarissa Ames Van Ness smiled mockingly at Adrian. She was so sure of her social and intellectual superiority, so certain of her ability to control her son. It was exactly what Adrian needed to convince him he was in love with Amanda Cadwallader.

Physically, Amanda was the total opposite of Adrian's dark, elegant mother. Amanda's face was long and angular, more sensitive than beautiful. Her slim body was almost boyish. Her streaming auburn hair proclaimed both her femininity and her western innocence. All of which made her attractive to Adrian.

Beneath his hyperactive intellect, Adrian was searching for a woman who would help him escape his mother's looming presence. He was emotionally exhausted by their alternating bouts of affection and anger. He did not, he could not, stop loving Clarissa Van Ness. But he could not resolve her apparent indifference to his father's fate.

Defying and irritating his mother—and enjoying every minute of it—Adrian continued to see Amanda. He struggled to change her mind about the war in Europe. But her California naivete was impenetrable. She simply insisted America had everything to lose and nothing to gain by entering the war. Her knowledge of European history was zero, her interest in it zero minus. She did not really argue. She believed. Adrian told himself it was part of her innocence. He even began to doubt his own arguments in favor of intervention.

They did not spend all their time arguing about peace and war. At the movies, Adrian teased Amanda about her resemblance to Mary Pickford, whose beatific smile and cascades of auburn ringlets had made her America's sweetheart. Amanda disarmed him by taking his hand and whispering. "I only want to be your sweetheart."

As spring advanced, they went for walks in the country and rows on the Charles River. Amanda was a fervent believer in exercise in the open air. On one of these excursions on the water, Amanda revealed more than an enthusiasm for California's scenery behind her smile. Adrian grew weary at the oars and suggested they tie up at a grassy spot on the river above Watertown. They ate sandwiches Amanda had packed and washed them down with iced tea. The rich May sunshine inspired Amanda to rhapsodies on California. In a month they would separate for the summer.

"Will you miss me?" Amanda asked.

"Yes," Adrian said.

"A part of you likes me—and a part doesn't."

"That's not so," Adrian said, vehemently trying to conceal

the truth from her—and from himself. His mother's critique of Amanda often troubled him.

Amanda flung herself into his arms. Her kiss was wilder, more intense, than anything Adrian had ever imagined. He was still a virgin. In his head women were divided into good and bad. Some of his fellow freshmen were already sampling what the bad ones had to offer in Boston's Scollay Square brothels. But Adrian had remained aloof from this ritual as well as the other forms of college friendship.

"There's nothing to be ashamed of," Amanda whispered. "Come to California and I'll show you there's nothing to be ashamed of."

Dimly aware that he was being invited to play Adam to Amanda's Eve, Adrian spent the summer in Maine resisting a procession of young women Clarissa considered more suitable than his California temptress. To his mother's almost visible distress, the romance resumed when school reopened in the fall of 1916. Not even Amanda's enthusiastic support of Woodrow Wilson's campaign for a second term on the slogan "He kept us out of war" diminished Adrian's ardor. There were more kisses on the Charles and more dinners on Beacon Hill at which Amanda jousted with Clarissa with growing skill.

Amanda reiterated her invitation to California, which acquired orgiastic overtones in Adrian's mind. For a while he almost lost interest in the war in Europe. Then the Germans began proving all the nasty things interventionists like Adrian said about them, sinking American ships and trying to turn Mexico into a hostile foe on America's flank. Woodrow Wilson's balancing act on the neutrality tightrope ended with a crash and America declared war. Adrian wondered if this spelled finis to his romance with Amanda.

He was surprised—and pleased—to discover a warrior maiden on their next date. Like many other pacifists, she had been swept away by the president's soaring call for America to wage a war without hatred or greed, to make the world safe for democracy. Her father had volunteered for the army the day he read Wilson's speech in the *Los Angeles Times*.

On a Saturday night two months later, Adrian was lounging in his room, enjoying the prospect of taking Amanda to dinner in Boston. One of his floor mates said: "Van Ness. There's a red-haired creature outside weeping and wailing to see you."

Behind Amanda in Harvard Yard a battalion of seniors was practicing the manual of arms with wooden rifles. Like most of America, the school was feverishly committed to the war. Tears streamed down Amanda's face. She clutched a telegram in her hand. FATHER KILLED TRAINING ACCIDENT STOP. RETURN HOME AT ONCE STOP. MOTHER VERY ILL.

Her tears stirred the guilt Adrian had felt the day they met, when he had mocked her pacifism. He was swept with a masculine desire to comfort this fragile, wounded creature. "Darling, it's terrible. My heart breaks for you. But you have me. You have me to take care of you. I love you," he said.

Adrian took Amanda back to Wellesley where sobbing friends helped her pack. He hired a taxi that took them to Boston where Amanda boarded a train in North Station for her return to California. He wiped away her tears and kissed her. "I'll see you in a month. Two at the most."

Adrian rushed to his mother's house on Beacon Hill and announced his plan to move to California, marry Amanda Cadwallader and complete his education in some local college at night. "That is an absolutely absurd idea," Clarissa said.

Before Adrian could begin to think of an answer, Clarissa outlined her plan for Adrian's life. "I want you to become a man of substance, Adrian. You can't do that growing oranges in southern California. You also can't do it with a woman like Amanda for your wife. A man of substance needs a wife who glories in his success as her success, who understands his ambition and defers to it."

Defer? Adrian raged behind his impassive expression. Is that what you did to my father? Is that what you call it?

"Your little California friend will never defer because she doesn't understand. She doesn't have a worldly mind, Adrian. I daresay no one in southern California does. One acquires worldliness painfully, through disappointment, yes, through pain. Through an awareness that there are winters as well as summers in every life, cold and snow and icy rain as well as sunshine."

"She knows pain now," Adrian said. "We both know it. We know what it means to lose a father."

Adrian's reply suggested more than the loss inflicted by death. It evoked the several ways he had lost Robert Van Ness. The implied accusation aroused his mother to fury. "Go to California if you want to. But you'll go without a cent of my money."

Adrian was stunned. For some reason—perhaps the unstinting way his mother had always given him money—it never occurred to him that she would invoke this ultimate weapon. He stalked out of the house and spent the next month in an agony of indecision. A letter from Amanda reported nothing but chaos and despair at Casa Felicidad. Her mother was having a nervous breakdown. Her overbearing older brother had taken charge of the orange groves and the household. She begged Adrian to join her as soon as possible.

Adrian spent a week composing a reply.

Dearest One:

Your letter tore at my heart. I wish I could rush to your side. But my mother is absolutely opposed to our marriage and has vowed to disinherit me if we go through with it. This leaves me in an impossible position. I can only see one solution: to submit and get my degree so that I can make my way in the world—which will, I hope, lead me with all possible speed to your side. Until that day, you have my undying love. Tell me I have yours.

Adrian showed the letter to his mother before he mailed it. It was a gesture of defiance but Clarissa chose to ignore it. She put her hands on Adrian's shoulders. "That is a manly letter. And a wise one," she said. "But I hope you don't mean that last sentence about undying love."

"I do."

With a stifled cry she threw her arms around him. Adrian

remained rigid, his arms at his side, refusing to return the embrace.

Clarissa kissed him on the forehead and let him go. Adrian retreated to the bathroom and wiped off the kiss with a cold washcloth. He knew it was an infantile gesture. But it had symbolic power.

Idealism thundered in Adrian's soul. He was too young to fight to make the world safe for democracy. But he could and would make love and honor his guiding principles. He would marry Amanda Cadwallader and teach her to be the wife of a man of substance. He would acquire enough of that substance to defy Clarissa Ames Van Ness forever.

THE LAST PATROL

From ten thousand feet in the cloudless blue sky of November 1918, the Argonne battlefield was a crazy quilt of green fields and toy farmhouses and the dun gouged earth of no-man's-land. Beside Lieutenant Frank Buchanan flew his wingmate and best friend, Captain Buzz McCall, who had painted death's heads inside the red, white, and blue circles on his wings. They had transferred from the Lafayette Escadrille to the American Air Service when the United States entered the war in 1917.

Around them droned a half-dozen other planes in loose formation. They were finally flying swift stubby-winged French Spads, a plane that could outspeed and outdive the German Fokkers. For months they had been forced to fly Nieuport 28s, a tricky unforgiving plane that had killed more American pilots in training than the Germans had killed in combat. It stalled without warning and the wings had a tendency to fail in a roll or dive.

There were no American-designed planes on the western front. The inventors of the twentieth century's miracle machine had barely advanced beyond the clumsy craft the Wright Brothers flew at Kitty Hawk, while the British, the French, the Germans, the Italians, all had fighter planes that could fly over a hundred miles an hour.

A burst of machine-gun fire on his left broke through Frank's gloomy meditation. It was Buzz McCall, telling him to wake up. Buzz was squinting above and behind them. At first Frank could see nothing. The trick was not to focus your eyes but to let them roam the empty sky. It was one of the first things a pilot learned on the western front. A cluster of specks rapidly grew and acquired color: at least a dozen Fokker Dr 1 triplanes with black crosses on their green wings.

Down they came out of the sun, hoping for surprise. In their eagerness they forgot that their three winged planes, having very little weight and a lot of drag, dove slowly. They were violating one of the modern world's fundamental laws, the machine must be obeyed before it will obey. The Americans had time to react.

Frank pulled back on the stick and shoved his right foot down on the rudder pedal. Up, up he soared into a loop. Just over the vertical he cut his engine and pulled the stick back sharply. There he was, slightly dazed by the gravity pounding his chest, behind the lead Fokker as the German came out of his dive. Frank's Vickers .303 machine guns hammered and two streams of tracers tore into the German's cockpit. The Fokker went into a writhing spin, an unmistakable death throe.

His fifth kill. He was an ace. He could hardly compare himself to Buzz McCall or Eddie Rickenbacker, who had five times that many victories. Moreover, he might soon be a dead ace if he did not do something about another Fokker on his tail. Red tracer bullets whizzed between his wings, snapping struts as Frank took violent evasive action, essing left and right, his brain turning to terrified mush.

Behind him the German abruptly spun out of control, smoke gushing from his engine. Buzz McCall hung on his tail, pouring extra bullets into him to make sure he was not faking. It was the tenth or eleventh time Buzz had saved Frank's life.

Around them the sky was crisscrossed by diving, rolling, spinning Fokkers and Spads. Buzz pointed below them, where two Fokkers were about to give a floundering American the coup de grace. Down they roared to pull out on the Germans' tails. Frank had a perfect shot at the Fokker on the right. He pressed the trigger. Nothing. Cursing, he grabbed a small hammer he wore around his wrist and whacked at one of the Vickers' outside levers, just in front of his windshield. The guns stayed jammed.

Buzz's first burst, short and deadly as always, set the other German on fire. He spun away, gushing smoke and flames. But Frank's German methodically blasted a stream of lead into the American's cockpit. Frank saw the pilot, a boyish Iowan named Waller on his first mission, shudder in agony. He shoved his Spad into a dive. The German, smelling blood, followed him. A thousand feet down Waller pulled out and tried to roll to the right. The German anticipated the move and caught him with another burst, riddling the cockpit. Waller spun in, exploded and burned.

A second later the Fokker pulled up into a twisting loop called an immelman, after the German pilot who invented it. He came down on Frank's tail. It was a maneuver the lightweight triplane was designed to perform. But Buzz McCall was waiting for him down below. He rolled over and fired a burst into the Fokker's belly while flying upside down. The German, probably wounded, banked away and fled for home.

Frank flew in a daze, not quite sure he was alive. Six American planes were still in the sky. They had lost two of their green pilots. At least half the replacements failed to survive their first mission. Hardly surprising, when the average life of all the pilots on the western front was six weeks. Below them were four, five, burning wrecks. His stomach churning, Frank dove with the survivors to waggle his wings above the fallen. In his head he heard his mother's voice hissing: *death machine*.

On the ground, Buzz threw his arm around him. "Good shootin' up there, Wingman," he said. "Too bad your lousy limey guns jammed and we couldn't save Waller."

"We're sending those kids up without enough training. It's murder, Buzz!"

"What's this, what happened?"

It was their squadron commander, a lean West Pointer named Kinkaid. With him was a handsome soldier in gleaming black riding boots and a broad-brimmed campaign hat tipped at a cocky angle. He had a brigadier general's star on his collar. Behind him trailed a photographer and several reporters.

"We ran into the flying circus and whipped their asses, Colonel," Buzz said. "I got two of them, Frank here got one. We lost two of the new guys—Waller and Kane."

"Two more kills," said the brigadier. "That means you're only three behind Rickenbacker. I'm Billy Mitchell. I came down to pin a medal on you, Captain."

Buzz remembered he was in the army and saluted the most popular general in the American Air Service. "Pleased to meet you, sir. This is Lieutenant Frank Buchanan. He got his fifth today. A real beauty."

Buzz described the way they had attacked the Germans as they came out of their dive. "That's the kind of aggressive tactics I want up there. That's the American style," Mitchell said.

They adjourned to the officers' mess, where champagne bottles popped and glasses were raised in a silent toast to the dead, then flung into the fireplace. Outside, the ground crews and pilots lined up in a semblance of military formation and Mitchell pinned a Distinguished Service Cross on Buzz McCall.

He added to the commendation a speech full of fiery prophecy. Fliers like Buzz McCall were demonstrating what Americans could do in the air against German veterans. "If this war lasts another six months, we'll wipe the Germans out of the sky. Then we'll show General Pershing and that circle of dunderheads he's got around him what air power can do for their infantry."

Flashbulbs popped, the reporters took notes. General Mitchell was already semi-famous for his running battle with

Pershing's staff, who scoffed at the importance of air power. Mitchell told them he was assembling a force of de Havilland bombers that would demolish enemy airfields and supply dumps and arms factories if the Germans rejected the Allies' armistice terms and kept fighting.

Two hours later, led by General Mitchell driving a black sedan at ninety miles an hour, the squadron headed for the nearby city of Toul to celebrate Buzz's medal. They started with dinner at the Three Hussars, the best restaurant in town. Fueled by more champagne, Mitchell talked about air power in future wars with visionary fervor. The plane would soon make the infantry and the warship superfluous.

"The bombers of tomorrow will make this war's attacks on London and Paris look like acts of tender mercy," roared the general. "They'll be no need to send millions of men to die in the trenches. The war will be over the moment one side achieves air superiority."

"Let's drink to that!" Buzz shouted. "Air superiority!"

Frank Buchanan lurched to his feet with the rest of his by now ossified squadron mates. "General," he said. "I hope you're not saying Americans—would bomb cities—kill women and children—the way the Germans—"

"The British are doing it right now in the Rhineland," Mitchell roared. "They dropped some bombs in a fucking schoolyard last week and killed about sixty *kinder*. Those things'll happen till we get better bombsights. Then—*plunk*— we'll be able to put a thousand-pounder down a goddamn factory chimney!"

After dinner, the squadron and General Mitchell adjourned next door to Madame Undine's, the best brothel in the city. It was stocked with enough champagne to drown an infantry division and enough mademoiselles from Armentieres and elsewhere to make Valhalla look like a Methodist camp meeting.

At midnight Frank found himself in bed with two dimpled whores named Cheri and Marguerite. They were sisters. Marguerite was going around the world, licking him from the back of his neck to the soles of his feet, while Cheri was rolling her tongue around and around his aching joystick. He was Craig again, happy, proud, indifferent to death. He passed out as he came in Cheri's mouth.

The party raged around him and in the blank darkness Frank dreamt of a plane with a fuselage as round and smooth as a gun barrel, a plane that swallowed its wheels after take-off and had only one wing, unsupported by struts. He leaped out of bed and stumbled over male and female bodies in various stages of undress to find a pen and paper and sketch it.

His mother hissed *death machine* but he defied her. This was a creature of speed and beauty, as vibrant with life as the Elgin marbles he had seen in the British Museum. It would make American pilots supreme in the air. That meant peace, not war.

"What the hell is that?"

It was Buzz McCall, glowering over his shoulder at the sketch.

"A plane we ought to build."

"You'd never get me to fly a fucking monoplane."

Louis Bleriot had flown the English Channel in a mono-plane. But he soon gave the design a bad name because his wings frequently fell off. Frank began explaining that the problem was not the single wing but its shape and its position on Bleriot's monoplanes.

"Let's go," Buzz said. "We've got the dawn patrol."

In a flash, as if the champagne fumes in his head had exploded, Frank was back in the dogfight. The motors roared, the machine guns chattered, the planes blazed and spun down to doom.

He could not go up again. He was not Craig, he was Frank, the younger brother with these beautiful creatures of the sky in his head. He had no confidence in either his luck or his skill as a pursuit pilot.

"I can't do it, Buzz. I don't want to die until I see this plane—other planes—in the air—"

"What the fuck is this?"

Buzz stepped back as if he wanted to get a better look at his contemptible wingman. "Why should I die?" he mocked.

"Do you think you're better than the rest of us, because you can draw pretty paper airplanes?"

Yes, Frank wanted to shout. He wanted to denounce everything, the war, the drunken parties at Madame Undine's, the dying. The endless dying. Before he could speak, Buzz hit him with a right cross that sent him hurtling across the room to crash into the opposite wall.

The next thing Frank knew he was on the floor and Buzz was shoving a foot his chest. "Are you comin'?"

Frank lurched to his feet. He was a head taller than Buzz but there was no thought of hitting him back. Buzz was Craig, curing another outbreak of momma's boyitis. "I'm sorry," he said.

"Nobody's gonna shoot you down as long as I'm up there with you," Buzz said. "We went into this fuckin' war together and we're comin' out together."

Buzz rounded up the rest of the patrol and they wobbled into the semi-dark street. Toward them panted Madame Undine, the fat blond-ringleted mistress of their revels. Her eyes bulged, tears streaked the layer of powder on her dumpling face. *"C'est fini!"* she cried. *"La guerre, c'est fini!"*

Frank threw his arms around Madame Undine and gave her a kiss. He was going to live. He was going to build the beautiful planes that flew in his head.

"Son of a bitch!" Buzz said. Peace meant he would never pass Eddie Rickenbacker and become the top American ace.

Behind him, General Mitchell looked even more disappointed. "What the hell am I going to do with all those beautiful bombers?" he said.

LOVE IN A COLD CLIMATE

The Negro jazz band in the SS *Berengaria*'s main salon was playing "There'll Be a Hot Time in the Old Town Tonight." In his mind's eye twenty-year-old Adrian Van Ness could see the dancers gyrating across the polished teak dance floor, the men in bright sports coats, the women in beaded dresses, their bobbed hair bouncing, their skirts revealing legs all the way to the knees and occasionally a silk-stockinged thigh.

Adrian wanted to be out there with the dancers. Instead he was standing on the main deck, holding his wife Amanda's hand while she fretted over the future health of a child they had yet to conceive. For a moment Adrian felt bewildered by the way life had catapulted him from carefree youth to husband and prospective father.

"Darling, I assure you England isn't an unhealthy country."

"Adrian, I can bear it for your sake. But what if the baby has weak lungs? All that dreadful fog and rain—"

"If the slightest problem develops, I'll quit my job in an instant and we'll take the first ship to California."

"I dread the thought of asking you that. I love you, Adrian. I'm terrified I'll make you unhappy."

The jazz band fell silent. It was past midnight. "Why don't you say good night to your mother?" Amanda said.

Adrian threaded his way through the tables to a corner of the salon, where Clarissa Van Ness was chatting with a sleek, gray-haired Italian nobleman. She wore a single strand of pearls around her swan-like neck, long white gloves, and a low-cut beaded black dress by Paul Poiret, the latest rage among Paris couturiers.

"Where's Amanda?" Clarissa said in her silkiest voice. "I was hoping you'd both join me for a nightcap."

"She's not feeling very well."

"Poor dear. I hope she gets her sea legs soon."

Everyone was being marvelously polite. Adrian's excuse avoided saying Amanda wanted to have as little to do with Clarissa Van Ness as possible, a sentiment that Adrian endorsed—and Clarissa ignored. She had blithely insisted on sailing with them to help Adrian launch his career as a merchant banker in London.

Her presence made Adrian uneasy. He wondered if she thought he carried his father's failure with him, like a virus. Did she plan to supervise his office conduct, his business decisions, to make sure he did not repeat Robert Van Ness's blunder?

Adrian had married Amanda in spite of Clarissa's desperate attempts to dissuade him. In fact, he had used her disapproval to wangle this opportunity to make himself a man of substance as rapidly as possible. He let Clarissa lure him to England last summer to renew their ties with Geoffrey Tillotson and other friends.

Tillotson's son Peter had been shot down and killed on the last day of the war. He seemed especially touched by Adrian's sympathy. Before long he was urging him to consider the possibility of coming to work for his family's merchant banking firm, Tillotson Brothers, Ltd., after his graduation from Harvard.

In the next year, Clarissa had mustered all her finesse to make this invitation as attractive as possible. She talked about the power and prestige of London's merchant bankers. She bombarded Adrian with stories from their glory days, when Byron celebrated them as men whose "every loan . . . seats a Nation or upsets a throne."

After a deliciously sadistic show of reluctance, Adrian accepted Tillotson's offer—and announced his plans to marry Amanda within a week of his graduation. A stunned Clarissa could only accept it with muted murmurs of regret. The wedding took place in Boston. Amanda's mother's mental condition had worsened, making Casa Felicidad, the family's Orange County home, unsuitable.

The newlyweds honeymooned for a week in Bar Harbor.

It did not take Adrian long to realize Amanda had changed. Her father's death, her mother's nervous collapse, had damaged her ebullient trust in the future, which had been one of the most appealing aspects of her innocence. She felt guilty about leaving her mother to the not very tender care of her half-brother. She had no enthusiasm for further clashes with Clarissa.

A northeast storm engulfed the Maine coast with freezing rain and wind for their entire honeymoon. Although a shivering Amanda offered herself wholeheartedly, even frantically, to Adrian, she kept apologizing for her failure to "let go," to make him truly happy. She blamed the awful weather and herself for not overruling her penny-pinching brother and insisting on a California wedding. Adrian, for whom self-control was basic, saw no virtue in letting go and could not understand her distress.

Amanda's dislike of Maine in June soon extended to worries about England's fog and rain. Adrian gradually realized she saw this sojourn in London as little more than an extended honeymoon before they moved to California. Adrian soothed her with vague promises and hoped she would like England in spite of her doubts.

Geoffrey Tillotson met the *Berengaria* at Southampton and they drove to London in his yellow Hispano-Suiza Cabriolet. Listening to him talk, Adrian had the heady sense of being at the vital center of the civilized world. Having just won the most stupendous war in history, England was the most powerful nation on the globe. India, South Africa, Iraq, Palestine, Persia, Bulgaria, Turkey, Greece—their condition, their fate, rested on decisions made in Parliament and 10 Downing Street—and in the banks where the financial resources of the empire were mustered.

There were some parts of the world that were not under English control. Adrian was surprised by a note of uneasiness in Tillotson's voice as he discussed Russia, where the Bolsheviks were on their way to winning a civil war and taking charge of the country. He was almost as disturbed by the emergence of an Italian socialist, Benito Mussolini, as a power in Italy.

"Communism—socialism—they're both demagogic rot—," Tillotson growled.

"I'm not sure that's true," Amanda said as the chauffeur eased the Hispano-Suiza to a stop in front of the Ritz Hotel. "In California we've seen the evil results of unrestrained capitalism. My father was one of the leaders in the fight against the railroad barons."

Clarissa's eyes asked Adrian what he thought of his California bride. In their room, Adrian told Amanda to keep her opinions to herself from now on. They went to bed angry, not the best beginning for an extended honeymoon.

The next day Adrian reported for work at Tillotson Brothers, Ltd. His American eyes were dismayed by the company's offices. The redbrick Queen Anne building was two hundred years old and looked it. A barely legible rusty sign next to the entrance was the only evidence of ownership. Inside there was a rabbit warren of extra floors and rooms and cubicles where aging clerks clipped stock coupons or entered mysterious figures in thick red ledgers. Cage-like elevators creaked and clattered.

In the oak-paneled partners' room, cravatted Tillotsons of earlier generations stared with aplomb from the walls. A halfdozen partners sat at polished mahogany tables, conferring with clients in low tones or reading the *London Times*. The stationery had the firm's address, 16 Old Jewry Lane, and the telephone number on it but not its name. Unobtrusive was the watchword of British merchant banking.

Geoffrey Tillotson helped the newlyweds find a comfortable flat in Mayfair on a tiny street called Islington Mews and proposed Adrian for the Garrick and the Athenaeum clubs. He arranged invitations to weekend parties at a halfdozen country houses. Usually Tillotson and Clarissa came to the same party and Geoffrey introduced Adrian to prospective clients. It was all so low-keyed, so casual, Adrian had no sense of being under examination.

His fear that Clarissa would breathe down his neck soon vanished. But his hope that Amanda would like England evaporated almost as fast. Deprived of her native sunshine, she got one cold after another. She sat around their flat shiv-

ering in two sweaters, gulping cough medicine, inserting
nose drops. This did not do much for their sex life. The ardor
Amanda had promised him in his Harvard days vanished in
tearful laments for California.

At work, Adrian filed routine letters from the African
loans department. Occasionally, familiar names from Anson
days relieved the tedium. Many of his former schoolmates
were in the army or the civil service in Nigeria, East Africa,
and other outposts. A letter from Kenya was especially welcome—it was from his Italian friend Ponty, who was running
a vast coffee plantation purchased by his family with some
help from Tillotson Brothers. He was still in love with flying.
He had a French-made Caudron R11 three-seater that he flew
all over East Africa.

Adrian lunched with Tillotson several times a month in
the partners' top-floor dining room and was told he was doing splendidly. Tillotson talked offhandedly about the firm's
recent investments in Chilean copper mines, South African
railroads, Canadian lumbering, explaining why each one
seemed a good idea. Invariably it came down to knowing
that up the road certain events or changes in government
policy would make the investment very profitable.

"A merchant banker has to be a bit of a crystal-ball gazer,"
Tillotson said. "Forethought. It's the key to success. Of
course it helps to know a bit more than the next fellow."

To acquire this inside information, Tillotson partners crisscrossed the globe, hobnobbing with politicians and business
leaders on every continent, sojourning for a year at a time
in Hong Kong, Melbourne, Singapore, New York. The firm
no longer invested much of its own money. It acted as a
middleman, bringing together potential lenders and borrow-
ers. Lately, the emergence of an aggressive Labour Party
preaching socialism in England inclined a great many people
to look abroad for safe places to put their money. Tillotson
thought a bright young American like Adrian Van Ness
might be just the man to encourage the worriers to make
their investments through Tillotson Brothers, who had a long
tradition of successful investing in the United States.

"We put two hundred million pounds into your country

during and after the Civil War," Tillotson said. "We did especially well on the Union Pacific."

"The railroad?" Adrian said.

"We built the bloody thing," Tillotson said. "Sent you the Irishmen to do the digging and the money for the rails and locomotives. Your great-grandfather did wonders with the money."

"My great-grandfather?"

"You Americans are unbelievable. You only remember what happened yesterday. My grandfather, Geoffrey Tillotson the third, advanced most of the money from here. Your great-grandfather, Congressman Oakes Ames, was the man who organized Credit Mobilier. Surely you've heard of that?"

Adrian could only shake his head. He had majored in European history at Harvard. "Hmm," Tillotson said. "Maybe I'm talking out of turn. Don't mention it to your mother."

Obviously trying to change the subject, Tillotson said: "What do you know about the airplane business in America?"

"There isn't any, as far as I know."

"There's bound to be one. Everybody in Europe's building planes and starting airlines. Even the bloody Germans. We've got four airlines flying the Channel and the French have two. We've put money into all of the British lines. Eventually they'll consolidate and we might well control the whole kit. The plane is the machine of the future, my boy. That's been the root of my interest in it from the day I saw one fly."

For the moment, Tillotson's remarks about Oakes Ames had more impact than his prophecies about the airplane. The historian in Adrian was chagrinned by his ignorance of his mother's family. On the way home from work, he stopped at the London Library and got out a book on Credit Mobilier. He read it with mounting astonishment until midnight.

Credit Mobilier was a holding company that had built the Union Pacific, a railroad that had a decisive impact on the outcome of the Civil War. Mobilier was also a conduit for massive bribes that Adrian's maternal great-grandfather,

Congressman Oakes Ames, paid to dozens of congressmen and senators to get the railroad government subsidies and a clear title to its right of way. When one of the promoters, feeling he had not gotten a fair share of the profits, sent a batch of Ames's letters to the *New York Sun,* a stupendous scandal erupted, which ended in 1869 with the House of Representatives voting 182 to 36 to "absolutely condemn the conduct of Oakes Ames."

In his astonishment, Adrian read quite a lot of this aloud to Amanda. At midnight, he decided he had to discuss it with his mother and rushed from his flat into a classic London fog. As his cab chugged though shrouded Mayfair, he began anticipating the first frank conversation he had ever had with Clarissa Ames Van Ness. Perhaps it would lead to an explanation of his father's ruin. Had he been persecuted because he was Oakes Ames's grandson-in-law?

Adrian bolted across the Ritz's long marbled lobby and rode to the fifth floor in the elephantine lift. As he charged down the red-carpeted upper hall, a door opened at the far end and a voice, which he recognized as his mother's, said: "Good night, my dearest."

A man's voice said: "I look forward to the weekend."

A few doors away was a room-service pantry. Adrian bounded into it and watched from its dark recess as Geoffrey Tillotson walked to the elevator, pressed the button, and departed.

Adrian did not confront his mother with this new, infinitely more stunning revelation. He was her son, with the same instinct for secrecy and evasion. He walked back through the fog to his flat, where he ignored Amanda's pleas to tell him what was wrong. He sent her to bed and sat in the small study composing a list of adjectives to describe his mother.

lascivious	profligate	lubricious
loose	amoral	hedonistic
adulterous	lecherous	disreputable

He decided he preferred *lubricious.* It best described the cold, concealed lust with which Clarissa and Geoffrey satisfied their appetites. Adrian stared out at the fog, seeing life for the first time with adult eyes. Tugboats hooted derisively on the Thames. Occasionally a larger vessel emitted a long, mocking moan.

In the bedroom slept his California wife whom he had married in his adolescent American idealism, never realizing that a different way of life awaited men of substance. If his mother had only had the courage to tell him. But she clung to her shameful secret, knowing he would condemn her in his ruined father's name.

Now Adrian saw the hidden purpose of the weekend house parties. They were all assignations between lovers like Geoffrey and Clarissa. Men of substance, men with forethought, parked their wives elsewhere and rendezvoused with lubricious women, while the middle and lower classes plodded through torturous moral lives.

The sheer duration of Clarissa's deception staggered Adrian almost as much as the fact. Geoffrey had been her lover when they watched Bleriot fly the Channel. For years before that, probably. All the years she had left her ruined husband behind her in New York to enjoy the company of a man of substance.

Substance? Money! That night the word was scorched into Adrian's brain. The word and its synonyms. Power, pleasure, freedom, lust, desire, fulfillment. And its antonyms: weakness, pain, humiliation, bondage, frustration, deception, loss.

In the morning, a snuffling Amanda begged him to tell her why he had not come to bed until dawn. Was he disturbed to discover he had an ancestor like Oakes Ames, a man as crooked and corrupt as the worst of the California railroad barons?

Adrian's arm froze in the act of raising his coffee cup to his mouth. His historian's brain shifted into gear. Crooked, corrupt? Oakes Ames, the bluff, blunt shovel maker from Massachusetts who had built the railroad that rescued the United States from dissolution?

Condemned by the hypocrites and thieves in Congress who took his money, Oakes Ames scorned them all and went home refusing to admit an iota of guilt. Here was a man who looked ruin in the eye and defied it. Who did not give a damn if the world considered him corrupt or disgraced. He was a hero who had saved his country.

In a flash Adrian saw an ancestor he could respect, even love. An ancestor who ignored—no, transcended—the approval of women. The fact that both Clarissa and Amanda condemned Oakes Ames, the one in her Boston silence, the other in her California naivete, was the best possible argument in his favor. Oakes Ames combined substance and heroism, money and patriotism, power and indifference to the vacuous morality of the herd.

"I don't think he was corrupt," Adrian said. "I think you need a different word for him. Effective?"

"He debauched Congress!"

"I suspect that was a contradiction in terms then—and probably still is one."

"Adrian—that's the crudest sort of cynicism. Is that what merchant banking does to you?"

"No. It's what history does to you," Adrian said.

DOWN BY THE RIVERSIDE

A few feet away, the Yellowstone River was a silent silver ribbon in the twilight. The snow-tipped peaks of the Bitterroot Range towered in the distance, cold, silent, serene. The frowning curly-haired young pilot sat with his back against a tree, his face toward the mountains. "The war was a disgrace," Charles Lindbergh said. "A national disgrace."

"In more ways than one, Lindy," Frank Buchanan said.

Fellow members of the Reynolds Air Circus, Frank and Lindbergh had spent the summer of 1922 barnstorming across Montana and Wyoming, risking their planes and their necks at county fairs and rodeos. Frank admired Lindbergh's skill as a pilot. There was nothing he could not make his

Lincoln Standard biplane do in the air. Inside loops, stall spins, rolling pullouts. Only Buzz McCall could match him. Two members of the circus had been killed trying to imitate them. Frank, flying a Curtiss Jenny, a leftover wartime trainer that he had picked up for fifty dollars and rebuilt himself, did not even try.

Lindbergh had been too young to get into the war. But he would have refused to fight, even if he had been drafted. He had inherited a violent opposition to it from his congressman father, who had written a book accusing the British and Wall Street of sucking America into the carnage. His father had been called a traitor and his political career had been destroyed, leaving Lindy with a deep contempt for popular opinion. Already detesting the war for his own reasons, Frank was delighted to add Lindy's populist litany to his creed.

When they were not denouncing the war, Frank and Lindy bemoaned the current state of American aviation. The public only seemed interested in the daring and spectacular side of flying. When two army lieutenants piloted a Dutch Fokker T-2 coast-to-coast in just under twenty-seven hours, Frank had been in San Diego when they landed. The city had gone crazy, honking car horns and blowing factory whistles. But no one seemed interested in using airplanes in any practical or constructive way.

Not even in the military could the advocates of air power make any headway. General Billy Mitchell was still predicting that the plane could make fleets and armies obsolete. No one paid the slightest attention to him, even when he proved it by sinking two obsolete battleships with two-thousand-pound bombs off the Virginia coast. The United States was manufacturing automobiles and vacuum cleaners and radio sets by the millions. Planes? A handful of stubborn believers in isolated hangars in upstate New York, central Kansas, and southern California were making a few hundred.

None of the plane makers was interested in the ideas Frank Buchanan had brought back from the three years he had spent studying aerodynamics and aircraft design with French and British manufacturers. So here he was, barnstorming.

"What are you going to do for the winter, Lindy?" Frank asked. "Head for California?"

Lindbergh shook his head. "I'm going home to make enough money to buy a better plane. First, though, I'm going to float down the Yellowstone to the mouth of the Missouri in that." He pointed to a big wide-bottomed rowboat tied to a stake on the riverbank.

"Not a bad idea. You want to improve it?" Frank pointed across the green grass of their camp to the main tent. In front of it, a tiny girl with streaming blond hair was grilling steaks on a bed of coals. "Take Sammy with you," he said. "Two weeks on the Yellowstone with her will blow the gloom out of your head."

Lindbergh pulled a fistful of grass out of the ground and studied the wet roots. "No. I need some time alone."

Lindbergh stalked down to the riverbank to inspect his boat. Frank Buchanan contemplated Samantha Soames against the backdrop of the Rockies. She was as beautiful—and as wild—as an eagle or a mountain lion on those looming slopes. She appealed simultaneously to Craig, the buccaneering pilot whose spirit Frank was sustaining, and Frank, the artist-designer who found beautiful women irresistible.

Sammy was a Wyoming rancher's daughter. Her father had kicked her into a snowdrift when he caught her in the bunkhouse with one of the hired hands. She soon decided aviators were more interesting than cowboys and wound up with Raynald Reynolds. He had made her America's first female wing walker—and his mistress.

Frank strolled over to the chuckfire. "I was just talking to the Silent Swede. Lindy. He says he's going to float down the Yellowstone in that boat and he wants you to come with him. But he doesn't have the nerve to ask you."

Samantha Soames flipped a three-inch-thick steak. "Ain't there a poem about a guy who goes to a girl to ask her favor for some third party?"

" 'The Courtship of Miles Standish' by Henry Wadsworth Longfellow."

"Yeah. Longfellow. I always liked his name. Do you think he was?" She grinned and flipped another steak. "Guess only

Mrs. Longfellow knew for sure. Anyway, there's this punch line in the poem. What was it?"

" 'Speak for yourself, John.' "

"Are you gettin' the message? Or do I have to hit you on the head with a sledgehammer? Daddy used to say that was the only way to get a steer's attention. Some pilots'r dumber than steers, I swear."

"I promised Buzz McCall I'd go to California with him."

"So? I like him too. If you go along with that sort of effrontery." Samantha grinned and flipped another steak. "Did I use that word right? I heard you use it the other night around the campfire. Somethin' about Reynolds havin' it."

"The effrontery to keep ninety percent of the money and only do ten percent of the flying."

Samantha held out a small, grimy hand. "Tell Lindy he's out of luck. I'm lookin' for some education. That's what I like about flyin' out with you and Buzz. You got lots of poetry and big words in your head. I figure Buzz'll take care of the other side of my ruined character."

Frank plucked a steak off the fire and strolled over to the tent he shared with Buzz McCall. He raised the flap and there was Buzz on his back, smiling at him upside down, not an unusual way of looking at things for a pilot. Buzz had both hands on the oversize breasts of a lady rancher who owned forty thousand acres near Fort Peck. She had been following them from show to show for weeks. Her husband had been killed in France.

"Come back in a half hour, sport," Buzz said.

From the darkening distance rose the incongruous sound of voices singing: "What a Friend We Have in Jesus." Booming above the mostly off-key chorus were the basso tones of the Rev. Abel Flutterman. Abel had been following the Reynolds Circus around all summer, preaching "the winged gospel" to the thousands of patrons the air shows attracted. According to Abel, who was five-five and weighed about three hundred pounds, the plane was proof that mankind had entered a new spiritual phase, in which they would surmount the evils of the flesh and achieve unparalleled purity of spirit. Frank sat down under a tree and listened to the sacred music mingling with the lady rancher's cries of ecstasy while he consumed the steak. Sweet music of the sort he soon hoped to be making with Samantha Soames. Buzz eventually emerged from the tent while the lady rancher used the more discreet rear entrance.

"She wants me to marry her," Buzz said, combing his jet-black hair. "She'll buy me any kind of plane I want."

Buchanan offered Buzz a chunk of steak. It was not the first nor would it be the last proposition of this sort Buzz received. His compact body emanated animal magnetism. Recklessness of an ultimate variety glinted in his gray eyes, flashed in his slanting grin. Why any woman thought she could domesticate him was a mystery.

"Sammy's coming to California with us. She says she can keep us both happy."

Buzz squinted though the deepening twilight toward the chuckfire. "Is that okay with you?"

"Sure."

"Reynolds won't like it."

"Doesn't that make it even more appealing?"

"What about next summer when we need the work?"

"Who knows where we'll be next summer? You could be back in the army. I could be running my own aircraft company."

"Yeah. Or we could both be on some bread line in Dubuque behind Billy Mitchell and the rest of the Army Air Corps."

Buzz was bitter about the way America had abandoned her fliers. General Billy Mitchell had recruited Buzz for the provisional air brigade that had dropped the bombs on the battleships to demonstrate the potency of air power. The brigade had been disbanded a week later. The Navy and Army brass had combined forces to smear Mitchell as a liar and a publicity hound.

A short figure in a black flight jacket, white scarf, and tan jodhpurs strutted up to them. Raynald Reynolds had flown for the British during the war and had acquired pretensions to being a gentleman. "Where are you lads winging it for the winter?" he said.

"Florida," Frank said. "Or Texas."

"I'm thinking of Mexico," Reynolds said. "They'd love Sammy down there. Mexicans adore blond hair. But she doesn't want to go."

"Maybe she's bored with the way you fly your crate like an old lady with rheumatism," Buzz said.

"I don't believe in taking unnecessary chances," Reynolds huffed. "I don't ask my pilots to take any either. You and Lindbergh take chances up there that aren't necessary to please the public. I've made that veddy clear."

"Veddy clear," Buzz said.

"I don't think I want you back next year, McCall. You're a disruptive influence. The same goes for you, Buchanan."

"Who knows where we'll all be next year?" Buzz said, winking at Frank.

At dawn the next morning Buzz and Frank bumped down the pasture that passed for an airfield. Sammy was in the front seat of Frank's Jenny; her suitcase was stashed in the backseat of Buzz's Spad. Reynolds came running out of his tent, pulling on his jodhpurs and gesticulating wildly. The combination resulted in loss of control of the jodhpurs, which collapsed to knee level, pitching him into a nose-first landing.

At five hundred feet, Buzz did one of his more spectacular loops, pulling out so low Lindbergh and other pilots who were emerging from their tents threw themselves flat to escape decapitation. As Buzz whizzed over the prone Reynolds, something pink fluttered from his cockpit: a pair of Sammy's panties.

Reynolds raced to his Sopwith Camel and took off in pursuit. The Camel's superior airspeed soon overtook Frank and Buzz. Reynolds pulled alongside Frank's Jenny, shouting *"I love you."* The words were drowned by the roar of the motors. But Frank had no trouble reading the Englishman's lips. Sammy paid no attention to him.

Buzz McCall did a double barrel roll that put him directly above Reynolds's Camel. *Whump*—his wheels crunched into Reynolds's top wing. *Whump*—he did it again. Spars and fabric flew off. The appalled Reynolds dove for safety. Buzz followed him down, firing the machine guns mounted on his cowling. He was shooting blanks, of course. All the planes were equipped with guns to simulate dogfights at the air shows. Buzz was only adding to Reynolds's humiliation.

Reynolds pulled out of his dive at about 1,000 feet with Buzz still on his tail. As the Englishman rolled to the left, the top wing on that side crumpled like a piece of wet cardboard. The Camel slid into a spin, whirling down, down toward the green earth. Frank heard Sammy cry: "Oh, my God!"

Reynolds never even came close to pulling out. He hit nose first and the plane exploded into a geyser of flame. "He murdered him," Sammy cried.

They landed outside a town in northern Idaho and telephoned the Montana state police to report the "accident." Sammy was so furious with Buzz, she would not go near him that first night. In Frank Buchanan's tent, she was almost as reluctant to let him touch her, especially when he tried to tell her Buzz had not intended to kill Reynolds.

Sammy wiped away tears. "It's just awful thinkin' of someone dyin' like that for no reason."

Having seen so many pilots die for no apparent reason in France, Frank was unable to share her grief. But he respected it. "You don't have to do anything for me tonight," he said. "I'll read you a poem instead."

He pulled out a thin volume with the word *Lustra* in large letters on the ocher cover.

"What's that word mean?" Sammy asked.

"It's Latin. *Lustra* are offerings to the gods to atone for the sins of the people."

He opened the book at random and began reading "Dance Figure."

> *Dark eyed, O woman of my dreams*
> *Thine arms are as a young sapling under the bark;*
> *Thy face as a river with lights.*

"Shhhhh-it" Sammy said. "Who wrote that?"

"Ezra Pound. A poet I met in England."

"Do you think my face is a river with lights?"

"There's light in it. Beautiful shimmering light sometimes."

"Effrontery." Sammy giggled. She rolled off her cot onto Frank's. "There's nothin' we can do for Renny, is there?"

She kissed him on the mouth. "Read me another poem by this guy Pound."

Frank flipped the pages of *Lustra*.

Woman? O Woman is a consummate rage,
But dead, or asleep, she pleases.
Take her. She has two excellent seasons.

Sammy kissed him harder. "I like that."

For the first time Frank allowed himself to admit how much he wanted this woman. Trembling with a summer's desire that a dozen other women had not satisfied, he lifted Sammy's blouse over her head and kissed the nipples of her small snub breasts. Her neck was wreathed in her golden hair. She kicked off her denim skirt and more golden hair gleamed in the moonlit darkness.

"You don't have to," he whispered, suddenly afraid he would disappoint her.

"It's my lustra," she murmured. She took his hand and placed it on the mound of yellow hair below her waist. "Can you find the right place down there?"

He found the place with no difficulty. "Hey," Sammy gasped. "We're gainin' altitude." She wrapped her small hand around his ecstatic penis. "Damn," she said. "Whyn't you tell me you had a stick this big? I would've been flyin' with you in July."

"I wanted to surprise you."

"Ready for some stunts, pilot?"

Her fragile body was so light, so limber, yet so taut with desire, so vivid with movement, Frank Buchanan almost spoke. He almost shoved aside Craig and said the unthinkable words, *I love you*. Did Sammy sense love there beneath his pulsing skin? Frank hoped so.

It was long past midnight when they subsided into sleep. At dawn they were awakened by the roar of Buzz's engine.

"Let's go, lovebirds," he shouted outside the tent flap. "We got a day's flyin' to do. The weather don't look so great to me."

Sullen cirrostratus clouds were covering most of the sky. That usually meant rain within twenty-four hours. They flew south across Wyoming and Colorado into Arizona. It was spectacular open country, with the Sierras towering on the right and endless miles of prairie and desert beneath them. A headwind blew the bad weather north into Canada, and they landed that night outside Flagstaff.

"Am I still on the blacklist?" Buzz asked, after dinner.

"Oh, I guess not," Sammy said. "A deal's a deal."

Frank was amazed by the pain he felt when Sammy disappeared into Buzz's tent. He ordered himself to grow up. He reminded himself of how often Buzz had saved his life on the western front. He tried to tell himself there was nothing special about Samantha Soames except that spectacular blond hair. She was like a hundred, a thousand other women who were crazy about pilots.

An hour later, Sammy was still inside Buzz's tent and Frank was pacing up and down in the desert beyond the glow of the campfire, barely able to restrain his rage. He finally went to bed and lay rigid on his cot, trying to think of other things. He did not know what time it was when Sammy lay down in the cot beside him.

In the morning Frank recoiled from Buzz's casual cheer. Sammy seemed almost as morose. Frank could not decide whether that was a good or bad sign. They flew across Arizona into California. Soon they were in the high desert, with its miles of scrub grass and lonely Joshua trees. They landed on a dry lake bed outside the tiny town of Muroc. Los Angeles was just over the San Gabriel Mountains, less than an hour's flying away.

A half-dozen people came out to inspect the planes but no one seemed interested in paying five dollars for a half hour in the air. Buzz could not resist taking two younger women up free. Around the campfire they discussed their prospects for making a living in California. The care and feeding of gasoline engines was expensive. Buzz thought Sammy would draw crowds as a wing walker. He had ideas for a series of hair-raising stunts, including a barrel roll with her on the wing and a midair transfer from his Spad to Frank's Jenny.

"Are you willing, Sammy?" Frank said. "We're asking you to take most of the chances."

"Sure," Sammy said.

That night Sammy came to Frank's tent and asked him to read her more poetry. He chose his favorite among Pound's translations from the Provençal, in which the troubadour tells his unfaithful beloved he will never find another woman like her, so he is going to select traits from a dozen women and "make me a borrowed lady."

"Why did you read that one?"

"I have a feeling I've lost you."

"Buzz is in his tent right now with one of the girls he took up today. Yet I'll come to him if he wants me. I wanted him the first time I saw him. It just grew and grew all summer. Why is that, Frank?"

"I don't know."

"I'll be good to you too. I really do want to learn some more poems and big words. Teach me another one now."

"Hedonist."

"What's it mean?"

"Someone who lives only for pleasure."

"That's Buzz, isn't it. Or is it me?"

"It's all of us."

Throughout the winter of 1921, Frank and Buzz and Sammy worked the great central valley of California, where people seldom saw planes. They fitted Buzz's plane with the foot grips and the wire that would enable Sammy to stand on his wing, only a few feet from the whirling propeller. The first time Buzz did a barrel roll with her in that position, her right hand holding the wire, the left held defiantly aloft, Frank almost lost control of his Jenny. But Sammy came out of the roll unfazed, smiling, her blond hair streaming behind her in the airflow.

The midair transfer was a tricky business in even a moderate wind. Sammy walked out on Buzz's lower wing and held up one finger. They both started counting to thirteen.

Precisely at that number, chosen by Sammy as a defiance of fate, she stepped gracefully, casually from Buzz's wing onto Frank's, and strolled to his front cockpit.

Thousands of California's farmers paid five dollars a head to see a beautiful woman risk death in an airplane. A man could never have attracted the crowds they drew that winter from towns like Grenada, Weed, Yreka, Tulare. At night there was love in the separate tents. Love that soon became as complex and dangerous as the stunts they were doing in the air.

Sammy wanted to respond to Frank's poetic vision of her. But she could not escape her dark compulsion for Buzz. That made her more and more contemptuous of her own character. Not a good frame of mind for a woman who was defying death in the air two or three times a week.

At first Buzz continued to take other women into his tent. He was trying to deny Sammy's growing power over him. Buzz began drinking harder. He was always a drinker, like most pilots. Drinking was part of the code, part of the way you controlled your fear and defied the groundlings. But this was a different kind of drinking. Buzz was using liquor to escape Sammy.

One night, outside Coachello, Buzz stumbled into the camp as drunk as Frank had ever seen him. "Sammy's not goin' near your goddamn tent tonight," he said.

"Did she say that?"

"No. I did."

"Why don't we ask her?"

"I won't ask her. I'll tell her. Just like I'm tellin' you."

Sammy strolled into the firelight with the groceries for dinner. "You're not fuckin' him any more. I just told him," Buzz said.

"I don't fuck him. I love him."

"No, you don't. You're saying that because you don't want to hurt me," Frank said.

"Shut up!" Sammy cried. "You're a pair of bastards. Why did I ever go near you?"

Long after midnight, Sammy slipped into Frank's tent and pressed her lips on his mouth. "I do love you," she said.

"I'm so sorry. I love the poems, the words. Teach me one more."

"Euphoria."

"What does it mean?"

"A feeling of great happiness. What we feel when we fly. What I felt the first night with you."

They made love one last time. Behind his closed eyes Frank saw Sammy on the wing, the blond hair streaming almost to the tail of the stubby Spad, a miraculous figure against the blue dome of the sky. Tomorrow or the next day or some day in the next week or month, one of them, perhaps all of them, would die if he tried to fight Buzz for her.

The next day they flew to Ukiah to participate in the town's annual rodeo. They went up to do their usual assortment of death-defying dives and spins and barrel rolls. As always the climax of the stunts was Sammy's wing walk. Frank thought she looked unsteady when she got up on the wing. With her feet in the grips and the wire wound around her right wrist, Buzz went into his barrel roll. Halfway around Sammy flew into the air and stopped only when the wire ran out.

She dangled there with Buzz flying upside down. If he rolled rightside up the wire might cut through the spars and fabric and amputate his wing. Frank went to full throttle and pulled under the swaying figure. Inch by inch, he moved closer, praying he would not slash her with the propeller. It required exquisite judgment to place the plane just far enough ahead of her to get Sammy's feet into the front cockpit.

"Now!" Frank roared.

She dropped into the cockpit. Below them, the crowd went wild. They thought it was part of the show. On the ground, Sammy could not explain it. When Buzz rolled, she had blacked out. The next thing she knew she was dangling by the wire. While the cowboys rode their bucking broncos, Sammy went in search of a doctor in Ukiah. She came back with astonishing news. She was pregnant.

"How could you let that happen?" Buzz shouted.

"I don't know. I guess maybe the diaphragm wore out. Or God wants us to have a kid."

"There are ways to get rid of it," Buzz said.

"Not in my book there ain't," Sammy said.

Frank could not believe Sammy's transformation over the next several months. She stopped wing walking and started going to church services and prayer meetings. She began urging Buzz to figure out some other way to make a living in aviation. She did not want their son growing up in a barnstormer's world. Buzz defiantly insisted he could make enough money to support them.

To prove it, Buzz developed a new repertoire of stunts that were so dangerous he did not even ask Frank Buchanan to try them. Buzz flew under highway bridges and through walls of fire, he did barrel rolls at twenty-five feet and landed the Spad on the roof of a speeding car. When they reenacted aerial combat and Frank shot him down, Buzz did not pull out of the spin until he was close to treetop level. Every show, Frank was braced for a crash that did not happen.

The baby was born while they were performing in Turlock. Who should be there to baptize him but the Rev. Abel Flutterman? He had bought himself a Jenny and was flying it around California spreading his winged gospel with spectacular success. Sammy brought the infant to a prayer meeting and Flutterman dunked him in a tin tub and pronounced him "a son of the sky." William Craig McCall (his middle name chosen by Frank) responded with a spluttering squawk.

A month later, Sammy said she was ready to start wing walking again. Buzz objected. His stunts were drawing big crowds all over the state. They did not need her help. Sammy insisted and as usual got her way—and then some. She announced they would do the stunt they had improvised on her last outing—a fall from Buzz's wing and a rescue by Frank.

They flew to Petaluma to help celebrate its claim to being the chicken capital of the world. Crowds had driven down from San Francisco and Sacramento to feast on the hundreds of pounds of broiling birds and enjoy the Buzz McCall Air Show. Up they climbed into an azure June sky, without a sign of a cloud. Onto the wing sprang Sammy to clutch the wire and wave exultantly to the sun, the crowd below, perhaps to God. Over Buzz went for the climactic barrel roll. Sammy flew into space.

The wire snapped. They had left it coiled in the rear cockpit of Buzz's plane for eight months. It had never occurred to them to replace it. They knew nothing about the tensile capacity of one-inch wound steel cable, its shelf life, its eventual fatigue. Down tumbled Sammy, her blond hair streaming. After her dove Buzz. Did he really think he could snatch her from oblivion?

A farewell word leaped into Frank's mind: *expiate*. Sammy walked on wings because deep in her woman's soul she could not forgive herself for the dark compulsion at the center of her wildness. She had hoped a child would atone for it. But she had found it necessary to go back to challenging death again.

Expiate. What would he and Buzz have to do to atone for their stupidity and arrogance and lust? In a frenzy Frank pounded his fists against his windscreen and cursed at the uncaring sky.

They were at a thousand feet when the wire parted. At two hundred feet Buzz overtook Sammy but there was no possibility of maneuvering the plane into position to stop her fall. Above them, Frank saw Buzz's outstretched arm reaching for that ribbon of yellow hair. He closed his eyes, unable to bear the sight of the woman and the plane going into the ground together.

When Frank looked down again, Sammy's body was on the grass, arms flung out in a final plea. Buzz was circling above her. Somehow he had pulled out of the dive.

Only as Frank landed did he realize that he and Buzz were the bereaved parents of William Craig McCall, already known as Billy—the son of the uncaring sky.

REALIST IN LOVE

It took Adrian Van Ness several months to absorb the discovery that his mother and Geoffrey Tillotson were lovers. Already adept at masking his feelings, Adrian was able to deal coolly, affably with both of them at business and on social occasions. But the revelation inevitably affected his feelings for his wife. From a figure of pity and sympathy, Amanda became a burden, a walking, talking mistake.

Amanda also changed her mind about him. Their disagreement over Oakes Ames meant a great deal to her. She brought it up again and again until Adrian finally told her he was sick of arguing about it. Having jettisoned idealism, he found it hard to grasp how much it still meant to Amanda. She blamed his fall from grace on Geoffrey Tillotson, whom she saw changing her sensitive poet into a hard-hearted banker—the sort of grasping amoral capitalist her father had fought in California.

Adrian also grew irked by Amanda's inability—he saw it as unwillingness—to adapt to their social life. When she accompanied him to house parties, she was intimidated by the upper class. She thought they were snubbing her. Adrian tried to explain the difference between English and American manners. "Just because they don't use your first name doesn't mean they're unfriendly," he said.

"I know when I'm being snubbed, Adrian," Amanda insisted. "You're so eager to kowtow to them, you barely notice it."

"There's no need for you to come. I'm perfectly happy to kowtow on my own," Adrian said.

A few weeks after that nasty exchange, Adrian was invited to a house party in Sussex. Amanda, wheezing and sneezing with her worst cold yet, stayed in London. The house was

Ravenswood, country home of Lord Elgin, chairman of the Cunard Line. It had a hundred rooms and at least that many servants. Around it were miles of woods and fields where guests shot grouse and hunted foxes.

The weather was cold and rainy. After unpacking, Adrian descended to the great hall and drank mulled wine before a blazing fire. A small dark-eyed brunette joined him, introducing herself as Beryl Suydam. She ordered sherry, remarking she was half frozen.

"What brings you here? Are you a member of the family?" Adrian asked.

"I was engaged to Lord Elgin's son, William. He was killed on the Somme."

"Oh. I'm—sorry."

"Don't be. It wasn't your fault. It wasn't anyone's fault. At least, that's what they want us to think."

"Are you inclined to blame someone?"

"Yes. But I don't know who."

Her bitterness coincided with Adrian's inchoate sense of betrayal and his deeper melancholy about history's pain. He felt an extraordinarily powerful attraction to dark, mournful Beryl Suydam. This was a woman who was grappling with more than a personal loss. She was trying to think about her pain historically, as Adrian had struggled to do since boyhood.

"What was he like—your fiancé?" Adrian asked.

"He was quite homely. A great lumbering bear of a man. But with the kindest heart, the most sympathetic nature I've ever seen. He was deeply interested in the social question. If he lived I think he might well have led a bloodless revolution in this country. He was not your ordinary aristocrat."

"A tragedy for you—and England," Adrian said.

"Beryl darling." Lady Elgin, a tall elegant blonde, clutched Beryl's hands and kissed her on the cheek.

Beryl introduced her to Adrian. "Are you married?" Lady Elgin asked.

Adrian reluctantly admitted he was. Lady Elgin sighed. "I drag Beryl to these parties because I want her to meet some eligible men. They're few and far between to her discriminating taste."

Beryl smiled gravely. "I'd like to pay a visit tomorrow. Will you come?"

Lady Elgin's good cheer disintegrated. "Oh, my darling girl. I don't think so. There's such a thing as too much sorrow. Edward's forbidden me to go there. I think he's right."

More guests arrived in the great hall. Lady Elgin regained her social smile and began greeting them. Among them were Clarissa Van Ness and Geoffrey Tillotson. Adrian enjoyed his mother's inquisitive glance at Beryl.

"What—where—are you going to visit?" Adrian asked.

"William's grave. It's about a mile away. On a lovely hill."

"I hate to think of you going there alone. May I come with you?"

"You're very kind."

"I lost some friends of my own on the Somme. From the Anson School. I'd much rather join you than make a fool of myself on horseback or shooting."

Adrian was a terrible shot and his enthusiasm for fox hunting was sharply curtailed by the memory of Robert Van Ness's fatal accident.

"Do you object to killing birds and beasts on principle?"

"If you think I should, I'll become a fanatic on the subject."

"I object to killing anything," Beryl Suydam said with sudden vehemence.

The next day, rain poured down but the shooters, the beaters, the whole party, struggled into macs and wellies and vanished into the drizzle. Adrian and Beryl enjoyed a second coffee before the fire and donned similar raingear for the walk to Viscount William Elgin's grave.

The rain stopped as they labored up the modest hill. An ancient cast-iron fence surrounded the two dozen graves, each guarded by a simple headstone. From the crest the rolling Sussex countryside, with its thick woods and pastures, was visible for several miles. Beryl opened the gate with a key and walked to William's grave.

"I used to bring flowers," she said. "I don't anymore. Maybe that's a good sign."

She did not kneel or say any sort of prayer that Adrian could detect. This was sorrow untouched by religious faith. Sympathy in its root meaning—the same feeling—stirred Adrian. He wanted to love or at least console this dark-haired wounded woman although history may have destroyed the very possibility of her loving him in return. For some reason he liked that idea.

The rain came down again. They walked back to Ravenswood while hunting guns thundered in the distance. William, the large-hearted nobleman with a social conscience, walked beside them, an invisible, formidable third. Adrian resolved to challenge him.

"Five years is a long time to mourn someone."

"It isn't just William's death. My father was a surgeon in France. What he saw there has left him a wreck. He can barely practice. I worked as a nurse, here. I saw some of the same things. I'll never forget what one man told me—the soldiers in the trenches hated everyone back here, enjoying the English way of life. We were their executioners."

"No you weren't. You were all—all of us—were—are—history's victims. Once you realize that, once you realize history's essential barbarism, you can begin to accept it—"

Beryl's face was almost invisible in the recesses of her hooded green mackintosh. "I like that idea," she said.

"It helps if you share the experience with another person."

"Where shall I find this historical hero?"

"He doesn't have to be heroic. We're talking about spiritual courage. That may occur in the most unlikely people— even in those who detest killing birds and beasts—and human beings."

Adrian yearned to tell her about his ruined father, his faithless mother, his naive California wife. But it was too soon. Beryl seemed to retreat deeper inside her green hood. They trudged silently through the rain, which had turned to a fine cold mist. Adrian sensed the third's looming presence.

"Have I made a fool of myself?" Adrian said.

"No," Beryl said.

That night after dinner Adrian sat down next to his mother and told her about the remarkable young woman he had met today. "She's very knowing," he said. "She tells me these house parties are really nothing but discreet assignations. Half the guests here are seeing each other illicitly, as the tabloids say."

"I'm sure that's an exaggeration," Clarissa said.

"Ah, here he is," Geoffrey Tillotson said, handing Clarissa a demitasse. "I've got a man over there who's ready to put a million pounds into an airline somewhere—Australia, America. Convince him of the glorious possibilities in your native land."

He nodded toward a rotund Liverpool shipping executive named Edward Jenkins. He had sideburns that reminded Adrian of his Anson headmaster, Mr. Deakwell.

"I wish I could stay in London a bit longer," Clarissa said. "But I must get home. There are so many things to do."

"I'm—I'm sorry to hear that," Tillotson said, sitting down on the couch opposite her like a man who has suddenly had a heavy sack dumped in his lap. Adrian strolled over to sell a paper airline to the man from Liverpool.

When a young man is angry at someone, it comes out in cruel ways. But retaliation never solves the deeper more dangerous anger at fate. That required a father's mediation—and a son's acceptance. For the time being Adrian had no father—and he was no man's son. He was at war with his world. As in most wars, the first victim was an innocent—Amanda.

LOOP THE LOOP

The Waco 10 biplane came in low and fast, just missing a line of eucalyptus trees. Frank Buchanan slammed the plane down for a rough three-point landing and bounced ten feet into the air. A crouching man scuttled beneath him. The

Waco came down for another tremendous bounce and headed toward a second line of eucalyptus trees on the other side of the field.

In a perfect imitation of a pilot who had lost control of his plane, Frank tore between two of the trees. He sheared off the right wings within two feet of the fuselage. The left wings lost only their tips. Still going fifty miles an hour, the Waco flipped on her side and Frank dove into the bottom of the cockpit to keep his head from being mashed into the dirt. The plane hurtled to a cracking, crunching stop, the propeller spewing up sod until it splintered.

Silence except for the *plop* of leaking gasoline. Frank struggled to unfasten his safety belt. Pounding feet. Hands reached to help him. They dragged him away from the plane, yelling "Are you okay?" He nodded. As far as he could tell, he still had the use of his arms and legs.

"That was great," cried the excited unit director. He was standing in an open truck with the cameras. "I can hardly wait to see the rushes."

Buzz McCall was waiting on the other side of the field, his arm around the picture's second lead, a sultry Theda Bara–type named Tama Moreno. "Nice going, sport," Buzz said. "Now we can have a party instead of a funeral."

It was the last stunt on their list for this movie, a comedy called *Loop the Loop*, about a rich idiot learning to fly. Tomorrow they would collect two thousand dollars for two weeks of risking their necks. They had wrecked four planes and come close to smashing a half-dozen more, flying them upside down under bridges and around telephone poles. As usual, Buzz had done the really dangerous stunts, leaving the obvious ones like crash landings to Frank.

They had gone into the movie stunt business after trying several other ways to make a living in aviation after Sammy's death. Frank had been adamant about getting out of the barnstorming game. He told Buzz it was Sammy's last wish and they had to fulfill it. That did not solve the problem of what to do with one-month-old Billy McCall. At first they tried boarding him with Frank's mother but her hostility to the boy disturbed Frank. She told him Billy was not a child of light or of darkness. She did not know what he was. They moved Buzz's widowed mother from Detroit and set her up in a house in Laguna Beach with the infant. It took six hundred dollars a month to pay the mortgage and support them—more money than most people were making from planes in the twenties.

At first they tried flying the mail. Their old barnstorming buddy, Charles Lindbergh, recommended it. The pay was eight hundred dollars a month, which left them enough to do some carousing—a must with Buzz. But the risks were so hair-raising, even he started to wonder if they were out of their minds. The planes had no instruments and a lot of the flying was at night. As a pilot came in for a landing, he had to listen to the sound of the wind whistling through the struts to estimate his airspeed.

Flying through clouds, pilots became completely disoriented and flipped upside down and spun to their dooms. There were no official weather reports. A pilot had to land and ask local farmers their opinion of what tomorrow might bring. Worst of all was the cold. Even with bulky bearskin suits, the below-zero wind whipping through holes in the base of the windshields was agonizing. Soon a pilot was so numb he no longer cared whether he lived or died. Many died. Planes crashed by the dozen. Twice Lindbergh escaped death by bailing out at the last second.

Buzz got a better idea. On a mail flight to Houston, he met the state's richest bootlegger. The gangster offered ten thousand dollars to build a plane big enough to carry two hundred cases of Scotch per flight from Mexico. Frank spent three months designing and constructing a gullwinged monoplane with this awesome load capacity. To his disgust the bootlegger refused to pay another thousand dollars for a decent engine. They had to settle for a motor from a Curtiss-Wright Jenny. The plane needed about a mile to take off and could barely maintain a survivable airspeed.

They wobbled back and forth from Mexico in this flying disgrace for several months, making money for their employer and a fair amount for themselves. One day they heard a strange sound, a sort of angry thud in the fuselage. "I'd swear that was a bullet," Buzz said.

Frank saw numerous white clusters of smoke on the ground. A lot of people were down there shooting at them. The bootlegger's friends apparently disliked airborne competition. After a few more trips the plane looked like a flying sieve. This did not improve its handling characteristics. Buzz decided it was time to try to get back into the Army Air Service, where dodging bullets would be an honorable profession if a war started.

Old friends such as Jimmy Doolittle and George Kenney, still flying World War I–vintage crates, told him to forget it. The Air Corps was the Army's unloved, unwanted stepchild. General Billy Mitchell was in imminent danger of being court-martialed for complaining about it. They flew back to California with about ten thousand dollars from their Scotch running and tried to find someone who would back Frank's monoplane with a real engine in it.

They built another version of the plane. But no one could see beyond the struts and wire biplanes being used by the army and the airmail service. Broke again, Buzz took charge and did the only thing that occurred to him—use his skills as a pilot to get a cut of the tidal wave of cash pouring into Hollywood. By this time Sammy had been dead almost three years—and he was also ready to enjoy the other commodity that Hollywood had in abundance: beautiful women.

Enjoyment was the watchword of the party to celebrate the completion of *Loop the Loop*. The festivities got going around 8:00. The movie company had rented all the bungalows around a small lake near Modesto. The star, a baby-faced blonde named Mabel Durand, had the biggest bungalow, of course. Everyone called it the Villa Modesto—not a bad joke, if you knew Mabel. Modesty was not among her virtues. The villa was party headquarters but they had the whole lake to themselves, which fueled an exorbitant excitement in everyone.

In Mabel's bathroom was a tub full of iced champagne. For those with cruder palates, there was Scotch, bourbon, and gin, all guaranteed to have genuine labels, direct from

Canada. Mabel's favorite bootlegger, a bullnecked Italian from San Francisco, had brought it in by plane earlier in the day. There was also plenty of cocaine on the side, delivered by a cheerful Mexican who was kicked out for daring to think he could snort with the Anglos.

Before everyone got too drunk, they had to see a rough cut of the film, which they spiced with exuberantly obscene comments. As usual, Tama Moreno had lined up one of the extras for Frank. She was a blonde from Texas named Gloria, a good ole cowgirl. She drawled about her heart bein' half out of her mouth when he crashed the Waco. After that gush of praise, conversation became a desperate struggle.

Buzz could never figure out why Frank wanted to talk to them in the first place. "Let them talk to each other," he said, a piece of wisdom that virtually echoed Craig.

By ten o'clock the party was taking off. Everyone was drunk and the grips were starting to snort cocaine. A black band was floating around the lake on a raft, playing New Orleans jazz. Buzz decided it would be fun to throw them into the water and see how well they played wet. Their British director organized a rowboat flotilla and commanded it Lord Nelson–style, screaming at every man to do his duty. They threw the terrified musicians into the lake, ignoring their pleas that they could not swim. Frank and a few others sensitive to race relations rescued them. They were left to shiver in their sodden clothes on Mabel's porch while the director staged a scene from *Anthony and Cleopatra*, the way he claimed it was played in ancient Egypt.

On a barge christened the HMS *Pussy*, Mabel and her ladies in waiting wore nothing at all. Floodlights were used to guarantee no one missed a detail. Mabel did a shimmy while her ladies Charlestoned around her. It was memorable. All that female pulchritude gyrating and jiggling in the white intensity of the ten-thousand-candlepower lights. "Hieronymus Bosch, Rabelais, Breughel—it beats them all!" the director shrilled.

Buzz commandeered a crew of stripped galley slaves in one of the larger rowboats who towed the HMS *Pussy* around the lake to massed applause from the drinkers and sniffers on shore. From another boat the director filmed the whole thing and shrieked he was sending it to *Ripley's Believe or Not* to claim the record for the most pubic hair in a single frame.

By midnight the orgy was in the stratosphere. The jazzmen had gotten into the champagne and cocaine and were playing very strange music, a dissonant assortment of howls and groans and wails. Buzz reeled past with his hand in Tama's black pussy. "Ain't this livin', Sport?" he roared. "I just fucked Mabel. Put in a good word for my ole wingman. Go for it, kiddo. She liked the way you crashed that plane."

Whether he took Buzz's advice, Frank was unsure. He dimly recalled swimming to the raft but the next thing he clearly remembered was a bungalow room with Gloria. She had shed her clothes and was telling him she liked to get on top. She liked almost everything, including Tama, who was in the room too, giving them instructions. Gloria and Tama went down on each other while half the crew, including Mabel and the director with his ubiquitous camera, screamed encouragement.

Suddenly a voice boomed in Frank's head. *Ain't this living?* It was Buzz's words but the voice seemed to belong to his brother Craig. Instead of the swaggering satisfaction in Buzz's question, the voice seemed mocking, almost contemptuous. Dazed, Frank slowly backed away from the two groaning, panting women on the bed. He shoved through the drunken crowd and stumbled to the shore of the lake in the darkness. *Ain't this living?* boomed the voice.

Pulling on a discarded shirt and pants, Frank wandered forlornly around the lake wishing he had hit the left-hand tree head-on in the Waco. Wishing, wondering, weeping in the darkness, while the jazzmen howled despair on the wind. Maybe the best thing to do was walk into the lake and abandon the mess he was making of his life.

He was sick of risking his neck for two hundred dollars a stunt, sick of crashing planes instead of building them. He knew why he could not find a backer to build the planes flying in his head. Most people found it hard to believe that Frank Buchanan, with his sloppy clothes, his rambling

swooping conversation, which could leap from planes to poetry to mystical religion in a single sentence, was businessman enough to run a company, pay his bills and produce a
given number of planes according to a contract.

For the past six months he had been begging Buzz to join
him in another try at manufacturing. Buzz had the toughness,
the leadership qualities, to get things done on schedule. But
Buzz had fallen in love with the movies. He had already
played a daring pilot in two films and Tama Moreno, among
others, thought he had a future as an actor. Frank knew what
he was really doing—using broads and booze to drown his
dreams of warrior glory—and forget Sammy and her son,
Billy.

Frank refused to forget Sammy—and to Tama Moreno's
barely concealed chagrin, he made sure Buzz did not forget
Billy. He insisted on a ritual weekly visit. He frequently reminded Buzz that Sammy did not want their son to become
a barnstorming bum like his two fathers. She would have
had the same opinion of stunt-flying bums. They made more
money than barnstorming bums but they were still moral and
spiritual disasters.

"Excuse me, mister. Have you seen my mother? The lady
was supposed to stay with me but she left me all alone and
there was all kinds of noises and I'm scared."

The voice belonged to a small figure a half-dozen cautious
feet away in the darkness. It was Cliff, Tama Moreno's six-
year-old son by a vanished husband. She took the boy on
location with her, claiming she had no relatives or friends to
mind him. He was one of the reasons she liked Buzz. She
thought he was the kind of father Cliff needed—a man's
man.

The little boy reminded Frank of Billy, the only person in
the world Frank loved at this forlorn point in his life.
"There's nothing to be afraid of," he said, putting his arm
around him. "You know me. I'm Frank. Buzz's friend. We'll
sit here together for a while and talk about planes. Do you
like them?"

"Sure."

"Would you want to learn to fly them some day?"

"I guess so."

"You're not sure?"

"If they crash you can get hurt—even killed—can't you?"

"Not if you're a good pilot."

Frank described the new planes that were appearing in the American sky—the Ford trimotor, the Sikorsky seaplane, lumbering creatures that were lucky to go 115 miles an hour. He told Cliff someday they would have planes that could whiz across the continent in a single day. Even fly the Atlantic and Pacific.

"Hey, Sport, where the hell have you been? We were gettin' ready to drag the lake."

It was Buzz, followed by Tama. The night sky was turning gray. It was almost dawn. Tama exploded when she saw Cliff. Why wasn't he in bed? He tried to explain as she dragged him back to their cottage on the other side of the lake.

"What's wrong, Sport?" Buzz asked.

Frank shook his head. He was not about to do a momma's-boy act and cry on Buzz's shoulder. He let the jazzmen wail their woes into the dawn.

Buzz sat down beside him. He understood what was wrong. Beneath his tough-guy act, he felt as lost and betrayed by the aviation world as Frank. "We'll figure something out, Sport. I promise you. I want to build those goddamn planes of yours as much as you do. Meantime we gotta keep eatin'."

Frank heard another voice saying: *we got to eat, kid*. It was Craig, speaking through Buzz, telling him he still cared.

A trumpet howled sardonically. Frank struggled for faith that he was being guided by a presence that would somehow help him survive these wasted years.

SON AND LOVER

"Now put your feet on the rudder controls," Adrian Van Ness said. "To keep level, the nose should cut the horizon just above the top of the engine cylinders. Press the stick and it goes above them. Pull and it drops below. You try."

"Marvelous!" Beryl Suydam cried. Adrian understood what she was feeling. Discovering you could control this strange creature in the sky was an extraordinary thrill.

Adrian and Beryl were two thousand feet above the green Wiltshire countryside in a de Havilland Moth, everyone's favorite sport plane. At Geoffrey Tillotson's urging, Adrian had learned to fly to impress potential investors in the aircraft business.

"For level flying we keep the wings parallel with the horizon. Move the stick to the left and the port wing will drop. Move it to the right and we'll come back again. Try."

Beryl dipped the left wing and they got a glimpse of the landscape Thomas Hardy had made famous in his novels about fate-haunted lovers. She moved the stick to the right and they were level again.

"Last we have the rudder. It's like a boat. We steer for a fixed point on the horizon. A gentle push with the left foot and the nose slides left. Reverse, and we recover. Try."

Beryl tried and the Moth veered dramatically left. Adrian straightened the plane and explained that the rudder was much more sensitive than the other controls. It did not have to contend with as much air pressure. He let Beryl handle the rudder again and she did much better.

"Easy, isn't it?" Adrian said. "Try a turn."

Beryl tried it and almost panicked. The nose wavered up and down, the plane skidded and sideslipped. Adrian took charge as they wallowed around. "Feel for the angle of the bank," he said, "Try again. Use your toes on the rudder. Nothing else."

Beryl obeyed and made a remarkably smooth right turn. She was catching on fast. "Adrian, I adore it!" she cried.

They cruised over the west country, Adrian pointing out places of interest below them. "Those are the Berkshire Downs to the north. That smudge is Reading. Now you can see the channel and the Isle of Wight. There's Southampton Water."

A liner was standing out to sea from Southampton. Adrian thought of his mother and her friends, plodding along on their boats and trains, and felt a gratifying surge of superiority. Geoffrey Tillotson was right. This was the machine of his generation. They were flying over the dull dismal past into the future.

In fact, they were flying to Ravenswood. The plane had become the smart way to arrive for a country weekend. In a half hour Adrian made a bumpy but adequate landing on the great lawn. A half-dozen other planes, most of them de Havilland Moths, were already parked in front of the house. As they taxied toward this impromptu flight line, Clarissa Van Ness and Geoffrey Tillotson stepped out of his Hispano-Suiza.

"What a marvelous surprise," Geoffrey said. Clarissa looked less pleased. A month ago, Amanda had returned to California. Seeing Adrian with Beryl confirmed a long-running rumor she had undoubtedly heard many times. But what could Clarissa say, when she was enjoying the amiable charms of her man of substance again? Adrian found his mother's dilemma deliciously satisfying.

For almost two years, Adrian had watched his marriage deteriorate, telling himself it was not his fault, it was a historical process in which he was unhappily participating. Amanda grew more and more melancholy at the prospect of a second winter in England. Her colds accumulated into the grippe and then into a bout of pneumonia—a very serious illness in the 1920s. In a flurry of guilt Adrian had asked Clarissa to return and nurse her back to health. She and Amanda spent the summer at the Tillotson house in Kent—

giving Adrian time to pursue Beryl Suydam in London.

She proved elusive. The ghostly third was a formidable antagonist. But Adrian, convinced he was a man of the future and time was his ally, was tenacious. Slowly, inevitably, Beryl's melancholy receded. Soon Adrian was her lover, visiting her flat in London at night, lying to Amanda about his long hours at the bank.

Finally came news from California that Amanda converted into an ultimatum. Her mother's mental condition had deteriorated so badly, Amanda's half-brother had placed her in a sanitarium a few miles from Cadwallader Groves. Violently distressed, Amanda reminded Adrian of his promise to quit his job and return to California with her if circumstances warranted it. Here, surely, were the circumstances. Her doctor had told her not to spend another winter in England. Her mother was being hounded into insanity by her monstrous brother.

Adrian calmly, coldly, declined to go. He said his career as a merchant banker was just beginning to prosper. It took years to accumulate clients. But he urged Amanda to go. In fact, he insisted on it. She had wept and asked him if he were going to divorce her. It was a painful moment. Adrian gave her the only possible reply. "No." It was a lie, of course. But men of substance regularly lied to their wives.

That night at Ravenswood, Adrian, Beryl and the other fliers came to dinner in their jodhpurs and flying jackets. Planes were the main topic of conversation at the table, upstaging the establishment of the Irish Free State and the jailing of the German agitator, Adolf Hitler, for attempting a coup d'état in Munich. Later, sipping brandy before the fire while his mother glared in the middle distance, Adrian turned to Beryl and murmured, "Can I come to your room tonight?"

Beryl understood the significance of accepting Adrian in her arms in this house. It would be a decisive break with her sorrow, with the ghostly third. "I can't make you happy. I have no happiness in me," she whispered.

Adrian was not listening. "I want to make *you* happy," he said.

That night for Adrian flight was a new gospel, an escape

from his empty marriage, a transcendence of the wounded naive adolescent who had sailed on the *Berengaria*. Flight fused with his desire for Beryl Suydam, his wish to heal her grief with his American faith in the future. Doubtful yet suffused with a wish to make an escape of her own, Beryl opened her arms to him. For a while that night in her room on Ravenswood's second floor, the ghostly third who walked beside her vanished.

The next day, while most of the guests shot grouse, Geoffrey Tillotson suggested a stroll through the woods. "A shame about Amanda going home like that," he said. "But our bloody climate is hard on Americans. She may well be better off in California."

He cleared his throat. "Your mother's a bit disturbed—as am I—about Beryl Suydam."

"Why?" Adrian said.

"The whole bloody family is full of socialist rot, dear boy. Socialist rot of the worst sort. Which makes her a bit inconsistent with your profession."

"We don't talk politics."

"You will, I assure you."

"I can handle politics quite nicely," Adrian said. "I'm not a fanatic on the subject."

"Not politics with a woman, old fellow," Tillotson said. "They add a dimension that can be quite devastating."

Adrian strode along, his eyes on the leafy path. "You and Clarissa don't talk politics? Is that the secret of your success?"

Now it was Tillotson's turn to walk a dozen paces in silence. He put his arm around Adrian's shoulder. "We must have a good talk one of these days."

Two weeks later, after a leisurely lunch, Tillotson led Adrian to a secluded corner of the Athenaeum Club's long lofty library. He ordered a turn of the century Sandeman's port and told Adrian how he had fallen in love with Clarissa Van Ness. His older brother's death in a climbing accident in Switzerland had brought him back from India, where he had been supervising Tillotson's numerous investments. He had married the daughter of a British civil servant out there and found her incapable of making the transition to social London. He was thrown on his own in society and seldom saw his wife, who preferred to remain "buried in Yorkshire."

When he met Clarissa Van Ness in 1898, Geoffrey Tillotson was a lonely man. She was a lonely woman. "Your father—her husband's—failure made him—how shall I say it?—less than adequate. Do you understand me?"

He finished his port in a nervous gulp and ordered another glass.

"Wrong as it was, her love has been the solace of my life, Adrian," Tillotson said. "And you, dear boy. I won't attempt to tell you what you mean to me now. Though I realize I don't have the slightest claim on you. I wanted to tell you immediately after your—your—mother's husband—your unfortunate father—I suppose you will always think of him that way—died. But your mother couldn't bring herself to do it. Of course you understand you must never tell her of this talk."

"Of course," Adrian said. He was too astonished to think or feel anything. He had just discovered Robert Van Ness was not his father. He was not the legitimate son of a failure, but the bastard son of a man of substance.

On a shelf behind Geoffrey Tillotson's head, illuminated mostly by the glow from the nearby fireplace, was a leatherbound book with a title in faded gold: *The Essays of Sir Francis Bacon.* The first man to write frankly about the pursuit of wealth and power. Thackeray had sat in this room writing *Vanity Fair,* another book that told how the world worked.

Something indefinable, an acceptance of the world's ways, filtered into Adrian's soul. It did not change his anger into milky benevolence. The wariness, the suspicion that life was a maze of secrets, would always be there. Along with a stubborn loyalty to the ruined speculator who had given him his name. But now this vortex of feelings belonged to a different man.

A man who saw himself telling Beryl Suydam he was half-English, ready to love her not as a visiting American but as a part of her own country, prepared to share its destiny with her at his side. For a little while, suffused with love and sonship, Adrian was no longer American.

A week later, Tillotson summoned Adrian to his office. "The chancellor of the exchequer—Winston Churchill—has asked me to form a commission to investigate our airline problems. We need a clever fellow who can find out how much money these confounded Europeans are losing whilst they pretend to prosperity. I'm quite sure the bloody beggars are all getting money from their governments. While our fellows are wobbling along on the edge of bankruptcy."

"I know someone who might be rather good at that," Adrian said.

Adrian was talking about his old schoolmate, Carlo Pontecorvo. He had returned from Africa when his father died in 1922 and assumed the family's ancient papal title. He was now Prince Carlo. But Italian politics had made his position precarious. His father, a believer in democracy, had opposed Mussolini and the Fascists had expropriated the family's estates in Calabria. They had been forced to sell their African lands at a catastrophic loss. In spite of his comparative poverty, Ponty was still passionately interested in flying. His letters to Adrian were full of descriptions of the latest airliners being developed by designers such as Antony Fokker and Gianni Caproni. He seemed to be in touch with all aspects of the European air world.

Tillotson approved the choice. "It's a job for a young fellow. Everyone in the business is young. Tell him we'll see that he's well treated for his time and trouble."

Ponty accepted Adrian's proposal by return mail. He planned to pose as the spokesman of a syndicate of investors who were considering the purchase of one or several existing airlines. He would refer doubters to Tillotson Brothers, who would confirm his authenticity. "I would also suggest setting up an account in the name of a third party in a Swiss bank," he wrote. "There may be a need for a certain amount of *douceurs*. Or as you Americans say, sweeteners."

Oakes Ames's great-grandson had no hesitation about suggesting all this, including the douceur account, to Geoffrey Tillotson, who approved it with a nod of his head.

Two months later, Ponty flew into Croydon Airport aboard a French Loire et Olivier Air Union biplane with reams of information on how much money all the European airlines were losing and how much their governments were paying to subsidize them. He also included some startling information on how Lufthansa, the German airline, was secretly training pilots for their military air force.

"Good job," Geoffrey Tillotson said after reading Adrian's digest of Ponty's espionage. "But we won't send this stuff to anyone in the government just yet. Let's take some of that Liverpool fellow's money and put two hundred thousand into Air France, two hundred thousand into Lufthansa and the rest into Alitalia."

"What about Lufthansa training military pilots?" Adrian asked.

"Forget that. It would raise hob with the stock," Tillotson said. "They're just playing the great game. As we'd be playing it if we lost the war."

Within a month, the British government announced a plan to consolidate the four faltering British airlines into Imperial Airways, with a government subsidy to keep it flying. Tillotson Brothers had, of course, bought into the company at bargain prices weeks before the announcement. Forethought at work again, Tillotson said, with his insider's smile. To reward their secret agent, a nice block of stock was signed over to Prince Carlo Pontecorvo.

Meanwhile, Adrian enjoyed Ponty's companionship. He combined aristocratic Italian good looks with a nonchalance that put men at ease—and if Beryl Suydam was a sample— women found enchanting. His stories of flying in Africa— crash-landing in the Nile, daring the downdrafts of Mt. Kilimanjaro—soon had him on everyone's list for dinner parties and country weekends.

On one of these outings, Beryl asked Ponty if he would give her flying lessons. Adrian's sporadic instruction had taught her the basics of flight but she had yet to solo. Ponty was evasive about his "commitments" in Rome. That night he took Adrian aside and asked him if he approved the idea.

"Why not?" he said.

"Learning to fly disturbs the equilibrium of many men," Ponty said. "I would be uneasy, if I were you, about its effect on a woman."

Adrian dismissed this warning as offhandedly as he had ignored Geoffrey Tillotson's concern about Beryl's politics. She had moved into his Islington Mews flat. True, she was working for a left-wing publishing house that seemed to specialize in books praising the Soviet Union. She was violently critical of the Conservative government that was ruling England. But Adrian saw this as a continuation of his contest with the ghostly third and avoided arguments by claiming an American should be neutral in British politics.

Within the week, Adrian and Beryl were airborne with Ponty in a biplane called the Lucifer 3 Seater. To Adrian's chagrin, Ponty was soon pronouncing Beryl a born pilot. She had the indefinable instinct that blended human and machine in the air. Adrian on the other hand was constantly trying to think his way through the process. The result was safe but clumsy flying.

Adrian simply did not understand Ponty when he urged him to "let the plane tell you what to do." The plane was an unthinking collection of struts and wood and metal that would kill him if it got a chance. Beryl had no such apprehension. She borrowed money from her father to buy a de Havilland Moth and was soon flying all over England, ferrying her authors to speaking engagements and participating in air shows, where she rapidly acquired a collection of prizes.

Adrian was not particularly troubled by Beryl's superiority in the air—until he began hearing more and more about a writer named Guy Petersham, who had been her late fiancé's roommate at Cambridge. He had just published a book about his visit to Russia. She invited him to dinner one night, along with Ponty and one of the half-dozen young Englishwomen who had fallen in love with the prince. Petersham arrived wearing baggy unpressed trousers and a dirty Shetland sweater. Tall, languid, he was totally convinced of his own intellectual brilliance.

For an hour he lectured them on Vladimir Lenin and Joseph Stalin as the prophets of the new age. "I begin to think the entire raison d'être of the slaughter of the Great War has been the creation of the Soviet Union. The war was the birth pangs of a new world."

"I've been led to believe America was the new world," Adrian said.

"Dear fellow," Petersham said. "You primitive capitalists are positively quaint."

You are positively asinine, Adrian thought. But he repressed the words. He did not like the excitement in Beryl's eyes.

"Communism looks to me like another name for fascism," Ponty said. "Both are disguises for the oldest form of government in the world—rule by the sword. I thought it was impossible for an Englishman to admire such a system."

"My dear prince," Petersham said. "You're a charming anachronism. If you stay around England long enough we may shoot and stuff you for some museum."

"Guy wants me to go with him to the Soviet Union on his next trip," Beryl said. "He thinks we can get permission to fly all over the country bringing a message of friendship from the British people. Do you think I'm up to it, Ponty?"

"If you fly in the summer, and they provide you with decent maps, yes," Ponty said.

His grave eyes met Adrian's. Were they saying *I told you so*? After the guests departed, Beryl cleared the table while Adrian poured the last of the wine into a decanter. "You're not really serious about that trip, are you?" he said.

"It's a once-in-a-lifetime opportunity, Adrian. A chance to see a part of the world I care about deeply. And perhaps set some records for overland flight."

"It's not a part of the world I care about," Adrian said.

"Perhaps you should. Perhaps you should at least let me explore it and find out if Guy is right about the Soviet Union being the only way to justify the war."

The third, the large-hearted noble ghost was back. Now his voice was more threatening, more formidable. Beryl Suydam was no longer the wounded woman he had met at Ravenswood. She had acquired a sense of mastery in the air and was prepared to demonstrate it on the ground. But Adrian was no longer the fatherless son, confused by his devious powerful mother. He spoke with a man's voice.

"I'm afraid I take a dim view of your spending three months in a foreign country with another man to explore an idea that I consider absolute trash."

"Maybe the trash is in your mind, Adrian. You talk about the plane as the symbol of our bright future. But what have you done with it here in England, with the help of your noble friend, Prince Carlo? Captured it for the ruling classes. Imperial Airways. Are you proud of helping to create that? The very name cries out exploitation."

"The ruling classes have the money. Planes cost a great deal of money. For the time being the rich will be their chief users. But America will change that. Look at the motorcar. Only a few hundred thousand people own one in Europe. In America there are millions of them on the road. The plane will go the same way."

"Bosh. You're lying to yourself. And to me."

"I love you. I've never lied to you. I try not to lie to myself."

Beryl began to weep. "I wish you'd taken me to America. Maybe this wouldn't be happening."

"I wish you hadn't met Guy Petersham. He's stirred up all the socialist rot in the bottom of your mind."

"Who told you that?"

"Never mind."

"It was your beastly boss, Geoffrey Tillotson. That man's a perfect example of what's wrong with this country. My father knew him in school. He was a snob then. The epitome of the ruling class."

"I disagree, totally," Adrian said.

"I know what I'm talking about. You don't," Beryl said.

Adrian felt like a man who had put his plane into a spin and failed to pull out. Instead of telling Beryl that Geoffrey Tillotson was his father, revealing himself as half-English and asking her to marry him, he was finding Tillotson's name the instrument of separation, desolation, loss. He was an outsider again, the American wog.

"You're talking about a man I—I admire. Admire deeply. Can you appreciate that?" Adrian said.

"I'm afraid I can't appreciate any such thing," Beryl said. "I'm afraid I can no longer appreciate anything you might have to say to me."

She packed her suitcases and departed. Adrian was certain she would be living with Guy Petersham within a fortnight. For a while he thought of taking a de Havilland Moth up to two thousand feet and pointing its nose toward the earth for a final dive. Ponty tried to soothe his turmoil with worldly advice. "She was charming, beautiful, sensual. But she was not a suitable wife, Adrian. She doesn't have a penny."

Ponty calmly explained the European view of the sexes. Next year he was going to marry Constance di Burgos, who would soon inherit huge swaths of southern France and Tuscany. She was a mousy woman with stringy hair and a will of iron. But her dowry made her an excellent wife. "The man who looks for love in marriage is naive," Ponty said. "Love is impermanent. Wealth—especially wealth in land—is what endures."

Ponty urged Adrian to investigate land values in California and reconsider his marriage with Amanda Cadwallader. Two thousand acres of orange groves might be the foundation of a comfortable fortune. "But don't teach her to fly," Ponty added with a grave smile.

One afternoon in the office a week later, Geoffrey Tillotson put his hand on Adrian's shoulder. "You're in the most awful funk, aren't you? Let's have a drink."

This time they went to the Garrick, smaller, more intimate than the Athenaeum in its Greek cathedral on Pall Mall. "Thought you'd be interested in this," he said and handed him a publicity release from de Havilland Aircraft. Beryl Suydam had just announced her plan to fly to Moscow in a DH Moth with Guy Petersham as her navigator.

"I knew her father at Cambridge," Tillotson said. "We were deadly enemies from the first days. Primal antagonism seems to be the only answer. It may go back to the Wars of the Roses. Or the Roundheads and the Cavaliers. The Tillotsons were royalists to a man. At any rate, it's not your fault."

Adrian said nothing. Tillotson sipped his sherry. "It's a blow, of course. But life is full of blows. Men carry on. Old Samuel Johnson probably put it best—'It does a man no good to whine.' "

Tillotson ordered another sherry. "It's time you thought about going back to America. You have a wife there. You ought to decide what to do about her."

Inwardly, Adrian bristled. Was Tillotson speaking as Clarissa's agent here? Or was he telling him it was time to accept another part of a man's task? Adrian's wound was too raw to think clearly about it. But he sensed pain, he saw sympathy in Geoffrey Tillotson's hooded eyes. He felt a father's love.

Tillotson began talking about their favorite topic, planes. With the formation of Imperial Airways, British commercial aviation was at a dead end. Imperial would buy only a few planes in the next decade. The other European airlines, secure in their state subsidies, would do no better. The sport-plane market was limited to the rich. The military market was hopeless. Grappling with massive unemployment, the British government had no money for weaponry of any sort. Parliament had actually forbidden the RAF to buy warplanes. There was only one place where the plane could multiply: America. He wanted Adrian to be there from the very beginning.

"You have an expression for it, from one of the generals in your Civil War. Get there first with the most?"

"I think it was firstest with the mostest. He was from Tennessee."

"Ah, yes. At any rate—I'll send you the mostest. I'm sure you'll put it to good use—for both of us."

"I'll try."

"Good-o." He slapped Adrian's knee. "There'll be other women. No reason for more than the normal regrets."

Adrian wanted to agree. But in his mind Beryl Suydam flew into a vast icy steppe of bitterness. Never again would

Adrian think of the plane as a mystical machine that blended love and optimism into a future aglow with happiness. But he retained a wary faith in its ability to make him a man of substance.

ONCE IN GOLCONDA

In the cockpit of his World War I Jenny, Frank Buchanan climbed into an overcast California sky that was a mirror of his mood. The year 1926 was drawing to a dismal close. He was still a movie stunt flyer, part of Buzz McCall's circus, crashing planes instead of building them. Admiral Richard Byrd had just flown over the North Pole. Americans applauded but they remained more interested in cars, bathtub gin, and the ever-rising stock market.

Frank was on his way to San Diego to see an Arizona rancher who might be interested in backing an aircraft company. Buzz was to join him if the man talked real money. Five thousand feet above Orange County the Jenny's motor sputtered and quit. Once, twice, three times, he tried to restart the ancient engine, while the crate began losing altitude. Below him he could see nothing but miles of orange groves and the winding Santa Ana River. He chose the river as preferable to a collision with an orange tree at forty miles an hour.

Keeping his nose up, he pancaked in the center of the river. Unfortunately, the Santa Ana was one of those California rivers Mark Twain said he fell into and came out dusty. The Jenny's wheels dug into the mud and the plane flipped. The impact simultaneously snapped Frank's safety belt and his forehead smashed against the windshield, knocking him cold.

The next thing he heard was a voice saying: "Put him down here."

Two solemn Mexicans deposited him on the grass. He was drenched in muddy water. Otherwise his situation was totally unreal. The air was thick with the scent of orange blossoms. A young woman with the kindest, saddest eyes he had ever seen was bending over him. Her auburn hair fell in thick ringlets down both sides of her rather long, narrow face. She was wearing a dark green riding outfit with a derby and a slit skirt.

"Are you badly hurt?" she asked.

"I may be dead. I can't think of any other reason for this heavenly vision."

She blushed. "I was riding along the riverbank and saw you crash. I'm Amanda Van Ness."

"Frank Buchanan."

When he tried to stand up, Frank discovered he had also bashed his knee against the instrument panel. The Mexicans helped him to Amanda's horse and she led him like a wounded knight down a broad green swath through the orange groves to Casa Felicidad, a turreted Victorian house made of white sandstone. A blond, impatient young man, who turned out to be Amanda's older brother, Gordon Cadwallader, called a doctor with a German accent who diagnosed a slight concussion and a badly bruised but not otherwise damaged knee.

For a week Frank recuperated between clean sheets, on a mattress stuffed with feathers. When he was not sketching planes, he talked with Amanda Van Ness. He soon learned she was separated from her husband, who lived in New York. Gradually, Frank picked up other details that explained the sadness in her eyes—her father's death in the war, her mother's breakdown. Her mother was confined to a sanatorium run by the German doctor. Her brother ran the family's orange groves—and Amanda. She intimated that she hated him and was often lonely.

She was different from Sammy, from the other women Frank had met and occasionally bedded. Her willowy body was not immediately erotic. She seemed barely conscious of her sexual identity. But beneath her sadness was an idealism Frank had never encountered before.

Brooding on her father's death, Amanda had become profoundly interested in world peace. She corresponded with peace advocates around the United States and the world. She was surprised and pleased to discover that Frank shared her detestation of war. "My brother says that proves I'm a fool," she said.

"When it comes to war, most people are fools," Frank said.

She wanted to found a peace colony at Casa Felicidad and import famous philosophers and religious thinkers to hold seminars on the folly of war. She read the numerous books that were appearing, ridiculing the idea that the World War was a crusade for democracy. She could recite statistics proving the arms and munitions makers had gotten rich on the blood of the soldiers on both sides.

Frank Buchanan agreed with everything she said. "We have a lot in common. Everyone thinks I'm a fool too. I design planes that will never fly."

"Show me some of them."

He took out some of his sketches. Amanda instantly grasped the thrust of Frank's vision—toward simplicity, clean lines, a stark modern beauty. Although she knew nothing about aerodynamics, her enthusiasm stirred Frank enormously.

"These planes are going to fly," Amanda said. "I can see them flying now in my mind."

"I'm afraid that's the only place they'll fly," Frank said. "I have no money."

"I'll get you money," Amanda said. "My brother is always looking for businesses to invest in. He hates growing oranges."

Alas, Gordon Cadwallader declined to entrust his money to a wandering movie stunt flier with no track record in the business side of the aircraft world. At the end of the week, Amanda had to confess she had failed to persuade her brother to risk a cent on Frank's planes.

They were sitting on Casa Felicidad's side porch, breathing air fragrant with orange blossoms. The flowering trees sighed in the warm wind. "I can't tell you how much I appreciate your—your concern," Frank said.

For a thunderous moment, Frank realized he could have said "love." He sensed Amanda Van Ness loved him in a lost despairing way that she could not admit. "Can I see you again?" Frank said.

"There's no point to it," Amanda said. "I—I can only wish you well—"

Her brother Gordon stamped up the steps to announce the Mexican orange pickers had hauled Frank's plane out of the river and deposited the sodden wreck on the back lawn. Frank had apparently recovered from his injuries. Would he come upstairs for a final examination by the doctor?

In the bedroom, the examination consisted of flexing his knee. "My bill is five hundred dollars. Can you pay me before you go?" the doctor said in his heavy German accent.

"No," Frank said.

"We may have to confiscate the plane and sell it for junk," Gordon Cadwallader said. "Unless you can repair it and fly yourself out of here in the next two days. In that case, I'll take care of the doctor's bill."

"You can't get rid of me that easily. I'm in love with Amanda. I think she's in love with me."

"I know she is. But I advise you—I urge you—to forget it."

Gordon let the doctor explain it. "Amanda has to lead a quiet life. Nervous disorders are rampant in her mother's family. Bad genes. She came very close to breaking down when she returned from England."

"I don't see what harm an occasional visit can do."

"If you had a steady job, there might be some point to it," Gordon said.

Frank put his Jenny back together with some help from the orange pickers, one of whom drove the Cadwallader truck and was a pretty good mechanic. While Amanda watched mournfully, the truck towed the Jenny to an open field and Frank took off. He swooped low over the house and released a stream of fluttering paper—watercolors of some of his planes, which he had stayed up half the night completing.

Frank flew to Clover Field in Santa Monica and tele-

phoned Buzz McCall to tell him he was through with stunt
flying. He hitched a ride to an abandoned film studio where
a man named Donald Douglas was building planes. He
showed the bluff, florid-faced Scotsman his sketchbook.
Douglas snorted and shoved it aside. "Not a damn one of
them will ever fly," he said. "But we could use some fresh
ideas. We're building float planes for the Navy and having
a hell of a time with the wings. If we make them too thick,
the plane has too much drag. If we go for thinness, we can't
put bombs on them."

Frank came back in a day with a wing that was a foot
longer and half the weight of the one Douglas had been using. By redistributing the center of gravity, it could handle
250-pound bombs with no problems. Douglas put him on the
payroll at twenty dollars a week. He himself was only taking
home twenty-two dollars.

Frank's ability to design wings spread through California's
small aviation community. In San Diego, a man named
Claude Ryan was putting together a monoplane rugged
enough to carry the U.S. mail. He borrowed Frank to solve
another weight problem. Ryan was easier to work for than
the gruff, dictatorial Douglas, but Ryan's idea of a plane
made Frank recoil. It was all squares and rectangles, like a
packing case with wings. Nevertheless, a Buchanan-
redesigned wing won Ryan a contract to build mail planes.

A few months later, in the spring of 1927, Frank got another call from Ryan Aircraft. The company had been taken
over by a young man named Mahoney and they needed help
on another wing. Frank cranked up his Jenny and flew to
San Diego, where the plane maker introduced him to an ex–
mail pilot named Charles A. Lindbergh. He was as slim and
boyish as the night they parted on the Yellowstone five years
ago. "Lindy's going for the New York to Paris prize. He
wants to use one of our planes but he's got some load problems," Mahoney said.

When they were alone, Lindbergh told Frank he was far
from happy with the Ryan plane but it was the best he could
get for the ten thousand dollars his backers in St. Louis were
ready to risk. Anyway, Lindbergh pointed out in his practical

Swedish way, the prize was only 25,000 dollars and it made
no sense to spend it all on the plane. When Lindbergh revealed he planned to carry an extra 300 gallons of gas in
special cockpit tanks, raising his total weight to 5,200
pounds, Frank urged him to forget the whole idea. Four men
had already died trying to cross the Atlantic.

Lindbergh calmly convinced Frank he knew what he was
doing. He was betting on the reliability of the air-cooled
radial motors that had replaced the water-cooled engines of
the World War. The rest was fuel management and naviga-
tion, which he planned to handle himself, saving the weight
of a navigator.

Frank went to work and in a week of concentrated effort
redesigned the wing for the N-X-211, as it was called in the
Ryan factory before Lindy christened it the *Spirit of St.
Louis.* He created a series of interior metal angles, easily
formed on ordinary shop tools, that solved Lindbergh's lift
problem with several hundred pounds to spare. Lindbergh
was at his elbow constantly, asking questions, making suggestions, checking Frank's computation of the plane's ratio
of lift to drag, the crucial factor in every design. Lindy had
obviously learned a lot about planes since his stunt-flying
days.

At the end of April 1927, they rolled the completed plane
out of the hangar and Lindbergh took it up for her first flight.
She performed well in spite of her ugly shape, bounding from
the runway in 165 feet. Frank stayed for the more important
load tests at San Diego's Dutch Flats airport. Lindbergh cau-
tiously added fifty gallons of fuel for each test, until they
reached the maximum load of 300 gallons. This time it took
the *Spirit of St. Louis* 1,026 feet to get off the ground, but
the wing did the job. Frank wished Lindy luck and headed
back to Los Angeles to resume his toils for Donald Douglas.

The next day he landed in the grassy field behind the Cadwallader orange groves. He had become a regular weekend
visitor, ignoring scowls from brother Gordon. Amanda welcomed him eagerly. "You look tired," she said as they drank
iced tea on the porch.

"I didn't get much sleep this week," Frank said. "I had to

design a new wing for a fellow named Lindbergh who's going to fly the Atlantic."

"Can he do it?" Amanda asked.

"I wouldn't be surprised," Frank said. "He's got it figured out to the last ounce of gas and pound of lift."

"If he succeeds, maybe you could take some of the credit and raise enough money to start your own company."

This had never occurred to Frank. Neither he nor anyone else in California considered Lindbergh's projected flight a significant event. Pilots were setting long-distance records all the time. Lieutenant Jimmy Doolittle had flown across the country in a single day in 1922. Two army planes had flown around the world in 1924. Two other army fliers were planning a flight from Oakland to Honolulu sometime in June.

"Look at this." Gordon Cadwallader strode onto the porch and threw a copy of the *Los Angeles Times* on the tea table. A streamer headline announced Lindbergh was halfway across the Atlantic and had an excellent chance of reaching Paris. Amanda read the story and gasped: "He's flying alone?"

Reading over her shoulder, Frank nodded: "All he has to do is keep himself awake."

"Now I know you can raise the money," Amanda said.

She told her brother that Frank had designed the *Spirit of St. Louis*'s wing. Gordon Cadwallader sat down and struggled to put a friendly expression on his usually sour face. "I've been studying the stocks of plane companies," Gordon said. "Compared to the rest of the market, they're all incredibly low. If someone like Lindbergh changed the way people think about planes, they could become the hottest investment in sight. If you agree to share the management with good businessmen, maybe we could start a company."

Beneath the table, Amanda took Frank's hand. She was telling him she was ready to start something more serious than a company. The gesture annihilated Frank's first inclination to explore Cadwallader's offer with Buzz McCall and a lawyer at his side. Frank held out his hand. "I can put us in business in a month."

For the moment Frank was ready to believe love conquered everything—even greed.

GOOD-BYE TO EVERYTHING

Martini in hand, Adrian Van Ness sat beside John Hay Whitney on a leather banquette in the elegant cabin of Whitney's Sikorsky Amphibian, one of the first business planes in America. Opposite the banquette, in a stylish wicker pullup chair, sat Jock's cousin, strapping Richard Whitfield, vice president of the New York Stock Exchange. They were all listening to Winston Churchill, the volatile British politician who had been England's chancellor of the exchequer for the past five years, tell how he had accidentally made a fortune in the stock market.

"My old friend Tillotson asked me just before I sailed if I had any money to invest and I told him I could always find two or three thousand pounds. I meant this was the limit for me and let it go at that. I had no intention of speculating. He went out and bought shares on margin in your aircraft stocks through this young rascal—"

He beamed at Adrian Van Ness and took a hefty swallow of his brandy and soda.

"I get off the boat and find out I'm a bloody millionaire. I'm tempted to call him Santa Claus but he's too young."

"There's no question, the market Adrian's made in aircraft stocks is one of the accomplishments of the decade," Richard Whitfield said in his clipped Locust Valley lockjaw way.

"I think the real credit belongs to one Charles E. Lindbergh," Adrian said.

There was more than a little truth to Adrian's modesty. Since the Lone Eagle flew the Atlantic, Americans had invested an astonishing four hundred million dollars in aircraft stocks. Airlines had sprung into operation in all parts of the continent. Manufacturers were eagerly building planes to meet their growing schedules.

"Nonsense," Richard Whitfield said. "You were the only man on Wall Street ready to do something about it."

The praise was equally true. Adrian, backed by Tillotson's money, had already bought into many of these airlines and aircraft companies at bargain rates—and was in an ideal position to become Wall Street's leader in financing new ventures through stock offerings.

It was hardly surprising that Adrian had become Richard Whitfield's favorite young comer. He was escorting Whitfield's older daughter, Cynthia, around New York. Adrian's yellow Hispano-Suiza roadster was parked outside the Whitfield Seventy-third Street town house two or three nights a week. He had put off indefinitely a reconciliation with his wife Amanda. He soothed his conscience by sending her a hefty check each month—and advising her brother Gordon on his investments. Recently he had helped Gordon make a million dollars selling a small aircraft company he had founded with a designer named Buchanan to United American Aircraft, a Detroit company that proposed to become the General Motors of the plane makers.

Very little of the airplane investments had yet to return a nickel but the paper profits were marvelous. That was the way things worked in America in the year 1929. You could buy town houses and diamond necklaces and Hispano-Suizas simply by displaying your stock portfolio to your banker. Stocks had been going up for eight years and there seemed to be no reason why they would not go up indefinitely. In the White House, President Herbert Hoover was confidently predicting the end of poverty. A jingle in the *Saturday Evening Post* summed up the national attitude, in which Adrian heartily, even defiantly, concurred.

> *O hush thee, my babe, granny's bought some more*
>   *shares,*
> *Daddy's gone out to play with the bulls and the bears,*
> *Mother's buying on tips and she simply can't lose,*
> *And baby shall have some expensive new shoes.*

Down came the Sikorsky Amphibian for a gossamer landing a few hundred yards from John Hay Whitney's dock.

The plane taxied to the pier and the copilot helped them debark. Cynthia Whitfield strolled toward them in gray slacks and a monogrammed white Bergdorf blouse, pouting. "Why didn't you wake me? I adore that plane."

Adrian smiled tolerantly. Vassar had taught Cynthia that most men were lunkheads. But Adrian did not particularly care what she thought of him. Cynthia was an appurtenance he needed to be a man of substance as successful as Richard Whitfield and possibly, in the not-too-distant future, as rich as John Hay Whitney, with his strings of polo ponies and racehorses and mansions in Cannes and Long Island and North Carolina and Florida.

"If you spent less time imitating Scott and Zelda you wouldn't have to sleep until ten-thirty every morning," Adrian said.

"What's all that about?" Churchill asked.

"A writer named Fitzgerald and his wife. Wrote a book about a gangster. Typical Irish moonshine," Whitfield said.

Churchill chuckled and they all trooped into the house for lunch. Adrian entertained them with tales of new air records. Two Australians had flown the Pacific, British flyers had winged nonstop from London to India. You could fly all over the Caribbean now thanks to enterprising Juan Trippe, who had launched an international airline named Pan American. Adrian basked in the glow of admiration these stories evoked.

Cynthia announced a determination to take flying lessons. Adrian coolly declared he was opposed to it. He said there was some evidence that frequent flying disordered a woman's body chemistry. They were studying the problem in Germany. It was a lie but Cynthia promptly lost interest in flight. As she left with the other females for tea on the terrace, Adrian lit a cigar and smiled at Mr. Churchill. Women were as easy to manipulate as the stock market.

The pain of losing Beryl Suydam had receded to a bittersweet memory. In fact, Beryl's fame as a long-distance pilot was worldwide since she flew from Moscow to Vladivostok. It added to Adrian's aviation persona when he casually remarked that he had given Beryl her first flying lessons.

The next day, Adrian sat in his mother's Fifth Avenue dining room, eating this sense of male superiority—and little else. Clarissa had come back from England only a week ago—and become an instant critic of the bull market. The burden of her speech was a grave warning to get most of his money into cash as soon as possible. She saw portents of the crash of 1893 everywhere.

"What does Geoffrey think?" Adrian said.

"He's as bad as you. Totally infatuated with the airplane. Irrational on the subject. He feels he's creating a monument to Peter, I think."

That remark made Adrian even less inclined to take her advice. With icy élan, he explained Wall Street to his mother. "They simply won't let the market go down," he said. "There's too much money at stake."

"They" were the big operators, the bankers and brokers who had loaned six billion dollars to speculators who had bought stocks on margin. Then there were the investment trusts, worth eight billion dollars. With such titans involved, the idea of a crash was ludicrous.

Clarissa Ames Van Ness raised her wineglass to her lips. Her hand trembled. "Adrian, for God's sake. I heard your—your father say the same thing thirty-six years ago."

Icy fury replaced icy élan. She was still mouthing the lie. For a moment Adrian almost told her he knew everything. He knew his real father. But forethought rescued him. He recoiled from the ensuing scene. What would he do if she wept and begged his forgiveness?

"You're talking about another century, Mother. You're hopelessly out of your depth. Do you know how much I'm worth, personally?"

"No," Clarissa Ames Van Ness said, her head bowed. She was still beautiful, even with age's wrinkles making their first inroads around her eyes and mouth.

"Ten million dollars."

Clarissa rang for the maid to take away their unfinished dinner. That done, she gazed at Adrian with something very close to loathing in her eyes. "I won't give you a cent if you fail. I won't go destitute into my old age to support your

New York arrogance. I told your father the same thing in 1893."

"Your compassion is overwhelming. It makes me think he was glad he ran into that tree limb. He may even have done it on purpose."

His mother struggled to her feet, knocking over her wine-glass. She was as white as the tablecloth. "I think we've said more than enough for one evening."

A month later, on October 24, 1929, Adrian stood in the visitors gallery of the New York Stock Exchange beside Winston Churchill, watching traders scream orders on the jammed floor. Huge blocks of stock in companies such as General Motors and Kennecott Copper were being thrown on the market. There were no buyers. Prices were in a ver-tical dive and "they"—the big operators and investment trusts—seemed powerless to pull them out.

With class A stocks dropping ten points an hour, it was almost a waste of time to ask the latest quotation on anything as speculative as airline and plane maker stocks such as United American Aircraft. They were already in the dust, mangled bits of wreckage.

"My boy," Churchill said. "We're both learning a lesson here today. There's no such thing as Santa Claus."

Adrian could not even muster a smile. All he could hear amid the frenzy on the exchange floor was his mother's voice tolling *ruined*. Was it his turn now to dwindle beneath her scorn? To live as her humble servant until fate or his own decision arranged an accident to remove him permanently from the scene?

Alone in his office, Adrian struggled to still the winged thing that looped in his chest. He was back in Anson, the American wog again. He was watching Beryl Suydam walk out the door, her radical shoulders squared. There was only one hope—his British father. The fountain pen slithered and slipped in Adrian's sweaty fingers as he composed the cable. CAN FIRM EXTEND FIVE HUNDRED THOUSAND POUNDS CREDIT? SITUATION GRAVE BUT GREAT OPPORTUNITIES FOR THOSE WHO STAY CALM.

He sat in his office for another two hours, watching the

stock ticker fall farther and farther behind. Richard Whitfield called asking Adrian if he could spare any cash. "I've had to sell out my Harvard roommate," he said. "He's threatening to kill himself."

Adrian's male secretary came in with the brown cable from London. "What should I do, Mr. Van Ness?" he asked. "I'm getting creamed."

"Sell," Adrian said, ripping open the cable.

DEEPLY REGRET MR. GEOFFREY TILLOTSON HAS RESIGNED AS MANAGING PARTNER EFFECTIVE IMMEDIATELY.

Ruined. He had hoped a reply that was even faintly encouraging would open his mother's checkbook too. Once and for all he abandoned that alternative. What was the other alternative? As he returned from the visitors' gallery, his secretary told him that eleven men had already committed suicide.

Adrian stared at the brown cable. Faintly, as if it were coming from a great distance, he heard Geoffrey Tillotson say: *Men carry on. It does a man no good to whine.* Adrian Van Ness was not the son of that ruined speculator of 1893, no matter how much sympathy he would always feel for him. He was the son of that hearty chunk of England, who stood with feet planted wide and told life to deal what blows it might, he would take them standing. He was the great-grandson of Oakes Ames, the flinty Yankee who had defied a world that pronounced him ruined.

Adrian summoned Bleriot's plane soaring over Dover Castle in 1909. He remembered Peter Tillotson in the Bristol Scout banking over Anson in 1912. He recalled the transcendence of flight above England, the sense of soaring above history into the future. He still believed tomorrow belonged to these miraculous machines.

The future. Forethought. He could hear Geoffrey Tillotson pronouncing them. The words would always have an English echo in his ear.

Father, Adrian whispered. *O Father.*

Although a winged creature looped in his chest, Adrian Van Ness would carry on.

Where, how? In the chaos of a collapsing economy, mere determination seemed futile. As he sat in his Wall Street office, his mother's presence uptown loomed above the skyline. It was only a matter of time before he succumbed to that invincible checkbook.

Unless he got out of New York. Unless he went someplace where planes were being made, some place Clarissa Van Ness would never follow him.

That was when Adrian remembered Amanda and Prince Carlo Pontecorvo's advice about those two thousand acres of orange trees in California.

GREED: THE SECOND ACT

While a half-dozen reporters watched, the gleaming white monoplane emerged from Buchanan Aircraft's dim main hangar into the brilliant California sunshine. The plane emanated modernity. Her sleek fuselage had a shark-like shape. Her streamlined engine cowling, her art deco wheel pants, added speed as well as beauty. The twin tail fins doubled her stability and maneuverability. Her 400-horsepower radial engine would enable her to fly twice as fast as the lumbering Ford Trimotors which most airlines were currently using. The multicellular wing, each cell a complex of metal angles, was so strong a steamroller could be driven across it repeatedly without damaging it.

"What's her name?" asked one of the reporters who had not bothered to read the publicity release.

"Lustra Two," Frank Buchanan said and explained the poetic allusion. He did not have to explain Lustra I. That plane was already well known to aviation writers. It had challenged the Lockheed Vega for the supremacy of the skies, setting records for speed at air races and on distance flights. Lustra

II was an attempt to take the basic design and convert it into a ten-passenger airliner.

"I'm in favor of changing it to Hot Pants," Buzz McCall said. "In a minute, you guys'll see why."

Buzz climbed into the cockpit and the engine rumbled. Minutes later, the Lustra leaped off the runway and whirled around Buchanan Field at 500 feet. At this dangerous height, Buzz did stalls and spins and banks that demonstrated the plane's amazing responsiveness. He opened her up to full throttle and whizzed across the airport again, a white blur, then all but turned her on her axis to slide in for a perfect landing.

"You're looking at the next generation airliner," Tama Morris (aka Moreno) said.

They were all working for Buchanan Aircraft—Buzz, Tama and her friend Gloria Packer, and several former mechanics from the Buzz McCall Flying Circus. Frank had hired them when Buzz agreed to take over as chief of production. Buzz and Tama had gotten married in 1929, shortly before the stock market crashed.

Frank had not had much difficulty persuading Buzz to take the job. His movie career had popped like a soap bubble in the sun as talking pictures arrived in 1927. Airplane movies went into eclipse around the same time when several stunt pilots died trying to fulfill impossible demands by directors who knew nothing about flying. The talkies had been fatal to Tama too. Her acting skills were rudimentary.

The reporters drank champagne in the hangar and peered at exhibits of the Lustra's wing structure and ultra-safe fuel system. Standing on the sidelines watching the party, a glum look on his foxy face, was their original backer, Gordon Cadwallader. Beside Cadwallader was Buchanan's chief financial officer, a small desiccated accountant named Arnold Appleby, from United American Aircraft, the Detroit company that had bought Buchanan, Lockheed and a dozen other aircraft companies in the bull market frenzy of the late 1920s. He was probably computing the cost of the champagne and the gasoline to fly the Lustra II for five minutes and adding it to his list of complaints in his daily memorandum on cutting costs.

It was March of 1930 and Wall Street showed no sign of reviving. United American stock, which had once sold as high as 70—close to what people had been paying for General Motors—was now valued at one and a half.

Beside the accountant stood Amanda Cadwallader in a flowery print dress, her shining eyes on Frank as he explained Lustra II's virtues to the reporters. Working under terrific pressure to produce planes that would make a profit in spite of the country's economic collapse, Frank had twice postponed their marriage. She had finally convinced him that she did not care whether he was rich or poor. They were to be married as soon as Lustra II was certified as airworthy by the federal government and she obtained her divorce from Adrian Van Ness.

Frank was determined to marry Amanda without a trace of Craig's misogynism in his soul. He had acquired a small library of books on the female body and applied his original mind to the problem of producing perfect bliss between husband and wife with the same passion for perfection he brought to the creation of a new plane. Their love would be as superior to the casual sex of the aircraft world as the Lustra II was to *Rag Time*.

"Tonight at our house—a real celebration," Buzz said, as the reporters departed.

"You're all invited," Tama cooed after the newsmen.

"I think we better have a talk," Appleby said to Frank and Buzz.

Gordon Cadwallader joined them in Appleby's office. Amanda was left to explore the cabin and cockpit of Lustra II. Appleby wasted no time. "We're broke," he said. "We can't even meet this week's payroll."

"The hell you say," Buzz roared. "We've sold twenty Lustra Ones in the last twelve months and we've got orders for another six."

"Whatever we've made on those transactions—which is damn little, with the salaries you're paying yourselves, has been requisitioned as an extraordinary expense to meet corporate financial problems," Appleby said.

"You son of a bitch!" Frank roared, seizing Appleby by the shirt. "You're robbing us to keep your Detroit friends driving around in their lousy Packards."

"Robbing is hardly the correct term," Appleby said, disengaging his shirt. "We own you, Mr. Buchanan. You are a division of United American Aircraft and we can do what we please with your cash."

"What about my stock?" Buzz cried. In the heyday of the bull market, with Lustras selling at the rate of three a month, he had put every cent he had into UAA.

"You're a very minor stockholder," Appleby said.

"We're all minor," Gordon Cadwallader growled. "UAA has twenty million shares outstanding."

"We're declaring bankruptcy and selling off our assets to satisfy class A stockholders and creditors," Appleby said.

"What the hell's a class A stockholder?" Frank said.

"You're looking at one," Gordon Cadwallader snarled. "I'll only get about ten cents on the dollar. You drew a salary while I got nothing. Not even a dividend."

"It was your idea to put us into that Detroit deal!" Frank shouted.

"You didn't complain when your stock was worth a half million dollars," Cadwallader said.

"You're robbing my company—my name," Frank said. "I'm going to sue the hell out of you."

"I don't think you have a case," Cadwallader said. "If you threaten me, I'll make sure you don't have a case."

"Consider yourself threatened," Frank said.

"You're not welcome in my house any longer."

"It's not your house. Amanda owns it just as much as you do," Frank shouted. "The same thing goes for those two thousand acres of orange trees. The day after we're married, I plan to have a lawyer go over the books of Cadwallader Groves and find exactly where the profits are going. Your days of intimidating her into being a silent partner will be over."

"You can hire all the lawyers in California," Appleby said,

in his infuriating drone. "This company is out of business, as of tomorrow morning. Notices will be posted, informing the employees before they leave tonight. Its assets and liabilities will be in the hands of the bankruptcy court of Los Angeles County within twenty-four hours."

"Why did you torment us—let us fly Lustra Two?" Frank cried.

Appleby grimaced. It was as close as he ever came to a smile. "Someone may want to buy the plane—and the design. Make sure when you leave tonight that all aspects of your design work will be available to prospective purchasers."

"The design of that plane is not for sale," Frank roared. "That came out of my head."

"Your head—as well as your hands—were working for United American Aircraft," Appleby said.

The enormous fact of his impotence, of all their impotences, descended on Frank. Gordon Cadwallader completed his humiliation. "Stay away from Amanda. Consider that a warning."

Gordon Cadwallader took a bewildered Amanda home. Frank retreated to the McCalls' house in Long Beach, where a funeral for Buchanan Aircraft lasted far into the night. Bootleg liquor flowed and everyone got very drunk. Frank awoke at noon the following day to find himself in a bed with Gloria Packer. "You looked so sad, Frank. I just wanted you to know I still cared," Gloria said.

Frank had tried to stay celibate for the last three years. It had not been easy, with Buzz for a partner. Ten-year-old Billy McCall appeared in the doorway with a pitcher of orange juice, intensifying Frank's guilt. Buzz had taken Billy into his household when he married Tama. "Any chance of a ride in Lustra Two, Pops?" he said, using the nickname he had given Frank years ago.

"No one's ever going to ride in Lustra Two if I can help it," Frank said.

Before he could execute his revenge, Frank had to extricate Amanda from her brother's custody. He drove to Long Beach Airport, where he kept his Lustra I. In a half hour he was circling over the white turreted Cadwallader mansion in Fullerton. Amanda stood on the lawn, waving to him. But it was Gordon Cadwallader who greeted him as he got out of the plane.

"I think we better have a talk," Gordon said.

"I'm through talking to you. I'm here to take Amanda away with me."

"If you really love Amanda, you'll do what I tell you. Get in the car."

They climbed into his Hupmobile Six and drove to the nearby mental hospital where Amanda's mother was an apparently perpetual patient. There were a half-dozen people on the lawn talking to themselves, wandering dazedly with glazed eyes. "It costs me five thousand dollars a year to keep her here," Gordon Cadwallader said. "If it weren't for Amanda's feelings, I'd have sent her to a state hospital years ago. She's my father's second wife. She never liked me."

Inside, they were greeted by Carl Farber, the German doctor who ran the place. He led Frank to the second floor and stopped before a door marked 13. He opened a small window and invited Frank to look inside. A woman with Amanda's russet hair and angular face paced up and down the tiny room. She sensed Frank's eyes on her and flung herself at the door. "Stop these men from tormenting me!" she screamed. "Tell my warriors where I am! Tell them Queen Califia is calling on them to rise again!"

"Mrs. Cadwallader thinks she's Califia, the mythical Amazon queen of California," Dr. Farber said. "An interesting schizophrenic delusion. It enables her to despise the entire male sex."

Back at Casa Felicidad, Gordon led Frank into his office, locked the door and set up a small motion picture projector and screen. He pulled down the shade and they sat in semi-darkness. At first Frank was bewildered by the flickering images. A dark lake, sodden Negro musicians stumbling ashore clutching their instruments, naked women on a barge. He realized it was the British director's outtake of the party at Modesto, after finishing *Loop the Loop*. There was Mabel

Durand doing a show-it-all shimmy while her ladies in waiting Charlestoned around her in the buff.

In the next frames Mabel was alone on the raft, stretched
on her chaise longue while various members of the cast and
crew rose dripping from the black waters of the lake to enjoy
her. One was unmistakably Buzz McCall. With his clothes
off, he looked part ape. Then another man, bigger than Buzz,
with pale skin and reddish hair that looked almost white in
the kleig lights. Frank watched himself, sick with shame.

Gordon Cadwallader stopped the camera. "I had a private
detective investigate you last year when it began to look like
you might actually marry Amanda. He picked this up on the
blackmail market. Do you think I should show it to
Amanda?"

"What do you want me to do?"

"Write her a letter, telling her you're bankrupt and you
think it best to stop seeing her."

Frank sat down at Cadwallader's desk and wrote the letter.
He stalked to his Lustra I and flew to Santa Monica, where
he found the Buchanan Aircraft Company hangar padlocked
and a notice of bankruptcy pasted on the doors. He borrowed
a sledgehammer from one of the other hangars, smashed the
lock and got into the cockpit of Lustra II.

Airborne, he roared above Los Angeles and its curving
boulevards. Gordon Cadwallader and United American Aircraft had stolen his happiness, his future. But they would not
steal Lustra II. Without this plane, Buchanan Aircraft was
worth nothing.

Pulling a parachute from beneath the copilot's seat, Frank
turned Lustra II's sleek nose east, toward the Mojave. Over
the desert, he shoved the controls forward, kicked open the
cockpit door and flung himself into space. By a miracle he
evaded the tail and his parachute soon opened. Beneath his
feet, the beautiful white plane exploded in a blossom of orange flame on the desert floor.

The sight made him feel guilty of a crime almost as brutal
as the one Gordon Cadwallader had committed against him
and Amanda. How could he ever explain it to Buzz and the
men who had worked on the plane, who loved it as their

creation as much as his? There was only one thing to do—
obliterate all trace of Frank Buchanan, the plane designer.
Hitching a ride back to Santa Monica, he began methodically
destroying the thousands of drawings and blueprints that had
gone into the creation of Lustra II and Lustra I.

He was interrupted by a woman's voice crying "Frank" at
the far end of the hangar. It echoed around him like a spirit
from the other world. He walked through the dimness to
confront Amanda.

"What does this letter mean?"

"It means I—can't marry you."

"Why?"

"I'm bankrupt. I haven't a cent. Surely your brother's told
you."

"He told me a great many things. I want to hear them
from you."

"What did he tell you?"

"He said this letter proved what he'd suspected all along.
You never wanted anything from us but money and now that
the money is gone—we're almost as poor as you these
days—you're no longer interested. You came out there today
to ask him for money and when he told you how little we
had you wrote this—this abominable letter."

She was weeping now. What could he say? Gordon Cadwallader was perfectly capable of showing her that film.
She might end up in Farber's sanitarium raving like her
mother. "That's something of an exaggeration. I still care for
you—"

"What else matters? I don't give a damn whether you're
rich or poor. I never have. I'd give myself to you right now
if I thought—"

She struggled to control the tears that were flooding her
voice.

"If I thought you were telling the truth."

She turned and walked slowly toward the open doors at
the front of the hangar. Sunlight blazed outside. A yellow
Lockheed Vega was racing down the runway to zoom into
the sky. The plane evoked his dream of soaring in this
woman's arms to new altitudes.

"Tell your brother I crashed Lustra Two. Tell him there's nothing here for him to sell."

It was better to play the madman. Better to be nothing but the stunt-flying bum who had plummeted into her life three years ago. Any humiliation, the worst possible disguise, was better than her seeing that film. His performance was a last twisted gesture of love. Weeping, cursing, Frank Buchanan went back to destroying his paper airplanes.

LOVE AMONG THE ORANGES

Six months later, Adrian Van Ness sat on the porch of Casa Felicidad, holding his wife Amanda's hand. California sunshine streamed down on them. The air was thick with the perfume of orange blossoms. For Adrian it was the scent of the promised land.

The situation was unreal but Adrian had grown used to unreality since Wall Street crashed. Clinging to his fragments of fatherhood from Geoffrey Tillotson, he had driven west through a landscape of pain. The Great Depression was twisting America on a continental rack. On the outskirts of city after city, homeless men lived in hobo jungles, clusters of tin shacks and empty packing cases. They crowded around fires in trash cans on street corners and glared at him as he drove past in his yellow Hispano-Suiza. He was frequently tempted to tell them the car was his last remaining asset.

Adrian went to California with only the dimmest idea of what he was going to do when he got there. Amanda and her orange groves were a faint hope, no more. When he wrote to explain why he was unable to continue the support money he had sent her since their separation, there had been no answer.

In Orange County, he discovered Amanda was, if anything, more forlorn than the woman he had sent home from

England. Her brother hinted there had been a romance that had recently expired. He urged Adrian to consider a reconciliation. He also filled Adrian in on the chaos in the California aircraft industry. Companies were going bankrupt and being sold at knockdown prices every third day. He added his personal tale of woe—the paper million he had lost in United American Aircraft. Adrian, who had lost ten times that amount in the same and similar companies, pretended to be sympathetic.

For a month Adrian had concealed his desperation and waited for a sign of forgiveness from Amanda. She had maintained a melancholy distance. With his money running low, he had decided to gamble on a frontal assault. "After the way I treated you in London, I have absolutely no claim on your affections," he said. "I see now I was completely under my mother's influence."

"I understood, Adrian. I was afraid it would happen."

"In the past month I've come to feel we never really separated. I feel as if we we've been sharing similar experiences. The pain of loneliness—and heartbreak. Will you take me back, Amanda?"

"Adrian I—I'm afraid the same thing would happen. I'm sure your mother still hates me."

"My mother's approval or disapproval no longer interests me. I doubt if we'll ever see her in California. The only thing that matters is the way I've regained my old feeling for you."

"I'm not sure what I feel—"

"Darling, I know you still love me. I admit—why should I deny it?—I've been trying to reawaken that love for the past month. Say yes."

Amanda wept and told him about her chaste romance with Frank Buchanan and his abominable behavior at its close. In her heart she felt she had been unfaithful to Adrian. Could he forgive her? Adrian considered matching the story with his far less platonic heartbreak with Beryl Suydam and decided against it.

"There's nothing to forgive," he assured her. "I hope someday soon I can give that bastard Buchanan what he deserves."

"Oh Adrian. Yes. Yes. Yes."

They kissed across the tea table.

That night, while Amanda waited upstairs, Adrian and Gordon Cadwallader met in the study and executed a legal document. For fifty thousand dollars, Adrian sold Amanda's rights to 50 percent of Cadwallader Groves. Adrian also agreed to take over the expense of maintaining Amanda's mother in Dr. Farber's sanitarium.

Upstairs, Adrian discovered that fifty thousand dollars was erotic, even if his trembling wife was almost its opposite. Amanda returned to his arms with a stifled, possibly regretful cry that only made him feel more powerful, more confident in the future, in spite of the comatose stock market and the doom-crying newspapers.

In the morning Amanda began packing for a second honeymoon on Catalina Island. Adrian told her they would have to delay their idyl for a day. He was due in bankruptcy court at 10 A.M., where he expected to buy the Buchanan Aircraft Company. "Then I'm going down to the factory, where I gather your former friend Mr. Buchanan is still lurking, and throw him out on his head."

Amanda kissed him fiercely. "Let me come. I want to see it!"

"No. Gordon tells me he may get violent."

"I *want* to come," Amanda said, displaying a willfulness Adrian thought life's disappointments had demolished.

Trained from birth to please women whenever possible, Adrian shrugged. "All right. But it may be unpleasant."

They drove to the Los Angeles County Courthouse with Gordon Cadwallader's lawyer, who was handling the legal details. The lawyer had told Adrian the business would not take five minutes and he was right. There were no other bidders. The balding judge obviously regarded Adrian as slightly insane as he banged his gavel and informed him that he was the sole owner of Buchanan Aircraft, including its debts and liabilities, for thirty thousand dollars.

Adrian shook hands with the lawyer and whizzed to the Buchanan plant in Santa Monica with Amanda beside him in the Hispano-Suiza. In the design and engineering offices at the rear of the main hangar, they found a swarthy man in a flying jacket and overalls cleaning out his desk. He looked at Adrian in his dark blue Savile Row suit as if he was a somewhat comic figure and introduced himself as Buzz McCall, the former chief of production.

Adrian informed McCall that he was the new owner and asked if Frank Buchanan was in the building. "He's been drunk for the last three months," Buzz said. "Ever since he crashed Lustra Two."

Adrian sat down slowly. Gordon Cadwallader had shown him the press clippings of Lustra Two's debut. They had convinced him that Buchanan Aircraft had a plane he could sell to the airlines.

"How long will it take to build another one?"

"That depends on when Buchanan sobers up."

"What do you mean?"

"He tore up all the designs. Ditto the blueprints. He did the same thing to the Lustra One files."

"I thought you had a half dozen orders for Lustra Ones." Again, Adrian was relying on Gordon Cadwallader's information.

"We did. Frank wrote letters, cancelling them."

"I'll sue him. I'll put him in jail," Adrian said.

Buzz shrugged. "You can probably do both. But it won't get you any closer to building some planes."

"There are other designers."

"Look at this before you start hiring someone else," Buzz said. "I found it in the mailbox when I came in."

It was a letter on the stationery of TWA, the new airline recently put together from the wreckage of Trans Western and several other lines that had collapsed since the stock market crashed. Adrian read it and handed it to Amanda.

Dear Frank: I have just taken on the job of consultant to TWA. They have financing from Howard Hughes, the Texas multimillionaire and are planning to buy quite a number of planes. I told them if it was at all possible, they should get a model with a Buchanan wing. Can your company produce a transport

capable of carrying 25 or 30 people within the next six
months?

Sincerely,
Charles Lindbergh

"You know Mr. Buchanan well, Mr. McCall?"

"Pretty well."

"Do you want to keep working here?"

Buzz shrugged. "I gotta work somewhere. I got a wife and
two kids."

"Tell him if he wants to save your job—everyone's job—
he should consider coming back to work as soon as possible.
Assure him I will let him have complete autonomy as chief
designer. I have no intention of changing the company's
name. Everyone knows Buchanan means quality planes. Tell
him I can sell planes better than anyone else in the country.
I know almost every airline executive in the business personally."

"I'll tell him," Buzz said. "I don't know whether it will
do any good."

"Tell the office people to report for work tomorrow,"
Adrian said.

Buzz nodded and swaggered out. Adrian sighed and turned
to Amanda. "I'm terribly afraid we'll have to postpone our
second honeymoon."

Amanda did not speak until she was back in the Hispano-
Suiza. As Adrian drove out of the Buchanan Aircraft parking
lot, she hissed a single word: "Liar."

REVELATIONS

For a long time that word *liar* encompassed all of them—
Adrian, Frank, her brother. Amanda did not know the exact
content of the lie. But she sensed its presence the moment
Adrian rehired Frank. She saw the cold-eyed banker she had

disliked in England. She was equally sure the contrite husband she had seen on Casa Felicidad's porch was a fraud.

She decided to leave them all. She was going to flee to New York, walk the streets, sell herself to men if necessary. She was going to escape California and its lies. Everything about it had become a lie, even the beauty of the land itself, its perpetual sunshine that denied the evil festering in the souls of men like her brother Gordon.

As she planned her escape, hoarding small amounts from the money that Adrian gave her to run their house in Westwood, only a few miles from the Buchanan plant, she had to struggle to retain her intuition of deceit. Adrian did everything in his power to annihilate it. He wielded arguments like a master duelist, portraying the golden future they would share, vowing that he had done nothing that any rational man would not have done when he discovered the truth about Buchanan Aircraft.

"The money!" Amanda raged. "Where did you get the money?"

"From your brother."

Adrian did not tell her how or why Gordon had produced the cash. He described it as a loan. She was even more confused by his repeated protestations of love. Still she refused to let him touch her. Adrian was not exactly importunate on this point. He was working fifteen hours a day, organizing a sales force, pleading with bankers for loans, trying to accommodate Frank Buchanan's erratic work habits.

Early in 1932, Amanda felt a presence in her body. She recognized it immediately as a child and knew in the next instant it was a girl. A few days later she met one of the Mexican pickers from Cadwallader Groves working in a grocery store in Westwood. Impulsively, she told him about the baby, then realized how strange the encounter was. Miguel had worked at Cadwallader Groves for over twenty years. "What are you doing here?" she asked.

"No more orange work," he said. "They cut down the trees."

She drove to Casa Felicidad in a wild rage. Sure enough, men were sawing down tree after tree. The landscape lay bare all the way to the river. Tractors were ripping up the stumps, leaving raw wounds in the green grass. The earth was being raped in front of her eyes.

"I won't let you do this!" she raged at her brother.

"It's none of your business," he said.

"I own half of it. I should have been consulted!"

"Adrian sold your half to me months ago."

A saw emitted an especially piercing shriek. For a moment Gordon almost lost his business aplomb. "Something like this had to be done soon," he snarled. "I mortgaged the place to the last tree to play the stock market. It's either drill for oil or let the goddamn banks grab it."

Amanda knew why there was a snarl in Gordon's voice. She knew why he had been secretly glad to risk Cadwallader Groves to make millions on Wall Street. She knew why he did not care about what he was desecrating here with his tractors and saws.

Gordon was destroying Eden. He was destroying the memory of their father and her mother walking naked among the trees, making love on the cool grass. Five-year-old Amanda had adored the lovemaking. She had clapped her hands and begged them to do it again. Seven-year-old Gordon had screamed *no* and had run frantically around the grove, clutching his dangling thing. Eden had made him afraid. It required courage to live in Eden.

Gordon was destroying Eden because there was evil in his soul. Adrian was his collaborator. He did not care if Gordon erected grimy rigs that spewed black stinking oil over the green grass where love had flowered in the sunlight. That meant there was evil in Adrian's soul too.

The wish to flee them all swelled in Amanda's throat with new desperation. But what could she do, where could she go with a child? The whole country was bankrupt. People were standing on endless lines to get a bowl of soup in New York and Chicago. Motherhood, motherness, consumed her.

She went home to Westwood and lay in bed remembering the loneliness of Casa Felicidad after her father died in the army and her mother retreated to her room and began to imagine she was Queen Califia, betrayed by her subjects.

For the first time Amanda thought about her mother's delusion. She had chanted songs about the cruel fate of Califia, abandoned as a prisoner, a victim, to the power of men. The words had a meaning for her. Now Amanda was in the middle of the same meaning.

Did her mother include her husband, Amanda's father, in her denunciations of male cruelty and lust? No, he was the exception, one of the rare ones who had no evil in his soul. Amanda had dreamt of finding Eden again with Frank Buchanan. Not at Casa Felicidad with Gordon watching. They would fly to it in one of Frank's planes.

She had been sure they could find another Eden in some remote canyon in the Cascades or the Sierras. They would swoop into it and strip off their clothes, strip off shame and civilization and discover the redeeming power of love.

What had gone wrong? Was Frank really no different from Adrian? Amanda could not believe it. All her instincts denied it. A hundred times, she got out the letter Frank had written, breaking his promise to marry her. She relived the conversation in the hangar. She wept. When Adrian came home at midnight, he found her in the kitchen staring at nothing, weeping.

He was profoundly, genuinely alarmed. When she told him Gordon had revealed his sale of her share of Cadwallader Groves, Adrian swore her brother had given her the most venal, the most atrocious version of the story. He had planned to raise the money from a bank, offering her share of Cadwallader Groves as equity, guaranteeing her continued half ownership of the property. He said he never would have taken such a step without her approval. But the bankruptcy court had moved the date of the Buchanan sale forward with no warning. He had been afraid to tell her before their reconciliation and there had been no time to tell her afterward.

It was almost convincing. Amanda discerned in Adrian's vehemence a kind of caring. She stopped crying. The child swelled in her belly, independent, indifferent to memory, regret, hatred. Amanda lived with Adrian Van Ness and the daily drama of Buchanan Aircraft's struggle to survive. It was impossible to remain indifferent to it. Adrian talked about nothing else. Her own happiness, the happiness of her child, was at stake.

With help from Buzz McCall, they had persuaded Frank Buchanan to come back to work and begin building another Lustra II for TWA. Adrian made an important contribution to the new design. Waiting at the Los Angeles airport one day, he watched a single-engined Varney Speed Line Vega take off, followed by a lumbering Ford Trimotor flying for Braniff. He suddenly remembered a story Carlo Pontecorvo had told him about how nervous single-engine planes made passengers on European airlines. He cancelled his flight and rushed back to the plant to persuade Frank to put two engines on the new Lustra II.

A day later, Adrian had sold the idea to Jack Frye, the president of TWA, and changed the plane's name to the SkyRanger. He disliked Frank's fondness for classical names, which few customers would ever understand.

The child grew. It leaped in Amanda's belly now, especially when Adrian put his hand there. Amanda permitted this much touching. She could not remove the word *liar* from Adrian's forehead. But she found it difficult to remain in a state of rage at him. He was so polite, so urbane, so determined to make her like him again. Amanda began to wonder if she could ever leave him.

A rhythm developed between the baby and the new plane at the factory. Both seemed to be growing on the same schedule. Adrian told Amanda he had promised a bonus to the workforce if the SkyRanger flew on or before the day his daughter was born. When Adrian invited Amanda to visit the factory in the middle of her eighth month, she could not resist the idea.

Inside the cavernous hangar, four dozen workmen swarmed around the ribbed fuselage, which rested on jigs, erector set–like metal platforms about six feet above the floor. It looked like the stripped skeleton of a whale on the deck of the *Pequod* in Melville's *Moby-Dick*. But this creature was coming to life. An obsequious smile on his tough guy's face, production chief Buzz McCall introduced her to foremen and riveters and machinists and explained that tomorrow they were going to give the SkyRanger her skin. Twin shells of lightweight steel would be glued together around the ribs.

"How many more weeks, Mrs. Van Ness?" one of the workmen yelled, as they departed. Amanda held up three fingers.

"We're way ahead. We're gonna finish this baby in two!"

In Adrian's office, she met Buzz McCall's dark-haired wife, Tama, who was, she cheerfully explained, Buchanan's publicity director.

"And office manager and payroll clerk and bookkeeper," Adrian added.

"This'll make a terrific story," Tama said.

A grinning little man with a flash camera materialized and began taking pictures of Amanda and Adrian, smiling, their arms around each other. Tama posed Amanda in the window of the office, so her bulging stomach was profiled against the light. "Terrific," she cried as the flashbulb popped again.

Amanda felt violated by the whole process. But she did not know how to protest it. Tama led her back to the assembly line, where Amanda posed with a half-dozen grinning workmen while the photographer blazed away.

The SkyRanger was completed in two weeks and rolled out for her first tests. It was a time of terrific tension for Adrian and everyone else. Would she live up to the promise of her design?

Precisely on the day her obstetrician predicted, Amanda went into labor. As she struggled to cope with the pains, she found herself hoping fiercely for a girl. She did not want a son. Adrian would corrupt him. She could protect a daughter from him. Confirming her intuition, the child was a girl.

"Do you have a name for her?" the formidable floor nurse demanded, as she filled out the tag for the tiny wrist.

"No," Amanda said, dismayed that she had never discussed it with Adrian. Would he name her Clarissa after his mother? She hated the name. She was afraid to use her own mother's name. She half-believed that names had power, that they carried meaning, fate, into a life.

"Where's my husband?" she asked.

"I have no idea," the nurse said, her opinion of Adrian's absence all too clear.

"He's here at last," Adrian said from the doorway of her room.

He kissed her limp hand. "I kept in touch by telephone. We were putting the plane through the final tests. She passed them all. The TWA people were there. They signed a contract for twenty planes on the spot."

"Marvelous. They want—a name."

Adrian took the tiny bundle out of the nurse's arms. She had been fussing and whining. She stopped and seemed to gaze up at him. "Do babies this young smile?" Adrian asked. "I could swear she's smiling."

"You are," Amanda said. The expression on Adrian's face was miraculous. It evoked the memory of her father's smile. The reality of unqualified love. She could never leave him now, Amanda thought. She might even learn to love him.

"Mr. Van Ness," said the impatient nurse. "Does the child have a name?"

"Victoria. Her name is Victoria."

The next day, Tama Morris arrived with a huge spray of roses—and her friend the photographer. Once more Amanda experienced the violated feeling, this time on her own and Victoria's behalf. Again she found it impossible to protest. Tama was so agreeable, so enthusiastic about the baby and the wonderful story and the wonderful news at the plant. Dark eyes aglow, she recited the dazzling figures. TWA was going to pay two and a half million dollars for the twenty planes.

A final blinding flash made Victoria whimper. "That's it, Roscoe, scram," Tama said.

The photographer fled as if he was afraid Tama might do him bodily harm. She lit a cigarette and sat down on the edge of the bed. "You're really glad it's a girl?"

"Yes," Amanda said.

"Why? Men get all the breaks in this world."

Propped on her white pillows, lying beneath the white hospital blanket in the white-walled room with thick white sunshine pouring through the window, Amanda contemplated

Tama's darkness. It was in her hair, her eyes, her olive skin—and those bitter words. Suddenly Amanda saw this beautiful woman's entire life. Her willfulness, her pride, her despair. She felt a kinship with her beyond the power of words, something she had never felt for another woman.

"Do you have any children?" she asked.

"A son by my first husband and a stepson by Buzz's first wife. They make me almost wish for a daughter. It'd be nice not to have to play drill sergeant all the time."

"Adrian seems pleased to have a daughter."

"Adrian's different. He's not your average flyboy. They think a woman's only good for one thing."

Amanda saw new darkness, new perils in Tama's soul. Tama inhaled her cigarette. "You're lucky."

Amanda's heart almost broke. Tama was explaining her fate to herself. Amanda wanted to offer her some consolation. "But you've got an important job."

"Nah," Tama said. "They just hired a man to be my boss. Some yo-yo from the *LA Times*. Adrian was nice enough to try to explain it to me, at least. It's a man's business. As if I didn't know that. It's a man's world. Even if you're Norma Shearer. You've still got some SOB studio executive telling you what to do."

Amanda saw how hopeless it really was. "Thank you for the roses," she said.

"Hey, it's the least we could do. You've gotten us more publicity this week then we've had in a year."

The next day, a totally unexpected figure filled the doorway: Frank Buchanan. He carried a gigantic white rabbit and a huge bouquet. "What a wonderful surprise," she said.

He kissed her hand. "Are you happy?" he said.

"Yes," she said. "Are you?"

He shrugged.

"I thought the good news about the plane would make you happy."

"That's my consolation. Not the same as happiness. I designed it for you—and this little creature—as much as for myself."

Suddenly she wanted to scream, rage at him. "I don't

know what you mean," she said, her voice empty and cold, her eyes averted.

"I would never have come back for any other reason. Adrian said he'd spent every cent he borrowed from your brother to buy the company. Everything you owned was at stake. I'm glad I came now. Consolation is better than nothing."

"I still don't know what you're saying!" she cried. She meant of course that he was not explaining the most important thing.

"What happened was entirely my fault," Frank said. "A— lamentable swinishness on my part. I deserve everything I've suffered for it. I only wish you hadn't suffered."

Suddenly nothing mattered, the child, Adrian's adoration of his daughter, the possibility of a happy marriage. Nothing mattered but the memory of that morning when Lindbergh was flying the Atlantic and she had taken Frank Buchanan's hand.

"I'm through with suffering!" she raged. "We're going to be very rich. I'm going to enjoy myself."

"I hope so," Frank said.

For the rest of the day, Amanda waited for Adrian. She wanted him to smile at Victoria again, to tell her more good news. But Adrian never appeared. She tried to feed Victoria but the baby could not get enough milk from her small breasts. "I knew she'd have to go on a bottle," the Valkyrian floor nurse said and carried the baby triumphantly away to the nursery.

Amanda lay alone in the white-walled room, watching darkness fall. She thought of Tama's despair, Frank's defeat, Adrian's smiling lies. She thought of her helplessness, her mother's madness, her brother's greed. When, how, could it change?

Darkness crept into the room. She did not bother to put on her bed lamp. She lay there, listening to wails and whimpers and random voices in the hall. When, how, could it change?

Califia could change it. Her mother sat beside her, wreathed in the golden light of Eden, telling her about Califia, when Amanda was five. What if Califia came by night to challenge the vile rule of men? She could enlist a million women like Tama, women who had been used for only one thing. A new army of Amazons would arise to reconquer California and restore the kingdom of women.

"Mrs. Van Ness. What in the world are you doing, lying here in the dark?" asked the floor nurse.

"I was thinking," Amanda said.

"There's only one thing you should think about," the nurse said. "Getting some milk in those breasts. I've brought you an extra glass for supper. Drink it all. If you can't nurse your baby, you don't feel like a woman. After all, it's what nature intended us to do. I've never seen a bottle baby who's been happy. They cry all the time."

Obediently Amanda gulped two huge glasses of foaming milk, while her keeper nodded approvingly. Califia was gone. But not forgotten.

BOOK THREE

BOOK THREE

MEN AND BOYS

Birdsong and sunlight. A beautiful spring morning. Half awake, Frank Buchanan imagined himself wandering through the green ravines of Topanga Canyon with his golden labrador, Winston. He wondered how long this unspoiled wilderness so close to Los Angeles would last if half the unemployed in America persisted in moving to California.

Wham wham wham. A fist was pounding on the front door. Winston was barking thunderously. Frank pushed himself up on one elbow. Jesus. There was a woman in his bed. What the hell was her name? Gladys? Gloria? She was a blonde. They were always blondes, in memory of Sammy. Never russets or even redheads. His pathetic way of honoring his chaste love for Amanda.

Where had this woman come from? Oh, yes. He had spent the weekend in Palm Springs, a little town in the Mojave desert, at a meeting of the Conquistadores del Cielo, the club Adrian Van Ness and other company presidents had organized to try to mold the airframe and engine makers and airlines into a group that could have some impact on the American psyche. Adrian had suggested the title to emphasize the airframe makers' largely California origins—and the grandeur of their ambitions. The conquistadores Frank had met in Palm Springs struck him as the biggest bunch of drunks he had ever seen. They had spent the weekend consuming immense amounts of booze and lamenting their imminent bankruptcy.

Frank's only pleasant moments had come when he watched Adrian trying to compete in the macho games the Conquistadores played—skeet shooting and archery from horseback, lancing targets à la the knights of the round table, running races with one leg strapped to a partner (Frank and

Adrian had been matched and—predictably—came in last).
But the gloom pervading the aircraft business far outweighed
the droll moments.

After growing at an astonishing rate in the first half of the
1930s, defying the otherwise depressed national economy,
the airlines were now in a fearful slide. Buchanan had
boomed along for a while on a flood of orders for SkyRanger
I and recently celebrated the rollout of SkyRanger II, bigger,
faster, with a pressurized cabin. But Boeing and Douglas had
both came out with competing models and Lockheed's Elec-
tra was also in the brawl. The future of SkyRanger II was
uncertain at best. All they had so far was an order for ten
copies from TWA.

If the rumors swirling around the company were true,
SkyRanger II might be the last plane Buchanan would produce. Frank remembered Amanda's defiant prophecy about
getting rich, five years ago. He wondered what she felt now,
on the edge of bankruptcy. Most of the time he tried not to
think about Amanda. It was too painful.

To console themselves, the floundering Conquistadores
had flown in a covey of girls for the last night of their desert
conclave. Each was a beauty, selected by their companies for
their willingness to brighten the proceedings for an hour or
two. The blonde in Frank's bed had obviously been one of
them. *Wham wham wham.* The fist pounding on his door was
not going away. Frank pulled on a pair of pants, telling himself he had to stop this drinking and random screwing. He
flung water in his face and stumbled to the front door, as the
fist continued to pound. Who could it be? A bill collector?
They usually pursued Adrian Van Ness and good luck to
them.

Wham wham wham. Had he made his monthly payment
on his car? He depended on his secretary for those details.
Was that her in bed? Marian? She was blond too.

He flung open the door and found himself face to face
with sixteen-year-old Billy McCall. Literally face to face.
Billy was no longer the cheerful chubby boy Frank had visited in Laguna Beach. He was almost six feet tall with solid
shoulders and a craggy face that blended innocence and dis-

illusion in a way that troubled Frank every time he saw him.

"I just had another go-round with Tama," Billy said. "I've had it with that bitch. I want to move in with you."

"Why sure. But—"

"I won't cramp your style. I just need a place to sleep. I got friends with wheels. I don't need an allowance. I got a job at the Long Beach airport."

"What about school?"

"The hell with school."

Billy was going to the public school in Westwood, one of Los Angeles's best. He studied just enough to stay one step ahead of expulsion. He was currently on his spring vacation.

"No deal," Frank said. "If that's why you're fighting with Tama you're going to have the same fight with me."

"I'm not fighting with Tama about school. I've had it with her lousy remarks. She never stops trying to make me look like a bum. While her big handsome momma's boy Cliff is always *wonderful*."

Frank waved him into the house. "You had any breakfast?"

Billy shook his head. Frank led him into the kitchen and began cooking bacon and eggs. As he was about to serve them, the blonde wandered in wearing his old army bathrobe. "Hi," she said. "Who's this?"

"My nephew, sort of," Frank said, winking at Billy. "I hate to admit it but I've forgotten your name."

"Sylvia. Sylvia Sydenham. My real name's Jones. You got some coffee? What the hell were they putting in those drinks?"

"I think it was gin."

The telephone rang. Tama Morris McCall's angry voice bored into Frank's throbbing skull. "Is Billy there?"

"Yes."

"You tell him to get the hell home here and simonize our cars. It's his turn. Cliff did it last month. If he doesn't have them both finished before sundown I'm going to tell his father what he called me."

"What did he say?"

"Never mind. It's too disgusting to repeat."

Tama had grown more and more proper as her movie career receded over the horizon. She could sound as straitlaced as a Midwest Methodist these days. Although her sex life was apparently still steamy. When Buzz married her, he had made it clear that he reserved the right to enjoy other women. Tama soon demonstrated two could play the reservations game. She had personally escorted Buchanan's contingent of beauties to the Conquistadores party.

"Give him until tomorrow on the simonizing," Frank said. "I'll take him for a ride in SkyRanger II and calm things down."

"That's no way to teach him discipline," Tama said. "You're going to ruin that boy, Frank."

"He doesn't look that bad to me."

"Put Sylvia on the line."

Sylvia came alive when she heard Tama's name. "Hi," she said in her brightest actress voice.

Her kewpie-doll face darkened. "Gee, Tama, I don't feel so hot. Does it have to be tonight?"

Sylvia sighed. "Okay. I'll be there. The Biltmore at six."

She slammed down the phone. "One of your goddamn airline big shots wants some more entertainment after he sees your wonderful new plane."

Billy shoveled down his ham and eggs. Frank avoided his eyes. Sixteen-year-olds should not be hearing the unlovely details of the way planes were sold.

"That SkyRanger II sounds like some plane, Pops," Billy said. "Where we going in her?"

Billy thought, ate, slept, drank, dreamt planes. He never read a book or magazine about anything else. He never stopped badgering Frank and Buzz to teach him to fly.

"No place in particular. Our savior and leader, Adrian Van Ness, wants to know how much money it will cost to fix some problems. We're going to run a few tests."

Frank regarded Adrian Van Ness with an unstable mixture of hostility and respect. He had rescued Buchanan Aircraft from oblivion. Adrian had also reclaimed the only woman Frank Buchanan had loved since Sammy. He struggled not to blame Adrian for that fact. But every time Frank saw

Amanda at a company party or rollout of a new plane, she looked unhappy. That made Adrian harder to like.

Frank gave Sylvia twenty dollars for a taxi and drove to the factory in his Ford. Billy fiddled with the radio and soon they were listening to an announcer describing an air raid on Madrid. "What about this civil war in Spain?" Billy asked. "Do you think the Russian planes can handle those German and Italian jobs? That Messerschmitt One-oh-nine sounds like quite a plane."

"The Polikaparpovs are pretty good fighter planes. The Russians have some first-class designers. I think they'll do okay."

"Who's gonna win the war?"

"The Loyalists, I hope."

"You mean you're for the Communists? Buzz says anyone who's for the Reds is a traitor."

"The loyalists aren't all Communists."

"Do you think we're gonna get into a war with the Germans or the Russians, Pops?"

"I hope not. People get killed in wars. I lost a lot of friends in the last one."

"You don't get killed if you're good enough. That's what Buzz says."

"I don't agree with him. We were lucky."

Billy looked disappointed. Buzz's bravado was much more appealing to a sixteen-year-old. "Buzz says if we don't start building some decent planes fast, we're gonna get wiped out. He gave me that book by Billy Mitchell. What do you think of it, Pops?"

"I'm afraid Buzz and the general could be right."

Last month Frank and Buzz and Adrian Van Ness had flown to Milwaukee for Billy Mitchell's funeral. He had died of heart disease but believers in air power like Buzz preferred to call it heartbreak. Frank had always felt uneasy about Mitchell's vision of the plane as the supreme weapon of war. But he knew too much about aerodynamics to ignore the progress the Germans and the Russians had made in designing fast, powerful fighters and bombers.

At the airport, Frank ordered the chief mechanic on duty

to gas up a SkyRanger II. While they were waiting for the tanks to fill, Frank got a motion-picture camera from the hangar. On the SkyRanger's wings were one of Frank's newest ideas, flexible flaps that could be extended to add lift in short takeoff airports. They were going up to shoot some film of how the flaps behaved in flight. They had developed a flutter problem during recent tests.

As they talked, Buzz McCall pulled up in his white Chrysler convertible with seventeen-year-old Cliff Morris beside him. Buzz parked the car beside the hangar and walked out to the plane with Cliff. The contrast between Cliff and Billy was remarkable. Billy was so blond and fair-skinned he sometimes looked bleached. Cliff had his mother's olive skin and black hair. He too was over six feet, with a Latin profile that had half the girls in Santa Monica palpitating, his mother claimed.

Frank liked both boys. Their personalities were as different as their looks. Outwardly nonchalant and easygoing, Cliff wanted badly to be liked. Billy seemed indifferent to everyone's opinion but his own and occasionally Frank's.

Buzz strolled up to Billy and without saying a word drove his left fist into his stomach. Billy gasped and bent double. Buzz clipped him with a right-hand uppercut that knocked him under the fuselage of SkyRanger II.

"What the hell was that for?" Frank said.

"Stay out of this," Buzz said. He dragged Billy out from under the plane by his shirt front. "Don't ever call your stepmother a name like that again, get me?"

"I get you," Billy said, blood trickling from a split lip. He glared at Cliff. "Did you tell him, you fucking momma's boy freako?"

"No," Cliff said. He was clearly baffled by Billy's dislike, which began the day they met.

"Tama told me. She was shaking and crying when I came home," Buzz said.

Frank sighed. It never seemed to dawn on Buzz that even a mediocre actress like Tama could make a man believe almost anything with a carefully calculated performance. Frank could practically hear Tama declaiming: *that kid is going up*

*in your new plane after insulting me while my son sits home?
What kind of a father are you?*

"Let's get going." Frank said.

He beckoned Billy into the copilot's seat and taxied out
for takeoff. The big plane leaped from the runway in thirty-
two seconds while Buzz took pictures of the flaps extended.
"The goddamn things are vibrating a foot and a half minimum," Buzz said.

Frank circled the field, touched down and took off again
three more times, while Buzz took more pictures. "We may
have to reposition the damn things," Frank said.

"Adrian'll shit a brick," Buzz said. "It'll cost at least fifty
grand."

"That's cheaper than a new plane, if the wings come off,"
Frank said.

"Worse things could happen," Buzz said. "Maybe
Adrian'd finally wise up and get into the right end of the
business."

For at least a year Buzz had been urging Adrian to start
building military planes. He had persuaded their designated
leader to attend Billy Mitchell's funeral to introduce him to
Army Air Corps brass.

"Could the wings come off now?" Cliff asked.

"No. We're putting the flaps up," Frank said, throwing a
switch that raised the flaps level with the wing's trailing
edge.

They soared over Los Angeles and up the coast toward
Santa Barbara. Frank shoved the throttles forward and the
Ranger was soon hitting her top speed, 320 miles an hour.
"Wow," Billy said.

He was used to flying. Frank had been taking him up in
his single-engine Lustra I since he was five or six. "She's all
yours, copilot," Frank said, relinquishing the yoke.

"Aye, aye, Captain," Billy said, his sore stomach and aching jaw forgotten. Frank looked over his shoulder at Buzz,
sitting in the flight engineer's seat behind them. Cliff Morris
was a few feet behind him in the observer's seat. Buzz was
watching Billy with unrelenting eyes. Was there fatherhood
in the tough-guy stare? Frank hoped so.

Billy swung the plane into a steep bank, then into a shallow dive. Frank had been letting him take the controls of his Lustra I for three years. "Beautiful!" he yelled as he leveled off.

"Can I try it?" Cliff Morris said.

"Sure. Let him take over," Buzz said.

Billy reluctantly surrendered his seat. Cliff obviously had no feel for how a plane handled. He put the Ranger into a clumsy bank and Frank had to rescue them before they slipped into a spin.

"What'd I tell you about keepin' the nose up?" Buzz said. He had been teaching Cliff in his Lustra I, a flyspeck compared to this muscular airliner.

"This is a lot more plane," Frank said, trying to comfort Cliff.

"Get outta the way," Buzz said to Frank. He planted himself in the pilot's seat and made Cliff follow him, hands on his copilot's yoke, as Buzz spun the plane into a banking turn that only a veteran pilot could handle.

"Now let's see you get us out of some real trouble," Buzz said.

He pulled back sharply on his yoke as the Ranger came out of the turn and the airspeed fell away. In ten seconds they tilted left into a spin. Buzz sat there, arms folded. "Pull it out," he said.

The airstream whined over the wing surfaces. The big plane began hurtling toward the blue Pacific. Sky and water blended in a whirling blur.

"Wow!" Billy yelled. "Great!"

He had the born pilot's certainty that he was indestructible. Cliff Morris sat there, his hands frozen on the yoke.

"Pull it out!" Buzz roared.

"I don't know how!" Cliff screamed.

"Then we're goin' in! I'm tired of buildin' planes nobody buys. Uncle Frank ain't good enough to get us out and neither is your wiseguy brother. You save your own ass in a plane. Nobody else's gonna do it."

For the first time Frank realized Buzz hated his stepson—and really loved Billy. But Tama would not tolerate a sign of it. Maybe he even loved Tama but he was afraid to let her know it because it might force him to disown Billy and favor Cliff.

Down they spun, close to being in serious trouble as the centrifugal force of the spin locked them in its grip. "I *caaaan't*," Cliff screamed, his hands over his ears as if he could not bear the sound of his own terror.

This was going much too far. Frank lunged over Buzz's shoulder and pushed forward on the yoke. "Stamp on that right rudder," he roared. Everyone rose a foot out of his seat and Frank's head almost hit the roof as the Ranger came out of the spin with two thousand feet to spare and roared toward the Pacific horizon.

"Whattya know," Buzz said. "The fuckin' wings stayed on."

Frank flew back to Santa Monica with Cliff Morris slumped in the copilot's seat. "You'll do a lot better when you get some lessons from an instructor who's not your father," Frank said. "Fathers shouldn't teach their kids to fly or drive."

"You wanta teach him, he's all yours," Buzz said.

"I'll teach both of them."

"I don't know whether I want to fly," Cliff said. "I'm not sure I'm good enough."

"I know I'm good enough," Billy said.

"You don't know a fucking thing," Buzz snarled. "You never open a book, you're flunkin' every subject in the curriculum and you think you're good enough to fly? How, why?"

"I just know it," Billy said.

"Flyin' takes brains. So far you haven't convinced me you've got any." Buzz glowered at Cliff. "It takes guts too. So far momma's boy here hasn't convinced me he's got much of that item."

Frank patted Cliff's shoulder. "You don't have to be as tough as he is. Adrian Van Ness thinks millions of people will learn to fly in the next twenty years. It'll be as common as knowing how to drive."

"I don't buy that idea," Buzz said. "Planes are gettin' faster, hotter all the time."

Frank hoped Buzz was wrong. He shared Adrian's belief that the plane would help create jobs and prosperity, like the automobile. So far it was a faith with few followers.

"You'll be surprised how fast you learn to fly," Frank said to Cliff. "Pretty soon you feel like you're part of the plane."

"I feel that way already," Billy said.

"Shut the fuck up," Buzz said.

Billy's face remained expressionless. But there were tears in his eyes.

THE GREAT GAME

Adrian Van Ness sat in his shabby office on the first floor of Buchanan Aircraft's main building watching their latest plane, a sleek stylish trainer for the Army Air Force, come in for a smooth landing. On his desk was an invitation to the spring meeting of the Conquistadores del Cielo. Beside it was a letter from Jim Redwood, Buchanan's sales manager, dolefully reporting he had failed to sell a single copy of SkyRanger II on his latest foray to New York.

Ruined whispered in Adrian's soul. He had begun to hate the bravura name the historian in him had selected for their trade association in 1935—the very year the bottom had started to fall out of the plane business. He watched Frank Buchanan climb out of the trainer and stroll across the tarmac, his arm around Billy McCall's slim shoulders. A few minutes later Frank took off with Cliff Morris in the second seat. The chief designer was giving teenagers flying lessons on company time. Why not, when the company had nothing to sell?

Buzz McCall stood in the doorway, a sketch in his hand. "Here's Frank's idea for the next-generation fighter," he said.

"It'll make that crummy P-Thirty-nine look like a Curtiss Jenny."

The P-39 was the current fighter plane of the Army Air Force. The bulky creature was inferior in speed and maneuverability to the fighters of every major power. Adrian pondered Buchanan's replacement—an angular craft with gull wings. "Who's going to pay for it?"

"I've practically got a guarantee—"

"Practically a guarantee doesn't pay the rent or the salaries or the taxes," Adrian said.

"Adrian—you gotta gamble to win in this business," Buzz said. "You gotta bet the goddamn company."

"It's easy to be a high roller with someone else's money," Adrian said. "Put this in a drawer until a war starts."

Buzz's recklessness was as unnerving to Adrian as Frank Buchanan's indifference to profit and loss. Both clashed with Adrian's belief in forethought. For the moment the dolorous facts were on Adrian's side. So far their plunge into the military plane business had been a financial disaster. They had sold only 150 trainers. Mockups of dive bombers, reconnaissance planes, fighters, cluttered the hangars. The Army and Navy procurement officers were delighted to encourage bold experiments. But other companies were competing for the same extremely limited appropriations. Don Douglas, an Annapolis dropout, had the inside track with the Navy. Boeing up in Seattle had a similar whammy on the Army.

Adrian's office intercom beeped. "Prince Carlo Ponte–something is here to see you."

Ponty was as handsome and urbane as ever. He was in California with his mistress, a Hungarian film star who was making a movie directed by the most lecherous mogul in Hollywood. "I am here to protect my investment," he said. He added a hilarious imitation of the mogul's assaults on the English language.

Ponty's sex life stirred envy in Adrian. He was usually too tired to do more than kiss Amanda when he stumbled home from Buchanan Aircraft at midnight. Amanda never even hinted she was interested in anything more amorous. They made love only when Adrian suggested it. Even in the bedroom he sensed an element of mockery in Amanda's manner. Again and again her eyes seemed to ask him why they were not rich. What had happened to his promises of a golden future as her compensation for turning Cadwallader Groves into a smelly, oozing oil field?

Yet Adrian struggled to keep his wife happy. He bought her expensive jewelry he could not afford. He swallowed her awful cooking. She had the power to make him miserable if she chose. She had daily access to the mind and heart of the one female in this world Adrian loved without reservations, his six-year-old daughter Victoria.

Ponty had married his French heiress. She seemed content to share him with other women—and with planes. He was known as the Italian Lindbergh for his record-breaking distance flights across Asia and Africa—and the elegant books he wrote to celebrate them. Like Lindbergh's books, his narratives combined high adventure with philosophy—in Ponty's case an uncompromising disdain for Europe's drift toward totalitarianism. He roamed the world to escape "the pygmies of the right and left."

Adrian had kept Ponty in close touch with the fortunes of Buchanan Aircraft. He was an admirer of Frank Buchanan's clean designs. "So, my old friend—how goes the profits and losses?" Ponty asked.

"Unless a miracle occurs, we'll be bankrupt in six months."

"I've suggested before, Adrian—and suggest again—you should see the whole world as your market."

Adrian sighed. "We're not a merchant bank. We don't have partners all over the globe, telling us where the deals are."

"That is something I would be happy to undertake. For old time's sake—and whatever douceurs you might be inclined to add. Breaking long-distance records is expensive. My wife's enthusiasm for financing me has distinct limits."

"I'm ready to add enough sweeteners to give you dyspepsia. Do you know anything we could go after right now?"

Ponty pointed to a copy of the *Los Angeles Times* on Adrian's desk. A black headline announced Adolf Hitler's agreement with British Prime Minister Neville Chamberlain at Munich, giving Germany the right to dismember Czechoslovakia. "Although the world sees it as a shameful surrender, the British are buying time. They've begun to rearm. But their aircraft industry has been starved for so long, they haven't the capacity to meet half their needs."

"Can you arrange something? My—my mentor, Geoffrey Tillotson, died two years ago."

His reputation ruined by the catastrophic losses Tillotson Brothers had suffered in the collapse of airline stocks in 1929, Adrian's English father had never returned to the business world. He had remained a stubborn believer in the airplane, writing Adrian letters full of praise for Buchanan's modest early success.

"It would be better for you to go yourself—and work through Winston Churchill. He's out of power but he's been calling for rearmament and has numerous friends in the military. I'd bring Frank Buchanan with you to deal with their design people. I would also contact your mother. She has many friends in English society. In these matters, every kind of influence helps."

Two weeks later, Adrian and Frank Buchanan were drinking tea with Clarissa Van Ness in her Mayfair flat. She had stayed in England almost continuously since Tillotson's death, saying she felt more at home there. They talked about Victoria, who had charmed her grandmother when Clarissa visited California last year.

On her home ground, Amanda had been an unruffled hostess. Clarissa even conceded a mild admiration for the scenery. But the visit had been marred by Adrian's desperate attempts to conceal the parlous state of Buchanan Aircraft. He had even rented a sleek black Packard for a week, ignoring the disapproval in Amanda's eyes. They had taken Clarissa to the best restaurants. But when they visited the factory, the charade had exploded. Outside Adrian's office, a small angry man in a derby declared he was not leaving until his client received three thousand dollars for a half dozen rivet guns purchased six months ago.

Clarissa had said nothing, of course. But *ruined* clanged

in Adrian's head like a fire alarm. He had slept barely two hours a night for a month after his mother went back to London.

Frank Buchanan was telling Clarissa about the radical designs they had experimented with when he worked at de Havilland before the last war. His favorite was a flying wing. It had the best lift-to-drag ratio of any plane he had ever seen. Clarissa beamed. "I remember my dear friend Geoffrey Tillotson talking about that. He put up a great deal of the money for de Havilland in those days."

"We're hoping to sell the Royal Air Force some planes," Adrian said. "We're seeing Winston Churchill at the Athenaeum tomorrow at five o'clock. Can you put in a good word for us with him or anyone else?"

"I sat next to Winston at a dinner last night," Clarissa said. "I'll be happy to mention your plight if I see him again. But I doubt if it will do much good. He could not be gloomier about his political situation. He blames a great deal on the Oxford Oath. That woman you used to escort, Beryl Suydam, was one of the leaders."

Beryl's name had an extraordinary effect on Adrian. Her radical politics had not prevented her from becoming one of the best known women in English aviation. Except for those euphoric days when he had been a Wall Street wonder, he had never been able to read about her record-setting flights without pain. Now, in the center of London, he was filled with old longing.

Adrian was familiar with the Oxford Oath, promoted by British left-wing intellectuals in the mid-1930s. Tens of thousands of students and professors and union members vowed not to serve England in another war. "No wonder Herr Hitler decided he could forget about the British and concentrate on intimidating the French and the rest of Europe," his mother said, glaring at Adrian as if it were all his fault.

"I hope the British and French don't expect the Americans to fight this time," Frank Buchanan said. "All we did was make the world safe for their revenge on the Germans."

"Keep your isolationism to yourself when we see Churchill tomorrow," Adrian said.

Back at their hotel, although he was exhausted by the two-day flight from Los Angeles, Adrian put through an overseas telephone call. It took an hour to complete the connection. Finally, Amanda's voice was on the line. "I suppose you want to talk to the birthday girl?"

In a moment, Victoria was on the line. "Hello, Daddy," she said.

An enormous tenderness swelled in Adrian's chest. "Hello, Gorgeous," he said. "Happy birthday. I'm so sorry I can't be there to give you a kiss."

Victoria said she loved her present, a paint set. She promised to paint him a whole fleet of planes. She asked him about England and hoped she could go there with him someday. Adrian told her they would visit all sorts of wonderful places—New York, Paris, London—when she was older.

"Mommy says we won't have enough money," Victoria said.

A flush of anger and anxiety swept Adrian. "Yes we will, Sweetness. I promise you we will."

Amanda came on the line. "At forty dollars a minute, I think someone should stop you two."

"Any news I should hear?"

"Douglas got a new Navy contract for some dive bombers. It's on the front page of the *Times*."

Adrian hung up and composed a cable to Buzz McCall, urging him to contact his fellow veteran of the air war in France, Colonel George C. Kenney, chief of Army production, and fan his envy of the Navy's decision to buy dive bombers. Frank Buchanan had a plane in his files that was superior to the Douglas plane in bomb load and speed.

Adrian realized he was hoping for the impossible, even as he wrote the cable. The Army had a new bombsight that was supposedly so accurate, it made dive bombers obsolete. That was why they were in bed with Boeing and their lumbering B-17 Flying Fortress, which was supposed to be able to shoot its way to distant targets without fighter escorts. That meant the Army was not particularly interested in fighters either.

Adrian went to bed and stared into the darkness, thinking of the future of Buchanan Aircraft. Amanda was right. After seven years of struggle, they had no money. This foray to England was their last gasp. It would be ironic if his attempt to become a man of substance ended where it had begun.

The following afternoon, Adrian and Frank Buchanan drank brandy in the lofty library of the Athenaeum Club with Winston Churchill and Major George Knightly, a trim mustached man in a blue RAF uniform. Adrian proposed their trainer, touting the Army Air Force's enthusiasm for it.

"I rather think we have all the trainers we need for the moment," Knightly said. "What we don't have is a light bomber. Do you have any ideas?"

"We've got a plane we call the SkyRanger Two," Frank Buchanan said. "I could turn that into a bomber for you in ten minutes."

Knightly pretended to set his watch. "Give it a try."

Frank seized pen and paper from a nearby writing desk and swiftly sketched the SkyRanger. Hurling technical terms that only Knightly understood, he redesigned the wings for extra strength and larger fuel tanks and reworked the interior to carry a 2,000-pound bomb load and a crew of five, with machine guns in the nose, tail, and a revolving top turret.

"How much?" Knightly asked.

"Two hundred and fifty thousand a plane," Frank said, looking warily at Adrian.

"Three hundred thousand," Adrian said.

"Umm," Knightly said. "I like it. If things go the way Winston thinks they will—you may hear from us."

"Any idea how many you'd want?" Adrian asked.

"Two hundred for starters."

Adrian barely managed to conceal his astonishment. Knightly was talking about six million dollars. "Surely you can spare a few thousand for the design work," Adrian said.

"Afraid not. We're counting every shilling at the moment."

"We'll manage it," Adrian said.

"Then we have an understanding."

Knightly went off to a staff meeting and Churchill ordered another brandy. "Is this man reliable?" he asked, eyeing Frank Buchanan.

"Oh, absolutely," Adrian lied, hoping Frank would keep his mouth shut.

"Your old friend Geoffrey Tillotson, whose loss I still regret, spoke to me of you now and then in matters more important than stocks and bonds. If war comes as I'm sure it will, you may be contacted from time to time by a small cadre we're sending over to offset German propaganda. I hope you'll be helpful."

"I'll try."

"Prince Carlo Pontecorvo will be handling matters in California."

Adrian, a student of the great game, wondered if Ponty's casual advice to sell planes in England and Churchill's prompt response were as accidental as they seemed.

On the ride back to the hotel Frank Buchanan was his usual erratic self. "Do you realize what he just asked you to do? The same goddamm stuff they pulled in the last war. Lindbergh's father wrote a book about it. They're going to drag us into it to save their imperialistic asses. Are you going to help them?"

"Yes," Adrian said. "So are you. The day we get home, I want you to go to work on designing that bomber. Hire twenty extra people if you have to. We'll finance it out of the trainer sale."

"Whose side are we on, anyway?" Frank said.

"Our side."

"Where is it?" Frank said. "Give me a moral or spiritual location."

"Beyond the rainbow," Adrian said. "Where the pots of gold are waiting."

"Why don't we make that our insignia?" Frank sneered.

"Not a bad idea. Give me a sketch."

In the lobby of the hotel, Frank grabbed a piece of stationery and drew a plane flying above a crescent rainbow. Adrian thanked him and put it in his pocket, deciding it was pointless to try to explain to his chief designer how little morality had to do with playing the great game, the hidden struggle for power that nations waged. Like Ponty, he felt a sentimental loyalty to England, a belief that despite her flaws she stood for something valuable. But the thrill of the game was a far more powerful motive.

At the hotel desk, the clerk handed Adrian a phone message. *Miss Beryl Suydam* 05-03-421.

"Not *the* Beryl Suydam," Frank Buchanan said, reading it over his shoulder.

"I met her years ago," Adrian said.

Upstairs, his hand trembled slightly as he picked up the telephone and gave the operator the number. "Adrian," Beryl said in that silky voice, unchanged by a decade. "A friend saw you in your hotel lobby. I couldn't resist calling you."

"How nice," he said.

"For one thing, you've got a plane that interests me. That SkyRanger? I think I could beat Howard Hughes's around-the-world record in it, with some help from the brilliant designer fellow you've got on your staff. What's his name?"

"Frank Buchanan."

"Yes. Could we meet in the next day or two?"

Adrian decided they would meet without Frank Buchanan. He was anxious to visit de Havilland and a few other companies where he had old friends. While Frank rode a train out of London, Adrian met Beryl at the Savoy Grill. She arrived in a flight jacket and slacks and the headwaiter refused to seat them. She led him to a small Greek restaurant in Soho, a place full of shadowy corners. Someone played a zither in another room.

Beryl had changed little physically. The face was still the same lovely oval, the dark hair still framing it in a twentyish bob. "You don't look a day older," Adrian said.

"You do," she said. "Your hair."

Adrian brushed self-consciously at his receding hair line. "They say bald men are sexier."

"You'll never be sexy, Adrian. But you'll always be attractive to women."

"Why?"

"Every woman likes to explore an enigma."

"I don't think of myself as enigmatic."

"You are. I didn't feel I could devote my life to solving you. Are you still married?"

"More or less. How about you?"

"You know I'm not married."

"Not even in love?"

"Not at the moment."

"You still think the Soviet Union is the hope of the world?"

"I've grown a bit more sophisticated. I think socialism is the hope of the world. Hasn't it arrived in Washington, D.C., under the flag of the New Deal?"

"Roosevelt isn't a socialist. He isn't anything. That's his problem."

"Perhaps it's your problem too, Adrian. Not being anything eventually becomes distressing."

"I'm not sure you're right about that. I know exactly what I want to be at the moment."

"What?"

"Your lover again."

Beryl did not display the slightest surprise or shock—which only made her more desirable. "Does that make any sense?" she said.

"We have quite a lot in common. Planes—memories."

Beryl raised her wineglass. "Let's rely on memories for the time being."

In Adrian's middle-class hotel off Picadilly, memory created a bittersweet aura. Beryl's skin was still wet, glistening from the shower as they embraced. He licked drops of water from her small rounded breasts. His hand moved easily, knowingly, up her firm thighs.

"I've had other women. But I've never loved anyone else," Adrian said.

"It's been the same with me," Beryl said.

Over a nightcap they talked about her flight around the world. She had a backer lined up, the publisher of the *Daily Mail*. Adrian assured her the plane would be provided free of charge. He would put Frank Buchanan in touch with her the moment they got back to California.

"You're such a dear," Beryl said, with a contented sigh.

"Tomorrow—dinner again?"

"Why not," she said.

It was the old Beryl without her radical animosity, her war wounds healed by time or the progress of socialism. Politics were not important, Adrian told himself. Love transcended politics as it transcended time and space.

The next morning, Adrian was awakened by a call from George Knightly, the RAF officer who had come to the Athenaeum Club with Winston Churchill. "Could you spare a few minutes for another talk about that bomber?"

"My designer's off in the country visiting friends."

"We can chat just as well without him."

Adrian was sure Knightly was going to beat his price down to nothing to help save dear old England's ass. He was not going to let sentimentality bankrupt him. He arrived at the Air Ministry determined to bargain hard for every shilling.

Knightly shoved a chair beside his desk and tugged at his mustache. "This is a bit awkward but it has to be done. I take it you're an old friend of Beryl Suydam? That explains the—er—reunion last night in your room?"

"Why is that any of your goddamn business?"

"It shouldn't be. I gather she's quite a piece in bed, if half the hangar talk I've heard is true. But the fact is, old boy, she's a Soviet spy."

"Absolutely ridiculous!"

"I wish it was. She's a marvelous flier. Quite a personage, you might say. But the evidence is rather overwhelming. Since you're going to be building a bomber for us, if things develop with Herr Hitler, I thought you should know."

"Can you prove this—this—slander?"

"This may be a bit painful. But you've asked for it."

Knightly took a folder out of his desk and handed it to Adrian. In it were a number of photocopied letters from Beryl to someone named Sergei. "You'd be most interested in the one on the bottom. She wrote it last night in the lobby of your hotel," Knightly said.

The letter was on hotel stationery.

Dear Sergei:
The fish bit the moment I dangled the hook. I'm sure I can

get you all you want on the light bomber in a week's time. He wants to marry me! That can be dealt with, of course. I'm inclined to go ahead with the round-the-world flight and see what else I can get from Frank Buchanan's files. I'll probe Adrian about that fighter plane tomorrow night.

Beryl.

"Sergei is her Soviet control. He's been working for us for several years."

Adrian was too dazed and humiliated to do anything but nod.

"We've no objections if you want to go on seeing her for a bit. You might pass on some rather useful misinformation to her. Multiply the number of planes we're buying by the order of five, say."

"Why?"

"We've reason to think it'll get to Herr Hitler via Moscow. The Germans have a covey of agents there. Trying to play the intimidation game a bit on our side. You might throw in some bull about orders with other plane makers. Heavy stuff."

"I see."

"She'll be doing her damndest to please you, old chap. Don't see how you can lose."

Knightly's smile sickened Adrian. The man of course had no idea what Beryl Suydam meant to him. For a moment, Adrian contemplated something much more vicious than repaying deception with deception. He imagined murder. He saw his fingers around Beryl Suydam's fragile throat, his thumb pressing hard on the hollow he loved to kiss. *Bitch*, howled a voice that did not belong to him. It wailed down from the stratosphere, where Beryl had found the strength, the guile, to make him a fool.

Forethought rescued Adrian. Outside the air ministry, he stared at the traffic on the Thames and told himself this was simply another phase of the great game. He had been given a license to enjoy himself. He would use it to the full.

For the next two nights, Beryl played Delilah to Adrian's cunning Samson. When she whispered *I love you* at the climax, his mask almost slipped, he almost reached for her lying throat. When she did it again the next night, Adrian almost believed it. He wondered if Knightly knew everything. Was this woman secretly pleading with him to rescue her from deception?

How could he speak? Knightly had warned him it was vital to keep Sergei's double agentry concealed. He would not live twelve hours if Beryl discovered it.

Beryl lit a cigarette while Adrian poured her a brandy. She curled up on the bed, oozing charm. "I've heard wonderful things about the planes you're making."

"'Want to make' would be better. We've had a hell of a time selling most of them. The competition is tough and the airlines are going broke. The Army and the Navy have no money. That's why this order for a thousand bombers from the British is a godsend."

"A thousand?" Beryl said. "I wonder where they're getting the money."

"I don't know and I don't care."

"What other planes do you have?"

"A pursuit plane. It can outfly anything in the air."

"I smell a speed record. Can you send me the plans?"

Adrian shook his head. "We're keeping that one in a locked file."

"Adrian. You can trust me. I might even help you sell it to someone else."

The lovely lips curled into a Cheshire-cat smile. She was devouring him in her lying mind. Adrian no longer had any doubt that Knightly was right. Still he could not let go of those whispered words. *I love you.* Was she, even in the slimy gutter of deceit, asking him to forgive her?

Adrian finished his brandy and told himself he was a fool. Take what you can get and forget the rest. Forget the soaring and adoring. From now on, Adrian Van Ness would enjoy his women without the emotional window dressing of love.

"I've got bad news," he said. "I have to go home tomorrow. A labor crisis."

He teased her left nipple until it came erect. "Once more for auld lang syne?" he said.

For a moment he was sure she knew. He wanted her to know. He let the coldness in his mind fill his voice, his eyes. But he said nothing. It would be much more satisfying to let her dangle on the hook of doubt for the next year as he made excuses about the round-the-world flight and fed her more misinformation about the light bomber and other planes. Revenge could be sweetened by time—and more nostalgic encounters in hotel rooms.

But there was still a corner of Adrian's soul where *I love you* whispered, where memory wept and hope mourned.

WHEN DREAMS COME TRUE

Adrian returned from his trip to England deeply depressed. Amanda assumed it was because he had failed to sell a single plane. When Victoria asked him if they could go to Hawaii over the Christmas holidays, he snapped "no" so harshly she burst into tears. He rushed out and bought her a seventy-five-dollar Shirley Temple doll, then excoriated Amanda in private for letting her daughter have delusions of wealth.

"We're not going to be rich, ever," he said. "Get that through your head. The aircraft business is a penny-ante game and it's going to stay that way."

"You're the one who talked about going to Hawaii," Amanda said. "You buy her the most expensive doll in the store. Then you tell me her delusions are my fault?"

"She's your responsibility. I don't have time to educate her. I wish I did."

"Gordon is forming his own oil company," Amanda said. "He called to ask if we wanted to buy any of the stock."

"We'll be lucky to pay the mortgage on this house," Adrian snarled.

"He's brought in another dozen wells. He's going to be a millionaire," Amanda said.

"Are you going to hate me for the rest of your life?"

"I don't hate you," Amanda said. "But you obviously have no intention of giving me a chance to love you, either."

"What do I have to do to merit that," Adrian said. "Grovel?"

"Give me some evidence that you want me to love you."

"I do!" Adrian said.

"For whose sake? Mine or Victoria's?"

She saw fear flicker in Adrian's eyes. She had read him correctly. Instead of admitting she was right, he retreated into sullen isolation again.

"Do I have to fill out a goddamn questionnaire?"

They went back to being antagonists in small things and large things. One of the large things was the drift toward war in Europe. Hitler swallowed Austria and Czechoslovakia, making the British politicians who favored appeasing him look more and more foolish. The British and French began rearming to meet the German threat. Adrian frankly, unabashedly welcomed the prospect of an explosion.

"How can you say such a thing?" Amanda gasped. For her it was a grisly replay of the First World War. All she could think of was her father's death, the destruction of Eden.

"Because it will be good for the airplane business," Adrian said.

"It will mean death, suffering for thousands, millions of people," Amanda said.

"I don't know any of them," Adrian said. "I can only sympathize with people I know."

"I'm not sure you can even do that," Amanda said.

Amanda of course had no idea that the Adrian who said those heartless words was the man whom Beryl Suydam had wounded. For the first time in years, she felt repelled by her husband. His good manners, his dislike of argument, had held such feelings at a distance. She was even more dismayed a few weeks later, when the newspaper informed her that the British had placed an unprecedented order for two hundred light bombers with Buchanan Aircraft. That day, Adrian came home brimming with good cheer. He had a huge teddy bear for Victoria and a string of pearls for her.

"I'm beginning to change my mind about the aircraft business. It may not be penny-ante after all."

"I don't want them," Amanda said, giving him back the pearls.

"Why, for God's sake?"

"I don't want to wear anything that comes from planes built to kill people."

"I always knew your intelligence was limited. This proves it," Adrian snarled. "These planes will defend decent people against barbarians. Do you want Hitler and his friends to conquer the world?"

It was too late to advance this rational argument. Amanda could only remember Adrian's declared indifference to slaughtering people. "I don't care who wins as long as we stay out of it," Amanda said. "This sort of thing—making planes for one side—will drag us into it."

Amanda was speaking out of the depths of her California self, in a voice that millions of Americans shared. To her, Europe was a land of literature and monuments, the dead past that could be explored from a distance but was not worth the death of a single American. Adrian, with his deep ties to England, could only respond with outrage. Seven-year-old Victoria watched, bewildered and tearful, as her mother and father insulted and reviled each other.

Amanda joined America First, an organization committed to keeping the United States out of any future war. Henry Ford, former governor Alfred E. Smith of New York, Senator Burton K. Wheeler of Montana were among its leaders. Its chief spokesman was aviation's hero, Charles Lindbergh. Adrian was infuriated but how could he object to a policy that Lindbergh was advocating? Polls showed 80 percent of the voters backed America First's call for strict neutrality. Earlier in the decade, Congress had passed a neutrality act which forbade the United States to sell arms to any country at war.

On September 1, 1939, huge headlines blossomed in all the Los Angeles newspapers, announcing that the Germans had invaded Poland. Two days later, Britain and France de-

clared war on Adolf Hitler's Third Reich. For Amanda that
only made America First's task even more important. Adrian
had other things on his mind. He rushed to Washington,
D.C., to wangle a change in the neutrality act, which forbade
him to ship his bombers to England.

Adrian came back to California with a self-satisfied smile
on his face. At his suggestion, Roosevelt had persuaded Congress to amend the neutrality act to permit the bombers to
be delivered, as long as they did not leave the country under
their own power. Adrian had found an airfield in North Dakota on the Canadian border. Buchanan pilots would fly the
planes there and Canadians would tow them across the border, where British pilots would be waiting to fly them to
England.

When Adrian described this coup at dinner on the night
of his return, Amanda denounced it as a criminal evasion of
the law. "Who did you bribe?" she asked.

"Do you realize where we'd be if we can't deliver those
planes?" Adrian shouted. "Bankrupt. Ruined."

"In a good cause, that wouldn't bother me in the least,"
Amanda said.

"It would bother the hell out of me," Adrian said. "Especially when the cause is brainlessness masquerading as idealism."

"Please stop, please!" Victoria cried, putting her hands
over her ears.

For Victoria's sake, Adrian and Amanda negotiated a private neutrality act. She would say no more about his bombers
and he would let her continue to support America First. A
few weeks later, Lindbergh came to Los Angeles to speak at
a rally. Amanda announced she was going and Adrian sullenly assented.

In the flag-decorated auditorium on Wilshire Boulevard,
Amanda was stunned to see Frank Buchanan in the front row.
"What are you doing here?" she said, sitting down beside
him.

"I could ask you the same question," he said.

"I'm sure Adrian is considering divorce. But I feel this so
strongly."

"So do I."

"But you're still designing those bombers. How can you live with that?"

"I'm here to prevent American boys from flying in them."

"I thought making them at all was reprehensible. Don't you think it puts us squarely on one side—against the Germans?"

"I hope not."

The pain in Frank's eyes made it clear that his conscience had asked the same question. She saw the anguish of his position and dropped the argument. She no longer despised this man. He seemed sad and lonely in his shabby flight jacket and tieless shirt.

Lindbergh gave a stirring speech, denouncing Franklin Roosevelt's attempts to evade the neutrality act and edge the United States into the war on England's side. He grimly declared Germany was going to win the war and there was nothing the United States could do about it but adjust to a world of new political realities. Amanda applauded fiercely, agreeing with every word of it. She noticed that Frank did not applaud. He sat with his arms folded on his chest, looking troubled.

Amanda drove Frank home to his house in Topanga Canyon, listening to him argue with himself. He was not sure Lindbergh was right about the Germans winning the war. He was unsure about Germany. Did Hitler's rampant anti-Semitism justify building planes for the British? Didn't every country have its anti-Semites? Could they possibly be right? His friend Ezra Pound, the greatest poet of the era, thought so.

Amanda said she disliked anti-Semitism as much as Frank—but she hated war. When they reached Frank's Topanga house, he urged her to stay for coffee. She sensed his loneliness. His anguish over the bombers was only a small part of his need for her companionship.

Inside the crude three-room house, she was appalled by the dirty clothes flung in corners, dishes piled in the sink. "Forgive my bachelor's style," Frank said. "I should have a woman come in once a week at least. But I can't afford it."

The words gouged her nerves. The chief designer at Buchanan Aircraft could not afford a cleaning woman? Frank saw the question in her eyes and began telling her what he did with his money. Some of it went to causes like America First. More went to Ezra Pound, whom he had been helping to support for years. More went to help Billy McCall, Buzz McCall's son, who was in college at UCLA. Buzz and the boy did not get along. Or, more precisely, Billy did not get along with Buzz's wife, Tama.

There was a mystery here, Amanda thought, as Frank Buchanan poured her coffee. This man was not the money-hungry manipulator her brother had portrayed. But how could she begin to search for the truth without telling him about her own unhappiness with Adrian? She knew what that might suggest to this lonely man. Anyway, how could she trust these intuitions? She was a naive woman, cut off from the politics of Buchanan Aircraft, the constant jockeying for power and money. She talked for an hour behind a shield of noncommittal politeness and went home troubled, full of inchoate wishes she could not even express to herself.

A month later, Hitler's armies swept into France and defeated the French and British in a few stunning weeks. Adrian went almost berserk with anxiety. He prowled the house from midnight to dawn, listening to the latest radio bulletins. He was terrified for England—and for Buchanan Aircraft. If the Germans bludgeoned the English into surrender, the 200 bombers already in production would never be paid for and Buchanan would be bankrupt.

In the middle of this turmoil, the first bomber came off the production line and was rolled out for a maiden flight. The desperate British decided to make it a symbol of their determination to fight on. They arranged for national publicity. Adrian was of course delighted but he still could not sleep and Amanda deduced that publicity was all the British were putting up. Nevertheless, to the press and public, Adrian was a picture of confidence and pride.

Amanda refused to go to the rollout celebration. Adrian almost exploded. "The British ambassador will be there with his wife! Harry Hopkins, Roosevelt's right-hand man, is fly-

ing out from Washington! The governor, both senators will
be there. I insist on you coming."

"I can be sick. Make excuses. You're very good at that."

"*I* want you there."

Amanda shook her head.

"I'll take Victoria instead."

"I can't stop you. But I think you shouldn't. She's too
young to understand any of this. All she knows is we seem
to hate each other."

"I'm taking her. I want her to see what her father is doing
to defend democracy. Let her figure out why her mother sides
with the barbarians."

On rollout day Amanda stayed home, working in the garden. It was a beautifully sunny June morning, without a
cloud in the sky. She listened on NBC radio, which was
devoting an hour to the ceremony. The British ambassador,
Adrian, California's governor, made brief speeches. Then the
announcer described the preparations for the test flight. The
test pilot and chief designer Frank Buchanan were introduced. Frank discussed some of the features of the bomber,
such as two counter-rotating variable pitch propellers on each
engine, which would add to the plane's stability.

"Are you going along, Mr. Buchanan?" the announcer
asked.

"I always go along on test flights of planes I design,"
Frank said. "I believe the designer ought to risk his own neck
to demonstrate his faith in his ideas."

The announcer described the two men boarding the plane,
settling into the cockpit. He let the audience hear the roar of
the two Wright Cyclone engines as they warmed up. In a
moment he was describing the takeoff, the climb. Suddenly
his voice changed tone. "Something seems wrong! The plane
is pitching and yawing up there. The pilot doesn't seem to
have complete control! He's trying to turn back to the field
but he can't do it. He's losing altitude fast!"

A roaring filled the sky. The plane was coming toward
her. Suddenly Amanda was in the cockpit with Frank and
the test pilot, as they fought to control the berserk machine.
Her body remained in the sunny garden but she was in the

careening plane, the thunder of the motors tearing her brain apart, hearing Frank shout to the test pilot. "Bail out! Bail out!"

The pilot leaped and his chute billowed like an immense question mark. Frank was alone in the cockpit. Amanda could see what he was trying to do, turn in a wide wobbly circle to head back to the Buchanan airfield, five miles away. But he could not do it. The plane roared over Amanda in her garden and tore through the top of a house on the next street, smashed through a half-dozen trees and cars and disintegrated. The wings ripped through two other houses and the fuselage hurtled down the street for another block.

Amanda saw the terrible things that happened to Frank in the cockpit. His seat ripped loose and he was catapulted into the windshield, then flung against both sides of the fuselage as fearsome forces smashed the plane back and forth in its passage down the street.

Amanda raced for her car. The swath of destruction on the next street made her brain reel. Two houses, three cars were on fire. Women and children ran toward her, screaming hysterically. Amanda roared through the burning debris to the plane. Flames were swirling inside the fuselage. A fire truck came clanging around the other corner. "The cockpit. Get him out of the cockpit!" she cried, as firemen spilled from the truck.

The fire was in the cockpit now. The firemen hesitated, afraid the plane would blow up. "Look!" Amanda cried.

Frank was on his feet, clawing at the cockpit window. Two firemen raced forward with a hose spraying foam. Another one hacked at the window and the metal around it with an ax. In two frantic minutes they had Frank out of the plane. His face and hands were seared black. Blood drooled from his nose. An ambulance arrived, siren whooping. Amanda climbed in beside Frank and they raced for the nearest hospital while an intern gave him oxygen and monitored his vital signs.

"He's not going to die!" Amanda said.

"If he makes it, I'm going to hire you as my full-time fortune teller," the intern said.

Frank was conscious. He stared dazedly at her. "What are you doing here?"

"You almost crashed in my garden," Amanda said.

"Tell Buzz it was the propeller. I knew those counter-rotating propellers were a bad idea—"

"Damn the propellers. Concentrate on staying alive," Amanda said.

Frank feebly shook his head. "My mother was right. Death machine. That's what she called it the first time she saw a plane."

"Damn your mother too,"Amanda said. "You're not going to die!"

Frank managed a feeble smile. "There's something—I want to tell you. I—never stopped loving you. Your brother forced me to—write that letter. He had a film of me—Buzz—we were all naked—a drunken party. I was ashamed—afraid it would hurt you—"

"I don't care," Amanda said, barely listening. "It's ancient history. You're not going to die."

She sensed, she knew, death was loose in Frank's soul, a huge black spider clutching him with multiple legs. She had to slay the creature.

At the hospital, they rushed Frank to the operating room. Buzz McCall and Adrian and others from the company soon joined Amanda. Gradually, she absorbed what Frank had told her in the ambulance. She looked at Adrian with a new, almost visible loathing. He must have been in the conspiracy. He must have known about Gordon's scheme.

Late in the afternoon, a grim-faced doctor in an operating-room gown gave them a gloomy prognosis. "His skull is fractured, his chest is crushed, both legs are broken, his pelvis is smashed. I'll be amazed if he lives until morning."

"He's not going to die," Amanda said.

The look Adrian gave her was loaded with suspicion and dislike. Buzz McCall and others were obviously curious about her passionate concern. She did not try to explain it away. "I want to see him," she said.

"I don't think that would be wise," the doctor said. "He's hanging on by a thread. Any disturbance—"

"I'm not a disturbance. I'm a friend. I will only stay ten seconds. I want to tell him something—that could save him."

"Is this some religious thing?" the doctor said.

"Yes."

"All right. Ten seconds," the doctor said, while Adrian glared.

Amanda stood beside the bed, trembling. Frank was a virtual mummy, his burned face, including his eyes, swathed in bandages, his chest encased in a cast. Instinctively she seized his hand. He groaned with pain. "Morphine," he said. "Please give me some more. I won't bother you much longer. The pain—"

"Frank," she said. "It's Amanda. I promise you, somewhere, somehow, we'll love each other again."

"Amanda," he said, half-sob, half-sigh.

Come war or Adrian's hatred or even the loss of Victoria, Amanda vowed she would create Eden with this man. They would find it somewhere in their California.

THE GREAT GAME II

Beryl Suydam stood beside Adrian in his office overlooking Buchanan's airfield as a green two-engined light bomber emerged from the factory. Adrian had christened it the Nelson in honor of the famous admiral who presided over Piccadilly Square on his soot-blackened pillar. "Such a beautiful plane, Adrian," she said. "I can't wait to fly the Atlantic in it."

"I can't wait either," he said. "I have reservations at the most beautiful hotel in California."

"That other plane—the pursuit plane Frank Buchanan is working on—that's the one I'd *really* like to fly."

"We should have a test model ready in about six months."

"Marvelous," Beryl said. "Another excuse to come back.

I've changed my mind about America. It makes me almost ashamed of the way we broke up."

"We were both young."

Was the contrition in her silky voice genuine? For the last year Adrian had tried to enjoy a different kind of satisfaction in his meetings with Beryl—the pleasure of deceiving a woman, of accepting her open arms, her inviting thighs, while inwardly a secret sharer laughed coldly. But it had not worked as well as he expected. Instead of a new dimension of power and pleasure, he was constantly listening, looking, for signs of genuine affection.

"I begin to think you Americans may be the hope of the world. With all your vulgarity, your materialism, there's an underlying honesty I find moving. Compared to the cynicism of certain other countries."

She was talking about her great disillusionment. In August 1939, just as the impending war canceled Beryl's plans for her around-the-world flight, Joseph Stalin signed a nonaggression pact with Adolf Hitler, enabling the German dictator to invade Poland and start his war with France and Britain with impunity.

The shock had left fellow travelers and worshipers of the future Soviet style numb. In an outburst of patriotism, many like Beryl joined the war effort. She was in California to ferry one of the new bombers to Britain.

"Americans can be cynical too," he said.

"Are you telling me to stop trying to save the world?"

"Perhaps. Just concentrate on saving me."

"Where is this wonderful hotel?"

"You'll see. I'll pick you up at the Beverly Wilshire at four o'clock."

Beryl departed and within five minutes she was replaced by a twitchy, suspicious Colonel George Knightly, Adrian's original RAF contact, who was at the plant supervising the delivery of the Nelson bombers. With him was the man in charge of British propaganda in California, Adrian's old friend, Prince Carlo Pontecorvo.

"I think she's changed sides," Adrian said.

"She's got some doubts, no question of that. But she's still

sending dear Sergei anything she can lay her hands on,"
Knightly said.

"Are you sure?"

"I only know what the intelligence boys tell me, old chap.
I urge you—indeed beg you—not to lose your head."

"Don't worry," Adrian snapped.

"We have two RAF pilots in town who flew against the
Germans in Norway," Ponty said. "Good copy. Can you line
up some press coverage for them?"

"I'll talk to our publicity director. Tell them to call his
assistant, Tama Morris."

"These blokes will do more than call her, if they get a
look at her. Whew!" Knightly said. "Is she as free with that
stuff as I hear?"

"I wouldn't know. I don't ask that sort of question,"
Adrian said. The memory of his humiliation at the air ministry made it hard for him to be polite to Knightly.

"Of course," Knightly said, dropping his pilot's persona
for his British officer's decorum. "I just thought she could
prove useful in certain situations, depending on her—er—
willingness."

"I'm inclined to reserve that willingness for the greater
glory of Buchanan Aircraft, thank you."

"Perhaps we should ask the lady herself?" Ponty said, with
a smile. "Or have you staked out a personal claim there too,
Adrian?"

"Not at the moment," Adrian said, struggling to regain his
savoir faire.

Knightly departed. Ponty stayed to discuss a dinner he had
persuaded Adrian to sponsor at which speakers were to call
for repeal of the neutrality act so the United States could
directly assist England. These legislative fits of pacifist hysteria had been signed into law by President Roosevelt before
war exploded across the globe. Adrian found FDR badly
lacking in forethought—a crucial requirement for presidential leadership.

There were times when Ponty acted as if Buchanan Aircraft was a department of his British propaganda machine.
In spite of the finesse with which his old schoolmate handled

such matters, Adrian was American enough to dislike the assumption that they were at His Majesty's service every time Ponty crooked a finger. His affair with Beryl inevitably sharpened this conflict.

Adrian was a tangle of emotions when he picked up Beryl at the Beverly Wilshire Hotel. With the Pacific rumbling and splashing almost beneath their wheels, they drove down Route 101A to the pink stucco La Valencia Hotel in La Jolla. The inner courtyard was full of fresh flowers in February. Their room looked down on La Jolla cove, one of the loveliest seascapes in California. The Pacific rushed against jagged rocks and cliffs. Beyond the cove, white beaches stretched north and south. La V, as everyone called the hotel, was where Hollywood's stars and directors and producers took their illicit loves.

They ate in the dining room overlooking the ocean. A full moon bathed the sea in golden light. Later, as they made love, Adrian found himself loathing the secret sharer who mocked their passionate charade. "I love you," he whispered, and meant it for the first time since their reunion night in London.

"I love you too, dearest dearest Adrian."

She meant it. As a man who had spent a great deal of time reading nuances of tone and emotion in women's voices, Adrian was sure he had just heard the real thing. "Let's put aside the masks," he said.

"Masks? What mask? Are you wearing one?"

Beryl's elbows were against his chest. She was suddenly a sharp object, even a dangerous one. "Has someone been telling you vicious lies about me? Your friend Mr. Churchill for instance? He's never forgiven me for my part in the Oxford Oath."

"Nothing of the sort," Adrian said. "I meant—you as a famous flier, me as an aircraft tycoon. I wish we could reach—some new depth. Something that blends the past and the present."

He was babbling but it had an unexpected impact on Beryl. She trembled, her elbows withdrew. She pressed herself against him. "Oh Adrian. I wish—I wish that were possible."

"Why isn't it?" he said.

"Dear dear Adrian." She spread herself on top him. "I love your awful American need for sincerity."

"Why is it awful?"

"Because the world has gotten on without it for centuries."

"I'll accept your insufferable condescension—in the name of love."

"Oh do, do. Wait for me. Be patient. I'll come. Someday, somehow, I'll come to you the way I was that night at Ravenswood. Hoping, wanting to believe in your indestructible American optimism."

For one of the few times in his life, Adrian lost his self-control. "You don't love Sergei?"

The silence was thunderous. He lay there watching her make the connections. She began to weep. "How long have you known?" she said.

"Knightly told me yesterday," Adrian lied. He cradled her in his arms and offered her more sincerity to mock. "I'll wait and wait and wait."

They drove back the next morning in the sunrise. Adrian was ready to believe the spectacular red-and-gold sky was being displayed only for them, old-new lovers on the brink of profound happiness. He felt triumphant, a conqueror of both women and politics, a master of the great game on his own terms. He was stealing a spy from the Russians, rescuing a patriot for the British-American alliance.

He dropped Beryl at the Beverly Wilshire and drove to the factory. Tama Morris was in his office, smiling slyly. "Where the hell was Beryl Suydam last night?" she said. "I had three reporters desperate to interview her."

"I have no idea."

"The doorman at the Wilshire said she was picked up by a balding guy driving a Cadillac."

"She'll be here soon. She's taking off at noon."

"That's what I told them," Tama said. "I just wanted to make sure the takeoff might not be delayed for a week or two."

"Patriotism before passion, that's my motto. But don't quote me," Adrian said, smiling. He found himself liking the idea of Tama knowing he had a secret sex life.

Beryl had already checked out the Nelson and flown it a half-dozen times. She stood beside the huge three-bladed propeller on the left motor and talked to the reporters about a woman's desire to help her country in a time of crisis. She had changed her mind about the war, she said. "I'm changing my mind about a lot of things. I attribute some of it to my seeing America, seeing democracy and freedom in the flesh, here."

Adrian smiled and kissed her on the cheek. He posed for a picture with his arm around her. Beryl waved good-bye and climbed into the plane. The big propellers turned, she taxied out and took off for the thousand-mile flight to the airfield in North Dakota, where the plane would be towed across the Canadian border. The field was a dangerous destination in February and Adrian found himself suddenly anxious for Beryl.

Sleep was impossible for him that night. He called the airport in North Dakota and was told it was snowing heavily and Beryl Suydam had not yet arrived. Two hours later, she still had not arrived. Premonition swelled to dread. Four hours later, Beryl still had not arrived and was now considered overdue.

The next afternoon, a TWA pilot flying a SkyRanger II reported seeing the wreckage of a green bomber on the slopes of one of the Sierras. It took a rescue team two days to reach the plane and radio back that Beryl Suydam, the queen of British airwomen, was dead. The cause? A faulty altimeter. The instrument had told her she was flying at twenty thousand feet when she was actually at twelve thousand—and the mountain was eighteen thousand feet.

Adrian had every altimeter in Buchanan Aircraft tested. All worked perfectly. Why had this one failed? He summoned production chief Buzz McCall to his office and asked him. "How the hell do I know?" Buzz said.

Buzz could have done it. He had killed twenty-three pilots on the western front in World War I. Adrian had heard him boast about strafing German trenches. If a British agent came to Buzz and said it was time to dispose of Beryl, Buzz would have simply nodded and agreed to maladjust the altimeter.

A sleepless night later, Ponty visited Adrian's office to ask Buchanan Aircraft to stage a memorial service for Beryl. "Go to hell," Adrian said. "Hold it at the British consulate in San Francisco."

Ponty sighed. "This is the last favor I will ask, Adrian. I'm flying back to England next week to help organize underground resistance in France and Italy."

"Did you have anything to do with fixing that altimeter?" Adrian said.

"My old friend," Ponty said. "I am not, strictly speaking, a member of British intelligence. But I understand certain things. Walls have ears. For those who play the great game, they have always had that peculiar quality—but now electronics makes the most private moments audible."

"It wasn't necessary! She was ready to change sides!"

Ponty lit a cigarette and looked out the window at a half-dozen new bombers waiting to be flown to North Dakota. "Adrian—surely you must know this arrangement between us and the Russians is a marriage of convenience that won't survive the war, presuming we win it. They are enemies of all the things we value. You and I can't really estimate what Sergei might mean to us in twenty years. You were wrong to sacrifice him. Wrong to place your personal desire ahead of history's imperatives."

Ponty put his hand on Adrian's shoulder. "Yet I understand, old friend. I understand why you did it. She was very beautiful."

Adrian wept. For Beryl and the self he had chosen to become, the boy, the man who vowed to learn history's lessons, to play by rules that only the powerful understood. "We'll stage—we'll hold the memorial service," he said.

To Adrian's surprise, Amanda offered to go to the service with him. As the British consul and a half-dozen British film stars praised Beryl's courage and patriotism, Adrian sat in a cockpit of private sorrow. Through the window he peered at his wife. Should he try to persuade her to love him again?

To his amazement, Amanda seemed to be thinking similar thoughts. That night as they were going to bed, she put her arms around him. "Adrian," she said. "I can see how much she meant to you. She was a woman you loved in England, I'm sure of it. She talked you into building those bombers. I know you're not religious and neither am I in the ordinary sense. But I do believe in the great precepts. The wages of sin is death. Doesn't this prove it?"

"I don't think it proves anything of the sort," Adrian said.

"Perhaps not. But I thought we might try to love each other again. All you have to do is tell me you won't build another warplane."

"I'm afraid I can't do that," Adrian said.

In a world already half engulfed by war, this naive woman was telling him to abandon the great game. Adrian vowed to go on playing it, to accumulate enough power and wealth to bar *ruined* from his soul, no matter what it cost him.

"I knew that would be your answer," Amanda said. "I had to ask the question."

For a moment Adrian sensed he was losing something precious—a chance to regain that youthful mixture of idealism and pity and desire that had drawn him to Amanda. So be it, he told himself. He was too absorbed by his grief and his determination to stay in the great game to wonder why his wife felt compelled to give him one last chance to love her.

AT WAR IN EDEN

On the third day of the year 1941, Amanda Van Ness put her nine-year-old daughter Victoria on the school bus and drove to Santa Monica Hospital to take Frank Buchanan home to his house in Topanga Canyon. He had made an amazing recovery from his injuries. Within a week of the crash, he was sitting up in bed reworking the Nelson bomber's design to give it the speed the British wanted without the extra propellers that had almost killed him.

The doctors warned him not to go to work for at least six months. Buzz McCall arranged for the work to come to Frank. Buchanan Aircraft was competing for dozens of contracts from the U.S. Army and Navy for every imaginable kind of plane. Congress, prodded by Franklin Roosevelt, had begun rearming the United States to deal with a world in which German power might be awesomely dominant.

For Amanda this only meant a renewed commitment to America First. Frank remained equally committed to keeping America neutral. He told Amanda that the planes he was designing would prevent a war because no one would dare to attack a strong United States. Amanda listened without argument, waiting for a sign that Frank was ready to respond to her declaration of love.

Frank was sitting on his hospital bed, dressed and smiling. Skin grafts had repaired most of the burn damage to his face and hands. His only disability was a limp. His right leg, which had been badly shattered, was still weak. He leaned on Amanda's arm as they walked to the parking lot. The temperature was in the seventies. The sun poured down and Amanda felt something—a voice or a single string of an instrument—begin to vibrate within her.

Frank was so quiet. He barely spoke as they drove through a changing landscape. People were surging into California by the tens of thousands. Clusters of houses were springing up on every other hillside. "From what I hear, half of them are probably working for you," Amanda said.

"Buzz told me they hired another thousand men last week," Frank said. "They're buying up all the houses on about four square blocks to expand the factory. Adrian predicts we'll go over ten thousand by the end of the year."

"He adores it," Amanda said. "I've never seen him so happy."

In a half hour they were winding through the green stillness in Topanga Canyon. There were no crowds of newcomers here; only a scattered handful of "settlers," as they liked to call themselves. In Topanga, Amanda could still imagine early California. That was another reason for the singing in her soul. Topanga was a place where Eden could be recaptured.

Up the steep road to Frank's house she climbed in second gear. "I've gotten experienced," she said. "A few more times and I'll apply for my pilot's license."

Frank nodded, smiling in an inward way that deepened the singing voice within her. Sunlight poured through the leaves of the sycamores surrounding the house. Inside, Frank stared in bewilderment. The place was immaculate. Books had been put on shelves, the bed was made, the closets were full of clean sheets and pillowcases. The floor had acquired flowery rugs. A painting, a Matisse-like view of sailboats off Santa Monica, hung on the bedroom wall.

"You did this?" Frank said.

Amanda nodded. "You're going to keep it this way. There's no reason in the world why a man without a woman has to live like an ape. What would you like to eat?"

"Waffles," Frank said. "Waffles and ice cream. I've been dreaming of waffles and ice cream ever since I woke up in that hospital room."

"Is that all you dreamt about?"

"No. I had a very strange dream, the first day. A beautiful woman stood beside the bed and promised to love me."

"That was unquestionably delirium," Amanda said. "There were no beautiful women in your room that day."

"Yes there was."

They stood there in the sunny stillness. The living room window was long and wide. They had left the door open. More sunlight, full of birdsong, wreathed them. "Oh my darling," Frank said. "Did you mean it? Or were you just trying to keep a wreck alive for pity's sake?"

"Would I be here if I didn't mean it?"

They were standing a dozen feet apart, speaking through the shafts of sunlight.

"What about Adrian? Victoria?" Frank said.

"Damn Adrian. He's a greedy swine who doesn't know the meaning of the word love. Victoria will be a woman someday. She'll understand."

The telephone rang. They stood there while the clang shat-

tered the sunlight, the birdsong, the singing in Amanda's
soul. Frank picked it up. "Velly solly," he said, "Missa Boocannon no here. This Chinee man who clean up slop. Missa
Boocannon come in from hospital and go out again. I tell
him to call you. Missa Van Ness? I write down chop chop."

He hung up and stood there, smiling. Amanda walked
through the sunlight into his arms. A wind swept through
the sycamores. The world shimmered. Amanda saw sunlight
breaking, exploding into great globules of vanilla light. She
swam up a milky river of hope and wish to Frank Buchanan's
arms.

She wept when she saw the purple patches of grafted skin
on his chest. "I don't want you to fly again. Ever," she said.

He promised her no such thing, of course. He presumed
it was wish, not reality, she was invoking. "Only with you
beside me," he said.

They lay on the sunny bed for a long time, savoring the
moment, touching only hands at first, then hair, then tongues,
lips. Then kisses, deeper and deeper and longer and longer,
kisses and caresses drawing her out of her self into a new
dimension. It was totally different from Adrian, the only
other man she had known. Adrian could not escape his
knowing self, his awareness of his performance. "Do you
like that?" he would ask. He wanted applause!

Frank wanted nothing but Amanda. He wanted what
Amanda gave him and gave Amanda what she wanted from
him without words, without hesitations and questions and
egotism. There were no selves, no divisions in the pool of
light in which they swam, only a blinding oneness that annihilated thought and fear and responsibility. Adrian and Victoria and her mother and father and even her dream of world
peace vanished. She was Frank and Frank was Amanda and
simultaneously they had ceased to exist. They had become
memories, rumors, beings beyond time.

Still her body spoke and acted and his body responded.
Hands and tongues and lips and hair and legs and thighs
touched and white fire leaped within the pool of light like
voices singing against a full orchestra. Amanda prayed for a
child. It would be a savior, a saint. She was losing faith in

Victoria, who reminded her of Adrian in too many ways, especially her willfulness.

The rational mind can explain this ecstasy, of course. Two people with a grudge against a third, two believers in love, two souls who had challenged death and won, two rebels against respectability and convention and habit. A lonely bachelor and a repressed, neglected wife. Tristan and Isolde reunited in spite of treachery and betrayal. Eden regained by an act of will, a surge of faith.

The analytic mind is a wonderful thing. But its logic cannot—in fact, must not—explain away what happened to Frank and Amanda in Topanga Canyon on January 3, 1941. Nor can the mind, if it feeds data into its brain cells for a million years, reproduce that wonder.

Finally there was consummation. A light richer and milkier than sunlight engulfed them. A golden light, shot through with shards of diamonds. As Frank's life, his self, his being leaped in her, Amanda broke the silence with his name. *Frank.* The word named everything in the known world. Happiness and unhappiness, victory and defeat, hope and despair. It embodied light and dark and warmth and cold and wealth and poverty. *Frank.* Everything was possible within the compass of those five ordinary letters.

They lay there, folded in the golden light, in each other's arms, for hours. They only spoke in fragments. Love. Life. Forever. Then Frank began to laugh. At first Amanda was shocked, almost frightened by the violence pouring out of his big chest until she realized what it meant. He was laughing at everything. At death, at Adrian, at Buzz McCall, at Adolf Hitler and Franklin D. Roosevelt. At the newcomers in their ugly houses on the hillsides.

He was Eden, California, laughing in its golden light at the rest of the world. She joined him, laughing, touching, kissing, laughing, weeping finally, both of them, weeping and licking away the salt tears. That was how the wonder ended, salty.

"Believe it or not," Frank whispered. "There's an earthbound part of me that has somehow survived annihilation and still wants those waffles and ice cream."

"With champagne?"

"Is there any in the house?"

"The refrigerator is full of it."

Frank opened a bottle while Amanda cooked the waffles. As they sat down and clinked glasses, the telephone rang again. Frank answered it and went into his Chinese routine. "No Missa Ran Ness. Missa Boocannon not here. But he come in and I tell him you called. He go out again and say he come to factory chop chop."

"You're not really going," Amanda said as Frank hung up.

"They're having all sorts of problems with the pursuit plane we're building for the army. It killed one of our best test pilots yesterday."

They ate the waffles and drank the champagne in silence. Light drained from the room. A colder wind sighed through the trees. Amanda saw she had loved without conditions and now could not impose them. This man designed planes for a living. Could she expect him to stop doing it because they had lived in Eden for a day? The best she could ask was a future of visits to Eden. She tried not to think of that as a diminution, a pollution of the golden light. But it was hard. Suddenly all she could remember was the salt taste of tears on her lips.

Eden remained Eden for the next few months. But other realities revealed a dismaying persistence, an indifference to the way the world had been transformed. Franklin Roosevelt continued to nudge America toward war. Adrian was his ally. He talked, thought, ate, breathed war and warplanes. That made Amanda redouble her struggle against the war. Scarcely a day passed without a rally, a seminar, a letter-writing campaign to congressmen. All diminishments of Eden.

Intensifying her anguish was the awareness that it was a losing struggle. Radio broadcasts and news films dramatized the merciless German bombing of London and Coventry and Liverpool, arousing sympathy for the British. Their local propaganda, often generated from the offices of Buchanan Aircraft, was relentless.

Frank began to drift away from his commitment to peace.

The pressure of work was enormous. They had built a new wind tunnel at the factory, the largest in America, and it was teaching him all sorts of fascinating things about airflow's effect on a plane's speed and stability. Another enemy to Eden.

Occasionally Frank deserted his wind tunnel and his designs to go to America First rallies, ignoring a directive from Adrian that forbade anyone in the company to support what he now called a subversive organization. But Amanda could see Frank's mind was dividing on the subject of peace or war. Germany's brutal use of airpower had aroused his male blood. He wanted to build planes that would enable America to strike back with the same savagery if Germany attacked us.

Another enemy to Eden, where division, disagreement, was intolerable, where a single string untuned could turn the singing into wails of regret. Still they met there on sunlit mornings and afternoons. Never at night. Amanda had acquired a dislike of making love at night. She blamed it on Adrian, who would never dream of taking the time to do anything during daylight hours but make money.

Adrian, unaware of Eden, remained maddeningly unpredictable. He was growing richer and more powerful each day and he wanted to share it with her and Victoria. They moved to a fifteen-room Tudor house in Bel Air, one of the most expensive sections of Los Angeles. They began going to dinner parties with wealthy descendants of the scoundrels who had looted California until her father and other honest men broke their political power in 1910.

More enemies of Eden. Amanda was barely polite to them. She tried to maintain a similar surface politeness with Adrian. But that was not easy. After a party, Adrian was sometimes amorous. She could not always refuse him. He was playing the patient, generous husband.

Almost instantly she saw it was a mistake. She had not realized how central her body was to the experience of Eden. She had attributed the ecstasy to California's sunlight, to Topanga's stillness, to Frank's lovemaking skill. She had to complete the performance with Adrian although her flesh shriveled at every touch.

"Is this the way it's going to be for the rest of our lives?" Adrian said when it was over. "Are you ever going to stop sitting in judgment on me?"

Amanda almost confessed Frank, Eden. But she realized Adrian would never tolerate it. She saw how dangerously she was living. She was trapped between Adrian and Frank. She was at war with herself in Eden.

The big war spread across another quarter of the globe when Germany attacked Russia. The newspapers, the radio, grew frenzied with it. Roosevelt flourished a map before Congress, reputedly proof that Germany planned to invade South America next. Amanda felt war rising like a scummy, frothy flood, its sickening surface lapping at the gates of Eden. America First announced another poll still showed 80 percent of Americans wanted to stay out of it. Buchanan Aircraft's Nelson bombers flew in droves to North Dakota to be towed across the border into Canada. Adrian came home to report that he had just signed a contract to produce Boeing's B-17 Flying Fortresses, a program that would virtually double Buchanan's workforce.

So they came to a sunny Sunday in December. Adrian was in Washington, D.C. to work out the final details of the B-17 contract. Victoria was at home with the housekeeper and a half-dozen friends, giving a pool party. Eden had never been milkier, more full of golden light. For a while Amanda forgot the carnage swirling around them.

Afterward, as they consumed their ritual waffles and champagne, Frank said: "I'm beginning to think we may stay out of this war after all. Even if the Germans eventually beat the Russians, they won't have the strength or inclination to attack anyone for a decade. By that time we'll be strong enough to maul them if they come our way."

"Last week Adrian predicted we'd be at war with the Germans and the Japanese before Christmas."

"The Japanese?" Frank said. "We're negotiating with them. I don't think they want a war with us. They're using themselves up in China, like the Germans in Russia."

Hope, love, his yearning for peace, were so visible on Frank's face, Amanda reached out to touch it. Never had she felt more whole, more certain that her life was complete.

The telephone rang. Was it Adrian? No, he was in Washington. But it probably was someone else from Buchanan, invading Eden with a problem in the design or engineering departments. Amanda brooded. She considered demanding the removal of that telephone.

Frank was on the phone. But he was not doing his Chinese houseboy routine. He was not doing anything. He was standing with the telephone clutched against his ear as if he had been turned into stone.

"Fly as many planes as possible to smaller airports!" he shouted. "Get all our design and engineering papers underground, as deep as possible. Bury them in a ditch if necessary. Stop the production line and send everyone home for twenty-four hours. We have to assume we're a primary target."

He put down the telephone and blinked into the sunlight. "Adrian was right," he said. "The Japanese bombed Pearl Harbor this morning. They sank most of our battleships. Maybe now our dimwit admirals and generals will start believing in air power."

War was in Frank's voice. Rage and revenge and death was in his name. The five letters no longer named everything beautiful in the world. Frank was part of the ugly flood that was swirling through Eden with all war's flotsam, gouged bodies and smashed homes and shattered planes.

Now Amanda knew what her mother had felt twenty-five years ago. She understood the undertow that had dragged her down into madness. It was not weak genes, as her vile brother Gordon claimed. It was the destruction of Eden. It made a woman welcome the obliteration of her mind, her memory.

"Don't," Frank said, trying to brush the tears from her cheeks. "I know how much this means to you—"

"It's the end of this. The end of us."

"Hitler, Tojo, Mussolini—all of them together can't do that."

Amanda shook her head. "The war will change everything. It won't be the same country. It won't be the same California."

"But we'll be the same."

"No. You've already changed. I'll change too."

"Maybe we won't see each other so often. But why should we stop loving each other?"

"The love won't stop. It will always be there. But we'll stop living in it the way we have this year."

"If I have anything to say about it, that won't happen."

Amanda watched him fling on clothes for the trip to the factory. "It's happening already," she said.

BOOK FOUR

THE YANK AND THE SKYLARK

"Geoffrey!" Sarah Chapman said, as the tall airman in his bomber jacket strode past her.

Geoffrey Archer squinted into the spring sunlight, simultaneously managing to look past Sarah—or through her—across the runways of RAF Bedlington. Geoffrey was what Sarah and her friends at St. Agatha's School called a Profile. Deep-socketed eyes that suggested haunted thoughts of lost love or suppressed sexual desires, a resolute mouth that intimated a readiness to face death with dauntless courage. (Romantic mush, but that was the way seventeen-year-olds thought in 1943.) At a dance at the Grantham Country Club for the pilots of the nearby air-base where he was training, Geoffrey had been Sarah's constant partner. Only when the band cut loose with a boogie-woogie beat did he abandon her—explaining that he detested American dancing. Sarah liked to jitterbug but she meekly agreed with his condemnation and sat out the jive, watching her friend Felicity Kingswood swirling her skirts to mid-thigh on the floor with a peppery Welshman.

At the end of the night, as they stood on the terrace drinking punch, Sarah had told Geoffrey a secret she had withheld even from her parents. She was planning to join the Woman's Auxiliary Air Force when she graduated from St. Agatha's next month. "The WAAFs are an absolutely rotten idea," Geoffrey said. "My brother says they do nothing but muck up procedures wherever they go."

Stunned and angry, Sarah had said good night to Geoffrey without a kiss and conferred with her friend Felicity, who downgraded Geoffrey from a Profile to a Poltroon. Now here they were, face to face again nine months later.

"Oh—hello," Geoffrey said.

"I didn't take your advice about the WAAFs, as you can see," she said, gesturing to her crinkly new uniform.

"Too bad," Geoffrey said. "Everything I've seen so far here at Bedlington has only convinced me my brother was right. You'd be doing much more for the war effort working in a factory or nursing in an army hospital."

Off he went into the sunshine, leaving Sarah in a stew of embarrassment and fury. She had been at Bedlington exactly one week and so far she had found very little that pleased her. Most of the pilots, those beings she had hero-worshiped since girlhood, seemed to share Geoffrey's opinion of WAAFs. Their aircrews and the ground officers at Bedlington were not much better.

Things had started going wrong the first day, when Sarah made the mistake of strolling in the front door of the former guardhouse that had been converted into the Waafery—their headquarters building where the CO and officers lived. The CO, who looked like the Queen Mum having a permanent tantrum, had excoriated her for such a breach of etiquette. Mere privates used the back door, as befitted servants. Imbued with a healthy detestation of England's class system thanks to her father and one or two radical teachers at St. Agatha's, Sarah had almost strangled with rage.

Worse, the so-called officers of the WAAF administrative staff were so foggy, they did not even know what an RTO— radio telephone operator—was. One suggested they go to the orderly room and learn to read timetables and absorb other information necessary to train railway transport officers.

Sarah and Felicity and three others were the first RTOs to reach Bedlington, and everyone, male and female, seemed baffled by their appearance. Someone finally sent them out to the Watch Office, a square box-like building on the edge of the airfield's perimeter where male RTOs talked to incoming planes over upright microphones. An officer wearing the rings of a squadron leader on his sleeve hemmed and hawed and confessed no one had warned him of their arrival. He suggested they take a weekend pass while he figured out what to do with them.

On fourteen shillings every two weeks, none of them had

the train or bus fare to go home—if they had the desire. Like Sarah, most of them had spent exhausting months convincing their parents to sign the waiver that permitted them to join up and they did not want to face inevitable interrogation and admit even a moment's disillusion.

Now Geoffrey Archer's epitome of male condescension! Steam all but flowing from her ears, Sarah stormed back to their brick hut filled with facing rows of iron beds and told Felicity about the latest insult. "Let's show the bastards we know where the grass is greener," Felicity said. "The Yanks are having a dance at Rackreath. They're sending over a bus to the village at seventeen hundred hours. Get on your war paint."

"Wizzo!" Sarah said, displaying her RAF slang in an ironic mode.

Best blues were pressed and buttons polished with Silvo (rather than Brasso) until they looked like the genuine expensive article. Shoes gleamed; freshly laundered shirts and collars were sacrificed without a murmur. Jane Newhouse was the only one with silk stockings. The rest of them had to tolerate the government's lisle. They all washed and set their hair and combed it just a little longer than the regulation length, so that it curled on their collars and below their ears. Sarah enjoyed the sensation of shaking her head and feeling her dark brown curls swing softly, loose from the ribbon she usually wore.

Finally came the makeup. Beneath her mother's puritanical eye, Sarah had never worn any. Felicity had introduced her to buying theatrical greasepaint for lipstick and eye shadow. It was much cheaper than commercial makeup and looked perfectly natural, if it was used with care. At Jane's suggestion—she was in her twenties and talked a lot about attracting men—Sarah blended a spot of greasepaint along her cheekbone to give her pale skin a bit more color.

A dash of Evening in Paris here and there and they were ready. They gamboled down Green Lane, an old Roman road that ran across the airbase and continued between low hedges and budding trees to the thatched roofs of Woodbastwick village. A tan U.S. Army Air Forces bus was purring on the narrow main street. They joined a dozen women from the village and rode across the wide Norfolk plain, as level and green as the top of a billiard table, past more villages like Woodbastwick full of the timeless tranquillity that inspired visitors to murmur "There'll always be an England." It was hard to believe that across the North Sea were ninety million Germans and their fanatic führer, determined to make that remark an anachronism.

War. Sarah could not quite grasp the horror with which her parents said the word. She knew her mother had lost two brothers in France during the Great War, as the textbooks called it—and her father had been shot down and badly injured in the Royal Flying Corps. But to her this second Great War was still an adventure, a marvelous opportunity to escape her mother's dominating grasp. Besides, they were going to win this time without so much slaughter. The Americans had come into the war early—instead of waiting until the last possible minute, as they had done in 1917. Her mother was quite bitter about the Americans for waiting so long the last time.

Sarah had no such prejudices. Individually, Americans were creatures she had only seen in the movies. Craggy-jawed cowboys in ten-gallon hats who said "howdy" instead of "hello"—or squat gangsters who said "troo" instead of "through"—or wiseguys who called women "Babe." She shared her father's admiration for their industrial and military might. As senior designer for de Havilland Aircraft company, he was awed by the statistics that emanated from Washington, D.C.. "Last month the Americans turned out three thousand planes," he said one night at supper, shortly before she left for the WAAFs. "Three thousand planes!"

That was twice what England could produce in a month. It meant victory was guaranteed. It entitled Sarah to regard her plunge into WAAFdom as an adventure, with no darker overtones. Mother could brood on England's losses, on another generation of broken hearts. She was eighteen and the world was enormously exciting. It teemed with brave men in hurtling planes, defying death and a vicious enemy. She loved them all—at least, she did until she met Geoffrey Archer and the assembled male supremacists and attendant female dodos of RAF Bedlington.

The American dance was in the Rackreath officers' club, in a big darkened room with a bar on one side and a band jammed against the opposite wall. The band was playing Glenn Miller's "In the Mood" with a wild intensity that made Sarah's flesh tingle. The whole room reverberated with the music and a cacophony of voices from the crowd of airmen around the bar. There was a frantic undercurrent to the voices and the jitterbugging couples on the floor. Everyone seemed to be flinging themselves into the party with something very close to frenzy.

There were no introductions, no formalities. The women trickled along the wall and stood shyly waiting for something to happen. It did not take long. The womanless drinkers around the bar stormed toward them in a cheerful, chortling mob. The village girls were snatched onto the floor like slaves off an auction block. It took a little longer to reconnoiter the WAAFs.

"Did anyone ever tell you you've got beautiful eyes?" said a deep confident voice. Sarah gazed up at one of the handsomest man she had ever seen. He was well over six feet with a profile that capitalized the entire word, a tough mouth and thick dark hair combed straight back à la Robert Taylor. "I think my nanny used to whisper that to me in my cradle," Sarah said. "After her, you're the very first."

It was such an obvious come-on, she felt her irony was justified. It was also a way of warding off the impact of his overwhelming maleness. He led her out on the floor before he bothered to introduce himself. "Cliff Morris, California."

She realized he was slightly drunk. That did not disturb her. Hard drinking and planes more or less went together. Her father often came home "snookered," as her mother called it. Her mother did not approve, of course. But her mother approved of very little.

"Sarah Chapman, Sussex," she said. "Are you a pilot?"

"Captain of the *Rainbow Express*," he said. "What are you doing in that uniform?"

"Not much of anything for the moment. But I expect to

be talking to pilots like you in a week or so—in the RAF. I'm a radio telephone operator, stationed at Bedlington."

"You may be talking to us too," he said. "A half dozen of our flying wrecks went into Bedlington after the last raid. You're fourteen miles closer to the North Sea. That can make a lot of difference when you're operating on one motor."

Totally unaware of what the Eighth Air Force was experiencing over Germany, Sarah expressed surprise. "The communiques are all so upbeat," she said. "Have your losses been heavy?"

Cliff Morris seemed to hold her a little closer, as if he needed warmth or comfort. "We lost a hundred and sixty-eight planes over Schweinfurt last week. In our bomb group the losses were fifty percent."

"My God. How many missions have you flown?" Sarah asked.

"Sixteen," Cliff said. "We were one of the first to get here. We've had the privilege of learning the hard way."

Sarah felt an enormous surge of sympathy. This man had come six thousand miles—from that state with the exotic name, California—to help fight England's battle. He was talking about the deaths of his friends—his own death—with the calm steady voice of courage.

"My father's a tremendous admirer of your bomber, the B-Seventeen," she said.

"Oh? You should see the list of things I just sent to my father—stepfather, actually—telling him what's wrong with the damn thing."

"Your father's in the aircraft business?"

"He's head of production for Buchanan Aircraft."

"Oh, I say. This is a coincidence. My father's with de Havilland. He often talks of the man who founded Buchanan—was his name Frank?"

"Frank Buchanan's practically my uncle. I've known him since I was six years old. My stepfather started the company with him."

"My father and he worked together before the first war, designing planes for de Haviland."

In the shadowy room, her eyes burning from the cigarette

smoke, the brassy music exploding in her ears, surrounded by the swirling swaying bodies of the other dancers, Sarah felt an aura envelop them, a compound of sympathy and fatality and attraction. Cliff Morris's arms crushed her against his broad chest as he talked excitedly about Buchanan Aircraft and its future. Planes were going to change the world after they won the war and Buchanan was going to be among the leaders in designing and making them. Frank Buchanan was a genius who would keep them perpetually ahead of the competition.

Into Sarah's mind flashed a vision of a dynastic marriage in the grand tradition. Her brother Derek would rise to power and fame in de Havilland while Cliff Morris rose to similar heights at Buchanan. She would be the link between them, urging each to greater and greater achievements, to better and better planes to defend the Anglo-American empire and preserve a peaceful world.

Cliff led her across the floor to a table where a half-dozen men were sitting with glasses of liquor in front of them. Five had English girls in their laps, two of them behaving amorously. "Hey, you bums," he said. "I found us a lucky charmer. This girl knows Frank Buchanan. Knows what a great designer he is. Wait'll you see the job he does on our flying coffins after he gets my letter."

He introduced Sarah to the crew of the *Rainbow Express*. They were a blur of names and titles—bombardier, waist gunners, belly gunners—except for two. One was the tail gunner, Mike Shannon. He was distinguished by his diminutive size—and the presence of her friend Felicity in his lap. The other man was the navigator, Dick Stone, who did not have a girl in his lap. Cliff drunkenly insisted Sarah should talk to Stone. "He doesn't think we should be bombing the goddamn Nazis," Cliff said. "Tell him what the bastards did to London."

Sarah did not know much more about what the Germans had done to London than anyone else who read the papers and listened to the radio. "Why don't you think we should be bombing the Huns?" she asked Stone, trying to make a semi-joke of it.

"I don't think anything of the sort," Stone said. He was a swarthy, square-jawed young man with horn-rimmed glasses that gave him a rather scholarly air. "I think we should be bombing them more accurately. To make sure we aren't killing women and children—or destroying irreplaceable cultural treasures. I'm all for bombing military targets."

"Isn't that what everyone bombs?" Sarah said.

"Miss Chapman—I don't want to upset you—but the British in my opinion are becoming mass murderers on a scale infinitely beyond Hitler's Luftwaffe. Your night raids on German cities don't have even a pretense of attacking military targets. They're terror bombing, pure and simple—or should I say impure and simply horrifying?"

Sarah was simultaneously angry and bewildered. It was the first time she had ever heard anyone connect morality and airplanes. Heretofore planes existed in a world beyond morality, the transcendent universe of the sky. They were an escape from the trivial groundling world of shoulds and shouldn'ts that her mother was perpetually invoking. She knew planes could be as maddening as an inconstant lover, as dangerous as a loaded gun. But she never thought of them as vessels of morality.

"See what I mean?" Cliff Morris said. "How would you like to have a navigator like this guy? To make it even worse, he's Jewish—you'd think he'd be cheering every bomb we dropped."

"Hitler and his crowd are anti-Semites. But I think the German people's anti-Semitism has been exaggerated," Dick Stone said.

"I'm not qualified to comment on their anti-Semitism," Sarah said. "But I think your opinion of the RAF should be reconsidered, Mr. Stone. I might even say the same about your comments on the Eighth Air Force. Captain Morris has told me about your terrible losses."

"Trying to bomb the lousy military targets he says we're missing half the time," Cliff said. "I say so what."

"Okay, okay," Dick Stone said. "I'll reconsider. I may even change my mind if Cliff reads Goethe's *Faust* and tells me how people who can produce that kind of literature should be bombed into extinction."

"I've read Goethe's *Faust*," Sarah said. "It's wonderful poetry, but I don't think the Germans have learned much from it. Wouldn't you say it's a warning against the danger of gaining the whole world and losing your soul?"

"I'd say Faust is a warning against loving a woman too much. A woman who seems to embody the whole world."

Dick Stone said this so softly, so calmly, in a voice that was such a contrast to the shouts and laughs and wisecracks flying around them, for a moment Sarah was ashamed of her reckless attack on him on Cliff Morris's behalf. The man was a *thinker*. At eighteen, she had never contemplated the possibility of a man who shared his thoughts with a woman. Men were like her father, creatures with short tempers, rough jokes, long obscure silences.

They sat down and Cliff poured Sarah a drink from a bottle on the table. It was her first taste of bourbon whiskey. Its sweetness made her think it was an American version of sherry—which her mother allowed her to sip at her graduation party. Anyway, Mother was a hundred miles away. She was on her own, an adult woman with a grudge against the RAF and an exultant sense of exploring a new world.

There were more dances, more drinks. More discussions with Dick Stone, who still lacked a girl for his lap. Someone explained that Stone had made the idiotic mistake of getting engaged before he left home and he was being faithful to his fiancée. "He's a veritable tower of rectitude," Sarah said, still feeling some of Cliff's hostility to the scholarly navigator.

"A tower of Stone," Cliff said. "Full of bullshit. Come on, Stone, take a drink, at least. I don't like it when I get drunk and you stay sober."

"I have too much respect for my stomach to put that rotgut into it," Stone said.

"The guy's a snob. That's his problem," Cliff said. "He thinks he's better than everybody else. He even thinks he's got a better stomach."

"Maybe it is," Sarah said. "It's made of stone."

"I've got stone feet too," the navigator said. "Want to risk a dance?"

Out on the floor, they swayed to a raucous version of "Don't Get Around Much Anymore." "Are you Jewish?" he said.

"Catholic," Sarah said.

"Ah. That explains your innocent look. You remind me of several very protected Jewish girls I knew in New York."

"Are you engaged to one of them?"

"As a matter of fact, I am. If she was here, I'd give her some advice. Instead I'll give it to you. Go home while the going's good. This party is bound to get wild."

"Leftenant Stone," Sarah said. "You are one of the most— most presumptuous men I've ever met. Why is it bound to get wild?"

"Because we're going back to Schweinfurt the day after tomorrow. A good half the people you see dancing around you won't be here next week."

"That only makes me want to stay! What kind of a shirker do you think I am?"

"I think you're a sweet beautiful girl who should have stayed home with her mother."

"If you knew my mother you wouldn't say that! For your information, Leftenant Stone, women are not going to accept condescension in any form after this war is won. We're helping to win it and we're going to demand respect as our reward!"

They returned to the table and Sarah declared her independence from Lieutenant Stone and his obnoxious advice by demanding another drink of bourbon. The room careened and she was on the dance floor doing a lindy with Cliff Morris. Her skirt was up her around her waist and she was laughing boldly into his handsome face. She felt as if she were in midair, performing a preternatural stunt. In the middle of her laughter she remembered what Dick Stone had told her about Schweinfurt and almost wept. Was it possible? Would half of these laughing young men die in burning planes the day after tomorrow?

Unthinkable. She wanted to be powerful enough to prevent

it. Another drink of bourbon and she was sure she possessed some sort of supernatural power. She would bestow it on Cliff, on the *Rainbow Express*, at least. If she could not protect them all she would protect him with her sheltering arms, her bursting heart.

They were outside in the cool spring night. A million stars crowded the incomprehensible sky. Dozens of couples were wandering across Rackreath Air Base, disappearing into the woods and fields that surrounded it. Air bases in England were inserted into the countryside with a view to doing as little damage as possible to existing farmland and orchards. The trees and grass were only a few yards beyond the runways.

"Dick Stone told me you're going back to Schweinfurt the day after tomorrow," Sarah said.

"I don't want to think about it."

"I want you to know I'll be thinking about it. Thinking about you. Praying for you."

"Praying?" Cliff said. "You'll be the only one. My mother stopped going to church when she was six. My old man—my stepfather—never went. How do you pray? I've never even tried."

"You—open your heart to God. You talk to Him."

"If He's there."

"He's there."

"You're the one I want to open my heart to. Can you open yours? I loved you the second I saw you coming in the door. I know that's a crazy thing to say. I know we've only been together a few hours. But when I look at you something like a prayer forms on my lips."

They were on a country lane between more low hedges. A sweet scent of new-mown grass rose from the fields. Nearby was the babble of a Wordsworthian brook. Cliff Morris took Sarah Chapman in his arms and kissed her for a long time. His hands moved slowly up and down her body, along her outer thighs, down her arms, over her breasts. "Say yes, Sarah, please. Say yes so I can get that plane off the ground the day after tomorrow. You can help me do it. With that prayer in your heart."

"Yes, oh yes, Cliff. Yes yes yes."

Off the lane the ground was soft, moist with night dew. Cliff spread his coat on the grass and slowly undressed her, whispering over and over: "You're so beautiful. You're so beautiful."

It was innocent, Sarah told herself. Her heart was over-flowing with compassion and pity. This gift of herself, this prayer of herself was the least she could offer this man who was facing violent death on England's behalf. Juliet would have offered herself to Mercutio, Ophelia to Hamlet if the plots had given them the opportunity. It was a Wordsworthian parable for the twentieth century, love among the daffodils beside a babbling brook.

Except for certain things that Wordsworth forgot to mention. The brook at ground level had anything but a sylvan breath. It was probably the sewer for one or several nearby villages. Nor did sweet William or sister Dorothy ever encounter this mass of maleness on top of her blotting out the stars, this tongue plunging into her mouth, until her lungs, her whole body was bursting.

Lawrencian. That forbidden genius whose books were smuggled into St. Agatha's with the risk of expulsion by certain girls who read them between the covers of other books in study hall, their eyes wide with astonishment and glee. Sarah had yearned to be one of the smugglers but all she had done was skim selected passages copied out and passed from hand to trembling hand. Were men that way? Was any woman that way? She simply could not believe it.

Now it was happening here in the Wordsworthian countryside, abandon in the daffodils. In a swift sure thrust Cliff entered her. With a flicker of pain came the flash of awareness that he had done this before; he knew exactly how to lay her down, open her thighs, lunge. Did it mean Dick Stone was right, she should have stayed home with Mother?

Like a daregale skylark scanted in a cage. Poetry was answering that obnoxious question. Her spirit, her heart was the skylark in the cage of home, of Mother's perpetual prohibitions, in the larger cage of St. Agatha's with its frowning nuns and old-maid lay teachers. It was her heart in the cage of her body, her timid heart, partaking now of male courage, from an explorer of the skylark's home, the sky. She was bursting out of the cage of girlhood into womanhood, adulthood, into the word that gave meaning to a woman's life— into love.

Marvelous thoughts but the reality somehow failed to live up to them. The brook's odors assailed her nostrils; Cliff was stroking her with drunken, careless ardor, his weight crushing her into the grass, his mouth against her throat. She tried to let go, to give herself to him, the night, the vanished sky. They were one thing, a kind of plane, soaring into faith and hope and trust—and prayer.

Yes, her prayer for him was on her lips, it flowed into his body. But she did not feel a similar flow from him. She wanted to soar with him, to hurtle beyond earth, beyond Lawrencian orgies into the happiness that belonged exclusively to those who conquered the sky. Nothing else could justify the sin they were committing, the implicit awful condemnation that was always in Mother's eyes when she argued against joining the WAAFs.

Before she could begin to soar Cliff gave a shuddering groan and came—a tremendous gush that lifted her at least to treetop level with a surge of inexplicable sweetness. She cried out with a wild mixture of pleasure and regret. The sky, the stars, remained blank behind his massive shoulders and head.

They spiraled down to the waiting earth. On the other side of the brook there were similar cries and groans of pleasure. Sarah found it somehow disillusioning to realize they were not the only ones in England performing this ancient rite. Earthbound ideas crowded her dazed mind. She had given herself to this man. She had surrendered what she had vowed she would never yield, without the certainty of deep and abiding love.

"What do we do now?" she blurted.

"We do it again," Cliff said. "Again and again and again. Whenever we get a chance."

For a moment Sarah almost wept. There was too much male delectation in those words. They revealed things she did not want to confront. "You do love me?" she said. It was almost a wail.

"Of course I love you. Get dressed. I'll drive you back to Bedlington. We've got a long day tomorrow getting ready for Schweinfurt. And a longer one the day after that."

"You'll be all right. I know you will. I know it!"

"Sure," he said. "Just remember. Be there to pray me down."

"I know you'll be all right!"

She was omnipotent again. Love's goddess, ruling the sky.

RAINBOW EXPRESS

"Grab your cocks and pull up your socks, here we go!" Cliff Morris shouted over the intercom.

Down the rain-slick runway at Rackreath Air Base raced the B-17E with a red, white, and blue rainbow painted below the left cockpit window. She was fighting for airspeed with two tons of bombs in her belly and a ton of high octane gasoline in her fuel tanks. In the pilot's seat, Cliff poured on the power. The four Wright R1820 Cyclone engines responded with a deepening roar. When the airspeed indicator read 110, he gently pulled back on the control column and *Rainbow Express*, all thirty-three tons of her, lumbered into the air for her seventeenth mission over Germany.

"Ain't she beautiful?" Cliff shouted over the intercom.

"She's got my vote," Mike Shannon whooped. He was hunched in his tail gunner's seat, watching the rest of the 103rd Bombardment Group take off behind them. No one else aboard the *Rainbow Express* said a thing. Their morale was as low as the rest of the 103rd, which was as low as the rest of the Eighth Air Force in the spring of 1943.

Below the cockpit, in the Plexiglas nose, navigator Dick Stone hunched over his charts and remembered what Colonel

Darwin H. Atwood had said when the 103rd Bombardment Group reported for training at Kearney Air Force Base in Nebraska in mid-1942. "Don't get the notion that your job is going to be glorious or glamorous. You've got dirty work to do and you might as well face the facts. You're going to be baby killers and women killers."

Tall and balding, Colonel Atwood had been a professor of modern history at Stanford before his elevation to rank and power. He seemed to carry history like a burden on his slumped shoulders. An unspoken pain lurked in his squinting eyes. If he did not know better, Stone would have sworn he was Jewish. Atwood knew all about the strategic bombing campaigns of World War I, which had killed hundreds of civilians in Paris, London, and German cities in the Ruhr.

Dick Stone was vulnerable to doubts about bombing German civilians. His paternal grandfather had been a professor of German literature at the City College of New York. Born in Germany, he was one of those Jews who were forever torn between admiration for its culture and dismay at its virulent anti-Semitism. He loved Goethe, Heine, Schiller and insisted on Stone learning German as a boy so he could read them in the original.

The pilots in the 103rd despised Colonel Atwood. For that reason alone Dick Stone was inclined to defend him—or at least take him seriously. Atwood had given some thought to what they were going to do over Germany. As far as Stone could see, none of the pilots had ever had a thought beyond their arrogant affirmation of their flyboy status and the inevitable superiority of the B-17.

Cliff Morris personified the goggles-and-scarf tradition Colonel Atwood struggled in vain to eradicate from the 103rd Bombardment Group. On their first flight Cliff had buzzed the field at fifty feet, missing the tower by inches, according to the terrified traffic controllers. Colonel Atwood threatened Cliff with a court-martial. "I was trying to give my crew some positive leadership," Cliff replied. "It's in short supply around here." When the outraged Atwood reported Morris to the commanding general, nothing happened.

Morris's stepfather, a World War I ace, knew bigger generals.

Everyone in the *Rainbow Express*'s ten-man crew except Stone soon worshiped Cliff Morris. He made them feel like fliers. They joined his campaign to outdrink and outscrew every other airman in the Eighth Air Force. Stone went along on their "reconnaissances" in Nebraska and in England but he remained aloofly sober and disdainful of the girls they picked up. He was a rabbi's son and he felt he owed his father moral allegiance, even if he no longer agreed with his theology. Rather than try to explain anything so complicated, he cooked up the fiction of being engaged to silence Cliff Morris and other needlers in the crew.

"Hey, Stone," Cliff said as they reached their prescribed height of 20,000 feet and plowed through the icy sky toward Schweinfurt. "You got Little Miss England so upset with your criticism of the RAF, she couldn't wait to show me how true blue she was."

"What was blue? Once you got rid of her uniform," said Beck, the bombardier, who preferred London prostitutes to nice girls.

"Her eyes, you miserable whoremaster. I didn't have to pay for it either. The old record is still intact."

Cliff was inordinately proud of his ability to seduce women. They all listened while he gave them a condensed version of his line with Sarah Chapman. He always talked about a seduction as if he were a movie director setting up a scene. Dick sighed and wondered what Sarah Chapman thought of it now, two days after she sobered up.

"You should have heard the stuff she babbled on the way back to Bedlington," Cliff said. "Something about a skylark in a gale trapped in a cage. She got so excited we stopped in a lane just outside the base and did it once more for good measure."

"Like a daregale skylark scanted in a cage," Dick Stone said.

"That's it, Shylock. What the hell does it mean?"

"It's from a poem by someone who feels spiritually trapped and discouraged," Dick said.

A groan filled the earphones. "Don't knock it, you fucking atheists. She's gonna pray us back," Cliff said. "We could use some prayers flying this miserable crate."

Back in the States during their training, when Cliff was not talking about girls, he talked about the B-17. Again and again he proclaimed it the best plane ever built. Family pride was partly involved. Buchanan Aircraft was turning out hundreds of the big bombers under a contract from the original maker, Boeing. Cliff had named their bomber after the Buchanan company symbol, a plane soaring over a rainbow.

Now no one, including Cliff Morris, was sure of the B-17's superiority, though he usually tried to disguise his doubts with bravado. On the first few raids over Germany their losses had been light. Everyone assumed the Germans were afraid to attack the Flying Fortresses, with their bristling array of machine guns. Alas, the Luftwaffe was only reorganizing its defenses, which had been devoted to defending the fatherland against British bombers by night. The American decision to bomb in daylight and prove the precision of the Norden bombsight and the invulnerability of the B-17 took the Germans by surprise. But not for long.

Soon the sky above their targets was thick with ugly black bursts of .88 millimeter shells. An .88 could knock out a Sherman tank. When it struck something as fragile as a plane, the results were horrendous. B-17s exploded into fragments, broke in half, spun down with wings or tails gone. Out of the sun hurtled swarms of Focke-Wulf and Messerschmitt fighters firing 20- and 30-millimeter cannons. Formations dissolved. B-17s began burning all over the sky or spinning down with dead pilots and copilots in shattered cockpits. Instead of the eight or ten planes that they had expected to lose on each mission, they started to lose sixty or seventy. Whole squadrons were wiped out.

People with mathematical ability soon estimated that only 34 percent of them would make it through the required tour of twenty-five missions. Colonel Atwood addressed this chilling computation with his usual candor. "I'll give you a little clue on how to fight this war. Make believe you're dead already. The rest will come easy."

On the B-17s plowed in two huge box formations. Below them, Europe was invisible as usual beneath its semi-permanent clouds. The weathermen said the skies would be clear but they had been wrong so often, no one even bothered to curse them anymore.

Dick Stone found himself thinking about Sarah Chapman again. Amazing how poetry could connect people. He still felt linked to his grandfather by certain poems by Goethe and other German writers that the old man had read to him. He identified with that poem by Gerard Manley Hopkins because he too felt trapped in a spiritual cage. In an odd way he also identified with the word *Catholic*, spelled with a small *c*. He could hear his grandfather saying: *catholic, that's what we all must become. That's what America is about, catholicity, diversity yet brotherhood.*

"Any fucking cultural monuments you don't want to hit on this run, Stone?" Cliff asked.

On a recent raid the primary target, Dusseldorf, had been invisible under heavy clouds and they had scattered to bomb secondary targets. Breaking through the overcast to get some idea where they were, the *Rainbow Express* saw a city full of church spires and eighteenth-century houses, with some factories on the outskirts. Dick Stone flipped his maps, did some rapid calculations of their airspeed and course and concluded it was Weimar, where Goethe spent most of his life. He urged Cliff not to bomb it. The place was a living museum. Cliff had bombed it anyway and was still needling him about it.

"Nothing to worry about but women and children," Dick said.

They droned on in subzero boredom for another two hours. Finally, navigator Stone informed Captain Morris they were less than fifteen minutes from Schweinfurt. Below them was a growing number of fleecy cumulus clouds. In ten minutes they began to darken into a gray cumulonimbus blanket. The weathermen were wrong again.

"Bandits at two o'clock!" screamed the top turret gunner, Smithfield. He was coming apart. He started firing his guns when the Germans were at least a mile away, hysterically holding the triggers down, instead of squeezing off three-second bursts. The planes were thick-bodied Focke-Wulfs. They did a barrel roll and came down ready to work on the outer edge of the American formation where the *Rainbow Express* was flying. It was known as the Purple Heart corner.

Smithfield was not the only member of the crew Dick Stone worried about. Cliff Morris was also showing signs of strain. He was getting drunk much too often at the Rackreath officers' club. Already a licensed pilot when the Japs bombed Pearl Harbor, Cliff had a personal motive for seeing action. His stepfather had told him a good war record guaranteed him a job at Buchanan Aircraft. Cliff had converted this promise into guaranteed jobs for all of them. But Cliff had never imagined that winning this pot of gold involved sitting behind a half inch of glass watching Focke-Wulfs closing on him at a combined airspeed of five hundred miles an hour, their wings aflame with machine guns and cannon.

Cliff shoved the *Rainbow Express*'s nose down, putting her into a shallow dive to give top turret gunner Smithfield a better shot at the oncoming Focke-Wulfs. The Germans' wings flickered fire. A slamming tearing sound, then a scream of anguish over the intercom. "Smitty's hit!" shouted the radioman.

"Get up there and man his gun," Cliff said.

The Focke-Wulfs rolled into a dive that brought them beneath the formation for another blast of cannon fire. A new cry of anguish. Dick Stone turned to find bombardier Beck slumped over his bombsight, blood gushing from his mouth. Dick dragged him aside and told Cliff he was going to bomb.

Cliff held the *Rainbow Express* on course while Dick flicked on the rack switches and the intervalvometer switch that controlled the spacing between bomb drops. He peered through the sight at the target area. The clouds were now shrouding Schweinfurt. But the bombers were all too visible on German radar. Up through the clouds hurtled a firestorm of .88 millimeter shells. The blue sky looked as if a madman was flicking gobs of intensely black indigo paint on it.

"*Marvelous Mabel*'s hit," shouted Mike Shannon from the tail. She had been flying directly behind them. A shell had

blown off *Mabel*'s wing. As she spun down the leggy blonde
on the fuselage below the name seemed to smile up at them.
"Not one goddamn parachute," Mike said.

Baby killers and women killers, Dick Stone thought, waiting for a break in the clouds to give him at least a glimpse
of their target, ballbearing factories on the outskirts of
Schweinfurt.

"Open bomb bay doors," Cliff said. A blast of freezing air
swept through the plane. Dick could feel the motors straining
against the extra drag.

A tremendous crash. Stone saw flames gushing from the
number-two engine. "We're in trouble," Cliff shouted as the
Rainbow Express lost airspeed. "Get rid of those goddamn
bombs. Now."

"I can't see a thing," Dick said.

"I said *bomb!*" Cliff said, pulling the CO_2 switch to douse
the fire in the burning engine.

Dick Stone's grandfather—or was it Colonel Atwood—
began reciting a poem in Stone's head. It was by the great
German Jewish poet, Heinrich Heine, asking his mistress to
listen to his breaking heart. He said the hammering sound
was a carpenter fashioning a coffin for him. Now the coffin
maker was in the sky and Stone's heart was hammering not
from love but a berserk mixture of fear and revulsion. What
if he refused to press the bomb release?

"Stone, I said *bomb!*" Cliff Morris roared.

Dick pressed the button and the four five-hundred-pound
bombs fell from their racks. He pressed a second button that
fired a white flare, a signal for the rest of the group to bomb
at the same time. God only knew what they were hitting in
Schweinfurt.

The B-17 soared up at least a hundred feet without the
bomb load. "Let's go home," Cliff said, banking the *Rainbow
Express* like a pursuit plane to make the tightest possible
turn.

"Bandits at two-three-four-five-six o'clock," screamed the
radioman. There were at least two hundred of them and they
all seemed to be heading toward the Purple Heart corner. A
wave of bullets and shells hurtled into the 103rd Bombard-

ment Group. Tail gunner Mike Shannon shouted reports of B-17s burning and exploding all around them. The *Rainbow Express* shuddered and groaned as she took her share of the bullets and shells.

Shouts from the waist. The radioman was dead, the second top turret gunner to go down. "Shannon, take over those guns," Cliff said. "You're having a goddamn vacation back there."

"Fire in the radio room," shouted one of the waist gunners.

"Number three engine's on fire," cried the copilot who was on his first mission. The regular copilot had been decapitated by a twenty-millimeter shell on their previous outing.

Smoke swirled through the plane. Dick Stone and the waist gunners used handheld extinguishers to snuff out the radio room flames, standing back as far as they could, praying they did not inhale any of the fumes, which were a deadly poison gas, phosgene.

Cliff used the automatic CO_2 in the wing to douse the number-three engine. That left them with only two engines. Their airspeed dropped below two hundred miles an hour. The surviving members of the formation soon passed them. They were alone in the sky with at least a dozen Focke-Wulfs barreling around them.

There were more slamming, tearing, clanking sounds as shells and bullets struck the plane. On the intercom Stone could hear Mike Shannon whooping: "I got one. I got one of the bastards."

A scream of pain erupted from one of the waist gunners. Stone realized it was only a matter of minutes before they went down. The rest of the bombardment group was on the way back to England, leaving the crippled *Rainbow Express* behind. The other planes were only obeying orders. There was no way to help a cripple. It was survival of the fittest up here in the enemy skies. Stone felt the detachment he had struggled to achieve under Colonel Atwood's tutelage slipping from his mind's grasp. Bombardier Beck's blood oozed from his dead body in a half dozen dark rivulets.

Death. He was going to die like Beck. He was going to turn into inert flotsam in history's stream. Garbage. Dust.

Nothingness. Before he understood what life, history, America, Jewishness really meant. A terrible cry of rage, of pain, almost burst from his lips.

Did Cliff Morris, in the cockpit of the *Rainbow Express,* know this? Or was it only Cliff's hand that knew what Stone was thinking and feeling, what everyone was thinking and feeling in the belly of the *Rainbow Express*? Was the hand protesting that mutual terror, that common dread as it reached for the switch that released the landing gear? Then and for years to come Dick preferred to think of it as an involuntary thing, as impersonal as one of the motor's throbbing pistons. Somehow that made it easier to accept.

Thunk. The wheels came down and the *Rainbow Express* almost fell out of the sky as her airspeed faltered with the sudden increase in drag. Did Cliff know what his hand was doing? Dick wondered. Lowering your wheels in enemy skies meant you were surrendering. You were agreeing to fly your plane to the nearest German airfield.

No one in the 103rd Bombardment Group had done this. But planes in other groups had done it. The Germans had captured enough B-17s to fly some into formations and cause chaos by opening fire just as the Americans were starting to bomb.

"What the hell's happening?" the copilot said.

"Shut up," Cliff Morris said.

"Like hell I'll shut up," the copilot said. "We've still got two engines and plenty of ammunition. Why the hell are we surrendering?"

"Yeah, Cliff. Why?" Mike Shannon said over the intercom.

Dick Stone did not say a word. He was paralyzed there in the navigator's compartment face to face with death and the realization that Colonel Atwood's solution was balderdash.

The Focke-Wulfs had stopped shooting at them. One of them pulled alongside the *Rainbow Express*'s right wing tip. A second one appeared off to the left. The first pilot hand-signaled Cliff to head northeast. He banked in that direction and Cliff followed him. The other Focke-Wulf stayed on their left wing-tip.

"Listen to me," Cliff said. "I'm trying to save our god-damn asses. When I say *go*, I want you to blast these two bastards out of the sky. Shannon, you take the guy on the right. Byrd, the guy on the left." Byrd was the ball turret gunner, curled in his glass sphere underneath the belly of the plane.

The other Focke-Wulfs were specks in the distance, pursuing the rest of the B-17s. Did fighting Germans justify this dirty double-cross? Dick Stone wondered. Were these two pilots who had accepted their surrender Jew-baiters and Nazis, out to rule the world? Or had they been in their second year of college like Dick Stone, more interested in literature than politics when the war exploded in their faces?

Still, Dick did not protest. No one protested. No one wanted to sit out the war in a German prison camp. Dick did not want to put his fate in the hands of something as murky as the Geneva Convention, which supposedly protected everyone, even a Jew, as a prisoner of the Nazis. Dick waited in silence, barely breathing.

"Now!" Cliff shouted.

The Browning machine guns clattered above and below the navigator's compartment. Dick saw the Focke-Wulf pilot on the right clutch his throat. The plane dropped into a spin, gushing smoke. Dick whirled in time to see the plane on the left spin in the opposite direction, afire. The pilot bailed out and hung there in his harness as Cliff retracted the *Rainbow Express*'s landing gear and dove for the cloud cover. The German shook his fist in rage as they roared past him.

The clouds remained thick all the way to the North Sea, a remarkable piece of luck. But when they emerged over the water, they found a half-dozen Messerschmitt 109s waiting for them. Cliff ordered the engineer to man the tail guns and they fought off a furious ten-minute attack, living up to their flying fortress nickname for once. Mike Shannon shot down another plane and Dick Stone, manning the nose gun in his compartment, amazed everyone, including himself, by getting a second as he pulled up after a head-on attack.

Cliff dove to less than 100 feet and let the Germans decide whether another attack was worth the possible cost. They tried one more pass and Mike Shannon got his third plane of the day. The 109s cut for home, probably reporting the *Rainbow Express* would never make it to England.

The plane was practically scrap metal. Mike Shannon counted over 200 holes in the fuselage. The horizontal stabilizer was hanging in shreds, giving them no elevator control. The ailerons were equally shredded. When Cliff tried to climb to a safer altitude, they almost stalled out. "Get rid of everything you can tear loose," he ordered.

They jettisoned the ammunition, the machine guns, their bulky flying gear, their boots, the fire extinguishers. Finally, at Dick Stone's suggestion, they dumped the dead bodies of Bombardier Beck, the radio man, and the top turret gunner out the bomb-bay doors. Coaxing maximum rpm's out of their two engines, one of which was making ominous noises, Cliff reached the Norfolk coast at treetop level.

There, almost under their wings, was RAF Bedlington. "Let's hope Sarah's saying her prayers," Cliff said. There was another, more realistic reason for landing at Bedlington. If that gasping engine quit now, it would not be a water landing, it would be on top of apple orchards, thatched roof cottages, it would be fire and explosions frying and rending their flesh.

"Hello Bedlington, this is *Rainbow*; do you read me? We've got a Mayday here. Request permission to land. Over-," Cliff said.

"Hello *Rainbow*, this is Bedlington," said a liquid feminine voice. "Receiving you poorly. Strength two, over."

"Need wind direction. Airspeed down to one hundred and ten," Cliff shouted into the microphone. "Designate runway immediately!"

"Wind from the west at ten. All runways open. Fire trucks spraying foam. Good luck!"

"We're going to make it, guys. We're going to make it!" Cliff shouted over the intercom.

In ten minutes they were over the field. The fire trucks had just finished spreading foam on the runway that ran southwest. The wings wobbled. Cliff fought them back to horizontal as they turned into the approach. Dick Stone saw a slim WAAF standing outside the Watch Office, her hands clasped together before her lips.

It was Sarah Chapman, praying them in. For a fleeting moment he felt a strange, wild gratitude—and a regret for his unbelief, which prevented him from sharing her plea to the faceless baffling God who held them in the palm of his omnipotent hand.

The runway rushed up at them. "Full flaps!" Cliff yelled and they pancaked in, skidding down the foam-covered runway to a shuddering, smoking stop. Fire trucks clanged toward them. The smell of scorched metal filled the plane. "Didn't I tell you guys this was one hell of a plane?" Cliff said.

As Cliff and Dick helped the vomiting copilot off the plane, Sarah ran toward them. "Oh, oh, oh!" she cried. Tears were streaming down her face. She flung her arms around Cliff and kissed him wildly. Standing to one side, watching the romantic spectacle, Dick Stone felt an odd, painful regret. Did he simply want those no-longer-innocent lips on his mouth? Or was he deploring the probability that she and Cliff would be inseparable now?

The surviving members of the crew were pounding Cliff on the back. Only the copilot, still green, and Dick Stone declined to join the celebration. Cliff's eyes explored the circle of faces with an almost preternatural wariness. For the first time Dick sensed something or someone trapped inside Cliff that he was trying to conceal.

For the moment they had a more immediate problem to conceal. What they had done over Schweinfurt was a violation of the rules of war, not to mention morality. In the circle of faces Dick Stone saw mutual guilt, heightened, somehow, by the adulation in Sarah Chapman's innocent blue eyes.

AMERICAN KAMIKAZES

Bless 'em all! Bless 'em all!
Bless the needle, the airspeed, the ball;
Bless all those instructors who taught me to fly—
Sent me up solo and left me to die.
If ever your plane starts to stall,
You're in for one hell of a fall.
No lilies or violets for dead strafer pilots,
So cheer up, my lads, bless 'em all!

The young American voices were bellowing these words off-key when Frank Buchanan emerged from Major General George C. Kenney's tent into the humid twilight of the New Guinea jungle a few miles from Port Moresby. "Thanks for dragging your ass out here to the end of the earth on such short notice, Frank. I wish I could give you something more concrete, like money. Or at least a medal," Kenney said.

"There's one thing you could do, George," Frank Buchanan said. They were old friends from World War I days. "Let me fly with the kids tomorrow. I always like to see how my planes perform under stress."

"You know as well as I do those bombers can't handle passengers. They've got enough weight problems."

"My nephew's copilot is down with malaria. They're going to give him some green kid who flew in yesterday."

"My ass will be in a sling with Richard K. Sutherland stamped on it if you get shot down."

Sutherland was General Douglas MacArthur's overbearing chief of staff. When he tried to browbeat Kenney the way he had intimidated other generals, Kenney had taken a blank piece of paper and drawn a tiny black dot in the corner. "The blank area represents what I know about airplanes. The dot represents what you know," Kenney said. Sutherland had not bothered him since that exchange.

Tomorrow the whole world would find out if Kenney knew as much as he claimed. He had taken over the Fifth Air Force with its reputation at zero and its morale at zero minus. Bombing from twenty thousand feet, their planes had hit almost nothing. Occasionally they attacked American ships by mistake. Kenney had fired five generals and a dozen colonels and totally revamped their strategy.

He had summoned Frank Buchanan to the Pacific to redesign the Samson light bomber, another plane Frank had created from the SkyRanger II configuration. It had more armor and more powerful motors than the Nelson version they had shipped to the British. Buchanan Aircraft was building hundreds of them at a new plant they had opened in the Mojave Desert.

Working with the crudest tools, but with dedicated mechanics, Frank had put eight fifty-caliber machine guns in the nose and bolted four more on the outside of the fuselage. All were fired from a button on the pilot's control wheel. Nose-heavy and loaded to the limit of their weight ratio, the Samsons required maximum skill from their pilots to keep them in the air.

Kenney added another requirement for his pilots: fearlessness. He announced the days of high-level bombing were over. They were going to come in at 150 feet or lower. For three months they had been practicing on a sunken ship in shallow water off Port Moresby.

Last night coast watchers and reconnaissance planes had reported a Japanese fleet carrying a full division of reinforcements heading for New Guinea, the key to the South Pacific. There was not a single U.S. Navy ship close enough to stop them. Kenney's strafers were the only available weapons.

"Come on, George," Frank said. "I want to see if Billy Mitchell was right when he said planes could sink a fleet."

Kenney could not resist this appeal to the hero of every U.S. Army airman. "Okay. Just don't tell anyone about it when you get back to the States."

Frank limped off to the tents of the 345th Bomb Group's

499th Squadron, better known as Bats Outa Hell. His right leg had still not entirely recovered from the crash of the Nelson bomber three years ago. He had wanted to die that day. The pain had been unbearable. Now he was volunteering to fly in what was basically the same plane at a near-suicidal altitude. But the pain had led to the miracle of regaining Amanda's love. Perhaps this flight, even if it ended in another crash, would reestablish a link with another person he loved.

He and Amanda seldom met in his house in Topanga Canyon now. He was away so often on overseas assignments such as this one. When he was in California, the pressure of work was all-consuming. Buchanan Aircraft had expanded a hundred, a thousand times. Proposals for patrol planes, heavy bombers, transports, poured in from Washington D.C.

But there was always the future, that almost mythical world of tomorrow, when the war was over and a victorious America was at peace again. What would he and Amanda do? Even before the war exploded, Frank had started to hate the furtive element in their love. He found it harder and harder to confer with Adrian Van Ness, to eat lunch and dinner with him—and on that very day, perhaps, make love to his wife.

Amanda belonged to him, not Adrian. Frank was absolutely certain of that on the spiritual plane. But in the everyday world of legality and custom she belonged to Adrian. Frank could not adjust his mind to a future of endless liaisons, perpetual deception. But he recognized Amanda's dilemma. Although she had talked bravely about risking Victoria's affection, she flinched from demanding a divorce from Adrian. Frank also had a dilemma—a deep reluctance to leave the company he had founded, to abandon the designers and engineers who had helped him create his planes—and would, he hoped, help him build even better ones after the war.

In front of the Bats Outa Hell tents, Frank listened to a short, slim hatchet-faced Texan describe his week's R&R in Sydney, Australia. "You go back and forth between satchel fever and sweet ass."

"What the hell are you talkin' about, Patch?" asked his younger more naive copilot.

"Satchel fever's like you and me gettin' us a couple of gals in Sydney and goin' to Mansion's Bar or some other pub and drinkin' and just sayin' anythin' in front of 'em. Then hustlin' the women back to our apartment for some more drinkin' and fuckin' and maybe in the middle of the night we switch women.

"But sweet ass. That's somethin' else entirely. That's when you think you've found the virgin, the one and only woman who hasn't been touched by any other male member of the human race. Then you take her to Bondi Beach the next day for a swim, and she sees McCall stretched out on the sand with two or three dames just as virginal breathin' perfume on him and you find out from the expression on your sweet ass's face that this California son of a bitch was there first!"

Captain Billy McCall had propped himself against a palm tree. His canteen—and all the other canteens—were full of Scotch from a case Frank Buchanan had brought with him. Billy smiled at Patch's complaint and Frank thought his heart would stop. He was remembering the four-year-old, the eleven-year-old, he had visited at Buzz McCall's mother's house in Laguna Beach.

Now Billy was wearing a hat with a fifty-mission crush and Frank could easily imagine the swath he cut through the women of Sydney. He had been cutting quite a swath through the girls of Santa Monica until he joined the air force. Women fell into his arms the way men had gone crazy over his mother.

"What's the word from the big brass, Pops?" Billy said.

"I'm flying with you. But it's a military secret."

"How come I don't get a copilot with five thousand hours' experience?" Patch groused.

A siren awoke them at 4:30 A.M. Frank sat in the operations tent looking at the sleepy young faces, remembering the haphazard briefings of World War I. This briefing was far more complex. They were going to fly almost five hundred miles down the coast to hit the Japanese fleet as it turned into a strait between New Guinea and New Britain.

Billy's bomber, named *Surfing Sue* after one of his Santa Monica girlfriends, awaited them inside the dirt revetment. She was black from nose to tail, with an evil-looking bat's head on the fin. Frank joined Billy in the walk-around to make sure nothing obvious was wrong with the plane. "Oh-oh," Frank said and pulled a screwdriver from the nacelle of the left engine.

"Jesus," Billy said. "Braun!"

His scrawny crew chief came running. "You forgot this," Billy said, handing him the tool. "Tomorrow Braun, I want you to get drunk and stay that way for twenty-four hours."

They climbed into the plane. "Braun got a Dear John letter yesterday. He hasn't slept for two nights," Billy said. "Imagine letting a chick bug you that much?"

"Sure. I felt that way about your mother."

He had given Billy a sanitized version of his love for Sammy.

"There's one thing I can't figure out in that story, Pops. Why she preferred my old man. It doesn't say much for her judgment."

The navigator, a chunky Tennessean named Forrest, informed Billy that he and the three gunners were ready to take off. The 1,700-horsepower motors split their eardrums as they burst into life. Many people swore they were the loudest engines in the world. "Any instructions for the co-pilot?" Frank shouted.

"Remember to flip the toggle switch that turns on the camera as we go over the target," Billy bellowed.

As squadron leader Billy led the other five planes to the runway. Ahead of them another squadron was taking off at thirty-second intervals. Billy's planes paused, roaring, belching, backfiring, as each pilot tested his engines one last time. "Kit Bag Leader to squadron," Billy said. "I'll circle a half turn to the left at two thousand feet. Follow me."

Thirty seconds after the other squadron's last plane took off, the green light in the ramshackle control tower flashed and Billy pushed the throttles to the wall. They hurtled down the runway toward a green mass of jungle five thousand feet away, bouncing wildly through chuckholes and dips in the dirt strip. Frank, who had his hands on the copilot's controls, could feel the elevators and rudder coming to life. At the halfway mark they reached the point of no return and it was up to Billy to get this seventeen tons of plane and bombs off the ground.

As the airspeed hit 120, he pulled smoothly back on the yoke and they cleared the trees by twenty feet. But they were by no means safe. The prop wash of the planes ahead of them had stirred the air like a giant eggbeater. Frank could feel the plane trying to fall off on her left wing, a common reaction to such turbulence. A novice pilot would try to right the plane with his aileron—an instinctive reaction, but one that would be fatal in this situation. The prop wash was momentary and when it vanished, the down aileron would throw the plane onto her side at virtually zero altitude. Good pilots like Billy repressed instinct and kicked the laggard wing up with the opposite rudder.

Frank was tempted to say nice going. Billy grinned at him, making it clear that he knew exactly what he had done right. They were both pros now. This was no boy sitting beside him.

They climbed laboriously to 2,000 feet to await the rest of the squadron. Forming up in a tight V formation they headed down the coast. Other squadrons of Samsons, Australian Beaufighters, and A-20s, designed by Douglas Aircraft's resident genius, Ed Heinemann, joined them. In an hour there were over a hundred planes around them, with the Bats Outa Hell in the lead. In another hour the navigator told Billy they were within fifty miles of the strait where they hoped to find the Japanese fleet.

"Let's ride some waves," Billy said. He switched on the intership radio. "This is Kit Bag Leader. We're going down to attack altitude."

Down, down Billy slanted *Surfing Sue*'s black nose until she was only 150 feet above the water. The other planes joined them, forming a wide arc, each squadron flying in the same tight V behind its leader.

"There they are!" Billy shouted.

Ahead Frank saw at least two dozen ships, a mix of troop transports and destroyers, spread across several miles of sea. "This is Kit Bag Leader," Billy said over the radio. "We'll take the ones at the end of the line. Good hunting."

Billy increased the propeller pitch to 2,100 rpms and moved the fuel mixture control from cruising lean to rich to give them maximum power. "Kosloski, watch for bandits out of the sun," Billy told the top turret gunner, as they headed for the transport that was bringing up the rear of the convoy.

They achieved almost total surprise. The guardian destroyers fired only a few rounds at them as they came in. Far above them, the Japanese air cover waited for the usual high-level attack. *Surfin' Sue* roared toward a black-hulled transport. Its decks were crowded with men. "Hang on!" Billy howled and pressed the button on the twelve fifty-caliber machine guns.

A stream of fire spewed from *Surfin' Sue*'s nose. Each of the twelve guns was firing 750 rounds a minute. That added up to the firepower of a battalion of infantry. The plane shook so violently, Frank would not have been surprised to see one of the engines fall off.

The blast of bullets from Billy's guns and the guns of the other planes in the squadron literally melted the superstructure of the transport before Frank's eyes. Most of the men on the deck never knew what hit them.

"Good shooting," Billy said. Ten seconds later he hit the bomb release and two of their one-hundred-pound bombs and twenty of their fragmentation bombs tore chunks out of the deck. Flame and smoke spewed from the transport and it went dead in the water

"Patch, Wilson, this is Kit Bag Leader. Follow me onto that destroyer," Billy said. "The rest of you finish the transport."

Billy banked to port, his wingtip all but touching the waves, and roared toward the long low-slung warship. Flames winkled from the muzzles of a dozen guns along the deck. This ship could fight back. A five-inch gun belched and Patch's plane exploded into a thousand fragments.

"You son of a bitch!" Billy roared. He was pure warrior

now. The expression on his face was one Frank had never seen before, jaw rigid, eyes bulging, mouth a slit. Billy pressed the button and the machine guns spewed fire again. Terrified Japanese flung themselves behind their gun shields. Parts of the destroyer's superstructure sagged and all but disintegrated under the firestorm of steel.

"Now," Billy said and pressed the bomb release. Two one-hundred-pound-bombs added to the chaos on the destroyer's deck.

Wheeling, Billy and his surviving wingmate came back for another run. This time, the gunners on the other side of the ship blew the wingmate out of the sky. Billy called on the rest of the squadron to join him. In five minutes there was no one alive on the destroyer's deck. She was drifting aimlessly, gushing flames and smoke. Billy planted the last of his hundred-pound bombs on her bridge.

"Skip bombers, this is Kit Bag Leader. Finish this guy off."

A trio of Samsons wheeled along the horizon and roared toward the destroyer. While their nose machine guns poured in the same blast of death, from their bays leaped five-hundred-pound bombs that bounded off the water into the hull. Three tremendous explosions blew half the ruined superstructure into the sea.

Carnage. Along the ten-mile length of the convoy, other destroyers and transports were sinking and burning. Japanese sailors and soldiers leaped from them into the sea, where they clung to rafts and drifted in open boats. "Take the swimmers. Even the score for Bataan," Billy said.

"No!" Frank cried.

"Orders, Pops," Billy said. "These guys don't surrender. If they get ashore we'll have to kill 'em all over again."

They dropped to less than fifty feet and the machine guns churned the water white around the hapless survivors. "This isn't war!" Frank cried.

"Yes it is, Pops," Billy said. "These guys shoot pilots when they bail out. They behead pilots who bomb their sacred homeland. What the hell's wrong with you?"

"Bandits at six o'clock!" yelled the turret gunner.

The Japanese air cover was roaring down from their high-altitude patrol to protect the convoy. They were much too late. Not a single troop transport was still afloat. Four destroyers had survived by fleeing over the horizon, leaving the soldiers to their fate. Billy Mitchell was right. A fleet could be destroyed by air power alone.

The Japanese wanted to prove that enemy air power could at least exact revenge. Samsons and Beaufighters plunged burning into the sea as the marvelously maneuverable Japanese Zero fighters zoomed around them. "Long-range fighters," Billy shouted, weaving across the water at no more than twenty feet. "Build us some long-range fighters, Pops."

"Zeke at eleven o'clock. He's trying to ram us!" the top turret gunner shouted.

Billy swung the plane violently to the right and the Zero crashed into the sea.

"I'm out of ammo," the turret gunner reported. He had used most of his bullets on the ships and swimmers.

"I only got enough for two or three bursts," the tail gunner said.

"Here come three more Zeros," the navigator said. He was in charge of guns in the waist but like most navigators had little gunnery training and was a lousy shot.

Billy raced for the shore of New Guinea and zoomed along the beach, still at twenty feet. The Zeros could not dive on him and pull out without plowing into the jungle. Ahead, Billy saw the mouth of a river. He banked into it and roared along its snaking surface, the Zeros still buzzing angrily overhead. The river made several turns around various mountains and the Japanese, low on fuel, gave up the chase.

Billy swung south toward their home base. They too were low on gas and he did not want to waste an ounce of it. Suddenly they were flying down a box canyon at minimum altitude. About a mile ahead was the ugly stone face of a mountain at least 2,500 feet high. "We better get the hell out of here," Billy said.

He pushed the props to 2,300 rpm, shoved the throttles to full power and started climbing. *Surfin' Sue* failed to respond.

Instead of going faster, the plane slowed to near stalling speed as it struggled to ascend.

"What the hell's happening, Pops?" Billy said.

"A downdraft," Frank said. "In the worst possible place."

"This thing stalls at one-thirty. I bet we're below that now. What's holding us up?" Billy said.

"I don't know. Maybe the spirit of Billy Mitchell," Frank said.

They were climbing but the mountain still blotted out the horizon. Frank began preparing to die in the jungle beside Billy. He could think of worse ways to go. At least he was with someone he loved. Maybe Sammy would be there to greet them on the other side. It would solve the dilemma of his future with Amanda.

"Jesus Christ!" Billy said. He was still pushing the engines to their limits. Instruments showed cylinder head temperatures creeping over the red line. Billy had the yoke jammed against his chest, trying to haul the plane over the top of the mountain by sheer physical effort. Frank could see the flat peak of the mountain now. They were going to hit about fifty feet below it.

"Full flaps!" Billy roared. "Give me full flaps. Fast."

Frank slammed down the lever and the flaps fell. *Surfin' Sue* ballooned straight up like a helicopter and they cleared the top of the mountain by ten feet. Billy had realized that by changing the shape of the surface of the wing, he could gain fifty feet of lift.

On the back side of the mountain, Billy quickly regained airspeed and roared back to the base at treetop level. "Do you think I'll always be able to get out of a tight spot that way, Pops?" Billy said.

"I hope so," Frank said. "But remember the saying, 'there are old pilots and bold pilots but no old bold pilots.' "

"Who wants to get old?" Billy said.

Over the base, Billy decided to celebrate their victory. He roared up to two thousand feet and rolled into a steep turn, which put the wings vertical to the ground. He cut the throttles, dropped the wheels and let down thirty degrees of flaps as *Surfin' Sue* started falling toward the jungle. Billy yanked the plane out of the turn, leveled the wings and was on the runway before Frank could get his breath.

General Kenney was waiting for them, his hands on his hips, as they taxied into their revetment. "If you weren't Frank Buchanan's nephew I'd have you court-martialed, Captain!" he roared. "You were never trained to do that in a bomber. I don't know many fighter pilots who'd land that way."

"It's a great way to build morale, General," Billy said. "I'll be glad to teach it to the whole bomb group."

"There's not a hell of a lot left of the group," Kenney said.

Three of the six planes Billy had led into the air that morning were at the bottom of the sea. Losses in other squadrons were equally heavy. Low-level bombing was murderously effective—Kenney had proved that. But it was also murderously dangerous.

"I hate to ask these kids to keep doing it," Kenney said that night in his tent. "But Bupp Halsey's got it right. He said you can't win a war without losing ships and you can't do it without losing planes either."

Frank said nothing. He knew Kenney was talking more to himself than to him, agonizing over a decision he could not retract.

"You lost a lot of your planes to Zeros, George," Frank said. "What you need is a good long-range fighter. I've got some ideas for one. They could use it in Europe to protect the B-17s too."

He began sketching a plane with a pointed snout and thin square-tipped wings. "Those wings will make her hot to handle on takeoffs and landings," he said. "But they'll let a pilot do wild things in the sky." Next came a long lean fuselage that would have room for twice as much fuel as the average fighter. The cruciform tail rode high above the body. "We've learned a lot in our wind tunnel," he said. "Putting the tail up there solves the flutter problem with this size fuselage."

"If I knew you had that plane in your head I would have court-martialed myself for letting you go up in that bomber!" Kenney said. "Go home and get to work on it."

Later that night Frank sat on the beach with Billy, getting

drunk beneath the starry Pacific sky, with the Southern Cross blazing in the center of the constellations. "Tell me the truth man to man, Pops," Billy said. "What happened to my mother? How did she die? I asked Buzz a hundred times and all he'd say was 'Don't worry about it.'"

Frank told him, leaving out his own anguish, though it was probably audible in his voice. "Buzz loved her, Billy. That's why he can't talk about it. He blames himself for it."

Billy was not interested in Frank's defense of Buzz. "It doesn't make any sense, does it? No more sense than poor old Patch gettin' creamed by that five-inch shell this afternoon while I make it back in one piece. What'd he do to deserve that, Pops? Why'd I make it back?"

"I don't know, Billy. War makes you realize how mysterious life is. How each of us is working out a destiny—how little we control it."

"I don't like it. Whoever's running the show is doing a lousy job."

Billy sprang to his feet and raised his fist at the dark glowing sky. *"Do you hear me up there? Are you listening, you fucking assholes? Tell the head asshole he's doing a lousy job!"*

Frank staggered to his feet, appalled by Billy's blasphemy. This was Sammy's son, the boy she had insisted on baptizing as a symbol of her repentance, her yearning to escape from her dark driven wildness to a life of caring love. With his dual nature, Frank understood it was not simply God Billy was cursing, it was all his failed fathers.

Frank saw he had to give Billy something more than the comradeship of terror and danger they had shared in the cockpit. That was Craig's love, older brother's love, a substitute at best for fathering love. In his desperation Frank offered his deepest and purest gift, his talent.

"Billy," he said. "You're a great pilot. After the war you'll fly planes that will go ten times faster and higher and farther than these crates. They're flying in my head now. I'll build them for you. I promise you."

With that pledge Frank knew he was abandoning Amanda, Eden, love in Topanga's green silence. He was accepting the

warriors' dark code, their love of danger, their fascination
with war and death. He was offering them his talent in Billy's
name, for Sammy's sake.

"I won't forget that, Pops," Billy said.

They clung to each other there in the New Guinea darkness, fabricating fatherhood and sonship, their only shield
against the misshapen world men and their gods had created.

MAN OF SUBSTANCE

Down the half-mile long assembly line Adrian Van Ness
strolled, smiling at his workers. He stopped to talk to a
woman riveter in slacks, her hair tied back by a bandana.
"How's it going, Muriel?" he asked.

"Pretty good, Mr. Van Ness. But we're gettin' kinda tired.
The overtime pay is great but after six months of twelve-
hour days—"

"I know. It's even tougher on the night shift. But we're
winning the war."

Muriel gave him a V for victory sign. "Anything that gets
my husband home faster is okay with me."

The Fox Movietone news announcer took over the narra-
tion. "The human touch," he said. "That's how Adrian Van
Ness and his company, Buchanan Aircraft, are setting records
in airplane production. Van Ness knows an amazing number
of his workers by their first names. When he isn't on a plane
to Washington, D.C. to confer with generals or admirals or
at an air base where his latest planes are being tested, he
walks these assembly lines, keeping in touch with his people
and their problems. This year Buchanan will turn out an
astonishing six thousand fighters and bombers, planes that
have proven they can outfly anything the Nazis and the Nips
can put in the air."

Tama Morris flipped off the projector and pulled up the

blinds on the big window overlooking the airfield. "Not bad?" she said, virtually uncoiling as she strolled across Adrian Van Ness's office. Her face, her figure were still remarkably youthful. A tight blouse accentuated the full breasts. Her legs deserved the black-market nylons Adrian bought for her in the east.

"You're a wonder," Adrian said, as she sat down beside his desk.

She was a wonder, in her own way. Not only did she get Buchanan reams of good publicity like the Movietone News feature, she also helped them sell planes in a less visible, more direct way. When generals, admirals, civilian bureaucrats, and congressmen began visiting Buchanan Aircraft with millions of dollars to spend, Tama reorganized the casual prewar dating service she had created to entertain visiting airline executives. She compiled a master list of women employees who were willing to keep these new VIPs happy in California. She also made sure her volunteers were rewarded with nylons, dresses, extra gas and ration coupons, if the visitor turned out to be too cheap or insensitive to leave a gift behind. Buzz McCall liked to say Frank Buchanan might design the best planes in the world, but Tama's volunteers sold them.

"We've got a problem with General Slade," Tama said.

Newton Slade was in charge of procurement for the Army Air Force's tactical branch. He had ordered a thousand copies of the long-range fighter Frank Buchanan had designed after visiting Billy McCall in the South Pacific. It was winning the air war in the skies over Hitler's collapsing Third Reich. Slade was about to order another five hundred, modified as fighter bombers.

"He needs a hundred thousand dollars to invest in some real estate in Santa Monica."

"Really?"

"Yeah. He says North American has a fighter bomber almost as good as ours."

"Why did he tell you all this? Is he afraid to come to me?"

Tama's eyes glowed with dark light. "We've gotten very friendly."

"What does Buzz think about that?"

"He couldn't care less. He's too busy screwing the whole assembly line."

"Oh? I didn't realize he was that ambitious."

"I'm not complaining. He doesn't care what I do, I don't care what he does. That was the deal I bought when we got married." She frowned and lit a cigarette. "One of these days I'm going to tell him to forget it."

"Why don't you?"

"Buzz doesn't let any woman walk away from him. I'm afraid he'd get me fired."

"That's a superfluous worry, as long as I'm around."

Adrian was certain Tama was not really worried about getting fired. She knew a man was stirred by having a woman ask for his protection. Adrian, a lifetime student of the feminine psyche, enjoyed the mating dance he and Tama were conducting.

For a year Adrian had mourned Beryl Suydam's death by working twelve-and eighteen-hour days. Gradually the pain had ebbed into regret. He began to see women as desirable again. But the pressures of his job and the fear of another wound made it a game he played mostly in his mind. In recent months he had begun to see Tama as the solution.

Her sultry reputation attracted him. But she was Buzz McCall's wife. What if Buzz suddenly played outraged husband? Even he stayed away from the wives of his fellow executives. On the other hand it would be a small step toward evening the score for Beryl. It might also deflate Buzz's ego, which had swelled to enormous proportions since the war began. He took credit for the avalanche of contracts from the U.S. Army Air Forces.

"How's Cliff?" Adrian asked.

"Still flying. I almost had a heart attack when he volunteered for another twenty-five missions."

"It was a remarkable thing to do. We're all proud of him."

"Do you think his English wife put him up to it? Could any woman be that crazy?"

"He might have done it for her. Love and idealism are easily connected when you're young."

Adrian understood Tama's relationship with her son. It was a crude version of his own involvement with his mother. It made him feel confident that he could deal with this woman. At the very least Tama would be a change from the tepid sex he got at home, when he got anything at all.

"Adrian—could you get Cliff transferred to this country? I can't ask Buzz. He'd have a tantrum. I'd be so damn grateful."

"I'll make a call or two. I can't promise anything."

"Thanks. What do you want to do about Slade?"

"Tell him to give me a ring tomorrow." He pulled an expense chit out of his desk and filled it out for five hundred dollars. "Buy yourself a new dress."

Tama strolled out the door, smiling. Adrian telephoned the president of the Los Angeles National Bank. He got through to him in ten seconds. These days Buchanan Aircraft kept a running account at the bank that seldom dropped below twenty million dollars.

"Joe," he said. "I've got an old army friend, Newton Slade. He's got a chance to make some money in Santa Monica real estate and needs a hundred thousand dollars. Can you get it to him fast, if he comes to see you tomorrow? Of course I'll cosign it."

Adrian buzzed his secretary. "Get me Hanrahan."

In a moment the rough voice of his new security chief was on the phone. Before the war, Daniel Hanrahan had been a career detective in the Los Angeles Police Department. Adrian had hired him at four times his detective's salary. With the company awash in money, Adrian used it to buy loyalty whenever possible. "Have we got a file on Buzz McCall?"

"You told me to run a file on everybody, Mr. Van Ness."

"Let me see it."

The government had ordered Buchanan Aircraft to hire a security chief. Adrian soon realized security was a good excuse to find out all sorts of useful things about his employees. Hanrahan arrived with the file in his left hand and handed it to Adrian. A remarkable feat if you knew the left arm, the stiff hand were plastic. A shell had blown off Hanrahan's real arm in a sea battle off Guadalcanal. It had been replaced by a prosthetic device designed by Frank Buchanan. Tama had gotten Buchanan reams of good publicity for this invention, which was being used to rehabilitate amputees all over the country.

Adrian opened Buzz's file. Hanrahan did not depart. He stood there, all two hundred pounds of him, feet spread wide. "What's wrong?" Adrian said.

"I don't intend to let one of those files out of my sight, Mr. Van Ness. Not even for you. You want to look at it, go ahead. But I'm staying here while you finish it."

Adrian read a sample page. *On August 18, 1944, at 8:31 P.M., Mr. McCall left the plant with two women, a riveter named Dora Kinkaid and his secretary, Helene Quinn. They drove to the Kit Kat Club in Long Beach where they met several friends, including Albert (Moon) Davis, Buchanan's chief test pilot. They had dinner and drinks and danced until 1:36 A.M. Leaving the club Mr. McCall was too drunk to drive and Miss Kinkaid took the wheel. They drove to her house in east Los Angeles, where a party was in progress. A glance in the window revealed a remarkable amount of nudity and orgiastic sex in every room. The party continued until 4 A.M.*

There was nothing to worry about from Buzz McCall.

"One other thing, Mr. Van Ness," Hanrahan said as Adrian gave him back the file. "The purpose of these files is to make sure there are no lapses of *military* security, no government secrets leaked. Is that correct?"

"Absolutely."

"Then I'm not obligated to inform you or anyone else about what you might call personal matters?"

"Definitely not."

"I'm glad we understand each other on that point."

Something—was it the intensity in Hanrahan's voice?—made Adrian uneasy. Did he mean matters relating to Adrian Van Ness's personal life? Adrian could not imagine what these might be. His personal life was humdrum to the point of boredom. He had a wife who spent far more time in hospitals working with amputees than she did with him. (Amanda had discovered Hanrahan in the hospital and recommended him to Adrian.) He had a thirteen-year-old daughter who adored him almost as much as she worshipped Frank Sinatra and was in all other respects a typical American teenager.

Adrian decided Hanrahan, a devout Catholic, was probably in a state of shock from discovering the sexual liberation of the aircraft world. Two days later, Adrian flew to Washington, D.C., to confer with Army Air Force planners at the Pentagon about a new military transport they were considering to carry supplies and wounded across the Pacific. The Japanese kamikazes had proven fearfully effective, blowing up hospital ships as well as warships. With B-17 production winding town, Buchanan had the capacity to build this plane.

As usual, Adrian took Frank Buchanan with him to discuss the design. He turned out to be the worst imaginable company. He was in a funk about the way the air war was being conducted over Germany and Japan. He said he did not object to the airplane as a weapon. He had resigned himself to that a long time ago. But the thousand-bomber raids on Berlin and Dresden were barbarism. Ditto for the firebomb raids on Tokyo and other Japanese cities. "If I'd known planes were going to be used to kill innocent civilians, I never would have designed one," he said.

"The terror raids were approved at the highest levels," Adrian said. "The Americans and the British fought over it for months. It finally went all the way to the White House. Roosevelt ordered us to go along with the British. You can't really blame them. The Germans did it to them first."

"Is that our morality? An eye for an eye? Surely we've advanced beyond the Old Testament. Even there, the prophets reminded Israel that the Lord said, 'Vengeance is mine.' "

"I don't see how it's any of our business. We're not running the war. Do you really want me to start lecturing the Air Force for killing civilians?"

"Someone should. I will, if I get a chance."

"Jesus Christ, you're as bad as Amanda. She carries on like this all the time. It's gotten to the point where I'm afraid to introduce her to a general or an admiral."

Buchanan buried his nose in a book for the rest of the flight. Adrian decided Frank was mortified to find himself being compared to a woman as feather-brained as Amanda.

Adrian skimmed the war news in the *Los Angeles Times*. In Europe, the end was in sight. The Americans were across the Rhine, battering their way into Germany. The Russians were rampaging in from the east. The Japanese were another matter. Although they were being pounded nightly by Boeing's B-29 superfortresses, they showed no sign of giving up.

In the taxi on the way to the hotel, Adrian tried to thaw Frank Buchanan by telling him about Tama's plea to bring Cliff home. Adrian thought Frank would applaud getting a friend's son out of the air war he was denouncing. Instead, the chief designer became enraged again.

"Let him take his chances like the rest of them," he roared. "She didn't ask to bring Billy home, did she? He's still bombing at fifty feet out there in the Pacific. Their casualties have been ninety percent. But they don't bomb civilians. Those Eighth Air Force crybabies have nothing to worry about. They've got fighter cover all around them now."

Adrian was undeterred by this explosion. He knew nothing about Frank's complex relationship with Billy McCall. He thought it was one more proof of his chief designer's eccentricity.

At the Pentagon, the five-sided fortress the government had erected on the Virginia side of the Potomac to house the War Department's brass, they conferred with the head of the Army's Air Forces transportation command, a tall cigar-smoking southerner named Mellow. He was enthusiastic about Clay's sleek, whale-shaped transport. He even liked the name Adrian had selected, the Skylord. But there were problems about going into production immediately. To explain them required a visit to General Hap Arnold's deputy chief of staff, Major General George Crockett.

They marched down the hall for what seemed a mile and a half to General Crockett's office. A short intense Texan, Crockett wore the crispest uniform Adrian had ever seen. He pumped Frank Buchanan's hand and praised the magnificent work his long-range fighter was doing over Europe and in the Pacific.

"We think we can end the war with Japan by strategic bombing alone," Crockett said. "To do it we need four hundred more B-29s. Can you go into production on them immediately? Boeing will give you everything they've learned. They've gotten the man-hours down to seventeen thousand a copy. A year ago it was a hundred and fifty-seven thousand."

"What about the transport? We can't do both," Adrian said.

"We'll sign the contracts for it and you can go to work on it the day after you deliver the four hundredth B-29."

"I thought you needed the transports for the invasion of Japan," Frank Buchanan said.

"There won't have to be an invasion if we can deliver the kind of stuff we laid on Tokyo a couple of nights ago," Crockett said. "We put three hundred and twenty-five Supers over the city, each with six tons of incendiaries. We burned out the whole goddamn joint. Take a look at these pictures."

He pulled some reconnaissance photos from his desk. Tokyo was a moonscape, with a random steel-and-concrete building such as the Imperial Hotel isolated by endless blocks of charred ruins.

"How many civilians did you kill?" Frank Buchanan asked.

"Hell, I don't know," the general said, missing the hostility in Frank's voice. "The Nips claimed eighty-four thousand but the Russian embassy estimated it at twice that. The temperature on the ground hit twelve hundred degrees fahrenheit. The last planes to bomb said there were whole streets that'd turned to red hot sludge."

The general smiled fondly at the photos. "We're gonna make these bastards cry uncle without sendin' a single Navy ship anywhere near the coast. The GIs and Marines can just play volleyball all day on Saipan or wherever and leave the war to us."

Air power, Adrian thought. They were all part of the mys-

tique. The planes they built were put into the hands of men
who were using them to settle an argument that had started
twenty years ago.

"Do you call incinerating a hundred and sixty thousand
civilians war?" Frank Buchanan roared.

"Jesus Christ, Frank," the general said. "Who's side are
you on? Didn't these bastards bomb Pearl Harbor?"

"I don't believe there were any women or children aboard
those battleships!" Frank shouted.

General Crockett's lip curled. "This here's war, Frank. It
sort of separates the men from the boys and girls."

Adrian seized Frank Buchanan's arm in a decisive grip
before he could bellow a reply. "I don't believe this is the
time or place for us to debate these difficult questions," he
said. "None of us here are responsible for the decision to
bomb Japan. As far as I'm concerned, speaking as the president of Buchanan Aircraft, we're ready to go to work on
those B-29s the moment you get us the blueprints."

Crockett glanced at the reconnaissance photos of Tokyo
for another moment, then banged the drawer shut. "Okay,"
he said. "We'll get 'em to you."

Back in General Mellow's office, Adrian braced himself
for a lecture on diplomacy. Instead, Mellow whacked Frank
Buchanan on the back. "I'm glad somebody told off those
bomber maniacs," he said. "There's a lot of us in the Air
Force who don't agree with what they're doing. When you
try to discuss it, they pull that men against the boys and girls
crap."

Adrian decided this was a good time to ask the general's
advice about getting Cliff Morris rotated home from Europe.
Frank glowered but said nothing. "Hell, that shouldn't be
hard," Mellow drawled. "Damn fool shouldn'ta been allowed
to go over twenty-five missions in the first place. Most pilots're so strung out by that time they start takin' off with
the flaps down and landin' with the wheels up."

Frank continued to glower while the general made a call
to a friend in operations. "They'll check his file," he said.
"Now—about my transports—I want a hundred of them by
June and I don't care how you do it. Those bomber blow-

hards aren't goin' to make the Japs surrender. Down in War Plans they're talkin' about invadin' Kyushu in September and the casualties are estimated to be five hundred thousand men."

"We'll see what we can do," Adrian said. "Buzz McCall has pulled off a lot of miracles for us. I think he can handle this one."

"How is that son of a gun?" the general beamed. "Still got a cock as long as a windsock?"

Adrian nodded. "Unanimous testimony of the entire female work force. Cliff Morris is his stepson, by the way."

On the way to the airport, Frank reopened the argument against bringing Cliff home. "Buzz will go wild when he hears about it," he said.

"I did it as a personal favor to Tama," Adrian said.

He was daring Frank to tell that to Buzz. Frank seemed impressed by the revelation, which suggested Adrian and Tama were seeing a lot of each other. That was exactly what he planned to do, Adrian decided. See a lot of Tama. In fact, every luscious inch of her.

Frank, Buzz, and the rest of the company plunged into a frenzied effort to get the B-29s and the Skylord into production, on top of the five hundred fighter bombers that General Newton Slade, happy with his Santa Monica real estate, had ordered on the same manic schedule. Adrian approved hiring another ten thousand workers if they could find them. That would give Buchanan a payroll of 101,000, making it the largest aircraft company in the world.

A week later, Adrian and Tama drove south across the San Gabriel River past the rambling white Pio Pico mansion, home of California's last Spanish governor. They followed Route 101 through the thick forest of oil derricks in Santa Fe Springs, Fullerton and Brea to the village of San Juan Capistrano. Tama had chosen it without explaining why. They rented a suite in a white-walled inn overlooking the ruined mission.

"I was born here," she said. "I used to walk with my mother in the mission grounds. My mother was Mexican. Does that bother you?"

"No," Adrian said.

Adrian began undressing her. He was full of triumphant desire. He thought of Beryl, of old sorrow, and dismissed it. He was beyond sorrow and regret now, the ultimate man of substance, with this beautiful woman eager to give herself to him.

Would she betray him too in some way? He could not imagine how. Tama let him lead her to a sunken tub where he bathed her as if she were an expensive toy. She was as beautiful as Beryl Suydam in a more ample American style. The dark triangle of hair below her belly was incredibly smooth and fine. Her olive skin gleamed when water flowed across it.

On the bed, after he had patted her dry, she responded to his kisses with sighs and cries that filled him with dark music. She was like an instrument he was playing, a kind of cello that emanated desire and a thousand deeper more intricate wishes. His hand found the little tip of love. She closed her eyes and trembled, her lips parted, the red edge of her tongue beckoned him.

"Are you really—or is it just—to even the score?" she whispered.

"What score? What are you talking about?" Adrian said.

"Amanda—and Frank."

Every imaginable kind of music vanished. A dozen memories coalesced. Hanrahan asking Adrian if he had to report personal misconduct. Hanrahan's amputated arm and Frank Buchanan's extraordinary interest in amputees and Amanda's devotion to them. Frank's abrupt silence when Adrian compared his tirade against bombing civilians to Amanda's monologues.

"Adrian," Tama said. "I thought you knew."

Of course she thought he knew. Everyone in Buchanan Aircraft knew. Why not the president? The presumption was completely logical, especially for Buzz McCall's wife. Why would she think his marriage was any different from hers?

No, that was too crude, the question had been asked out of that sea of secret sorrow that flowed through every woman, that invisible web of yearning for ideal love they wove around every man, even when their own minds mocked the idea.

"Adrian," Tama sobbed. "I didn't think anything could hurt you. You're always so calm, so aloof."

Women. Women. Adrian stumbled to his feet and stared out at the ruins of San Juan Capistrano. The crumbled walls were an image of his self. Behind him there was a thud of footsteps and Tama had her arms around him. "Adrian, Adrian," she whispered. "You don't know how much it means. You cared. You really cared. I've never met a man who cared that way. Not a man like you."

He shook his head. It was hopeless. He was fated to be tortured by women. Tortured and mocked and humiliated like ruined Robert Van Ness. Not even success protected him.

"Now we can really begin," Tama whispered.

She turned him, faithless, passive, to meet her kiss. Nothing happened, of course, as she revolved her gleaming black pussy against his inert stump. He was an amputee. Why couldn't she see that? Why didn't she leave him alone with his misery?

Tama did not seem in the least surprised or disappointed or offended by his plight. She led him back to the bed, step by step, her tongue deep in his mouth and drew him down on top of her. Then the slithering began, the coiling and uncoiling of that sinuous body, that electric tongue as she traveled up and down the moonscape of Adrian's flesh and finally took the still indifferent stump in her mouth. Around and around the doleful little snout her tongue revolved.

Amazing things began happening inside the burnt shell of Adrian's desire. He found himself imagining a thousand positions from some primeval Kama Sutra—he had never read the famous book itself. He saw himself taking Tama with inexhaustible desire in every imaginable way. He saw his tongue probing the pink flesh beneath the black frond of silky hair between her thighs.

He could never love this woman. She had no education, no taste, no refinement. But in some profound and triumphant way she was a woman and he would love that womanness, he would mingle his regret and humiliation and success and achieve an approximation of love and an acme of desire. He would be a man of substance with a woman every other man desired.

Yes, yes, he whispered, as his penis, a stump no more, plunged deep into Tama's darkness. Yes Yes Yes. A man in spite of all of them. A man with the power to betray and humiliate in turn.

"Oh, Adrian, love me, really love me." Tama whispered. "Tell me you do—now."

"I do, I do," Adrian lied.

The room filled with a triumphant roaring. The 400 B-29 Superfortresses that would soon roll off the assembly line in the Mojave thundered across the Pacific to sow flaming death over Tokyo and Yokohama. Adrian accepted that too. He accepted the life he was living in the middle of the twentieth century. A player of the great game. A conqueror of women and nations.

LOVE AMONG THE RUINS

Horns hooted, whistles blew, sirens howled, guns boomed, planes zoomed overhead doing loops. The war in Europe was over. Germany had surrendered. Amanda Van Ness heard the news in the amputee ward of Wainright Army Hospital in Long Beach. Around her, young men, some without arms and legs, expressed little emotion. Europe was not California's war. In the Pacific, men were still dying aboard ships and on islands where the Japanese continued to resist in spite of two years of defeats. In the skies above Japan hundreds of planes, many of them made by Buchanan Aircraft, dumped tons of bombs on city after city.

Amanda tried to banish the bombers from her mind as she left the hospital and drove through California's sunshine to Topanga Canyon. Although gasoline was supposedly rationed, the boulevards were clogged with cars full of whooping celebrators. But Topanga was still immersed in green silence. In five minutes, she was driving up the steep hill to Eden.

The word had a sad hollow ring now, like the sound of a temple bell in the abandoned monastery of a forgotten god. Amanda prowled the empty rooms, remembering happiness, how palpable it had been for a while. In Frank's study, she pondered a sketch of the immense transport plane he had designed, with room for two decks of beds for wounded men.

Frank was somewhere in the Mojave Desert testing a new kind of plane, a bullet-shaped creature that spewed flame from its tail. It had a new engine and a new fuel that might revolutionize flying. He was always somewhere else, even when he was here, lying beside her. His planes flew in his head, sowing death and devastation over half the world. They flew in her head too, sowing devastation on Eden. On their love.

She tried not to think of the last time they had talked about it, when he came back from New Guinea. He had turned into a different being before her eyes. Darkness oozed from his pores, his skin had seemed to grow swarthy as he roared his memories of the first war at her. How Americans had died flying bad planes and he was not going to let that happen again. Young men like Billy McCall and Cliff Morris deserved a chance to live and if she wanted to think of him as a murderer so be it. He thought of himself as a savior. It was blasphemous and sad.

She picked up the telephone and dialed her own number. "Victoria? I just wanted to make sure you got home from school in one piece. The city is going slightly crazy over the German surrender.

"No. You can't go downtown. It'll be full of drunken sailors and soldiers."

Victoria was fourteen. A very precocious fourteen. The war had vulgarized everything. Crooner Frank Sinatra sold sexual hysteria to every teenage girl in the country. They necked with sailors and soldiers on buses and had sex in the city parks.

A distant rustle of the temple bell. Go, it said. Go in peace if possible. Eden was over. Treasure its memory. It was never more than a dream, a hope. Now you have to find your way back to Adrian. You've abandoned him for almost four years.

If abandoned was the right word. Adrian was so self-contained Amanda never felt he needed her. Even when he was mourning his English mistress, Beryl Suydam. But Amanda had been indifferent to him for a long time and he knew it. He was uneasy at her independence from him. Recently he had begun making sarcastic remarks about the time she gave to her amputees.

It was time to try to return to his territory, to live within his domain again. It would be difficult at first. Her indifference to Adrian could so quickly turn to hatred. She would risk it for Victoria's sake. She was another reason for Eden's decline and fall. Motherhood and Eden did not mix.

What would happen to Frank? She would go on loving him, of course. Perhaps they could resurrect Eden for a few precarious hours some place, some time. But it could never be here. This place throbbed with the thunder of Wright Cyclone engines, with the crunch of exploding bombs, with the screams of dying women and children.

On Frank's design table was a letter from Billy McCall. It described a daring flight across a thousand miles of the Pacific to bomb Japanese ships in Saigon. The letter exulted in the destruction they had wreaked. Billy said he hoped they had a chance to do a similar job in Tokyo harbor soon. He talked about how many Japanese he had killed to even the score for all the men in his bomb group who had died in their wave-top attacks.

Amanda recoiled from the hatred in Billy's soul. War had entered his bloodstream. He would bring it home with him. She dreaded what it would do to Frank. Amanda knew why Frank loved Billy. There were no secrets in Eden. He knew about Amanda's first Eden, the orange blossoms in the dawn. He even knew her temptation to a dream life with Califia, a confession that had disturbed him almost as much as her revulsion at the bombing. She knew about Craig, Frank's long struggle with his dark spirit.

Sad how absolute honesty between lovers made love more imperiled. But so perfect, so unstained, for a little while. No matter what happened to her for the rest of her life, she had lived in Eden. She had tasted the forbidden fruit of innocence and hope and now she was ready to be an American wife and mother again.

Farewell, whispered the temple bell as Amanda closed the door.

She drove down more boulevards clogged with cars, past sidewalks jammed with cavorting soldiers and sailors. At home, Victoria was on the telephone, telling her best friend, Susan, daughter of a Warner Brothers mogul, what a freak her mother was. "She's prehistoric. I mean your mother's living in the nineteenth century but mine's prehistoric."

A pound of lipstick and rouge on her face, Victoria announced she was going downtown no matter what Amanda said. "I'm not going to *do* anything. I promise you absolutely I'll be a virgin on my wedding day."

"You're not going anywhere. Invite Susan over here."

"She's going downtown. Her mother's getting one of the studio security guards to escort us."

Amanda shook her head.

"Mother, it's a great historic moment! I want to see it."

"It's a lot of vulgar people doing vulgar things."

"They're not vulgar, they're happy. Something you couldn't be if you lived a thousand years."

"I'm not that morose, am I?"

"Yes, you are. I'm going going gone!"

She left, all but smashing the windows with the slam of the front door. Amanda stood in the silence, helpless. What was going to happen to Victoria if she insisted on making her voracious will her dominant trait? No man would tolerate it.

Adrian came home for dinner, an event in itself. He was somewhat drunk, even more unusual. "We've been celebrating," he said. "Victory through air power. Planes beat Hitler."

"Hurrah," Amanda said.

"You don't agree?"

"I have no opinion."

"Where's Victoria?"

"Helping sailors celebrate downtown."

"You let her go?" Adrian shouted.

"I tried to stop her. I'm not a policeman. Perhaps you should hire one for her."

"I couldn't afford it. I'm spending too much money hiring them to watch you."

They were in the sunken living room of their Hancock Park house. Adrian had hired a decorator who had chosen California mission furniture. Huge slatted chairs and couches made of dark woods, with red upholstery. Amanda had wanted blue but Adrian ruled in favor of the decorator. It was not a restful room. Not a *living* room, in Amanda's opinion. Now it was a trap. The red pillows oozed blood.

Adrian knew.

She had wondered more than once what he would do if he found out. Frank had told her there were rumors floating through the company. People were watched and followed all the time to make sure no military secrets were being leaked. Which led, of course, to all sorts of other secrets being discovered.

"How long have you known?"

"Years. I let it go on because it kept you quiet and Frank Buchanan happy. Lockheed, North American, have offered him tons of money to switch jobs. He's a genius."

The glee on Adrian's face was horrendous. Her husband had sold her, sold his wife for profits, money. Unspeakable. But how could she protest? She had betrayed him. He was entitled to this or any other kind of revenge.

"Do you want a divorce?"

"Of course not. I loathe the very idea of divorce. That's the coward's solution to unhappiness."

"I wasn't going to see him again."

"Why not?"

Amanda shrugged. "Why did you decide to tell me now?"

"The war is as good as over. We're going to reduce Japan to rubble in a few months. They'll surrender and decorum will return to our lives. I will no longer be able to tolerate my wife being screwed by my chief designer."

Amanda sensed this was a lie. The exultance in Adrian's eyes suggested that he had been aching to speak and liquor and events had combined to make this moment irresistible.

"I have a dossier on you two a foot thick. It's crammed with details. Even a few pictures. If you ever see him again, I'll show it to Victoria."

She saw what Adrian was doing. Sentencing her to a life with him as his spiritual and moral prisoner. She heard the clang of a cell door, she breathed the rank odor of the dungeon. In the distance, the temple bell of Eden tolled one last time.

Adrian made a dinner reservation at the Ambassador Hotel for twenty people. Buchanan's executives were celebrating victory through air power. "Get dressed," Adrian said. "You're coming with me. I need you for ceremonial occasions. Otherwise, you're superfluous. I've got a woman who's ten thousand times more satisfying in bed than you."

It was Tama. Amanda was sure of it. She remembered the bitterness at the core of her spirit and wondered how Adrian had subjected her. Simply for money? Or revenge against her loathsome husband, Buzz McCall?

Amanda breathed the overpowering sweetness of Califia's perfume.

Madness, warned her mother's voice. But it was also freedom.

Smiling, Amanda went upstairs to dress for the celebration.

POWER PLAYS

His head still aching from the champagne he had drunk to celebrate the victory over Germany, Adrian Van Ness flew to Muroc Air Force Base in the Mojave Desert, where Frank Buchanan was testing a rocket engine using liquid hydrogen fuel in a silver bullet of a plane, nicknamed White Lightning. No one was sure what the next generation plane-engine configuration would be. A half-dozen aircraft companies had experimental models flying out of Muroc, some using hydrogen, others kerosene in a jet engine developed by the British.

Frank Buchanan was exultant about their progress. He thought hydrogen was an ideal fuel for a plane engine. It was odorless, powerful. Unfortunately it was ten times more expensive than kerosene but Frank was sure they could solve that problem. Adrian was not so sure. He watched White Lightning fly at a speed close to six hundred miles an hour after it was launched from a pod beneath a B-29 bomber.

The amount of money being spent was breathtaking. But it was all on that wonderful World War II invention, the cost-plus contract, so there was no reason to wring his hands. Uncle Sam paid for everything designated as costs and Buchanan still got the plus—the fixed fee. Anyway, he was not here to fret about money or even to check out White Lightning.

He brought a case of California champagne with him to help the Buchanan team celebrate the end of the war in Europe. After a liquid lunch, he strolled to the small office at one end of the hangar where Frank Buchanan was designing planes that might utilize what they were learning from White Lightning's high-speed flights. Frank began discussing compressibility—the phenomenon that buffeted a plane almost to pieces as it approached the speed of sound.

"Interesting," Adrian said. "By the way, will you please stop screwing my wife?"

The desert glare filled the end of the hangar. In the center of it stood the white plane with its stubby wings and burnt black tail section. It would be hard to conceive a more perfect setting. Here was the resident genius, being permitted to spend a hundred thousand dollars a day to indulge his fantasies of future flight by his admiring boss. Now, with pain and sadness in his heart, the boss reveals the awful truth he has accidentally discovered.

"Who told you that?" Frank said, perhaps trying to gauge the value of a denial.

"She did," Adrian said. "It finally got to her conscience. Sounds old fashioned, I know. But she's been worried about Victoria's—proclivities, shall we say? It gradually dawned on her that she couldn't very well preach to her daughter while she was committing adultery herself."

"I love Amanda," Frank said. "You have to understand that. I was afraid she'd begin to feel this way. Are you going to divorce her?"

Adrian shook his head. "I don't intend to ruin my daughter's life by exposing her to such an ugly truth at the age of fourteen."

"I suppose you want me out of the company as soon as possible."

"There's no need for you to leave if you promise me you'll never touch Amanda again."

"Of course," Frank said. He was utterly, totally crushed.

It was all so convincing, for a moment Adrian almost believed his own invention. It was true, he did not want to expose Victoria to a messy divorce. But the rest was a carefully calculated performance, infinitely superior to sputtering outrage and angry dismissal. He now had Frank Buchanan in his grasp forever. No one else would ever make a plane designed by this strange combination of genius and fool.

Back at the plant in Santa Monica, Adrian conferred with Buzz McCall and the treasurer, a big bulky man named Thompson, whom he had hired away from Lockheed. The B-29s were in full production and Buzz had somehow found enough workers to produce Newton Slade's five hundred fighter-bombers at the same time. The last of these were rolling off the assembly lines and work would soon begin on the Skylord transport.

Buzz was all business, urging Adrian to put more money into jet engines as well as the rocket engine Frank was testing, telling him to use his influence with General Slade to get their hands on one of the jet fighters the Nazis had deployed in the skies over Germany in the final months of the war.

Buzz unquestionably knew Tama had become Adrian's mistress. If it had any impact, he concealed it behind his usual swagger. Probably a better index of his feelings was his reaction to Adrian's attempt to have Cliff Morris brought home. The moment Buzz heard it, he had gotten on the phone to Mellow and other generals and bullied them into forgetting it.

Thompson was telling them how much money they would have to pay in excess profits taxes when the door burst open. Tama stood there, tears streaming down her face. "Cliff's gone!" she cried. "He went down over Berlin three nights ago!"

When she saw Buzz, Tama went berserk. "Are you happy now?" she screamed. "Are you glad you killed him, you rotten bastard?"

"When I get home tonight, I want you out of the house," Buzz said.

Treasurer Thompson fled and Adrian telephoned General Slade at the Pentagon. The general got through to Rackreath Air Base and talked to someone who told him other pilots had seen parachutes from the *Rainbow Express* as it spun down into burning Berlin.

Adrian spent the next two days consoling, calming, a frantic Tama. On the third day, Newton Slade's oily voice crooned over the wires from the Pentagon. "Adrian. Cliff's okay. He and two other guys got out. They came down behind the Russian lines."

A month later, Cliff flew into Los Angeles aboard a TWA SkyRanger II with his British wife, Sarah. Adrian found her shy but charming. He gave Cliff high marks for marrying the daughter of the chief designer of de Havilland Aircraft, the best plane maker in England. Cliff was undoubtedly coming to work at Buchanan after the war and the connection could be useful.

Tama outdid herself with a publicity extravaganza that got Cliff and Sarah on the pages of every major newspaper in California. It was climaxed by Cliff taking delivery of the two hundredth B-29, which they named the *Rainbow Express II*. He and Sarah, in her WAAF's uniform, took off on a savings bond tour, along with a half-dozen other air heroes. Offhandedly, Adrian checked with Newton Slade and made sure Cliff would not be assigned to bombing Japan. With the end of the war in Europe, there was no shortage of pilots.

Tama filed for divorce from Buzz and she and Adrian resumed their weekly visits to San Juan Capistrano. Adrian's ardor mounted with Tama's ingenuity. He had never met a woman for whom sex was both love and a game. Her sense of humor, which was almost nonexistent verbally, seemed to emerge in bed. He also discovered something less entertaining. For Tama, sex meant not only pleasure but power.

She announced she wanted to be Adrian's executive secretary. She said it would give her more authority over her volunteer escorts. Adrian saw it would also give her power over a lot of other people. Soon no one would get to see Adrian Van Ness without consulting her. He finessed this move by doubling Tama's salary and insisting no one could replace her in the publicity department.

Adrian was more amenable to Tama's penchant for sharing gossip about the shortcomings of Buchanan's executives, suggesting promotions and demotions. It did not take him long to notice most of these stories were directed against Buzz McCall.

Buchanan's production chief maintained a stable known as Buzz's beauties, who did very little work on the assembly line when they showed up at all. Others in his department were imitating his example. Tama shuddered at what might happen if the story got into the newspapers.

Buzz was not the sort of man who sat quietly, letting any woman, above all his ex-wife, ruin him. He marched into Adrian's office one day with Frank Buchanan beside him. "I hear someone's tellin' you my guys are exploitin' the ravishin' beauties we got on the line," he said. "I checked into it and found a couple of bozos were guilty. I fired them yesterday. I got an idea to make sure it doesn't happen again."

Adrian was forced to admire his effrontery. "I'm listening," he said.

"Frank here's movin' out of his house in Topanga Canyon.

He's ready to sell it to us for practically nothin'. I think we should convert it into a club for our top guys—where they can relax without anyone tellin' stories about them. A club where guys call the shots and the women don't have nothin' to do with Buchanan. We'll pay everyone's dues, just the way we pay your dues and mine at the Conquistadores del Cielo and other clubs."

"What do you think, Frank?" Adrian asked their chief designer.

Frank was drunk. Tama had told Adrian that Frank was drunk alarmingly often lately. He was not taking Amanda's loss well. "You haven't heard the best part of it," he mumbled.

"The women ain't gonna wear a goddamn thing. It's gonna be the ultimate in realistic advertising," Buzz said.

"Can you find enough of them to do that?" Adrian said, momentarily staggered.

"Sure. They had a speakeasy like it in Kansas City I used to drink at when I flew the mail for a while in the twenties. This is Los Angeles. The canyons are full of dames who'll take it off in ten seconds to get a part in a picture. We'll pay them plenty to take it off permanently. I guarantee you they'll like it. We'll have twice as many applications as we can handle."

"Let's understand a few things," Adrian said. "First of all, we never had this conversation. Frank here doesn't know a thing about what you're planning to do with the property. This was your idea and we approved it without asking any questions."

"Sure," Buzz said, defiance flashing in his gray eyes. "You can do me the same kind of favor."

"What?" Adrian said.

"Tell Tama all about it."

The Honeycomb Club—a name suggested by Frank Buchanan—enraged Tama and simultaneously demoralized her. Adrian realized time was the enemy here as well as Buzz. Like many Californians, Tama found the approach of middle age terrifying. Buzz's ability to defy it, to continue his unlimited access to young women, was more than an affront, it was a judgment on Tama's fading youth. She clung to Adrian with almost frantic ardor, not quite able to believe his assurances that he found her much more desirable than some naive twenty-year-old.

In the Pacific, the B-29s pounded Japan. The war surged toward a climax. Something similar surged in Adrian's blood—a new sense of dimension and pathos and pride. There seemed to be nothing that the conquerors of the sky could not have for the asking. Buzz McCall's descriptions of the Honeycomb Club turned the executive dining room into a passion pit. Adrian, determined to avoid any hint of approval, declined to visit it. He sought his climaxes with Tama in San Juan Capistrano.

"Your choice," she would whisper. "Tell me what you want to do."

At first Adrian's ideas were mundane. But as the summer of 1945 wrapped southern California in a haze of heat and humidity, he became more ambitious. One night in August he said: "Tie you up."

He was amazed by the words. They came out of an unknown part of his mind. Tama liked it. Giggling, she let him spread-eagle her on the bed and tie her wrists and ankles to the walnut bedposts. Adrian knelt beside her and Tama added touches out of her silent movie repertoire. She whimpered and begged for mercy, she writhed in mock fear.

The barrier Adrian maintained between his ego and his desires crumbled. A fist began to pound inside his chest. A red film filled the room with sunset light. His penis was a sword of revenge and celebration. It was more than Buzz McCall's ex-wife on the bed. It was woman in all her maddening ambivalence and ambiguity. His hands clutched Tama's breasts until she cried out with pain and pleasure.

Tama enjoyed it as much as he did. She loved and hated men in almost the same proportion that Adrian loved and hated women. They were a fusion of hatred and love emitting the energy of a hundred suns. "More, more," she begged. "Hurt me a little more."

Grunting, growling, Adrian seized fistfuls of her ample rump. His penis was spewing fire like the White Lightning rocket plane. He was a hydrogen engine annihilating himself and this woman. He and Tama had become a machine driving pleasure, pleasure, great thundering waves of it, thick and foaming as Pacific surf, through Adrian's soul. He could not stop, it would never stop, it was eternal, they were reaching some shore wreathed in red light.

Of course it was not eternal. Adrian was not a machine. An hour later, he lay on top of a whimpering, laughing, writhing Tama, his penis a dry aching stalk.

"Adrian, Adrian, make me the happiest woman in the world."

"Yes, yes, anything."

"Fire Buzz. Fire him even if Frank Buchanan goes with him."

Overreach, overload. The Adrian of desire was gone. The Adrian of intellect and forethought reappeared. He had lost control. He was in danger of losing another kind of control. He did not like it.

"Did I spoil it?" Tama asked, clinging to him. "I couldn't help it. It just came out."

"No, no," Adrian lied. "You couldn't spoil anything that beautiful."

"I'm afraid of what Buzz will do to Cliff. He's always hated him."

"I'll take good care of Cliff. Don't worry."

That night Adrian lay awake for hours brooding about women, the maddening way in which money, history, politics, entangled and so often strangled their love. Would he ever find one who loved him without a secret agenda in her head? Was part of it his fault? He remembered Amanda in freezing Maine yearning to let go. Was that what they wanted? He had let go tonight and where had it gotten him? Back to his first trauma, mother love.

The next morning a sleepless Adrian felt depressed, distant from a still-amorous Tama. As they drove back to Santa Monica he turned on the car radio to avoid conversation. A newsman's voice said: "The White House announced that sixteen hours ago an American airplane dropped an atomic bomb on the Japanese city of Hiroshima. President Harry S.

Truman described it as a device that harnessed the power of the sun. The president said the United States had spent two billion dollars to produce it."

"My God," Tama said. "Did you know about this, Adrian?"

Adrian's first reaction was outrage. How could he not have known this secret, after spending so many hours in wartime Washington? Why, how, had the generals ordered an extra four hundred B-29s when a single plane was about to drop more explosive power than all four hundred combined? He raced to the factory at suicide speed and called General Crockett in Washington. The general ruefully admitted that he had known no more about it than Adrian.

"But it don't really matter whether it was one plane or four hundred," he said. "We did the job, Adrian."

Victory through air power, Adrian thought. But there was something wrong with this victory. At lunch in the corporate dining room, Frank Buchanan voiced the thought Adrian had deflected. "It's a disgrace."

He was drunk again. That should have made him easier to dismiss, but Adrian discovered the contrary. The drunkenness reiterated that Frank was speaking not only for himself but Amanda.

"It's a victory that couldn't have been achieved without an airplane," Adrian said. "Anyone who criticizes it shouldn't be working in this industry. I find it rather sickening to see a self-appointed moralist ready to lecture the rest of us. May I ask what your qualifications are when it comes to morality, Mr. Buchanan?"

Frank slumped in his chair, reduced to silence. "Adrian's right," Buzz McCall said. "It's what we've said from the start. We could win the war without the goddamn Army and Navy and we've done it."

"By incinerating women and children," Frank said.

"I don't like that part of it any more than you do," Buzz said. "But what were we supposed to do when the bastards wouldn't surrender?"

"You would have dropped that bomb?"

"If I got an order, yes."

"That's where you and I part company."

For a moment Adrian wondered if he could fire McCall and keep Buchanan. At some deep level, did Frank loathe Buzz as much as he did?

Frank lurched to his feet and pointed a trembling finger at Adrian. "I predict we're making a horrendous mistake, getting in bed with the generals. We didn't start out to build planes for them. We built them because we loved flying. Because we wanted to create a better world, not blow it up. People aren't going to forget a plane dropped this bomb. We're going to be haunted by it for the rest of our lives."

He's right, whispered the historian in Adrian as Frank reeled out of the dining room. But the words could not be spoken. Adrian Van Ness was the president of the world's largest aircraft company. He could not let this bizarre eccentric, whom he had reduced to his obedient servant in perpetuity, tell him what to think, much less force him to eat his words in public.

Adrian's eyes traveled past the faces of the two dozen executives at other tables. Among the designers, all Frank Buchanan disciples, he saw anxiety on almost every face. Around Buzz McCall and his production engineers he saw only contempt. On the other faces the dominant emotion was consternation.

"I don't believe a talent for designing planes includes an ability to predict the future," Adrian said. He raised his wine-glass. "To air power," he said.

"Second the motion," Buzz McCall said, hoisting his Scotch.

There were no objections to the toast. Everyone drank to air power. "Incidentally," Buzz said. "I've been on the phone to the Pentagon. They're cancelin' everything on the books but fifty B-29s. Unless someone starts another war real quick we're gonna have to fire fifty thousand people next week."

Ruined clanged in Adrian's soul. "Peace, it's wonderful," he said.

MOONLIGHT

An immense moon dangled above Los Angeles, bathing the city and the beaches and the boulevards in its pale yellow light. Amanda Van Ness paced the rooms of her empty house. For three months the world had been at peace. She was sure Adrian spent his nights in Tama's arms, although he claimed to be grappling with the horrendous problems of converting Buchanan Aircraft to a builder of commercial planes. Victoria was always out with her fellow teenagers. Amanda was alone most of the time.

Alone but not lonely because in the darkest corner of her soul, Califia lay in an ivory casket, her golden sword in her pale hands. Amanda vowed she would not utter the fateful word that would awaken her. Memory would warm her heart. Those years in Eden would be her refuge.

For centuries, the moon had summoned lovers to rendezvous. Amanda thought of it gleaming on the forest of grimy oil derricks that Cadwallader Groves had become. She thought of it shining through the sycamores in Topanga Canyon. When Frank was away during the war, she often drove there and sat on the porch, bathing in the glow, relishing the silent affirmation of Eden.

Why not go again? Why not touch the memory? It would help keep Califia in the tomb. Adrian had told her Frank had sold the house and moved to another canyon. If someone else was living there, she would explain that she had spent four happy years in the house and was simply returning for a look at it. She would be content to sit in her car for a few minutes in the moonlight. The most nervous householder could hardly object to a forty-five-year-old housewife sitting in his driveway for five minutes.

Amanda drove out Santa Monica Boulevard to the coast
highway and swung north beside the ocean. Santa Monica
was full of young people with ebullient eyes, laughing
mouths. They were Americans, winners of the greatest war
in history. The future belonged to them. She wondered if
among them there were a few like her, for whom the victory
was a wound.

Oh, Father, with your dream of a world reborn as Eden.
Maybe to wish for too much happiness was the worst sin. Perhaps your daughter has learned the lesson of survival. Happiness preserved in the memory, like the beautiful butterflies
you used to catch and mount in glass cases on Casa Felicidad's
walls.

On the coast road the moonlight was incredibly bright.
People were driving without headlights. The ocean undulated
like an immense shimmering carpet. The narrow entrance to
Topanga appeared on the right. In five minutes she was ap-
proaching the road to Frank's house. She shifted into second
gear for the steep climb.

Up the slope labored her 1940 Ford to burst into a clearing
twice the size of the one Amanda had known. Half of it was
a parking lot filled with at least two dozen cars. Frank's
house was gone. It had been replaced by a hangar-shaped
building, the front painted gold and illuminated by concealed
searchlights. There were a half-dozen oval windows cut in
the side walls. Amanda walked to one of them and looked
inside.

A beautiful dark-haired woman was bending low, serving
food to a bald, grinning fat man. The woman was naked.
Amanda recognized the man. It was Moon Davis, Buchanan's chief test pilot. Next to him, an equally obscene grin
on his face, was Buzz McCall, Buchanan's production chief.
Beside him, leering drunkenly, sat Frank Buchanan. In the
distance were a half-dozen other beautiful naked women
serving food to other members of the Buchanan hierarchy.

Amanda did not know how long she stood there in the
moonlight watching them swill their liquor and chomp on
their steaks and ogle the naked women. She looked for
Adrian but could not find him. That was hardly a consolation.

He was unquestionably a steady customer. But Frank! His presence meant he not only approved, he had collaborated in this desecration of Eden.

Amanda drove home through the moonlight, blinded by tears. It was a miracle that she reached her Hancock Park driveway alive. In the house, the moonlight continued to flood her mind. Everything in her life was revealed with scarifying clarity. All the truths she had suspected and tried to banish, the truths that she had hoped love would keep at bay.

Women were men's victims from the dawn of time. From the days when they oiled their bodies with frankincense and myrrh to please a pharaoh to the gift of their fidelity to lying medieval troubadours to their public prostitution in the celluloid world of Hollywood, they were always victims, exploited, used, abused. Only once, in a dim past before male historians began to write their lies, was there a country where women reigned.

The land of Califia. California before time began.

In the theater of her mind, this land would be reborn. Slowly, solemnly, Amanda descended to the ivory casket and spoke the word. *Awake*, she whispered. *Awake, my queen.*

The casket opened. There lay Califia in her silver robes, clutching her golden sword. Her dark-blue eyelids fluttered. The wide sensual mouth trembled. She opened her eyes and spoke. *Did someone call my name?*

Almost blinded by the moonlight streaming from Califia's eyes, Amanda fell to her knees. *Your servant, summoning you to restore the reign of women, my queen.*

Will you obey my commands?

Yes! Yes!

The ecstasy of surrender flooded Amanda's soul with the radiance of a thousand moons.

Then I will arise and ride the winds of night with you. All our deeds will be done in darkness. In the dawn you will resume your disguise of the faithful wife and I will retire to my tomb.

Yes! Yes!

With a smile, Califia stepped from the casket and held out her hand to the kneeling Amanda.

Arise. Let us seek out the worst of the oppressors and design fitting punishments for them.

Dazedly, Amanda imitated Califia and stripped naked. Together they walked through the silent house to the lawn, where a gleaming silver plane awaited them in the moonlight. At the controls, also naked, was Tama! She too was a servant of Califia! She too had the knowledge of oppression that opened the secret door in the female soul. She smiled a welcome to Amanda and they soared into the moonlit sky.

Amanda chose their first target, the club on Topanga's ridge where women were groveling naked before the conquerors of the sky. Down, down they swooped to let Califia and Tama see the obscenity with their own eyes. The rage it ignited there! It was a flame in Amanda's heart. *What will their punishment be, my Queen?* Amanda asked as they circled above the building.

I will lay my most terrible curse on them, Califia said in a voice that had the thunder of surf in Pacific caves. *They will labor and labor but they will never profit, they will never know happiness with a woman again. They will emanate a stench that drives women mad, a foulness that inspires revenge and retaliation in sunlight and moonlight.*

They swooped down again and Califia aimed her golden sword at the building. A terrifying yellow flame leaped from the tip and surged in the window, enveloping everyone in the room. Amanda could see the skulls and the bones beneath the revelers' flesh. The yellow flame sank into all of them, a divine electrocution that left them looking like putrefying corpses.

Amanda rejoiced until her eyes found Frank Buchanan. Frank! The five letters that had once encompassed a world. That too was being destroyed by Califia's vengeance. For a moment grief tore at Amanda's heart. Was Frank truly among the guilty? Was he too a victim of Buzz McCall, Adrian? It was too late to ask Califia for mercy. She could only weep as he too joined the ranks of the living dead.

Amanda awoke with sunlight streaming in the window. It was almost noon. Adrian was in the doorway frowning at her. "I'm going to work, even though it's Saturday," he said.

"Since when have you taken to sleeping in the raw?"

She said nothing. She was terrified that she might betray Califia.

"You can sleep any way you please—but you ought to get under the covers—or shut the door. It's not a habit I want Victoria to acquire."

She knew what he was thinking. That was the way she had slept with Frank. He was right, of course. Just in time she remembered her promise to be a dutiful wife by daylight. "I won't do it again," she said.

Adrian walked over to the bed and kissed her. With a terrific effort she managed to accept the touch of his loathsome lips. "You could also get pneumonia. It got quite chilly last night."

"Thank you for taking such good care of me."

From the darkness Califia whispered: *Well done, my good and faithful servant.*

For a moment Amanda wondered if this was freedom or a new more terrible bondage.

It was too late to do anything but obey. *Thank you, my queen.*

As Adrian regarded her with his usual condescension, Amanda slowly regained her joy. All the atomic bombs and flying superfortresses in the world would not protect this man from Califia's vengeance.

BOOK FIVE

WELCOME TO CALIFORNIA

Sarah Chapman Morris sat on the patio of her south Los Angeles tract house in the February sunshine, reading a letter from her mother. It was one long lament about everything that was wrong with England. The country was bankrupt, freezing, starving. The winter of 1946 was the coldest in memory and the winter of 1947 was no better.

Sarah's two-year-old, Elizabeth, tugged at her sleeve. "Want a cookie, Mommy. Cookie—and ice cream."

Why not? Sarah could not get over living in this land of abundance. She scooped some creamy dark chocolate chip ice cream into a dish and put a chocolate chip cookie beside it. She fixed another dish for herself—with two scoops. They sat out on the patio eating this delicious mid-afternoon treat.

"Can I have a bite?" called her neighbor, Susan Hardy, from her patio. She also had a two-year-old—a boy—staggering around.

"Come on over, we'll have a party," Sarah said. Susan's husband worked at Buchanan Aircraft as a designer. That in itself was a bond. Cliff was already working there two days a week, making calls with the head of the sales department. When he graduated from UCLA next term, he would go to work full time.

Sarah liked Susan because she was so American. She was utterly totally disrespectful about everything. She called President Harry S. Truman "the haberdasher." She was equally contemptuous of the governor of California and its two senators. "Pointy-heads," she called them. She called her husband "the Hardy Boy," a reference to a series of books for adolescents. She never stopped complaining about the long hours he worked—and frequently hinted that instead of de-

signing planes at midnight he was seeing other women—
which did not seem to bother her.

A Vassar graduate, class of 1942, Susan was just that
much older than Sarah to give her a voice of authority. She
was a chunky woman, with a strong sensual mouth, over-
generous breasts, and a heavy bottom. She smoked continuously, dropping ashes into everything. Some probably fell
into her ice cream but she slurped it down nonstop. Susan
leaned back, lit another cigarette and sighed. "California! It's
so goddamn boring!"

She was off on one of her favorite topics, comparing Los
Angeles and New York, where she grew up. There was no
comparison, in Susan's opinion. Los Angeles had no Broadway theater, no decent restaurants, no art museums, no department stores worth patronizing—nothing. "I've been
much too busy to be bored," Sarah said.

"What are you going to do when you finally get Cliff
through college?"

"Oh—I don't know. Have another baby, probably."

"You're the one who should be going to college."

There was some truth to that. Cliff had absolutely no interest in the required history and English and French courses
he was taking. Sarah had written all his term papers. She had
even written a paper for one of his economics courses. He
was getting a B.S. in that weighty subject. "But I don't have
a job waiting for me at Buchanan," she said.

"He may not have one either, from what I hear," Susan
said. "They're in a lot of trouble."

Sarah simply could not believe it. The biggest plane maker
of the country that had built a thousand planes a month—
with Buchanan frequently accounting for half of them—
could not possibly go bankrupt. The English aircraft business
was in the doldrums, like the rest of England. But that was
understandable, if regrettable. Flying to California had given
Sarah a sense of the immensity of America. Gazing down
from the plane at the endless miles of prairies, the snowcapped mountains rimming them, she had felt awed, even
privileged to find herself part of this tremendous nation.

"How's your mother-in-law treating you these days?"

"She still hasn't called me Sarah."

"Be nice to her anyway. She reminds me of my mother. The kind of woman you shouldn't cross. Because she'll never forget it."

Susan did not have much respect for her ultra-dignified mother. She made upper-class New York sound as stuffy and proper as England. From that viewpoint, she was glad to be in California, where there was no proper way of doing anything. Susan's father, who had died in World War I a few months before she was born, was the only person she respected. Sarah sometimes wondered if his loss was the real reason for Susan's anger at the United States of America. In the name of her dead father she seemed to be determined to take a man's jaundiced viewpoint on everything. That made her a passionate student of office politics at Buchanan Aircraft, a subject that definitely included Sarah's exotic, irritating mother-in-law, Tama Morris.

By this time Sarah knew sultry sullen-eyed Tama was the mistress of Buchanan's president, Adrian Van Ness. She had divorced Cliff's stepfather, the company's production chief, Buzz McCall, more or less formalizing the arrangement. Hints and prods from Susan had prompted Sarah, after weeks of hesitation, to ask Cliff about it. Was it true that Tama exercised enormous power inside Buchanan—not only from her special status but because, in Susan's words, she "knew where the bodies were buried"? Cliff had stared at her in astonishment, then burst out laughing. Flustered, Sarah had asked Cliff in her earnest English way if bodies were literally buried somewhere. "How the hell do I know?" he snarled.

When he was in the mood, Cliff could be incredibly charming—the ebullient swaggering flyboy she had loved and married in England. When he was not in the mood he was about as charming as a tarantula—a creature she had encountered in her bed on their American honeymoon in Mexico in 1945, paid for by Tama.

It was absurd but sometimes Sarah suspected her mother-in-law of putting—or at least wishing—the insect beneath her sheets. There seemed to be an irreducible wall of hostility between her and Tama. It apparently had something to do with Cliff volunteering for those extra twenty-five missions over Germany. Tama seemed to think that Sarah had put the idea in his head, when she had actually wept and begged him not to do it. When his insistence on continuing to fight what he called "our war" had been a crucial part of her decision to leave the WAAFs and marry him. She felt compelled to equal such courage, such sacrifice, with the gift of herself. Most of the time, their marriage still lived on the emotional capital of those extra twenty-five missions.

Susan began talking about Adrian Van Ness. Her mother had known him in New York. She told Sarah about Adrian's unsavory father and aloof Boston-born mother and the rumors of infidelity and criminality that had swirled around them. She added far more specific rumors about the insatiable sexual appetite of Buzz McCall, Tama's ex-husband—and his friend Frank Buchanan, the company's resident genius who had reportedly seduced Adrian's wife, Amanda.

Sarah listened to these stories with an odd mixture of disbelief and indifference. The victorious war seemed to insulate them from the failures of the older generation—and give them a sense of ownership of the future. At Cliff's suggestion, Sarah had invited Frank Buchanan to dinner a month ago. She liked him instantly; he so much resembled her father—a man without guile because his heart and soul were absorbed by creating planes. She found it hard to believe such a shy, diffident unworldly man was capable of seducing another man's wife.

Sarah had invited the Hardys to the dinner, a gesture for which Susan was enormously grateful. She was sure it had a lot to do with the Hardy Boy's rapid advancement at Buchanan. Susan disagreed with Sarah's assessment of Frank. Even in those prefeminist days, she found it hard to believe any man was without guile. That made her even more curious about Amanda Van Ness. Susan begged Sarah to quiz Cliff about her but inquiries produced nothing but grunts and snarls.

Now, her ice cream consumed, her cigarette glowing, Susan began speculating about Amanda. She was probably a nonentity. After all, she was a born Californian. They had nothing upstairs but sunshine. But Amanda was rumored to be immensely wealthy. Her brother was becoming one of the country's premier oil tycoons. Maybe Frank Buchanan had seduced her, hoping to get his hands on her money so he could take over the company and get rid of Adrian Van Ness, whom he seemed to hate.

Susan's ruminations were interrupted by a metallic *rap-rap* of the brass knocker Cliff had installed on the front door, his one contribution to beautifying their jerry-built bungalow. Sarah opened the door to confront a huge awkward man with the most Irish face she had ever seen. He introduced himself as Daniel Hanrahan, Buchanan's director of internal security. At the moment, he added, he was functioning as a chauffeur. Mrs. Van Ness was in the gray Lincoln parked at the curb. She wondered if she might pay a visit.

Bewildered and a little scared, Sarah agreed, if Mrs. Van Ness would give her five minutes to straighten up the house. She rushed to the patio to tell Susan Hardy the news. Susan flung dirty towels in the hamper, kicked toys under the couch and shoved the unwashed lunch dishes under the sink while Sarah frantically applied some makeup and put on a decent dress. As Susan tiptoed out the kitchen door, the knocker rapped again and Hanrahan ushered Amanda Van Ness into the house.

She wore her russet hair braided tightly around her long narrow face, giving her an oddly severe, almost witchy look. "I'm here for a very special reason," she said. "I want to see Tama's granddaughter."

Sarah plucked Elizabeth from her crib and carried her into the living room. "Can she sit on my lap?" Amanda said.

"Of course."

Sarah gravely introduced them and deposited Elizabeth on Amanda's lap. The little girl gazed up at Amanda's solemn face and smiled shyly. "She brings back such memories," Amanda said. "My daughter is sixteen now. Completely impossible. Adrian plans to send her to England for college. He says an American school will let her run wild."

She suddenly glared at Sarah as if she were responsible.

"I hated England. I hated everything about it. Do you like California?"

Sarah managed to stammer an affirmative.

"Every woman should like California," Amanda said. "It's a sensuous, sensual climate. A world where women belong. Women don't belong in a country like England, where it's freezing and raining ten months out of the year."

Sarah murmured something defensive about enjoying summers in Sussex. Amanda glared again. "That was where Adrian used to go to meet his mistress."

She gazed at Elizabeth and her manner softened remarkably. "I'm so glad this little creature will grow up a California woman."

Sarah said something about planning to stay in California as long as Buchanan Aircraft had a job for her husband. Amanda glared again. "They'll always have a job for him. Tama and I will see to that. But that's not why I'm here. I want you to try to raise this child as a true California woman. A creature with no dependence on a man. Can you do that?"

Amazed, Sarah could only murmur she had not thought about it. "Begin thinking about it!" Amanda said. "You're a woman. Haven't you found out already how much humiliation that involves?"

She clutched Elizabeth close to her and spoke over her tousled dark head. "You think Tama isn't humiliated? Her whole life has been one long humiliation. Like mine. If it weren't for this man, I'd be a prisoner in my own house. He understands. He *knows* exactly how humiliated women are at Buchanan Aircraft."

Hanrahan turned his hat over and over in his hands and murmured something about getting back to work. Unaware of the security chief's debt of gratitude to Amanda, Sarah could only stare in astonishment, mutely asking the Irishman why he had brought this madwoman into her home. Hanrahan seemed aware of her opinion but he did not attempt to defend himself or quiet Amanda Van Ness. It never occurred to Sarah that most of what Amanda said that day might be the truth.

HOME IS THE HERO

"The best thing about the Excalibur, Captain Rickenbacker—"

"Call me Eddie, for Christ's sake."

Sweat congealed the armpits of Cliff Morris's Hathaway shirt as he tried to regain his poise before Eddie Rickenbacker's hard impatient glare. Cliff's stepfather, Buzz McCall, had the same eyes. Fighter pilot's eyes. Killer's eyes. Rickenbacker had been the top American ace in World War I, with twenty-six victories.

The year was 1948. Buchanan Aircraft's Excalibur, the plane that was supposed to create an "empire in the sky" for U.S. airlines, flew in four colors on an easel Cliff had set up in Rickenbacker's fifty-first-floor Rockefeller Center office. The whirling propellers on the four 3,500-horsepower Pratt and Whitney engines seemed ready to pull it off the page and send it roaring around the ceiling. Cliff was planning to flip through the booklet to pages displaying the luxurious interior, the sophisticated cockpit design, the huge baggage compartment.

"With a two-hundred-seat capacity, we estimate annual profits per plane of—"

"Two hundred seats!" The president of Eastern Airlines fell back in his leather cushioned swivel chair and growled with exasperation. "Buzz. The goddamn plane's too big. We're flying SkyRangers half empty. What the hell do we want with this whale?"

Buzz McCall was standing by the window, looking west across New Jersey toward California. His presence was an index of Buchanan's growing desperation as they struggled to survive in the post–World War II aviation world. Buzz had resisted coming to New York to see Rickenbacker. With some justice, he claimed he had his hands full trying to deal with the chaos on Buchanan's shrinking assembly lines.

Jim Redwood, the vice president for sales, tried to rescue the situation. He was Cliff's height, six-foot-four, with a face full of dewlaps from too much Scotch whiskey. "Eddie—our figures show a steady upturn in the market. Come 1950 there'll be an explosion. With twenty of these planes you could put National and Braniff out of business."

"If you're wrong they'll put me out of business while I'm trying to service a five-million-dollar debt. Thanks but no thanks, guys."

Buzz cursed steadily in their long ride down in the whooshing elevator. Out on the sidewalk, he jammed his finger into Cliff's chest. "The next time you get an idea like this, come to me with it, not our famous fucking marketing genius Adrian Van Ness."

Last month, *Newsweek* magazine had run a cover story on Adrian, hailing him as a model of the new postwar executive, a man who combined an uncanny instinct for the marketplace with a profound grasp of the latest technology. Ignoring the help he had gotten from Hitler and Tojo, the magazine told its readers how Adrian had brought Buchanan from bankruptcy to the biggest plane maker in the nation. Ironically, the journalists puffed him just as he was falling on his face. Betting on a steep rise in the flying public, Adrian had built the Excalibur, the biggest airliner in the world—and started selling it a month after the postwar recession sent passenger numbers plummeting.

Adrian was the toast of the aircraft business, while Buzz grappled with the thousand and one problems of Buchanan's transition from war to peacetime production. From a hundred thousand workers churning out five hundred planes a month, Buchanan had shrunk to eight thousand workers making—if they were lucky—two hundred planes a year. Adrian had put Buzz in charge of the firing—which made him the most hated man in the company.

"I'm sorry, Buzz," Jim Redwood said as they strode through the noonday crowds toward Fifth Avenue. "I thought it was worth a try. It was my idea as much as Cliff's."

"That makes you a pair of assholes," Buzz said. "Dragging me across the fucking continent to kiss Captain Eddie's ass. If my war had lasted another month I'd have passed him in the numbers game and I'd be up there running that airline and Eddie'd be a garage mechanic in Milwaukee."

"I don't know what the hell we're gonna do with this plane," Redwood said. "Rick was pretty much our last hope."

Buzz whirled on Redwood. He knew they had sold a grand total of ten Excaliburs, all to TWA because the airline's eccentric owner, millionaire Howard Hughes, liked big planes. But Buzz could never tolerate defeatism. "Listen. We're gonna sell that plane somewhere. Maybe the army if the country wakes up to what the Russians are tryin' to pull—"

He pointed to a Daily News headline: BERLIN STILL FREE. President Truman had responded to Russian attempts to drive the Americans, British, and French out of Berlin with a massive airlift.

"If they had fifty Excaliburs redesigned for cargo, they could keep Berlin supplied till doomsday. Instead they got half-asleep pilots makin' two flights a day in C-Forty-sevens. It's just like the last war. The goddamn government makes do with yesterday's planes and the whole aircraft business stands still."

Back at the Waldorf, the desk clerk handed Cliff a telegram. He ripped it open and read: SARAH HAD A GIRL AT 6:30 A.M. TAMA. "Good Christ," he said, showing the message to Buzz. Sarah was not supposed to deliver for six weeks.

"Another girl?" Buzz said. "When you gonna stop shootin' blanks?"

"Hey. Adrian's got a girl. He's nuts about her," Jim Redwood said.

"Adrian's a fucking—aristocrat," Buzz said, avoiding Cliff's eyes.

The averted eyes, the momentary hesitation in his voice, convinced Cliff again that Buzz regretted losing Tama to Adrian. It had nothing to do with affection. He had been unfaithful to Tama with a hundred other women over the past ten years. It was the loss of face, of power, that the switch implied. The rearrangement was part of the new game the war had created. Buzz was no longer the only hero around, the tough guy who made Cliff and even Adrian twitch when he looked at them. The war, a new generation of pilots, had put things in perspective. Buzz was the ace no one remembered, the guy who came in second to Rickenbacker in France flying funny-looking planes that barely went a hundred miles an hour.

He could handle Buzz now, Cliff told himself. He had told that to Tama with not a little anger when she announced her affair with Adrian and said he had promised to protect Cliff from Buzz. A man with forty-nine missions over Germany did not need protection.

Except when he fell on his face. When an idea went sour, the way things had just gone with Rickenbacker. Anxiety swelled in Cliff's belly. Buzz would not let him forget that fiasco for months. Cliff silently cursed Adrian Van Ness and his oversized plane. He forced a smile and socked Buzz on the shoulder. "Hey listen, Grandpa. At least I can still get it up," he said.

In the room Cliff telephoned the plant and heard the good-bad news from Tama. "Sarah's okay. The baby only weighs four pounds. They've got her in an incubator. I've never seen anything so tiny. How did the meeting go?"

"Lousy. He practically threw us out."

"The son of a bitch. I'll tell Adrian."

For a moment Cliff felt five years old. When was Tama going to stop running his life? He slammed down the phone and called the hospital. After the usual delays, a weary Sarah came on the line. "Honey, I'm sorry I wasn't there," Cliff said. "How do you feel?"

"Tired. How did things go at the big meeting?"

"Lousy."

"Oh, Cliff, I'm so sorry."

"Don't worry about it. How's the kid? Tama says she's so small you can hardly see her."

"She'll be all right. They do wonders with preemies these days."

"What'll we name her?"

Cliff had wanted a boy so badly, they had not even discussed girls' names.

"I like Margaret."

She had named their first girl Elizabeth. "What are you trying to do, turn us into a royal family?" Cliff said.

"I just like the names. Tell me about the meeting."

"There's nothing to tell. He hated the plane. It's an oversized lemon. A grapefruit."

Anxiety crawled in Cliff's chest. How many cross-examinations from the goddamn women in his life did he have to swallow? "I think you should get out of sales. This plane is making you look like—what's the word?—a loser," Sarah said.

"Listen. You have the babies. I'll worry about my goddamn career."

He slammed down the phone and stood there cursing. Why the hell had he married the daughter of an aircraft executive?

Buzz charged in, suitcase in hand. "Come on. I got us on the noon balloon out of Newark. An Excalibur."

"I thought we were going to stay until tomorrow. I've got a date with Dick Stone, my navigator on the *Rainbow Express*."

"Call him and cancel it. Let's go. We've only got an hour. I want you and Redwood there when I talk to Van Ness. We've got to convince him this plane is hopeless and figure out another move fast."

Cliff called Dick Stone and blamed the cancellation on the unexpected birth. Dick was cheerful about it. "What's the kid's name? I want to send a present. I can get it wholesale."

"The baby-wear business is good?"

"The money is great, the business is shitty. How's the plane business?"

"The exact opposite," Cliff said.

"I may call you one of these days."

"I told you, I'll kick the door open—if it's still there to kick."

Forty-five minutes later, Cliff and Buzz and Jim Redwood stood in the art-deco departure lounge of Newark Airport. Around them were about a hundred fellow businessmen in broad-brimmed felt or Panama hats, many wearing the new nylon cord summer suits, with white shirts and dark ties. Among the men were a dozen or so women wearing hats of assorted spiral shapes, blouses with large balloon sleeves and skirts that covered their knees, the "new look" of the previous year. Cliff preferred the tight skirts of the war years.

"I got a weird letter in the mail yesterday," Buzz said, trying to pass the time. "Written in words clipped from a newspaper. It said something about a dame named Califia who's gonna cut my throat. There's probably a lot of dames'd like to do that—but I can't place this one."

"Maybe it's one of Tama's movie names," Jim Redwood said. Everyone knew about Tama's vendetta against Buzz.

"Trans World Airlines Flight 607 to Los Angeles departing from Gate 16," gargled the invisible announcer.

The Excalibur sat on the runway looking twice as big as Cliff remembered it. He found himself eyeing the plane, wondering if someone had ground-tested the engines, checked the fuel lines, the electrical systems. In his seat, he listened tensely as the pilot turned over the motors, waiting for the throaty roar that announced the right fuel mixture.

Nothing to worry about, he told himself. Nothing to worry about. TWA was a first-class airline with good pilots. Down the runway they thundered, the huge engines sending vibrations of power through the fuselage that surpassed anything Cliff had ever felt aboard a B-17. He found himself bracing his legs against the footrest as if he expected a crash. *Nothing to worry about.*

Clunk the wheels retracted. The Excalibur dipped and wobbled slightly as they hit some turbulence. Pinpoints of sweat sprang out all over Cliff's body. It all came back every time he flew, the way they had become pariahs. The *Rainbow Express*'s copilot had told a friend about the double-cross they had pulled over Schweinfurt and the story spread through the 103rd Bombardment Group. Whenever the 103rd flew the Purple Heart corner, the Focke-Wulfs and Messerschmitts seemed to attack with special fury. The rest of the group started blaming their losses on the *Rainbow Ex-*

press. The thing hung over them like a gigantic hoodoo, tormenting everyone in the crew.

Inevitably, the story got to their commanding officer, Colonel Atwood, who hauled them into his office and raved about court-martials and perpetual disgrace. "We'll volunteer for another twenty-five," Dick Stone had said. Before Cliff could say or do anything, all the others volunteered. That had left Cliff no choice. He had to join them for another nine months of gambling with death over Germany.

Cliff took a deep breath. Now was the time to finish it. They had evened the score. They had flown another twenty-three missions. On the twenty-fourth, the *Rainbow Express* had taken a direct hit over Berlin. Didn't that even the score? Getting blown out of a plane clutching your parachute, somehow strapping it on as you fell toward the burning city beneath you? Yes, Cliff told himself. It evened the score.

"Jesus Christ, you're still jumpy in a plane, ain't you," Buzz said.

"I'm just jumpy for a drink," Cliff said.

Suddenly Cliff wanted to tell Buzz what had happened over Schweinfurt. Instead of the old antagonism, the submerged quarrel for Tama's love, they finally had something to share as men. Buzz had risked death in the air on the western front. Maybe he would tell him what happened over Schweinfurt was all right.

For a moment the words crowded into Cliff's throat. Across the aisle Jim Redwood, eager for his first Scotch of the day, buzzed for the stewardess. "What'll it be, guys?" he said.

Jim would never understand what he wanted to tell Buzz. The sales chief was always introducing Cliff as his "assistant war hero," reciting his number of missions, his miraculous survival over Berlin. Cliff let the moment pass.

The Excalibur climbed to 27,000 feet and the captain told them their route to Los Angeles. The stewardesses brought them their drinks. A tall sinewy redhead who wore her blue garrison cap at a cocky angle got their attention. "There's a live one," Cliff said. Her partner, a short chipper brunette, was not bad either.

On they flew into deepening dusk. The Excalibur's fuel tanks were big enough to skip landing at Chicago, a standard requirement for other cross-country flights. The stewardesses served dinner. Cliff asked the redhead if she lived in Los Angeles.

"Mayn-hattun Beach," she said, with an accent that had to be Tennessee or Kentucky.

"We work for Buchanan Aircraft in Santa Monica."

"As a test pilot?" she asked.

"No. In sales."

"If you see someone named Billy McCall tell him Cassie Trainor says hello."

His stepbrother's name filled Cliff's throat with bile. But years of practice enabled him to conceal it. "Say hello to his father, Buzz," he said.

Cassie eyed Buzz skeptically. "You don't look like him."

"He took after his mother," Buzz said.

"Billy must be quite a pilot. He likes to test *everythin'* to the limit of its structural capacity," Cassie said.

"I know all about it. I'm the same way," Cliff said.

"It runs in the family," Buzz said.

Billy had just become a major in the newly created U.S. Air Force. Recently Buzz had brought him to California to help them test an experimental jet Frank Buchanan was developing at Muroc Air Base in the Mojave Desert.

"There's some sort of club you belong to?"

"The Honeycomb Club. Maybe you'd like to work there. The hours and the pay are a lot better than this job," Buzz said.

Cassie's penciled eyebrows rose. "So I've heard."

Cliff could almost feel the heat. Cassie had cut loose. She was on her own in California, playing the big-girl game. A lot of stewardesses went this route. There was no limit to what they would try if you got them early. Timing was important. It did not take long for a woman to get her heart broken and turn morose, sullen, bitchy.

Cliff considered himself a student of women. Even a collector, a connoisseur. Cassie's down-home drawl added a touch of fire, a suggestion of sultry southern blood. She was ready to do things Cliff could never suggest to Lady Sarah, his private name for his English wife.

"You ready to go for some of that tonight?" Buzz asked Cliff, as the stewardesses began serving after-dinner drinks.

He had been planning to get Cassie Trainor's phone number for future reference and go to the hospital to see Sarah and the baby. But Buzz's offer was not something Cliff could afford to turn down. It implied Buzz was ready to forget about dragging him to see Captain Eddie—if Cliff forgot about how crudely his old pal rejected him. It even suggested a sort of truce between them, an admission that Cliff was a man now, ready to play games with women Buzz's way. "Sure," Cliff said.

By the time they landed in Los Angeles, twelve hours and ten minutes after leaving Newark, Cliff and Buzz had dates with Cassie and the chipper brunette, whose name was Barbara. Cassie offered to find a date for Jim Redwood but he did not feel in a celebrating mood and went home.

"What the hell's the matter with Redwood?" Cliff said, as they waited in the terminal for Cassie and Barbara to change out of their uniforms. "Sometimes I think he's queer. You can't get him interested half the time."

"A dame broke his heart years ago," Buzz said. "It happened to me with Billy's mother. I swore I'd never let it happen again."

On that point, he and Buzz were in agreement. Exactly where that left Sarah was something Cliff did not think about very often. Sarah was part of the war, something he had brought home, along with the forty-nine missions and the memory of Schweinfurt.

With Buzz in charge of the party, they headed for the Trocadero, a place Cassie and Barbara considered as prehistoric as the Great Pyramid. They ate the terrible food and drank a lot of wine and ogled the aging screen stars. Buzz tried to impress Barbara by claiming he had dated some of them in his stunt-flying days. On the way out he squeezed Gloria Swanson's arm and gave her a big hello. To Cliff's surprise, she smiled and said: "Hi, Buzz."

At ninety miles an hour they hurtled up the coast highway

to Buzz's house in Pacific Palisades. There they persuaded Cassie and Barbara to audition for the Honeycomb Club. Barbara had good breasts and a dark wild pussy but she was shy about taking off her clothes. Cassie had no inhibitions about that or anything else. She was an instant winner. Sex popped out of every pore of her long lithe body.

Barbara and Buzz went for a swim in the pool and Cassie continued her audition with Cliff in Buzz's king-sized bed. She was just drunk enough to let him do anything and enjoy it. It was beautiful fucking, exactly the way Cliff liked it. Almost impersonal, so you could concentrate on the performance, the electricity in every touch, every thrust. Yet not completely impersonal, not like whorehouse sex. Pleasure, not money was the payoff. Cliff was proud of his ability to please a woman.

Power was almost as important. With each stroke, each moan of desire, their failure to sell the Excalibur dwindled, the world outside the walls of the bedroom was somehow less threatening, less relentless. Clifford Morris was in absolute control here, a man defying luck, eluding memory and rules, a kind of outlaw.

Finally, there was no more juice in the joystick. They lay side by side laughing, fondling. "Am I as good as Billy?" Cliff said.

"You're better," Cassie said. "You're more fun. You didn't scare me."

"How did he scare you?"

"Never mind."

Billy knew zilch about how to acquire a woman. That was what Cliff liked to do. Not just screw them and walk away à la Buzz. He liked to come back for seconds, thirds, fourths, fifths, to arouse flutters of love, to toy with the possibility of loving them in return.

"Billy's still out at Muroc testing one of our planes. Why don't you call him right now and tell him I'm better?"

"Why not?" Cassie said.

Cliff found Billy's number in Buzz's address book. Cassie dialed him and said: "Hey, Billy. You probably don't remember me. I'm just some stewardess you fucked one night

in Manhattan Beach. I'm here with Cliff Morris and I want
to tell you—"

Strange things began happening in Cassie's body. She
shook as if she was having convulsions.

"I want to tell you—"

The tremors became more violent. Cliff grabbed her, afraid
she was going to fly off the bed.

"I want to tell you—"

Cassie flung the phone against the wall and curled into a
ball. She bit the back of her hand and sobbed and sobbed.
"What the hell's the matter with you?" Cliff said.

Cassie rolled over on her back and smiled at him.
"Nothin'," she said. "Get me a drink and we'll go for the
record."

"Some other night," Cliff said, putting his hand on her
damp pussy in a comforting—and acquiring—way.

DOES OOO WUVUMS WIDDLE ME?

"Mr. Stone? Mr. Pesin wants to see you immediately."

It was around five o'clock on the day Cliff had called to
cancel their dinner date. The vice president of nothing in
particular at Pesin's Baby Wear was sitting in his office reading a symposium, "Religion and the Intellectuals," in the
Partisan Review. For the past three weeks, Dick Stone had
not had time to do much reading. No one at Pesin's Baby
Wear had time to do anything but entertain buyers.

Twice a year they invaded New York like a horde of Visi-
goths, insulting, demanding, cajoling, sneering, greedy for
tickets to Broadway shows, free dinners, exotic sex. Everyone
on the executive level of Pesin's Baby Wear, the comptroller,
the production chief, the vice presidents, the designers, were
all hurled into the task of keeping these obnoxious provincials
happy. As son-in-law and heir apparent to the business. Dick

Stone was expected to be more jovial, more amusing, more charming than anyone else.

Pesin's Baby Wear was grossing about ten million dollars a year, reason enough, in the opinion of most people, to be very very charming. Sam Pesin had made this obvious more than once, in what he called little hints.

This afternoon, Sam was pondering the usual rush-hour traffic jamming Seventh Avenue when Dick Stone walked into the office. Sam was a short energetic man who disliked the word *energetic*. He maintained energetic people were usually dumb. *Dynamic* was the word he preferred. Last year he had put up most of the money for a testimonial dinner at which the Seventh Avenue Association had hailed him as the dynamo of the baby-wear business.

"Maybe it's time we had a talk," Sam said.

"I'm listening," Dick said.

"It's not about the grandson. I can wait another year for him. It's about the business. Your attitude toward it."

Trouble, Dick thought. He had been half-expecting it since he declined to escort a half-dozen buyers to the Copacabana last Monday. He had given them the name of the headwaiter and a guarantee they had a front table. All they had to do was sign for anything they wanted to eat, drink, or squeeze. But the headwaiter had gotten a bigger tip from someone else. Instead of topping it the schnooks had left in a huff.

"Greenberg's buyer, Shapiro. He went home without giving us a single order. He never even came back to shake hands good-bye."

"That's too bad."

"Too bad? That's two hundred thousand dollars' worth of bad. They've got stores from one end of New England to the other. The same thing happened with Levitt. He's always good for fifty thousand dollars. He's got everything in Pennsylvania south of Lancaster in his pocket. Nothing."

"Is it all my fault? Or is it possible that there's something wrong with this year's line?"

"There's nothing wrong with this year's line that some dynamic selling couldn't fix. What the hell happened to you

Monday night? How come you left those people on their own at the Copa?"

"Nancy and I had tickets to *Death of a Salesman*."

"Oh, this is beautiful. You go see a show about a goddamned failure written by a smartass Communist while our clients are left standing around the Copa with their fingers up their asses. Is this what an MBA does for you?"

"I tipped the headwaiter fifty bucks. Is it my fault if he's a fink?"

"It's nobody's but your fault. But it's only a symptom of an overall thing. An overall attitude, Dick. I brought you in here when you married Nancy. I was frankly delighted to have a guy with brains, a hero who bombed the Nazis no less, on the payroll. But I expected some gratitude. Some dynamism. You don't seem to really *care*, you know what I mean? You just seem to be going through the motions."

"You're right," Dick said. "I don't care. I don't give a shit whether yellow or blue is the in color for bibs this year. Or whether dresses for one-year-olds should have lace collars. Or whether the Lone Ranger should be on our overalls. I not only don't give a shit, I don't give a fuck."

At six-one, Stone had about eight inches on Sam Pesin. He had added twenty pounds to his burly thick-necked body since the war. The dynamo of the baby-wear business did not make a sound as his berserk son-in-law strode out of the office.

Dick squeezed into the packed F train at Sixth Avenue and 42nd Street and rode under the East River. What the hell was happening to him? Was he losing his mind? Was his father finally getting to him?

His father had been disappointed by his decision to go into business. His high marks in college, his intellectual interests, had led Rabbi Saul Stone to expect his only son to choose a profession—the law or medicine or academe. Dick did not completely understand the decision himself. It had something to do with an inchoate desire to become—or remain—part of the American world in which he had participated as an airman. He liked being an American first and a Jew more or less second. His father, worried about the number of Jews marrying Christians in his congregation and elsewhere, had nodded impatiently when Dick tried to explain this to him. "Just be sure you marry a nice Jewish girl," he had said.

Was that why he had married Nancy Pesin? Dick wondered as the F train groaned and creaked through the East River tunnel at ten miles an hour. It had seemed logical in so many other ways. She was in the top third of her class at Barnard, a reader and something of a thinker. She had a good disposition and her figure was definitely A+. Inheriting Pesin's Baby Wear was a not-unpleasant prospect. It dovetailed with another inchoate desire—to acquire enough money to pursue a career as a writer and thinker in the *Partisan Review* league.

At last the F Train was through the tunnel, rocketing toward bucolic Forest Hills. Dick walked to the apartment house through the warm June dusk, wondering if Sam Pesin had called his daughter to complain about her ungrateful husband. Nancy had passed little hints of her own about Daddy's dissatisfaction.

Up to the third floor in the shiny new high-rise off Queens Boulevard. The aromas of a half dozen dinners mingled in the hall. Veal cordon bleu, his nose told him the minute he opened his door. Nancy was on the telephone in the kitchen, gassing with her best friend and fellow Barnard graduate, Helene Feldman.

"It's the most devastating experience I've ever had in the theater."

She was talking about *Death of a Salesman*.

The living room had an oriental rug on the floor, prints from the Museum of Modern Art on the wall, traditional furniture from Sloane's, except for an immense television set in a mahogany case in front of the window. A Christmas gift from Daddy. In the dining area, the table was set, with a spray of fresh tulips in a vase in the center of it. A shaker sat on the coffee table with martinis for two. What could he complain about? Dick wondered. Wasn't this the American dream come true? Wouldn't Willy Loman call him a lucky SOB?

"Oh—here's my one and only. I'll call you tomorrow, *dollink*."

Nancy hung up and emerged from the kitchen, smiling broadly. She was wearing a frilly apron over a dark red dress inset with panels of blue. The energy she put into getting good marks at Barnard now went into being the compleat housewife, with a touch of upper-middle-class chic. "Here he is, home from the garment wars to his little balaboosta," she bubbled.

She threw her arms around him, nestling her body as close as possible and kissed him on the lips. Her tongue played around his mouth. "Does ooo wuvums widdle me?" she gurgled.

From the sky above them came the distant grumble of a plane landing at La Guardia Airport. The apartment house was only a block from one of the approach patterns. "No," Dick said.

The word spoke itself. It was an eruption, an explosion of memory and impulse and desire. He was back in Sam Pesin's office telling him he did not give a fuck and simultaneously in his father's temple in Rego Park listening to him compare the metaphor of the promised land to Thomas Jefferson's pursuit of happiness. He was on the telephone hearing Cliff Morris tell him the plane business was great.

Nancy had not used baby talk when he dated her, nor when they began sleeping together, in her last term at Barnard. She had been passionate but shy in those encounters. The baby talk had started on their honeymoon. Dick soon discovered it had deep roots. Sam Pesin talked that way to his daughter whenever they met. *Does oo wuvums Daddykins?* he would gurgle. Why had it suddenly become intolerable?

Nancy stepped back. Dick could see her thinking: how could he mean that? Not love this beautiful apartment, the great dinners I cook for him every night, followed by equally scrumptious screwing? Not love the perfect deal I've handed him? All he has to do is put up with the dynamo for another ten years or so and take over and run the business his way? No?

"I've had it with your father and I've had it with you and

your stupid baby talk," Dick said. "I want a divorce."

Nancy's pretty face puckered like a two-year-old. Wailing, she fled into the bathroom. Dick sat down on the couch and tried to think about what he was doing. He was frightened by his inability to understand this defiant inner self, this Samson who was ready to pull down the walls and ceiling.

He could only compare what he had just done to volunteering for another twenty-five missions to get the stench of Schweinfurt out of his soul. That too had seemed an act of insanity. It would have been easy enough to blame the whole thing on Cliff Morris and let Colonel Atwood court-martial him, as he had been longing to do since training days. Only their tail gunner, Mike Shannon, seemed to understand why Dick had volunteered. Mike had been the first member of the crew to follow his lead. Where did these explosions of anger or need or morality—Dick did not know what to call them—come from?

He had no answer to the larger question. He only knew the source of this convulsion, the root of the *no* he had just snarled in his wife's face. It was the sense of being swallowed by Jewishness again. He wanted to be part of the American world of 1948, the America that had just won the greatest war in history. Instead he was stuck in a Jewish corner of New York where he felt as separated from the rest of the country as if he had emigrated to Israel.

Dick heard Cliff Morris telling him the plane business was great and the pay was shitty. Why did that appeal to him? Was there a moral dimension in those words? Or was it simply the fact that the airplane business was in California, as far away from New York as he could get?

Or was there some unfinished business between him and Cliff, something to do with those five minutes over Schweinfurt in a plane built by Buchanan Aircraft, five minutes that distorted and confused something deep in his soul—maybe in both their souls?

With an angry shake of his large head, Dick Stone told himself to cut the bullshit. When he got going he was worse than his father the rabbi. He was a goddamn mystic.

He strode into the bedroom and began throwing clothes in

a suitcase. If Cliff Morris welched on his promise, he would talk his way into Buchanan on his own. Or into Lockheed or Douglas or North American. One way or another, he was on his way to California to get into the plane business.

PEACETIME BLUES

In his split-level house in south Los Angeles, Cliff Morris was awakened by his three-year-old, Liz, giving him a big wet kiss. "You smell funny, Daddy," she said.

"I feel funny too," Cliff said. "They call it a hangover."

He gulped aspirins and drove to the hospital, surprising Sarah. "I haven't even combed my hair," she said.

Cliff was tempted to tell her that would not make much difference. Sarah had gained about thirty pounds with this latest baby. The trim brunette who filled out her WAAF uniform in all the right places at Thorpe Abbots Air Base had almost vanished in rolls of fat. She swore she was going to lose weight—a song Cliff had heard before. Sarah could not resist six ounces of heavy cream on her breakfast cereal and a half pound of butter on every slice of bread.

Fat or thin, Sarah still wanted to know everything that was happening at Buchanan Aircraft. What were they going to do if the Excalibur did not sell? Was there a market for it abroad? Could they reduce it in size? Cliff's replies were curt. He did not know the answers. He was in an impromptu training program, supposedly learning the aircraft business, while the company tried to cope with its postwar poverty. Her executive-level questions only reminded him of his insignificance.

He took a look at the tiny creature sleeping on her stomach in the incubator and drove to the Buchanan plant in Santa Monica. He remembered the way the windowless sandstone buildings always took him by surprise in his boyhood. They suddenly appeared in the middle of a neat neighborhood of one-family stucco houses, as if they had been built there by mistake. The plant now sprawled over a dozen blocks, most of it a series of hangars only one story taller than the houses around it. In the center was a hexagonal six-story tower built during the war years, with a top-floor dining room enclosed in glass. The whole place was separated from the neighborhood by a high chain-link fence.

The retired LA cop at the desk in the bare main lobby gave him a cheery hello and signed him in. Cliff clipped a badge to the handkerchief pocket of his suit coat and strode down the dim central corridor. On the left behind a blue-painted brick wall was the factory. On the right was a maze of narrow corridors leading to offices.

In the engineering and design departments rows of men bent over desks and drawing boards. They all wore identical white shirts and solid-color ties. Artificial ceilings had been inserted to lower the hangar height of the building. Overhead fluorescent lights cast a cold silver glow on the desks and their occupants. The men were mostly silent, concentrating fiercely on their tasks. Cliff did not envy them. In spite of their expensive engineering educations, they were as expendable as the assembly line workers. Thousands of them had already been fired in the great postwar cutback.

Cliff finally reached the tower in the center of the building where several flights of stairs led to an office that had the same low-budget look. Tama Morris was sitting behind another secondhand desk, wearing the usual tight nylon blouse. She had a weight problem too but she controlled it by fierce dieting. The scars of a recent face-lift were visible at the edges of her carefully combed dark hair. Thanks to willpower and the doctors, she looked younger than Sarah.

"Hi," Cliff said. "Anything I should know before I see the great man about our disaster in New York?"

"There's a big decision coming up on that goddamn plane Frank wants to build."

Cliff had seen a drawing of the plane; it was bizarre—all wing and no tail or fuselage. "Does he really think that thing will fly?"

"I think he's trying to wreck the company. First the Excalibur, now this monstrosity."

"The Excalibur was Adrian's idea."

"I didn't hear you say that. I hope you don't say it again."

As usual, Tama was playing Adrian's game for him, blaming his mistakes on other people.

"Incidentally," Tama said. "Do you know anything about this?"

She pulled a letter from her desk drawer. It was written with words clipped from a newspaper or a magazine. For Tama's name separate letters from headlines were used. *Beloved TAMA do not despair. You will be freed from your bondage soon. CALIFIA.*

"Did Sarah send this? Is it her idea of a joke?" Tama said.

"It's some nut. Buzz got one a couple of days ago from the same dame."

"You're sure it's not Sarah?"

The hostility between Tama and Sarah was one more irritation in his life. Women! Cliff retreated to his office where he found a stack of phone messages from local airlines in search of replacement parts for their fifteen-year-old Sky-Rangers. As he returned the calls, he could hear Jim Redwood in the next office, trying to sell the Excalibur to Pan American for their South American routes.

Another call—this one not so routine. Dick Stone was on the line asking Cliff to get him a job at Buchanan. Could he do it? Did he want him around? Old Shylock could be a difficult character. But he could be an ally. Sarah was always telling him to build alliances with people his own age. "I'll see what I can do, Dick. I'll call you back tomorrow."

At twelve o'clock a whistle gave a long low hoot and the assembly line went to lunch. The executives headed for their dining room on the top floor of the tower. As Cliff and Jim Redwood strolled in, a new Excalibur took off from the company field, the roar of its motors rattling the glasses in the well-stocked bar.

About a dozen men in rumpled dark business suits were standing in two clusters on the other side of the room, drinks in their hands. One group were designers, the other engineers. As usual they were not speaking to each other.

Cliff and Jim each ordered a glass of the house single-malt Scotch, Inverness. Most people thought it tasted like week-old rainwater but Buzz McCall said it was a man's drink. Adrian backed him because it was cheap—and he never drank it. Cliff and Jim headed for the engineers, who were grouped around Buzz.

"Where the hell did you go last night?" Buzz said. "When I came back from the pool Cassie was horny as hell. I had to satisfy her and Barbara."

"He's full of shit," Jim Redwood said. "He passed out in the pool and almost drowned. Barbara had to rescue him. She called me this morning and told me all about it."

Buzz threatened to slug him but Redwood just grinned. He had been an all-American tackle for UCLA in the twenties. "I thought we were going to talk to Adrian," he said.

"I talked to him by myself. I told him what I thought of wasting my time trying to sell a plane we never should have built in the first place. We ought to be concentrating on military stuff based on that jet Billy is testing at Muroc. If we get something like that into the Air Force we'll have enough money to develop two new airliners. But first we gotta get our resident genius to cooperate."

He glowered toward the bar. "Frank wants to talk to Cliff about that goddamn flying nightmare he's trying to build."

At the bar, Pat was surrounded by six of seven of his favorite designers. In contrast to the prevailing crew cuts, his reddish brown hair flowed over his ears and partway down his neck. Instead of a business suit, he wore an ancient leather flight jacket, which was cracking in a half-dozen places.

"Cliff," Frank said. "I heard about your latest frustration in New York. Since we don't have a plane to sell—and you're in a sort of training program—would you be interested in working with me as project manager of a new plane we hope to get into production? It's called the Talus."

"I might be," Cliff said warily.

"This plane could change the history of aviation. It's completely different from the planes you flew during the war.

They used most of their engine power to overcome the drag of their fuselages and tails."

"Sounds like you're going to break the sound barrier and then some," Cliff said.

"There's no such a thing as a sound barrier," Frank said. "There are only underpowered, badly designed planes that can't survive the buffeting they take at very high speeds."

"That's verbiage, Buchanan, and you know it," roared Buzz McCall from his cluster of followers.

"No, it's intuition. Something an engineer doesn't believe in, until the facts hit him between the eyes."

"Intuition," Buzz growled, striding toward them, backed by his entourage. "That's a designer's name for something that can't fly until an engineer tells him how to make it work."

"You're telling me, I suppose, that the Talus won't fly?"

"Not without killing a lot of people."

"We'll see who's right in a month or two," Frank said.

"If I have anything to say about it, nobody'll see a goddamn thing!" Buzz roared. "We've got enough problems with the plane that could save our asses, if you'd only get to work on it. Billy's risking his neck every day flying it and you're ignoring him to work on your crazy castrated gooney bird."

"White Lightning is a research tool, not a production model. We're learning a lot about flying in the ionosphere."

"While we go broke on the ground," Buzz said.

"If we'd built the Talus instead of the Excalibur, we'd be ten years ahead of everyone else," Frank said.

"Bullshit," Buzz bellowed.

"Even if we fail, we'll go down gloriously, contributing to the advance of flight."

"Fuck glorious failure," Buzz said. "I'm for staying in business first, last, and forever."

" 'Sacrifices must be expected,' " Frank said. "Do you recognize those words, Cliff?"

Cliff shook his head.

"Otto Lilienthal said them in 1896, shortly before he died of a broken neck trying to demonstrate his erroneous prin-

ciples of aerodynamics. Without his two thousand glider
flights the Wright Brothers would probably still be trying to
get off their sand dune at Kitty Hawk. Otto was a brave man,
even if he was a German."

By this time a waitress in a tight black cocktail dress had
served everyone another round of Inverness. Cliff told himself he had to learn to pace his drinks to get through these
lunches. Frank was only warming up. They drank to the Talus. In spite of Buzz's refusal to toast a "dead kraut," the
designers downed another round to Otto Lilienthal.

"Gentlemen. I'm sorry I'm late," Adrian Van Ness said,
somewhere on the outer fringes of the crowd.

"You're always late," Frank said. "Is it a way of reminding
us of your importance?"

Antagonism flickered between Frank and Adrian every
time they met. By this time everyone knew why. It was the
company's dirty secret, never mentioned above a whisper.
Giving up Amanda Van Ness had filled Frank with bitterness. It came out in unexpected explosions of temper and in
a reckless insistence on the right to experiment with radical
new designs like the Talus.

Everyone sat down at a long table in front of the window
overlooking the airfield. Two waitresses began serving hot
dogs and baked beans. Gone were the war days when they
feasted on black market lamb and steak. Everyone except
Adrian Van Ness drank more Inverness. A waitress served
him red wine.

More drunken arguments broke out at various points between engineers and designers. Jim Redwood said Pan American still might buy twenty Excaliburs. Everyone sneered.
Jim had given them too many blue-sky promises.

"I want to take Cliff out of sales for a while to keep things
organized on the Talus prototype," Frank said.

"Who said we're going to build that?" Adrian said.

"I did," Frank said.

"Do you have any idea how much we're losing on the
Excalibur? Lockheed is killing us with this talk of a Super
Constellation. Douglas, Boeing are both bringing out
hundred-seat models."

"All the more reason to gamble on something radical," Frank said. "Something those play-it-safe boys wouldn't try in a million years."

"How much will it cost?"

"Four—five million—for the prototype. Overall development shouldn't go beyond twenty million."

"What do you think, Jim?" Adrian said, turning to their sales director.

"I vote no. It may fly but it won't sell," Redwood said, avoiding Frank's eyes. They were good friends. "It's too experimental. It looks like a fucking boomerang. People are scared to death of jet engines. The goddamn things don't have propellers."

"It won't be experimental when it breaks the speed record from here to New York," Frank shouted, bringing his fist down on the table with a crash that sent Inverness cascading toward the ceiling. "I guarantee you this plane will outclimb and outfly every commercial airliner in the sky."

"We don't have five million dollars to spend on a fantasy," Adrian said.

"Borrow it!" Frank roared. "High finance is what you're good at, isn't it? Call up one of your Wall Street friends."

"I don't have any Wall Street friends anymore," Adrian snapped. "As far as they're concerned, we're back to being a cottage industry. The war's over. We've saved the world for the goddamned automobile."

For a moment Adrian's eyes met Cliff's. He seemed to be trying to ask him for something. Support? Sympathy?

"Mortgage the real estate then," Frank said. "This plane has to be built. If I can't build it here, I'll go elsewhere."

Adrian finished his wine. "We had some money in the bank until we ran into trouble with Excalibur." He drummed his fingers on the tabletop.

"The Talus will have a hundred seats in a cabin roomy enough to jitterbug in. At six hundred miles an hour," Frank said.

"Six million an hour is more like it," Buzz said. "Don't you have any idea how much fuel those jet engines use?"

"They'll solve that problem within a year—two at the most."

"That's not what I hear from Curtiss Wright. They don't see any future for jets except in pursuit planes," Buzz said.

"Then I don't see any future for Curtiss Wright," Frank said.

"All right," Adrian said. "We'll build a Talus prototype. Providing Buzz gets the Air Force into the act to put up at least half the money."

"Absolutely not," Frank said. "I don't agree to that condition. I made a promise to myself never to build another bomber. We don't need one. We've got the atomic bomb and no one else does. The B-29 can take care of anyone who threatens us for the next twenty years."

"What if the Russians get the bomb?" Adrian said. "From what I hear in Washington, they grabbed more German scientists than we did when the Reich went kaput. They've built a pretty good imitation B-29—that Tupolev Tu4—the one they call the Bull."

"What about the White Lightning? A jet derived from that design could put us back in the big time," Buzz said.

"We don't need fighter planes any more than we need bombers," Frank said.

"I predict we're gonna need bombers and fighter planes—a lot of them—to deal with Joe Stalin and his pals," Buzz said.

"It's your sort of mentality that's created the cold war," Frank said.

"Listen to the guy!" Buzz exploded. "He's a fucking Communist."

"Let's be kind to our old friend," Adrian said. "His problem is political naivete."

"You can call me any name you please," Frank said. "Are we going to build the Talus?"

Adrian's eyes roved the table. Cliff thought he saw some sort of message pass between him and Buzz. "Maybe we ought to humor the crazy bastard," Buzz said.

"I want it designed for prop as well as jet engines," Adrian said. "I agree with Jim about the public's attitude toward jets."

"To the future," Frank Buchanan said, raising his glass of Inverness. His designers rose with him, each at least as drunk.

"Aren't you going to join us?" Frank called to Cliff.

"You bet," Cliff said, lurching to his feet. Only then did he discover neither Buzz nor Adrian nor Jim Redwood was with him. It was too late to sit down without looking like a fink. He found Adrian's eyes again. They were stony.

The hell with him, Cliff decided. The hell with Tama too. Who knew what could happen if Frank pulled this plane off? It was a gambler's business. He and Frank might start telling Adrian and Buzz what to do.

"I predict it will kill a lot of people," Buzz said.

"Sacrifices must be expected," Frank said.

"Remember, you'll be operating on borrowed money," Adrian said.

Cliff Morris wondered if he ought to call Dick Stone and tell him he was crazy to come anywhere near the Buchanan Aircraft Company.

MYSTERY BUSINESS

Six weeks after he walked out on Nancy Pesin, Dick Stone trudged off a Douglas DC-6 at Los Angeles airport with Irwin Shaw's *The Young Lions* under his arm. A smiling, crew-cutted Cliff Morris mashed his hand. They got into Cliff's white Buick convertible and in a few minutes were on a six-lane highway, roaring along at eighty-five miles an hour. "How do you like this?" Cliff said. "It's the Hollywood Freeway. They're going to build a whole network of these things."

"How many people do they lose on it each week?"

"A half dozen or so. Everybody drives fast—it's the western approach to things. Fast cars, fast planes, fast women."

"I'm ready for all three."

"I can't believe it. Old Shylock is busting loose."

"Yeah," Dick said. He had never liked the Shylock joke. "What happened between you and Nancy?"

"Diarrhea of the mouth."

"Is there a dame who doesn't have that problem?"

"I'm hoping to find one."

"It may take you the rest of your life."

"I'll wait."

"I've thought about splitting a couple of times. But we've got two kids now."

"Hey, I'm not trying to start a fashion."

Cliff's reaction gave Dick an instant attack of guilt. Maybe he should have tried harder with Nancy—asked her to come to California with him. Maybe distance would have eliminated the baby talk. But Sam Pesin had too much money to eliminate the source of it.

"How's business?"

"If you didn't have an MBA, I couldn't have gotten you near the place. We've made a couple of wrong moves. It's part of the sport, you know? You bet half the company on a plane. We did it on the Excalibur, a double-decker transcontinental job. Nobody wants to go near it."

"What's wrong with your marketing people?"

"Marketing, schmarketing. In this business we operate on hunches. Rabbits' feet. Everything gets decided in Adrian Van Ness's head. Other companies aren't that different. Nothing happens at Douglas until Don Douglas makes up his mind. At North American Dutch Kindelberger came back from Washington the other day with a three-million-dollar contract on the back of an envelope. He couldn't read it until he sobered up."

"Don't you have a chain of command?" Dick asked.

"Sure," Cliff said. "Most of the time someone's trying to wrap it around some other guy's throat and pull it tight. This is a man's business, Dick. You've got to learn to talk back, fight dirty, play rough."

"Are you still in sales?"

"There's nothing to sell. I'm a project manager on a new plane. It's the damndest thing you've ever seen. All wing and no fuselage. If it flies I'm a hero. If it crashes I'm a bum."

They rocketed off the freeway down a ramp to a broad boulevard, where the traffic moved much slower. Eventually they reached Cliff's ranch house in a development that rambled up and down a half-dozen hills. It looked like a transplant from Long Island or Westchester—except for the palm trees on the streets and the mountains looming in the distance.

"Here's your home away from home," he said.

As Cliff helped carry his bags up the walk, a beaming Sarah Morris opened the door. "Dick," she said in her low liquid voice that brought back the years in England. "How good to see you."

Cliff dumped his share of the bags in the hall. "You two behave yourselves while I try to calm down a couple of designers who want to assassinate half the engineering department," he said, heading back to his car.

Sarah had gained over forty pounds and looked much too matronly to keep a lothario like Cliff Morris happy. Dick dismissed that unpleasant thought as she led him into a living room full of inexpensive furniture. "I see you're reading *The Young Lions*. What do you think of it?" she asked.

"It's ten times better than *The Naked and the Dead*. I especially liked the German side of the story."

"I agree on both counts. I hoped Mr. Mailer would teach me a bit about the American male, a mystery I need to penetrate. I'm afraid all I learned were naughty words."

"Do you still read Gerard Manley Hopkins?"

"Hopkins?" For a moment she looked blank. "Oh, that poor old Jesuit. No. How did you know I ever read him?"

"You—you mentioned him to Cliff—the night we met. The first night."

She gave him a peculiar look. Did she remember where and how she had mentioned him to Cliff?

" 'Like a daregale skylark scanted in a cage,' " he said.

Sarah's eyes came alive. " 'Man's spirit in his bonehouse, meanhouse dwells.' Yes. Yes. I remember how much I used to love that passage. I don't remember mentioning it to Cliff."

She made a wry face. "I can't imagine ever reciting poetry to Cliff. It's a sad commentary on how quickly romance vanishes, I suppose."

She served him tea and scones covered with an inch of butter and another inch of raspberry jam. The tea was deliciously strong, brewed in the pot as only the English make it.

"I don't know why we revolted because you taxed this stuff. I would have paid gladly," Dick said.

Sarah nodded, pleased. She stirred in some milk and sugar. "It must have been very painful—getting divorced."

Dick shrugged. "The worst part is wondering how you got involved in the first place. How you could have made such a dumb mistake."

There was a painful pause and Dick wondered if Sarah was applying the words to herself. He changed the subject to California. How did she like it? She struggled to be enthusiastic but ended up saying she had many acquaintances but few friends.

Her daughters awoke from their naps. Elizabeth, the three-year-old, was a little beauty. Dick felt a pang at the sight of her. If he had stayed with Nancy, would they have had a child like this?

Eventually Cliff came home and banged Dick on the back and told him Adrian Van Ness was looking forward to meeting a guy with an MBA. Buchanan was having a tough time right now like the rest of the industry but the coming decade was going to be stupendous. This hot air contradicted most of what Cliff had said in the car driving from the airport. Was he sorry he had told the truth the first time? Or was he talking for Sarah's benefit? If so, he was wasting his breath.

Gone was the adoration with which Sarah had gazed at Cliff at their wedding, just after he had volunteered for another twenty-five missions. Her tight mouth made it clear she was all too familiar with Cliff's tendency to talk big. It made

Dick feel better about his decision to flee Nancy Pesin. Was seeing, knowing too much, an enemy of love?

Dinner was pleasant. Cliff talked sports, Sarah talked books. Dick was able to keep them both happy. He wondered what they would have said to each other if he were not at the table.

At midnight, in bed in the guest room, Dick listened to the rising wind. A Santa Ana, Cliff Morris had called it. A weird California phenomenon that swept down from the mountains and across the deserts with near hurricane force, hurling cars off highways, blowing roofs off houses. Tomorrow the weather would be hot and sticky.

Dick found himself remembering his father's distress when he appeared at his parents' house in Rego Park the night of the cosmic no. On the stairs going up to his old bedroom, his father had seized his arm. "Why such bitterness?" he cried. "It is something I've done?"

Dick almost tried to explain one last time. A new metaphor flared in his mind. The last mission over Berlin. Leaping from the doomed bomber. It was a kind of birth—like a butterfly from a burning chrysalis. But it would have been futile. He could not talk frankly to the rabbi. He had become a professional advice giver, a spokesman for Jewishness.

He looked past his father at his mother and was shaken by what he saw there. Her face was sad but her eyes said: *go*. In a flash he saw deep into his parents' marriage. She did not want him to be a secular replica of this pompous man she no longer loved. How did she know that Saul Stone, the articulate boy she had fallen in love with one teenage summer in Bradley Beach, New Jersey, would become a verbose Reform rabbi?

In another flash, Dick saw the evolution. His grandfather had abandoned his Orthodox faith for the glory, the power of modern culture, in particular the German culture into which he had been born. His son, reacting against the father as sons have a way of doing, had doubled back to Reform Judaism, trying to hold the old and the new together. His son had repudiated him—for what? Was it for another faith, Americanism? Maybe freedom was a better name.

Dick drifted down into sleep in the middle of these thoughts and dreamt he was flying through the darkness on a gigantic arrow, to which he clung with total desperation. A hand was seizing his shoulder, trying to tear him off. He fought with amazing fury to resist it. "Wha—?"

Cliff Morris was shaking him awake. "Hey, Navigator. You got a telephone call."

"Your mother gave me the number," Nancy Pesin Stone said. "I just want to tell you one last time what a rotten no good son of a bitch you are."

A fugitive from Jewish wrath and pain, Dick Stone was almost afraid to meet Adrian Van Ness the next morning. What if he turned out to be an anti-Semite? He could hear Sam Pesin chortling, his father mocking him with his compassionate smile.

To Dick's immense relief, Adrian Van Ness was exactly what he imagined a Protestant aristocrat would be like. Urbane, unhurried, he slouched in the big leather chair behind his desk, wrinkles of quizzical surprise on his forehead because Dick had recognized the paintings by Klee and Matisse on his wall. "I picked them up in Paris in the twenties. You're the first person who's even known they were serious paintings," he said.

Cliff Morris squirmed and said nothing. Dick smiled, pleased at being recognized as a fellow member of the shadowy brotherhood of the elite, those with superior taste, judgment, wisdom. He was only a novice in this undefined unrepresentative band. But he was eager to grow in wisdom and age and grace.

"We could use someone with an MBA to bring a little order out of our chaotic accounting methods," Adrian Van Ness said. "Basically we spend money on developing new planes and take in money for planes we've sold and add things up at the end of the quarter to see how we're doing. That frequently leads to rude shocks. For your first assignment, I want you to take a look at one of our biggest, riskiest projects, the X-49, also known as the Talus."

"What is it?"

"Some people call it a flying wing. I call it a headlong

catastrophe," Adrian said, his hooded eyes flickering toward Cliff.

"Why don't you stop it?"

"You'll find out the answer to that question by going to see the man who's designing the thing."

A surly Cliff called Frank Buchanan's secretary, who reported he was in the wind tunnel studying some aerodynamic problems in the Talus. "Let's go meet the rest of the big shots," Cliff said.

They found Buzz McCall on the factory floor conferring with a foreman. They had to talk above the rattle of rivet guns, the shriek of metal cutters. "You're the navigator?" Buzz yelled.

"That's right," Stone shouted.

"Now you're going to play cost cutter?" Buzz bellowed. "Come see me tomorrow in my office. We'll discuss the next layoff. Then you can go explain it to the union."

"We've got some pretty tough unions in the garment industry," Dick shouted.

Buzz looked at him if he had just confessed he was an embezzler and went back to talking to the foreman. "Don't let it bother you," Cliff said as they retreated to the office side of the building. "He treats everybody that way."

The treasurer, a big easygoing man named Thompson, welcomed Dick as an ally. "It isn't easy to track costs in this crazy business," he said. "You've got to prorate guys selling planes at the 21 Club in New York and birdbrains on the assembly line connecting hydraulic controls backwards. Then there's Tama's stable. That's one we've got to cover under miscellaneous. And the Honeycomb Club. That's ten feet under miscellaneous, in never-never land."

Thompson grinned at Cliff as he said this, apparently presuming he had already explained all this to Dick. Outside the treasurer's office, Dick asked for the explanation. Cliff wryly told him how Tama's stable of willing women employees helped sell planes.

Welcome to the United States of America, Dick thought, recalling his repugnance when he escorted Pesin Baby Wear buyers to whorehouses in Harlem.

"And the Honeycomb Club?"

"We'll let you see that for yourself one of these nights when Frank's in the mood."

Cliff hoped Frank Buchanan would join them for lunch in the company dining room. But he stayed in the wind tunnel. Dick met a half-dozen lesser designers and as many engineers. He was amazed by the acrimony flickering between the two groups. He was even more amazed by the amount of Inverness Scotch everyone consumed. Dick's first taste brought tears to his eyes. He had no intention of swallowing another drop until Buzz McCall wondered if all Jews were timid drinkers. Almost strangling, Dick matched him belt for belt.

"Believe it or not, eventually you get to like the swill," Cliff said.

After lunch Dick wobbled through routine security and physical examinations. Security chief Hanrahan only seemed interested in whether he had any Communist relatives. Owlish Kirk Willoughby, the company doctor, wanted to know if he had been to the Honeycomb Club yet. When Dick said no, he asked him to send him a memo on his first impressions. He was collecting opinions.

Cliff called to report Frank Buchanan had finally emerged from the wind tunnel. Five minutes later, Dick sat in the chief designer's cluttered office listening to him sneer: "An MBA? What does that stand for? Master of bullshit? Nothing personal, but I have a rather low opinion of so-called business schools. I don't think they can teach you anything helpful about making planes. I've never gone near a university. Neither has Jack Northrop or Ed Heinemann, the best designer at Douglas. Can you explain why this uncanny gift should suddenly manifest itself in the human race?"

The man was everything Adrian Van Ness was not. Passionate, sincere, childishly enthusiastic. All traits Dick Stone, the rationalist, considered dangerous, although he had adored them in his grandfather. But it was one thing to enjoy passion and enthusiasm in a professor of literature at the City College of New York and another to approve them in a man who was supposedly in business to make money.

"Stop and think about it for a moment," Frank Buchanan continued. "Our teachers were two self-educated mechanics who ran a bicycle shop in Ohio, Orville and Wilbur Wright. Can you imagine anything more unlikely—except the story of the Savior being born in a manger?"

"I don't happen to believe in the Savior," Dick said.

"I don't either, in any literal sense," Frank Buchanan said. "But you can't be Jewish and not believe in some of his ideals. They're all in the Old Testament."

"I'm sorry," Dick said in a softer tone. "My father's a rabbi but—he didn't persuade me."

"Maybe I can, before we're through," Frank said. "I was brought up to believe all the great religions reflect the same spiritual truths. Reading poetry taught me everything in the material world is an emblem, a shadowing forth of a spiritual world. That's what makes the plane so important. In spite of the way we've already abused it, I still think it can become a symbol of our ascent to a new spiritual synthesis."

Dick Stone cleared his throat. He was not here to discuss metaphysics. "That's very interesting. Mr. Van Ness wants me to review the Talus's costs and do an analysis of them. Estimate future outlays, that sort of thing."

"You can't do it. We're building a plane, Stone, not an automobile or locomotive!" Frank roared. "We don't know what she'll run into up there in the sky. You've flown. Don't you remember days when the plane got thrown all over the horizon? When she shuddered and yawed and groaned like a man on the rack?"

"As far as I was concerned, it did that every time we flew," Dick said.

"I know what you mean. I flew in World War I and I was terrified every moment. The peacetime sky isn't quite as deadly but it's full of mysteries. Forces that reveal themselves in new ways every time we challenge them in a different airplane. That's why you can't worry about costs, you can't start whining about budgets. By the way, can you fly?"

"No."

"Take my advice and learn. It will help you deal with a

lot of people in this business, especially our chief of production, Buzz McCall."

Dick found himself confused by the mixture of hostile and friendly signals in this encounter. "Mr. Buchanan," he said. "I promise you that nothing in the job I'm going to do will interfere with your goals."

"You shouldn't make promises like that when you're working for Adrian Van Ness," Frank said.

His bitterness shook the reassurance Dick Stone had felt in Adrian Van Ness's office. The sky was the not only place where they were exploring mysteries. There seemed to be almost as many loose inside Buchanan Aircraft.

MOTHER KNOWS BEST

The doorbell rang just as Sarah Chapman Morris was sitting down to lunch. She was ravenous. Perhaps it had something to do with nursing. She remembered overeating when she nursed Elizabeth. On her plate was a ham and cheese sandwich—double slices of both with mayonnaise and lettuce on well-buttered white bread. For a side dish she was finishing up some macaroni left over from dinner. For dessert there was chocolate pudding she had made for the children two days ago; it should be eaten before it spoiled. She asked Maria, her Mexican maid, to answer the front door. It was probably some magazine salesman.

Into the dining room stalked her mother-in-law with a huge pink rabbit. "Oh, isn't that sweet," Sarah said, jumping up to kiss her. "Can I give you some lunch?"

"I never eat lunch," Tama said. "How's the baby?"

"Just fine," Sarah said. "Would you like to see her?"

She put the macaroni in the oven and they went upstairs. In the nursery Elizabeth was playing mother with Margaret, who now weighed ten pounds and was thriving. Liz was pretending to read a copy of *Winnie the Pooh*. Tama gave her a perfunctory kiss and picked up Margaret. "She's looking more and more like Cliff," she said.

The baby's hair was dark and she did seem to have Cliff's fine nose. But she had the Chapman family's blue eyes. Sarah decided not to point this out. Lately she had begun trying to conciliate her mother-in-law.

Tama put Margaret back in her crib. "Maybe I'll have a cup of coffee," she said. "Black."

Sarah served the coffee, rescued the macaroni and resumed her lunch. She sliced the sandwich and licked some oozing mayonnaise off her fingers. Tama sipped her coffee and said: "Do you know where Cliff spends a lot of his time these days?"

"He's been awfully busy with this experimental plane—"

"He spends it with a redhead named Cassie Trainor. He met her on the plane the night after Margaret was born."

Sarah tried to read Tama's expression. Was she mocking her? Sympathizing with her? The wide dark eyes were opaque, the heavy-boned, strong-jawed face expressionless. Sarah suddenly remembered Amanda Van Ness's visit, a year ago, when she told her all the women at Buchanan Aircraft were humiliated. Was this some sort of initiation?

"How do you know this? Did he tell you?" Sarah said, all interest in food gone.

She had wondered more than once if Cliff was faithful. They did not make love nearly as often as they had in England during the first year of their marriage. It was an impossible subject to discuss with your husband. It was also impossible to check up on a man who had a hundred excuses for his absences. She knew from her own experience that everyone in the aircraft business worked horrendous hours. She had barely seen her own father when he was involved in designing a plane.

"Of course he didn't tell me," Tama said. "I had security check him out. Dan Hanrahan and I are old friends. He runs security checks on my girls all the time."

Although she knew how Tama's girls helped sell Buchanan's planes, her casual reference to them shocked Sarah.

The woman had no shame! But Sarah was much too absorbed by Tama's revelation about Cliff to give the girls more than a passing reproach. "Why are you telling me? Wouldn't it be better if I didn't know?"

"Not if he stays married to you. I can't figure out what you've got on him. It sure as hell isn't sex."

"Really! I know you've always disliked me. But I can't see why you've chosen this moment to become completely rude—"

"Whether I like you or not has nothing to do with it. You're married to my son. I happen to *love* him. Last night you entertained Dick Stone, a guy who knew you in England. What do you think went through his head when he saw you?"

Tama strode into the living room and came back with a framed picture of Sarah and Cliff on their wedding day. She pointed to the slim WAAF and said: "She's turned into a fat slob. That's what Dick Stone thought."

"This is insufferable!" Sarah cried. "I refuse to listen to another word. Please leave my house this instant."

Tama ignored her. "Stone is the sort of guy they're going to start hiring at Buchanan, if they make it into the next decade. People from your generation, who judge a man by the looks of his wife as much as by his own looks or his ability on the job. Cliff's got everything he needs to go to the top of this company. But he can't do it with a fat slob for a wife."

"My weight gain is connected to having children," Sarah said, almost strangling with indignation. "It's a natural thing. My mother gained weight the same way and never lost it."

"And I bet your father's got a couple of Cassie Trainors in his past—and maybe in his present."

"You really are insufferable!"

"Cut out the Greer Garson act and listen to me. Do you think you're the first woman who married some guy during a war and then found out he's not Mr. Perfect? I married Cliff's father in 1918 when I was sixteen years old. When he came back from France I realized I couldn't stand the sight of him. He got me pregnant before I got up the nerve to dump him and the Catholic Church."

"This is irrelevant. I still love Cliff."

"If you were telling the truth you wouldn't be standing there forty pounds overweight. I've still got that letter you wrote me when we both thought he was dead. All that baloney about always remembering his heroism. Not one word about the possibility that he was still alive somewhere in Germany. I figured it out on the spot. You were glad he was dead."

"No!" Sarah said, tears of shame mingling with the rage already blurring her eyes. The woman was an uncanny monster. How, where, did she acquire the skill to uncover that secret sin, unspoken, unconfessed, unadmitted to anyone?

"I want to love him. I try to love him," Sarah said. "But he makes it so—so difficult. Now—telling me this—you've made it impossible."

"Whether you love him or not isn't the point," Tama said in the same merciless voice. "Your responsibility is to those two kids upstairs. They're going to have enough trouble being women. You want them to have a failure for a father?"

"I try to talk to Cliff about the business. He isn't interested in my opinions."

"That's because you're about as subtle as a kick in the shins. You want to run him. Meanwhile you're turning into Margaret Rutherford in front of his eyes. You can't get a man's attention with ideas. You want to help Cliff get somewhere? Stop eating. Get down to a hundred and ten pounds and buy yourself some decent clothes. Look like a young executive's wife. Talk like one. Smile. Tell amusing stories. Charm the socks off guys like Jim Redwood and Adrian Van Ness. You can do it. They like that English accent. They think it's classy. Especially Adrian. He's nuts about everything English. He worked in London in the twenties."

"I—I don't know what to say," Sarah said. "Except to—to—express my astonishment at your utter lack of consideration for my feelings. Now—would you please leave?"

She turned her back on Tama—something she hadn't done to anyone since she was five. It was childish but the awful thing was, she felt childish. She felt reduced to the shy stammering creature she had been in grade school by this overbearing woman, so much older, yet still possessing the sheen of youth.

Tama walked past her to the table and picked up her gloves and purse. "When you calm down maybe you'll be glad I did this," she said.

Tama strolled to the mirror over the sideboard to check her makeup. "You may not think so right now but you can do it. This is America, not England, where you go on doing the same stupid things for five hundred years because that was the way your mother and father did it. In America we believe you can change your life, create yourself. You know what my mother did for a living? She washed clothes for the Anglos in San Juan Capistrano. My father weeded their gardens—when he felt like working. You want to know what it's like to be Mexican in California? Pick up some dirt and put it in your mouth."

Tama dug into her purse for her car keys. "Now my name is Morris instead of Moreno and I'm driving that car out front. I've got a five-figure salary and an unlimited expense account and one of the most powerful men in California, maybe in the country, in my life. You may not approve of my morals but it's a hell of a lot better than ironing shirts."

She pushed the dark wave on her forehead firmly into place and smiled at Sarah. *Smiled.* Sarah could not believe the woman's effrontery. Tama strode to the white Cadillac convertible at the curb. Sarah wandered dazedly around her house. On the second or third circuit, she passed her uneaten lunch. She dumped it into the garbage. She opened the door of her white American refrigerator and stared at the glowing interior. In the center sat the chocolate pudding.

She reached out a trembling finger and put a speck of it in her mouth. Tama had it all wrong. Sarah was only trying to make up for those five horrible war years when there was no sugar, no sweets, no pleasures that were not forbidden, sinful.

She had sinned for England. She had opened herself to Cliff, to the cascades of pleasure he sent surging through her body. She sinned for England and the only sweetness available in a world at war and told herself it was love.

But it was, it was, it was love. Love was offering, gift, commitment. She had lived all three, she was Elizabeth Barrett Browning plumbing heights and depths, a Bronte heroine clutched by dark desire. Now she was trying to deny it all, get back to Englishness again in suburban Los Angeles. Enjoy afternoon tea and scones and sweets and occasional sex with her preoccupied husband.

Oh God, oh God, oh God, Tama was right. She was recreating her mother's life with a tiny change to make herself feel progressive, modern. She would be more involved in her husband's business. More participatory. She must have gotten the idea from a *Good Housekeeping* article on how to live happily ever after.

Sarah found herself in the living room staring at the portrait of the slim bride in the WAAF's uniform. *Like a daregale skylark scanted in a cage.* Was that why Dick Stone had asked her if she still read Gerard Manley Hopkins? He was seeing an English skylark in a cage of fat?

Sarah went back to the refrigerator and threw the chocolate pudding into the garbage. She poured the heavy cream she used on her fruit desserts down the sink. Out went the whipped cream, the jams. She transferred chocolate chip cookies, macaroons, and other snacks from handy jars to the back of her kitchen cabinet.

Finally there was nothing left in the cabinets but condiments and canned fruit and nothing in the refrigerator but milk and veal for dinner and salad greens and an array of baby food. She seized a jar of spinach, untwisted the cap, and spooned some of the mush into her mouth.

"Mommy," Elizabeth said, wide-eyed in the doorway. "Why are you eating that?"

"I'm playing a game with myself," Sarah said. "It's called growing up. I'm going back to being a little girl like you and then I'm going to grow up all over again. Fast."

"That sounds like fun," Elizabeth said. "Is it an English game?"

"No. It's American," Sarah said.

HONEYCOMB

Dick Stone spent the rest of his first week at Buchanan Aircraft acquiring an office in the executive tower and a blond secretary named Regina who helped him requisition some secondhand furniture and a used dictating machine. At Adrian Van Ness's suggestion he began analyzing the company's financial records. He also began educating himself in the intricacies of the aircraft business. This meant asking engineers, designers, purchasing agents, and foremen innumerable basic questions. Most people were delighted to explain their sometimes arcane specialties, especially the engineers, who felt no one appreciated them. He listened to endless horror stories of idiocies they had prevented the designers from perpetrating on various planes.

Late Friday afternoon, Cliff Morris called and told Dick to meet him in Frank Buchanan's office. The chief designer was in a more cheerful mood. "This fellow swears you're not one of Adrian Van Ness's finks," he said. "He's persuaded me to introduce you to the Honeycomb Club. Did you pick up any Greek history in your marvelous MBA course?"

"A little," Dick said.

"That's where the club's name comes from. From the same story that gave me the name for the Talus—the life of the great Athenian designer, Daedalus. Talus was his nephew. Daedelus murdered him because the boy was on his way to surpassing him. I chose the name for our new plane to remind us how often original ideas are destroyed in the name of the great god profit."

"Hey, Frank, be careful," Cliff said. "That's my god you're bad-mouthing."

Frank smiled and continued his explanation. "Daedelus

and his son Icarus were our first fliers. They fled to Crete after murdering Talus. King Minos made them virtual slaves, creating buildings and machines for his nation. Daedalus decided to escape and he designed wings for himself and Icarus.

"He gave the boy the first aerial advice. Fly the middle course between the sea and the sun. But Icarus, like many a pilot since, became drunk with the exaltation of flight. He soared into the upper air, where the sun melted the wax on his wings. They fell off and he plummeted into the sea, atoning for the murder of Talus. Isn't it marvelous the way these old myths contain fundamental spiritual ideas? Contrary to appearances, you don't get away with murder or anything else in this life."

Again, Dick was struck by Frank Buchanan's resemblance to his grandfather. He had heard the same passionate rendition of *Faust*, *Till Eulenspiegel*, the *Niebelungenlied* from him. He made the stories meaningful in the same way, linking them to history and experience.

Buchanan shrugged into an old flight jacket. He summoned two designers about the same age as Dick and Cliff. Sam Hardy was short, thin and scholarly looking. Jeff Hall was angular and wry. They trooped downstairs to a battered prewar blue Ford. Sliding behind the wheel, Frank headed west through the gathering dusk to the coast road, continuing to talk about Daedelus. "Like the fliers of today, he was a worshipper of Aphrodite, the goddess of love. In Sicily he designed a temple in the shape of a golden honeycomb for her on the promontory of Eryx. You're about to visit the California version of the shrine."

Buchanan swung onto a two-lane highway that wound between steep-sided hills. "Topanga Canyon," Jeff Hall said. "The Greenwich Village of Los Angeles."

"Where I'd be living if I wasn't married to the Nightstalker," Sam Hardy said.

They turned into a narrow dirt road with thick woods on both sides and rocketed up an almost vertical hill into a parking lot. Before them in the glow of concealed searchlights sat a building with a distinct resemblance to an airplane hangar. Swinging doors spun them into a lobby that was painted gold; the walls and ceiling were scalloped like the inside of a honeycomb. A slim smiling redhead strolled toward them, wearing nothing whatsoever.

Stone stared in disbelief. Nothing! Not even a G-string.

"Hello, Frank," she cooed and kissed Buchanan on the cheek. "And Cliff—I hope you're not mad at me for saying no the other night."

Cliff patted her smooth tan rump. "You know how to fix that, Madeleine."

"Too late," she said, strolling away with Frank Buchanan's flight jacket. "Billy said he's going to have 'private—keep out' painted right here." She pointed cheerfully to where Cliff's hand had been a moment before.

Everyone laughed. Dick thought Cliff's jollity was forced. They sauntered into another gold-scalloped room where about two dozen mostly crew-cut men were drinking at a long bar and at scattered tables. A shapely brunette, also wearing nothing, was plinking out "The Darktown Strutters Ball" on a baby grand. Moving around the room carrying trays of drinks were a half-dozen other women, redheads, blondes, brunettes, each beautiful enough to land a long-term Hollywood contract, all of them in the same costume. Redoubling the dreamlike quality was the way none of the drinkers was paying the slightest attention to them.

"I remember the first time Buzz took me here, when I came back from Germany," Cliff said. "I thought I was dead and in some sort of flyer's heaven."

"We better explain the rules to Dick," Frank Buchanan said. "The club is dedicated to Buzz McCall's cherished belief that there are only two things worth doing, flying and fucking. The latter is not permitted on the premises. However, none of the girls works two days in a row. They're always available for late-night appointments, or matinees the following day. Presuming you strike their fancy as much as they strike yours."

"Where do they come from?" Dick asked.

"From all over the country," Cliff said. "Most of them are trying to get into the movies."

"A doctor checks them every week, so you don't have to worry about catching anything but hell from your wife if she finds out where you've been," Sam Hardy said.

"Do they get paid?" Dick asked.

"Plenty. It all comes out of the membership dues," Frank said. "The company pays the money directly to the club, just like the oil companies do for the stuffed shirts at the California Club."

"That's the most exclusive club in L.A.," Cliff explained.

"It's all a tribute to the cost-plus contract, one of the noblest inventions of the mind of man," Sam Hardy said.

"What are you drinking, boys?" asked a throaty voice. Dick Stone looked up into a pair of coned breasts, topped by luscious dark red teats. There was a woman's face above these charms, of course, with a strong-boned, western look. But in his state of shock Dick could think only of anatomy.

"We'll all have the usual, Cassie," Frank Buchanan said.

They drank Inverness at a deadly rate. Dick became more and more detached from reality. Frank Buchanan asked Cassie for a pencil and paper. He and the two young designers began sketching revised versions of the Talus. At first it resembled a boomerang, then a V-shaped projectile. Then the wing swelled and merged with a fuselage, creating a bat-like shape. The engines, eight of them, were on the back of the wing.

"The idea is to put most of the plane in the wing. Or most of the wing in the plane," Frank said. "It will take time to figure out which way to go."

A rotund totally bald man with a black cigar clenched in a corner of his mouth slapped Frank on the back. "Now what crazy goddamn thing are you cooking up?"

"A plane that flies without engines. On wish power," Frank said. He introduced Moon Davis, Buchanan's chief test pilot. With him was Harry Holland, introduced as the second best designer at Douglas, which, Frank added, smiling broadly, "wasn't saying much." Holland had lines like crevasses in his face, making his gray crew cut even more incongruous. "Seriously, Harry, why didn't you put the

wings where the tail is on the DC-6? You could have added
a hundred knots to its airspeed."

"Because Don Douglas would have kicked my ass into
Long Beach Harbor if I suggested it," Holland said.

"You're a slave to a tyrant, Harry. Rise up. You have
nothing to lose but your paycheck."

"I didn't have the nerve to start my own company, Frank."

"I didn't have the brains to keep mine."

Hours seemed to pass. Dick kept seeing Cassie's coned
breasts, forgetting who they belonged to, wanting to touch
them, until Cliff whispered: "You want to play halfsies with
her? There's more than enough to go around."

"Sounds good," Dick said, even though he did not really
think so. He wanted to make his own selections. He eyed the
other women. A brunette with soft rounded breasts reminded
him of Nancy Pesin. That made him feel guilty for a moment.
But too much was bombarding his senses to give guilt or
any other emotion a chance.

The conversation swirled around planes of all sorts: World
War I Spads, helicopters, bombers. Buchanan and Holland
insulted each other's taste in fuselages, wings, tails. Buchanan drew a sketch of a Douglas airliner, making it look like
a drunken bumblebee. Holland retaliated with a sketch of the
Buchanan Excalibur that turned it into a flying dinosaur.

"At least we're not as bad as those myopic bastards at
Boeing," Frank said, "Have they ever produced a decent-
looking plane?"

Never, everyone agreed. Boeing had never produced a
decent-looking plane and never would because it rained too
much in Seattle. Their brains were waterlogged. Only Lockheed was admitted into the fraternity of aviation geniuses.
Occasionally they produced a passable plane like the P-38.
Frank even conceded Kelly Johnson, Lockheed's chief designer, knew more about tails than he did. They drank a toast
to Alexander Kartveli, Republic's chief designer, for the P-
47, which Frank pronounced the best fighter of the war. Dick
noticed they did not drink to any engineers, salesmen, or
company presidents.

Dick was close to passing out when they finally hailed

Cassie to order dinner. While they read the short menu, Cliff told Cassie that Dick was famous in New York as the man no woman could satisfy. "Now, that's a challenge," Cassie said.

Dick smiled drunkenly at her. It was all unreal. Six weeks ago he had been living a conventional life. He was a husband, supporting a wife, planning a family, moderating his desires like a good middle-class citizen and dutiful son. A single word had sent him hurtling across the continent to this lotus land where there seemed to be no limit to desire and satisfaction. It was so free it was scary.

One of Cassie's breasts was in his mouth. His tongue revolved on that dark red teat. He was free to do that some night soon. His hand roamed those firm thighs, that auburn pussy. There were no obligations, no prohibitions, no guilt. Incredible.

He ordered steak like everyone else. "Buildin' up your strength?" Cassie said.

"I'd say you're being challenged, Dick," Sam Hardy said. "With Cassie satisfaction is guaranteed."

"Unto exhaustion," Moon Davis said.

"You're just a dirty old man," Cassie said and swiveled away, her compact rump rippling.

"Now there's the kind of flutter I admire," Davis said. "Why can't you work some of that into your goddamn planes, Frank?"

"Because you'd never keep your eyes on the controls," Frank said.

They ate thick steaks washed down by more Scotch. Frank Buchanan began assaulting an idea Adrian Van Ness had launched in *Newsweek*'s profile of him, a lightweight vehicle he called the People Plane. With savage sarcasm Frank mocked the idea of a plane in every garage. "People kill themselves by the thousands driving cars. Can you imagine what they'd do flying planes? Of course, that wouldn't bother Adrian any more than it bothers those vultures in Detroit. Some people will do anything for money."

Cliff reminded Frank he used to agree with Adrian on the

People Plane. "I don't agree with Adrian about anything. On principle," Frank roared.

"Douglas is fooling around with the same idea. We call it the Convertiplane," Harry Holland said. "It's half-helicopter, half-propeller driven. If you think flying a jet's dangerous you should try getting that thing back on the ground."

There was a commotion at the entrance to the dining room. A big blond man in a blue Air Force uniform was standing there, his arm around Cassie and Madeleine. "Billy!" Frank bellowed.

All around the room heads turned, expressions changed, as the other drinkers and diners and waitresses turned to gaze at the newcomer. On the women's faces was a range of emotion from patent envy to suppressed desire. On the men's faces rueful admiration was almost universal. This was obviously a celebrity. He seemed to know it too, as he strolled toward them. The grin on his face was supremely reckless, the eyes coolly defiant. He doesn't give a damn for anything or anyone, Dick Stone thought, in a burst of intuition he would confirm many times in the next twenty years. How do you get that way?

In a moment Dick was shaking hands with Major Billy McCall. Frank Buchanan flung one of his long arms around him. "You're looking at a test pilot that can fly anything we put in the air," Frank said. "The best goddamn pilot alive today."

"Hey Pops, careful," Billy said. "Lindbergh's still around."

"So's Eddie Rickenbacker, Jimmy Doolittle, and Buzz McCall," Frank roared. "The claim still stands."

He gazed at Billy with an affection that would have made Dick Stone flinch. His conscience would have immediately asked him how he could possibly deal with such unstinted love. But Billy accepted it as offhandedly as if it were a pat on the back.

"You guys thought you had it tough over Europe. This kid flew ninety-seven missions in the Pacific, bombing at fifty feet," Frank said.

"Twenty-five feet, Pops. Let's keep the record straight," Billy said.

"Yeah. We've heard all about it," Cliff Morris said. In his drunken daze, Dick Stone had trouble including him in his field of vision. On Cliff's face was not an iota of admiration. In his eyes were the polar opposite of affection. He looked at Billy with an odd mixture of loathing and—was it fear? Yes, Dick decided. His intuition, probably the only part of his alcohol-soaked brain that was operating, concluded it was definitely fear.

"What's this bullshit about Madeleine being off limits?" Cliff said.

"It's her idea, Big Shot, not mine," Billy said. "Can I help it if she only likes jet pilots?"

Billy took a swallow of Cliff's drink. "The fact is, you haven't really flown until you wrap your legs around a jet engine."

"How about around Madeleine?" Harry Holland said.

"She comes close. We put my Lustra on autopilot and tried it the other day at ten thousand feet. Sensational."

"Hey," Dick said. "Do you and Madeleine give flying lessons? That's one I'd like to take."

"In a couple of months Billy's going to become the world's fastest human," Frank said. "Our experimental jet, White Lightning's going to hit twice the speed of sound."

"Or they're going to scrape what's left of me off the desert floor with a spoon," Billy said, all traces of self-satisfaction vanishing from his face and voice. "That crate's been doing strange things in the sky. Haven't you gotten my reports?"

"I'm sorry, Billy. I've been working day and night on this new plane, the—"

"Read those goddamn things, Pops. Especially the one about tumbling from seventy to seventeen thousand feet before I figured out what to do."

"Fifty-three thousand feet!" Frank said, shaking his head. "But you pulled it out."

"Next time I may not be so lucky."

"Yes you will," Frank said. "There's absolutely nothing that can destroy your luck."

"Maybe," Billy said. "But read those goddamn reports anyway, Pops."

"I will, I will," Frank said. But when Billy joined them for several Inverness nightcaps, Frank spent most of his time talking about the Talus. Billy listened with cool indifference. At times he almost seemed bored and made little attempt to conceal it. Dick Stone was baffled by his refusal—or was it his inability?—to return Frank Buchanan's lavish affection.

Meanwhile, Sam Hardy conferred with a tall blonde named Tess about her availability. She was very cool. "Sam's problem is negative sex appeal," Cliff said.

"He's got an awful case on her," Frank said. "I'm beginning to wonder if this club is a good idea for some people."

Hardy returned to the table and ordered a double Inverness. "The bitch is treating me like my wife," he said.

At 1:45 the lights began to blink. Cliff reassured Dick that he was not passing out. It was closing time. They staggered to the door where Madeleine asked Billy to wait for her. Cliff Morris watched, glowering. Billy whispered something in Cliff's ear. Dick was standing next to them and caught the word "Cassie."

"Yeah. But ask her now, wiseguy," Cliff said.

Outside, Dick wondered who was going to drive. Frank Buchanan did not look up to it and neither did anyone else. "Pilot!" Frank roared. "We need a pilot."

Out of the darkness rushed a middle-aged Mexican. "I'm right here, Mr. Buchanan," he said.

"This club thinks of everything," Dick said.

"That's how you build planes. You try to think of everything," Frank said.

"Then you test them and find out how much they forgot," Billy said.

"I thought strafer pilots didn't worry about that sort of thing," Cliff said.

"Fuck you, Cliff. Come on out and fly it tomorrow," Billy snarled. His rage seemed out of proportion to Cliff's minor needle.

"We'll do something about it. I promise you," Frank said.

Sam Hardy slapped Billy on the back and began reciting a poem.

Wrinkle wrinkle little spar
Up above the yield so far.
Away up in the sky so high.
I sure am glad that I don't fly.

The other designer, Jeff Hall, did a little dance around Billy and added a stanza.

Sputter sputter little jet
Out of fuel would be my bet
Fuel consumption way too high.
I sure am glad that I don't fly.

"Fucking designers," Billy raged. He grabbed Hardy by the tie and began swinging him in a circle that would have sent him sailing into downtown Los Angeles. Dick Stone and Cliff Morris managed to rescue the choking victim before the crash landing took place.

"We'll fix it, Billy. I promise you," Frank said, acutely distressed.

"It's serious, Pops." He glowered at Cliff. "I bet this bastard has been throwing my stuff in the circular file, hoping I'll get splattered."

"Cliff wouldn't do a thing like that. It's my fault, Billy."

Crazy, Dick thought. Coming close to murder about a plane after spending the night talking wings and tails and rates of climb and more or less ignoring ten or fifteen beautiful naked women. Love in the aircraft business might turn out to be more complicated than it looked at first.

THE DAWN OF FLIGHT

Cliff Morris sat in his sunny dining room frowning at the front-page story in the *Los Angeles Times*.

WHITE LIGHTNING SETS
NEW ALTITUDE, SPEED RECORDS

With Air Force Major Billy McCall again at the controls, a Buchanan Aircraft experimental plane, called White Lightning by its aficionados at Muroc Air Force Base, streaked to another new speed record of 1,315 miles an hour yesterday. Launched from a B-29 high above the desert, the almost wingless rocket plane was a white blur in the cloudless blue sky as it whizzed down the prescribed course. Last week in the same plane, McCall set a new altitude record of 89,916 feet.

"I lost another four pounds last week," Sarah Morris said.

"Huh? Oh—great," Cliff said.

"I'm down to a hundred and thirteen pounds—only three pounds more than when we were married," Sarah said.

"Great. You look great," Cliff said, without raising his eyes from the paper.

Sarah did look a lot better than the fat woman he had seen in the hospital eighteen months ago, when Margaret was born. But Cliff had too much on his mind to get very excited about it. Billy McCall was setting altitude and speed records, rapidly becoming one of the most famous test pilots in the country, while he was project manager of a plane that might vanish without a trace. The Talus program was awash in problems. Frank Buchanan was threatening to quit the company. The U.S. Air Force was demanding to see a demonstration of the Talus's supposedly unique powers six months ahead of schedule.

"That's wonderful news, isn't it—about Billy McCall setting another record."

"Wonderful news for who?" he grunted.

"For Buchanan Aircraft. Isn't it?" Sarah said, blinking her blue eyes in that plaintive way that set his teeth on edge.

"Yeah," Cliff said.

"Will you be home for dinner tonight?"

"I doubt it. I may be out at Muroc for a couple of days, in fact."

There was a long pause. "Is that the truth?" Sarah said.

"Sure it's the truth. Why the hell shouldn't it be the truth?"

"Because the last time you stayed overnight at Muroc, you came home with matches from the Casino on Catalina Island in your pocket."

"I told you—we flew there to unwind—get some fresh ideas from the sea breezes. This plane is driving us all nuts."

It was not the first time Sarah had implied Cliff was unfaithful. It invariably infuriated him. He was not ready to become an old married man. But the arguments—and the unspoken threat of a divorce—made Cliff realize Sarah was important to him. Her admiration for his heroism in the air over Germany was an emotional insurance policy he did not want to lose. She was a kind of emblem of his war record, the most important achievement in his life.

He pulled her out of her chair and kissed her. "I swear to you—I've got nothing on my mind but you, the kids and this plane."

And Cassie Trainor, he silently added, thinking of that slinky slithery body in Manhattan Beach; fucking her at 3 A.M after watching her moving naked around the Honeycomb Club in that bold, languid way. Laughing. Cassie was always laughing while he did it. She made him laugh too.

Sex was so dumb sometimes. The crazy positions you tried for the hell of it. Sometimes it was better in the dark, when it was all feeling. Cassie liked it in the dark and she liked it in the shower and in the tub and on her terrace looking out at the dawning ocean pretending not to notice what he was sliding into her from behind.

Then the call to Billy. Last night she had called him while he was inside her. He stroked her while she told Billy how (*gasp*) much (*ooh*) better Cliff *wasssssss*.

Jesus. Where did all that come from? With his arm around his wife. Was it the contrast? Could he get Lady Sarah to become Cassie? Get her to stop making sex some sort of sacred performance, complete with classical music on the phonograph? It was amazing, how much she had changed when the war ended. When she wasn't kissing a lover who was liable to die the next day.

He remembered trying to get Sarah to take her clothes off and hang around naked in the beach house they had rented in Laguna in the summer of 1945. On hot days Tama had seldom worn anything in their house at Redondo Beach when he was a kid. Lady Sarah had been *horrified*. The way that snooty little English nose twitched. *Horrified*. Maybe he should have insisted on it. Torn off her clothes and screwed her on the rug.

Cliff did not like the way Sarah was looking at him. There was nothing in her eyes, not even anger. She seemed to be holding everything back. Maybe he should cut it out. Drop Cassie. But not for a while. He kissed Sarah on the cheek.

"I'll call you."

"Don't bother."

"Okay. I won't bother."

He drove swiftly down the boulevards to the Hollywood Freeway, listening to the news on the car radio. Truman was cutting the defense budget again. Douglas Aircraft had just laid off 4,000 workers, Lockheed had axed 8,000, Northrop wasn't saying how many but it sounded like it could be the whole company. Maybe Billy McCall had the right idea, staying in the Air Force.

At ninety on the freeway Cliff wondered where they would all be if it were not for Adrian's pull in the Pentagon. He had gotten them ten million dollars to turn the Talus into a bomber. Frank had called Adrian dirty names but Cliff and Buzz had convinced him that if he wanted to see his plane fly, they had to go this route. It was, of course, the way Buzz and Adrian had planned to go from the start. They knew the plane would never make it as an airliner.

An hour later, Cliff and the rest of the team were on the way to Muroc in an Enterpriser, a Buchanan two-engined plane aimed at the short-haul airline market. It was an old SkyRanger refitted with new Wright Cyclone engines. Jim Redwood had sold about eighty of them last year on the telephone. But the profit margin hardly made it worth the trouble.

Dick Stone sat beside Cliff in the front row of the Enterpriser. Dick had shared Cassie Trainor last night. Cliff liked the idea of sharing a woman. A lot of guys did it at the Honeycomb Club. Buzz said it cut down on the chances of things getting romantic—the last thing most guys wanted.

Across the aisle Buzz was trying to soothe Frank Buchanan. "If it passes all the tests, we've got ourselves a contract that could revolutionize the whole business. A billion goddamn dollars. That's what they're gonna commit to a new bomber. Later we can turn it into an airliner in about ten minutes of redesign. We could get so rich it'll be disgusting."

"It isn't ready. We're risking the lives of the test pilots. I don't like losing control of the plane this way," Frank said.

"You're not losing control of a goddamn thing. I've got these Air Force guys in my pocket."

That was not entirely true and Buzz knew it. If the generals were in Buzz's pocket they would not be flying out to Muroc for tests they knew were premature. Something was cooking in Washington that made Cliff uneasy. Buzz did not want to admit that the Air Force was full of guys who had barely heard of World War I, much less Buzz McCall.

"How was Cassie?" Cliff said.

"Okay," Dick said.

"Okay? Sounds like she wore you out, Navigator, and you don't want to admit it."

"Actually, she couldn't get enough of me. She says she's sticking to Jewish cock from now on."

"Yeah. I bet your balls are aching. That broad could use up the whole UCLA football team."

Dick smiled in that superior New York way Cliff had disliked during the war. Was he working on Cassie to give him the same treatment he was giving Billy?

"She's turning into the star of the Honeycomb Club," Buzz said, implying she was one of his girls. Cliff happened to know Cassie had turned him down twice.

In a half hour they landed at Muroc Air Force Base in the Mojave Desert. It was not a big operation. A half dozen hangars and four or five planes of various sizes sitting on the flight line, a dozen or so Quonset-hut barracks and some officers' housing sprawled around a long low operations building. The natural scenery was far more spectacular. The empty desert stretched to the snowcapped Sierras without a single house or even a road in sight.

Billy McCall was waiting for them in front of the operations building in his blue Air Force uniform. "How's the fastest man alive?" Cliff said as they shook hands.

Billy acted as if that was the dumbest question of the year and led them down a couple of corridors to an office where an Air Force brigadier general named Johnson Scott was shooting the breeze with two colonels. Scott was a stocky man with a hard mouth and squinting eyes. He did not look more than thirty-five years old. "About time you guys got here," he said. "Before we go any further on this thing, let's decide whether we're operating on Air Force or civilian time."

"Air Force, General," Buzz said. "We had a little problem with our plane."

He introduced Dick and Cliff as Eighth Air Force veterans. The general grunted. A fighter·pilot, he had no use for bomber jocks. But when he heard Frank Buchanan's name, his expression warmed. He began telling him how much he loved flying the long-range fighter Frank had designed toward the end of the war.

"I want to go on record with a warning that this plane isn't ready for extensive testing, General," Frank said.

"We can't wait, Mr. Buchanan. Congress is ready to vote some real money for a new strategic bomber now that the Russians have an atomic bomb. If we sit around waiting for the perfect plane the stupid bastards will forget all about the problem."

The Russians had exploded their first atomic bomb two months ago. This breakthrough had demolished most of Frank Buchanan's resistance to turning his plane into a weapon.

"I've been telling the general what a hell of a plane he's got," Billy McCall said. "I've applied to fly her in the next round of tests."

"I've been talking to your current test pilot," Scott said. "He makes this thing sound like the second coming."

"Correction," said a voice from the hall. In came Moon Davis, Buchanan's rotund chief test pilot, zipping up his flight suit. He was getting pretty old to be testing planes but

Buzz would not let anyone talk about retiring him.

"I didn't say anything about the second coming," Davis protested. "I just told the general how this plane came into being. The Lord said unto Frank Buchanan, make me a vehicle swifter than the sun and lighter than the wind. And the dawn of a new age of flight began."

Buzz grinned nervously. "They say enthusiasm wins wars, General."

"So I've heard," Scott said. "But it doesn't pass appropriations. Let's get to work, gentlemen."

They climbed into a pair of jeeps and rode down the flight line to the Talus. She squatted in the glaring desert sun, simultaneously real and unreal. The tail was a minuscule fin, the fuselage was nonexistent. The plane had become a huge wing, two hundred feet from tip to tip. In the center a cabin bulged like a thyroid eye.

Cliff invited Dick Stone aboard to see the interior. Contrary to appearances, there was an amazing amount of room inside. The cabin was big enough to house a ten-man crew, with bulky radio and radar equipment, a bombsight and other war-fighting gear without the slightest crowding. Behind the compartment there was ample space for bomb racks.

"I've flown in it," Cliff said. "It's the greatest experience I've ever had in the air."

The most terrifying experience was closer to the truth. The plane had slewed and yawed all over the sky. Frank had yet to solve a lot of the stability problems.

Moon Davis came aboard with his copilot and flight engineer and Frank Buchanan. They went over the tests they planned for the flight. "Let me add something to impress Scott," Davis said. "He's out to kill this thing, Frank."

"That may be—but we aren't ready to do anything spectacular," Frank said. "I want to solve some of these problems with the engines and their position on the wing. We may have it wrong. I suspect they're underpowered. I wish I'd stuck to my hunch and insisted on using jet engines. But Adrian and everyone else screamed about costs so much—"

Cliff sensed Moon was not listening to Frank's plea for caution. They debarked and Davis warmed up the engines.

The whole plane vibrated as he shoved them to full throttle. Satisfied, he taxied to the runway.

Down the long concrete ribbon Moon whizzed to lift off in one of the sharpest climbs Cliff had ever seen. The Talus made a B-17 look like an overloaded dromedary with wings.

"How do you like that, General?" Cliff said.

"Not bad," Scott said.

"It's got eight tons of iron in the bomb bays," Cliff said. "We're trying to simulate the real thing."

General Scott grunted.

At about five thousand feet, the huge aluminum creature leveled off and banked sharply to the left and right as it roared over the base. It was an eerie sensation, seeing it in the sky.

"If we flew it over L.A., they'd evacuate the city," Cliff said. "They'd be sure the Martians were coming."

"I'd be the first guy on the freeway," Dick Stone said.

Davis proceeded to put the Talus through a series of dives and climbs and banks. He cut two engines on the left wing and flew perfectly straight and level. He cut two on the right wing and duplicated the performance. "It could fly on two engines from here to New York," Cliff said.

Moon shoved the throttles to full. The Talus streaked for the distant mountains, wheeled and came back across the air base at top speed. "Four hundred miles an hour," Buzz McCall said. "With underpowered engines. The B-36's max speed is 416—with ten goddamn engines."

Convair's B-36 was the Talus's chief competitor. It was a totally unoriginal plane, an overgrown World War II bomber.

"What's the ceiling?" Scott said. "Have you solved that problem?"

"Watch."

Moon Davis was climbing now, a steady remarkably steep climb, until he was the size of a butterfly in the glaring azure sky. "Leveling off at thirty thousand feet," Davis said over the radio that stood beside the hangar door.

He banked, dove, climbed in the near stratosphere, where thin air frequently caused stability problems for standard-shaped planes. "Now, General, to show you what this plane can do, watch closely," Moon said.

Down came the Talus in a series of spirals until it was about five thousand feet above the air base. Davis leveled off and began doing stunts. Chandelles, rolls, it was dazzling—until he tried a loop. "No!" Frank Buchanan cried.

Over the vertical the huge plane came and down in a dive. Now, Cliff thought, now, pull it out. Davis tried. But the left wing crumpled under the forces he had unleashed, the motors ripped free and the Talus slid into a roaring whirling spin that sent it into the brown desert with a stupendous explosion and a fireball of flame.

"That wasn't on the checklist!" Frank cried. "Why in God's name did he think he could loop a thirty-ton plane?"

"Goddamn it," Buzz said. "Goddamn it." He said it about a hundred times as the fire trucks clanged across the dry lake bed to spray foam on the wreckage. There was no hope for Moon Davis or his crew. It would be a miracle if they could even identify the bodies.

Flying back to Santa Monica, everyone was glum. Buzz poured Inverness and they drank a toast to Moon. "He put some great planes in the air," he said.

Buzz took responsibility for the crash. "I told Moon to try it," he said. "We had to do something wild to get their attention."

"It was partly my idea," Billy McCall said. He had hitched a ride to Santa Monica with them. "I want to fly it, Pops."

He smiled mockingly at Cliff, who could hardly object to Billy as a test pilot now. Ordinarily he would have done everything short of assassination to keep him out of the project. Cliff wondered if he had just seen his career explode and burn on the desert floor. He heard himself telling Dick Stone that if the Talus succeeded he was a hero and if it failed he was a bum.

"What happens now?" Dick asked.

"We've got another prototype almost ready to roll out," Frank Buchanan said.

"You'll keep testing?"

"Of course we'll keep testing. You can't let these setbacks throw you," Frank said.

"I haven't seen a plane yet that didn't kill at least three pilots," Buzz said.

"Sacrifices must be expected?" Cliff said.

"Exactly," Frank said, pleased that he remembered the phrase.

Include me out, Cliff thought. But how? They landed at Buchanan Field in the dusk. Billy hitched a ride to the Beverly Wilshire Hotel with Buzz. No doubt he had some beautiful piece waiting for him there. Cliff got into his car and thought about driving home to tell the story of the crash to Sarah. There would be the usual dumb questions, then plaintive wifely sympathy, maybe some symphonic sex at bedtime.

Nuts. He wanted Scotch, he wanted fucking, fucking, fucking until the anger and frustration and fear drained out of him. There was only one woman who could give that to him. Cliff shoved a coin in the pay phone outside the main hangar. "Hello, Cassie?" he said.

SOARING LESSON

Sarah Morris was dressing for Buchanan's annual Christmas party, the major social event of the company year. She should be brimming with Dickensian cheer. But Christmas in California, with the temperature at seventy-five, was too bizarre to foster the traditional impulse to God bless everyone. That meant cheer depended on one's inner resources, on words like *love* and *faith*. At the moment, Sarah was very low on these emotions.

Sarah had completed Tama Morris's program to redesign her English daughter-in-law as an American wife. She had lost fifty-eight pounds and was keeping her weight at 110

with heroic dieting. But the program was a failure in the
romance department. That was the main reason for Sarah's
lack of Christmas cheer. A perfunctory performance in the
bedroom once a week or so was still the most she could
expect—and Cliff seemed to think she should be grateful for
that. Several times recently she had to remind him that ten
days or two weeks had passed without a touch or a kiss.
Meanwhile there was a steady supply of evidence that other
women were getting plenty of both.

At this point in Sarah's unChristmasy meditation, her husband emerged from the bathroom in his underwear and
pulled a shirt from his dresser. He shoved his arms into it,
flipped a tie under the collar and began buttoning the neck.
"Christ!" he said. "There's enough starch in this collar to
straighten Mulholland Drive."

"I keep telling Maria—but it doesn't do any good. Maybe
she wants to make Anglos suffer."

"I thought you Brits were good at dealing with the lower
orders."

"Speaking of shirts," she said. "The one you wore last
night was covered with lipstick. Would you mind telling me
how that happened?"

"Business," Cliff said.

"Funny business?"

"I was out with an Air Force general trying to keep him
interested in the Talus."

"And you each had one of Tama's volunteers with you?"

"Mine got a little drunk. She was practically lying on top
of me in the backseat. But I didn't do a goddamn thing to
her. So help me. I don't fool around with the help. Tama'd
give me hell, for one thing."

"But if I give you hell it doesn't matter?"

"I'm getting pretty bored with it. I've told you before—
you don't have to worry about me leaving you. If I get
tempted now and then, it's strictly a passing fancy. Christ,
this is the twentieth century. You can't expect a man to be
absolutely faithful."

Sarah almost burst into tears. She could not deal with this
presumption of infidelity. For a while she had tried to com-

pete with these invisible women. She spent hours studying
herself in the mirror, trying to think of new ways to use
makeup, change her hair. She prowled the department stores
looking for bargains in the latest styles.

What did she get for this devotion? A demand for less
starch in his shirts. Sarah stared at her husband in her
dressing-table mirror. He looked ridiculous, the stiff collar
making his neck bulge. How, why, had she ever fallen in
love with this arrogant playboy?

Strangling in his over-starched shirt, Cliff drove them at
terrifying speed down the Hollywood Freeway and out Santa
Monica Boulevard to Buchanan Field, which was already
crammed with parked cars. All Buchanan's employees were
invited to this annual bash. The tradition apparently stretched
back to 1929 or 1930 when Frank Buchanan had run the
company with a lavish optimism the Great Depression had
soon dimmed.

One of the biggest hangars had been cleared, except for
the company's tiny experimental rocket plane, White Lightning, in which Billy McCall had recently set several more
records for speed and altitude. It perched on two wheels like
a defiant insect. The thin swept wings, the rapier nose, gave
it a menacing look, even on the ground.

Standing nearby in his Air Force uniform was the record-
breaker himself. People swarmed around him, slapping him
on the back, asking him questions. Sarah had met Billy at
these Christmas parties and once or twice at other Buchanan
ceremonies. She knew her husband did not particularly like
him. Today, that made her all the more inclined to chat with
him. Billy was unquestionably one of the handsomest men
she had ever seen, almost as tall as Cliff and much younger
looking, even though they were roughly the same age. Sarah
decided it was the blond hair, the fair skin.

"Congratulations from your sister-in-law, Sarah," she said,
holding out her hand.

"I haven't forgotten you," Billy said, giving her hand a
brief squeeze. "I may be dumb and a little deaf from flying
Samsons too close to the water, but I'm not blind."

"Is that a compliment?"

"It's a fact," Billy said, smiling.

"I've been following your exploits."

"I don't deserve any credit for them. I just switch on the rockets in this excuse for a plane and go along for the ride."

In the distance, a band began to play. There was a wooden dance floor at the far end of the hangar. "Want to risk a fox trot?" he said.

They moved onto the uncrowded floor to the latest hit, "Mona Lisa." "That's you," Billy said, as the singer began gushing the saccharine words. "Mona Lisa."

"Why?"

"The way you smile. It's different from most women's. Sort of wary—and mysterious."

"Appearances are deceptive. I'm neither."

"It's a mystery to me how you've stayed married to Cliff."

"You don't like Cliff very much, do you?" Sarah said.

"I don't like him at all."

"I happen to love him."

"Come on. You loved a wartime hero. A pilot. Now you're stuck with a salesman on the make. You must feel like you've gotten into the wrong movie halfway through. But it's not too late. There's a real pilot waiting to fly you into the wild blue."

"Who, may I ask?"

"You're dancing with him."

"Really," Sarah said.

"Really," Billy mocked. "I can usually get into Los Angeles on a day's notice. Buchanan and a couple of other companies keep a suite reserved at the Beverly Wilshire, in case they want us test pilots for some publicity. Just call this number—"

He palmed a card from his pocket and slipped it into her hand. "I'm ready when you are."

"I admire your nerve, Major," Sarah said. "But not your morals."

"Think it over," Billy said. "At the very least, you'll get even."

It took Sarah a moment to realize Billy knew all about Cliff's romps with other women. Cliff probably bragged about them. The band switched to "That Lucky Old Sun" and Billy swung her into a smooth lindy. Whirling at the end of his muscular arm, Sarah's bewilderment changed to cool decisive lust. Why not dispense once and for all with her adolescent ideas about love and partnership and see herself for what she really was—a young, attractive, neglected wife who was being propositioned by one of the two or three most famous pilots in America?

"You're a beautiful woman, Sarah," Billy said.

It had been years since she heard those words from her husband. "You're a rather handsome man, Major," she said.

A big hand seized Sarah by the shoulder and spun her out of Billy McCall's grasp. "Maybe it's time I danced with my wife," Cliff said.

He put his broad shoulders between her and Billy. "What's that wiseguy telling you about me?"

"He's predicting you'll be CEO of Buchanan in fifteen years," Sarah lied.

"Not if he can help it," Cliff said.

For the rest of the party, Sarah felt Billy's eyes on her. Every time she turned her head, so it seemed, there he was in the middle distance studying her, a small smile on his face. Even when she was talking to Adrian Van Ness, answering as well as she could his offhand but probing questions about how de Havilland Aircraft was doing.

Beside Adrian stood Amanda Van Ness, wearing a gauzy blue gown out of the 1920s or 1930s. Sarah's friend Susan Hardy had pointed her out earlier in the party as an example of a born Californian's total lack of style. "How are Tama's granddaughters?" Amanda said. "You must bring them both to visit me one of these days."

"They're—fine," Sarah said, abruptly flung back to her memories of Amanda's visit. "They're on their way to being very independent women. Already they ignore everything I tell them."

"Good," Amanda said. She whispered in Sarah's ear "Its more important for them to ignore their father. They need to consider men *superfluous.*"

Adrian Van Ness goodnaturedly asked if Amanda was telling her he had a weakness for English women. Was he aware of his wife's bizarre opinions? Sarah wondered. Probably. But he ignored them. Sarah could not imagine anything disturbing Adrian's self-assurance.

For the third or fourth time her eyes found Billy McCall. He was standing alone, raising a drink to his lips. Sarah felt warmth gather in the center of her body. It was amazing how he could make something that simple an erotic gesture. She grew irked by Adrian's questions, which presumed her strong interest in English aviation. She was not English anymore. She was completing the process of growing up American. Maybe Billy McCall was her graduation present.

At home on Christmas Day, confronted by her two daughters and her husband and mother-in-law, Sarah told herself to forget Billy McCall. It was absurd. She was a mother and a kitchen helper, a slavey. The Morrises ate and drank what she and Maria had spent ten hours preparing for them as if they were California nobility.

Tama congratulated Sarah on charming Adrian Van Ness. "He talked about you for a half hour last night at my place."

Tama's reference to my place made it very clear that adultery was par for the course in Buchanan's executive suite. But Billy McCall was still out of the question, Sarah told herself, washing a sinkful of dishes later in the night.

The next morning at 10 A.M. the telephone rang. "This is your friend the pilot," Billy McCall said. "Just wanted to make sure you didn't lose that number."

She hung up. Out of the question. If Cliff made a single tender gesture, if he made love to her with even a hint of his old wartime ardor, she would forget it.

Instead, there was another late-night return to the nest reeking of a different perfume and a call around midnight on New Year's eve explaining that an office party had "gotten out of hand" and he would not be home at all because he was too drunk to drive. In the background she could hear women laughing.

On New Year's morning, the first day of 1950, the beginning of the second half of the century, Sarah fed the children and took down the Christmas tree. The rituals of motherhood and family completed, she went upstairs to the bedroom where she had slept alone on New Year's eve and dialed Billy McCall's number.

"This is Sarah," she said. "Are you still flying that route into the wild blue?"

Two days later, her husband in the Mojave Desert, her daughters asleep, her reliable Mexican maid, Maria, in charge of her house, Sarah drove up Los Angeles's main street, Wilshire Boulevard, to the hotel that shared its name, and walked to a white lobby phone.

"May I speak to Major McCall, please?"

A pause while the operator found the number and she had one last chance to flee. There was something so tawdry about coming to his room like a prostitute. Then Billy's voice was on the line. "Sarah? I'm on the other side of the lobby."

He strolled toward her in casual California clothes, the shirt open at the throat. Sarah felt another rush of warmth. The blond hair reminded her of several boys on whom she had teenage crushes; then the raw-boned western face. He was a remarkable blend of English and American good looks.

Was she feeling sexual desire for the first time? Were the feelings she had experienced with Cliff a kind of spiritual immolation? Do you have to grow up American to want a man? Sarah's heart pounded. She could not turn back now.

"I figured we'd go for a plane ride first," Billy said. "A friend of mine's got this place in the desert near Palm Springs."

They drove to Los Angeles Airport, where Billy kept a dark green single-engined plane. He told her it was a Lustra, one of Buchanan's first aircraft. He had rebuilt it himself and installed a new engine. Behind the cockpit he had created a miniature sitting room with a cushioned swivel chair, a couch and a small bar. In minutes they were soaring over the lights of Los Angeles and then over the darkness of the desert toward a horizon filled with stars. "I love to fly at night," Billy said.

Some random lights appeared below them. Billy talked to someone on the radio and a half-dozen more powerful lights came on, illuminating a single runway. He landed without even the hint of a bounce and left the plane beside a small control tower. They walked to a station wagon in a nearby parking lot and drove a few miles into the desert to a house surrounded by a high adobe wall.

Billy unlocked a carved wooden gate and they entered a dark courtyard. He touched a switch just inside the gate and lights glowed around a rectangular pool with two chaises beside it and a bathhouse at the far end. The mission-style house remained in darkness a few dozen feet away.

Billy disappeared into the house and returned with a bottle of Scotch and some ice. "First we get just a little drunk," Billy said, pouring her a generous splash.

"To dull the conscience?" Sarah said.

"To forget about getting even," Billy said. "That's the wrong reason for coming here."

They sat down side by side on chaises facing the pool. Sarah sipped her Scotch. It burned deep in her throat. "Tell me what it feels like to go thirteen hundred miles an hour," she said.

"Like hitting a home run and scoring a touchdown in the same day."

She shook her head, dismissing these male metaphors. "Make me see it, feel it. The whole thing."

Billy hunched forward, balancing his glass on his knee. He picked it up and stretched out on the chaise. "You never know if the goddamn plane is going to explode. Two have, already. They didn't even find pieces of the pilots. With our model, it's twice as likely to happen because we're relying on rocket fuel. We were supposed to get jet engines but Westinghouse never came through with the power."

He took a hefty swallow of Scotch. "It's like flying down a tunnel of fire. Any second you expect to disappear. Your body feels like it's already vanished. You're scared in a new way, different from combat. You feel like you're going down God's throat and He doesn't like it. Afterward you just want to get drunk."

He smiled briefly at her. "That's the bad flight. Want to hear about the good flight?"

"Yes," Sarah said.

Billy poured himself more Scotch. "The altitude flight. That's the good flight."

He lay back on the chaise again and his voice dwindled to a murmur. "The first boost that pulls you away from the B-29 is nothing to what you get when you ignite all four tubes at thirty thousand feet and start to climb. The altimeter goes up a thousand feet a second and suddenly you're at sixty thousand feet. You can feel the difference. She doesn't want to fly in that thin air. But she does as long as you've got that power in the tail. You keep going up, up with nothing but a little aileron throw to keep the wings steady. Then you're at seventy-six thousand and the rockets sputter off."

"It's perfectly quiet?" Sarah said.

Billy nodded. "You've left the world. There's only this blue-black sky and you and the plane. You feel her vibrations as if they're happening in your own body. At the same time you're incredibly aware of your body. As if it's part of the inside of the plane. You can feel every cell, every muscle, every ounce of fluid. They're awake, alive in a different way inside you. Everything you see is somehow more intense. Black is blacker, white is whiter. You feel like you're on the edge of the unknowable."

"You're not afraid?"

Billy's voice almost faded against the desert wind blowing at the gate, the bubbling water in the pool. "Fear seems independent, a ghost sitting on your shoulder. It doesn't belong to you anymore. You don't feel the slightest concern for the future. Everything is now. Nothing has any meaning but this experience. The stuff on the dials, the rocket pressures, the altimeter, the angle of attack light, are meaningless. You stop worrying about everything. You have this feeling that no matter what the dials say, the ship is going to keep flying."

Billy reached out and took her empty glass. "That's what I want us to have tonight. An experience like that."

For a moment Sarah was afraid. She banished it. She breathed Billy's courage, his faith in surviving the unknown. Her dominant emotion remained curiosity. Billy had not mentioned the word *love*. She wondered if this was a new kind of man she was confronting, a being indifferent to old ideas and feelings.

"First a swim," Billy said. He stood up and began undressing. Zip, flip, he was naked. His penis was a long dangling tube. "Come on," he said, lifting her to her feet. Unbutton, zip, slip, and she was naked too. Billy picked her up and walked slowly down the steps into the pool.

The water was incredibly cold. He lowered her into it and let her go, then dove deep beside her. She watched him swim underwater to the other end of the pool, each stroke a smooth flowing motion that shot him forward in the green depths. She dove and imitated him. Water flowed against her breasts, thighs. Up she came, gasping for breath. He drew her to him, his hands moving casually around her body. "Isn't this great?" he said.

He kissed her, his tongue crowding her mouth. She moved against him in the bubbling water. It *was* great or at least exotically different. What was she feeling? Sarah told herself to stop worrying about it. This was a man, a pilot, this was California, the beginning of her flight into unknowable freedom, into becoming a grown-up American woman. She was a being unto herself, Sarah, neither Chapman nor Morris. She was severing all the connections here, all thoughts and feelings for parents, husband, daughters.

They swam to the other end of the pool and Billy carried her to a chaise, where he carefully toweled her dry. "Are you using a diaphragm?" he said.

"Yes."

"Take it out. What we're going to do was designed by God. He didn't factor in diaphragms."

She went into the bathhouse and removed the diaphragm. Returning, she walked toward him with a lightness, a fearlessness, that amazed her.

Billy drew her down on the chaise and began playing with one of her nipples. Then his hand traveled down her body and grazed the hair on her mons. Again and again the tips of his fingers, then his palm, passed through the hair, producing shivers of pleasure in her belly and thighs.

"Hair is an extension of the skin," Billy whispered. "Do you like that?"

"Yes," she said.

"I think you'll like this even more."

He wet his fingers with his own saliva and began caressing her clitoris. "Just let go, stop thinking about everything," he said. "You're a woman, that's all you need to know. This is what makes you happy."

Waves of warmth began surging through Sarah's body into her throat. She began to sigh and shiver against him. "We're only at thirty thousand feet," Billy said. "We haven't even fired the rockets yet."

He began sweeping the inner wall of her vagina with his index finger, stopping at various points that seemed to treble the pleasure pounding in her body. "Oh," Sarah cried. "Do that again. Again!"

"That's the Grafenberg spot," Billy said. "He was one of the pioneer sex pilots."

Curving across her mind like a shooting star was the realization that Billy was flying her, she was his plane. But it did not matter. She was past caring, past thinking, all she wanted was more of those knowing fingers. "Don't look at me, just look at the stars," Billy said.

He took her hand and wrapped it around his penis. It was huge, pulsing. She gazed into the night sky while pleasure cascaded through her body. She was coming. It had been a year, perhaps two, since she had an orgasm with Cliff.

Billy scooped the creamy ointment from her labia and spread it across her lips. "Ambrosia," he said. "The food of the gods. You want some of mine?"

A stream of clear fluid was oozing from his penis. It was not semen. She did not know what it was. She took some on her fingers and put it in her mouth. It had no taste.

"It's coming without coming," Billy said. "It takes will-power—and practice."

His forefinger was still moving deep in her vagina, his thumb was stroking her clitoris. Now his tongue was in her mouth, then curling from her nipples down her breasts. "I think you're ready. You must have been in the mood. I've never seen anyone climb so fast," he said.

"Yes, yes, ready," Sarah gasped.

He lifted her on top of him and his penis filled her with new pleasure and something more profound, a sense of absolute surrender to every motion, every touch. Her whole body was in orgasm now. Her thighs, her breasts pulsed, a mist enveloped her eyes.

"Let go, let go of everything," Billy said and began moving inside her, each thrust sending new pleasure surging through her body and mind. There was no longer any distinction between these two realities. Sarah had receded from Chapman and dismissed Morris. She was in a world of pure feeling where only Billy McCall, the spaceship of her body beneath his hands, was real.

Billy was coming now too, she could feel the vibrations in his chest. Both his hands were on her breasts, massaging them firmly, steadily. He smiled up at her from the level chaise. "Isn't it great?" he whispered in the same low intense voice he had used describing his flight in the rocket plane.

He drew her down for a kiss that consumed her. His penis moved up her vagina as his tongue filled her mouth. In slow, careful syncopation they reversed again and again. Sarah began leaving the world. Her eyes saw nothing but the black sky and its infinity of stars. She was up there with transcendent beings, beyond fear and anxiety, soaring through the night on a fuel she had never encountered before. "Now," Billy said. "Now. Are you ready?"

"Yes, yes, yes!"

He came with a shuddering growl, clutching her breasts, holding her at arm's length, simultaneously apart and together, a new kind of human vehicle. Sarah vanished in this final eruption. There was no self at this altitude, only woman, man, primary words, primary beings. Again and again and again Billy came until the green water in the pool, the stars above it vanished in a wild wish that it would never end. She was inside something vast and smooth, a universe of black satin and simultaneously outside it, gazing down on the shining pool and their entwined bodies, glowing like

stars. She was nowhere and everywhere, blinded and visionary, forever lost and eternally found to be the woman she
had imagined, brave, proud, free.

When Sarah opened her eyes Billy was lying beside her,
his fingertips moving slowly across the damp hair of her
mons. "Now we glide down in nice, long spirals," he said.
"In a half hour we'll be ready for another swim and a midnight supper."

This time the swim was more dreamlike. They emerged
from the pool, put on terry cloth robes and sat down at a
redwood table behind the chaises. Billy brought cold chicken
and California champagne from the house. "I had a feeling
you were ready for something like that," he said. "After five
years of Cliff."

"Can't we leave him out of it?"

Billy shrugged. "We can try."

He raised his champagne. They touched glasses and Billy
smiled. "Take a look at your eyes," he said.

She examined them in the mirror of her compact. She was
appalled. The lids were a dark blue. They looked bruised.
"They're engorged," Billy said. "That's what eye shadow is
all about."

"How did you find out so much about women?"

"Frank Buchanan taught me most of it. He gave me books
on physiology, sex techniques. It made sense. Before you fly
a plane, you spend a lot of time studying the manual, finding
out how she works, how far you can push the flight envelope.
Why not do the same thing with a woman?"

"That's what we were doing? Pushing the envelope?"
Sarah said.

"We were way up there," Billy said. "I haven't found
many who can go that high. Want to do it again before we
go home?"

For a moment, desire seized her, the stars beckoned. But
Sarah found something in her soul resisting Billy. "Now that
I'm back on earth, I think I'll stay here for a while."

"Suit yourself," Billy said.

He was stunningly, brutally indifferent. There were endless numbers of women out there waiting to be flown. Was

she wrong to let him go? Desire or its echo in memory clutched at Sarah's throat. She was almost ready to change her mind.

"I've never had English pussy before. I'm gonna look for more," Billy said.

He was still smiling but he knew he was hurting her. That meant she had hurt him by saying no. She was glad she had said it. She was almost proud of her power to hurt him. She did not seem capable of arousing any other emotion in him.

Suddenly she wanted to rage at him, fling food and dishes. *I gave myself to you. I gave you everything.* She wanted to scream it in his face. She wanted to run howling into the desert to repent her surrender, to escape the temptation pulsing in Billy McCall's cock. What was happening to her?

She did none of those violent things, of course. A determination to match Billy's cool uncaring produced a frozen politeness. Sarah hated it almost as much as she feared the other impulses. What was she doing? Was she rejecting the greatest love of her life—of any woman's life? Was it waiting behind Billy's smile for the woman who risked everything to penetrate his uncaring?

No, no. It was all insane. What did those warfare words have to do with love? She still believed love was gift and gratitude, sharing and sympathy. For Billy these words did not seem to exist. It was all mockery, skill, daring. If this was the kind of love he found in the sky, she wanted none of it.

And yet, and yet—she wanted it. She wanted that ascent again, that shuddering fulfillment.

They flew back to Los Angeles in the dawn. "How do you feel?" Billy said, as the rising sun burst over the Sierras, filling the sky with vivid red.

"Good," Sarah said. It was defiant. But it was true. She felt good.

"How about a little aerial celebration?"

Billy reached over and tightened her seat belt. Without another word he leaned on the half circle of wheel in his hands and the left wing went down and they went somersaulting over it. Sarah felt all the blood in her body bulge into her face. It seemed ready to explode through her skin. Ahead of them she saw the coast of California rotating like a gigantic seesaw, sliding up and down. Then gravity slammed her against the seat and her heart was being crushed into a small rectangle and her intestines were flattened like ribbons and her thighs stripped of all sensation. Upside down now and slowly revolving with the Pacific sluicing the other way, pouring water over Alaska and the Pole.

"Like that?" Billy said.

"Yes," Sarah said, all defiance now.

They rolled in the opposite direction this time. The San Gabriel mountains crumbled into the illimitable desert and her eyes bulged with gravity. Her teeth were jammed into an eternal grimace. At any moment she thought she might bite chunks from her lungs. A whining roar from beyond the planets filled her ears.

They were level again. "What was that?" Sarah asked.

"Barrel rolls," Billy said.

It was more than a celebration. He was giving her a small sample of what he confronted when he pulled a plane out of a 10 or 11 g dive. He was letting her know his art was written with his blood and bones and flesh. He was revealing some of the things he had omitted in their ascent.

Now Billy was all business, clicking overhead switches and checking dials and talking to air traffic controllers at Los Angeles Airport, scouring the sky for other planes. They landed in the same smooth effortless way without saying another word. He walked her to the parking lot where she had left her car. She offered to drive him to the Beverly Wilshire. He said he would get a cab. They stood there in the rosy light while a DC-6 thundered down a nearby runway.

"Should I call you again sometime?" he said.

Sarah's whole body went hot and cold and hot again. "It was wonderful but—maybe not."

That was a ridiculous attempt at compromise. Say something else, something that will let him call you and somehow give you the right to refuse. But there were no second chances with Billy. "Okay," he said.

He stood there for another moment, the smile not quite as confident, his eyes almost sad. A force more powerful than will or ideas flung Sarah against him. She crushed her lips against that unyielding mouth.

Sobbing, she fumbled in her purse for her car keys. Billy found them for her. "See you around," he said.

FREEDOM FLIGHT

"Will it work in Moosejaw?"

Frank Buchanan's shout made the fluorescent lights in the plasterboard ceiling vibrate. Sam Hardy, the designer in charge of the ailerons on the Talus, trudged out of Frank's office looking as if he would be happy to impale himself on the nearest sharp object. Dick Stone did not know exactly what was wrong but he knew Frank was talking about Moosejaw, Canada, where the temperature was 40 below zero most of the winter. Ailerons had to work in that sort of weather—and in desert heat and equatorial humidity.

It was 8 P.M. and no one in the design department—at least the part of the department surrounding Frank Buchanan's office, where he kept his brightest people—showed any sign of going home. The designers called the area the Black Hole, after the infamous torture site in Calcutta. Some years later, when astronomers used the name for the mysterious time warps in space created by dead stars, the designers said both meanings were true.

Dick sat in his office just beyond this fluorescent-lit arena tapping data into a new machine he had persuaded Adrian Van Ness to buy, a Miller McCann computer. People in the design department used it too. It saved them hours of slide rule computations. That was one among several reasons why Dick had moved his office out of the executive tower to the edge of the Black Hole.

His main reason was his desire to learn as much as possible about the complications of creating a new plane. By now he knew a lot. He understood the perpetual struggle to anticipate problems like the weather in Moosejaw. He saw why there were so many designers needed to back up Frank Buchanan. He created the original concept of the plane. But every square inch of the creature had to be harmonized with the rest of it. A tail, a flap, a window, required hundreds of drawings by teams of men.

Each day Frank held design conferences with the leaders of the teams. There was a standing rule that nothing on the plane could be changed if those whose work it affected had any objections. If the man in charge of the landing-wheel system wanted to extend the struts an inch or two for what seemed to him a very good reason, everyone concerned with that area of the plane had a vote—and it was frequently negative. The resulting brawls could be spectacular.

That was only round one. When the engineering department began changing things, proclaiming this or that solution would not work, a firestorm of rage invariably swept the design department. The test pilots also had their say. Most of the time they complained about the cockpit, which was never designed to their complete satisfaction. Invariably, because Buzz McCall was a pilot, the engineering department backed them up.

Day after day, Dick was appalled to see thousands of blueprints representing ten times that many man-hours dumped in wastebaskets. Wind-tunnel tests, using scale models, often forced rude reevaluations on everyone, designers and engineers. These were the "unknowns" that only became apparent once a plane was exposed to some of the stresses it faced in the sky. When the real thing began to fly, there were likely to be more shocks—"unk-unks"—the unknown unknowns that revealed hidden flaws in the design or unidentified forces in the sky.

But no one in the Black Hole, even those who got the Moosejaw bellow several times a day, really complained. Frank Buchanan was working longer hours than men half his age. His enthusiasm for the Talus, his vision of a new kind of plane that would surpass in efficiency and safety everything now in the air, galvanized everyone.

Dick's telephone rang. "This is Kirk Willoughby," a voice said. "Remember me? The company sawbones? You haven't sent me that memo on the Honeycomb Club."

"I don't get it. Are you working for Dr. Kinsey on the side?"

"Just collecting opinions, pro and con. Believe it or not, some people think we ought to shut it down. They're afraid to say it in public because Buzz McCall will call them pansies. I'm also worried about its effect on the women. A lot of people have been getting letters from someone who calls herself Califia. She sounds a bit homicidal to me. We'd have a hell of a mess if someone got murdered and the tabloids got their hands on the story. Can't you see the headlines? Cost plus sex at Buchanan Aircraft."

Dick hung up and computed his latest cost projection on the Talus. It was so appalling, he decided not to show it to Frank Buchanan. It would only trigger another tirade on the futility of predicting costs on a radically new plane. At 10 P.M. Dick left the designers burning the midnight fluorescence in the Black Hole and drove down the boulevards to his one-bedroom apartment in Manhattan Beach.

He had moved into the Villa Hermosa, a complex of three-story buildings a few blocks from the ocean. Most of the residents were airline pilots, stewardesses, and middle-level aircraft company executives. Almost all were single. Dick was amazed by the offhand way everyone slept around. Sexual liberation pervaded all branches of the aircraft business.

As he drove through the warm California darkness, the cool sea wind caressing his face, Dick felt desire gathering in his belly, crowding his throat. Cassie Trainor would be waiting for him beside the pool tonight. For the past six months he had been sharing Cassie with Cliff Morris. That meant she agreed not to date anyone else from the Honeycomb Club.

For the first three months Dick had liked it. Cassie just seemed to want to screw. That was all Dick wanted to do too. He did not want to think about it. He wanted to enjoy this strange new world of sexual freedom on its own terms. Cassie was tireless. If he wanted to do it two, three, four, five times a night she was perfectly agreeable. She was always ready for one more. "Come on, go for the record," she would whisper mockingly. "Show up the Big Shot."

That was her nickname for Cliff. She had begun to talk about him and other members of the club. It broke Dick's concentration on pure physical pleasure and made him think about the whole arrangement. He was not interested in going for records or showing up his friends. Some members apparently thrived on this sort of stuff.

Dick changed to bathing trunks and found Cassie lounging beside the pool, the social center of the Villa Hermosa. She was listening to a TWA copilot describe his latest narrow escape trying to land in Pittsburgh or Chicago or Raleigh. "The fog was so goddamn thick the propellers sliced it like it was sausage meat. We had enough ice on the wings to throw a skating party—"

"Wait'll you see the Talus," Dick said. "No worries about ice, ever again. We've got heating coils in the wings that melt it at the flip of a switch."

"Is that supposed to excite me?" Cassie drawled. She was wearing a blue lastex two-piece bathing suit. The bottom half was cut to the minimum, making her long tawny body resemble a Modigliani painting.

"I thought heat excited you," Dick said.

"Just about anything excites Cassie," said Sue, a Pan American stewardess who was currently sleeping with the copilot. She was a honey-blond with a hefty wide-waisted torso and good breasts.

"What excites you?" Cassie said. "A full planeload of ginks lookin' up your dress?"

"No," Sue said.

"Then shut up about what excites me."

"Sorry," Sue said.

"Maybe you excite me," Cassie said. "Maybe that's where I'm goin'."

"Not tonight, I hope," Dick said.

She looked at him with surprising distaste. "No. Not tonight," she said. He realized Cassie was drunk. It was not the first time she had showed up this way. But it was the first time booze had not put her in a good humor.

"I think I'll take a swim," Dick said. He did two laps in a lazy Australian crawl. "Come on in," he called to Cassie.

She was still working on Sue. "Why the hell don't you get a job where you get paid for doin' it?" she said. "That's why you're on the goddamn plane but they don't pay you any real money for it."

"I think you ought to try diddling yourself for a change," Sue said.

With a lunge worthy of an offended tigress, Cassie raked Sue's face with her nails. The stewardess screamed and fell into the pool. Cassie dove on top of her and held her head under the water. "Hey, you're drowning her!" the bewildered copilot yelled and leaped on top of Cassie to rescue his girl. After a lot of thrashing he managed to pry her hands off Sue's throat.

"Get her out of here," Sue screamed, clutching her bleeding face.

Appalled, Dick led Cassie to his apartment. "What the hell is the matter?" he said.

"Nothin'. Nothin' for you to worry about," Cassie said. She pulled off her bottom, slipped out of her top and stood there, hands on her hips, naked. "Let's do it," she said.

"Wait a minute," Dick said. "Wait a couple of minutes. I'm not exactly in the mood after seeing you practically commit murder."

"Ain't that too damn bad. I thought you were a war hero. Forty-nine missions with the Big Shot? Why should you be bothered by a little friendly killin'? In case you're interested, this is my forty-ninth mission for the Honeycomb Club. I've been keepin' a record. Maybe you've noticed I'm kind of interested in records."

"I have noticed that," Dick said. "But something's gone wrong. You were flying high until tonight."

"How the hell would you know?"

"I guess I wouldn't. I thought you didn't want to talk about anything."

"I don't," Cassie said. "Let's fuck. I'm ready when you are."

It was the first time Dick had heard a woman say *fuck*. It only confirmed how disturbed, maybe crazy, Cassie was. "I'd like to know what's wrong first."

"Nothin'!"

"That's obviously bullshit."

Cassie walked over to the window and stared down at the pool. "It's a sort of anniversary. But I can handle it."

"What happened?"

"I met somebody three years ago today. He broke my goddamn heart. That's all. You don't care. You'd rather have it without any heart. Isn't that what all you bastards want? A nice smooth fuckin' machine?"

"I thought if you liked it and I liked it—"

"What's there to like? After the first couple of dozen times you start to feel dead down there. You start to feel death creepin' up through your whole body. Pretty soon you actually want death to show this certain bastard what he's done. You know he doesn't care but that doesn't matter. You think maybe it'll make him care—and that's all you want."

Cassie started trembling from head to foot. "Hey," Dick said. "Hey." He put his arms around her. "Hey, listen. It isn't that bad. It can't be that bad."

Cassie had crossed some sort of boundary. She had exceeded some sort of tolerance in her soul. For a moment he wondered if she was Califia, the woman who had sent threatening letters to half the executives at Buchanan. "Listen," he said. "We don't have to do it. Let's just lie down and let me hold you for a while."

He led her into the bedroom, his arm around her waist. It was strange. He did not have an erection. Until tonight, he could not look at Cassie naked without getting aroused. Touching her stirred instant desire. Was it all in his head? Dick wondered. Was the other Cassie, the fucking machine with the blank smile and mocking eyes, an ultimate expression of male freedom? While this Cassie, a woman in pain, was something else?

They lay down in the double bed, face to face, his arms

around her. Gradually Cassie stopped trembling. But her tears continued for a long time, a silent bitter stream, eventually soaking the pillowcase. "Why did this guy break your heart?" he said.

"I don't know," Cassie said. "I don't think anybody ever knows till it happens, do they?"

"That's the way it works in novels," Dick said. "But in real life we usually get some warning signals and back off."

"Is that supposed to make me feel better? Tellin' me it's my fault?" Cassie said.

"I don't mean it that way. I'm trying to help you think about it. Look at it objectively."

"Just hold me. That helps more than anything."

They lay there, listening to laughter and shouts and splashing from the pool. Airline people lived on such crazy schedules, there were swimmers at all hours of the night. Often Dick was awakened at 3 A.M. by water polo contests between copilots and flight engineers, with stews cheering on the sidelines.

"Are all Jews this nice to women?" Cassie said.

"I don't know. I sort of doubt it," Dick said.

"You're the only one I've ever met this close. I never saw one in Noglichucky Hollow."

That was Cassie's Tennessee birthplace. She often compared it to Al Capp's Dogpatch. "Why did you leave that garden spot?" Dick asked.

"The only man I cared about got killed in the Pacific. He was a strafer pilot. You ever heard of them?"

"Sure."

"Bravest of brave. Not like you Eighth Air Force cowards bombin' from twenty thousand feet."

"We had some worries at twenty thousand feet. Focke-Wulfs and Messerschmitts," Dick said.

"That's why this other guy broke my heart. He was a strafer pilot too. I guess I thought I was sort of touching Joe. Then I found out all he wanted to do was fuck me silly. Jesus."

Dick held her a little tighter, trying to say he was sorry.

"You don't give a damn about all this. Why're you listenin'?"

"I like you."

"You mean you like to fuck me."

"I like to do that too. But I like you for other reasons."

"What are they?"

"You're honest. You say what you think."

"I don't, most of the time. Tonight it all came out."

"That's still worth a decoration. People aren't brave all the time."

"I like you too, Dick."

"Why?"

"Because you listened tonight."

Cassie began kissing him. Sad, gentle kisses at first, her tongue just touching his lips. Her hands roved his body with the same melancholy tempo. He let her make all the moves, sensing that she wanted to offer herself without immediate response from him. Soon her lips and her tongue began following her hands. She licked him like a cat, sighing, occasionally weeping.

He began to swell. Desire throbbed in his chest. But it had a different timbre. There was an ambiguity in the center of it. Part of Cassie's soul was reaching out to his soul in the California darkness. From simple screwing they had come to that perilous word, *like*. It was an unknown in the magical freedom of the air fraternity. Were there unknown unknowns waiting over the horizon, hidden in words like love?

"Oh. Oh," Cassie sighed as he entered her. "Oh Dick."

It was the first time she had used that name. Until tonight she called him Stone or when she was feeling wry, Mr. Stone. He liked it. He liked the tenderness, the sadness that was intertwined with the pleasure. He liked the sense of entering a new dimension with this woman. Was it another stage of California freedom or the beginning of its loss?

"Oh now, Dick, now, come now," Cassie whispered.

It was the first time she had spoken to him about her desire. It was the first time he had thought about coming as something more than a physical release, a nice climax to the athletic performance. He came and came and Cassie melted in his arms. She cried out with a wild compound of pleasure and sadness and triumph. Had he somehow helped her to escape the hollow in which she had been trapped by war and grief? Dick did not know. He only felt a kind of awe at the unknown through which they were both moving.

For a long time Cassie lay in his arms, silent except for deep, slow sighs. Then she said: "I don't want to see the Big Shot anymore."

"So? Tell him. Isn't that the way the Honeycomb works? You're free to say no."

"He won't like it. Especially if I stay with you. He'll hold it against you."

"Maybe you ought to get the hell out of that club," Dick said.

"Why?"

"Because you're too smart. You can't not think about it."

Cassie chewed on that for a while. "Yes I can," she said.

Was he disappointed? Dick wondered. Or relieved? "Tell Cliff. I can handle him if he gets sore," Dick said.

"Good luck. Do you want to see me again, in spite of my persistence in whoriness?"

Dick sensed he was being tested. "Yes," he said. "If you feel the same way."

"Call me when you're ready," Cassie said.

The next morning, after Cassie departed for her own apartment a few blocks from the Villa Hermosa, Dick wrote a memo for Dr. Kirk Willoughby.

The first time I went to the Honeycomb Club I felt like some rich boys had invited me into their secret tree house. It was full of expensive toys you could not find anywhere else. They told me I could do anything I wanted with these toys. After all, a toy can't feel anything. The other day a surprising thing happened. One of my toys started to cry. Now I'm not so sure I want to play at the Honeycomb Club any more.

HOME TO ROOST

Sarah Morris went through the routine of mothering her two daughters, assisted by fat, earnest Maria, her Mexican maid. But Maria, the children, the house, the sunbaked streets of south Los Angeles, remained unreal. Again and again she was with Billy McCall at 81,000 feet, on the edge of the unknowable.

Perhaps the most curious thing was the disappearance of her rage against her husband. Was it some kind of ultimate sexual contentment? Or was it the satisfaction of revenge?

She did not know the answer. She only knew she alternated between being curiously happy and desperately unhappy. The happiness seemed to seize her spasmodically, when she least expected it—when she was giving the baby a bath or reading a book to her older daughter. *Happy.* A voice seemed to whisper it from a distance, almost mockingly—but not quite. Billy?

After lunch, the sleepless night caught up to her. She toppled into bed and found herself wide awake. She went over and over the scene in the airport parking lot until she convinced herself Billy was going to call her again. She told herself she did not want him to do it. The next moment, the thought of his voice on the telephone made her body dissolve. If it wasn't love, what was it? Lust? She had been taught that lust was vile, ugly, brutal. What she had felt with Billy had been none of those things.

What was it? She had to give it a name. She finally called it freedom. She had done something daring—more daring than marrying Cliff Morris in war-torn England. There was more courage in her heart than she had suspected. Why did she like that idea? Was she a test pilot by temperament? A test pilot of the spirit?

For the first time she faced the truth about the night Cliff had been reported missing over Berlin. She had wept briefly in her mother's arms. But in her heart she had been secretly relieved, she had felt an awful shameful gratitude. Tama and Billy were right. Why not admit it to herself? She had married a war, not a man, and she had been glad she did not have to spend the rest of her life with him. What kind of a woman was she?

English pussy, Billy whispered mockingly. He was hateful. But fascinating. Who knew what ideas he would bring back from 90,000, 100,000 feet?

She got up without sleeping, put on lipstick and went shopping for groceries in one of the new supermarkets. More American freedom. A thousand choices and no one telling her what to buy. What had she bought in the desert? Infidelity as a way of life? Could she become Billy McCall's mistress?

She sensed something special had happened to him too. Perhaps that was part of his anger. He hated the thought of a woman having power over him, even the power of giving him pleasure.

Pleasure. *Pleasure*. The word was inadequate. All the words in Shakespeare's language, her mother tongue, were inadequate to describe what she had found in the American desert. She was a *wanton*. She was a *bitch*. All the words she had read in books and never dreamt of possessing were suddenly part of Sarah Chapman Morris's American self.

What about love? What about that supreme value in every woman's life? Was it possible that Billy loved her? Was there a moment in a man's soul when pleasure crossed some boundary into love? She knew so little about how a man thought and felt. Cliff was still mostly a mystery to her.

Back in the house, she noticed an anxious look on Maria's face. "You hoosban', he call. Be late," she said.

"Don't worry about it," she said. She had not expected Cliff until tomorrow.

Maria hesitated. "He call—this morning too. I no tell you."

"That's all right," Sarah said. Sometimes Maria was too

conscientious. She was so anxious to do everything right. It was almost embarrassing, the way the Americans had made the Mexicans so humble. It reminded her of stories she had heard about native servants in Kenya and India.

She ate dinner and watched television for a while. It was all so stupid—grinning game-show hosts and comedians telling fourth-rate jokes. She turned it off and read *Pride and Prejudice* for the third or fourth time. She adored Jane Austen's prose. It reflected the English world her characters inhabited, also so controlled and measured. While this American world seemed to have no visible boundaries, no signposts or rules.

At ten o'clock she turned on the television news. A handsome talking head told her about American plans to counter the threat of Russia's possession of the atomic bomb. Then came a commercial featuring dancing soup cans. Then the talking head again reporting "another tragedy in the Mojave." A Buchanan Aircraft experimental plane had crashed, killing its three-man crew. A previous model of this top-secret bomber had plunged into the desert six months ago.

A half hour later, Cliff's keys jingled in the front door. The sour look on his face was predictable. "How are you?" she said, kissing him briefly on the mouth.

"Lousy," he growled.

"I just heard the bad news—another crash."

"Yeah."

"Will they scrap the program?"

"I don't know. What've you been doing?"

"Baby tending. House running. A big market for my services."

"Is that all?"

"What else do you think I might be doing?"

"Fucking someone!"

It was the first time he had ever used that word in front of her. The first time she had ever heard it, except once, by accident during the war, when she had overheard two pilots using it.

"I really don't know what you're talking about," she said. "I got back from the Mojave this morning. I called the house. Maria gave me some bullshit story about you staying with friends."

Maria had been trying to warn her.

"I—I had a call from an old school chum. She's in town doing a movie. We sat up so late talking I decided to stay with her rather than drive home half-asleep."

She could not believe the intensity of her deceit. She launched it without a moment's hesitation. Why didn't she just tell him she was playing the infidelity game? Remind him it was the twentieth century.

"What's her name?"

"I don't ask you these questions."

"What's her name?"

"None of your business!"

It was outrageous. She hated him. He was invading her desert idyll with his vulgar jealousy. "Let me rephrase the question. What's *his* name?"

"Billy McCall!"

She did not see the hand. It seemed to come from nowhere. He seemed to be standing too far away to hit her. But the hand came whirling to smash her in the face and send her hurtling across the living room. Her head struck the rug with a terrific thud and she lay there, unable to move, engulfed by a new emotion: shame.

She had known from the moment Billy propositioned her on the dance floor. She had known by the pool in the desert. This was the one man her husband could not tolerate as his rival. Cliff's choked raging words were superfluous. "Anybody else—I wouldn't give a fuck—anyone—anybody."

He stood over her, berserk. She wondered if she was about to die. She felt strangely indifferent to that possibility. She almost welcomed it. Would it even the score for her unholy gratitude at the news of his death over Berlin?

That had been a sin. It was a sin to secretly rejoice over the death of a man she had promised to love. She had sinned again last night with Billy.

She wanted Cliff to hit her again. She would welcome a beating that would reduce her to a pleading blob. It would clean her slate, it would leave her empty and calm in another kind of freedom, the opposite of Billy's soaring. The inward calm of the penitent prisoner in her cell.

Something completely unexpected began to happen. Her husband was kneeling beside her, saying "Oh, Oh, Sarah. Oh Jesus, Sarah." He picked her up and carried her to the couch.

Something even more amazing began to happen. Kneeling beside the couch, Cliff began blubbering. Tears and sobs. This six-foot-four hunk of masculinity was crying like a two-year-old.

The room was still spinning. A shrill telephone seemed to be ringing inside Sarah's head. "Stop. Stop, please," she said. "You hurt me so much I just wanted to hurt you back."

He wiped his streaming eyes with his handkerchief. "My career's going down the tubes with that goddamn plane. Isn't that enough hurting? Were you going to tell me he's better than I am?"

A terrible understanding gathered force in Sarah Chapman Morris's soul. Part of it was guilt, part of it was painful wisdom. This tower of male muscle and bone, this Charles Atlas who could knock a woman twenty feet with a swing of his mighty arm, was a psychological ninety-seven pound weakling. In a world without a sense of sin, it was still possible to acquire a misshapen soul.

"He isn't as good," Sarah said. "The whole thing only made me realize I love you. I was sorry I tried it."

She was saying farewell to ascent, farewell to little deaths on the edge of the unknowable. Farewell to Billy McCall, who thoroughly deserved it. She hoped it would be a long time before he found someone able to climb as fast. She was accepting a substitute for love—pity.

No. That was too brutal. She was going to create a different kind of love, a blend of sympathy and nostalgia and honor. Especially honor. That was the best part of it. She had made a pledge to this man in the country church outside Rackreath Air Base in 1943. She was honoring that pledge now—with this lie.

It was better than Billy's way, better than his uncaring freedom. Sarah had to believe that part of it. Billy did not care. If Billy cared she was forever undone. She was still

enough of a romantic, enough of a Catholic, to disapprove
of uncaring freedom, in spite of its enormous temptation.

Cliff was carrying her upstairs to their bedroom. It was a
sad parody of Billy carrying her into the pool where she had
been baptized in his new lonely faith. Her husband was
pressing a cold washcloth on her face. "I didn't mean it," he
said. "I was out of my mind."

It poured out, his fear and hatred of Billy, the certainty
that he was going to resign from the Air Force eventually
and join the company, where he would have Buzz McCall's
backing—and Frank Buchanan's. Adrian Van Ness would
die or retire and Billy would demolish his boyhood enemy.
"All my life I've tried to be nice to the bastard. He goes right
on despising me."

Sarah tried to convince her husband he was allowing himself to be haunted by a myth. "You have more brains than
he has, more personality. He can only do one thing. Fly a
plane."

"In the business we're in, nothing else matters."

"He could get killed next week."

"He won't. The bastard's got a charmed life."

"So do you," she said. "Forty-nine missions. Doesn't that
prove something? You're lucky too."

"You're not lying? He wasn't better?"

"I'm not lying. He wasn't better," she said, the edge of
mockery enabling her to tell the lie without a tremor. "I
wouldn't have done it if you hadn't made me so angry about
other women."

Romantic in spite of everything, she was still yearning for
fidelity. "You don't know what it's like in this business—
people think you're queer or henpecked if you walk away
from it."

He was his stepfather's son. Buzz McCall had put his mark
on Cliff Morris as profoundly as if he had implanted him
with his genes. Why wasn't Billy marked in the same way?
Where did he get that incredible desire to explore the unknowable? Why was he so endowed with freedom and its
corollary, courage?

While this man, her husband, chased women into bed because he did not dare to defy the conventions of the plane business. For a moment an awful sadness sucked at Sarah's soul. She was learning too much. She wanted to drown her mind in blankness. She resisted the impulse. She was not going to despair. She had proven to herself and Tama that she had willpower. Now she would prove she had another kind of power. If Tama could change herself from a Mexican washerwoman's daughter into Adrian Van Ness's mistress, maybe Sarah could change Tama's son from a spoiled play-boy to a serious husband and a successful executive.

"I want you to walk away from it for my sake," Sarah said. "I want you to promise me you'll try. If you want my love, you've got to make that promise."

There was a long silence. Was he saying farewell to some-one he cared about? Someone he loved more than this de-manding English bitch? "I promise," Cliff said.

She kissed him and began unbuttoning his shirt. "Do you want me?" she whispered.

"Yes," he said.

Were they crossing a boundary? Sarah wondered. One of those unmarked American zones just beyond the erogenous where love began? She could only hope so. "I want you most when you want me," she whispered. "It's like music. Two instruments playing. You meant so much to me in England. Make me feel the same way here in America."

They were both naked now. Cliff's fingers were deep in her English pussy. Sarah's breath came faster and faster. My God, maybe he *was* better than Billy! She kissed the pulsing tip of his penis, something she had never done before. Will-fully, powerfully, she rolled him onto his back and mounted him, a position they seldom used—and never on her initia-tive.

Cliff rotated his palms on her nipples until they were as erect, as erotic as his penis. "You've been my luck from the start," he said. "No matter what I did with anyone else, she never meant anything to me. You're the only one I ever cared about."

Some antenna in her mind, perhaps stirred by a tremor in his gaze, made her suspect that was a lie. But it was a loving lie. As loving as the lie she had told him about Billy. It was enormously confusing. Love on a bed of lies.

"From the start I saw us as a team," he said, stroking her as he spoke, sending surges of pleasure through her body. Sarah summoned pity, she summoned hope. "We are, we are," she said.

From somewhere deep in her soul a caustic voice whispered. *You'll do your part. He won't even try.* Was it Billy McCall? Go to hell—or heaven—you smiling bastard, Sarah replied while her husband clutched her to his chest and came with a shuddering rush.

Power. The word whispered in Sarah's soul. She had just exercised, demonstrated, her power over this man. He had prostrated her with a swing of his mighty hand. Even that humiliation had become part of the power she had just acquired. Sarah lay in her husband's arms wondering if once a wife tasted such power, she could ever let it go.

"By the way," Cliff said. "You're not sending those letters to Tama, are you? The ones signed Califia?"

"No."

"They're driving her nuts."

Good, Sarah thought, delighted to hear her chief rival was faltering. Was she on her way to becoming an evil woman, in spite of her repentance? Life in America was incredibly complicated.

VORTEX

High above the Mojave Desert, a new version of the Talus roared through its latest tests, looking more than ever like an illustration from a science fiction novel. The entire plane was now a wing. Not a trace of a fuselage remained. Around Cliff four Air Force generals shook their heads in disbelief. "Give me three hundred copies and the Russkies won't say boo for twenty years," one said.

Three hundred copies at a million a plane was three hundred million dollars. With spare parts and the usual overrides in a cost-plus contract, they were talking about a half billion dollars. Cliff Morris, project manager of the Talus, could claim a lot of the credit for pumping that much money into Buchanan Aircraft. It was incredible the way his life had turned around in the last three months.

In Cliff's mind it was all connected to an amazing event. He had fallen in love with his wife again. The feeling seemed part of a current suddenly swirling through him and around him since their night of rage and reconciliation. Everything had been clicking, flowing, flying.

Frank Buchanan had switched to jet engines and solved most of the Talus's stability problems. The plane zoomed through one checkout after another, demonstrating speed, maneuverability, endurance—and its greatest asset, its phenomenally low drag-to-weight ratio. No other plane in existence could match it as a weight lifter.

The rest of Cliff's life seemed to reshape itself in the same magical way. A nervous Cassie Trainor told him she did not want to see him anymore. She was going to move in with Dick Stone. Two months ago he would have been furious. Now he just patted her on the behind and wished her well.

Sarah had shut off that stupid phonograph. She said she wanted to make her own music. She greeted him every night with ravenous eyes. After they made love they lay in bed, talking about the company, his ambitions, the Talus, Frank, Buzz, Adrian. He told her everything.

Sometimes she helped him see things he had missed. Mostly she told him how good he was at this project manager's job. He was good at bridging gaps between people. Maybe it was because he was big and looked like he had the answers. People trusted him. He was a war hero.

Each day he went to work without the old crawling anxiety in his belly. It was amazing. Was Sarah some sort of sorceress? At times the wartime hunch that she was his luck swelled to cosmic proportions. She was his guide, his priest-

ess, his goddess. The boyish devotion he had once felt for
his mother was transformed into something close to adoration of his wife.

There was only one thing wrong. Up there at the controls
of the Talus was Billy McCall. Every time Cliff saw him, a
flicker of his old fear revived. Beneath the fear was a cold
unforgiving rage. It was one thing to play sex games with
chippies like Cassie Trainor. Billy had seduced his wife. Yet
Cliff had to pretend he knew nothing about it, he had to go
on exchanging jokes and taunts with Billy in the same old
way.

Billy was flying the plane that could make Cliff the crown
prince of Buchanan Aircraft. Sarah told him again and again
that this was cause for glee, not grief. But something dark
and sullen at the bottom of Cliff's soul refused to accept it.
He did not want Billy McCall to give him anything, even by
accident. He did not want to owe even a shred of gratitude
to the arrogant bastard.

Sarah did not understand how men hated each other. How
deep it went, how impossible it was to forgive because to
ask it or offer it would be a confession of weakness. He could
forgive her, of course. He had forgiven her as she had forgiven him for that murderous slap.

Down, down came the Talus in a beautiful approach, not
a hint of a yaw or a wobble. The tires kissed the runway as
lightly as the wheels of a Piper Cub. It was hard to believe
they were watching a thirty-ton plane carrying eight tons of
simulated bombs. Cliff thought ruefully of how many times
he had thumped the *Rainbow Express* onto the runway at
Rackreath.

The generals murmured admiringly. Buzz McCall and
Frank Buchanan accepted another round of congratulations.
Cliff could see nothing but Billy and Sarah on a couch or
bed somewhere engulfed in a green mist. The gleaming silver
plane, the empty mocha desert, the distant mountains, vanished. He stood there, paralyzed until General Scott clapped
him on the shoulder.

"You ready to do some selling in Washington? We'll back
you with everything we've got."

"You bet," Cliff said, his tongue thick and dry in his mouth. He watched Billy taxi smoothly down the runway toward them. In a moment he was climbing out of the plane with his copilot and flight engineer. "The thing flies itself," Billy said. "You just got to tickle its clit now and then."

Inverness flowed on the old SkyRanger they flew back to Santa Monica. As far as they could see, the Talus was as good as sold. "I gottta hand it to you, wingman," Buzz McCall roared, holding out his glass to Frank Buchanan. "I thought it was a piece of fucking insanity the first time I saw it but you've made me a believer."

"I couldn't have done it without you. Without all of you," Frank said. He lurched down the aisle to pound Billy on the back. "Without this pilot at the controls."

He thumped Cliff's shoulder. "Without this *executive* pulling it all together. Adrian thought we were going to fall on our goddamn faces. Didn't know we were a family! Band of fathers—and brothers."

Frank whacked others on the back too. One of Buzz's engineers, Bruce Kelly, who ran things at the Muroc end of the line, designer Sam Hardy who had solved all sorts of problems with the Talus's ailerons. Dick Stone, who had made the cost estimates low enough to keep Adrian at bay. Frank talked exultantly of getting to work on an airliner version within six months.

"That's when we're really going to start lying about costs," he chuckled, winking at Dick.

They were so high on Inverness and anticipation they barely noticed when the plane landed at Buchanan Field. They piled out and gazed at a satisfying sight on the flight line. No less than nineteen copies of the Talus roosted there, some ready to fly, others waiting for the jet engines Frank had persuaded the Air Force to let them try.

"Let's head for the Honeycomb and pick out the best pussy on the list," Buzz said.

"Why not?" Billy said.

"Why not indeed?" Frank said.

Cliff took a deep slow breath. "Sorry," he said. "I've got to get home."

Buzz could not believe his ears. "What the fuck? Have you gone queer, Big Shot?"

"No. Married," Cliff said. "I've gone married." His face was flushing. His whole body felt like it was melting. Billy McCall was grinning at him.

"What's wrong? Afraid you're going to draw Califia?" Buzz said. Everyone had decided one of the girls at the club was Califia. Buzz liked the idea of screwing a woman who might murder you before it was over. He said it was better than stunt-flying.

Cliff struggled for breath. He could handle Buzz. If Billy said something he was going to knock him into the Pacific Ocean. "You're absolutely right," Frank said, squeezing his shoulder. "I wish I had a wife to go home to."

"I was going to let you try Madeleine tonight. That's how good I'm feeling, Big Shot," Billy said.

"She's all yours," Cliff said.

"I'm worn out. I think I'll head home too," Dick Stone said.

"Jesus," Buzz said. "Respectability is spreading like a fucking plague. Let's get the hell away from these pansies."

Cliff realized Frank and Dick Stone had tried to help him. It was a small comfort. He drove home in a daze. Had he really done it? Had he made a total asshole of himself for Sarah Chapman Morris's sake? Buzz would never let him forget it. Billy would be telling him all about Madeleine's cries and sighs for the next month. He must be going crazy to let a woman—a foreigner who knew absolutely nothing about Americans—mess him up this way.

He parked the car in the driveway and trudged slowly across the lawn to front door. Sarah met him just inside, her eyes shining. "I hope you've got good news," she said.

"Pretty good," he said.

"Mine is very good. I'm pregnant."

It was the current again. Carrying him in the right direction. His response came from somewhere outside his mind. "It's going to be a boy."

"I'm sure of it too."

They made the tenderest love of Cliff's life that night. Sex

had never been tender for him. He never thought of women
as fragile. He liked them big and muscular. Maybe it was
because there was so much of Tama—and he saw it all in
the Redondo Beach house. Sarah was fragile, especially that
night. She was like a precious object, a vase or a statue that
a harsh touch could smash.

He did not even want to do it at first. "I'm afraid I'll hurt
the kid," he said.

"You won't. I want you. I want you more than ever."

He rested her on top of him again. It was beautiful and
slow and almost sad. He kept thinking of what Billy was
probably doing with Madeleine, what Cassie Trainor might
be doing for Dick Stone. Why couldn't he have both worlds?
Why was Sarah inflicting this choice on him? For a moment
wisps of the green fog drifted through his mind, he saw her
with Billy. But he concentrated on loving Sarah, on the current that was carrying them both toward some sort of special
happiness.

Afterward they talked about the Talus, the hopes it was
igniting. The day after tomorrow Billy was going to fly it to
Washington. Adrian Van Ness and the top people from the
project team were going to join him there and display the
plane to senators and congressmen. The Air Force was going
to back them with all the influence they could muster.

They could not fail. The current was irresistible now. Cliff
rubbed Sarah's stomach and said: "What'll we name him?"

"It's your choice if it's a boy."

"Charles. But I'm going to call him Charlie."

Princess Elizabeth, England's future queen, had just
named her first son Charles. Tears streamed down Sarah's
face. "Oh Cliff, I do love you. No matter what happens in
the future, let's never forget these three months."

"Don't worry about the future," Cliff said. "It's going to
get better and better."

Sarah sighed. "You Americans are all such optimists."

The next day, the chill in that comment made it difficult
for Cliff to share the ebullience of the Buchanan team on the
flight to Washington. Over the Rockies, he noticed Adrian
was not joining the celebration. He sat alone, looking out the

window of the Lockheed Super Constellation.

"What's the boss worried about?" Cliff said, sitting down beside him.

"The usual thing a boss worries about. Money,"

"Won't this contract take the pressure off?"

"It would—if we get it."

"Is there any doubt? Our only competition is that ridiculous B-36. The other day General Scott called it a B-29 with elephantiasis."

The boss managed a smile. "Maybe I'm worried about the government's overall policy. It doesn't seem to have one. We're drifting from event to event. While the Communists take over huge chunks of the world."

"Like China."

Adrian nodded. "The Democrats will never recover from that one unless they do something dramatic with the defense budget. Stay sober when we get to Washington. Talk to people your age—majors, lieutenant colonels, congressional aides. Sometimes they know more about what's coming than the people at the top."

"Sure," Cliff said, flattered that the Adrian was confiding so much to him.

They landed at National Airport and ensconced themselves in a pair of suites at the Shoreham. The next day at Muroc Billy climbed into the jet-engine version of the Talus and streaked across the nation in four hours and twenty-five minutes. He came within twelve minutes of breaking the transcontinental speed record, which had been set by a Lockheed P80A "Shooting Star"—a fighter plane.

Billy roared over Washington and landed at Andrews Air Force Base in Maryland. The afternoon papers carried pictures and front page stories. The next day, President Truman inspected the Talus and remarked, "This looks like one hell of an airplane. We ought to have some."

Everyone at Buchanan could almost hear the rustle of money. The Air Force announced it was interested in buying four hundred copies. That would put the contract close to a billion dollars. At the Shoreham, Billy was the center of a nonstop party for senators and congressmen from the armed services committees, Air Force generals, and Pentagon officials.

Cliff remembered Adrian's orders to stay sober and listen. Standing with two Air Force lieutenant colonels, he heard one say: "this thing fits beautifully into NSC 68."

"What's that? A new way to sink the Navy?" Cliff asked.

The Navy and the Air Force had been battling ferociously over their share of the budget in the consolidated Department of Defense. The lieutenant colonel grinned and shook his head. "Top secret for the time being. We're still putting it together. A new policy statement."

They flew back to California that night. On the plane, Cliff told Adrian about NSC-68. "Interesting," Adrian said. "NSC stands for the National Security Council. It's one of Truman's better ideas. They're supposed to advise the president on defense policy—instead of letting a lot of kitchen cabinet pals make up his mind for him, Roosevelt-style."

In California, the ebullience continued to build. Buzz McCall drew up plans for rehiring 20,000 workers. Frank Buchanan put the design department to work on converting the Talus to an airliner. Jet engines still guzzled too much fuel to make a commercial plane profitable. They would have to go back to props, which meant a lot of expensive changes. Jim Redwood talked to Cliff about joining him in an expanded sales department as second in command.

The Air Force continued to test the Talus at Muroc. Other pilots found it a difficult plane to handle. Perhaps they lacked Billy McCall's skills—or his determination to make the plane perform for Frank's sake. There was a third crash, killing another three-man crew. But three crashes were not considered excessive for a radically new plane. Frank was sure another redesign of the ailerons would solve the problem.

One hot day in June of 1950 Cliff was summoned to Adrian Van Ness's office. He charged up the stairs wondering if the good news from Washington had finally arrived. The CEO was standing at the window, looking down on Buchanan Field, where nineteen completed copies of the Talus now sat on the flight line. "I've got a little present for you," he said.

He handed Cliff a check for a thousand dollars. "A bonus for staying sober in Washington and hearing about NSC 68. It's the most important state paper since the Monroe Doctrine. It proposes a policy to deal with the Communist threat. It's what they call a forward strategy—a network of bases around the world that'll support our allies and enable us to meet a Soviet challenge wherever and whenever it appears. Do you see why that could be very important to Buchanan Aircraft?"

Cliff nodded. "Air power. That's where we're ahead of the Russians. Most of those forward bases will be for planes. We'll need fighters to defend them, transports to supply them."

"Exactly," Van Ness said. "After I finished reading NSC 68, I slept for eight hours. It's the first time I've done that since the war ended."

Adrian moved some papers around his desk for a few moments. "But it doesn't mean our worries are over."

He moved a few more papers. "How's the Talus doing? Buzz tells me you've still got those stability problems."

"Frank thinks he's got them licked."

"I want the reports on it. All of them. Don't say anything about this to Buchanan."

There was a hostile sound to the way he used Frank's last name. "Why not?" Cliff asked.

"Because you just got a direct order from me not to," Adrian said.

"What's going on?"

"A lot of things I can't explain to you."

"Mr. Van Ness—Adrian—" Cliff was never sure which name to use. "I think I'm entitled to an explanation. I've put a year and a half of my life into this plane."

"If we don't get this bomber off our backs, we'll have to lay off three or four thousand people—and you'll be one of them."

"I thought it was worth a billion dollars if the Air Force

buys it!" Cliff gasped, trying to comprehend what Adrian was saying.

"The powers that be in Washington, in particular the Secretary of the Air Force, don't want to buy it. They prefer Convair's B-36. Do you know who Floyd Odlum is?"

"He's head of Convair."

"The Secretary of the Air Force vacations regularly at his house in Palm Springs. Consolidated's going to build the B-Thirty-six in Texas. The Speaker of the House of Representatives, Sam Rayburn, is from Texas. One of the slickest, crookedest operators in the U.S. Senate, Lyndon Johnson, is from Texas. They want that billion dollars to go to Texas, not to California."

"Why the hell should we let them do that, if their plane isn't as good as ours?"

Adrian Van Ness smiled briefly. The flash of bitter humor exposed Cliff to a world of power and intrigue that he barely knew existed. "I've been told by the Secretary of the Air Force, personally, if we encourage our friends among the generals and pilots to fight for our plane—and they could fight very effectively—we'll never get another contract from the Air Force or the Navy or the Marines. We'll be back to trying to sell planes to airlines that don't need them."

"So you're going to give the Secretary the stability reports and he can use them to beat the Air Force generals' brains in when they complain?"

This time Adrian Van Ness's smile was almost pleasant. "I begin to think I haven't misjudged you after all, Cliff."

"Yes you have. I don't buy it. If Frank knew about this, he could fight back. He could give them data that proves we've solved most of the problems. Or will in a couple of months."

"That won't do him or you or me any good. It will just make the blood flow on both sides. Consolidated has the votes—in the Pentagon and in Congress. What is there about growing up in California that makes people so naive?"

Cliff felt a flush of anxiety and humiliation. Adrian was talking to him as if he were a child. Cliff heard Buzz sneer *momma's boy.* "I'm trying to educate you, Cliff. You could go a long way in this company," Adrian said. "We need someone with a good personality and no moral principles worth mentioning."

Cliff tried to choke down that compliment. It was so oblique, it was not easy to get down his throat. He gulped and gulped, trying to make excuses for Adrian Van Ness. Maybe if you were born rich it was hard to treat people as equals. Maybe it had something to do with graduating from Harvard.

"It's for the good of the company," Adrian said. "It's even for Frank's good. He's got years and years of planes to design for us."

"But he loves this plane," Cliff said. "It's the most original thing he's ever created."

"Frank gives every plane that ultimate rating. He tends to think in extremes. You have to learn to use people like him. And people like Buzz, for that matter."

With an inrush of regret Cliff realized Adrian Van Ness had him figured exactly right. He would do this rotten thing. He would help Adrian sabotage the plane Frank Buchanan had worked on day and night for eighteen months. He would betray a man who had been his second father and friend.

Why? Was something missing inside him? Was this another moment of truth like the one over Schweinfurt? Cliff twisted away from answering that question. Courage had nothing to do with it. Adrian was right. It was for the good of the company. He was bending before the power of the Pentagon and Congress and making Cliff bend before his power. That was the way power worked.

For a moment Cliff thought of Sarah and the current of love that seemed to be carrying him toward some special happiness. What did that mean now? "Get moving," Adrian said. "I need those stability reports before the end of the day."

Cliff nodded obediently. He was being sucked into a vortex that swirled invisibly around Adrian Van Ness the way knots of force swarmed around a wing and fuselage in flight.

He had watched them testing models of the Talus in the wind tunnel, charting these vicious unpredictable unknowns. He had learned a lot about building airplanes in the last eighteen months. Now he was learning how they were destroyed.

LAYING ON OF HANDS

Dick Stone sat before his computer putting together a cost estimate for redesigning the Talus as an airliner. Frank Buchanan burst into his office with a painting of the plane soaring over the Rockies. "We need a new name for it," he said. "Something dignified—but with commercial appeal."

"How about the Aurora," Dick said. "Didn't Moon Davis say it took him back to the dawn of flight?"

"Wonderful!" Frank said, whacking him on the back.

Frank wandered around the Black Hole, showing the painting to everyone. He returned to tell Dick the name had won unanimous approval. "Now all we've got to do is sell it to Adrian Van Ness. He thinks naming planes is his prerogative."

About a half hour later, Cliff Morris dropped into Dick's office. "How's it going?" he said.

"Great," Dick said. "I'll have an estimate for the airliner version ready by the end of the day."

Cliff closed the door. "That may be premature. We're having some problems with the bomber. It takes more than a good design to sell a plane to the government. We need some help from you."

"Who's *we*?"

"Adrian Van Ness and your old buddy."

That was supposed to impress Dick and to some extent it did. "We want you to revise your cost estimates on the Talus," Cliff said.

"Scale them down to the minimum?"

"No. Raise them to the maximum."

"What the hell's the point of that?"

"Look. Trust me. I can't explain everything right now. A maximum evaluation would be very helpful with the problem we're having."

"How about a minimum explanation, at least?"

"It's—it's got something to do with keeping Congress happy. Adrian wants a high and a low so no one will scream if we come out on the high side. Don't mention it to Frank. He won't understand the politics. It'll only upset him."

Dick put together an upscale cost estimate that brought the Talus close to two million dollars a copy. It was not hard to do, since Frank was still grappling with some unknown unknowns in the plane's controls. At lunch the next day, Adrian Van Ness smiled arcanely at him and squeezed his arm. "I appreciate that estimate," he said. "It's nice to have another realist at work around here."

Dick did not get the point but he nodded and smiled back, not inclined to dispute a compliment from this WASP, which for him at this point meant White Anglo-Saxon Paragon.

At home, he continued to enjoy Cassie Trainor. She was still working at the Honeycomb Club, playing a defiant game with him, daring him to love her in spite of her refusal to take his advice. He played the game right back, dating other women whenever he felt like it. He was not quite ready to love Cassie but he liked her more and more. She entertained him with impersonations of horny airline passengers and panting Buchanan executives. Cassie had developed a contempt for the male sex that was invigorating, as long as it did not get personal.

On weekends, they did not see as much of each other because Dick spent Saturday and Sunday in the air with Billy McCall in his dark green Lustra I. Billy had been surly at first. He made it clear that he was teaching Dick to fly strictly as a favor to Frank Buchanan. Like most pilots, he had a low opinion of navigators, except when he needed one. Frank had apparently told him it was important to keep the computer guru happy so he would send Adrian Van Ness only soothing reports.

Billy loved flying too much to remain surly in the air.
From the start he taught Dick the way Frank Buchanan had
taught him. Frank called it the laying on of hands. For the
first several hours Dick simply kept his hands on the yoke
and imitated everything Billy did, while he explained it. By
now Dick had mastered taking off and landing and other
elementary maneuvers, such as the turn and the climb and
the dive. Today they were going to explore something more
ambitious: spins.

Ten miles at sea, Billy began his lecture. "An airplane is
a three-axis all-attitude vehicle," he said. "It can be flown in
any attitude accidentally or on purpose. I want you to be able
to fly this baby upside down, in an inverted spin if necessary.
I want you to be able to handle every kind of spin in the
vocabulary."

He proceeded to put the plane into an oscillatory spin, a
translational spin and a flat spin, which Dick later learned
was usually fatal in a single-engine plane. Each time they
pulled out with Dick's sweaty hands on the yoke and numb
feet on the elevators while gravity threatened to pound his
chest cavity to jelly.

Returning to the Buchanan airport, Dick made a classy
landing, lining up the plane in the middle of the runway in
spite of a tricky crosswind. Billy pushed back his fifty missions cap and socked him on the shoulder. "You're ready to
solo," he said. "Only thing left to discuss is philosophy."

"What do you mean?"

"What you believe is up there in the sky. You think there's
a Big Air Traffic Controller who's gonna take care of you
when you get your ass in a tight spot?"

Dick shook his head.

"You don't think there's anything up there?"

Dick nodded.

"You're wrong," Billy said, staring at the northeast runway, where a blue Cessna was taking off. "There's two ladies
up there. The Lady of Luck and the Lady of Death. They go
for some guys, no one knows why. Sometimes guys go for
them. No one can figure that one out either. Except they're
both beautiful."

The Cessna's right wing dropped alarmingly. The pilot was obviously a student. Billy paused while the instructor jerked the plane level and climbed for survival. "Sometimes you can feel the Lady of Death's hands resting on top of yours on the throttles. The Lady of Luck just watches and smiles. Pretty soon you figure out she doesn't give a damn. Only thing to do then is laugh in both their faces."

Billy smiled bleakly and socked him on the shoulder again. "Now you're ready to go. Take her down to Laguna and back," he said. "Keep an eye out for other planes. They'll be a lot of them around today."

The Lustra was a very forgiving plane. It lifted off the runway as if it were part balloon and in ten minutes Dick was at five thousand feet, about five miles off Long Beach. He looked around him and felt a loosening in the center of his chest.

Freedom! He could go north or south, climb into that azure sky or dive toward that dark blue sea. He could loop or roll if he had the nerve. The sky filled his eyes. He owned it. He owned that burning sun and that iridescent blue dome, he owned the ocean and the coast line with its thousands of little houses and tiny boats in narrow harbors. He even owned that big-bellied Southwest Airlines DC-3 plodding toward him en route from San Diego to San Francisco or Seattle.

Dick banked and dove and climbed. He did not try any loops or snap rolls or immelmans. He was an unstable mixture of courage and caution. Having seen a few planes crash, he knew how dangerous flying was. The stunts could wait for a little more confidence.

Closer to shore, he swooped low enough to watch the surfers riding the big waves. He wondered if he might see Cassie. She often surfed at Laguna. Sure enough, there she was. He recognized the streaming auburn hair, the long lithe body swaying on the board as it slithered and bounced down the almost vertical incline while the white mountain of water crested just behind her.

That did it. Dick lowered the nose, picked up speed and

hauled on the yoke to climb into the blank blue sky and go over the vertical into his first loop.

Cassie recognized the plane. She paddled out on her board and stood up to wave. Dick did three snap rolls and came out of the third one with the nose much too high. He was within a whisker of stalling into a probably fatal spin at five hundred feet.

Sweating, he roared up to a thousand feet for another loop and a few chandelles. He was on his way to becoming the hot pilot of his repressed dreams. Screw those punctilious medical bureaucrats who had turned him into a navigator because he had astigmatism in one eye! Dick Stone was flying in California.

Back at the airport, Dick's landing was not quite so classy. The crosswind was blowing harder and he almost hit the runway with his left wing. He pancaked to safety. Billy frowned but the Lustra was undamaged. He signed Dick's log book and they adjourned to a nearby bar to celebrate.

Billy drank hard as usual. He was in a lousy mood. "You know Sarah, Cliff's wife?" he asked.

"Sure."

"What do you think of her?"

"Nice woman. Smart."

"How's she put up with him? I mean—do you think she really loves him?"

"I don't know," Dick said, his loyalty to Cliff tying his tongue. "Women are funny about that sort of thing. You have some reason to doubt it?"

Billy shook his head. It was hard to tell whether he was saying yes and it did not matter, or no and he did not care. Dick wondered if there was a third possibility.

He drove home in a boozy glow, hoping Cassie would be there to help him celebrate his first solo. Not only was she there, she had a bottle of champagne in a bucket and frosted glasses in the freezer.

"How did you recognize the plane?"

"I've flown in it," she said.

"Oh."

Cassie smiled mockingly. "Jealous, Mr. Stone? I can't believe it."

"Curious."

"It didn't work out. I didn't want to fly as high as Billy likes to go."

Dick decided it was none of his business. "You'd rather hang around with a nice, unimaginative front-office man? Dull, normal sex once a week?"

"That's right," Cassie said. "I hate excitement."

He started undressing her. She was only wearing shorts and a pullover shirt. In ten seconds she was naked. Dick ran his hands down the firm breasts, the supple belly, into the warm luxurious pussy. "You're a bitch," he said. "Why the hell do I like that sort of woman?"

They spent most of Sunday in bed. Dick drove to work in a state of semi-exaltation. Was he falling in love with Cassie? She was unquestionably American. You could not get more American than Noglichucky Hollow, Sevier County, Tennessee.

He put Cassie out of his head and looked forward to telling Frank Buchanan about soloing. He was pretty sure Frank would tell Buzz McCall at lunch. He wanted to see the surly surprise on the SOB's swarthy face when he found out the navigator had turned pilot.

Dick never got a chance to say a word about soloing. When he walked into the design department, the place looked like the mental ward at the county hospital. People were tearing up blueprints and cursing and pounding their desks and glaring out the windows as if they might jump, even though they were on the first floor. "What's wrong?" he asked.

"They've canceled the Talus," Sam Hardy said. "The fucking Secretary of the Air Force awarded the contract to Convair's B-36. It's the goddamndest decision I've ever heard. Even the Russians can build a better plane than that lumbering behemoth."

"Where's Frank?" Dick said.

"Upstairs arguing with Adrian Van Ness. Trying to keep something alive."

Dick wondered if his cost estimate had anything to do with

the disaster. Had he exaggerated too much? Where was Cliff Morris?

Frank appeared in the doorway to the corridor with tears in his eyes. "It's all over," he said. "Not only have they canceled our contract. They've ordered us to destroy all nineteen of the prototypes we've built. Today. They want them chopped up by sundown. They want all the tools, jigs, designs destroyed. They want to wipe the Talus off the face of the earth. Adrian's surrendering to the slimy bastards. For the good of the company."

"Why?" Dick said, more and more appalled at what he may have helped to do. "What's their reason?"

"Stability problems. Somehow they've gotten their hands on our internal reports. Did you ever give them to anyone, Dick?"

"Never."

"No matter. It's easy enough to rifle files at three A.M. Adrian may have done it himself. He's perfectly capable of it."

Frank turned to his demoralized staff. "I'm quitting. I don't intend to spend the rest of my life designing planes for lying politicians to destroy. I advise you gentleman to imitate my example as soon as you can afford it."

"Wait a second, Frank," Dick said. "We're not going to let you do this. There's a hundred other planes waiting for you to design."

Emotion drained from Frank's face. "That's what Adrian just said."

"Dick's right, Frank," Cliff Morris said. He threaded his way through the empty desks. "Adrian's right too, even if he is an SOB."

Frank found it hard to believe Cliff was defending Adrian. "Cliff, you're hoping Sarah will have a son, aren't you?"

"Sure."

"If he does, you'll love him in a special way, won't you?"

"Sure," Cliff said, growing more and more uneasy.

"You'd be in despair if he were killed?"

"Of course, but—"

"This was my son."

"I'm quitting with you," Sam Hardy said. "We'll start another company." Dozens of similar declarations swept the Black Hole.

"Let's do some drinking on my expense account before we go," Frank said.

The designers departed for the Honeycomb Club. Dick wandered into in his office and discovered Cliff was there waiting for him. "Do I get the maximum explanation now?" he said.

"The problem didn't go away. We—we never had a chance," Cliff said.

Dick stared at his blank computer screen. Things began coalescing in his head. "Especially after you gave Adrian all the reports about the stability problems and my upscale cost estimate."

"Dick. You've got to be realistic. This is a business, not a goddamn experimental flight laboratory. Adrian's traded that plane for a promise of an order for two hundred Excaliburs, redesigned as troop and cargo transports. So Frank's heart is broken for a while. He'll get over it."

A week ago, a month ago, Dick Stone might have nodded and agreed with these words. But something remarkable had just happened to him. He had become a pilot. He had learned to fly in a plane designed by Frank Buchanan. He had been taught by a pilot who had learned from Frank by the same mystic laying on of hands.

"I'm sorry. I don't like the sound of that. I don't know exactly why."

"You better learn to like it if you want to keep working for Adrian," Cliff said. "He wants you to wipe out everything you've got on the computer about the Talus. Then we'll go to work on my files."

"No!" Dick smashed both his fists down on the desk. "I won't do it. I won't let you do it. Don't you have any appreciation for this plane? What it means—not just to Frank but to the whole history of flying?"

"I appreciate it as much as you do," Cliff said. "But I appreciate keeping the goddamn company in business too."

"I'd rather stand on Hollywood and Vine with a tin cup."

"That won't be necessary," Adrian Van Ness said.

He paused in the doorway, smiling sardonically. "Maybe Dick is right," he said to Cliff. "We'll just pretend to destroy the files. We'll tell the SOBs in Washington we've wiped them out to the last comma. What's another lie in this messy business? We've got an underground vault we built during the war in case the Japs bombed us. We'll put them there. But you both have to promise me not to tell Frank Buchanan. As far as he's concerned—the wipeout was total."

"Why?" Dick asked, not even trying to conceal his contempt.

"You can't trust an emotional basket case like Frank."

Slumped on the couch, Cliff nodded wearily. Adrian Van Ness turned to Dick. How did he know he was vowing to tell Frank Buchanan the truth? "You agree, Dick? Or would you prefer an actual wipeout?" Adrian asked.

Adrian's smile made everything perfectly clear. He was the man in charge. Dick nodded numbly. Now he knew what Frank Buchanan meant about making noble promises when you worked for Adrian Van Ness.

Was this a second laying on of hands? Not if he could help it, Dick vowed. In his head a voice whispered: *What do you think of California freedom now?*

TRIO IN BLUE

She had lost him, Sarah thought, watching her defeated husband slouch across the lawn to his white Buick convertible. The destruction of the Talus had ruined something less visible but far more important between her and Cliff. She had failed to comfort him, reach him, last night as they made love. She was four months' pregnant. But that had not made the difference. She felt a new—or old—distance between

them, a strange, almost bitter withdrawal to the status of perfunctory husband again.

An hour later, helping Maria hang the wash in the back-
yard, Sarah was startled by a swooping plane. She looked
up in time to see the green Lustra zooming straight up into
the blue sky and tipping into a loop that turned into a spin
that flowed into a half-dozen snap rolls.

How did Billy know? She watched him inscribe himself
against the sky like the rhythmic line of a modern abstract
painter. Intricately doubling back on himself, exploding into
effervescent heaps of loops, he wrote coded messages in lazy
barrel rolls and unbelievably intricate inverted spins. It was
painting and music combined in a dance of death-defying
skill. She could almost hear the orchestral crescendos as he
stood the plane on its tail, its back, its wingtips. She saw
him at the controls, gravity pounding at his chest and brain.

Sarah wanted to be with him. She wanted to share the
danger and the exaltation. But she knew she could only do
it by calling that scribbled number on the card Billy had
given her five months ago. He would never call her. He
would only send her this coded declaration of his mastery of
the sky. A terrible sadness seeped into her soul.

Cliff Morris and Dick Stone spent the day storing the records
of the Talus in the underground vault. They did not have
much to say to each other. There was no trace of Frank
Buchanan or his designers, which added to the sense of desolation as they collected blueprints and reports and stuffed
them into boxes.

That night Cliff called Sarah and told her he would be
working late. He and Dick Stone went looking for Frank
Buchanan. He was not at the Honeycomb Club. In fact, no
one was at the Honeycomb Club. The place looked as if it
had been hit by a couple of fragmentation bombs. A tearful
Madeleine, wearing slacks and a sweater, told them the designers had started a brawl with the engineers that wrecked
the place.

Madeleine said Frank and Billy McCall and a half-dozen
designers had left there last night so drunk they could hardly

walk but they insisted on driving Frank's Ford. She hoped they were not dead at the bottom of one of Topanga's ravines.

They took Madeleine along and drove to Frank's house in Las Tunas Canyon, several miles north of Topanga. They found their heroes were not dead but were all drunker than they had been the night before, if that was possible. Cassie Trainor and a half-dozen other women from the Honeycomb Club were trying to console them.

Cliff accepted some Inverness and told them he and Dick had stored the records of the Talus against Adrian's orders. "Who knows what'll happen in the next couple of years? Adrian might change his mind. Or a new secretary of the Air Force might decide to go for it," he said.

Cliff looked steadily at Dick Stone, waiting to see if he would let him get away with the lie. He said nothing. Was he here for the same reason? To regain a few shreds of his manhood?

"Your loyalty is touching, Cliff," Frank said. "But nothing can alter the fundamental facts. Our plane is lying in pieces in some junkyard in El Segundo or Long Beach. Getting drunk is the only sensible response. Join us."

He refilled Cliff's glass to the top with Inverness. Across the room, Cassie Trainor smiled at him. She had her clothes on. But Cliff's imagination undressed her in a flash of desire. He was quite certain that if he drank this Scotch and joined the party, Cassie would soon be wearing nothing and so would he.

In another flash Cliff saw Sarah mounting him. He saw the delight in her eyes, the pleasure of being on top, in control. Was that where the current had been carrying him? She was no longer his magic princess. He was here to regain another kind of current, the sense of being a man among men, even if they were writhing in defeat. A man who fucked beautiful women for consolation. Cliff began drinking the Inverness.

Night and day blended with music and laughter and a trip to Malibu Point, not far from the mouth of Las Tunas Canyon, where Cliff and Billy demonstrated the art of riding killer waves and several designers who tried to imitate them almost drowned. Cassie was also very good on the board. "How about riding something else for old time's sake?" Cliff said.

"Sure," she said, smiling past him at Billy.

After a lot more Inverness, Cliff and Dick joined the designers in a vow never to work another day for Buchanan Aircraft Company. Cliff was pretty sure no one would remember it when they sobered up.

Much, much later, Cliff was on a bed with Cassie. She was telling him he was better than Billy while his hand roamed her auburn pussy making her laugh and sigh. They tried it in every position and she liked it more and more. He was so drunk he could keep it up forever. Finally she was on top, crying *Oh Oh Oh* with each thrust.

In a flash Cassie changed from a laughing, drunken dream girl riding up and down on Cliff's equipment to Sarah with sadness in her eyes. In another flash Sarah went from sad to witchy, to the snarling, whining, jealous wife of a year ago. Who had done it? Who had switched the reel and changed this movie from a farce to a possible tragedy? Who had changed Cliff Morris from a drunken bachelor to a louse of a husband?

Frank Buchanan was standing beside the bed, telling Cliff to go home, it was all right for a bum like him to live this way but Cliff had a wife, children. Behind Frank, Dick Stone stood in the doorway with a frown on his face. Was he sore about Cassie? Was he telling him to listen to Frank?

Frank. There was only one thing to do. He had to confess what he had done. He had to tell him. Cliff shoved Cassie aside and sat up, almost weeping. *I looted the files. I gave them to Adrian. Without telling you.* But another face in the doorway stopped him before he could speak.

"Pops is right," Billy McCall said, his arm around Madeleine. They were in bathing suits, just back from another swim at Malibu Point. "You got to man the home front, Big Shot."

"Home front?"

"While we bachelors go fight another goddamn war."

Billy flipped on the radio beside the bed. An announcer began babbling about an invasion of South Korea by North Korea with thousands of tanks and planes. American planes were trying to help the South Koreans. President Truman had announced the United States was going to support them with everything in its arsenal.

Madeleine and Cassie started to cry. "Come on," Billy said, putting his arm around both of them. "It isn't so bad. I can't wait to fly a jet in combat."

"We don't have a decent jet fighter," Frank said. "Nothing that can handle MIGs, if the Russians come into the war."

"Get to work, Pops," Billy said. "Don't let Califia jinx this one."

To everyone's astonishment, Frank started to weep. "I'll try, Billy. I'll try," he said.

Cliff drove home in a daze to find an enraged, almost hysterical wife. "Where have you been? I called your office and they said no one had seen you for two days."

"I was with Frank Buchanan. He's coming apart over the Talus cancellation. I was trying—"

He realized the impossibility of telling Sarah the truth. She would forgive nothing—neither the betrayal of Frank Buchanan nor the betrayal of her with Cassie.

"Trying what?" Sarah cried.

"Honey, listen, calm down. You're upset about this thing in Korea. Unless it turns into World War III I'm not going to get drafted. A war's good for the plane business. We'll do okay. We'll be fine."

"I'm not upset about the war. I don't care whether you go or stay," Sarah said.

"In that case maybe I'll go," Cliff said.

"I take it back," Sarah said. She clung to him, sobbing. "Oh, Cliff, I need you. I need you so much."

It was the first time she had ever used that word, need. It made Cliff wonder what had happened to his wife during the two drunken days he had been trying to regain his manhood.

Dick Stone drove slowly home to Manhattan Beach with Cassie Trainor, listening to excited radio newsmen reporting massive tank-led assaults by the North Koreans and the continuing collapse of the South Korean army.

"Are you sore at me?"

"I didn't particularly like finding you in bed with Cliff."

"It was seeing Billy," Cassie said. "I couldn't help it." She stared out at the dark ocean for a moment. "He was the one I told you about—the strafer—on Joe's anniversary."

She was confessing a wound. But Dick was unable to muster any sympathy. The new war was hardening his emotions. He was back in the 103rd Bombardment Group accepting Colonel Atwood's announcement that everyone, even Dick Stone, was going to die.

"I'm tired of what you can't help. Maybe it's time you started blaming yourself instead of God or fate or whatever the hell you talk to in the sky over Noglichucky Hollow."

"Maybe you're right," Cassie said, gazing sadly out at the sea.

"Quit that goddamn Honeycomb Club."

"Then what?"

"I don't know. Go to college, maybe. You can go free here in California."

"What's the point? We could all get blown up tomorrow."

"So what? You go on living the best way you can. You're not doing that. You'd rather feel sorry for yourself."

"I'd rather have you feel sorry for me. But all you do is preach me self-improvement sermons," Cassie said.

"You've got a self that needs improving."

"So do you."

"I know," Dick said, thinking of his surrender to Adrian Van Ness.

The telephone was ringing as they walked into Dick's apartment. It was none other than Buchanan's president, sounding very impatient. "Where have you been?" he said. "I've been trying to get hold of you for hours. Get up here as soon as you can. This war in Korea means we have to move fast."

Dick roared up the coast highway to Buchanan Aircraft's headquarters. Adrian Van Ness was in his office with Buzz McCall. They were both looking angry. "The war means we can bid on a contract for two hundred new transports for the Air Force," Adrian said. "With the Excalibur still in limited production, we're years ahead of everyone. We can convert it overnight. I want you to go to work on the costs. Buzz will give you the data."

"Goddamn it, Adrian, there's more to this than profits," Buzz said. "Maybe we ought to get the Talus back on the burner. We owe it to Frank to at least try."

Adrian shoved papers around his desk. "I don't feel we owe Frank Buchanan anything. He's disappeared for the last three days. Half the design department has gone with him. The rest of them are sitting down there getting drunk on company time. The man is an anarchist. I should have gotten rid of him years ago."

"We're not gonna sell the Excalibur as is," Buzz said. "The Air Force wants more range and speed. We'll have to put those new turboprop engines on it. They're the best thing that's come out of the jet-engine research. We need Frank to design a wing that can handle those engines. You can't get along without him, Adrian. As usual."

For a moment Dick thought Adrian was going to snarl a curse at Buzz. But his voice remained calm. "Then get him back. He'll listen to you."

Buzz lit a cigarette. "Adrian, sometimes I don't think you belong in this business. You don't know how to gamble. When's the last time you flew a plane?"

"I don't know. Nineteen twenty-five, I think. When I left England."

"You should have kept flying. That's the only way to keep the instinct alive. Every time you step into a plane you're riskin' something. You've got to risk the fuckin' company the same way. Bet it on something new out there. It's a sporty game, Adrian. A game for real men."

Buzz blew smoke in Adrian's face. "That flying wing turned out to be a hell of a plane. You never should have let those Texas pricks destroy it. We did something rotten when we let that happen, Adrian."

Adrian's hooded eyes swung toward Dick. He seemed to be saying something to him. Something very confusing. A kind of plea or apology. The eyes returned to Buzz. "I thought you blamed it on your ex-girlfriend, Califia. The one who wants to kill us all."

"She's another reason for fighting back. I can't stand the thought of a dame jinxing us this way."

"You really think they have supernatural power?"

"I don't know whether it's supernatural. But some of them have power," Buzz said.

"I guess I should start worrying. She's writing to me too. Threatening me with all sorts of exotic punishments. Like strapping me to the propellers of an Excalibur and starting the motor."

Buzz did not even try to smile. He took Califia seriously. "Can't security find that dame?" Dick said. In a corner of his mind he was still worried she might be Cassie.

"She's smart as hell," Buzz said. "Mails the stuff from different boxes all over L.A."

"Getting back to the real world—will you talk to Frank?" Adrian said.

Buzz stubbed out his cigarette. "I'll talk to him. Not for your sake or my sake. Those kids flying World War II crates over Korea are gonna need some new planes."

Buzz strode out, slamming the door. It echoed through the empty building as if a bomb had exploded. Adrian Van Ness gazed after him with undisguised hatred on his face. It took him a full minute to control himself. "Get to work, young fellow," he said with a forced smile. "I'm sorry to ruin your evening. Were you involved in something pleasant?"

"I would have been if you'd called ten minutes later," Dick said.

Adrian stared at the door Buzz had just slammed. "We don't have room for sentiment in this business," he said. "I can be as sporty as Buzz at betting the company. But I don't think we should do it if we have a safer choice. Don't you agree?"

This time Adrian was unquestionably reaching out to him, claiming him in some subtle and totally unexpected way. Dick let him know he was not accepting the offer. "I'll get to work," he said.

Four hours later, a weary Dick Stone knocked on Adrian Van Ness's door. Buchanan's president was walking up and down the office, listening to a multiband shortwave radio on his desk. "This is Mercury Two confirming a red alert," a deep voice said. "All leaves are canceled. Pilots will report to their duty bases." The radio added instructions for Air National Guard and Air Force reserve units.

"It's a real war all right," Adrian said. "Truman's sending in a division of infantry. We've already started bombing North Korea. What do the figures tell us?"

"Assuming Buzz's data is correct we can produce two hundred transports at five hundred thousand a copy. We can make as much money on that plane as we could make on the Talus."

Dick's cold monotone made it clear he was still on Frank Buchanan's side. "Put in an expense chit for five hundred dollars for the night's work," Adrian Van Ness said.

Dick drove back down the coast highway in the cool final hour of the night, the war news crackling out of the radio like slivers of steel. There were still a fair number of cars and strollers along the ocean in Santa Monica and Venice. In the Villa Hermosa compound in Manhattan Beach, a volleyball game was going strong in the shallow end of the pool, girls against boys. He looked at the tanned lunging bodies, the laughing faces and wondered how many of the men might soon be dying on Korean hillsides, how many of the women might be weeping in lonely apartments.

In his bedroom, he found Cassie prowling up and down like a caged panther, listening to the radio. "Our guys are gettin' creamed," she said. She was wearing his dark blue bathrobe, a wedding present from his mother.

Dick flipped off the radio. "The hell with it."

Cassie eyed him warily. "You feel like it?"

He nodded. He needed her. He needed the touch of a woman's flesh to defeat the way the new war was restoring the old one to memory. "I'm sorry about what I said in the car. I understand about Joe and Billy. I'm glad you told me."

"It's the war. I feel bad about it too," Cassie said, slipping out of the bathrobe and wrapping her long arms around him.

Suddenly Dick was kissing his ex-wife, remembering what she had meant: life, pleasure, the future, all the things he had consigned to oblivion in order to fly those forty-nine missions without coming apart. He had finally obeyed Colonel Atwood's injunction to think of himself as a dead man. But it had been a hard order.

Now he finally understood. Nancy Pesin had been the resurrection of Richard Stone. Perhaps first he had needed to be reborn as a Jew before he could resume his American journey. Perhaps he had been too cruel in achieving the second birth. But birth, life was full of pain, some of it necessary.

Oh, woman woman woman. He kissed the tears on Cassie's tan cheeks, he plunged his hands deep in her thick auburn hair. She was clinging to him, murmuring: "Dick, Dick, I think I love you. Will you let me love you? Will you try to love me? I'll quit the club. I'll think about goin' to college."

"Good, good," he said, unable to respond with love. Was he clinging to his California freedom? He was beginning to think it was an illusion.

As Dick came he saw Adrian Van Ness standing in a dark corner of his mind, smiling at them. Did those hooded eyes contain some sort of supernatural knowledge or power?

No. He was smiling because the war was going to make Buchanan Aircraft prosperous again. From even deeper darkness, a voice whispered this was wrong. It wounded the intensity of Dick's coming, his taking of Cassie Trainor in the name of many loves. The voice, perhaps also the sum of many voices, won- dered if he deserved happiness as long as he worked for the Buchanan Aircraft Company.

WARRIOR

Frank Buchanan stood beside the single waterlogged bomb-pitted concrete runway that constituted Suwon Airfield, his eyes obsessively scanning the icy blue Korean sky. The runway stood in the middle of a sea of mud. Snow and mud intermingled on the hills sloping down to the field. He felt like a man simultaneously living two bad dreams.

One was his own life, full of anguished yearning for Amanda—and snarling hatred for Adrian Van Ness. Buzz McCall and this new war had lured him back to Buchanan Aircraft. But nothing could persuade Frank to talk to Adrian. That partly explained his inability to deal with the rest of this bad dream—the fear that Amanda was drifting into madness. He knew she was the source of Califia's letters. But he did not know what to do about it. The day before he left for Korea, he had telephoned her. His voice triggered an explosion of rage that left him bewildered and appalled. She seemed to hate him and Adrian with equal ferocity.

The other bad dream was the war in Korea. Unlike the global brawl with Germany and Japan, this was a war about which most of America seemed indifferent. No one gave the men who were risking their lives any glittering slogans, like making the world safe for democracy or fighting for the Four Freedoms. Few reporters got enthusiastic about a struggle that had turned into a stalemate.

Twenty-five miles away, in the front lines along the border of North Korea, a half-million American infantrymen were confronting a million Chinese. Only America's control of the air had enabled the infantry to survive the enemy's overwhelming numerical superiority. Relentless pounding by light and heavy bombers had reduced Chinese supplies to a trickle, leaving them incapable of mounting an offensive.

Most of the planes fighting this crucial part of the war were propeller-driven B-29s and B-26s from World War II. But the decisive struggle for air superiority was taking place far away, along the Yalu River border between Russia and North Korea. Billy McCall was up there now, leading eight F-86 North American Sabrejets from the 337th Squadron into unequal combat with Russian-built MIG-15s. The jet engine was on its way to transforming air warfare—and the entire world of flight.

Each day, the American pilots took off from Suwon and other fields and flew over the desolate mountains and valleys of North Korea to the Yalu. From there, they could look down on hundreds of MIG-15s, parked in gleaming rows beside 7,200-foot-long runways on their airfields across the river. But the Americans could not bomb or strafe them. That might bring on a wider war with Communist China, the politicians in Washington said. As if a million men trying to kill Americans was not a war about as wide as wars could get.

Frank returned to the 337th operations room to listen to Billy and his friends discussing the situation. First came Billy's voice: "This is Black Leader. Thirty-six lining up at Antung."

"Hell, only twenty-four takin' off at Tatungkou," drawled another voice, a Floridian who was Blue Leader, head of another squadron.

"It'll be at least three for everybody," grunted the nasal New England voice of White Leader. "I count fifty at Takushan."

Antung, Tatungkou, Takushan were three of the sacrosanct Chinese airfields. They placed the MIG-15s only minutes away from attacking the B-29s and B-26s pounding the Communist supply lines in Korea. If the MIGs got at these World War II planes, it was no contest. Their gunners could not deal with planes flying at 684 miles an hour, armed with .23- and .37-millimeter cannon. It was up to the American jet pilots to keep the MIGs out of North Korea.

Flying from bases two hundred miles away, the Americans never had more than thirty minutes of fuel on which to fight.

In all of Korea, they only had fifty Sabrejets to confront an estimated five hundred Chinese MIG-15s. In almost every fight, the Americans were outnumbered four or five to one.

Minutes later, the radio erupted with battle language. "Honchos at six o'clock," Billy said. Honchos were MIG pilots who wanted to fight. Everyone was sure they were Russians. Two days ago, Billy had shot one down and proved it. When the pilot ejected, he lost his helmet and his blond hair streamed in the wind.

Then came the fragmented cries and shouts of combat.

"Break left, Black Leader. Honcho on your tail."

"Break right. I got him. I got him."

"Reverse and pick us up at three o'clock!"

Frank was in the swerving, diving, twisting Sabrejet with Billy, feeling the terrific force of 5g turns that can wipe out a man's mind like a blow on the head, swiveling his neck 360 degrees to see MIGs diving on them at seven-hundred miles an hour, cursing the Sabrejets' inability to outclimb a MIG or outturn him above 25,000 feet. Tormented by the exhaustion of taking this high-speed punishment day after day, while the Communists had enough pilots to send fresh teams into the air.

For Frank, worst of all was the knowledge that he could have given Billy a better plane if he had not thrown his heart and soul and the entire Buchanan design department into the dream of the flying wing. He denounced himself as a self-indulgent poseur. He was here to make amends, to find out from the pilots themselves what they needed to restore American superiority in the air.

Frank listened, hungry for the sound of Billy's voice, as the dogfight ended as abruptly as it began. The overall commander for the day's operations reported: "Flights reforming and returning—all MIGs chased across the Yalu." Then Billy came on reporting a rough engine. "I think I've got part of a MIG in there," he said. "He blew up only about two hundred yards ahead of me and I flew right through the debris."

With calm efficiency, he climbed to 40,000 feet and told everyone to relax. He was only eighty miles from the base now and could glide in if the engine flamed out.

Frank hurried to the control tower to watch the squadron land. Billy's wingman, a twenty-two year old from Georgia, did an exultant victory roll before getting into the landing pattern—announcing he had gotten his fourth MIG. Billy had shot down eleven. In a few minutes Billy appeared overhead, coasting serenely, a silver sliver against the blue sky. Behind him came two other pilots making deadstick landings. In five minutes everyone was on the ground, heading for the operations room for a debriefing.

Frank limped after them on his bad leg and listened as Billy described a new MIG tactic. Usually the Communist pilots stayed high to take advantage of the MIG's superiority above 25,000 feet. The Americans had grown used to looking for contrails left by jet engines in the thin upper air. Today the Communists had positioned another squadron well below the contrail height to pounce on the Americans while they were watching the higher trails.

"From now on we've got to keep some sections low," Billy said.

"Does that mean we get one day off every fifth week instead of every fourth week?" his wingman asked.

"It means you're getting up tomorrow to run three miles instead of two."

The pilots ran every day. Like prizefighters, they had to stay in shape to handle the pounding of the g forces. Billy's wingman was notoriously reluctant to take any exercise.

The briefing over, the celebration began. They had downed four more MIGs today. Billy's victory raised his score to twelve—one of the highest of the war. They piled into jeeps and headed for the Korean capital of Seoul, twenty miles away. Frank rode beside Billy, remembering Buzz driving at the same reckless speed to the bars and brothels of Toul in World War I. Planes changed but pilots remained pilots.

Two hours later, in a smoky nightclub known as the Mocambo, Frank heard far more about the Sabrejet and air-to-air combat than he could get in an official briefing. "We need a plane that can let us hunt them instead of the other way around," Billy said.

"We can build one—but it'll be tough to fly," Frank said.

"The wings will have to be even thinner than a MIG's. It'll be a flying gun platform, pure and simple, like the MIG."

"Why don't we have one right now? I thought that's what we were trying to put together in the White Lightning."

"We were—but the Air Force wasn't enthusiastic. Americans are always trying to combine everything in one plane. An interceptor close support attack heavy bomber that can fly around the world without refueling."

"Where the hell did those Russian meatheads get that beautiful MIG airframe, Pops?"

"The same place we got the design for the Sabrejet—from the Germans. They're the ones who proved you needed a swept wing to get a plane above five hundred miles an hour."

"What about the engine?" Billy's wingman asked. "I thought we made the best engines in the world. But those MIGs can just run away from us anytime they feel like it."

"The British make the best engines," Frank said. "The MIG has a Rolls Royce Nene. The Labour government sold fifty-five of them to the Russians in 1946."

"That wasn't too smart, was it," Billy said.

"The British are in a state of mental and spiritual collapse," Frank said. "They've canceled one brilliant airplane after another since World War II ended. They didn't have a plane to put the engine into."

Korean bar girls swarmed around them. The wingman was telling one how he shot down his fourth MIG. She smiled and ordered champagne for both of them. Everyone but Billy had a girl. He glowered at the wingman, who was using both hands to demonstrate the way he dove, upped his flaps and got his MIG as it roared past him.

"I've lost two wingmen so far. I'm gonna lose him too. He doesn't take it seriously up there. Sometimes I think flying these jets should be limited to old crocks like me, Pops. The goddamn things are so fast, they respond to the slightest touch. And there's no sound. The noise is all going the other way. You start to think you're indestructible, like Superman."

"Maybe it would help to have a plane that makes the pilot concentrate on staying alive."

Billy nodded. "I like that idea. Then we got to figure out what to stay alive for. The land of the free and the home of the brave? Seems to me nobody back home gives a shit whether we're living or dying out here."

"Some of us do, Billy. More than you'd think, from the newspapers."

Billy pondered their images in the bar's cracked mirror. He and Frank both looked shattered into a hundred pieces. "How can this be happening, Pops? Explain to me why we're out here with fifty planes fighting the other guys with five hundred and fifty?"

"It's an old American tradition, to disarm after every war we fight."

Billy looked saturnine. He was no longer a boy. He was still a flier, still convinced flying was the only worthwhile thing a man could do. But fighting this war had turned him into a man who was angry at his country. That was a far more dangerous anger than the anger at God that had occasionally flared in his soul in New Guinea. Frank felt the same anger permeating his own soul, inflaming his mind, clouding his judgment.

"If I get through this thing in one piece, I'm gonna do everything I can to make damn sure this doesn't happen again," Billy said. "I'm not gonna salute and say yes, sir to the politicians. I'm gonna say fuck you, sir. I'm not the only pilot who thinks that way."

"Maybe we can team up. If we can design some guts into Adrian Van Ness."

"How are things back at the Honeycomb Club?"

"Not the same since Madeleine quit. They've got a new manager—a dyke who bullies the girls. They don't stay long enough to get to know them. Doc Willoughby's campaigning to close it. He says it's wrecking half the marriages in the company. Where did Madeleine go, anyway?"

Billy ordered another Scotch. It was rotgut stuff, made in Japan. "Good old Madeleine," he said. "She was something."

"Where did she go?"

"You really want to know?"

"Why shouldn't I?"

"Makes me look like a heel, Pops."

"Why?"

Billy called for a pen and scribbled an address. "Go ask her."

Frank hailed a pedicab and the grunting driver dragged him along the freezing avenues to a narrow alley near the city's central market. Frank knocked. The door opened and there stood Madeleine. But it was not the smiling glossy-haired glowing woman who used to greet him at the Honeycomb Club. This Madeleine wore a face dulled by alcohol and unhappiness. "Frank!" she said. "What are you doing out here?"

"Trying to help win this stupid war." He held up the scrap of paper. "Billy gave me your address."

She invited him into a tiny apartment, barely warmed by two laboring space heaters. Moisture oozed from the walls. Dirty dishes and pots filled the sink. "I followed him out here," Madeleine said. "I love him. I thought he loved me. Instead he gave me a thousand dollars and told me to go back on the next plane. I haven't done it. But the money's running out."

She started to weep. "What's wrong with him, Frank? He made me so happy. I thought I made him happy."

"You did. You did," Frank said. "But—"

What? He did not know what was wrong with Billy. Did flying at mach 2 make some men unfit for ordinary happiness? Was Billy living out his brother Craig's dictum on women: they're only good for one thing? Frank no longer believed that. But he had not been able to make happiness with a woman part of his own life. Nor had Billy's other father, Buzz McCall.

Was Billy, in that peculiar symbiosis a son can contract from a father, imitating him and Buzz in a deeper, lonelier way? Marrying himself to the Air Force and a struggle to keep it on the cutting edge of flight, while a swelling bitterness demolished his soul?

"Do you want me? Is that why you're here?" Madeleine said. "He sends people here all the time. I've thrown them all out. But I'll make an exception for you."

Frank took several hundred dollars out of his wallet and crushed it into her trembling hands. "Go home," he said. "He can't help it. Bad things are happening up there in the sky. That's where he lives these days. It isn't your fault."

"I love him, Frank!"

Gazing into Madeleine's once beautiful face, Frank Buchanan had a wrenching intimation that this was not the last time he would hear this cry from a woman trying to understand the mystery of Billy's flight from happiness.

Brill, and several hundred out of it Bel's other two
children. Arthur must internalize Deckard; he was, the
order knew that place in this polity, an intention an eye
Dan Simmons a true that were. It left it your will
love him; bleakly.

Christ, one Ne Bood, a poor sound of one whom Bill,
mean baths withtopang, I sald that this this was now the last
fingers again that they go into a mad man trying to mind
and his sheave of 9HSE Buck hymn forest.

BOOK SIX

BOOK FOUR

SCORPION

Champagne glass in hand, Adrian Van Ness stood in the doorway of the Buchanan Aircraft chalet at the 1955 Paris Air Show watching Major Billy McCall streak overhead in the company's new supersonic jet, the Scorpion. Around Adrian stood a cluster of Air Force generals and executives from Pratt & Whitney, builders of the jet's engine. "That almost makes me wish we still had a war in Korea," one of the generals said. "I'd love to see that thing up against a MIG-15."

Adrian murmured agreement. Everyone declared the Scorpion the most audacious airplane ever built, a marvel of lightweight construction and design. It had already set six world speed and altitude records. It could outclimb, outdive, outturn every fighter plane in the world, sending designers in other companies reeling back to their drawing boards.

Frank Buchanan had created the Scorpion after spending three months in Korea with Billy McCall and other pilots. Unfortunately, the war it was designed to fight had ended. The Communists had abandoned their plan to unify Korea at the point of a gun. The cold war continued, of course.

The Scorpion had also set a record for killing pilots. Six had died in the testing process, exploring what happened to an airframe at Mach 2. Many more had died learning to fly her since she became operational. The Scorpion did not tolerate mistakes. The thin, astonishingly short swept wings had inspired some people to call it a missile with a man in it. A pilot who forgot his flaps on a final turn to land never got a chance to correct his error. An engine failure left the Scorpion with the aerodynamic characteristics of a bathtub.

Although the generals admired the plane, the Air Force was not rushing to buy large numbers of it. Their current order was a puny hundred copies. But Adrian had an answer to that problem: he was selling it to the rest of the free world—with the help of Prince Carlo Pontecorvo.

Ponty had emerged from World War II as a hero of the underground resistance to Naziism. He had helped organize the continental struggle with British guns and money and finally led one of the most successful guerrilla groups in his native Italy. His book, *Code Name Zorro*, described dozens of narrow escapes in night drops, ambushes, and near-betrayals.

While Adrian struggled to keep Buchanan aloft in the turbulent postwar world, Ponty had been absorbed by the fight to beat back communism in Italy and France. He had been a conduit for millions of dollars funneled into the contest by the Central Intelligence Agency to support politicians with the courage to resist Moscow's collaborators. Now, with the left wing thrown on the defensive by the surging prosperity of the 1950s, he was in an ideal position to become Buchanan's roving representative.

Buchanan had brought planes to other Paris Air Shows, of course. It was the preeminent event of the aviation world. Every nation that either made planes or bought them poured into the City of Light for a wild week of partying and dickering and eyeing the competition. Le Bourget Airport became a sort of world's fair of aviation, with the latest model airframes and engines on display or roaring overhead.

Adrian returned to the air-conditioned interior of the chalet as Billy McCall began doing a series of stunts over the field that had the grandstands shouting applause. In a sitting room Ponty was watching Billy on closed-circuit television. With him was Frank Buchanan, Buzz McCall, and florid General Heinz Gumpert, second-in-command of the West German Air Force. "I wish we could get him to train our pilots to fly your plane that way—without fear," Gumpert said.

"It's the only way to fly any plane," said Buzz McCall.

"Especially this one," Ponty said.

Six months ago, Ponty had persuaded the West Germans to buy no fewer than four hundred Scorpions. Harsh necessity had required the victors of World War II to rearm

Germany. Risk aside, it was painless. They had billions in surplus marks from their miraculous economic revival, enough to buy the west's latest weaponry.

Adrian was not especially surprised to learn the deal involved that old reliable lubricant, douceurs. Last month, Ponty had coolly informed him three million dollars should be deposited in a certain Swiss bank. He would withdraw appropriate sums to reward the German politicians and generals who had participated in the decision to buy the planes. The great-grandson of the man who bought up the entire Congress of the United States to build the first transcontinental railroad smiled his agreement. He had brought the money to Europe and dispatched Dick Stone to Zurich to deposit it yesterday.

Adrian's daughter Victoria joined them, wide-eyed at Billy's aerobatics. "He can make that plane do anything!" she cried, as Billy put the Scorpion through a climbing roll with flaps and landing gear extended, no more than a hundred feet above the runways.

"It's not supposed to be able to do *that*," Frank Buchanan groaned.

Now twenty-four, Victoria had not inherited her grandmother Clarissa's regal beauty nor her mother Amanda's winsome femininity. In low heels, she was almost as tall as Adrian. Her Englishy tweeds, a style he currently favored, made her resemblance to him almost dismaying. Adrian told himself there was something plaintive, even appealing about her homeliness. She made no attempt to disguise it with makeup or high fashion. Far more important to Adrian was her intellectual sophistication. She had spent the past four years at Somerville, one of Oxford's colleges for women. She had become a good minor poet and had an admirable grasp of English and American history and literature.

Adrian had sent her to school in England for a number of reasons. The sloppy, sulky postwar California teenager with nothing but pop music and movies in her head had driven him to outbursts of rage. But the main reason had been his deteriorating marriage—and his affair with Tama Morris. Whole weeks passed without him and Amanda discussing anything more significant than the weather. She never displayed the slightest interest in probing his vague excuses for spending two or three nights a week at Tama's Malibu cottage. With Victoria at home, this kind of routine would have been unthinkable.

Victoria was also well on her way to getting her name into Clarissa's will—something Adrian would never do as long as he stayed in the aircraft business. That was another reason Adrian had sent her to England. Victoria, of course, had no idea that she was a weapon in this lifelong power struggle.

On the TV screen the Scorpion was replaced by the plane that was creating an even bigger sensation at this year's show—the jet-powered British airliner, the Comet. It was a sleek swept-wing affair with four Rolls-Royce Avon engines. The pilot made a swooping pass over the grandstand, banked and climbed to 10,000 feet almost as fast as the Scorpion.

As if it were a cue, Clarissa entered the sitting room. She had let her hair go white, which added a grace note to her hauteur. She wore only black suits and gowns now, heightening the play of light on her proud, lined face. "That's the sort of airliner you'd have in production right now, Adrian, if you'd listened to me," she said.

"I told him exactly the same thing," Frank Buchanan said, without turning his head in Adrian's direction. In the five years since the cancellation of the Talus, they had yet to exchange a civil word. Most of the time his chief designer communicated through memos or messages carried by Cliff Morris or Dick Stone.

"Jets guzzle fuel," Adrian said. "The flying public has no confidence in them."

"I'm looking forward to flying on her," Clarissa said, as the Comet continued to perform in the sky above Le Bourget.

"I wouldn't, if I were you," Frank Buchanan said.

"Why?"

"That crash off Calcutta worried me."

"A woman my age doesn't fret about sudden death, Mr. Buchanan. In some ways it would be a blessing."

"Grandmother!" Victoria protested, tears in her eyes.

"I like your mother. She reminds me of my own. Indomitable," Ponty said.

Adrian heard the irony in Ponty's voice. He had met Ponty's mother. She was a dragon in the operatic Italian tradition, an interesting contrast to Clarissa's controlled severity. Women! Incredible how they haunted a man's life.

The sale of four hundred Scorpions to the Germans had encouraged Ponty to introduce Adrian to someone else who could help them sell planes in Europe—and possibly in America. Madame George was a thin gray-haired French woman with a severe smoker's cough and watery red eyes. Madame explained in excellent English the advantages of using one of her girls to persuade a potential customer. The fee was five thousand dollars. Adrian had recoiled—until he met several of the girls.

They were the most exquisite women he had ever seen, all perfectly groomed and dressed with Madame George's infallible good taste. They were well-read and au courant politically. Panache seemed to characterize all of them, a serene self-assurance that was never grossly sexual but was subtly, persistently erotic. Ponty had chosen his latest mistress from Madame George's collection and he advised Adrian to consider doing the same thing.

"It's not inexpensive, of course," the Prince said. "The girl must have a suitable apartment, charge accounts, an air travel card. But you could pass most of the expenses through the company, no?"

No, Adrian thought, although he assured Ponty he would consider it. He already had a mistress who was quite enough for a busy man with only a moderate sex drive to handle. But he had to admit to himself that Madame George's girls made Tama Morris look shopworn—or maybe just worn.

That night, in Tama's room at the Crillon, Adrian asked her if she thought Madame George's girls were worth the price. Tama scoffed. "We could bring six or eight of our girls over here for five thousand dollars," she said. "They could have a great time and do us a lot more good."

Adrian sighed. More and more, Tama showed her limitations, mental as well as physical. She was provincial. California did not travel to Paris. He had discovered this at the last two air shows. At home he had grown more and more weary of Tama's compulsion to play office politics. Even before he met Madame George and her girls, he had begun to think it was time to shed Tama.

"I'm going to use them for people at the top," Adrian said. "People the Prince can reach. They expect something more than a quick lay."

"You get some liquor into our girls and they'll do anything," Tama said. "They're from California. They don't have any inhibitions."

"Maybe the buyers do. They're getting more sophisticated—like the planes. That's something I've been trying to explain to Cliff."

Cliff and Jim Redwood had been trying to sell an upgraded version of the Excalibur with very little success. "People don't want a 1940s plane in 1955," Tama snarled. She was always ferocious when Adrian criticized Cliff.

"Maybe I don't want a 1930s woman in 1955," Adrian said.

"There's plenty of other people who do," Tama shouted. "Anytime you want to take a walk, go ahead. I'm sick and tired of playing *Back Street* for you. If you had any guts you'd have divorced your creep of a wife and married me years ago."

"Thank God I'm not impulsive," Adrian said, stalking to the door.

"Adrian!"

Tama was standing at the French window overlooking the Place de la Concorde. In her lacy pink negligee she was a parody of the movie queen she had never become. She looked frightened—and old. "I didn't mean any of that, Adrian."

"I did," he said, slamming the door.

WENN DAS HERZ AUCH BRICHT

She was the most beautiful woman Dick Stone had ever seen. Tall, with chestnut hair that shimmered in a glowing aura around her high-cheeked, fragile-boned face. Her expression was mildly bemused, even disdainful, the wide oval eyes unillusioned. For the first time Dick was glad he had come to the Paris Air Show.

He worked his way through the jammed salon of the Buchanan Chalet, squeezing past U.S. Air Force generals and Royal Air Force air marshals and German Air Force colonels and their wives and/or mistresses. Occasionally, his quarry disappeared behind a pair of massive military shoulders. From the opposite side of the room, he saw Billy McCall moving in the same direction. But Billy got waylaid by one of the more routinely beautiful women who thronged the room and suddenly Dick was standing in front of her without the slightest idea what to say.

"Can I help you?" he said. "I sort of work here."

"For the Americans?"

"I am one," Dick said, mildly flattered that she did not think so at first glance.

He had spent the past six weeks in Germany working out the financial details of the sale of four hundred Scorpions to the Federal Republic's air force. It was the first time he had returned to Europe since he had bombed it in the *Rainbow Express*. A strange atavism had seized him as he walked the streets of Munich and Bonn. The land of his ancestors had spoken to him with a confusing mixture of menace and affection.

By now, Dick and the rest of the world knew about the Holocaust. He knew that one of the worst concentration camps, Buchenwald, was only a few miles outside Weimar, that paradigm of kultur he had objected to bombing. He wondered what his grandfather would think of his schizoid fatherland now.

"I was told to look for General Heinz Gumpert," she said.

Dick knew the suave ex-fighter pilot well. He was the West German Air Force's vice chief of staff. They had spent many hours negotiating the complex problems of training pilots to fly the unforgiving Scorpions, teaching ground crews to maintain them, subcontracting to German companies the rights to make spare parts and some of the sophisticated electronic equipment in the plane. He had found the general agreeable but formal—and a tough negotiator. Every time a Scorpion crashed—they seemed to go down at the rate of one a week—he demanded a new concession from Buchanan Aircraft.

"The general's in the far corner, describing how he almost shot me down at least a dozen times during the war," Dick said. "Why not let me get you a drink first?"

"You were a bomber pilot?" she said, with just the slightest accent.

"A bomber navigator," Dick said, steering her to the bar.

She ordered a vermouth cassis and smiled a thank you as he handed it to her. Close up, she was even more beautiful. Her neck was rather long and supple, her body a landscape of subtle curves and planes. She was wearing a clinging mocha silk dress with thin straps that left her shoulders and arms bare and revealed most of her long spectacular legs. Her only jewelry was a gold-link bracelet on her right wrist.

"A very scared navigator," Dick said.

"Not nearly as scared as those you were bombing," she said.

"You were—are—German?" he said.

"I lived in Schweinfurt," she said.

"We bombed it many times," Dick said.

"Every time I prayed you would hit our house and destroy us all. But you never did."

"Why?"

There was a pause. In the depths of her wide gray eyes

Dick thought he saw contempt. "Do you know Heine, the German poet?" she asked.

"My grandfather used to read him to me."

"How odd. So did my grandfather."

Suddenly she was someplace else, miles from this crowded room full of important people. The cool commanding line of her mouth broke and Dick thought she was going to weep. She sipped her drink and the mask of blasé uncaring returned. Softly, casually, she recited:

Anfangs wollt' ich fast verzagen
Und ich glaubt ich trüg es nie.

Dick knew the verse.

At first I thought I could not bear
The depths of my despair.

He also knew the lines that followed it. He spoke them as softly as she had spoken hers.

Und ich hab' es doch getragen—
Aber fragt mich nur nicht, wie?
Yet O yet I bore it.
Never never ask me how.

"Do they also apply?" Dick asked.

"Yes," she said, smiling as if it were all a joke.

"Are you an old friend of General Gumpert?"

"I have never seen him before in my life."

She smiled serenely at his confusion. "Madame George has asked me to make his stay in Paris more enjoyable. Most Germans—especially those who fly planes—tend to be uncultured. They need guidance, counsel in reading French menus, touring the Louvre—"

Her mockery was exquisite—and touching because it included herself. The reference to Madame George explained everything to Dick, of course. In the past week he had paid astonishing sums to Madame George for the services of her beautiful creatures. He should have known—in fact, he must have known—this woman was one of her stable.

The word *stable* suddenly seemed impossible or at least intolerable. "Americans need just as much cultural help, perhaps more," he said.

"Oh, no. You are the conquerors. Have you not mastered culture too?"

"Not really," Dick said, smiling. "What's your name?"

"Amalie."

The name of Heinrich Heine's first great love.

"Why do you live in Paris?"

He was fumbling for conversation, trying to prevent her departure to General Gumpert.

"Because Madame de Stael said here a woman can live without being happy."

"Can I see you again, after you've improved the general's culture?"

"Why?"

For the first time in his life, Dick spoke to a woman without even an attempt at calculation, saying exactly what leaped to his lips. "Because you're so beautiful."

A wisp of a smile played across her mouth. It was impossible to tell if she was pleased or bored by the compliment. "Are you Jewish?" she said.

"What difference does that make?" he snapped.

She shrugged. "You don't look it. But then, what is a Jew supposed to look like? I've never quite understood that question."

"You're Jewish?"

"I'm not supposed to answer that question. Or better, it should never come up."

Cliff Morris slapped Dick on the shoulder. "Hey—is this General Gumpert's dinner date you're monopolizing, Stone?"

"I'm afraid so," he said. Dick began to introduce her to Cliff and realized he did not know her last name.

"Borne," she said.

The name of one of the many German Jews Heinrich Heine both hated and admired. Dick watched Cliff lead her through the crowd to General Gumpert, whose angular face was consumed by anticipation at the sight of her.

Cliff drifted back to the bar. "Two more fucking Scorpions crashed this morning," he said. "Adrian told Madame George to send us the top of the line."

For the rest of the party, Dick could not take his eyes off Amalie Borne. Occasionally her eyes strayed around the room but she never missed a beat in her conversation with Gumpert. The general was obviously absorbing immense amounts of culture.

The party began to wind down. Dick realized he had lost all interest in finding himself a date for the night. There were plenty of available women, journalists and public relations assistants and models from a dozen nations at the air show. With a little effort, a man could line up a different adventure every night. He turned his back on Amalie Borne and retreated to the bar to order Buchanan's favorite, Inverness single malt Scotch.

Dick drank the swill and brooded about his erratic love life. He had talked Cassie Trainor into going to college and she wound up getting a full scholarship to Stanford, putting an end to their nights and weekends at the Villa Hermosa. Cassie had wept at the thought of leaving him—but she took the scholarship. Now they were occasional lovers—she had others in Palo Alto, Dick was sure. He had more than a few among the swinging singles of the Villa Hermosa.

He felt a hand brush his suit-coat pocket. When he turned, Amalie Borne was going out the door with Gumpert and Adrian Van Ness and Tama Morris. In his pocket he found a small white card with a telephone number on it.

Dick called the next morning at 10:30. A maid with a heavy French accent was barely polite. It took several minutes to persuade her to let him speak to Miss Borne. Amalie's dusky voice finally came on the line. Dick suggested lunch at Verfours, a five-star restaurant. She said it might be better if they lunched at her apartment. Natalie, her cook, was making a bouillabaisse.

The apartment was in the fashionable Faubourg St. Germain, in one of those huge buildings with immense doors reinforced by black-iron grillwork, guarded by a concierge. The elevator rose with the serene majesty of an ascending balloon. The French maid greeted him at the door with a frown. She was about forty, with the face of a gorgon on Nôtre Dame. She led him down a short hall to a sunny living room, where Amalie was seated on a dark red couch, wearing a blue peignoir. A bottle of champagne tilted in a silver ice bucket on a nearby secretary.

"I hope you don't mind," she said. "I hate to go out to lunch. Dressing to Madame's standards is too exhausting to do more than once a day."

"Of course."

"After lunch we'll roam Paris a bit, if you're in the mood. I walk a minimum of five miles every afternoon. What do you do for your aircraft company?"

"I keep track of the money."

"Ah. A man of importance."

"Not really. I have very little say on how it's spent."

"But you will, eventually?"

"Possibly."

"What is your fascination with planes? You like to live dangerously?"

Dick shrugged. "The test pilots are the ones who take the real chances."

"From what General Gumpert was saying last night, everyone who flies your planes takes chances."

"That's true of the plane he's buying. It's very fast and very dangerous."

"And you enjoy the vicarious encounter with death this plane creates?"

"Not really."

"You don't despise the Germans? You haven't deliberately sold them a plane that will kill their new pilots?"

"No."

"You're not here to find out if General Gumpert was sufficiently entertained to forget the recent crashes?"

"No!"

She smiled as if this was amusing. "Would you like to open the champagne? Or shall I call Annette?"

"Allow me."

The wire was recalcitrant. It took him five minutes to free the cork. Finally they raised their glasses and Dick said: "To Heinrich Heine."

"*Ich grolle nicht*," she said, referring to one of Heine's most famous love poems, which began: *I won't complain although my heart is breaking.*

"Tell me how and why you lived in Schweinfurt during the war."

"You know the story of Anne Frank, the girl who hid in a Dutch attic? I lived a similar existence in Schweinfurt. The Nazis took my parents away to a concentration camp in 1939 when I was eleven. My mother left me with their dearest friends, the Starkes, whose house was at the end of our street. They hid me in their attic for the entire war."

"Why did you pray every time we bombed Schweinfurt that we'd kill them—and you?"

She gave him a puzzled smile. "I don't understand?"

"You told me you did that—at the air show yesterday."

"Oh! It was so noisy. You must have misunderstood me. I prayed the very opposite. Those dear devout people saved my life. I told the whole story to General Gumpert last night. He broke down and wept. Imagine? A famous fighter pilot, with one hundred and fifty kills to his credit, weeping in this very room, after his fourth bottle of champagne, because I made him ashamed to be a German?"

She's lying, Dick thought. I'm not going crazy. That is irony you are hearing, savage irony of the sort Heinrich Heine used in his prose, when he was demolishing an enemy. "Remarkable," Dick said. "Perhaps you should write a book. It might make some people think better of the Germans."

"Perhaps I will when I'm old and feebleminded. Are you married?"

"No."

"I thought all Americans married at twenty-one and had dozens of children."

"I'm divorced."

"You must tell me what went wrong. I collect misalliances. It's helpful as well as amusing."

"My wife talked baby talk to me. I couldn't stand it."

"Why didn't you simply tell her to stop?"

"I didn't think she would—or could. She was a Jewish princess."

"You mean she was spoiled by indulgent parents."

"That's part of it."

"I had parents like that. You should have been more understanding, compassionate."

He shook his head. "She made me realize I didn't want a Jewish wife."

"Why not?"

"That's hard to explain. My grandfather went to his grave in 1939 believing German anti-Semitism was a passing thing, a minor flaw in a nation that had produced the greatest music, the greatest literature, the greatest philosophy of modern times."

"My grandfather—and my father—believed the same thing," Amalie Borne said.

"I want to prove to myself—and perhaps to others—that Jews can be Americans first—now that Germany's failed them."

"Fascinating," Amalie Borne said.

For the first time, Dick felt he had gotten her attention. It was also the first time he had ever tried to explain his feelings about Jewishness in such detail to anyone—including himself.

Amalie held out her glass for more champagne. "But ultimately perhaps as foolish as the dream of German assimilation?"

"Perhaps. But people in the plane business like to live dangerously."

The fishy, garlicky odor of bouillabaisse began to fill the apartment. Annette opened a table before the sunny windows and they sat down to steaming dishes of it, with a Puligny Montrachet which Annette opened with a flourish that made Dick ashamed of his struggle with the champagne. They discussed recent German literature, notably the Catholic novelist Heinrich Böll, whom Amalie urged Dick to read. "Among his many virtues, he never was and never will be a Nazi," she said.

The wine flowed and Dick asked her how she came to Paris. For a moment she seemed to ponder what to tell him.

"An American general brought me here—and left me when his wife arrived, after the war. For a while I almost starved. Then I met Madame George and began my ascent. I'm now as spoiled as my father ever dreamt of making me. Somewhere I like to think he's smiling."

"Considering what you went through during the war, you're entitled," Dick said.

She laughed and his body almost dissolved. It was more than her beauty, it was the mystery, the aura of hidden pain that surrounded her. Absurd romantic ideas crowded Dick's brain. He would rescue her from the degradation of one-night stands with macho slobs like Gumpert. He would take her to America, convince her it was a refuge she could trust.

Over dessert of *profiteroles au chocolat*, Amalie proclaimed their mission for the afternoon: to see Heinrich Heine's Paris. Germany's greatest romantic poet had lived in the City of Light for the last twenty-five years of his life in protest against the anti-Semitism and conservative politics that kept him in a frenzy of ambivalence about his fatherland.

They began with a stroll down the Champs Elysées, the poet's favorite boulevard, where he and his friend Balzac used to parade arm in arm. Then a taxi whirled them to the site of the glove shop in the narrow Passage Choiseul where Heine had met Mathilde, the nineteen-year-old peasant girl who would dominate—and ultimately destroy—his life. "I come here often to try to understand the way fate waylays a man," Amalie said.

"He loved her."

"He loved a great many women. Too many. Mathilde was woman's revenge. She was all body and no mind."

Another taxi took them to streets where the poet and Mathilde had lived—Rue d'Amsterdam, the Grande Rue des Batignolles, the Avenue Matignon, where he died. In each site, Amalie meditated on Heine's erratic, erotic life. Gradually

Dick saw him looming over her, part guardian angel, part idol, part threat.

"He was an old-fashioned romantic," Dick said as Amalie recalled the poet's last love affair with the adventuress he called Mouche.

"What does that mean, exactly?"

"He fell in love with almost every woman he met."

"We moderns don't believe in love?"

"Not that effervescent kind. We're more inclined to make distinctions. Sex is not the same as love."

"How profound. Tell me more, Mr. Stone."

Confused by her sudden hostility, Dick blundered on. "We—we Americans anyway—believe in falling in love with one woman—and hoping the love will grow deeper and richer and more powerful as life goes on. For romantics falling was the most important part of love. I prefer the American approach."

"That's so naive," she said, looking up at the sagging shutters and crooked windows of the half-dozen nineteenth-century houses still standing on the Avenue Matignon. Once more Dick sensed he had gotten her attention.

"I don't know," he said. "At the end, didn't Heine wail, *'Worte, Worte, keine Taten!'*—words, words, no deeds. That's the verdict on romanticism in my opinion."

"You don't understand romanticism—or me!" she said, springing out of the taxi and striding down the street.

In his bad French, Dick told the driver to pursue her.

They kept pace with Amalie while he leaned out the window, reciting the rest of Heine's disillusioned cry: *"Immer Geist und keinen Braten/ keine Knödel in der Suppe."*—Always spirit and no roast, no dumplings in the soup.

"You're disgusting," she said. "Disgusting and naive."

"How about dinner at Verfours tonight?"

"I'm engaged."

"Tomorrow night?"

"Don't you have airplanes to worry about?"

"They can wait. I've fallen in love with you. But I want to get beyond Heine."

"There's nothing beyond him. There never will be!"

They continued to creep along beside the striding defiant Amalie for another block, while other taxis and cars beeped angrily behind them. Dick cheerfully recited more Heine. *"Lass mich mit gluhnden Zangen kneipen, Lass grausam schinden mein Gesicht."* Let me be pinched with red hot tongs, let my face be flayed from my skull, only do not make me wait any longer.

As they approached the Champs Elysées, Amalie's frown vanished. When he tried *"Noch einmal, eh mein Lebenslicht,"* in which the poet prayed that before his "life's light" was extinguished, he would be blessed once more by a woman's love, she capitulated and got back in the cab. They did not say a word all the way back to her apartment. As she got out she said: "What time, at Verfours?"

Verfours said a reservation was *impossible.* A face-to-face conference with the headwaiter and 150 dollars created a table. On the way back to his hotel, Dick realized he was supposed to be at a reception for Buchanan Aircraft at the West German embassy. He arrived as the party was breaking up. General Gumpert was still there, however, and was impossible to avoid.

"That was a fascinating creature you found for me last night, Dick," he said. "She spoke better German than I did, in spite of being born in Corsica."

"We thought you'd find her interesting, General," Dick said. "Will you be seeing her again?"

"We were supposed to go to Verfours tonight but she's ill."

"Too bad."

"You've heard about the new crashes? The newspapers are going to crucify us, I'm afraid."

"I believe it was one of Germany's aeronautic pioneers who said sacrifices must be expected."

"Does that include my career?" Gumpert said.

"I hope not, General."

Behind his soothing manner, Dick was thinking: *Fuck you, you Nazi bastard.* He was appalled. Did Amalie Borne have something to do with it? Had she reawakened a primitive Jewish identity in his soul?

Prince Carlo materialized to rescue Dick, an irony in itself. Dick instinctively disliked this urbane aristocrat. The Prince put his arm around Gumpert's shoulder. "Never be discouraged by a defeat in love, General. Tonight we'll go to a little place I have in the country, where complaisance is guaranteed. Would you care to join us, Stone?"

"No—I have a previous engagement."

That could easily get him fired from Buchanan Aircraft.

The Prince walked him to the door, sighing over the problems of the Scorpion. He was going to need more money—a great deal more—to deal with it. Adrian Van Ness had authorized another draft of three million dollars. Would Dick see that it was deposited in the Swiss account tomorrow?

Dick fled to his hotel for a hasty shower and a dash to Verfours, where Amalie awaited him at their table, chatting with the headwaiter in flawless French. They were apparently old friends. After champagne cocktails, they feasted on truffles and pheasant under glass and a raspberry tart whose crust seemed mostly air.

Amalie insisted on hearing more about Dick's love life. Mixing irony and humor, he described the liaisons, the weekend flings, the one night stands of the Manhattan Beach aeronauts. He portrayed them as delayed adolescents—and did not mention Cassie Trainor.

"Now, like Heine when he encountered Mathilde, you're weary with debauchery and long for the simple affection of an unspoiled heart?" Amalie asked.

"You could say that. But I wish you wouldn't."

"How fortunate that we met," Amalie said. "Perhaps I'm was wrong about fate being a dark presence in our lives."

After dinner they lingered over a forty-year-old brandy Amalie selected. Dick tried not to look at the bill as he handed the waiter his American Express card. It probably exceeded his salary for the month.

They rode back to the Faubourg St. Germain through the mostly deserted midnight streets. A soft rain had fallen while they dined; the macadam gleamed beneath the lampposts. At the apartment, Amalie fumbled for her key and Dick stood by the cab, wondering if he should pay the fare. "Ten francs, *s'il vous plaît,*" the driver rasped, perhaps trying to tell him that any Frenchman who escorted a woman this beautiful to her apartment would follow her upstairs if he had to climb the facade.

Dick paid him as the heavy door groaned open. "I have more of that brandy," Amalie said.

He kissed her as they walked into her apartment. She did not resist, but she did not respond, either. "It's all wrong," she whispered. "You must know that."

"I only know I love you."

"Shhh. Annette doesn't approve of you."

"Why not?"

"You're too young. You can't possibly be rich enough."

"I'm not."

"Oh. Can't you see, can't you hear?"

"I only see a beautiful woman who doesn't believe in American love."

" '*Lieb Liebchen, leg's Händchen aufs Herze mein.*' Do you know that verse?"

"Yes," Dick said. It was the Heine poem that had resounded in his head over Schweinfurt, about a lover's hammering heart becoming a psychic coffin.

"That's the literal truth about me. *Nicht worte, worte.* The truth."

" '*Tobende eile mich treibend erfasst,*' " Dick murmured, kissing her neck. *A wild unrest is desolating me,* another line from one of Heine's cries of romantic despair. Did he mean it? Was she using the other line to tell him of a twentieth-century despair? Dick only knew he could not retreat now. She was mystery and memory, Jewishness and the guilt of the navigator of the *Rainbow Express.* He pressed his lips against her pulsing throat and she seemed to crumple against him. The straight firm body dissolved into helplessness, sadness.

Undressed in the shadowy lamplight, she was a landscape, a country of love. A flat soft stomach descended to full thighs, ascended to coned breasts. She reached out to him like a plaintive child as he lay down beside her. "*Kommt, kommt,*" she whispered. "*Kommt feins liebchen heut.*" Come,

come, come sweet love today. It was from the first verse of one of Heine's most famous song cycles.

Entering her was the most profound moment of Dick Stone's life. He felt like a conqueror of space and time, returning to the old world in his grandfather's name with a new and bolder love for it, an American love that could both master and transform its tormented history. Amalie gave herself without reservation, shuddering, sighing, almost sobbing and at the climax retreating into a dark silence, to emerge with a small final cry.

After another five minutes of silence, she whispered: "The brandy is in the armoire in the living room."

He returned with glasses and the bottle. She drank some and held out her arms to him again. "Now, now," she whispered. "Now must come *worte worte*. Now that you've had the meat, Heinrich."

In the same slow insistent whisper, she began telling him the story of her six years in the attic at Schweinfurt. Accepting her had been an impulsive act of charity on the part of her parents' friends, the Starkes. Soon she became a dangerous burden. Their attitude began to change. She could hear them arguing in the bedroom below her. Herr Starke wanted to turn her in, Frau Starke urged him to wait until Germany won the war.

Then Germany began to lose the war. The Starkes' son, who was the same age as Amalie, was killed on the Russian front. Mrs. Starke had a stroke during one of the air raids. Herr Starke, who was one of the managers of the ball-bearing works the *Rainbow Express* tried so often to destroy, began visiting Amalie in the attic with less than compassionate motives.

"He always reviled me while we did it," she whispered. "*Judenshit*," he would say. "*Juden Juden Judenshit*. Every other obscene word in the language."

Unreality seized Dick's mind. The way Amalie was whispering the story somehow seemed more bizarre and horrifying than the story itself. Dick wanted it shouted. He wanted it broadcast over loudspeakers so that everyone in Germany, from General Gumpert to Heinrich Böll to Chancellor Konrad Adenauer could hear it. He wanted it put on every radio and television network in the United States. He wanted the entire world to confront the story of Amalie Borne.

"Now do you see how impossible it is for us?"

"I only see the impossibility of anything but marrying you, living with you for the rest of my life."

"The Prince would never permit it. He would ask for your job, your head."

"What does he have to do with it?"

"I'm his mistress. Who do you think pays for this apartment, for Annette, for the cook?"

"And he'd send you to Gumpert for—"

"He had confidence in my ability to elude Herr General."

"You're making this up."

"I wish I were. I wish I could convince you how much I'm risking at this very moment. There must be a risk for you too."

"The hell with that. I can't believe you prefer to be kept by that titled crook when you could come to America with me—"

"I don't believe in your America. What I see of your countrymen here in Europe makes me think you're no better than us. Possibly worse, because you lie to yourselves about your goodness and virtue."

"That has very little to do with whether two people love each other."

"I'm not at all sure you're right. In fact I suspect you're wrong."

Desperation clutched at Dick's throat. She was eluding him. "When can I see you again?"

"There's no point to it. Think about what I've said, what I've become—and you'll understand." She kissed him gently on the lips. "I'm sure you will. You're an intelligent man."

In the meantime, Dick realized, they—or at least she—would have this Heinesque romantic memory. He struggled into his clothes and trudged into the dawn, resolved to defeat both the Prince and the poet.

The next day, the last day of the air show, Billy McCall led a squadron of U.S. Scorpions in aerobatics that were the

sensation of the week. Spain, Portugal, Italy, all expressed
an interest in acquiring the plane. Adrian Van Ness was ecstatic. Everyone on the Buchanan team was pressed into
charming the new customers. Dick found himself taking a
Spanish general and his wife to dinner at the Ritz. As they
chatted about Mexico and California, which the general had
recently visited, there was a stir at the other end of the long
narrow dining room. Amalie and Prince Carlo sat down at a
table, along with Adrian Van Ness and another of Madame
George's girls, almost as beautiful as Amalie.

The encounter only redoubled Dick's resolve to convince
Amalie of the possibility of American happiness. The following day, he telephoned her apartment. Annette answered.
The moment she recognized him, she flung a stream of hostile French over the line from which he extracted the absence
of Miss Borne. He rushed from the hotel to the nearest flower
shop, bought two dozen roses and rode to the Faubourg St.
Germain in a steady rain, almost suffocating himself and the
driver with the scent in the airtight cab.

The concierge allowed him to ascend when he displayed
the telephone number in Amalie's handwriting. But Annette
barred the door, insisting Miss Borne was not at home. In
fact, she was not in Paris.

"Where is she?" Dick practically shouted, hoping Amalie
would hear him.

"Rome."

He retreated forlornly into the rain. At the Buchanan Chalet, exhibits were being dismantled, photographers, French
public relations people, were waiting to be paid. Dick wrote
out checks and tried to join in the exorbitant cheer that the
success of the Scorpion had created. Adrian Van Ness came
by, looking almost effervescent. "Did you get that money to
the Prince?" he asked.

"I'll do it by the end of the day."

"Good. He's off to Rome, where I think he'll need it. You
can't get anything done in Italy without spreading a lot of it
around."

"So I hear."

"He took that fabulous girl with him. He and Madame

George have been feuding about her. She wanted a villa in Cannes. He was resisting the cost. So Madame sent her to entertain General Gumpert. The next night, Ponty heard she was at Verfours with some American."

Adrian smiled in a strange, almost wistful way. "You get a whole new idea of worldliness when you spend some time with Europeans."

The next day as Dick was checking out of his hotel, the desk clerk handed him a letter. The handwriting was strange—almost a child's scrawl. He stuffed it into his pocket and did not read it until he was aboard the plane. On sky blue paper was one of Heinrich Heine's best known love poems. But it was not a testament of love here. Amalie Borne was asking him, one last time, to understand.

Ich grolle nicht, und wenn das Herz auch bricht,
Ewig verlor'nes Lieb! Ich grolle nicht.
Wie du auch strahlst in Diamantenpracht,
Es fällt kein Strahl in deines Herzens Nacht.

I shall not complain, although my heart
        is breaking
Love forever lost! I shall not
        complain.
However much you gleam in the diamond's
        glow
No light can reach the darkness in your heart.

The DC-6 labored west toward America against a strong head wind. The pilot told them they would be at least a half hour late.

No, Dick thought, as the engines throbbed in his head, no. He refused to understand. He would somehow penetrate the darkness in Amalie's heart. She would be his talisman of forgiveness for the bombs, for abandoning Jewishness, an emblem of hope and triumph.

Dick did not realize he was like a pilot trying to land at a strange airport in night and fog, talking to air traffic controllers in a language they did not understand.

QUEEN OF THE NIGHT

With a hundred million dollars' worth or orders for Scorpions on the books, Adrian Van Ness should have left Paris a happy man. Instead, he was miserable. De Havilland Aircraft had picked up at least two hundred orders for Comets and the British were suddenly the world leaders of commercial aviation. Frank Buchanan blamed it on Adrian's timid refusal to build a jet-powered airliner and was whispering "I told you so" through all ranks of the company, making Adrian look like Casper Milquetoast.

Tama kept throwing contrite looks at him but he ignored her. Their affair was over as far as Adrian was concerned. He might even end her connection with Buchanan Aircraft if he could think of a good reason. Madame George's girls had made him feel sexually invulnerable.

Adrian's main concern was what to do about the next generation Buchanan airliner. The Scorpion's sales gave them the money to build one. If he hoped to keep Buchanan in the major leagues with Lockheed, Boeing, Douglas, he had to make a decision soon. To jet or not to jet, that was the question. Buzz McCall sat next to him halfway to California, arguing for a jet. He showed him a Frank Buchanan sketch of a plane twice the size of the Comet with the Pratt & Whitney engines they were using in the Scorpion in pods on the wings.

Adrian resisted the idea. Part of the reason was personal. A few rows ahead, Frank Buchanan sat talking to Dick Stone. The back of Frank's head was a kind of statement of his persistent contempt. Adrian saw Buzz as Frank's spokesman, with no opinion of his own worth discussing.

"I don't think we should rush into this," Adrian said. "I want to commission a survey of the public attitude toward jets. I'm not sure people want to fly at six hundred miles an hour."

Buzz saw the survey as another proof of Adrian's basic problem: lack of nerve. "Adrian, Americans want to go as fast as possible. Even the car business understands that. Why the hell do you think they've decorated the fuckin' fenders and hoods and grilles with all those fins and streamline effects? They want to make them look like planes."

In California, the debate continued to rage through the usual drunken lunches in the executive dining room. Frank and Buzz converted everyone, even young people like Cliff Morris and Dick Stone, whom Adrian hoped he had brought into his executive aura. One day, after a particularly vitriolic (and alcoholic) lunch, at which a jet had been favored by a five to one margin, Adrian went back to his office teetering on the brink of decision. Something deep in his mind still resisted the idea of admitting Frank Buchanan was right.

His secretary buzzed him. "Victoria is calling from London."

"Hello, darling, how are you?" Adrian said.

"Haven't you heard the news?" Victoria cried. "Grandmother's plane crashed. Everyone died. She's gone!"

Within minutes, Adrian had the British embassy in Washington on the telephone. They ruefully confirmed that a Comet 3 en route from Naples to London had crashed off the island of Elba. "No survivors?" Adrian said dazedly.

"None, I'm afraid. The ambassador, I'm sure, joins me in expressing our deepest regret."

Adrian hung up and sat motionless behind his desk for a long time. The whine of a jet engine out on the airfield meant another Scorpion was about to be flight-tested. As it rose to a shrill wail, Adrian tried to absorb the meaning of Clarissa's death. He told himself a fifty-five-year-old man did not fall apart over the death of his eighty-three-year-old mother. But for Adrian it was a primary event. He felt like someone who had spent most of his life guarding a door against a dangerous intruder. Now the door had swung open to reveal no one was there.

Or was it the other way around? Had he, all his life, been

trying to burst into a guarded room and now, suddenly, the door was open and the secrets he had been determined to discover, the oracle he had been longing to interrogate, had vanished? He was free in a new mysterious way he had to explore.

Should he divorce Amanda and marry Tama? No, that had never been more than a remote possibility and now it was out of the question. He began to understand his involvement with Tama in a new way. In his imagination, he had seen himself introducing her to his mother as his wife, relishing the shock and dismay on Clarissa Ames Van Ness's face. Tama's middle-class taste, her sensuality, were polar opposites of Clarissa's standards. Of course, he had never done it because he also loved his mother.

And feared her.

And hated her.

And pitied her.

Adrian struggled to place all his emotions on the table so he would know, like the gambler who was getting ready to bet his money and his life, the status of the deck. Was he free of Clarissa's accusing voice, free of *ruined*? When it wailed in his head now would it belong to no one in particular? Could he ignore it if he chose?

The decision, the great decision to jet or not to jet, was part of this new freedom. Should he bet the net assets of the company on a plane that had just crashed?

No. In some unassailable blindly superstitious corner of his mind, Adrian felt his mother's death was a retribution—and a warning. He had spent his life rejecting most of her advice. Now she had died aboard the world's first jet airliner, the plane she had wanted him to build. It was an omen no one in the aircraft business, where fate so often seems to be sitting in on every hand, could resist.

It was also an irresistible opportunity to use his presumed grief with masterful effect. He called in Frank Buchanan and Buzz McCall and told them the news. They were appalled and sympathetic, of course. Adrian nodded and briskly turned the conversation to business. He predicted that this crash, the second Comet to go down this year, would cast a fatal shadow over the plane. One more crash and it would be out of business. "I seriously think it could finish jet-powered air travel for twenty years," he said.

Instead of an intercontinental jet plane like Boeing and Douglas were building, Adrian had a better idea. "At the last meeting of the Conquistadors, at least three airline presidents told me they needed an intermediate range plane that could take off from La Guardia and other small airports. Let's build one for them—with turboprops."

Pratt & Whitney had produced this compromise between a jet engine and a propeller. Buchanan had used it successfully on the Excalibur-derived transports they had built for the Air Force at the start of the Korean War.

"I like the idea of an intermediate plane," Frank said. "But why not make it a jet? The Comet isn't crashing because of its engines. It's the pressurized cabin. The Brits didn't take into account the effect of the extreme changes in air pressure at the altitude a jet flies. It's metal fatigue, not engine failure that's bringing them down. They're just disintegrating up there in the sky."

"You're telling me to build a plane that may kill people the way that thing just killed my mother?" Adrian shouted.

"All right," Frank said. "I'll give you your turboprop."

Buzz and Frank departed, shaking their heads. Adrian strode up and down the office in a terrific state of agitation. "The son of a bitch, the son of a bitch," he kept saying. He realized his reaction made no sense. What was happening to him? Had he lost his emotional bearings?

At home, Adrian found Amanda working in the garden. Beneath a large old-fashioned sun hat, she looked oddly youthful, as girlish as when he first met her. "My mother's dead," he said. "She died in the crash of the Comet."

"I know," Amanda said. "Tama called to tell you how sorry she was. She wants you to call her."

Amanda patted earth around a newly planted bulb. "Are you going to marry Tama now?" she said in a dry, almost toneless voice. She had begun talking that way about a year ago. Adrian thought it was another way of telling him how much she hated him.

"Why should I do that?"

"You don't love her?"

"I don't know what you're talking about."

"Adrian—I've known for years. I was glad. For her sake. For yours. I knew you only stayed with me because of your mother."

"That's not true!" Adrian shouted. "It was for Victoria's sake. For your sake too—if you only gave me a chance to show it instead of crawling into bed with that slob Frank Buchanan."

"That was meant to be, Adrian. There was nothing either of us could do about it."

"I did something about it."

"I knew you would."

"What the hell is the matter with you? Why don't you talk to me like a human being, an adult woman, instead of in that voice of the living dead?"

"Call Tama. She needs you," Amanda said and left him there in the garden.

He called Tama. She was at her Malibu beach house. He could hear the surf crashing. She was out on the deck with the white telephone in her hand. "Adrian," she said. "I called to tell you how sorry I am about your mother. How sorry I am about everything. Will this—make a difference, Adrian? I mean—will you feel free to—"

"I've always been perfectly free to do what I pleased. What I've done—and haven't done—are for very good reasons," he said.

"Oh, God Adrian, I haven't been able to eat or sleep since that argument in Paris. I didn't mean any of those stupid things I said. I love you. Doesn't that make any difference? Can't you forgive me?"

"There's nothing to forgive. I was unpleasant too. I'm afraid our little fling has just run out of gas."

"Little fling? Adrian—it's been almost ten years. I divorced Buzz. I've told you what you mean to me. Told you and told you."

"I know. But you don't mean that to me. You never have. You were—very helpful. I needed you badly when it began."

Adrian was trying not to be cruel and failing miserably. He could not control the anger at women that lurked deep in his soul. "It might be best if you left the company, Tama. It's not a healthy situation for either of us. I'm sure you can get more money doing the same thing at Douglas or North American. Everyone says you're the best publicity woman in the business."

"Adrian!"

"I'm only being sensible, Tama. I'll arrange for severance pay tomorrow. It'll be very generous, I assure you. If you invest it well you'll never have to work again."

"Adrian!"

The telephone was a wonderful invention, Adrian thought, as he hung up. It enabled a man to say things to a woman he could never say face to face.

Adrian showered and dressed for dinner in his usual deliberate fashion. He put on one of his new pink shirts—a daring style that some people thought might replace white as the color of choice—and one of his newest Savile Row suits. A resolve—a wish—was growing in his mind and heart. A decision to reorder his life. Victoria would be coming home in a year. Why not bring her into a house where her father loved her mother, his wife, in a new profound way?

Wife. Why did his mother's death give that word new depth and resonance? *Wife*—was Amanda the victim of his long bitter need to fend off Clarissa Van Ness? Had he kept her at the same taut arm's length in his mind and heart? Was it possible that he was now free, not to take a mistress selected by Madame George, but to love his wife?

At dinner he talked about Victoria. He praised her intelligence, her cheerful disposition, her budding gifts as a poet. He gave Amanda more than her share of the wine. Over dessert, with the housekeeper safely clanking pots in the kitchen, he took Amanda's hand and made his plea. He told her about his ruined American father, his discovery of his English father, his mother's obsessive attempts to control him. He confessed the whole truth about selling her share of Cadwallader Groves to her brother.

"This has been the most momentous day of my life. I've

seen so much. Especially how I've let my quarrel with my mother hurt us. I've only known one way to deal with a woman—warily, fearfully, if you prefer the whole truth. That's why I could never find a way to explain our reconciliation in 1931—I mean really explain it. I should have insisted on the absolute truth that I've always loved you and money had nothing to do with it. But I couldn't do it. Pride— that spirit of defiance my mother stirred in me—was always in the way. Now I'm free to ask you to forgive me. Can you—will you?"

"What about Tama?"

"Forget Tama. She was never more than a consolation."

Amanda's eyes blazed with unnatural light. "That is more unforgivable than all the rest of it, Adrian. Forever unforgivable!"

"Why?" Adrian gasped. He had no idea Tama Morris meant anything to Amanda. As far as he knew, they had not met more than a dozen times.

Amanda tore her hand away and flung back her chair. Another emotion seemed to overwhelm her. She trembled violently. Tears ran down her cheeks. "Oh, Adrian," she said. "If only you'd said this years ago."

She fled to her bedroom. Adrian retreated to his study in a near frenzy. There would be no sleep tonight or any other foreseeable night. His stomach ached. He gulped antacid pills and poured himself a tumbler of port. For a long time he sat on the terrace watching the planes land at Los Angeles International Airport. He tried to think of a name for his new turboprop.

Starduster. Yes, he liked it. Lockheed named their planes after stars. This claimed the whole galaxy. He poured himself more port and decided maybe the Prince was right. One of Madame George's girls was the way to go. He could set her up in New York. It would be easy to keep it a secret from everyone, even Victoria.

But it was Amanda's love he wanted. A love he had neglected, denied, abandoned. It was the only way he could ever expiate the enormous echoing guilt that was throbbing in his belly now when he thought of how much unhappiness he had caused Clarissa Ames Van Ness.

An hour or two after midnight, the telephone rang. It was Dan Hanrahan, Buchanan's chief of security. "Adrian?" he said. "I'm at Tama Morris's house. I think you better get out here right away."

"What's wrong?"

"She's dead. Killed herself."

A full moon splashed ironic gold on the heaving Pacific as Adrian drove down the boulevards and up the coast highway, his brain clutched in an icy fist. *It's not your fault*, he repeated to himself. *It's not anyone's fault.*

Buzz McCall opened Tama's front door. The last person Adrian wanted to see. Buzz looked like a man who had just fallen out of a plane without a parachute. "I found her," he said. "I called Dan."

Buzz struggled to control himself. Adrian could not believe it. The ultimate tough guy, bawling. "She's in there." He pointed to the bathroom.

Hanrahan was taking photographs of Tama. She lay in her big oblong tub—her Roman tub, she used to call it. Her heavy-lidded eyes were open, staring sightlessly at a photograph of her and Adrian which had been taken at the rollout of a Buchanan plane. The water in the tub was dark red.

"Did she cut her wrists?" Adrian asked.

Hanrahan shook his head. "A knitting needle in the heart." He handed Adrian a letter. "I found this on her pillow. She left one for Buzz and another one for Cliff."

Adrian opened the envelope and read the bold scrawl. *I can't prove my love in any other way I guess so here goes. I'm too old to start hopping from bed to bed the way I lived before I met you. If there's another place I hope we meet there so you can say you're sorry. Tama.*

"What did she say to Buzz?"

Hanrahan dug the letter out of his pocket. *If you weren't such a louse I'd have come home to you with my broken heart. But I knew there was no point to it. I really loved you in the old days but you ruined it. Good-bye, you bastard.*

"Cliff's still got his," Hanrahan said.

"He's here?"

"She called them both before she did it."

"What do we do?"

"Call the cops. But I think you better talk to Cliff first. He said some wild things when I first got here."

Adrian handed both letters to Hanrahan. "Burn them," he said.

He walked into the living room to find Buzz and Cliff glaring at each other. Cliff must have been walking on the beach. His shoes were soaked and sandy. "You're a pair of bastards," Cliff shouted. "All you ever did was fuck her around."

"Shut up," Buzz snarled. "If you were a man instead of a fuckin' crybaby maybe she'd have asked you for help."

"Prick!" Cliff shouted and hit Buzz with a terrific round-house right that sent him hurtling across the living room through the glass doors to the deck. Cliff lunged after him. Buzz struggled to his feet just in time to get another punch in the face that sent him crashing through the deck's bamboo railing onto the beach below. Cliff jumped on top of him screaming, "Prick! Prick!"

Hanrahan started after them. Adrian seized his arm. "Let them fight it out," he said.

It was no contest. Buzz was almost sixty years old and he was only half Cliff's size. Cliff pounded him to the sand again and again in the ghostly moonlight. In Adrian's eyes each punch was a demolition of Buzz McCall, the swaggering sultan of the assembly line, the man who called him a coward, who had possibly—no, probably—killed Beryl Suydam.

Cliff finally knocked Buzz into the surf, where he seized his stepfather by the throat and began drowning him. "Now," Adrian said and Hanrahan leaped to the beach and rescued Buzz. The security chief took the battered loser home and Adrian descended the familiar ladder to the beach and put his arm around Cliff, who stood with his back to the house, watching the white combers rumble toward them in the darkness.

"I loved her," Adrian said. "We had a nasty fight in Paris.

It was partly about business. I decided it wasn't working anymore and told her I wanted her to leave the company. With generous severance pay of course. I had no idea anything like this would happen. She never gave a hint, I swear it, Cliff. Not a hint. She was always so independent, proud."

"Yeah, proud," Cliff said, rubbing his eyes with a fist like a three-year-old.

"Cliff," Adrian said. "I'm going to do my best to make this up to you—and to myself. You've always had a great future with this company. But now—"

Cliff bowed his head, struggling to control his grief. The surf sent ghostly fingers up the beach toward them. "We're going to build a new commercial airliner. I'm going to make you the project manager. Then I'm going to switch you to sales when we start selling it. So you can get maximum credit for it."

"Thanks, thanks," Cliff said.

It was marvelous what you could do with power, Adrian thought. You can triumph over grief, regret, guilt—even hatred. At least, he hoped he was triumphing.

The next morning, Adrian told Amanda about Tama's death. He did not want her to read it in the newspaper first. He also wanted to find out more about her friendship, relationship, whatever it was, with Tama.

Amanda told him nothing. All she said, over and over, was: "Adrian, the time has finally come. You'll have to pay a price for this. A terrible price."

"I didn't do anything that a thousand other men haven't done! I did it for your sake! Because I love you. I've always loved you. I wanted to come back to you."

Whether it was true or not, Adrian now believed it. He was desperate for some kind of resolution, for relief from emotions that were tearing him to pieces. At the office he dictated a statement about Tama Morris's "tragic death," expounding on her years of "stellar contributions" to the company.

That night Adrian brought home a huge bouquet of roses for Amanda. She ignored them. She also continued to ignore his questions about her friendship with Tama.

"How did she die?" she asked.

Adrian told her. Amanda smiled. "A true warrior," she said.

"Warrior?" Adrian said.

Amanda refused to say another word. Adrian began to grow alarmed. But he did not know what to do. He was almost as irrational as Amanda at this point. He spent the night in his study, dictating his conception of the Starduster. It would carry 175 passengers and a crew of six at 450 miles an hour. It would have a cruising range of 2,700 miles, just short of transcontinental. He dictated letters to nineteen airline presidents, all members of the Conquistadores del Cielo, asking their opinion of the profitability of such a plane.

Adrian went to bed at three A.M. so exhausted he was sure sleep was only an eyeblink away. But the vision of Tama in the bathtub's crimson water loomed in the darkness. Her husky voice whispered: *Love me, really love me, Adrian.*

I'm sorry, Adrian whispered to the heedless ghost.

A sound in the darkness. Someone had stumbled into a chair a few feet from the bedroom door. Adrian reached for the gun he kept in the drawer of his night table at Dan Hanrahan's suggestion, when Califia started sending him menacing letters. Hanrahan had also taught him how to use it.

Footsteps came toward the bed. A figure was outlined against the starlit window. Adrian rolled out of bed and crouched behind the night table. "Who's that?" he said.

"It's Califia, Adrian, come to avenge her beloved Tama and all the women you've degraded in your vicious clubhouse with its golden face."

Amanda? Adrian switched on the light and almost dropped the gun. His wife was standing at the foot of the bed, naked, a long carving knife in her hand. Somehow she had cut herself across the top of her right breast, a deep slice that had already coated the breast and half her torso with oozing blood.

"What in Christ are you doing?" Adrian screamed.

"I'm going to kill you, Adrian. In Tama's name. Only then can Califia sleep content in her gold-and-ivory tomb."

She walked toward him, the knife raised. "I can use this," Adrian cried, brandishing the gun.

"Bullets can't harm Califia. She's immortal," Amanda said in the toneless voice that had been irritating Adrian for months.

She rounded the corner of the bed and lunged at him. Adrian thrust the lamp in front of him for a shield and the knife sank into the green shade. Amanda pulled it out and tried to raise it again for another thrust. With a snarl Adrian shoved the lamp in her face, knocking her onto the bed. He dove for the knife arm and they wrestled wildly across the double bed, Amanda screaming now, a shrill wail worthy of a jet engine.

In the melee Amanda received an ugly slash on the neck below her left ear but she continued to do her utmost to kill Adrian. He finally seized her wrist with both hands and smashed it against the other night table. The knife flew free but he still had a madwoman to contend with. Amanda clawed at his eyes, kicked, kneed, all the while shrilling her war cry.

Cursing, terrified, Adrian wound her into the sheet and shouted for their Mexican housekeeper. She stood in the doorway, bug-eyed at the blood-smeared bed, the wrecked lamp, the knife. "Call Dr. Kirk Willoughby," he said. He gave her the number from memory. "Tell him it's an emergency. *Emergencia!*"

She scampered away and he was left with Amanda raving. "Kill me. Kill me now!" she screamed. "I want to die like a warrior in the service of my queen. I don't want to spend another hour as a prisoner of you loathsome men."

"Shut up!" Adrian jammed his hand over her mouth and pressed the sheet into the wounds on her neck and breast, stanching the flow of blood.

Kirk Willoughby found him in this position when he arrived. Adrian told him what had happened and begged him to deal with Amanda without calling a hospital ambulance. He dreaded what people in the company and the aircraft business would say if the story got into the newspapers.

"They'll think I attacked her," he said.

"You'll both be attacked by Califia, Queen of California, the moment I free myself," Amanda screamed, resuming her wild thrashing.

Amanda kicked and spit and clawed furiously at Willoughby when he tried to approach her. "We'll be glad to submit to your royal whims, your highness, if you'll let us tend to your wounds," Willoughby said.

"Bring Sarah Morris to me. The mother of Tama's granddaughters. I have a message for her," Amanda said.

Willoughby's eyes sought Adrian's. He nodded. He was ready to do anything to satisfy this madwoman. He called Cliff Morris and told him to bring Sarah to the house. Thanks to the freeway, they arrived in fifteen minutes. Adrian explained Amanda's delusion and advised Sarah to pretend to be a subject of Queen Califia.

By that time Willoughby had given Amanda an injection of morphine and stitched her wounds. She was propped against the back of the bed, looking weirdly regal with the sheet robed around her. She seemed pleased to see Sarah, who could only stare incomprehensibly at her.

"You must explain to your daughters exactly what happened tonight," Amanda said. "I was distressed to see that my breasts had grown back and resolved to amputate one, as an example to my followers. I wanted to be sure none of us would ever be enslaved in their gold-smeared club in Topanga Canyon. The loss of blood weakened me and I was unable to kill the chief scum bearer, Amanda's husband. Will you tell them that?"

"Yes, your majesty," Sarah said.

"Assure them my followers haven't deserted me. They're out there in the night, waiting to be summoned. But I've failed them with my weakness for male vileness and luxury. I never should have signed even a temporary truce with them. I've paid a terrible price for it. I've lost my dearest truest follower, Tama. You knew her and loved her, didn't you?"

"I did, your majesty," Sarah said. "She was a wonderful woman."

"I let him destroy her," Amanda said, glaring at Adrian. "I watched and let him destroy her because I thought she was happy. I didn't believe any woman could be happy with this monster but I let her try. I let her die of unhappiness. Now I want to die too."

"We'll talk about it tomorrow, your majesty," Willoughby said. He had called an ambulance from a private sanitarium in the San Fernando Valley. The attendants were at the door. Strapped to the stretcher, Amanda left them screaming: "Tell your daughters they can kill Califia a thousand times but she'll always return!"

Adrian thanked Sarah Morris and got her and Cliff out of the house as quickly as possible. He did not like the way she was looking at him. There seemed to be an unspoken accusation in her eyes. He ordered the housekeeper to clean up the bedroom and retreated to his study. Around him lay the pieces of his personal life, like the wreckage of a crashed plane.

Adrian banished the mess from his sight and whispered the name of his new airliner: "Starduster." It was going to make a billion dollars for Buchanan Aircraft. Did that justify Tama's sightless stare, Amanda's blood-soaked madness, Sarah Morris's accusing glare?

Of course not. The two things had nothing to do with each other. He was a man who made planes and had trouble with women. The two things had nothing to do with each other. Nothing! For a few desperate minutes, Adrian almost believed it.

WHAT DO WOMEN REALLY WANT?

Starduster, Starduster, Starduster. She was sick of it, Sarah Morris thought, as her husband orated another aspostrophe to the plane that was going to make their fortune. Usually she tolerated these monologues at the dinner table. Why was she irked by a Saturday morning version? What was wrong with her? Didn't she want to make a fortune?

Already, the Starduster had doubled Cliff's salary. They had moved from south Los Angeles to a stone-and-stucco house on the upper slope of the Palos Verdes peninsula, with a marvelous view of the ocean. It was a nice place to live, washed by sea breezes, largely free of the noxious gases that created smog attacks in the rest of Los Angeles.

Maybe her alienation was simply British. While the Starduster gathered momentum, her father and his colleagues at de Havilland were frantically trying to find out why the Comet had disintegrated in midair three times. They were conducting enormously expensive tests that were driving the company to the edge of bankruptcy. Her mother related the doleful story to Sarah in weekly letters. When she tried to talk to Cliff about it, he had gloated—yes, gloated—over the Comet's failure. In a flash her English self, her English pride, had been reborn inside her American persona.

"*Bzzzzzzz.*" Her six-year-old son came racing into the living room flying a scale model of a B-17 in his upraised hand. He rounded the couch and a wingtip caught a lamp shade. The lamp toppled onto a vase and water and tulips spewed all over the couch. "Oh!" Sarah cried, seizing him in a near death grip.

"It's okay, it's okay," Cliff said. "He didn't mean it. Right, Charlie?"

"Right," Charlie said, twisting away from Sarah. The mockery in his green eyes, the curve of his smile, left Sarah shaking inside. Was she looking at Billy McCall's son? The rest of Charlie diminished the fear. He had jet-black hair and a physique that seemed closer to Cliff's thick-boned body than Billy's lean sinewy frame. But Billy's father, Buzz McCall, was thick-boned and dark to the point of swarthiness.

Cliff was oblivious to the resemblance. Charlie was his son, the light of his life, the reason he went to work every morning with a smile on his face. Charlie and the Starduster. They had transformed Cliff's life, rescued him from the morose, sullen husband who had emerged from the destruction of the Talus. Sarah told herself she should be grateful for that. But gratitude kept eluding her. Maybe it was because another secret separated her even more brutally from Cliff's happiness.

It lay upstairs at the bottom of her jewelry box. A letter that had arrived the day after Tama committed suicide. On the blue-bordered page were three words: *I was wrong*. Sarah knew why Tama had killed herself. Cliff had choked out the awful story the night of her death. The next day the letter arrived, addressed to Sarah.

Since that day it arrived again and again in Sarah's mind. *I was wrong* reverberated through her soul. Wrong about what? Sarah asked. The answers were endlessly puzzling and often demoralizing. Wrong about what a person can accomplish in America? Wrong about the power of love? Wrong about Cliff? Wrong about leaving her first unloved husband, Cliff's lost father, disobeying the injunction of the Catholic Church? Wrong about trusting Adrian Van Ness? Wrong about redesigning Sarah Chapman to be an executive's wife?

Some—perhaps all—of these questions caused sadness to seep through Sarah's soul. She awoke in the gray predawn light and prowled the rooms of her house. She stood in the doorway and contemplated her two daughters and her son, blissfully asleep in the peaceful year 1957 and wondered what their futures would be. It was the age of Ike, the general and president who ruled a prosperous, self-satisfied America. She read magazines that declared the family was the natural center of a woman's life, the only social entity to which she should ever belong. The editors of the *Ladies Home Journal* told her that an incredible 97 percent of American women had taken marriage vows.

Where did that leave Tama's *I was wrong?* Where did it leave Sarah? Another voice answered that question. *Humiliated*, Amanda Van Ness whispered. It was a year since she had been summoned to her audience with Queen Califia in Adrian Van Ness's blood-smeared bedroom. The episode still partook too much of a nightmare to think coherently about it. But it had engraved Amanda on Sarah's consciousness as a primary being, a symbolic woman. Again and again she found herself returning to Amanda's first visit to their tract house in south Los Angeles, when she had warned Sarah and her daughters against humiliation.

Sarah had told no one about her midnight visit to the Van Ness house. But everyone in the company soon knew about Amanda's breakdown. Susan Hardy said Buzz McCall had gotten the story from the Mexican housekeeper, whom Adrian had fired a week after the incident. Buzz claimed Adrian had known Amanda was Califia, the woman who had sent threatening letters to half the executives in the company. Buzz claimed it was a plot to close the Honeycomb Club. For Susan, the discovery of the existence of the club had been a humiliation. Sarah, more sure of her ability to match the Honeycomb's women in the bedroom, had only been dismayed. Now she wondered if she too should feel humiliated in the name of other women who felt that way.

After helping Sarah clean up the mess on the couch, Cliff headed for another weekend of work on the Starduster. Charlie and his sister Margaret went off to a play group at the country club, and Elizabeth, now a precocious fourteen, vanished in a swirl of hair spray and mascara with a troop of equally precocious girlfriends. Sarah helped Maria make the beds and then went out on the porch to read *The Lonely Crowd*, a book that argued Americans were shifting their values from inner moral codes to the opinions of those around them. Sarah suspected they had been doing that since 1776—but California was a giant laboratory that seemed to prove every word of the sociologist's argument.

Grrrr. Her concentration was broken by another plane, this one's motor not created by the voice of a six-year-old. Over the ocean, a green monoplane was tracing a Jackson Pollock line against the blue sky, rolling, diving, looping, spinning in and out of near disaster again and again, carving the air into forms that built wildly, musically on one another. There was a rhythm to it, violent, spasmodic, that found an echo in Sarah's inner ear. It resembled the new music, rock and roll, which her daughter Elizabeth found exhilarating and Cliff found infuriating. The pilot ended his performance with the most dangerous stunt in the aerobatic book, a *lomcevak*. He climbed almost vertically until he stalled and then tumbled down, tail over nose, wing over wing as if he and the machine had simultaneously gone berserk. He regained control less than fifty feet off the water and roared skyward for a farewell loop.

Sarah gripped the railing of the porch with both hands, feeling as weak, as feeble as a ninety-year-old. Billy McCall was back in Los Angeles. Whenever he arrived, he announced his presence to her this way. It had become a cruel game they played with each other. The next time she saw him at a Buchanan party or ceremony, she would smile and tell him how much she enjoyed his performance. He would nod and tell her he was working on a whole new repertoire out in the desert.

I was wrong. What was Tama telling her? Wrong to cling to Cliff and her children, in spite of the sadness that washed through her body like a tide of sludge? Wrong to trust her body to deliver happiness? Wrong to be born a woman? Maybe that was the fundamental mistake.

That night when Cliff came home Sarah kissed him and said: "I want to learn to fly."

"What?" He looked at her as if she had gone insane.

"I've always wanted to learn. Will you teach me?"

He shook his head. "I haven't flown a plane since I left the army. You know that."

"You could brush up easily enough. Then you could teach me."

He started to get angry—or ashamed. "Sarah—we've got three kids to raise. Flying is dangerous. Dangerous as hell."

"How can you say that? When you're busy trying to sell the whole world on how safe it is."

"The airlines are pretty safe. But flying around in a private plane isn't. Unless you do it all the time and keep your skills sharp. That's why I gave it up. I didn't have the time. Or the money."

He was lying. He gave it up because he was afraid of it. How did she know that? Was Billy McCall whispering it to her? "Why the hell do you want to learn?" Cliff asked, trying to control his exasperation.

"For the thrill of it! Because I've got three kids am I condemned to being a hausfrau for the rest of my life?"

"I sure as hell hope you're going to stay around and raise them. Flying isn't thrilling once you learn. Did you ever talk to an airline pilot? They're bored stiff most of the time. It's like driving a truck."

"Dick Stone seems to think it's still thrilling."

"That's because he flies up to Palo Alto to see a girl who likes doing it at ten thousand feet."

Sarah shook her head. "He loves it. You can see it on his face, in his eyes, when he talks about it."

"I don't care whether you love it or hate it. You're still not entitled to risk your neck learning how to fly—with three kids to raise."

She could not tell him she wanted to invade Billy Mc-Call's sky, she wanted to face him as an equal. That was the only way she could respond to his challenge. The other way, the telephone call for another flight to the desert, was the really ruinous choice. That would separate her from Cliff, the children, forever. Dying in the wreckage of a plane would not do that. It would leave her enshrined in their hearts as a cynosure of courage, a martyr of the air.

I was wrong, Tama said. *Humiliated*, Amanda whispered.

Sarah glared at her husband, fighting despair. "I want to learn!" she said. "I'm going to learn! If you won't teach me I'll find someone else."

Cliff kissed her on the forehead as if she were a tired child. He put his arm around her and chucked her under the chin. "Okay," he said. "You can take your first lesson on Charlie's twenty-first birthday."

He was eluding her. The Starduster was taking him away from her in a new way. The collapse of the Talus had thrown him backward to the sullen playboy. Now he was moving ahead or beyond her, on a wave of pride, confidence, that she could not share, that she almost resented. Why couldn't she rejoice in his renewed American optimism?

I was wrong, Tama said. *Humiliated*, Amanda whispered. The words dislocated everything. "I'm going to fly someday. I really am!" she said.

A week later, on another sunny Saturday after Cliff had

gone to work, a cable arrived from England. FATHER KILLED IN CRASH. FUNERAL TOMORROW. DON'T TRY TO COME. MOTHER. A transcontinental transatlantic phone call told her the rest of the story. Working overtime on the redesigned Comet, her father had spent the night before last at the factory, getting snatches of sleep on a cot in his office. Everyone else was doing the same thing, including the engineers who were installing new wing flaps. They had to disconnect the aileron controls to do this and in their exhaustion reattached them backwards.

The next morning, her father and three members of his design team went up to test the flaps. A crosswind caused the plane to yaw. The pilot tried to compensate with the aileron. The wing responded in the wrong direction. He applied more pressure and the wing struck the ground. The plane cartwheeled across the airport into a line of trees, killing everyone aboard.

I was wrong, Tama whispered. Sarah threw herself on the bed and wept for the rest of the day. She was still weeping when Cliff arrived around four o'clock. He had heard the news at Buchanan. He held her in his arms and told her how sorry he was. "You see what I mean about planes being dangerous?" he said.

She wanted to scream insults at him. He was using this tragic accident to destroy her wish, her hope, for freedom. He was frightening her into being an inferior, a passenger, for the rest of her life. *Humiliated*, Amanda whispered. Would she end up like her, locked in an asylum?

Somehow this justified more tears. She wept all night and into the next day. She realized her grief made no sense. She had never been close to her father. He was seldom home. But he had always been cheerful and affectionate with her, especially when she was little. He called her Lamby. It was a silly name from a game they used to play. She would sit in his lap and insist she was his lamby pie. He would pretend to eat her.

Cliff was right about the danger of flying. There was a very good chance that she might kill herself trying to become Billy McCall's equal. But that only seemed to justify more tears. She thought of Lamby and Billy and Tama's letter and Amanda's fate and wept and wept for a world hopelessly out of joint. Her father was dead, his jet plane in ruins, while the Starduster carried Cliff farther and farther away from her.

Frank Buchanan came to dinner and tried to console her with memories of her father from their friendship in England before the first World War. He talked about going to Ezra Pound's apartment in Kensington, where they gave an assembly of poets a lecture on aerodynamics. Her father had fallen in love with one of the poets. Frank intimated it was not a platonic attachment. That only made Sarah remember Tama's suggestion that he probably had a secret love life. She burst into tears and fled to her bedroom.

After a week of almost continuous weeping, Cliff became seriously alarmed and asked Dr. Kirk Willoughby to arrange a meeting with a psychiatrist. Dr. Eric Montague looked a lot like Willoughby. He was losing most of his hair. His skin was pink, his face round and bland. He gave Sarah pills that stopped the weeping but she remained intransigently gloomy. She declined to tell him why. She said it was none of his business.

"You have to put your life in perspective, Mrs. Morris," Dr. Montague said. He talked a lot about perspective. He seemed to think that was Sarah's problem. He assured her getting the right perspective on her life would banish her depression. He urged her to tell him all her secrets. It was the only way to achieve perspective.

I was wrong, Tama said. *Humiliated*, Amanda whispered. How could she trust any of these Americans, even ones with English names like Montague? She would tell him nothing. Especially about Billy McCall. She clutched that pain to her private heart with absolute ferocity. She would use the pills to defeat the gloom and become a dutiful mother and wife again. She would stick to her diet and remain as attractive as possible and every time she saw Billy McCall she would hope he was—what was the American phrase?—eating his heart out.

Yes. She liked that. She had eaten her own traitor heart in defiance of him. She hoped in the end Billy would be an

empty man, flying planes faster and faster and faster to nowhere.

I was wrong, Tama said. *Humiliated*, Amanda whispered.
From now on Sarah would be right, right, right. Nobly, sac-
rificially right in the name of private righteousness. No one
would ever humiliate her again.

SAVING THE QUEEN

On the third floor of the Buena Vista mental hospital, Adrian
Van Ness peered through the one-way mirror at his wife.
Amanda strode up and down the small bare room shouting
orders to an invisible army of Amazon warriors. "We must
ride, my darlings. We must ride to revenge our beloved
Tama!"

She was naked as usual. She refused to wear clothes. The
wounds she had inflicted on herself still scarred her throat
and breast. With a sigh Adrian retreated to the office of the
hospital's director, a tall, owlish German named Farber.
Amanda's mother had died in this asylum. Willoughby had
brought her here because he hoped Farber's experience with
the mother might give him some insights into Amanda's
breakdown. That was now a failed hope.

"The prognosis remains the same?" Adrian said.

"I'm afraid so," Farber said.

For a year, Amanda had alternated between periods of par-
anoid calm and episodes of manic frenzy. They had tried the
new psychotropic drugs on her but they had had almost no
effect, beyond calming her. The delusion that she was Queen
Califia remained intact.

"You both recommend the operation?" Adrian asked.

"I have reservations, moral and medical," Willoughby
said. "For one thing, it's irreversible."

"That's part of its beauty, my dear fellow," Dr. Farber said.

"There are alternatives. Every month they announce a new drug," Willoughby said.

"But they don't affect the delusion," Farber said. "Whereas on this point the medical evidence is overwhelming in favor of our other alternative."

Willoughby said nothing about a third alternative but his eyes accused Adrian. Frank Buchanan had begged Adrian to let him take Amanda away with him and nurse her back to sanity. He vowed to devote the rest of his life to the task. Adrian demurred. He wanted Frank to devote the rest of his life to Buchanan Aircraft.

"Will I be accused of—of mutilating her?" Adrian asked.

"Of course not. It is still a medically respectable operation," Farber said in his heavy German way. "It does not threaten the life or health of the patient. The recovery rate is above ninety-five percent."

"She won't be a zombie, will she? I don't want a zombie for a wife," Adrian said.

"Not if the operation is a success," Farber said.

They were talking about a prefrontal lobotomy. It was a very simple operation from a surgical point of view. Amanda would be anesthetized and a steel needle, about the size of a ten penny nail, would be pushed through the front of her brain. The delusion that was consuming her would vanish. If it worked, she would be a docile woman for the rest of her life, capable of happiness albeit on a reduced scale.

The operation appealed to Adrian for several reasons. Victoria was coming home from England and he dreaded the idea of her seeing her mother in her violent Queen Califia state. A tranquilized Amanda, living at home with her husband and daughter, was immensely preferable to this madwoman in her cell.

The operation appealed to Adrian even more as an act of power. Amanda had escaped him by her flight to madness. He liked the idea of recapturing her, even though it meant keeping her as his wife for the rest of their lives. Adrian's profoundly conservative instincts had no quarrel with that idea. Perhaps most important, it put Amanda forever beyond Frank Buchanan's reach.

"Do it," Adrian said.

Willoughby grimaced, suggesting he still preferred Frank Buchanan's option. Adrian found ironic satisfaction in the doctor's pain. It was a preview of what Frank would feel. On the way back to the factory, Adrian tried to appease Willoughby with some news he knew the doctor would approve. "We're closing the Honeycomb Club," he said.

For several years Willoughby had been telling Adrian the club was a mistake. He had documented numerous broken marriages and an unacceptably high rate of alcoholism among its members. Amanda's homicidal diatribe had forced Adrian to accept his responsibility for it. "I expected a tantrum from Buzz McCall but he didn't say a word," Adrian said.

"He hasn't sobered up since Tama died," Willoughby said.

The next morning at Buchanan Aircraft, Adrian confronted another decision laden with future insomnia attacks: the design and production plans for the Starduster. It was a beautiful plane, of course, as beautiful as anything the company had ever built. But it was expensive. The SkyRanger, the pioneering all-metal plane that had saved the company in the 1930s, sold for fifty thousand dollars. The Starduster's price tag was 3.8 million dollars. The development costs would be a minimum of twenty million dollars—and Frank Buchanan's memorandum warned of unknowns in the turboprop engine that could significantly raise this figure.

Adrian sat there, contemplating the design. The huge Allison engines seemed to dwarf the short wing. Was this another hot plane like the Scorpion, which was still killing a pilot a week in Germany? His chief designer assured him it was the opposite—a plane that any decent pilot could fly safely. The monster propellers—fourteen feet long—would sweep a tremendous airstream under the short wings. The wing itself was a completely new airfoil, remarkably low in drag-to-weight ratio.

The net assets of Buchanan Aircraft—the value of its buildings, equipment, and property—were no more than thirty million. To build this plane, Adrian Van Ness would have to bet his company on his salesmen's ability to sell it to the world's airlines. That in turn depended on whether it could compete with the long-range jets that Boeing and Douglas were building.

As Adrian sat there contemplating the plane that could destroy him, he saw Amanda, sedated, her skull shaved, on the operating table. Dr. Farber approached, his thyroid eyes glittering above his face mask. He saw the terror in Amanda's eyes—and the rage.

Adrian shuddered and almost became ill. But he continued to watch in fascination as the steel needle was pressed against Amanda's temple, then slowly, steadily, tapped into the frontal lobe.

It was over. He had become this woman's master. His docile wife who would henceforth symbolize his mastery over all women—and most men.

That morning in the spring of 1957, Adrian Van Ness could with some justification have been called insane. His mother's death, Tama's suicide, Amanda's madness had catapulted him into a new spiritual dimension, a world of desperate, haunted need.

Suddenly he saw how he could guarantee the Starduster's success. He rushed up the two flights of stairs to the glass-walled executive dining room. Frank Buchanan and his designers were in their usual huddle around the bar, Buzz McCall and his engineers disdainfully drinking before the opposite windows. Cliff Morris, Dick Stone, and others were in smaller groups. Everyone turned to the door as Adrian entered, their eyes bright with anticipation.

Adrian walked over to Buzz McCall, the man who had told him he had no guts because he canceled the Talus. "How are things going with the SkyMaster program?" This was another generation of big transports they were building for the Air Force.

"Couldn't be better. We're two months ahead of schedule."

"Good. We're going to need half your engineers for the Starduster."

"Are you changing the design?"

Adrian shook his head. "We're going to have the most elaborate preflight testing program in the history of aviation. We're going to sell this plane on the basis of its safety! By implication, we're going to be telling people that the jets aren't as safe. The Starduster's going to be the only plane in the world that can claim it's crash proof."

"I don't think you can—or should—say that about any plane," Jim Redwood said.

"I agree," Buzz McCall said. "Until you get perfect pilots, planes are always gonna crash."

"I intend to say that about this plane—and prove it!" Adrian said.

He pointed to Buzz McCall and his engineers. "I want you to come up with tests no one's ever tried before. I want someone to attack the fuselage with an ax while it's under pressure—to prove it won't disintegrate like the Comet. I want landing gear strong enough to carry six tons more than the plane's gross weight. I want those wings twisted on racks, loaded with tons of sandbags and put into simulated four-hundred-mile-an-hour dives. I want a one-sixteenth scale model put through a hundred thousand wind tunnel tests. Forget about costs. Just concentrate on proving that this is the world's safest airplane!"

"Brilliant!" Jim Redwood boomed.

"Fantastic!" cried Bruce Simons, their raffish public relations director, who drank almost as much as Redwood.

"I like it," Cliff Morris said.

Adrian appreciated but discounted this praise. Redwood, Simons, and Cliff were all students of the power curve. For some reason he did not entirely understand, he wanted Frank Buchanan to say something even more extravagant. But his chief designer turned away without a word.

After lunch, Frank caught Adrian at his office door. "How's Amanda?" he asked.

The question unnerved Adrian more than a challenge to his plans for the Starduster. "The same. But I have some hopes of bringing her home soon. They've developed a new therapy that seems effective."

"What is it? Another drug? I have grave reservations about them. I question whether we should let the doctors play God with other people's minds."

"It—does involve drugs," Adrian said, an evasion at best.

"My offer still stands, Adrian," Frank said. "I feel I'm as responsible as you."

"I don't think either one of us is responsible," Adrian snapped. "It's an inherited disease."

"That's a trivial explanation," Buchanan said. "I prefer a spiritual answer. She's in revolt against the real world because between us we've made it intolerable for her."

"I have no such guilty feelings," Adrian lied. "Maybe I should have spent more time with her. But I had an aircraft company to keep alive."

"Are you sure she's not worse? All last night I heard her calling my name. This morning, around six A.M. it suddenly stopped. I wondered if she'd died."

"She's quite well," Kirk Willoughby said, from the doorway to the stairs. "I saw her this morning at the sanitarium."

"I'm—glad to hear it," Frank said and retreated down the stairs.

Willoughby followed Adrian into his office. "Is she all right?" he said.

"She's out of the anesthetic and quite calm. She recognized me. She didn't react negatively when I mentioned your name. She smiled when I mentioned Victoria."

"When did they do it?"

"Very early. About six A.M."

Adrian struggled for calm. "Do you believe Buchanan's story? Do you believe in psychic communication?"

"No."

"It's done. We can both live with it, can't we?"

"We can try," Willoughby said.

Two days later, Dr. Farber was on the telephone, informing Adrian that the operation was a "complete success." Adrian soon learned that the medical world measured success in ways quite different from the aircraft business. Amanda emerged from the surgery tranquilized, her violent fantasies obliterated. In fact she was so passive she refused to get out of bed for the first several days. But firm nursing soon overcame this reluctance.

Amanda had another reaction that Farber said was not unusual in lobotomies, although it seemed bizarre to Adrian—extreme tactile sensitivity. She screamed in agony when an adhesive bandage was removed. She could not endure even the slightest squeeze of her arm, her hand. In a word, her skin was so sensitive to pain she was untouchable.

"There is one other problem," Farber continued in his bland professional way. "About thirty percent of those who have lobotomies became extraordinarily outspoken. Their inclination to physical violence vanishes, but in an interesting compensation, they develop a tendency to make cruel and tactless remarks. Amanda seems to be among this thirty percent."

Was that a mocking smile in Willoughby's eyes? For a moment Adrian was tempted to get a new medical director. "In the aircraft business, we call these unpleasant surprises unk-unks," Willoughby said.

Two weeks later, Adrian brought Amanda home from the hospital. When he arrived to pick her up, Dr. Farber revealed a final qualification of the completely successful operation. "I think she can deal with most social situations. But I must make one recommendation. I don't think she can handle sexual intercourse. Aside from the pain you might cause if you touched her too aggressively, it might arouse memories in the deepest part of her psyche. We don't really understand how the brain—the mind—works."

For a moment Adrian hoped Willoughby would challenge Farber on this prohibition. But Willoughby said nothing. Did he think Adrian Van Ness was getting exactly what he deserved? Was he sitting in judgment on him in Frank Buchanan's name? Struggling for composure, Adrian took Amanda home. Around-the-clock nurses guaranteed her safety. She was quiet and completely submissive. She spent most of her time watching television, mostly game shows and sitcoms. She had no interest in the news. When she asked why she could not remember so many things from the past, Adrian blamed a head injury in a car accident.

A month later, Adrian decided Amanda was well enough to attend Buchanan's Christmas party. Her presence was especially important this year. The pièce de résistance in the center of the hangar was a gleaming white mockup of the Starduster. Everyone tramped through it while new employees were told in heroically sentimental terms the story of how the first SkyRanger rolled out six weeks ahead of Victoria Van Ness—and flew to glory. Everyone hoped Amanda was casting an equally favorable aura on the Starduster.

Amanda wore a ruby red Balenciaga chemise selected by Adrian. Older employees swarmed around them to shake her hand. The foreman of the work gang on the original Sky-Ranger, now the assistant manager of their Mojave Desert plant, was among them. He had brought along a picture of the original party. There stood Amanda, eight months pregnant, blinking into the flashbulbs. She looked at it and said: "I was pretty, wasn't I, Adrian."

"Yes," Adrian said.

"But you were rather vile looking, even then."

Everyone laughed. They thought she was being funny.

By far the happiest man at the party was Frank Buchanan—for the first hour. He kissed Amanda and said the new Starduster would be finished twelve months ahead of schedule, to celebrate her recovery.

After two attempts to talk to Amanda, Frank drew Adrian aside and snarled: "What've you done to her? What've you and Willoughby done?"

"Done?" Adrian said, glancing nervously around to make sure no one was within earshot. "We've cured her. Brought her back from a raving madwoman—"

"She doesn't remember me. She doesn't remember anything. I told her I was going to send her a copy of Pound's newest *Cantos*. She didn't know who he was! Ezra Pound! The greatest poet of the twentieth century! She doesn't remember Helen Hunt Jackson, Mary Austin—none of her favorite writers."

"She's had severe memory loss," Adrian said. "It's not unusual after acute psychosis."

"You're not telling me the truth, you bastard," Frank said.

He had a full glass of Inverness in his hand. "I dare you to tell me. I want to know where the woman I loved has gone."

"I loved her too, a long time ago," Adrian said. "I tried to love her again but it was impossible, thanks to you. Now it's impossible for both of us. But I promise you, as a man of honor, I'll take care of her for the rest of our lives."

Frank looked over his shoulder at the mock-up of the Starduster. "After a crime like this—a crime in which I'm willing to admit I share—do you think that plane will fly? Do you think we're worthy of it? Do you think the guardians of this universe will permit it? All I see in that plane is doom, Adrian. Death and doom!"

Eight hours later, at 3:30 A.M., Adrian sat in his study, unable to sleep, haunted by Frank Buchanan's words. For the hundredth time he rejected them. Why was he listening to a maniac's ideas about spiritual rewards and punishment? Adrian closed his aching eyes and saw the Starduster soar skyward on her huge propellers. This was the plane of his manhood, his liberation from the petty power-plays of Buzz McCall and his world of military procurement, of fawning over generals and politicians. The plane that would trump the jets on which millions were being gambled at Boeing and Douglas and Convair. The plane that proclaimed his supremacy over every man and woman in his universe. He was in command of his fate at last, a true conqueror of the sky.

DYNAMIC COUPLING

On a hot August day in 1958, Cliff Morris watched the first Starduster roll out of Buchanan's main hangar in Santa Monica. A band played and thousands of the men and women who had worked on her cheered. "You're looking at a plane that will sell a thousand copies!" Adrian Van Ness roared into the microphone.

Cliff had never seen Adrian so wound up. Gone was his usual aloof air of command. He was closer to a southern stump speaker whipping the faithful into a frenzy. Over and over, he called it the safest plane in the world.

Beside him on the platform stood his wife, Amanda, in a powder blue suit. She stared into the distance, barely listening to Adrian. Their daughter Victoria, back from England with a British accent that almost matched Sarah's, wore a forced smile that suggested she would rather be someplace else. She had matured into a tall, thick-bodied young woman with Adrian's heavy face and wary eyes and her mother's auburn hair.

Adrian was telling the faithful they had orders for 150 Stardusters on the books—worth a reassuring 380 million dollars. He had wanted two hundred—the shortfall was an index of the ferocious competition they were getting from Boeing and Douglas, who had salesmen prowling the country bad-mouthing Adrian's turboprop in favor of the pure jets their companies were developing. Adrian, playing cheerleader, made the 150 orders sound like a vote of confidence.

Goodwin J. "Goodie" Knight, California's governor, said the plane made him proud of the state, the aircraft headquarters of the nation. Eddie Rickenbacker, chairman of Eastern Airlines, who had ordered fifty copies, said he could hardly wait to put it to work. C. E. Smith, the balding benevolent dictator who ran American Airlines, added a similar apostrophe.

While everyone drank champagne, Cliff took Sarah and the children through the passenger compartments to the cockpit. "Wow," Charlie said, gazing at the array of instruments. "Is this more stuff than you had on the *Rainbow Express*, Dad?"

"About six times as much," Cliff said.

"When can we fly in her?" Elizabeth asked.

"Maybe when we go skiing in Colorado next Christmas," Cliff said.

"Let's hope it's as safe as they say it is," Sarah said. "I'm glad we don't have to fly in it for a while."

Cliff almost growled with irritation. He had a very large

personal stake in this plane. Adrian had not only made him the project manager, he had put him in the office next to his own, with a new title, Assistant to the President. "This is the safest plane in the entire world," Cliff said.

Cliff was not just echoing Adrian Van Ness. He had seen the incredible things they had done to guarantee the Starduster's durability. They had fired four-pound carcasses of electrocuted chickens out of a compressed air cannon at the cockpit windows at 450 miles an hour to make sure the outer glass and inner vinyl panes were tough enough. They had hurled frozen ice balls—make-believe hailstones—into the engine air-intake ducts to see if they caused damage. They had loaded tons of sandbags on the wings and vibrated them in the company's wind tunnel to guarantee they were strong enough to support the big turboprop engines. The Starduster had passed every test.

"Every aircraft company wants to believe that about a new plane," Sarah said.

Cliff knew she was really talking about the de Havilland Comet. He had sensed her hostility to his recital of the Starduster's virtues from the day he went to work on it. Adrian's decision to make safety its greatest virtue had sharpened her antagonism. It was more than the Comet and her father's death struggling to redesign it. Something else had gone wrong between them.

Sarah never stopped picking at him. She said his ties were too loud and bought him a whole new set. She decided he was getting fat and put him on a protein diet. She wondered why he never read a book. She told him he was too old to be driving a convertible and nagged him into buying a sedan. Yet in the bedroom, she was a tigress. She thought he was a no-taste numbskull but she wanted him almost every night. Was it part of that word, *need*, that had erupted the night the Korean War began?

Like most husbands, Cliff had no idea what was happening in his wife's psyche. He did not know he was in a bitter inner war between Sarah's traitor heart and her marriage vows. He was never home when Billy McCall wove his coded messages in the sky. "I was talking to Frank Buchanan before the ceremony," Sarah said. "He seems awfully dubious about this plane."

Cliff ground his teeth. In private and now in public, Frank had been incredibly negative about the Starduster. He said he was proud of its design but he was sure it would never be a success. No one understood the reason for this uncharacteristic gloom. Dick Stone and others theorized it was a residue of bitterness from the destruction of the Talus.

One month later, the first ten Stardusters started flying for Eastern Airlines. Another ten would be delivered to American in the next thirty days. Braniff, Northwest, were next in line. It was time to build on this sales momentum. A week later Jim Redwood and Cliff flew to Chicago and picked up the first New York–bound flight of an American Airlines Starduster. The plane was almost full and the chief pilot could not stop praising it over the intercom. He told the passengers the Starduster was the fastest-climbing, best-handling plane he had ever flown. He invited Jim and Cliff into the cockpit and thanked Cliff for making a number of changes a committee from ALPA (the Airline Pilots Association) had suggested. "Usually you arrogant bastards ignore ninety percent of what we say."

Back in their seats, Jim said: "You've got to hand it to Adrian. He's always thinking ahead."

"Yeah," Cliff said, with minimal enthusiasm.

Cliff had not completely forgiven Adrian for Tama's suicide. For a while he had carried her farewell note in his wallet. *I'm sorry to say good-bye this way. But I know you can take it like a man. That's all I ever wanted you to be—a man.* He had finally torn it up and told himself to stop thinking about it. Lately he tried to see the Starduster as a final gift from Tama, a flying carpet to the success she had always wanted for him.

The landing at La Guardia was pure powder puff. It was hard to believe the pilot was putting a four-engine plane on the runway. At the Waldorf, they unpacked and Redwood suggested a late supper at "21". They were halfway through their thirty-dollar steaks when one of the owners strolled over to them. Redwood had long made the restaurant his New York headquarters.

"Bad luck about your new plane, Jim."

"What plane?"

"The Starduster. One just crashed in south Jersey."

The steak congealed in Cliff's mouth. "What the hell should we do?" Redwood wondered. He was thinking of tomorrow, when they were scheduled to call on TWA to sell Stardusters.

"Let's find out if it's more than a rumor," Cliff said.

He telephoned Buchanan Aircraft and asked for Adrian. "His line's been busy for the past hour," the operator said.

"Get me Frank Buchanan."

In a moment Frank was on the line. "It was an Eastern plane. No survivors," he said. "Ten days after the plane went into service. I knew something like this was going to happen."

"Jim Redwood and I will go down there and see what we can do."

"Good idea. It will save us the price of flying someone from here."

The Starduster had crashed in farm country not far from Camden. By the time they got there the site was swarming with state troopers, local police, and officials from the Civil Aeronautics Board. The man in charge was the CAB's regional investigator, a tall, thin deadpan type named Jeremiah Coyne. He shook their hands and said: "Take a look. It ain't pretty. They never are."

In the headlights from a half dozen police cars they could see hundreds, perhaps thousands of pieces of Eastern Flight 915 scattered across a vegetable field—strips of torn aluminum and yellow insulating material and chunks of the seats and tail surfaces. Mingled with the metal and plastic were pieces of human bodies—a leg here, an arm there. In a tree near the farmer's barn dangled two headless corpses, upside down. The stench of burnt kerosene and scorched metal and seared flesh lingered in the humid air.

"This thing didn't crash," Cliff said. "It disintegrated."

"That's about right," Coyne said. "We just found the left

wing and the engines in the woods, a mile and a half from here."

"Are there any witnesses?" Redwood asked.

"The farmer and his wife were awake. He says they heard a weird sound—a sort of high-pitched whine—then a terrific explosion. The next thing they knew pieces of the plane started raining out of the sky."

Jim Redwood seized Cliff's arm and led him back to their car. His face was shiny with sweat. The grisly debris of the crash had made him queasy. "This isn't our job. Let Buzz send a couple of his engineers out here to pick up the pieces. We've got important appointments tomorrow."

The next morning, Cliff watched Redwood bombard executives at TWA with statistics on the Starduster's projected performance. They listened politely, agreed that it sounded like a marvelous plane—but said they would wait to hear the results of the CAB investigation of the New Jersey crash. "Midair disintegration is not exactly the sort of thing that suggests a crash-proof plane," TWA's brusque president, Jack Frye, said.

A disheartened Jim Redwood decided to return to California. Cliff Morris called Adrian Van Ness and told him he wanted to stay with the CAB investigation. "Go ahead," Adrian said. "I'm sure it's pilot error. Maybe you can stop ALPA from blaming it on the plane. That's their favorite tactic."

There was an hysterical trill in Adrian's voice. His legendary calm had seemingly vanished for good. Cliff called Frank Buchanan and told him what the farmer had said about the high-pitched whine just before the explosion.

"A runaway propeller at supersonic speed might cause that sound," he said. "But it wouldn't tear off a wing. Those are the strongest wings I've ever put on a plane. Only God could tear those wings off!"

In a warehouse on the outskirts of Camden, the CAB investigators began trying to put the pieces of Starduster YP448, its Buchanan serial number, back together. It was a slow, disheartening job and mostly it told them what had not happened. There was no evidence of an inflight fire started by a tire blowout or a hot wheel brake. The fire definitely occurred after the wing broke off. Had the pilot attempted a violent evasive maneuver to avoid another plane? The Federal Aviation Authority reported no plane had been within ten miles of the doomed Starduster.

In desperation, Jeremiah Coyne convened a meeting of every expert he could think of, including officials from the Army's Bureau of Aircraft Accident Research and the Los Angeles FAA personnel who had given the Starduster its airworthiness certificate. For five days they hurled possible causes at each other and discarded them. "If this lasts another day," the pilot who was representing Eastern cracked, "we may decide the accident never happened."

Cliff Morris flew back to California to report the impasse to Adrian Van Ness. "Pilot error," Adrian snarled, pacing his office like a man about to face a firing squad. "That damn fool tried some stunt to show off the plane."

"The pilot had over forty thousand hours in his logbook," Cliff said. "He was fifty-six years old. He wasn't the damn fool type."

"Every pilot's a damn fool when no one's watching."

Cliff went home to confront an unhappy wife. "I missed you so much," Sarah said.

"I know. But I'm trying to solve a problem that could put us out of business."

She turned away as if she were stifling a nasty reply. *You're getting what you deserve for your hot air about safety.* Was that what she was thinking? It did not make for loving thoughts. For the first time in his life, Cliff said he was too tired for sex and went to sleep with a cold good night kiss.

The next morning at the office, Cliff toiled on an interim report on the New Jersey crash for the engineering department. His telephone rang. "Cliff," Frank Buchanan said. "Another one's gone down. An American flight. Over Iowa."

At lunch the gloom in the executive dining room was thicker than any conceivable smog attack. Adrian Van Ness sat at the head of the table like a zombie. "Are you going to keep on yelling 'pilot error' now?" Frank Buchanan asked.

"It's possible," Adrian said, clutching his wineglass. "Co-incidences happen all the time. We don't even know why this one crashed yet."

"It's another wing failure. I feel it in my gut," Frank shouted. "But it's impossible. That wing was designed to handle every stress known to aeronautical science. Am I right, Buzz?"

"Yeah," Buzz said. He was drinking Invernesses by the gulp.

"How do we know that's true?" Adrian snarled. "Maybe the chief engineer was too drunk to read the report that warned us of the problem."

"If you're right, the man who sent in that report can have my fucking job, as of now!" Buzz roared, glaring at his engineers. There were no takers.

Again, Cliff volunteered to represent Buchanan at the crash site. At Los Angeles Airport, he had tickets on American's Starduster Special flight to Chicago. The man ahead of him on the line asked the clerk: "What kind of plane are you flying?"

When the clerk told him, the man said: "I'll take TWA."

In Iowa, Cliff shook hands with Jeremiah Coyne again. The CAB had ordered him to ignore his regional title and take charge of the crash site. "If you thought New Jersey was bad, get a grip on your nerves," he said.

American's Flight 444, en route from Chicago to Denver, had been flying through apparently perfect weather—blue sky, virtually no wind. About twenty-five miles south of Sauk City, two loud explosions startled farmers for miles around. Looking up, they saw a huge cloud of ugly black smoke. Out of the cloud hurtled Flight 444, minus both wings. Down came the smoking fuselage in a vertical dive to smash into a cornfield at approximately seven hundred miles an hour.

Cliff stood at the edge of the crater the Starduster had dug. It was forty feet deep and at first glance the 100-foot-long fuselage had disappeared in it. Jeremiah Coyne told Cliff that beneath the swirling smoke the long silver tube containing

some seventy-three men women and children had been tel-
escoped to less than thirty feet.

As Cliff gulped air to control his stomach, a thin sallow-
faced man with bloodless lips walked up to the rim and cried:
"Propeller fatigue. It causes more crashes than anything else
and those CAB bastards cover it up every time." He merged
a dozen reporters into an audience and made a speech about
corruption in the CAB and Federal Aviation Authority.
"They're tools of the aircraft companies," he yelled.

"That's the local congressman," Coyne said. "The son of
a bitch will say anything for publicity. We haven't even
found the goddamn propellers yet."

The similarities with the New Jersey crash were numerous
and chilling. The wings had come down some two miles
from the fuselages's crater. The breakup had apparently happened with no warning. There was no record of a distress
signal, which every veteran pilot would send if he had an
engine fire. "The biggest difference," Coyne said in his un-
dertaker's drone, "is clear air turbulence. We've got reports
from two pilots who said they ran into a lot of it just before
the crash. An Air Force jock riding a B-57 almost got his
head rammed through his canopy."

In his pilot days Cliff had encountered some mild clear air
turbulence. It was one of the most treacherous phenomenons
of flight. Without any warning, a plane could collide with a
swirl of air that knocked it up or down or sideways. It was
like hitting a pothole in the sky. But the Starduster was built
to fly through such obstacles with no more than an "oops"
from the pilot to reassure the jangled customers.

Once more Cliff participated in the grisly ritual of collecting pieces of the smashed plane and watching the CAB's
experts sifting it for clues. In a week they were at the same
impasse they had reached in New Jersey. Something had torn
the wings off the Starduster. But no one could explain how
or why it happened.

This did not stop Jeremiah Coyne from coming up with a
solution. "Ground it."

"Let's not do anything until I have a chance to talk to the
man who designed this plane, Frank Buchanan," Cliff said.

Frank's name was enough to check the rush to execution. Cliff flew back to California with the news and Adrian summoned the top brass to his office. He seemed dazed, unable to comprehend what was happening. Instead of taking charge, he let Cliff make his trumpet-of-doom report.

Buzz McCall was inclined to accept the sentence. "They grounded the DC-6s in 1948 for six months," he said. "It didn't ruin them."

He was recalling a series of disastrous midair fires on Douglas DC-6s caused by a misplaced air scoop that sucked gas into the heating system during a fuel transfer from one wing tank to another.

"Grounding will ruin this plane and this company," Adrian said.

"There's only one alternative. Limit the airspeed," Frank Buchanan said. "Cut it to two hundred and fifty."

"That's slower than a DC-6 or a Constellation!" Adrian said.

"I know that. But it will keep the plane in the air. Meanwhile let's launch the biggest emergency research program in aircraft history to find out what's wrong," Frank said. "If we sit here and wait for the CAB to tell us, we'll deserve to be out of business."

"How much will it cost?" Adrian said.

"I have no idea. If I were you I'd go to the nearest moneylender and tell him you want a line of credit as wide as the Mississippi at its mouth and twice as long."

Adrian's face was a grimace of pain. "All right. I'll call the CAB."

On the way downstairs, Frank seized Cliff's arm. "Find out if there were any modifications made on the engines or the wings of any of the planes since they went into service."

Cliff found there had been one fairly important change made after delivery. Passengers sitting near the huge propellers had complained of vibrations. The engineers had tilted the nacelles of the engines slightly, which in turn altered the angle of the propeller blades. Presto, the vibration vanished. Buzz's boys had checked with design before doing this and

Frank Buchanan's initials were at the bottom of the page beside *approved*.

When Cliff reported this to Frank Buchanan, he smiled forlornly. "That's our first clue," he said. "Now we're ready to find out why the Starduster has been crashing. We'll give it a scientific name. But the real reason will be unnameable, Cliff. It's a punishment for Adrian's evil will, his indifference to moral laws."

The ferocity of Frank's hatred for Adrian made Cliff his defender. "I've got reasons to dislike him too, Frank," he said. "But there's a whole company at stake here. Thousands of people's lives will be messed up if we go broke—including my own. Let's find that scientific explanation for their sakes."

"Are you ready to risk your life to find it, Cliff? I sense so much evil swirling around this plane—it's going to be very dangerous."

Cliff thought of Tama's farewell note. *Be a man*. Maybe that too was part of the gift she was trying to give him with the Starduster. "I'll take my chances if you will," he said.

Two months later, Cliff sat in the cockpit of a Starduster, strapped in by two sets of seat belts, as the plane headed for the Sierra Wave, a piece of sky above the Sierra Nevada Mountains famous for its turbulence. At the controls was Lieutenant Colonel Billy McCall, borrowed from the Air Force at Frank Buchanan's request. Frank sat beside him in the copilot's seat. Frank had insisted on Billy. He seemed to think he had some special power to resist the forces that were trying to destroy the Starduster.

Day after day for weeks now, they had flown Stardusters into the Sierra Wave, subjecting the planes to turbulence more violent than anything an airliner would ordinarily encounter in the sky. The company's two thousand engineers then virtually dismantled the planes to study the effect of this extraordinary stress.

In a half hour, the jagged snowcapped Sierras loomed on the horizon. By this time they had acquired personalities. They were a tribe of evil giants, spewing murderous winds. "Hang on!" Billy shouted as an updraft sent the airliner bouncing a thousand feet. A second later, a howling wind shear cut the air from beneath the wings, leaving the propellers clawing in a near vacuum. They dropped straight down like a stalled helicopter for three thousand feet.

To Cliff's amazement, they did not slide into a spin. Somehow, Billy kept the plane perfectly trimmed. "Jesus, Pops, I'm glad you thought of asking me to this party. I haven't had this kind of fun since the old White Lightning rocket plane days," Billy said.

"Get back up to twenty-five thousand feet," Frank said. "We're going to give these wings the ultimate test today."

In the passenger compartment, the seats had been replaced by sandbags weighing 97,000 pounds, the full gross load of the plane. Billy slowly climbed back to 25,000 feet, relit the cigar clenched in the corner of his mouth and asked: "Now?"

"Now," Frank said.

They dove into that cauldron of violent air, down, down with the airspeed needle rising up the dial in weird counterpoint to their descent. Past 400 miles an hour, past 425, the Skyduster's top speed, toward 500 miles an hour, probably faster than any commercial airliner had ever gone before. The raw brown slopes of the Sierras hurtled toward them.

"Pull it out," Frank said.

"Hold together, you son of a bitch!" Billy howled and hauled on the yoke. The motors literally screamed in protest. The fuselage did a conga. The wings flapped as if they were made of feathers. The g forces hammered at Cliff's brain. The memory of Schweinfurt swelled in his belly. But he fought his panic with new weapons. Tama's farewell message: *Be a man.* Knowing his son Charlie would remember him dying this way. A wild resolve to prove he was just as tough as Billy McCall.

Memory, fear, love, hate coalesced in the plane's roaring struggle to survive the Sierra Wave's turbulence. The next thing Cliff knew Frank Buchanan was asking him: "What kind of stress readings did you get on the outer wing?"

They were still alive. The wings had stayed on.

"High," Cliff said, handing him the numbers he had just

copied with a shaking hand from the dials of the special instruments in front of him.

"That's an understatement," Frank said, studying the figures. "That part of the wing is taking ten times more bending force than the rest of the wing. Who could believe that would happen from tilting a motor a few inches?"

Back they flew to Buchanan Field. "One more trip like that and they're going to need a spoon to get me out of this plane," Cliff said.

"Hey Big Shot, you're doing okay," Billy said. "I'm starting to believe you really flew those forty-nine missions over Krautland. I always thought Tama made it up for a press release."

"We're finding something new on every flight," Frank said. "Today could be the breakthrough. I'm betting those outboard engine nacelles will show us something."

Along with risking his life, Cliff was accumulating a graduate education in aerodynamics from Frank's inflight lectures. By now he knew there were a hundred different kinds of flutter that could attack a plane in flight. Designers had learned to check it in various ways so it did not explode into an uncontrolled spasm that ripped steel struts and aluminum skin to shreds. They were trying to find out if a new unsuspected kind of flutter had gotten loose in the Starduster's wing.

Billy roared in for his usual perfect landing at Buchanan Field. Buzz McCall and his engineers swarmed around the plane. "I thought so," Frank said, pointing to the struts holding the nacelles of the outboard engines. Two of them had bent inward from the g forces of the dive.

"The same sort of bends on the engines from the New Jersey crash," Cliff said.

"Exactly," Frank said. "In the Iowa crash, there were two struts broken. On to the wind tunnel. Cliff, ask Adrian to join our demonstration."

It was getting dark but Frank Buchanan had long since stopped paying attention to the clock. So had Adrian Van Ness. Cliff found him in his office conferring with Winthrop Standish, the company's solemn, hawk-nosed attorney. The families of the victims of the two crashes were suing the airlines and Buchanan for millions of dollars. Adrian was trying to fend off the suits, clinging to his theory of pilot error.

Adrian greeted Cliff with a bleak smile. "You're back from the Sierra Wave in one piece. That's the good news. Any bad news?"

"Frank thinks we've got it figured out. He'd like you to come down to the wind tunnel," Cliff said.

"What's going to happen down there?" Adrian asked.

"I don't know exactly."

"That's part of your job—to find out in advance, Cliff. So I can deal with it. Forethought. You can't use it without information."

"Frank isn't giving out any information."

Cliff found it difficult to sympathize with Adrian's fear that Frank would use the Starduster to diminish his power in the company. Those trips to the Sierra Wave had built something hard and cold into the center of Cliff's self. He was risking his life to save this plane. It made him impatient with Adrian's obsession with personal power.

In Buchanan's wind tunnel Adrian and Cliff found a one-sixteenth scale model of the Starduster sitting on a special mount, which could be manipulated to simulate movements in actual flight. Carefully, Frank Buchanan sawed through some of the struts and braces on the two outboard engines. They then adjourned to the control room and turned on the wind while Billy McCall "flew" the model from a panel in front of the window.

"When I drop my hand, pull up the nose and cut the air-speed," Frank said. "That's what the pilot probably did in Iowa when he hit clear air turbulence."

The wind whooshed through the big gray tunnel for another minute, the miniature Starduster bouncing in the turbulence. Frank's hand dropped, Billy jerked the model's nose up and cut the airspeed fifty knots on his toy throttle. Before their appalled eyes, the small Starduster suddenly shook like a bone in the mouth of an angry dog. Thirty seconds later—Cliff was timing it on a stopwatch at Frank's orders—both wings snapped off.

Frank switched off the wind. It died away like the moan of an angry ghost. "Whirl mode," he said.

"What is it?" Adrian said. He looked as if he were barely breathing.

"An extremely rare type of flutter. Two physicists wrote a paper on it in 1938. I'd forgotten it like everyone else until the wings started coming off."

Even Billy McCall, who thought he could handle anything he encountered in the sky, was aghast. "Why, Frank?" Buzz McCall said. "Why didn't it just damp out like it would on any piston plane?"

"Because the Starduster has turboprop engines," Frank said. "Those turbines are spinning at thirteen thousand revolutions a minute. The propellers are turning at a thousand. The whole thing is a giant gyroscope. The moment a jolt broke or bent one of those weakened struts, the engine started to wobble. That started the propeller wobbling and the whole vibration was transmitted to the wing, which was built to flutter at three vibrations a second. Whirl mode, for some reason, slows down from ten to five to three cycles per second. The moment both the wing and whirl mode got to three per second you got—"

"Dynamic coupling," said Frank's favorite designer, Sam Hardy.

"Exactly," Frank said. "What happens when a high musical note breaks a glass tuned to the same vibration level."

"Dynamic coupling," Buzz muttered. He shuffled out of the wind tunnel building like a man who had suddenly aged twenty years.

"It's not your fault," Frank called after him. "It's not the fault of anyone who built the plane. It's the sort of thing that can happen when you play God with other people's lives—and call a plane crash-proof."

"That's not true!" Adrian Van Ness cried, backing away from Frank as if he were some sort of supernatural being. "I've never done anything that wasn't for the good of this company. I've lived for this company! Are you going to listen to me or this madman?"

Billy McCall was smiling, enjoying Adrian's terror. Buzz McCall was gone—wiped out by believing whirl mode was a curse Tama had put on him. The rest of the executives, mostly designers, swayed in the firestorm of emotion between Adrian and Frank Buchanan. Someone had to take charge. It was like flying the *Rainbow Express* over Germany. You had to be a leader whether you liked it or not, whether you believed in what you were doing or thought it was mostly insanity.

Cliff Morris knew he looked like a leader—and he knew how to act like one. In that compressed room, with an explosion about to blow the company apart, he was the only man with some faith in the future. He still believed in the Starduster. It was Tama's gift to him. It had already given him a new sense of manhood.

"Wait a minute!" he roared. "Wait a minute! We've got a problem to solve. This isn't a courtroom. It's not the Spanish Inquisition either. Let's all go back to our offices and sit down and try to solve it! It's either that or start looking for other jobs."

"He's right," croaked a perspiring, trembling Adrian Van Ness, his eyes full of gratitude. That was the moment Cliff knew he was on his way to becoming president of Buchanan Aircraft.

GOING SUPER

Hatred—he was surrounded by hatred, Adrian Van Ness thought, staring into the darkness at 3 A.M. the next morning. The idea steadied him. Hatred was a force, a kind of airflow. He would use it to soar above the haters on wings of guile.

Insomnia added a dry, cold clarity to Adrian's mind. He

had sat at the dinner table last night and confronted Amanda's mindless hostility. He remembered the moment of decision, when he had ordered the nail driven into her brain. Did this woman—or any other woman or invisible spiritual entity in the universe have the ability to harm him? No, Adrian decided. Although the world was frequently incomprehensible, he did not believe it was controlled or even occasionally manipulated by invisible powers.

Amanda was counterbalanced by his daughter Victoria. Her presence reminded him of Buchanan's first breakthrough to prosperity. If there was such a thing as luck, she was his talisman of good fortune. He told her nothing about the crisis at the company, of course. But he drew strength from her plaintive sympathy for his public woes with the Starduster.

Philosophy aside, Frank Buchanan had demonstrated Adrian's pilot error theory was nonsense. Their design was responsible for killing 120 people. They, not the airlines, could be liable for all the damages in the pending lawsuits. If this information in its present version got out, they might be headed for the nearest bankruptcy court. As a crucial first step he had to regain Frank's support for the plane.

He summoned Cliff Morris and Dick Stone to his office. "Do you agree with Frank—that I'm responsible for the Starduster's crashes?" he asked.

They both shook their heads. He discounted Cliff's sincerity, although he was grateful for his support. He had sentimental ties to Frank and was, like most salesmen, a believer in luck. Dick Stone's negative was the one Adrian valued. He was a fellow believer in the intellect's cold unillusioned view of the world.

They discussed how to persuade Frank Buchanan to fix the Starduster's fluttering wing. Cliff volunteered to talk to him. Before the end of the day he was back with good news. Frank was ready to cooperate. "He even came up with a name for the redesign program—Project Rainbow."

"How much will it cost?" Adrian said, ignoring the gibe in Project Rainbow.

"He's discussing it with Dick Stone right now. It'll be damn expensive, you can be sure of that."

The success of Project Rainbow required someone who
did not get drunk at lunch and stay ossified for the rest of
the day. Adrian hired an executive from North American and
put him in charge of the engineering department. Buzz
McCall sat in his office, a ghost of the swaggering son of a
bitch who had intimidated everyone for two decades.

At Dick Stone's suggestion, Adrian decided to let Bruce
Simons tell the whole truth about Project Rainbow. Bruce
called in TV and newsreel cameras to film the one hundred
Stardusters in service as they flew to Buchanan Field and
had their motors stripped and wings rebuilt. Simultaneously,
Adrian told Buchanan's lawyers to negotiate a settlement
with the airlines, accepting a 50 percent liability in the damage suits. The costs were terrifying but the Scorpion was still
in production and bankers were impressed by Project Rainbow's boldness.

The CAB demanded a few more trips to the Sierra Wave
to convince them that whirl mode was under control in the
Starduster's redesigned wings. They declared Project Rainbow a success and lifted the speed restrictions on the Stardusters already in service. There were celebrations in the
engineering and design departments. But Adrian, reading the
memorandums from salesmen in the field, did not join them.
In spite of Bruce Simons's heroic publicity effort, the public
refused to fly on the plane.

Nevertheless, Adrian pressed grimly ahead. He hired a
half-dozen veteran plane salesmen to push their troubled
product. He sent Cliff Morris and Bruce Simons out to support them with hoopla and advice. They soon grew weary of
hearing "yes, but" from airline executives when they swore
the new Starduster was worry-free and certain to regain the
public's affection. The coup de grâce was American Airlines,
which had an option to buy another forty copies. They canceled the order and refused to talk to anyone from Buchanan.

In desperation, Adrian himself flew to New York and
joined Cliff and Jim Redwood in a final plea to American's
boss, C. E. Smith. Adrian brought Dick Stone with a briefcase full of cost projections to prove how many millions the
Starduster could save, compared to a jet. He even borrowed

Billy McCall to give the airline brass a chance to shake the hand of a famous test pilot and hear him describe what the new Starduster could do. They arrived at American's headquarters equipped with a motion picture camera and screen, to show Smith some of Billy's adventures on the Sierra Wave.

Adrian knew they were licked when they walked into Smith's office and confronted glowering red-faced Bill Horton, the airline's resident son of a bitch. "C.E.'s had to fly to Tulsa," Horton growled. "What the hell have you got in mind? You look like you're ready to show me *Gone with the Wind.*"

"We want to prove the Starduster is not gone with the wind, Bill," Adrian said.

"If you can do that, you can also sell me some beachfront property in Arizona," Horton said. "Don't embarrass yourself and me, Adrian. The plane is dead. Kaput. Let me show you something."

He pressed a button and a movie screen slid down the wall. Another button and onto the screen roared a swept-wing four-motored jet airliner with American markings. "That's the Boeing 707," Horton said. "We'll have forty of them in service next fall."

Five minutes later, the Buchanan team stood on the Avenue of the Americas, beaten men. *Ruined* crooned in Adrian's head. "Gentlemen," Adrian said, "You are now privileged to experience failure. They say it can be good for the soul. So far my encounters with it have made me doubt that."

"Adrian," Cliff Morris said. "You give me some money and support and I'll sell this fucking plane overseas. I'll sell enough to break even on this thing. I swear it."

"Breaking even was not exactly what I had in mind," Adrian said.

"It's better than going broke."

This was the tougher, more determined Cliff who had emerged from the Sierra Wave and saved Adrian from humiliation at Frank Buchanan's revengeful hands. But Adrian doubted his ability to penetrate the maze of a foreign culture to sell a commercial plane overseas. Perhaps teaming him with Prince Carlo was the answer. Ponty could deal with the subtleties, Cliff could provide the hard American sell.

At the "21" Club the young men drank Inverness and Adrian drank Sherry and listened to Billy McCall talk about the problems of the Strategic Air Command, where he was flying a Convair B-58 Hustler. It was the first bomber to hit Mach 2, twice the speed of sound. Billy had nothing good to say for it. The plane had escape capsules that could chop off a man's hand if he was not careful when he ejected. At Mach 2, the skin temperatures reached 130 degrees in the nose, threatening to cook the pilot. To slow down from supersonic to subsonic speeds, the pilot had to transfer fuel to keep the aircraft in balance, a frequently fatal maneuver. In fact, the Hustler had already killed more pilots than the Scorpion.

"After all that," Billy said, "the goddamn thing is too small. It can't carry enough bombs to do anyone serious harm."

"What do they need?"

"A supersonic bomber that won't kill pilots and can deliver a real load," Billy said. "They're going to ask for bids on it in a couple of months."

"I'm not sure I can interest Frank Buchanan," Adrian said. "He's vowed never to design another bomber. Can you talk him into it?"

"Sure," Billy said.

Adrian saw anxiety in Cliff's eyes. Interesting. Cliff did not like Billy's intrusion into the company's business. Adrian filed the insight for future reference. "A supersonic bomber could become the model for the next-generation airliner," he mused. "It's only a question of time before we go super there too."

"I don't give a damn what you do in the airline game," Billy said. "I just want one thing understood. If the politicians try the sort of shit they pulled on the Talus, we fight."

"Agreed," Adrian said, mentally reserving the right to change his mind.

"Let's all shake on that," Dick Stone said.

Disconcerted, Adrian had to shake hands all around. He

would have to give Dick a lecture on the need for greater detachment.

None of them realized they were entering a nightmare that would haunt them for the next twenty years. Nor did Adrian Van Ness, smiling hopefully at Billy McCall, foresee he was face to face with heartbreak.

LIMA BLUES

"Hemingway," Prince Carlo Pontecorvo said, banking the Starduster so that it was practically flying at a 180-degree angle along the flank of Machu Picchu. "I've hunted with him often. He too is haunted by his mother, who cast fundamental doubts on his manhood. It's an extremely common affliction. It requires a man to repeatedly look death in the face."

Sarah Morris was sure the belly of the plane was grazing the slope of the mountain. She got a swooping glimpse of the ruined palaces of the Inca kings. Her face and other parts of her body turned to rubber and bulged in unpredictable directions as the g forces sucked at them. Below the narrow saddleback on which the lost city stood, precipices plunged to a raging brown river. Around them loomed black snow-streaked mountains waiting to devour the bits and pieces of the Starduster.

The restored wings shuddered, the big engines whined as the palaces and the mountain itself vanished in swirling clouds. Cliff Morris, sitting in the copilot's seat, looked back at Sarah. "How do you like this?" he said.

He's afraid. Sarah read the fear on Cliff's face with a wife's practiced eyes. He's afraid but he isn't showing it. That's the way men deal with it. "I love it," she said.

The man who had forbidden her to learn to fly because it was too dangerous was now letting this corrupt aristocrat risk both their lives to sell this abominable plane. The Prince was not cleared to fly the Starduster. But the Prince thought he was cleared to fly anything, ride anything, sail anything, shoot anything, climb anything, love anything. He was the ultimate nobleman, the creature that a thousand years of Europe's civilization had strained and groaned and bled to produce. Sarah loathed him. She hated what he was doing to Cliff. She hated the male arrogance the Prince personified. The Prince and Adrian Van Ness were two of a kind.

I was wrong, Tama whispered. Wrong about trusting men like the Prince and Adrian Van Ness? Undoubtedly. With the help of Dr. Montague's pills, Sarah had achieved a bitter stability in defiance of them all—Cliff, Billy, Adrian, even her father, that missing person in her life who had done nothing to help her understand men.

"I didn't see *anything*," Amalie Borne said, filing her fingernails in the observer's seat beside Sarah. She was another example of Europe's decadence. The more time she spent with Amalie and the Prince, the better Sarah understood why England had always remained aloof from the continent, why so many Americans were isolationists.

The Prince banked in a wide circle and dove at the mountain again as if he were determined to commit suicide. He peeled away at the last second, leaving their hearts, stomachs and lungs behind. Sarah struggled to raise her eyelids, to hold up her head, heavy as a chunk of granite, against the g forces. Again she saw nothing but a blur of trees and crumbling walls. "That's much better!" Amalie said.

They flew on to Lima, the capital of Peru, where the Prince allowed Buchanan's assigned pilot to land the plane with the chief pilot of Peru's airline in the copilot's seat. Landings, unless they were in jungle clearings or on crevasse-gashed glaciers, bored him. He lectured them on the history of the place as they looked down on broad white beaches and the sprawling city in the lush splendor of the Rimac Valley, seven miles from the sea. "When the American pilgrims were sitting down to their first Thanksgiving dinner, wondering if they could survive another year of semi-starvation, Lima was a hundred years old, the capital of Spain's overseas empire."

What was he telling them? Lima was part of Europe, which entitled him to include it in his personal imperium? Something like that, Sarah was sure of it. She had become sure of a lot of things on this trip.

At Jorge Chavez International Airport they were greeted by a smiling delegation of Peruvian airline executives and their brothers or brothers-in-law in the ruling political party. They trooped through the Starduster exclaiming at its roominess, its comfort. No one said a word about its penchant for crashing. Its reputation as a jinxed plane had failed to penetrate South America.

With the help of the Prince, Cliff was rescuing his reputation as a jinxed executive. From Mexico south to Brazil and Argentina, then over the Andes to Chile and Bolivia and now Peru, he had sold an astonishing 150 Stardusters. It was exactly the sort of plane they were looking for south of the border, where there was not enough money to lengthen airport runways to handle jets.

Cliff had invited Sarah to join him in Santiago for a celebration when they sold their 150th plane. He explained that the Prince was along to impress the South Americans, all of whom doted on European nobility. But Sarah took one look at Amalie and suspected more complex, less moral motives.

That night, on the top floor of Cesar's Hotel, looking down on Lima's ghostly white Plaza de Armas, where Conquistador Francisco Pizarro once strutted, Cliff told Sarah the Prince was also along to dispense bribes to the executives who bought the planes and the politicians who supplied their state-run airlines with the money. There was not a hint of concern or contrition in his voice. He tried to make it sound clever, amusing.

"You could go to jail!" Sarah cried.

"Not a chance," Cliff assured her. "There's no law against bribing foreigners. Everybody does it. There isn't a country in the world where the guys in charge don't expect a piece of the action when they buy something as expensive as a plane."

As a convincer, he told her how they had already sold almost a thousand Scorpions to Germany, Holland, Spain,

Portugal, the same way. "I still think it's wrong," Sarah said.

"We're rescuing this plane, maybe the company, from oblivion," Cliff snarled. "Adrian sent the Prince along to make sure I didn't have another flop on my record. He knows three strikes are out in any game. You want to keep shopping on Wilshire Boulevard? Be nice to the Prince. And Amalie."

"Does she sleep with them?"

"I don't ask. The Prince handles that part of it. Most of the time I don't think so."

I was wrong, Tama whispered. Was she asking Sarah to tell Cliff not to trust Adrian Van Ness? She could see how much the Prince subtracted from Cliff's accomplishment. He could see it too, she was sure of it. But he was telling himself he still deserved most of the credit for the 200 million dollars in orders they had already rolled up. He had brought her down here to sell her the lie.

They spent the weekend in the forty-room mansion of the suave chairman of the board of Peruvian Airlines, who spoke perfect English and talked nonchalantly with the Prince about Cannes, Antibes, Portofino. The house was in the center of an immense valley, fifty miles from Lima. Cliff made love to her in a bed that looked as if it belonged in the palace of Versailles. He did not even mention the Starduster. He had decided to be indifferent to her disapproval. As his big body crushed her into the mattress, Sarah thought:. *Now I know how it feels to be fucked*. Amanda Van Ness whispered: *humiliated*

Cliff did not have the slightest idea what she was thinking. Afterward he cradled her in his arms and talked about moving to a bigger house in Palos Verdes, on the bluffs. In the morning they stood at the window and gazed at the mountain-rimmed valley with its terraced miles of coffee trees. "He owns it all," Cliff said.

"Why do you have to bribe him?"

"He likes Yankee dollars."

"Did Amalie sleep with him?"

"Jesus Christ!" Cliff said. "Maybe you better go home. The kids probably miss you."

Sarah heard the rest of the sentence. *But I won't*. She was swept by confused regret. After the struggle to solve the Starduster's crashes, she had found a new Cliff Morris in her house, neither the sullen playboy nor the husband who sought her advice, but a man who had discovered something inside himself that he liked, in spite of the Starduster's commercial failure.

Sarah had liked this man too. She liked the way he played basketball with Charlie in the yard when he came home from work, the way he was noticeably kinder, more patient with the girls. She realized he had done something that helped him play a father's role, especially with Charlie.

Now he was doing something he hoped Charlie would never do, something he could not admit to him. He had wanted her to know about it—and forgive him. No, more than that, he had wanted her to collaborate with him, rejoice in his clever corruption, his friendship with the Prince and his elegant whore.

I was wrong, Tama whispered. "Maybe I should get home," Sarah said. "When's the next flight?"

"I'll find out," Cliff said.

She was saying no. She was refusing to join him. She might be doing more than that. She was feeling something that had been growing in her since his refusal to let her fly and his cunning misuse of her father's death. She was telling him she no longer cared about his planes.

Where did that leave Billy McCall and his coded messages in the sky? Receding, receding over the far horizon, dwindling to a speck of memory, regret, contempt. She was freeing herself from both these Americans, with their strange ability to turn admiration into its opposite, to turn her inside out, to crush her heart and mind with g forces and contorted appeals for love.

Sarah saw the sadness in Cliff's eyes. And the fear. He hated what she was telling him. But she also saw the cold resolve. Whatever he had learned out there on the Sierra Wave, he was no longer afraid of his fear, his self-doubt. Maybe he was not even afraid of losing her.

Suddenly Sarah wanted to find out if that was true. She wanted to show him she still cared about the memory of those three months when they had loved each other without reservations, the months that ended with her discovery that she was pregnant with Charlie. She wanted him to know she remembered that time, no matter what she felt about his planes. "I'm sorry," she whispered.

Cliff stood at the window, staring down the valley toward history-laden Lima. "I am too," he said.

MORALITY PLAYS

Upside down in his Aero Commander, Dick Stone flew cheerfully over the dark green surf-washed cliffs near Cape Mendocino, in Humboldt County. "How do you like this?" he asked.

Cassie Trainor laughed. "You're a maniac at heart!" she shouted. You could not scare Cassie.

Aerodynamically, Dick was becoming a very good pilot. Psychodynamically, he was a mess. For three years, he had flown to Palo Alto to see Cassie as she majored in American Studies at Stanford. He had watched her self-confidence grow as she discovered that coming from Noglichucky Hollow did not limit her ability to think and learn. Outwardly, Cassie turned into an all-American girl not unlike her classmates in their brass-button blazers and pleated skirts.

Dick was fascinated by the Stanford scene, shot through with California sunshine. These western Americans seemed to have discovered the secret of life without angst. They were so good-natured, so well-intentioned, so confident that a future of married love, hard work, babies, success, would create happiness. Their optimism, their laughing serenity, seemed to confirm his decision to become a complete American, to abandon the Jewish side of his hyphen. But beyond the sunshine stood Amalie Borne, whispering: *Never ask me how.*

Dick banked the Aero Commander and headed out to sea. Climbing to ten thousand feet, he turned to Cassie and said: "Time for the autopilot?"

Cassie was already taking off her clothes. There was a mattress spread out on the cabin floor. Dick set the autopilot's slave—a tiny claw that fastens onto a heading—and waited a moment to make sure the plane was obeying its robotic commands. Then he struggled out of his pants and shirt. It was not easy to undress in a plane and it was even harder to dress. But in between there was an unforgettable reward.

It was part feeling, the vibration of the metal skin, the roar of the motors and the rush of the airflow, and part idea, knowing where you were, hurtling between the sky and the earth at 150 miles an hour. It was a marvelous blend of sensation and power. Cassie called it angel love. She said it was the way angels would do it, if they had bodies.

For Dick there was an even more important idea at first. He was challenging Billy McCall for supremacy in Cassie's soul. He was daring Billy's two ladies of the sky to make a move on him. He was blending danger and love to prove how much he wanted to make Cassie free and happy.

It had worked, it had broken Billy's spell. By now it had become a ritual. But it could not free Dick Stone from Amalie Borne's spell. She was always there in the shadows, mocking his attempt to be a macho American lover.

Lately he had begun to imagine him and Cassie as two lovelorn robots in a science fiction movie, two machines who had accidentally acquired the ability to love each other. He thought of his penis as a piston operating with the same methodical frenzy displayed by the gleaming metal rods in the Aero Commander's growling engines. They were parts of the plane, extensions of technology, not two fleshy warm caring bodies and souls.

Insanity. He had only seen Amalie Borne once in the last three years, at the 1957 Paris air show. Again their eyes had met across a crowded room. But this time Dick read the enormous sadness in them. She had left for Rome the following day without speaking to him.

Why was he being haunted by a woman who disdained him? Amalie answered the question with a mocking sigh: *Never ask me how.*

Cassie was above him and Dick had both his palms pressed against the hard teats of her coned breasts, while the engines pounded between his shoulder blades. He raised his head and rotated his tongue on the teats. Cassie bit the bone and flesh on his shoulder. The blue sky stared in both windows. Off to the left and right he could see the propellers whirling. He put both hands on her firm smooth rump and moved her up and down. Her tongue slithered up his neck and into his mouth. He breathed the perfume of her auburn hair, the sweet deodorized smell of her flesh. "Dick, Dick," Cassie cried. "I wish it could last forever."

There was a romantic answer to that question. Will you marry me and make it try to last almost as long as forever? But Dick could not say the words. Did Cassie expect them, want them? Money was not a problem. He was now the assistant treasurer of Buchanan Aircraft. Cliff Morris had rescued the Starduster from red ink by selling two hundred copies in South America. Cliff thought he could do almost as well in the Middle East. The design department was in a frenzy, working on a top-secret supersonic bomber. The Lady of Luck might not give a damn but she was smiling on Buchanan Aircraft.

He came and came and came and Cassie cried out with joy and raked her nails across his chest. There was still a delicious blend of desire and animosity in their lovemaking. She was still a creature to be tamed, mastered. She still resisted surrender—which made it so much sweeter when she came.

Sighing, Cassie put on her slacks and blouse and Dick got his pants and shirt back on and they flew north along the Santa Cruz coast to the Santa Lucia mountains, with the Hearst Castle sitting in the middle of their huge rocky faces like a rich child's toy. They had flown all over California in the last three years, seeing it from the air in all its immensity and splendor. From Muir Beach, a sliver of white sand between dragon's jaws of green crouching headlands to the great Central Valley with its stupendous swaths of fruit and vegetable farms to Death Valley's narrow wasteland.

He was heading for their favorite site—the winding serenity of the Russian River as it descends between green hills to the sea at Jenner in Sonoma County. Soon they were swooping over it at 1,000 feet. "It's what heaven must look like," Cassie said.

"I thought you didn't believe in heaven anymore," Dick said.

"That changes my mind," Cassie said, gazing down at the looping ribbon of water.

For a moment Dick wondered if this was more important than the love they had just consummated on autopilot. He had shared his ownership of California from the air—the word *ownership* kept forcing itself into his mind—with this woman. Could he ever do it with anyone else? Amalie Borne? That might be a betrayal of Cassie far worse than sexual infidelity.

They landed at the small airport on the outskirts of Palo Alto and Cassie helped Dick tie down the Aero Commander. They drove to a roadside restaurant in Cassie's 1950 Ford and discussed her future. She was going to graduate in four months. What did he think she should do? Could he get her a job at Buchanan?

Again the unspoken question dangled between them. "You might be better off at Douglas or Lockheed. If you're set on the aircraft business."

"Why?"

"The Honeycomb Club. People remember you."

Instantly, he hated himself for saying it. "Is that what's wrong? Is that what's worrying you?"

"Nothing's worrying me."

"That's not true. We haven't been honest with each other—in the old way—for a long time. A couple of years. We talk about American history and literature. But never about us."

"Maybe there isn't anything to talk about," Dick said.

"Really?" Cassie said. "You mean that?"

Dick was hating himself, the conversation, more and more.

How could he lose control of the situation this way? "We're not exactly romantic lovers."

"Whoever said we were?"

She had him. All the cards were in her hand. All the pain too. "Look, I don't mean any of this the way it sounds. I like you a hell of a lot. I wouldn't have spent all this time with you—"

"Maybe you're tired of starring in *Pygmalion*. Especially now the statue's startin' to talk back."

"You've been talking back since the night I met you. I like it."

"But you don't want to marry someone from the Honeycomb. It wouldn't fit the executive image. Is that it?"

"In this business? Are you kidding? It could make me the next president."

She did not like that either. Her eyes were bright with tears. A nerve pulsed in her temple. "I guess I'd just like to hear you say you love me."

There it was. The trump card of the 1950s, played between the heavy coffee cups and the thick plates of this roadside restaurant in the last year of the decade. "I do. But I'm not sure about the rest of it. Can you give me more time?"

"Sure."

He picked up her hand and was shocked to see how badly she had been chewing her nails. One or two fingers were raw, bitten to the quick. Maybe it was not as easy to become an all-American girl as some coeds made it look at Stanford.

Three days later, Adrian Van Ness called Dick into his office and told him to withdraw four million dollars from the Los Angeles branch of the Swiss bank in which they had set up a special account during the 1955 Paris Air Show. "The Prince is at the Ambassador. Take it over to him. It's for the Starduster sales in South America. Carry it on the books under extraordinary expenses."

So much for Cliff Morris's miraculous sale of two hundred planes, which he was celebrating all over Los Angeles, along with his promotion to sales vice president. Something deep in Dick's nature opposed this way of doing business. But he could not resist the way Adrian took him into the inner circle of the company's policies. It was a level of trust that no one else had achieved. It was Adrian's way of saying people like them, intelligent, sophisticated people, understood the way the world worked.

Dick could not decide what troubled him most, his own inner resistance or the way Adrian Van Ness seemed utterly unbothered by the bribery. Knowing nothing about Adrian's early commitment to Oakes Ames and his epic example of making ends justify means, Dick fell back on uneasy rationalizations. The money went to foreigners to keep Americans working. Buchanan was not breaking any laws. They were not even losing money for the stockholders—the bribes were merely added to the cost of the planes.

Dick brooded on these conundrums as he drove to the Ambassador with the four million dollars in his briefcase. At the desk in the ornate lobby, the clerk told him the Prince's line was busy. He wandered down a corridor full of shops— jeweled Swiss watches, the latest fashions in furs, dresses, shoes. A figure in the dress shop froze him to the deep-piled carpet. A tall woman with a mane of flowing chestnut hair. Amalie Borne.

Of course it made sense. The Prince was here. Why should he leave her in Europe with the meter running? Dick stepped into the shop. "It's nice to see some foreigners have a conscience," he said. "I bet before you're through with these shops, fifty percent of our lend-lease debts will be settled."

She turned, her smile arch—but pleased. "You're absolutely right," she said. "But I gather it can't be done without your assistance. Why aren't you upstairs? Your arrival has been anxiously awaited all morning."

"The line is busy."

"He's on the phone to his wife in Milan or his mother in Rome. He calls them every day."

"How admirable. It makes me feel guilty. I haven't called my mother in six months."

"Such schadenfreude. You ought to be ashamed of yourself."

"Can I buy you a cup of coffee?"

"You can do more than that. You can help me carry these dresses to our suite."

"I'm not interested in three way conversations."

"Why not? They allay suspicions."

He let the smiling saleswoman pile three large boxes on his arms and followed her to the elevator. "What sort of a tip can I expect?"

"If by tip you mean advice—I've already given you all I have."

In the suite, the Prince was just finishing his telephone call. "Ciao, Mamma," he crooned. "Ciao." He kissed the receiver and hung up.

"I encountered this old friend at the desk when I picked up our mail," Amalie said. "We met at the Paris Air Show. He took me to Verfours for dinner, saving me from starvation when you abandoned me for some disgusting Germans."

"I'm happy to see you again, Dick," the Prince said. "You have the full amount? Some of our friends in South America are growing rather urgent."

"It's right here," Dick said, handing him the briefcase.

The Prince opened it to make sure the amount was correct. The money was in five-thousand-dollar bills. "James Madison has such an engaging visage," the Prince said.

"I've already counted it," Dick said.

"We're flying to New York today," the Prince explained. "Then on to Rio. Any mistakes might be inconvenient."

"Of course."

"I'm taking an apartment in New York. At the Waldorf Towers," Amalie said.

"Oh?" Dick said. "I seem to recall you detested Americans."

"That sounds just like her," the Prince said, briskly shuffling through his mail. "She specializes in outrageous opinions."

"All of which are based on experience," Amalie said.

"If you come to New York, give us a call, Dick," the Prince said. "We won't be there often but we'd enjoy seeing you. Especially if the circumstances are as pleasant as they are today."

Dick knew he should say something equally ironic. But he looked at Amalie and said nothing. "This new supersonic plane—will it be ready soon?" the Prince asked.

"According to rumor, yes," Dick said.

"Business will be brisk. I hear the British and the French are working on one. And the Russians. If they can steal someone's plans."

"But not the Italians?"

"Lately our talent seems confined to cars."

"And women?" Amalie said.

The Prince smiled. Dick was mute. All his feelings for this woman were being aroused again, after he had struggled so long to banish them. She was boldly inviting him to visit her in New York, converting the Prince into her mouthpiece. What did it mean?

"Now you may buy me that coffee you offered when we met downstairs," she said.

"I'll call room service, darling," the Prince said.

"No. You have your usual long distance calls to make. I can't be witty while you're talking business. Didn't you notice that in South America?"

The Prince shrugged. "Pay no attention to anything she says, Dick."

In the lounge, Amalie ordered Coffee Amaretto. "He's so charming. And so disgusting," she said.

"Why don't you leave him?"

"I dislike complicated decisions."

"I still have that note you sent me."

She smiled, her eyebrows lifting. "It was a deft ending to our story, don't you think?"

"It wasn't a story."

"Dear Dick. Dick. It was."

"What do you mean?"

"I'm not Jewish. I'm Polish. I worked in Schweinfurt as a forced laborer throughout the war. I met Madame George there. She was in the same precarious situation. We agreed that if we survived, we would arrange to live splendidly after the war. She conceived the idea of telling men stories to enliven our friendships. I was practicing on you. It worked rather well, you must admit. I passed it on to Madame and another girl has used it on a Jewish banker from New York with great success."

"You're lying."

"I wish I was. I would have long since hired a writer to tell it to the world. It might make more money than that simpering little goody-goody, Anne Frank."

"I still think you're lying."

She shrugged. "Think what you please. Tell me what Adrian Van Ness is like."

"He's very shrewd—and he doesn't have a moral bone in his body."

"Does he have a mistress?"

"Not at the moment, as far as I know. His wife's had some sort of breakdown. He devotes a lot of his time to her."

"Is he generous?"

"Yes, on the whole."

"I dislike your reservations. I prefer simplicity in a man."

"Why are you so interested?"

"I'm at his disposal when I'm in New York. I suspect it may turn out to be the other way around. When he is in New York, I'll be summoned from Paris, Rome, wherever I happen to be."

"Why? Are you and the Prince separating?"

"No. He simply can't afford me any longer. His wife has been speculating on the Paris Bourse. She's mortgaged a great many of her estates and has no cash to spare. He depends almost entirely on Buchanan for his livelihood these days."

"He's selling shares in you!"

"You put it crudely—but I suppose it's true. I'm an asset. I suggest impossible dreams to men. They believe your planes fly without crashing."

"Will you be in New York soon?"

"Tomorrow. I have no intention of going to South America again. I found their food atrocious, their wine abominable, their men vile, their women pathetic. The whole continent is drenched in the despairing knowledge that they're doomed to perpetual inferiority to the Yankee colossus. I found myself believing you Americans may rule the world in spite of your naïveté."

"I'll see you in New York, next week."

"I'll make you miserable."

"I'll make you happy."

Did he really believe it? Was he ready to betray Cassie Trainor, abandon his all-American girl for this mocking elusive woman who clutched sadness to her being like a second skin? Dick was catapulted back to his first fantasies of what it would be like to bomb Germany. He had imagined himself hunched over his maps, giving the pilot headings in a calm, intense Hemingwayesque voice. Reality had been horrifically different. His heart had pounded, his voice had croaked and trembled.

Was it a warning? Perhaps. But the plane was already in the air. He was on his way to a strange country on a mission of redemption, not destruction. Wouldn't that make a difference?

In his heart Dick already knew the answer. He was rewriting the ethics of betrayal as Adrian Van Ness rewrote the ethics of selling planes. The consequences might be bitter. But he accepted the risk in the name of that elusive word, love.

BOOK SEVEN

WAR GAMES

A gasp ran through the crowd as the great white plane emerged from the main hangar of the Buchanan plant on the edge of the Mojave Desert. No one had ever seen anything like it before, except in science fiction magazine illustrations. It was two hundred feet long and weighed three hundred tons. A stiletto fuselage tapered to a flat span of triangle wing surface set above an engine intake duct the size of a hotel hallway. Head-on it resembled a winged creature out of the dawn of time, craning its beaked head toward the light. Everyone realized they were looking at the most original airplane ever designed—the BX experimental bomber, the Warrior.

"This one's gonna make history," Lieutenant Colonel Billy McCall said, throwing an arm around Frank Buchanan.

"It almost made me history," Frank Buchanan said. Only a few people inside the company knew how much inner agony this creature of the sky had cost their chief designer. He had been profoundly reluctant to build a plane that delivered nuclear weapons. No one but Billy McCall, implicitly reminding Frank of the promise he had made in New Guinea, could have persuaded him.

Thanks to Billy's early warning, Buchanan had a running start on the competition when the Air Force issued an invitation to six aircraft companies to submit designs for Weapon System 151. The requirements for the plane were mindboggling. It had to be able to fly at mach 3, have a global range, carry 25,000 pounds of bombs—and be able to land on existing runways. Four of the six companies blanched and decided not to bid. Only Boeing and Buchanan competed and they both submitted designs that were so complicated, the Air Force suggested scrapping the project.

At that point, Frank Buchanan discovered an obscure technical paper published by the National Advisory Committee for Aeronautics that proposed an aircraft flying at supersonic speeds could belly-slide on the shock wave it was creating, like a surfer riding just ahead of a big comber. Frank asked for a forty-five-day extension of the competition and lashed himself and his equally exhausted fellow designers into an immense effort to incorporate this principle, called compression lift, into their design. Buchanan won the contract to produce two prototypes.

Adrian Van Ness took one look at the plane and uttered a prophecy of his own. "That's the supersonic airliner of 1965."

"I was hoping someone would say that," Frank murmured, looking past Adrian as if he did not exist. He was still unable to speak his name without loathing.

"You better start building a new factory," said burly square-jawed General Curtis LeMay, head of the Strategic Air Command. "I want two hundred and fifty of these by 1963."

Two hundred and fifty planes at thirty million dollars a copy was 750 million dollars. With the usual follow-ons for spare parts it was a billion-dollar contract. "Will that fly in Washington?" Adrian asked.

Since the end of the Korean War, each year had seen bruising battles between the armed forces over the shrinking Pentagon budget. So far, the Air Force had won most of the fights. General LeMay reflected this momentum in his answer. "We'll make it fly."

Cliff Morris did not have the slightest doubt that Curtis LeMay could deliver on this promise. To him and other veterans of the air war over Germany, LeMay was an almost mythical figure. He had devised the tactics that enabled them to survive and frequently flew in the lead plane to sustain their sagging morale. He had crowned his wartime achievements by creating the Strategic Air Command, whose mission was to warn the Russians against any more Korean-type adventures. Currently equipped with subsonic B-52s built by Boeing, SAC's strategy of intimidation seemed to be working. As the year 1960 began, communism was quiescent throughout the world except for some sporadic guerrilla fighting in a remote southeast Asian enclave called Vietnam.

Cliff could see why General LeMay was ecstatic over the Warrior. It could cruise at 2,200 miles an hour at 70,000 feet, giving it an 800-mph advantage over any fighter plane known to exist. It could fly 20,000 miles without refueling, eliminating the fleet of vulnerable flying tankers that the B-52s needed for global warfare. If it was not the ultimate weapon, it was as close as anyone had come to it yet.

"Now all you've got to do is pray your bloody Congress doesn't go missile crazy," said a weary English voice on Cliff's right.

Everyone looked at Derek Chapman—and at Cliff—with an uneasy mixture of dismay and dislike. Cliff found himself wishing there was some way he could make Derek disappear, instantly. He was turning into a hoodoo, an albatross, a walking, talking intimation of bad luck.

Unfortunately, Derek was his brother-in-law. Making him disappear was impossible. Short, stocky, and balding, he seemed an affable, tolerable relative when he showed up in California, wondering if he could get a job in Buchanan's design department. Frank Buchanan was delighted to hire this son of his old British friend. Derek joined the department in the final stages of the superhuman effort on the Warrior and made some valuable contributions to positioning the canards, the small tail-like wings on the nose that enabled the plane to achieve compression lift.

But Derek's conversation soon gave everyone the creeps. He brought with him from England a tale of woe that sent chills through Buchanan Aircraft. He talked endlessly, bitterly about the way England's aircraft industry had been decimated by the emergence of the missile.

Last year, Russia's German rocket scientists had beaten America's German rocket scientists in a secret race and fired a capsule called *Sputnik* into orbit around the earth. Nikita Khrushchev, Russia's new strongman, had proclaimed his missiles made American bombers obsolete and the Soviet Union was the number one global power. In the United

States, this development had no immediate impact on the aircraft industry, beyond inspiring several companies to set up missile divisions. In England, where budget problems were far more severe, the minister of defense had canceled virtually every advanced aircraft in development, sending a half-dozen companies lurching toward bankruptcy.

It was unthinkable, Cliff told himself. It could never happen in America. A plane like the Warrior represented all Frank Buchanan and his cohorts had learned from the experimental rocket planes, the Talus flying wing, supersonic fighters like the Scorpion, the agonizing research into flutter to rescue the Starduster. When Buchananites looked at the BX's sweeping cursives and sharp obliques, they thought of the test pilots who had died in earlier planes, the designers and engineers who had collapsed with heart attacks or heartbreak when their ideas or their endurance failed them. They felt the pride of creating another leading edge in the history of flight.

The Air Force was equally unenthusiastic about missiles, as Cliff Morris had learned in more than one drunken evening with Billy McCall and his fellow colonels. Hot pilots all, they were horrified by the thought of turning into the silo sitters of the sixties. They had put on their uniforms to fly planes and they refused to believe that a hunk of hurtling metal with a fire in its ass and a computer for a brain could replace them. The Warrior was their answer to the missile.

These were the emotions vibrating through Buchanan Aircraft and the Air Force in the weeks after the Warrior rollout. Billy and a half-dozen other pilots began putting the plane through a series of tests that made everyone more and more euphoric. Never had they seen a prototype perform more precisely on or above its specifications. Heat problems were nonexistent, thanks to the exotic metals such as titanium Frank had used for the skin. At supersonic speeds there was not a hint of flutter or buffet.

Cliff frequently flew with Billy and enjoyed coming home to tell Sarah and the kids that he had been to Chicago or Hawaii and back that day. They got to Chicago in less than an hour, to Hawaii in less than two. Frank gave him a model of the plane for Charlie. Cliff solemnly swore him not to show it to anyone, because it was still top secret. Charlie loved it, of course.

Sarah watched, unenthused. "Why are you making him a pilot?" she said. "He may not be any good at it." Charlie did not do well in math or science in school.

Cliff curtly informed Sarah he was not necessarily making the kid a pilot, he might be making him an airline or aircraft executive. "I hope not," Sarah said.

Since their disagreement in South America, they had been observing a Korean-style armed truce. It frequently broke down, with Charlie often the battleground. Cliff's solution was brutal but effective. He stayed away from home as much as possible, using his new title of sales vice president as his excuse. He spent weeks on the road schmoozing with Air Force contacts in the Pentagon and at Wright Patterson Air Force Base and engine honchos at Pratt & Whitney and General Electric, getting a line on the latest thinking in the field.

In Washington Cliff began picking up some very bad vibes on the future of the Warrior. Back at Edwards (formerly Muroc) Air Force Base, Billy McCall bitterly confirmed the rumors. "They're talkin' about junkin' it, just like they did the flyin' wing," Billy said. "The gutless son of a bitch you've got for a boss will probably go right along with it."

"Not if I have anything to say about it," Cliff said, remembering Adrian's pledge.

Cliff reported the bad semi-news to Adrian and was encouraged by his reaction. "We've got to keep that plane alive," Adrian said. "It represents our chance to take the world commercial market away from Boeing and Douglas when we go supersonic. I'll talk to some people at the White House."

Adrian had been chairman of the California Business Executives for Eisenhower in both elections. He had some chits to play. A week later, as the big plane roared through a series of high-altitude tests, he telephoned Cliff. "Get all the pertinent data together and reduce it to one page. That's the most Ike ever reads about anything. Be at LAX tonight.

We're flying to Georgia to settle the Warrior eyeball-to-eyeball."

Twenty-four hours later, Cliff sat in a pine-paneled room at the Augusta National Golf Club, listening to Air Force General Nathan Twining, chairman of the Joint Chiefs of Staff, tell President Dwight D. Eisenhower why America needed Buchanan Aircraft's Warrior bomber. Beside Twining sat General Curtis LeMay. Behind them was a row of colonels and lieutenant colonels, including Billy McCall.

Adrian Van Ness and Frank Buchanan sat beside Cliff, ready to expand the one-page memorandum on the Warrior's performance envelope, if the president requested it. Dick Stone was also on hand with a briefcase full of financial information. Ike was flanked by his Secretary of Defense, Neil McElroy, and his science adviser, Dr. George Kistiakowski.

McElroy backed Twining with a strong plea for the Warrior, even if it never dropped a single nuclear bomb. He saw enormous possibilities for it as a reconnaissance plane, a military transport—and a commercial carrier. Cliff sensed Frank Buchanan's tension, as the president listened, deadpan. "I'm allergic to using military funds to develop a commercial plane," Ike said.

The astonishment on most faces was unforgettable. For a moment Cliff was sure Frank Buchanan was going to ask Ike where he thought Boeing got the 707 jetliner. All you had to do was glance at their military planes to see the connection. Anyone in the room could have told this man, who was supposed to have access to every piece of pertinent information on any subject under the sun, that leapfrogging from military to commercial models and back again was what the American aircraft business had done since its foundation. But the power of the presidency silenced everyone, even Frank.

"Mr. President," said Air Force Chief of Staff General Thomas White, "We need this plane because we think a flexible defense is basic to the nation's security. A bomber is under the control of a man, not a computer, like a missile. It can be recalled. It can take evasive actions, improvise avenues of attack. It can force the enemy to deploy defenses that absorb a lot of his energy and attention."

"You've got Boeing's B-52s for that job," Eisenhower said.

"They're subsonic, Mr. President. Their highest speed is 620 miles an hour. This plane can go three times that speed! We've got a plane that represents the greatest breakthrough in aerodynamics, in the whole science of flight, in two decades. We can't dismiss it. We can't afford to do that. The morale of the Air Force is at stake here!"

"It's your job to worry about the morale of the Air Force," Ike growled, his ground soldier's animus showing. "Mine is to worry about the economy, the morale of the whole country. It may be a great plane but a missile can do its job as well or better. That's all there is to it."

Cliff found himself thinking about Sarah's moral outrage at bribing half of South America to sell the Starduster and half of Europe to sell the Scorpion. Didn't this justify it? There sat the president of the United States, dismissing the greatest plane ever designed by an American. Consigning it to the junkyard. Where did that leave Boy Scout ideas like patriotism, loyalty, integrity? Adrian's attitude was the only one that made sense. You had to survive in this business by making your own rules.

Dr. Kistiakowski, Eisenhower's science advisor, now waded in. He dismissed General White's argument about the virtues of a plane versus a missile. If anything, the plane was more vulnerable. The CIA had recently reported alarming improvements in Soviet radar and antiaircraft missilery. They now had weapons capable of destroying a plane at 70,000 feet, no matter how fast it was going.

Cliff turned expectantly to his hero, General LeMay and his cohorts, expecting a furious counterattack. Instead, the generals and the colonels looked dumbfounded. The CIA had not said a word to them about such developments. It was Cliff's first glimpse of the way the American defense establishment operated, not as a team but as a collection of warring tribes.

The meeting broke up with the Air Force and Buchanan

Aircraft in disarray. "Now maybe you'll understand why I chopped up the Talus," Adrian said to Frank Buchanan as they rode back to their hotel in downtown Atlanta. "You see the stupidity, the arrogance, the infighting we have to deal with? The quality of the plane is irrelevant."

"I wish I'd taken my mother's advice and stuck to painting pottery," Frank said.

As they sat in the hotel bar gloomily sipping Scotch, Billy McCall joined them with General LeMay. "What's the next step?" Frank Buchanan asked. "Do we chop it up?"

"Like hell," LeMay said. "That goddamn plane is gonna fly or I'm gonna get court-martialed. That fucking infantryman knows as much about air strategy as I do about molecular biology. He's only gonna be in office another fourteen months. There's two political parties in this country and the other one is looking for an issue to beat Ike and his boy Tricky Dick next year. This plane could be it. What we want to know is, will you guys cooperate?"

"What do you want us to do?" Adrian said.

"Spend some money," LeMay said. "We're gonna bring congressmen out to fly in that bomber by the dozen. We want you to make sure they're well entertained."

"Can you protect us if Ike starts canceling other contracts?"

"We'll try," Lemay said. "But we can't guarantee anything."

Adrian looked at Cliff and Dick Stone. Was he remembering his pledge to fight for the plane? It was hard to read his impassive face. Was he thinking of his billion-dollar Starduster dream that would have made them independent of this gut-shredding political game? Probably. "We're with you," he said. "Cliff here will be in charge of the reception committee."

Cliff sat with Frank Buchanan on the flight back to California. "I'm amazed," Frank said. "I never thought Adrian had this much guts."

"He wants that supersonic airliner," Cliff said, trying to play peacemaker.

"So do I," Frank said ruefully, as if it pained him to agree with Adrian on anything.

First on LeMay's invitation list was the Senate Majority Leader, Lyndon Johnson, who was running for president. The tall, stooped Texan came to the Mojave factory on a swing through California to try to line up money and support. He had a memo in his hand when he got off his Air Force plane. "Is this bullshit or the God's honest truth?" he said, handing it to Cliff.

The memo was a hymn to the power and beauty of the Warrior. It declared the bomber was the issue that could make Johnson president. "The truth, Senator," Cliff said, raising his right hand. "I wrote it myself."

Cliff introduced Johnson to Billy McCall and they took a walk around the Warrior, as it crouched on its eight-wheeled landing gear in the desert sunshine. "That's the damndest plane I've ever seen," Johnson said. "Looks like a bald eagle with its neck stretched."

"Wait'll you fly in it, Senator," Billy said.

"You couldn't get me into that thing for all the gold in Fort Knox," Johnson said.

"I hope you have time to watch her go up," Cliff said.

Johnson shook his head. "I'm meetin' eleven oilmen in the Bel Air Hotel in exactly one hour. But this thing—it's got my support."

"We were hoping we could entertain you in other ways, Senator," Cliff said. "Buchanan's got some of the best-looking girls in Los Angeles on the payroll."

"Don't worry about me, son. I can get my own pussy anytime, anyplace," Johnson said.

The next day, the *Los Angeles Times* carried a story announcing Senator Johnson's "all-out backing" of the Warrior. "This is the greatest plane of the century," he said. "If we can't afford to build this plane to defend ourselves, we don't deserve to remain a free people. General Eisenhower is showing his age when he dismisses it as nothing more than a manned missile. I've flown in it. I've witnessed its miraculous technology in action. I am going to urge the Congress of the United States to fund it, no matter what the president says."

Cliff came home in a celebratory mood. He suggested cocktails on the patio before dinner and told Sarah the inside story of Johnson's endorsement. "We didn't even have to pay anyone overtime to entertain him," he said.

"You're still doing that?" she said, implying that Tama's stable should have died with her. "It's sickening to think a man like him is running for president. He sounds as bad as the Prince. Is his endorsement worth anything? You can't trust him, can you?"

"I'm getting awfully tired of your sermons on morality," Cliff said. "Did it ever occur to you that you're hopelessly out of your depth?"

"Did it ever occur to you that I might like a husband with some integrity, some genuine pride in what he's doing?"

"I've got pride," Cliff roared. For months he had tried to ignore the anger he had felt about her judgment on the Starduster sales. This new disapproval seemed to justify unleashing it with compound fury. "I've got all the pride I need. I'm proud of the plane. I'm proud of the way we're selling it. You don't build planes in a fucking convent school and you don't sell them in a church."

"Shhh, the children will hear you," Sarah said.

"Let them hear me!" Cliff shouted. "I'm not ashamed of what I'm doing. You're the one who should be ashamed, trying to undermine me with them, with myself. Trying to destroy my self-confidence. You're worse than your goddamn brother. He's sitting around telling everyone we're going down the tubes the same way you stupid limeys went, chopping up planes because the Russians found out how to shoot off a goddamn rocket."

She was trembling. Her eyes were swimming with tears.

"Maybe Derek—and I—can't help trying to tell you the truth. It's a bad habit among us stupid limeys."

He saw how impossible it was going to be to talk to her about anything from now on. "I'm sorry about the limey stuff. Let's forget it."

The next day at lunch Adrian congratulated Cliff for the

Johnson endorsement. "You can expect a visit from the mick from Massachusetts within the month," he said.

Adrian was talking about Senator John F. Kennedy, who had recently announced he was a candidate for the White House. Showing the built-in prejudices of his Boston ancestry, Adrian found it hard to believe any Irish-American could be presidential material. Within two weeks, the Kennedy office called to arrange a visit. A week later, JFK bounded off another Air Force plane and seized Cliff's hand with an almost lethal grip. "Where is this superbomber?" he asked.

Cliff introduced the senator to Billy McCall and he promptly recited three of the four records Billy had set in high-altitude flight. Billy grinned. "You must have had a hell of a briefing."

In the desert sunshine Kennedy seemed almost unnaturally youthful. Compared to him the drooping Johnson looked like an old man. As they rode down the flight line, Kennedy said: "We've got a mutual friend who says hello."

"Who?"

"Your old tail gunner, Mike Shannon. He's handling my campaign in New Jersey. Doing a great job. He told me what a hell of thing you did over there. Going for another twenty-five missions."

Cliff managed to grope his way past the memory of Schweinfurt to embellish the myth. "That's what happens when you fall in love with an English girl."

"Still married to her?"

"More or less."

Kennedy grinned. They understood each other. They were men of the world. A good feeling. Cliff's hopes soared. Shannon was a good omen all by himself.

The Warrior awed Kennedy. He walked around it twice. "It flies?" he said.

"Want to find out for yourself?"

"You bet. Should I make out a will?"

"Not to worry," Billy said. "We've got a parachute for you."

"What happens when you bail out at mach three?" Kennedy asked as they strapped in and Billy turned the engines over.

"You lose your head," Billy said. "And your legs and your arms and anything else that happens to be stickin' out."

"Let's go," Kennedy said.

It was as wild a ride as Cliff Morris had ever had in the bomber. Billy sent her right up to the red line, 2,273 mph. He took evasive action against imaginary fighters, rolling right and left, diving from 70,000 to 50,000 feet. Kennedy never showed even a quiver of nerves. "Where the hell are we now?" he said, looking down at the clouds obscuring the earth beneath them.

"Over Alaska," Billy said. "We'll be home in an hour."

On the ground, Kennedy thanked them and said: "I hear you fellows are good at other kinds of entertainment."

"We do have that reputation, Senator," Cliff said.

"What have you got that I haven't seen?" Kennedy said. "Lyndon told me you fixed him up with the greatest night of his life. But that raunchy bastard has no taste worth mentioning."

To avoid duplication, Kennedy let Cliff flip through his address book. It was full of names of movie stars that left him momentarily speechless. "Johnson's girl was one of our best," Cliff said. "But she's a little old for you. I've got another one from the top of our A list—"

"I'll be in meetings till about eleven tonight. Tell her to come by my room at the Bel Air around midnight," Kennedy said.

"She'll be there," Cliff said.

Kennedy flew on to LAX and Cliff got on the phone to Adrian. He told him how much the senator liked the plane—and what he expected for the evening. "She can't be one of the secretaries, Adrian. Have you got anything special in reserve?"

"I've got someone in New York. She can be here by eight o'clock. One of Madame George's girls."

The next morning, Cliff phoned the Bel Air from his office and got through to Kennedy. "I just wanted to make sure everything went all right on the entertainment front."

"It was special, all right. Where did you find her? I'm putting her in the front of my book," Kennedy said.

"Are you going to make a statement about the plane?"

"It's being typed."

Cliff had barely hung up when his secretary somewhat nervously informed him there was a woman who wanted to see him. She had asked to see Adrian Van Ness, who was in a meeting and had shunted her to Cliff. Ten seconds later, Cliff was face to face with the angriest, most beautiful woman he had ever seen. Amalie Borne glared at him and said: "Mr. Morris. Did you have anything to do with arranging my introduction to the famous Senator Kennedy?"

"In a way."

"I have a message I wish you would deliver to Mr. Van Ness. I am not a whore. I resent being treated like a whore. If I am ever treated this way again by you or Mr. Van Ness I will retaliate with every resource at my disposal."

"What the hell happened?"

"I have no intention of discussing it with you. Simply give him my message—and also tell him I have bought a few things at the hotel. The bills will signify in a very small way my outrage. I knew in my heart I should have nothing to do with you Americans."

Later in the day Cliff found Adrian Van Ness and passed on Amalie's message, including the warning about bills of outrage. Adrian told him not to worry about it. He showed him a copy of the *Los Angeles Examiner* with Kennedy's endorsement of the Warrior on the front page. "She got results. No need to worry about the bills if we land the contract."

Cliff could not resist finding out what sort of bills Amalie had run up. He told the story to Dick Stone over lunch and asked him to check with the accounting department. He was amazed by Dick's reaction. "You approve using a woman like that to sell this goddamn bomber?"

"Christ, you sound like Lady Sarah. I spent two months in South America with Amalie. She didn't exactly impress me as a Girl Scout."

"I met her in Paris. She's telling the truth. She's not a whore!"

"She works for Madame George, doesn't she?"

"You have the moral sensibility of a hound dog, Captain."

"If I'm reading you right, you're making a big mistake, Navigator. Stay away from that broad. She doesn't play by the usual rules."

"We're not talking baseball!"

Cliff was amazed by Dick's fury. It was out of character. "Hey, listen. Between her and Cassie Trainor, when it comes to dames, your taste doesn't exactly run to Snow White. I don't get this moral outrage act. Calm down and find out how much she charged us for being treated like a whore. Maybe that'll change your mind."

Later that afternoon, a memo arrived from the assistant treasurer.

TO: Cliff Morris

RE: Entertainment expenses for the BX Bomber.

    According to bills received today from the Ambassador Hotel, the following charges were made to the account labeled Adrian Van Ness Extraordinary: one white mink coat, $50,000. One Chinchilla coat: $85,000. One bracelet inlaid with diamonds and rubies, $65,000.

                                        Yours Truly,
                                        Richard Stone
                                        Ex-Moralist

WOMAN TALK

In the splendid new terminal TWA had recently built at Los Angeles International Airport, Sarah's brother Derek looked shabby and prematurely old—a veritable image of his once powerful country. Derek was going back to England after less than six months in California. His wife and daughter had already departed. He had stayed to complete some assignments at Buchanan.

"I'm thinking of writing a book," Derek said. "Aborted. About all the wonderful planes our idiotic government canceled. What do you think?"

"Do it," Sarah said.

Perhaps it would get the disappointment out of his system. He was so bitter. It was the real reason he and his wife had soured on California. They had soured on their country, their lives. He said he was going back to renew the struggle for the lost planes. But he was really fleeing the casual abundance, the assumption of unlimited success that pervaded America. He told Sarah he was afraid he would end up hating Americans and he did not want to do that. He did not think they were bad people, on the whole. Just spoiled.

His decision to go home stirred special pain in Sarah. She had encouraged Derek to come to California. She had persuaded Cliff to get him a job. She saw now it was a desperate attempt to cling to her English self, that moral idealist who had said no to Cliff in Peru. But it had not worked. Derek was so bitter, his wife was so intimidated by California's casual manners and morals, they had only made Sarah realize how American she had become.

"I've been meaning to ask you—but never quite found the courage," Sarah said. "Was Father faithful? Or did he have his girlfriends, like so many aircraft people over here?"

"I think he sowed a few wild oats. Most men do. But I doubt if he did much in his later years. He didn't have time, for one thing." Derek smiled bleakly. "Painful to say, but the damn planes get more attractive than women in the long run."

His Boeing 707 began boarding passengers. "Come see us," he said, kissing Sarah on the cheek.

She stood on the terminal's sunny upper deck watching the plane take off. What would he have said if she suddenly announced she was going with him? She was leaving them all—American husband, daughters, son. She imagined herself yielding to some drastic impulse like that more and more often lately.

She hated the way she and Cliff had drifted apart again to become polite, slightly hostile strangers. She wondered if he was faithful during his weeks on the road. She doubted it but she did not have the energy, the anger, to accuse him.

She rode an escalator to the lower floor, oblivious to the faces flowing past her. "Sarah!" called a woman's voice.

It was her old friend Susan Hardy. She lived several blocks from them on Palos Verdes. Her husband Sam was ascending on the design side at about the same pace Cliff was rising on the sales side of Buchanan. Susan had the same wicked tongue and disillusioned view of men and California. She had continued snacking in the afternoons and drinking hard in the evenings. She was now at least fifty pounds overweight.

"I've got an hour before my flight," she said, hefting a bag. "Feel like a drink?"

"I'd love some tea."

Susan gave her a wry look. Sarah could almost hear her thinking: goody-goody. They found a restaurant that served both liquor and tea. At the last minute Sarah decided she would have a Scotch and soda after all.

"Where are you going?" she said.

"New York," Susan said. "I'm going home to talk it over with my mother. I think I've had it with Mr. Five by One."

That was one of her milder epithets for her husband. For a while Sam and Susan had made a kind of revue of their alienation. But it had grown less amusing as it became clear they really did not get along and the humor was mostly serious insult.

"I'm so sorry."

"Nothing to be sorry about. Under California's wonderful new community property law, I'm going to take him for fifty percent of everything he owns. Then we'll see how much he spends on his Las Tunas Canyon cunt."

Why did you marry him in the first place? Sarah wondered. Why didn't you try to hold him? Lose weight, control your tongue? Appalling. She was applying Tama's approach to this bitter, unhappy woman. But Sam Hardy was not Cliff Morris. He was a thin, balding man with pipe-stem arms and a scrawny neck.

Was she still in love with Cliff on some fundamental physical level that transcended the hostility, the alienation that flickered between them? She remembered the night of reconciliation, his whispering *you're my luck* when he was inside her. She had loved that idea. It appealed to the mystical streak in her soul.

"He met her at the Honeycomb Club," Susan continued. "He set her up in this house that cost twice as much as ours—"

Swept by self-reproach, Sarah tried to listen. A woman was sharing her pain and she was thinking about herself. Her egotism was shameful. Sarah could only shake her head while Susan told her about Sam Hardy's obsession with this beautiful woman.

"She can barely stand the sight of him, dates other men—but takes his money."

"How awful," Sarah said.

"It's not that bad," Susan said, knocking down the last of her Scotch in a barroom swallow. "I'd rather see a woman sticking it to the bastard that way than the kind of thing that usually happens. Have you heard about Madeleine West, one of Billy McCall's ex-girls? She followed him to Korea and back to this country. He wouldn't even look at her. She became a drunk, a streetwalker. Last month she drove her car into the desert, soaked the cushions with gasoline and struck a match. Died like a test pilot."

"My God."

"Some women are vulnerable, Sarah. I'm glad I'm not one of them. I hope you aren't. I haven't heard anything about Cliff lately. Have you got him under control?"

"I hope so," she said, gulping the rest of her drink.

Susan departed for New York. Sarah drove slowly home to Palos Verdes thinking about the woman who had immolated herself in the desert. They were all loathsome! Cliff, Adrian Van Ness, even Dick Stone. But none of them could

equal the loathsomness of Lieutenant Colonel William
McCall.

I was wrong, Tama whispered. For the first time Sarah
began to suspect she knew what it meant.

SCHEHERAZADE AT WORK

"I arrived at the great man's room at midnight, as directed.
He was on the telephone. He interrupted his call long enough
to tell me to take a shower and lie down on the bed in the
next room. Only the supposedly enormous importance of my
visit persuaded me to stay. He was still talking on the phone
when I came out of the bathroom. I lay there for ten minutes,
listening to him debate with someone named Bobby whether
or not to support your wonderful plane.

"Finally he strolled into the room, pulled down the sheet
and examined me as if I was a cadaver on a slab. Five
minutes later I was back in the bathroom. I took another
shower. Never in my life have I felt so unclean! When I
came out, he was on the telephone again, trying to arrange
a date with another woman. He blew me a kiss as I departed."

Dick Stone lay beside Amalie Borne in the rose-and-gold
bedroom of her Waldorf Towers apartment, listening to her
describe her visit to John F. Kennedy. They were both naked.
On the television screen at the foot of the bed Walter Cron-
kite and other talking heads were excitedly reporting the
1960 election returns. The race between Kennedy and Richard Nixon was still too close to call.

As far as Buchanan Aircraft was concerned, it was a no-
lose situation. Kennedy's support for the Warrior had forced
Nixon to abandon Eisenhower's cancellation and promise to
build the plane. Nixon had stumped through California the
day before the election, telling everyone the Warrior would

provide an unbeatable defense against Soviet Russia—and 20,000 jobs.

On a chair in the corner was another briefcase full of James Madisons for the Prince, two million dollars' worth. He was arriving tomorrow to pick it up. After several false starts, intensive lubrication had persuaded the government of Italy to buy 150 upgraded Scorpions as fighter bombers. Frank Buchanan did not approve of burdening the plane with the extra weight—it would make it even more lethal to fly— but Adrian Van Ness decided not to turn down a hundred-million-dollar contract.

Dick was no longer worrying about the ethics of overseas bribery. He was more troubled by the moral perceptions of Amalie Borne. *I'm not a whore*, she had cried—and paid herself 175,000 dollars for the humiliation John F. Kennedy had inflicted on her. Dick's normally controlled, reflective self wavered in the violent emotions this woman stirred in him. He still believed the story she had told him in Paris was true. But tonight, after dinner at the Chambord with two bottles of wine, they had made love and she told him a different story.

She was the illegitimate daughter of Rudolf Hess, the Nazi leader who had fled Germany to England early in the war, supposedly to try to arrange a truce with England in return for a promise to depose Hitler. "That's why I prayed for your bombs to destroy Schweinfurt," she whispered in the shadowy bedroom, while taxis honked on Park Avenue forty floors below them.

She described growing up in a Germany that regarded her mother as twice a pariah, as the woman who had seduced Hess from the arms of his faithful wife—and urged him to go to England to try to rescue Europe from Hitler's madness.

Bewilderment sucked at Dick's brain. He was not psychologically equipped to deal with a woman like this. Was she simply crazy? Or was she compelled to create myths because the truth was too unbearable to remember?

"Now this Irishman, this case of satyriasis, is going to be your president," Amalie said, as the television cut to Kennedy's headquarters and he expressed confidence in eventual victory. "But you don't care, do you? As long as he funds your bomber."

"I care a great deal. I'm not a slave of the business. I have other hopes and dreams for myself, the country."

"What are they? Tell me? I collect illusions."

"Let's talk about us instead."

"Another illusion. How much money do you personally expect to earn from this bomber and other planes you hope to foist on the warmongers of this world?"

"I have no idea. I'll be happy with a reasonable amount."

"There is no such thing as a reasonable amount of money." Amalie pointed to the briefcase in the corner. "Is that a reasonable amount?"

"That depends on what you want to do with it."

"Would it be reasonable for us to take that two million dollars and disappear? Go to South America or Lebanon? Would you do that for me?"

"You'd spend it in six months and I wouldn't be able to make any more. We'd starve."

"I've starved before."

"Are you serious?"

"Are you?"

She was challenging him to abandon his career, his respectability, for her. He wanted her to do the abandoning, to join him in rational affection, reasonable happiness. How could he convince her it was possible? "I'm serious about loving you in the real world."

"You don't love anyone else? Some American or Jewish girl? I hear a frantic note in your voice, as if you were using the absurdity of loving me to escape her."

"I was fond of one woman I met in California. I still am. But it doesn't compare to my feelings for you."

"Does she want to marry you?"

"She did for a while. Now she's getting more interested in literature."

That was not entirely true. Cassie was teaching freshman English at Oxnard, a small private boarding school for girls north of Los Angeles. But she was still waiting for him to make up his mind about the step beyond saying he loved her.

His excuses were growing more and more fraudulent. She knew something was wrong—and he did not have the courage to tell her what it was.

"Do you really see me as a housewife pushing a vacuum? Shopping at the supermarket? Changing diapers?" Amalie said.

"There are servants who can do those things."

"You don't have the courage to say yes. You knew I'd laugh in your face."

"I have the courage to love you. You're the one who doesn't have the courage to believe it."

"Take me again. Slower this time. You're the only man in years who's aroused me."

They made love while the dark TV screen stared at them like the blind eye of fate. An eye that refused to blink shut, no matter how many buttons were pushed or pulled. The touches, the kisses, were simultaneously sad and joyous. When it ended with the same small cry, Dick felt strong enough to challenge God himself. "Now tell me the truth. Admit what you said in Paris was true."

"How many times do I have to deny it? As your reward for that half hour of happiness, I'll finally tell you the truth. I'm not German. I'm Swedish. I was recruited by Madame George on a visit to Stockholm. I speak excellent German because that's what we were all taught in school until 1944, when it dawned on everyone that Hitler was going to lose. Then we started studying English. I devoted six months to mastering Heine because Madame George insists all of us must know at least one major writer so we can discuss him intelligently. Heine was perfect for me because he was Jewish. I was able to make so many German industrialists squirm as I quoted him. It never dawned on me until I met you that he could be used in other ways."

"Why would you take up such a life? What did it offer you?"

"Money—and a chance to prove to my father what I contended throughout the war—that the Swedes were the whores of Europe."

Dick turned on the television set. Nixon had carried California, proving his switch to the Warrior was good politics even if—according to rumor—it infuriated Eisenhower. But Kennedy was carrying another crucial state, Illinois. "It's going to be President Kennedy," Dick said.

"I'll say this much for him. He has a reasonable amount of money," Amalie said.

They went to sleep and Dick dreamt he was walking beside Amalie down an arcade of shops, immensely longer than the little alley in the Ambassador Hotel in Los Angeles. It stretched over the horizon and Amalie methodically bought fur coats and diamond bracelets and pearl necklaces. She piled them all in the trunk and front seat of a gleaming red Ferrari that he was driving slowly behind her as she went from shop to shop. At the fifth or sixth stop, as Amalie piled a dozen pairs of shoes in the narrow backseat, she pointed at him and burst out laughing. Dick looked down and realized he was naked.

In the morning, he awoke exhausted—and reckless. "Are you going back to Europe with the Prince?" he asked.

"I doubt it," Amalie said. "Our partnership is becoming precarious. He leaves me in New York more and more. I see now why he agreed so cheerfully to this apartment. Italian men are incapable of speaking directly. They delight in sending messages in invisible ink."

Dick casually extracted fifty thousand dollars from the Prince's money and announced they would go shopping to celebrate their engagement. Amalie was not amused. "You're teasing me," she said.

"I'm serious," he said. "I want to see you spend a reasonable amount of money."

"I know exactly where to go."

They strolled up Park Avenue to Fifty-fourth Street and east to an auto showroom that featured Italian sports cars. A red Ferrari sat in the window, a gleaming creature so sleek, so curved, so powerful looking, it was a fusion of masculine and feminine. Dick bought it for 45,000 dollars and an hour later drove it up Park Avenue to Ninety-sixth Street. Amalie drove it back to the Waldorf Towers and parked it in the garage.

Madness. He had crossed some sort of boundary, exceeded some kind of altitude limit with this woman. He was no longer Richard Stone, the astute guardian of Buchanan's finances. He was no longer the rabbi's son, with ethical principles drilled into his bones. Maybe it had something to do with knowing too much about everything. About the plane business, about the new president of the United States, about Amalie Borne.

Two hours later the Prince arrived, looking somewhat tired. He explained that negotiating bribes with Italians was the most exhausting process in the world. There was always someone else to be paid—cousins, uncles, in-laws. But the deal was still set, if Buchanan agreed to a new wrinkle. The planes would be assembled in Italy.

Dick saw no objection but he checked with Cliff Morris to make sure. Cliff cleared it with Adrian and called back. "Nixon just conceded," he said. "Kennedy's the president. I think it's great. I trust him more than Tricky Dick."

"Yeah," Dick said with obvious unenthusiasm.

"Still brooding about Amalie? Have you seen her?"

"She's right here," Dick said.

"Ask her what she thinks of sleeping with JFK now. She may be getting invitations to the White House."

"She says JFK's got your problem. Satyriasis."

"Fuck you."

In the next room, the Prince was looking confused. He had just finished counting the money. "We seem to be a little short, Dick. With the added costs I've mentioned, my share of this arrangement will barely pay my barber."

"It must have been a mistake at the bank," Dick said. "I'll take care of it today. They have a branch in New York."

"Please enter it in the books as such," the Prince said. "I would not want to give Adrian the least impression of dishonesty."

"Don't worry. I'll take full responsibility."

"I'm to stay here in this dreadful city," Amalie said. "My lord and master thinks I will be happier here. He promises to return in a month. In the meantime I must rely on you for entertainment, Mr. Stone."

"I'll do my best," Dick said.

The Prince smiled. But his eyes betrayed a certain lack of amusement. "Madame George sends you a thousand kisses," he said to Amalie.

"Tell her I return every one," Amalie replied.

"She's her favorite," the Prince explained to Dick. "Ever since the war, no one has come close to her in Madame's affection. Others come—and often go abruptly. Madame can be severe."

"Our love is mutual—and undying," Amalie said, informing the Prince that his threat had failed.

The Prince began talking about the significance of Kennedy's victory. It would mean billions for Buchanan on the Warrior bomber, of course. But it was the Warrior's descendant, the supersonic airliner, that the Prince was urgently awaiting. In other respects, he wished Nixon had won. The Republicans guaranteed American stability. The Democrats were a party of political adventurers.

Dick barely listened to the Prince's monologue. He gazed at Amalie's beautiful face with its impenetrable glaze of smiling disillusion and told himself love was there behind the mask. Love that would somehow outshine the diamonds and restore the wonder and pity of that night in Paris. Love that would enable him to be an American and a Jew in a way that was beyond the gift of Cassie Trainor or any other all-American girl.

CAPITOL PUNISHMENT

"In the councils of government," President Dwight D. Eisenhower droned, "we must guard against the acquisition of unwarranted influence, whether sought or unsought, by the military industrial complex. The potential for the disastrous rise of misplaced power exists and will persist. We must never let the weight of this combination endanger our liberties or democratic processes."

"The son of a bitch," Adrian Van Ness said. "He'll make me a registered Democrat yet."

It was January 7, 1961. Dick Stone and Cliff Morris were in Adrian's office, along with a half-dozen other Buchanan executives, watching Dwight Eisenhower's farewell address to the nation. General Curtis LeMay had told them not to miss it. He said the word was out that Ike was going to get even with the Air Force for defying him on the Warrior bomber.

"That idea is going to haunt us," Adrian said. "Every loudmouth who wants to take a cheap shot at the aircraft business will use Ike as his authority."

Cliff was inclined to be skeptical. "Our guys are in the White House and he isn't," he said. "Isn't that what counts?"

"Let's see if they're our guys before we start celebrating," Adrian said.

Again, Cliff put Adrian's attitude down to his WASP prejudices against seeing an Irish-American win the presidency. Cliff was equally unimpressed by Dick Stone's loathing for Kennedy. So he wasn't the world's most considerate lover. Cliff suspected a lot of Dick's antipathy was ethnic rivalry. He was sore because a Jew didn't get there first.

The prospect of a billion-dollar contract for the Warrior was not the only reason Cliff liked Jack Kennedy. His election also had an unexpected warming influence on his marriage. Suddenly there was this wonderful idealist in the White House, telling everyone in Churchillian accents that it was time to do battle for freedom around the world. Suddenly the Warrior, even the Scorpion, did not seem quite so tainted by Adrian Van Ness's amoral methods.

Naturally, Cliff did not say a word to Sarah about Kennedy's sex life. He had stopped sharing almost everything like that with her. He seldom had anything to say about his work, period. She seldom asked about it. Their marriage was polite, tranquil—and empty.

Cliff did not worry about it very much. He was working too hard. There were always some congressmen or their aides in town to inspect the Warrior and enjoy the pleasures of Los Angeles, escorted by several of Buchanan's willing secretaries. Adrian supplemented midweek entertainment with weekend cruises aboard an ultramodern 150-foot yacht, the SS *Rainbow*.

On the night of JFK's inauguration, Cliff summoned Sarah and the kids around the TV screen to watch the news reports of Kennedy's speech. He had heard it in full at work—everyone was hoping he might say something about the Warrior. Cliff was genuinely moved by Kennedy's peroration, telling the world that a new generation of Americans was taking charge of the country, a generation that would pay any price, bear any burden, in the defense of freedom.

At work, everyone had cheered and slapped each other on the back, assuming that the price included a billion dollars for the Warrior. At home, hearing it again, the speech had a much more personal meaning. The hundreds of hours of boredom and fear in the *Rainbow Express* acquired purpose. Cliff Morris had helped to create this triumphant generation that was taking charge of the world. He held Sarah's hand and said: "Doesn't that make you proud of being an American?"

"Yes," Sarah said. "I think I finally feel like one."

Her expression reminded Cliff of the way she looked in England during the war—simultaneously innocent and sexy. That night, as they went to bed, he reached out to her and she responded to his kiss in the old yearning way.

"Maybe we ought to try to forget some things I've said—and you said," Sarah whispered.

"That sounds great to me," Cliff said.

For a little while they were lovers again.

In the morning at breakfast, Charlie asked Cliff if JFK was a better president than Eisenhower. "He's better than Ike and Truman and Roosevelt," Cliff said. "And maybe better than Lincoln and Washington and Jefferson too. He's going to tell the Russians where to go and he'll give us the money to build the greatest plane in the world."

"The Warrior?" Charlie said. "Any chance of a ride in that thing, Dad?"

"Maybe."

"I've made up my mind. I definitely want to be a pilot."

Cliff glanced uneasily at Sarah, fearing the abrupt end of their newfound harmony. But she only smiled and said: "You'll change your mind a lot about what you want to be before you're twenty-one."

Everything was possible in John F. Kennedy's America.

One week later, Cliff Morris sat in a plane to Washington, D.C., rereading with disbelief a story in the *Los Angeles Times*. KENNEDY ADMINISTRATION CANCELS NEW BOMBER. With sarcasm dripping from every word, Adrian Van Ness had told him to find out what happened—and see if there was any possibility of rescuing the situation. Buchanan had kept ten thousand workers on the payroll, sitting around doing almost nothing, while they waited for Kennedy to get elected and the billion for the bomber to arrive.

By four o'clock Cliff was in Curtis LeMay's office in the Pentagon listening to his bitter explanation. "It's the gang of Harvard whiz kids Kennedy's installed at the Pentagon," he said. "They put the data into a fucking computer and it came out *m-i-s-s-i-l-e*. You won't believe these double-domed characters. They wear glasses eight inches thick and they're about thirty years old. They sit there telling Curtis LeMay he doesn't know what he's talking about."

"I'm here to find out if we should lay off ten thousand workers tomorrow," Cliff said. "It's costing us about ten million bucks a month to keep them playing cards and shooting craps on the assembly line."

LeMay chomped on a cigar and growled: "You keep right on paying those guys. You can get it back from the contract. We're gonna fly that bomber. I don't give a goddamn what a bunch of fucking Ph.Ds who never saw a war say. We'll go up to the hill and get it this spring. You ever met Carl Vinson?"

Cliff shook his head. He had heard of the legendary chairman of the House Armed Services Committee, who was now eighty years old. "Truman wanted to make him secretary of defense," LeMay said. "Old Carl turned him down. He said he'd rather run things from where he sat. He wants that fucking bomber. But the first thing you've got to do is build some of it in Georgia."

"Why?" Cliff said.

"Because that spells *j-o-b-s*," LeMay said.

No further explanation was necessary. It was obviously the Air Force's answer to *m-i-s-s-i-l-e-s*. "That's a big decision," Cliff said. "I'll have to talk to Adrian Van Ness."

"Talk fast. We haven't got a day to waste," LeMay said. "While you're at it, talk to him about opening a plant in Oklahoma."

"Why?"

"Because Bobby Kerr, the head of the Senate Finance Committee, is from the fucking state. If necessary we'll throw in another Air Force base to make the bastard delirious."

"Can I make the call from here?" Cliff said.

He sat down outside LeMay's office and called Adrian. He got the idea instantly. "We'll be ready and eager to open plants in Georgia and Oklahoma. The extraordinary size of the Warrior program will require that sort of decentralization. You might mention that there'll be a vast expansion in the future, when we go from the bomber to the supersonic transport."

"I'll do that. In the meantime, ship me Dick Stone and a ton of data on the plane. We'll start selling it on Capitol Hill tomorrow morning."

Dick arrived that night with the data. They headed for the White House, where their old crewmate Mike Shannon now had an office in the West Wing, in charge of congressional liaison. The pintsized Shannon had become a scaled-down Jack Kennedy, complete with the haircut and one-button suit. Everything but a Boston accent. They adjourned to the Jockey Club, the best restaurant in Washington, and compared notes on the last fifteen years of their lives.

Shannon had married Teresa, the girl of his lovelorn *Rainbow Express* dreams and found out she was a nun. He had stashed her and four kids somewhere in Maryland. "How the hell is Lady Sarah?" Shannon asked Cliff. "You still getting it on with her?"

"About as much as you are with Sister Teresa," Cliff lied. He could never resist being one of the boys. "Stone here's the only guy who's done it right. Still a bachelor."

"That's because he's a Jewish atheist. No worries about sin," Shannon said.

"Is that right?" Cliff asked, remembering Dick's fury over Amalie Borne.

"Just guilt. Jews don't even have to commit sins to feel guilty," Dick said.

They finally got around to the bomber. Shannon explained it all very carefully to them. The president hated the idea of canceling it. He was Irish and a promise was a promise. But Robert McNamara, the secretary of defense, was not Irish in spite of his name. He had canceled the plane without clearing it with Kennedy. That had left the president in a very negative frame of mind.

"If you can get some support in Congress, you won't find anyone in the White House fighting you. Do you get the idea?" Shannon said.

"How about a little fighting in our favor?"

"I might manage some guerrilla stuff," Shannon said, with a knowing grin.

"To the *Rainbow Express*," Cliff said, raising his Scotch.

There was a split-second of hesitation before Shannon and Dick Stone raised their glasses. Cliff realized they were both remembering Schweinfurt. They were avoiding his eyes. Especially Navigator Shylock. *You son of a bitch, you wouldn't be here if it wasn't for me.* Cliff almost shouted the words in his face.

Shannon inadvertently rescued them. "Jack wonders if you've still got that dame he met in L.A. on the payroll. Amalie Borne? Can you fix him up?"

Cliff smiled wryly at Dick. "Sure. If she's willing."

"Let me know. We've got a back door to the White House Jackie hasn't found yet."

At the hotel, Cliff got on the telephone to Adrian Van Ness, even though it was 4:30 A.M. in California. Could Amalie Borne be persuaded to spend another night with JFK?

"I don't think there's a woman alive who can resist the

most powerful man in the world," Adrian said. "Just in case, tell her she can buy any fur coat in the store at Bergdorf's if she keeps him contented."

Cliff called Amalie at 7:45 A.M. the next day. "I'll be delighted to see your president," Amalie cooed. "Tell him to call me about arrangements."

Adrian was right, as usual. Where did that leave Dick Stone? Cliff decided to tough it out with him. At lunch he said: "I called your dream girl in New York. She said she'd be delighted to see JFK again."

"I'm not surprised," Stone said. "She collects examples of how low people can sink. Especially Americans."

"I don't get it," Cliff said, although to some extent he understood it all too well. It was not that different from Sarah's disgust with the way they did business overseas.

"She's in despair," Dick said. "She lives in a state of despair."

"She sure as hell doesn't act that way."

"That's one of the interesting things about despair. I've been reading up on it. It's totally different from depression. It's liberating. Once you give up all hope, you're free to do anything."

"Women are nuts," Cliff said.

"Maybe we're the crazy ones. We just happen to be running the show," Dick said.

Each day before Cliff hit the congressional trail, he called Sarah in Los Angeles. Each day he heard loneliness eating away the feelings they had rediscovered the night of Kennedy's inauguration. It was very confusing and upsetting. He was here in Washington because Jack Kennedy had broken his promise to build the Warrior. Covertly, he was helping the Kennedys sabotage McNamara to build a plane that the secretary of defense, theoretically Curtis LeMay's commander, had canceled. It was double-crosses inside doublecrosses, with a touch of mutiny.

Maybe Dick Stone was right. Maybe they were the crazy ones. But the plane had to fly. Everything depended on it. Every day, Adrian Van Ness was on the telephone reminding him of that fact.

Sometimes Billy McCall flew in to join Cliff and Dick Stone to see a congressman or senator who was into airplanes and wanted to talk to the famous test pilot. At the end of the day they regrouped in Cliff's room at the Shoreham Hotel and considered how to entertain themselves for the evening. Frequently Mike Shannon joined them and recruited some girls from his little black congressional liaison book for fun and games.

In his head, Cliff resisted and regretted the idea in advance. But it was impossible to explain without getting a sneer from Billy and squawks of disbelief from Shannon and mocking smiles from Dick Stone, who seemed to take savage pleasure in watching him go along with the gang. At times Cliff almost believed Dick knew he did not want to do it and was forcing him to play the game by Kennedy rules in revenge for Amalie.

Sometimes, in bed with one of Shannon's stable at the very moment of climax, Cliff would be seized with drunken regret. He would whisper a plea that he wished Sarah could hear: *I'm sorry.* At other times he remembered the night in Lima and exulted in the impersonality, the virtuosity of the fucking; it was a defiant throwback to his bachelor youth.

Meanwhile, Mike Shannon was assuring him that they were making excellent progress in their double-cross campaign on Capitol Hill. More and more congressman and senators were starting to wonder if McNamara knew what he was doing when he canceled the Warrior. Mike was in there pouring subtle salt on the tails of the more difficult birds. General Curtis LeMay also had a swarm of lesser generals and colonels working at it.

Then came the morning Cliff opened his copy of the *Washington Post* to find the front page black with disastrous headlines. President Kennedy had tried to overthrow Fidel Castro. The expedition was a fiasco. The attacking force was barely 2,500 men and their only air support were some World War II Douglas Invader bombers that Castro's jets shot down in about twenty seconds.

Cliff called Mike Shannon to find out what happened. His voice shook as he told the story. "Adlai Stevenson talked the president into canceling the air support for those poor bastards. The plan called for a squadron of Navy jets to go in there and blow Fidel's planes away. All he had were some T-33 jet trainers. Without them, the Invaders could've bombed the shit out of Castro's troops and turned the whole battle around."

Shannon ranted on about the influence of Stevenson and his circle of "fucking idealists" in the Kennedy administration. Cliff had more important things on his mind. "What does this do to our hearings on the Warrior?"

Shannon told him to forget about the Warrior for a year. It would take them at least that long to regain their leverage with Congress. "We're still spending ten million a month on those cardplayers and crapshooters in California," Cliff said.

"Give me a couple of days. I'll find something for you."

Shannon set up a lunch with Carl Vinson and a congressman from Iowa, whom Mike called "the Creature." He turned out to be the man who had stood beside the second Starduster's grave and blamed it all on the FAA and bad propellers. The eighty-year-old Vinson was sympathetic to Buchanan's plight in a courtly if somewhat fuzzy way. He told the Creature to get out the current list of defense projects and see if there was something in it for Buchanan.

Cliff took one look at the list and almost started to palpitate. It was a preview of what the Air Force, the Navy and the Marines were going to buy for the next five years. Skimming it, Cliff saw a hundred-million-dollar Navy request for ninety antisubmarine planes. The aircraft had to be big enough to carry a couple of tons of electronic gear, fast enough to get out to the deepest part of the ocean in a hurry, and slow enough to all but hover over the trouble spot.

"We've got a commercial plane that fits that description as if it was designed for it. The Starduster."

"One of them crashed in my district!" the Creature said. "We can't send our boys in blue out to sea in an unsafe plane."

Cliff labored to point out that the redesigned Starduster had been flying for two years without a crash. The Creature continued to agitate. Finally, Chairman Vinson said: "Down, boy. Let's have a couple of admirals decide how safe it is."

The Creature departed and Carl Vinson poured Cliff a glass of the best bourbon he had ever tasted. "Don't pay any attention to that fellow," he said. "He ain't worth a cup of warm spit. But he knows how to get elected and you've got to deal with him."

Vinson sipped his bourbon and studied Cliff with eyes that were no longer fuzzy. "Son," he said, "don't ever be ashamed to ask for money to build a good plane. This is the richest country in the world. Also the most thoughtless, wasteful, foolish. No one can imagine the United States of America losin' a war. But I can 'cause I come from a country that lost one. My Daddy fought for the Confederacy. He used to sit and talk by the hour about how sure they were that the pusillanimous Yankees could never lick 'em."

Congressman Vinson poured himself more bourbon. "You know how much this country spends on alcohol?"

Cliff shook his head.

"Ten billion a year."

"On cigarettes?"

Cliff shook his head.

"Seven billion a year."

"On hair spray and cosmetics and jewelry?"

Cliff shook his head.

"Seven billion a year."

On and on went the list of trivialities on which Americans spent billions, Vinson scribbling down the numbers and sipping his bourbon. Finally, without benefit of an adding machine, he added it up: fifty billion dollars a year.

"That's why it don't bother me much to spend a couple of hundred million on a good plane."

The next day, Cliff got an urgent call from the Creature. He said he had found new evidence that the Starduster was still unsafe. Cliff raced to the Congressional Office building in a cab, taking Dick Stone along for a backup.

In his office, the Creature announced he did not really have any hard evidence. In fact, his mind could easily be changed. "I've been hearin' rumors about a certain tall dark beauty Jack Kennedy's sneakin' into the White House. French. She does things only the French know how to do. How about fixin' me up for a night with her?"

Cliff contemplated the congressman's sallow, wide-pored cheeks with their overlay of five o'clock shadow. His chest was sunken; his wrists had odd bony knobs. He brushed at a cowlick and grinned expectantly.

"I wish I could do it," Cliff said. "But she's gone back to Europe. I think Jackie got wise to her. Jack told her to get out of the country for six months."

In the corridor, after hearing the congressman whine ominously about the Starduster for another ten minutes, Dick Stone said: "Thanks."

"Forget it," Cliff said. "We've got old Carl Vinson on our side. He tows that asshole around so he won't have to keep taking out his glasses to read the fine print on things."

Within two weeks, a team of admirals flew to Los Angeles to look at the Starduster. Within another month, Buchanan had the contract and Cliff and Dick Stone were splitting a fifty-thousand-dollar bonus. Cliff decided to fly home to celebrate. Dick preferred New York—and Amalie. He really had a bad case. Cliff gave him Buzz McCall's old lecture about not letting any woman get to you but it was a waste of breath.

Poor Buzz was not a very good example for anyone these days. He got drunk at lunch and stayed that way in his back office, where a few old loyalists visited him pretending to ask his advice, trying to make him feel like he was still in charge. Adrian kept talking about firing him but he was afraid Frank Buchanan would quit with him. Frank still blamed the Starduster crashes on Adrian. He said Buzz was an innocent victim.

Cliff boomed into Los Angeles aboard a 707 feeling ten feet tall about the bonus and the new career for the Starduster. The kids greeted him with yells of glee. Sarah's smile was more wary. What was wrong now? Out on the patio, he sipped his martini and tried to find out. "You look like you've got some news you don't want to tell me," he said.

"In a way, I have. Billy McCall is going to marry Victoria Van Ness."

For a moment the yard, the blue California sky above them seemed to contract to the cockpit of a spinning plane. How could she sit there smiling in that ridiculous way when she had just told him his career was ruined, his dream of becoming Buchanan's president was shredded, his life was a smashed burning wreck? Was she *glad?*

"Don't be afraid. We can handle it," Sarah said.

Her eyes were unnaturally bright. She looked happy in an odd wild way that Cliff had never seen before. That night in their bedroom Sarah made all the moves. She was as inventive as Cassie Trainor at the crest of her Honeycomb days. "Stay calm, keep your head. We'll destroy them. I *promise* you," she said, as he came.

They were together again. Cliff could sense a current flowing between them. But it was different from the old soaring tenderness. This current had a dark acrid quality; it cleared the passages, like Inverness scotch. It would take Cliff a long time to figure out what it was.

SERPENTS IN THE SKY

As he came.

As she came.

And *went*. Went went went went

Out of that familiar bedroom. Away from the soothing sound of the Pacific surf.

Went went went went streaking over the mountains into the desert. Metempsychosis. The transfer of the soul. It was happening as Sarah came and went.

She was in the desert becoming another woman. Leaving behind a different woman in her husband's arms. A soulless woman. Her soul, the source, the vessel of love and hate, her soul had entered Victoria Van Ness. Everything you read and see and hear from that woman henceforth belongs to Sarah, *is* Sarah. At least, that is what Sarah henceforth wanted to believe.

With the men and their endless deceptions of themselves and each other, Sarah had merely penetrated their souls, peered dispassionately into the accumulated darkness and confusion. But with Victoria it was entrance, becoming, acquiring. There was no alternative. Otherwise, Sarah could not have tolerated the idea, much less the reality, of Billy McCall marrying Victoria Van Ness.

It began in the desert, in the doorway of a little shack, not much bigger than the Watch Office at Bedlington Royal Air Force Base where Sarah had talked to pilots in distress. Into the boxy little building she had walked to discover Billy McCall and Victoria Van Ness. Behind Sarah in the desert sun stood a covey of congressmen and their wives, *oohing* and *aahing* at the sight of the Warrior's winged immensity.

Sarah had followed Mike Shannon into the shack, unable to resist another encounter with Billy. She was wearing a thousand-dollar violet Dior suit. Her hair had been done, her face and body oiled and massaged that morning at Monsieur Jacques, the best beauty salon on Rodeo Drive. Earlier in the morning the scale had said 110—exactly what she weighed when she broke the altitude record with Billy ten years ago. She wanted him to see all of her, she wanted him to eat another piece of his frozen heart.

Instead she found him telling Shannon he could not entertain the congressmen and their wives in the Warrior. He was taking a vacation—his first in years. He was going to Catalina Island for the weekend. Billy had turned to Victoria Van Ness and asked her if she liked Catalina.

Victoria glared at Sarah, a paradigm of defiance, of naïveté, of shame. "I love it," she said.

That was when Sarah divided. When the soulless part of her fled back to her bedroom to create inventive sex with her bewildered husband and her soul entered Victoria, became her willful, innocent, angry, driven self on the way to immolation and despair. Turning away in anguish, Sarah's eyes had found a distant Joshua tree. She had raised her metaphorical arms like that dumb plant and sworn eternal hatred and revenge.

Is all that perfectly *clear?* Now we can tell how it happened calmly, consecutively, the way stories are told.

The romance began aboard the SS *Rainbow,* the yacht Adrian had bought to entertain congressmen, Air Force generals, airline executives, and other visiting VIPs in the struggle to keep the Warrior alive. Adrian pressed Victoria Van Ness into service as a hostess. Amanda's unpredictable, mostly hostile tongue made her an impossible candidate for this crucial task. She was liable to say almost anything about Adrian, the plane, or the country. When she was aboard, Frank Buchanan became almost as unmanageable.

Victoria had come home from England a troubled young woman. She was very intelligent but her education had been almost entirely literary. Adrian had supervised it from a distance, trying to keep her mind uncontaminated by the hatred of capitalism that infected so much of British academic life. He wanted her to be a cultivated woman in the tradition of the previous century, indifferent to politics and business. It was an impossible dream and he did not come close to achieving it.

Instead, he got an amateur poet with an intense interest in business and politics, which she understood in a literary, emotional way, like most British (or American) members of the intelligentsia. Adrian, no longer a member of the intelligentsia, barely noticed this. He was far more satisfied with something else Victoria had brought home—4.5 million dollars from Clarissa's will.

Adrian was somewhat nonplussed to discover that there was a clause in the will forbidding Victoria ever to loan a cent of her inheritance to her father. Adrian explained it away (he thought) as an old, long-since-irrelevant quarrel. A father with a company grossing a half billion dollars a year hardly needed to worry about borrowing money. He did not know that while he was at work, Amanda told Victoria the clause proved his own mother did not trust Adrian. It was another proof—Amanda was always looking for proofs—of his hatefulness.

After five years in England Victoria found herself a stranger in a strange land. Los Angeles in the late fifties and early sixties changed faster in a half decade than most cities changed in a half century. Her friends were scattered; new dances, new music, new styles, pervaded the shops and nightclubs and beaches. Even more disturbing was the discovery that her father wanted her to be his companion, his social colleague, in her mother's place—as well her mother's keeper.

This was not a conscious decision on Adrian's part. Such things seldom are. He was living from week to week, month to month, like most people, hoping Amanda might somehow become the docile, polite wife he had envisioned when Dr. Farber recommended the lobotomy. Ninety percent of his time and emotions were consumed by the travails of the Warrior and other more mundane crises.

Buchanan had become a company racked by labor problems. Without Buzz McCall to keep the unions in line, there was a walkout a day on the assembly lines. The engineering department was also in chaos. Many of Buzz's best people deserted to Boeing and Douglas, who were building the commercial planes Adrian hungered to produce.

There was no hope of Buchanan penetrating the airline market now. Boeing's 707s ruled the transcontinental and transatlantic skies, with Douglas's DC8s not far behind. Buchanan was trapped inside the military industrial complex—unless the Warrior flew and catapulted them into the lead for the next-generation airliner, a supersonic jet that could cross the Atlantic in three hours and the Pacific in six. The possibility sat inside the angular, beaknosed fuselage of the Warrior. Is it so surprising that a man as driven as Adrian found it difficult to think coherently about his daughter's problems?

One of the most frequent weekend guests aboard the SS *Rainbow* was Lieutenant Colonel William McCall. Senators and congressmen and their aides liked to chat with a man who had flown planes higher and faster than anyone else— and was a Korean War ace in the bargain, with fifteen Migs on his escutcheon. Billy did not enjoy being ogled and verbally pawed this way. The more he saw of legislators swilling Buchanan's booze and gorging themselves on the gourmet meals served by the *Rainbow*'s French chef, the more disgusted he became with the government of the United States of America.

The *Rainbow* usually cruised off Baja California. Sometimes Billy would fly a Scorpion down to an airstrip the Pentagon, with the cooperation of the Mexican government, had carved out of the rugged desert on that arid peninsula and give the VIPs a demonstration of his readiness to risk death at supersonic speeds, sending the plane spinning, rolling, looping around the sky like the aerial equivalent of a dervish.

It was hardly surprising that Victoria Van Ness, a lonely young woman with a lifelong fascination for planes, would soon find Billy McCall the most attractive man she had ever seen. He seemed to be all the things her smooth, loquacious, lying father was not. Fearless, dedicated, indifferent to wealth (Frank Buchanan told her a lieutenant colonel made less money than a riveter on Buchanan's assembly line)—all the attributes an idealist could admire without reservations.

One night in the spring of 1962, the SS *Rainbow* cruised serenely through the placid waters of the Gulf of California. In the main cabin, six congressman were dining on pâté de foie gras and Alaska king crab. The one even his fellow congressmen called the Creature was drunk and pawing the hapless secretary Adrian Van Ness had assigned as his escort. On deck, Lieutenant Colonel Billy McCall picked out the constellations: the Great Bear, the Little Dipper. A full moon cast a swath of gold from the horizon to the hull of the ship.

Beside him Victoria Van Ness said: "Thinking of landing in a crater up there, Colonel?"

"Nope. Too old," Billy said. "I volunteered but they turned me down."

They were talking about the race to beat the Russians to the moon, which President Kennedy had announced as one of the objectives of his administration. "That's hard to believe. I would think they'd want the best pilots they could find," Victoria said.

"They turned Chuck Yeager down too."

"How old are you?"

"Thirty-nine."

Victoria Van Ness sighed. "I'll be thirty this year. Now, *that's* old."

Billy laughed. "I know what you mean."

They were silent for a moment. "I guess you can't stand the congressmen either," Victoria said.

"They're pretty boring. But it's part of my job to stand them, these days."

"They disgust me. It's like watching pigs at feeding time. How much did it cost to fly them out here?"

"Oh, counting my salary and my copilot's and engineer's and the fuel—maybe fifty thousand dollars."

"The more I learn about the plane business, the less I like it."

"How about the planes? Do you like them?"

"I love planes. I love flying. The Warrior is the most awesomely beautiful aircraft I've ever seen."

"You're all right, then. If you didn't care about the planes, I'd know we were in trouble."

"Why?"

"Aren't you going to own the company someday?"

"I have no idea what arrangements Daddy—my father—has made in his will. I'm not a businesswoman. Unlike you, my future is a question mark."

"What's my unquestioned future?"

"Someday you'll be chief of staff of the Air Force."

"Not a chance. They've got kids coming out of the Air Force Academy who know twice as much as I'll ever know about engineering or aerodynamics."

"You're teasing me. Frank Buchanan says you know as much about airplane design and engines as anyone in the country."

"Seat-of-the-pants stuff. I can't talk the game. Except maybe some folk wisdom like, 'if it looks like a good plane it probably will be a good plane.' "

"Would it surprise you if I told you I love you?"

There was a very long pause. The ultimate pilot, the man

who always knew exactly what to do in a flight emergency, did not know what to say, think, feel.

"I know you prefer beautiful women. Am I wasting my breath?"

"What do you mean when you say you're in love with me? What's it like?"

"I think about you day and night. I have trouble sleeping. I have a sudden impulse to smash windows. Or burst into tears. I write poetry about you."

"Let's hear some of it."

Victoria turned away from him and spoke the words to the dark Pacific's starry sky.

"There are too many horizons.
The sky keeps bending into question marks
While the clouds proceed, somnolent as cattle
Into the pastures of the night.
In the farthest stratosphere, a man conspires
Lonely as a hero in a myth.
Jung says we must go beneath the rainbow.
I say beyond it
Always always always beyond it
Where angels laugh at folly
And weep genuine tears."

"Would you repeat that?" Billy said.

Victoria recited the poem again.

"That's beautiful," he said. "That's almost as beautiful as flying. Have you flown in the Warrior?"

"No."

"We'll see if we can work it out. It's the most fantastic experience I've ever had."

"I've loved you for a long time, girlishly. You're extremely handsome and you make planes like the Scorpion do miraculous things in the air. But since I've come home, I've stopped being girlish. You're the only man in this business besides Frank Buchanan who seems to have retained a shred of integrity. You smile and talk flying with slobs like the congressmen and crooks like my father but I sense you're as lonely as I am."

"You've got that all wrong," Billy said.

Of course Victoria had most of it right but it was too painful for Billy to admit. At thirty-nine, he was heading into middle age without thinking about it, relying on the same instinctual skills that had enabled him to survive in the sky. He had no children and no special woman in his life. The result was a profound loneliness. Billy dealt with it stoically, the way a warrior deals with pain.

His lifestyle simultaneously deepened and disguised his loneliness. His good looks had weathered well. There were bleak Gary Cooperish lines in his face and skeptical wrinkles on his brow. He remained irresistible to women of all ages. His enthusiasm for flying them had not significantly diminished. A certain boredom, a first cousin of loneliness, was beginning to bother him. He told himself it was just getting to be a long time between wars.

The problem that made Billy's loneliness hard to bear was his anger. It lurked beneath the surface of his relaxed cocky manner, revealing itself in sarcasm and occasional flashes of temper. But it was always there in his personal sky like a blue storm swirling off the jet stream, invisible until it struck.

"Let's think about it," he said. "Let's fly together first and think about it."

Victoria fled to Frank Buchanan. He was the invisible third in this explosive equation. Victoria had, like most women, found his honesty, his spontaneity, his love of poetry, irresistible. She had confided her feelings about Billy to him and he had urged her to be bold, to be a modern woman and speak first.

That night, Frank too was boycotting the congressmen. He sat in his stateroom sketching a design for a supersonic airliner. "It didn't work!" Victoria cried. "All he wants to do is give me a ride in the Warrior. He's treating me like a teenager!"

"That's a very significant first step. Be patient. You're just like your mother. You expect miracles on demand."

Did Frank find secret savage satisfaction in encouraging

Victoria Van Ness? Unquestionably. But he was also thinking about Billy, whom he continued to love without reservations, a fathering love that grew stronger as Buzz McCall receded into negligibility in both their lives. What could be more marvelous (and more savagely satisfying) than the prospect of Billy retiring from the Air Force as a general in five or ten years and becoming president of Buchanan Aircraft with the backing of the majority stockholder, his wife?

Frank made sure that the Warrior had a busy schedule in the coming week. The big plane was being used in an Air Force–funded research program called HICAT, an acronym for High Altitude Clear Air Turbulence. Everyone from NACA, the National Advisory Committee for Aeronautics (forerunner to NASA) had become seriously concerned about the discovery of clear air turbulence in the stratosphere. If a supersonic plane was going to be developed, the location and magnitude of this menace had to be explored. It was bad enough to hit CAT at low or medium altitudes in a prop plane. Hitting it in a supersonic jet would magnify the impact a hundred times. It was the difference between a car going over a bump in a driveway and a bus hitting a boulder on a high-speed highway.

Frank had absolute confidence in the design integrity of the Warrior. So he did not have the slightest qualm about assigning Billy to investigate one of the toughest problems confronting supersonic flights over the North Pole, a phenomenon called the Polar Night Vortex, which contains winds of up to 380 miles per hour. It also tends to have sudden seasonal drops in temperature of as much as forty degrees, creating awesome windshears. Meteorologists using pictures from weather satellites and data from sounding rockets had been able to locate this jet stream in a general way. Billy was ordered to cruise close to it and see what sort of HICAT he encountered. The Warrior was loaded with gear to monitor its force and the impact on the plane's surfaces.

"I gather Victoria Van Ness has spoken to you about flying in the Warrior," Frank said. "She won't be able to do it once it goes back under Air Force control. Why don't you take her up on the next flight?"

"Won't her father have a goddamn fit?" Billy said. "This is sort of dangerous, Pops."

"Her father doesn't have to know about it." Frank paused to let Billy absorb the message he was sending. "You don't need a beautiful woman for a wife. It usually complicates things."

That afternoon, Billy invited Victoria on the flight. The next morning, she arrived at the Mojave field almost an hour early. Billy matter-of-factly found her a flight suit. "Did you tell your father where you're going?" he said.

"No. I hope you don't feel compelled to file a report."

"I never feel compelled to do anything," Billy said.

Victoria sat in the observer's jump seat behind Billy and the copilot, an easygoing Texan who was properly impressed by the boss's daughter. Into the stratosphere the big plane soared while the mach needle climbed up the dial toward 3. There were slight jolts as they went through mach 1 and 2. The loudest sound in the cockpit was duct rumble, which Billy had explained in advance. It was created by pressure fluctuations in the engines as air entered them at supersonic speed. Otherwise, the ride was unbelievably smooth and quiet. The thunder of the huge motors was flung miles behind them as they cruised on the shock waves the nose canards drove beneath the wings.

"Sixty thousand feet," the copilot said. "Getting close to the top of the ride, Billy."

"Here comes the hard part," Billy said. "Make damn sure you're belted in, Victoria."

"Don't worry about me," she said. "Look at that sun! The horizon!"

The morning sun was a burning white disc, filling the blue-black sky with incredibly intense light. The horizon ahead of them seemed infinite. Billy did not have time to admire the scenery. He was concentrating on leveling off at precisely the correct pitch attitude. A mistake would create weightlessness, a scary phenomenon he did not want Victoria to experience.

They eased into horizontal cruise at mach 3 without losing contact with gravity. Billy explained what might have happened. "That's gonna be one of the problems if they turn this big baby into an airliner. A half degree off pitch and the martinis'll be floatin' against the ceilin'."

Victoria laughed. "I love that idea."

"Come to think of it, so do I," Billy said.

They roared toward Alaska in search of the Polar Vortex. Billy talked to meteorologists in Fairbanks and Point Barrow to find out what they were learning from their weather balloons about the jet stream's current location. His copilot plotted a course to bring them parallel to it for a two-hundred-mile run.

"You can't see this thing," Billy said. "That's the spooky part of it. It's like playing games with a huge invisible serpent in the sky. Are you belted in real good, Victoria?"

"I'm practically part of the seat."

"Are you having a good time?"

"The time of my life."

"Here we go," the copilot said.

Victoria gazed out the cockpit window at a sky of perfect blue. She had never seen anything as pure, as serene, in her life. But somewhere in its light-filled heart the jet stream coiled, hurling vortices that smashed against the giant bomber with a ferocity that made her face, her neck, ache.

"Put it on autopilot?" the copilot said.

Billy shook his head. The autopilot was one way of dealing with turbulence. It relieved the pilot of the struggle for control of the plane. But Billy did not trust a spinning gyroscope to do his thinking for him when he was on the edge of the unknown.

Suddenly they hit a windshear unlike anything Billy had ever encountered before. It sent the bomber into pitchdown—the nose dropped below the horizon—and simultaneously scythed away a column of air a mile wide beneath the wings. The Warrior plunged into a dive that took them over the red line on every instrument on the panel.

"We're hitting mach 3.5," the copilot gasped.

"Pull!" Billy shouted, hauling on the yoke with all his strength. The copilot imitated his example. It had no visible effect. They were going straight down, seventy tons of bomber headed for the frozen earth.

Some three miles down, the Warrior hit the bottom of the shear and responded to the controls. "Hang on!" Billy said. The wings rose, the fuselage groaned, the engines "unstarted" with a series of violent jolts as their internal shock waves readjusted themselves to normal flight. The g forces smashed Billy down in his seat and almost tore his brain apart. But he hung on to the yoke.

"Are we going back up there?" the shaken copilot said.

Billy looked over his shoulder at Victoria Van Ness. For the first time it occurred to him that she had not made a sound. Most other woman he knew would have been blubbering and wailing by now. Victoria was smiling. "Are you game for it?" Billy said.

Victoria nodded. They climbed back up to 70,000 feet and completed their jolting two-hundred-mile run along the edge of the vortex. Billy banked the Warrior into a 160-degree turn and headed back to the Mojave. On the ground, Victoria sat in Billy's office while he wrote a report of the flight. As he finished, in charged Mike Shannon.

"Hello, Miss Van Ness," he said. "What brings you out to the desert?" They had met on the SS *Rainbow*. Shannon was a frequent weekend guest.

"A supersonic ride in a top-secret plane," she said.

"She's some crate, isn't she?" Mike said. "Billy. I've got that load of congressmen out on the runway. Remember I called you about them? Are you ready to go up?"

"Can't do it, Mike. We'll have to reschedule it for tomorrow. Talk to Frank about it."

"What the hell's wrong?"

"I'm taking a vacation, Mike. The first one in years."

That was the moment when Sarah Chapman Morris appeared in the doorway. From Billy's point of view the timing could not have been more delicious. In the violent incandescence of the next five minutes, Sarah saw he knew exactly what she was feeling and he was still determined to win their long, mutilating struggle for spiritual supremacy. What he did not know, what he would never know, was Sarah's power to become Victoria Van Ness, to be the secret lover inside her awkward clumsy body, to live in the manic fire of her imagination until she won, won, won!

Two hours later, Billy circled over Santa Catalina Island in his green Lustra. The white twelve-story casino presided over the yachts in Avalon's picture-postcard harbor. The sand of Pebbly Beach gleamed against the blue-black Pacific. The interior valleys were lush with tropical foliage. It was a miniature continent.

"Remember the song?" Billy said. "I lost my heart in Avalon?"

"It's one of my favorites," Victoria said.

Billy flipped the Lustra into an inverted spin. The island, the sea, whirled inside Victoria's head as if it were being stirred by a giant whisk. "How did you know we were going to pull that bomber out?" he said, as they hurtled toward the water.

"I just knew," Victoria said, as calmly as if she were riding along Wilshire Boulevard in her red Triumph convertible. "I knew you'd do it."

"If that shear was another mile deep, no one could have done it."

"It wasn't," she said.

Billy pulled the Lustra out at 250 feet and asked for clearance at the island's airport, at the head of a deep canyon northwest of Avalon. The air traffic controller said there wasn't a plane within ten miles. He whipped the Lustra into a 180-degree turn and came in much too fast. He had to burn his brakes to stop before they rolled off the runway.

"That's the worst landing I've made in twenty years," Billy said. "And it's all your fault."

Victoria smiled. "Will you to teach me to fly?"

"Sure," Billy said.

Billy and Victoria spent two days on Santa Catalina Island. Travel writers call it the nearest thing to Shangri-la in California. That would make it the ultimate unreality in a world where realism has never been in large supply. Billy rented a thatched cottage on Papeete Beach, site of a dozen South Sea movies. In those days it included abandoned movie sets, such as the Continental Hotel in which Jean Harlow had played Sadie Thompson.

They made soaring love beneath the palm trees, they swam in the looming surf. Billy flew Victoria with a concentration, an intensity, he borrowed from memories of other women, from the metaphor of their flight together. She was an assignment given to him by the one man who could persuade him to do anything. In his instinctual, intuitive way he sensed the combination of hatred and love in Frank Buchanan's soul that was animating them. Billy saw it as another unknown, another serpent to challenge in the sky of the future. He had the same attitude toward the serpentine realities that awaited them on the mainland.

For Victoria those forty-eight hours of love became the fulcrum of her life. She had no idea love involved such a shocking surrender of the deepest self. Her previous encounters with poetry-quoting Oxford dons and randy fellow students became instantly insignificant. She now belonged to Billy in an absolute way that transcended—but did not abolish—her father's will to power and her mother's rage for moral purity.

How Victoria affected Billy is a question that people still debate. Unquestionably he became something different from the Billy McCall who had laid a thousand women without caring—except for a few who touched something inside him, usually, as in Sarah Chapman's case, quickly smothered by his anger.

Victoria dared Billy to become a being he had been taught to dismiss with contempt. "I want to be your wife, I want you to be my husband," Victoria said. "*Husband.* It's the most beautiful word in the English language. One of the oldest. It goes back beyond English to ancient Norse and German, *hus* meaning 'house' and *bondi* meaning 'to dwell.' I want to dwell in your house, in your heart, I want to live there forever."

"*Bondi*," Billy said. "That's the name of a beach in Sydney. Not many husbands there. Or wives."

Husband. It was the most unnerving challenge Billy ever faced—infinitely more unsettling than exploring the stratosphere in rocket planes or supersonic bombers. Billy responded to it in the only way that interested him, in the only way he knew. He made it dangerous.

Billy had no idea just how dangerous a sky inhabited by Sarah-Victoria-Amanda would become. No one did. Not even Sarah. For the moment she swooped hungrily above Catalina, a lonely cormorant, feeding on the last shreds of her hateful heart.

BILE

Adrian Van Ness vomited his lunch and dinner into the toilet bowl. Pain throbbed in his chest. His head pounded. *Ruined* whined in his soul in a new more menacing way. Was he having a coronary? It had been a day of shocks—the worst day in his life. It made his discovery of his mother's infidelity, even the stock market crash of 1929, seem insignificant.

First had come a report from Cliff Morris on the ferocious struggle for the Warrior bomber. Congress, defying Secretary of Defense McNamara and his whiz kids, had voted a hundred million dollars to build another ten copies. It was a compromise, far short of a commitment to the billion-dollar program General Curtis LeMay had wanted. The secretary was still using the power of his office and the mathematical wizardry of his aides to try to kill the plane.

Then Morris delivered the shock. It was of earthquake proportions. McNamara, with the Kennedys' approval, was abolishing the cost-plus contract. In all future Defense Department contracts with airframe and engine companies, the contractor would have to deliver his product within the limits of his original estimate—and pay any cost overruns out of his own pocket.

This amounted to a whole new way of doing business,

piling on a military aircraft design the same gut-wrenching risks that a new commercial plane required a company to swallow. For something as experimental as the Warrior bomber, it meant betting the company three or four times over if future testing revealed unforeseen problems—the unk unks almost every plane contained.

"Can't you talk to your boy wonder from Massachusetts?" Adrian shouted.

Wretchedly, Cliff Morris confessed his mounting disillusion with the Kennedys and the whole Democratic Party. "It's a can of worms and no one knows what happened to the lid. I think maybe Jack left it under Marilyn Monroe's bed. One thing's for sure, most of the time he doesn't pay attention."

"He's paying attention to Amalie Borne. She's been to the White House five times. I'm paying her bills in New York and he's getting all the action," Adrian snarled.

Cliff's only vestige of good news was a report that the Pentagon, in line with JFK's drive to beef up conventional forces, was looking for a new close support plane, something subsonic with a high-load capacity and plenty of endurance. Maybe Frank Buchanan had something in his files from the Korean War that they could wrap around a jet engine.

"What about a new transport—something really big?" Adrian said. Attack planes were small, compact, and cheap. The current one being used by the Navy was a Douglas job called Heinemann's Hot Rod, after their chief designer. It was so small pilots claimed you did not strap into it—you strapped it on.

"I'm working on it," Cliff said. "But LeMay is so in love with our goddamn bomber he doesn't want us to think about anything else. He's going down fighting on the thing and there's nothing we can do but go with him."

All this was only a prelude to the ultimate shock. Adrian had come home for dinner at 8 P.M. to find Amanda in an unusually cheerful mood. Most of the time she either ignored him or glowered sullenly and asked questions about the "accident" that made it so difficult for her to remember many things.

"For once I have some good news," she said.

"Oh?" Adrian said.

"Victoria is going to be married."

Adrian felt five, perhaps ten years older in ten seconds. Struggling for aplomb, he sat down, tossed a leg over his knee and said: "Who's the lucky fellow?" He half suspected he was hearing a fantasy from Amanda's damaged brain.

"Billy McCall. I told her I was a little disappointed that she was marrying a man whose profession was bombing people—but on the whole, considering how dim I thought her chances of marrying anyone were, I think it's good news, don't you?"

"Shut up, for God's sake," Adrian snarled and stormed upstairs in search of his daughter.

He found Victoria lying on her bed, staring dreamily at the ceiling. "Is it true?" he said.

"We love each other," she said. "We spent the weekend on Catalina together."

"It's a mistake," Adrian shouted, losing all his vaunted self-control.

"I thought you'd feel that way. That's why I didn't discuss it with you."

"The man's a mental vacuum. All he can talk about is planes."

"He talks about them wonderfully. Better than you, Daddy. Better than anyone. Haven't you watched the way those congressmen listen to him? He's authentic. Real—in a way most men can't even approach."

Adrian heard the reminder that he needed Billy if he had any hope of getting a billion dollars to build the Warrior. But he still could not control his chagrin. "It's romantic nonsense. Sleep with him for six months if you want to—you have my permission. But don't marry him."

"I told you—I *love* him."

"I heard you—and I hope you heard me. Most love is an illusion. Give it six months either to solidify—or dissipate."

"We're getting married as soon as possible."

"Why? Why such an idiotic rush?"

Victoria sat up and glared at him with Amanda's eyes, full

of her old ominous intensity. "Otherwise I'll lose him. And if you keep talking this way—you'll lose him too. I'll see to it."

Adrian was meeting his willful match. Stunned but still frantic, he retreated. "How did this happen? I have a right to know."

She told him everything without reserve, including Frank Buchanan's role. Adrian saw it all in the worst possible light, of course. He was ashen, trembling, by the time she finished. "I thought you loved me," he said. "I thought you at least loved me."

He was really saying, how could you betray me to my enemies? But he had never explained how or why Frank Buchanan was his enemy. Victoria heard the words as an old-fashioned reproach for deserting him.

"I do love you!" she cried. "But you can't expect me to stay ten years old for the rest of my life. Besides—"

Victoria was about to tell him how much she loathed the way he did business. But she saw how wounded he was already and let pity deflect her anger into a more ordinary reproach. "Do you really expect me to be your creature indefinitely? To wait until you're ready to dispose of me to the man of your choice? Some superannuated character like Prince Carlo?"

"I never dreamt of such a thing."

What had he dreamt? Finally Adrian was forced to confront the halfway house in which his fears and his hopes had trapped his fatherhood. He had confessed too much to hold his daughter's admiration and not enough to win her forgiveness. Wretched, wretched, a wretched performance for a man whose gift was forethought.

Adrian flushed the vomit down the toilet and stumbled back to bed. In the doorway of her bedroom stood Amanda in a long ruby night robe, her russet hair streaming down her back. She smiled and said: "My poor husband. Can I get you anything?"

For a moment Adrian struggled with a terrifying inrush of fear. Was this woman in touch with some sort of supernatural power that enabled her to inflict pain and disappointment on him? Were all women in some profound way enemies to a man's deepest hopes? Rationality trembled in a swirl of terror. Adrian fled to his room and called Kirk Willoughby. He came to the house and found nothing physically wrong with Buchanan's anguished President.

The next day, Adrian retreated into acquiescence, even into apology with Victoria. He had no other choice. He struggled to welcome William Craig McCall as his son-in-law. He tried to impose reason—his word for control—on the situation.

"What are you going to do? Where are you going to live?" he asked his daughter, as wedding plans went forward.

"That's up to Billy," Victoria said.

"You're going to be an Air Force wife? Have you seen the houses they live in on most bases? You'd have more room in a Starduster."

"I remember Mother telling me we were never going to be rich, that I should adjust my expectations to realities. I was very proud of her for asking me to do that. It made me feel grown-up, serious."

"Are you going to have children?"

"Not right away. Billy doesn't want any—as long as he's test-flying."

"You don't fly forever, even in the Air Force. It would make much more sense if he retired and came to work here. He could do it in stages. He could be the air force manager for the Warrior program, assuming we get the contract—and then transfer to the civilian side."

"I'm not sure that's a good idea. I'd rather see him work for some other aircraft company."

"You're not being realistic. Each company has a different personality. This is the one he knows. Where he has friends—"

Victoria struggled to trust the secretive, subtle man she called Daddy and thought of as father—an infinitely more awesome word. Adrian struggled to control his anger. Neither succeeded. "I think you'll find he needs protection for a while at least," Adrian said.

"That's ridiculous!"

"Pilots are like athletes, very naive about the world outside their planes. When you spend your life in the military, that only adds to the naïveté."

In one of those bizarre but all too common repetitions, Adrian was sowing doubts about Billy deep in Victoria's psyche in much the same way his mother had undermined Amanda. Victoria felt the doubts as wounds, inflicted in revenge. Her mother, listening in the distance, let her outspokenness run rampant as soon as Adrian left for work.

"Isn't he perfectly hateful?" Amanda said. "I'm sure he was this way before my accident. I can't remember exactly why I hated him but now I'm sure I was right."

HEART OF DARKNESS

Outside the window, Saint Elmo's fire flickered along the wings of the Pan Am 707 as they approached Africa. Dick Stone found himself wishing it was a real fire, not one of nature's electrical stunts. Beside him, Amalie Borne read *Elle*, the French fashion magazine, relentlessly tearing out page after page of dresses she intended to buy in Paris.

It was insane, his doomed irresistible love for this woman. By now he had embezzled over three hundred thousand dollars from Buchanan Aircraft to buy her dresses and diamond necklaces and gold bracelets. The withdrawals were carried on the books as extraordinary overseas expenses, part of the millions handed over to the Prince and other agents. Buchanan's auditors had long since accepted these expenses as perfectly legal under American law. There was no immediate danger of being caught.

For someone with Dick Stone's conscience, punishment was almost superfluous. He was his own accuser, judge, and victim. He seldom slept more than four hours a night. He rarely looked at another woman. His airline and aircraft friends at the Villa Hermosa called him the hermit. Cassie Trainor wrote him sarcastic letters from Oxnard. Dick wrote evasive replies to Cassie and long letters to Amalie, full of bad imitations of Heine, or meditations on America and Europe, desperately trying to explain what was happening to him—while compounding the disaster.

In return, Amalie wrote him savagely detailed descriptions of her visits to the Kennedy White House, each as demeaning as her original encounter with JFK in Los Angeles. She told him, without moderating a phrase, how important this was to her career in Europe, where Kennedy, after his 1961 visit to Paris with Jackie, had become a near-mythical figure. Madame George had a waiting list of over twenty cabinet ministers, bankers, industrialists, generals, who were begging for a chance to escort her to Cannes, St. Moritz, Amalfi. But she stayed in New York, because she loved Richard Stone—and was certain her price would continue to rise.

By now Dick had learned to deconstruct the word *love*, to see how strangely Amalie dealt with its elements. Sacrifice was part of love, was it not? She sacrificed money, fame, for his sake. But the arrangement was strictly temporary. Next week or the week after, love might end as abruptly as a sleeper awoke from a dream—or a nightmare. Forever was not part of Amalie's love, except as a possibility. It was not exiled from the palace but it was not permitted in the throne room either. Forever watched wistfully from a dim alcove, awaiting a summons that might never come.

Fidelity was an exile in the strictly literal sense. But it was allowed to reenter the country under an assumed name, to travel in a dozen different disguises, all designed to wrench the heart. Fidelity sidled onstage as a thought at moments when obscene acts were being performed. It slithered past as a sigh when the bedroom plunged into lonely darkness. It pirouetted as a robed, hooded dancer while headwaiters bowed and Château Haut-Brion was poured.

Desire was never an exile but postponement was its constant fate. Love was not sovereign in Amalie's world. It was a deposed queen without offspring or supporters, a creature for whom tears were shed, fealty pledged—without the slightest hope that these rituals would achieve anything significant. The world was ruled by darker powers. These could only be propitiated by deception, endless, perpetually charming deception.

Dick had renounced, once and for all, his desire to know the truth about her past. She had forced him to capitulate, to accept her as a woman who seized the foreground of his vision and held it by her force and guile and affection and disdain and lust and beauty and intelligence and indifference and concern and laughter and tears.

A dozen, two dozen more words could be added to that sentence without exhausting the catalogue of Dick's love. The words and their multiple meanings trooped over the green horizon into Africa, as the big plane roared up the mouth of the Congo toward Brazzaville. The Prince was there, awaiting them and the money Dick had in his briefcase. Pontecorvo and Cliff Morris had sold eighty-two Stardusters in sixteen African countries.

En route to California with the orders, Cliff had eaten dinner with Dick and Amalie the night before they left New York. The former commander of the *Rainbow Express* talked about his adventures flying in Ethiopia, the Congo, and other countries with pilots who had trouble reading the English words on the dials. As usual, Cliff omitted the Prince's role in his triumphal progress.

Clearly seeing a rival on the horizon, Cliff devoted much of their dinner to sarcastic comments about Billy McCall's imminent marriage to Victoria Van Ness. He tried to make marrying the boss's daughter the equivalent of moral turpitude. Dick, his brain sodden with Amalie Borne, barely listened.

Amalie announced she was coming with Dick yesterday as he was packing his suitcase. "Why?" he said, resisting the idea of the Prince regaining her.

"There's no need to worry about sharing me with him," she said. "Didn't I tell you he's impotent? Some say the Gestapo gelded him. Others think his mother is responsible. Still others say he prefers six-year-old choirboys, like his ancestor, Pope Innocent."

As usual, Dick capitulated. He could not stop her from flying to Brazzaville with her own money. Now they were circling above the mixture of squatters' shacks and gleaming white skyscrapers that constituted this typical African capital. They drove down roads that were narrow causeways through seas of mud to the Intercontinental Hotel, where the Prince greeted them with his usual cordiality.

"Ah, Stone," he said. "Never did I dream that the Santa Claus of my life would turn out to be Jewish. I risked my life a great many times to save Jews from the Germans. Do you think you're my reward?"

"Perhaps."

"But what have I done to deserve this?" he said, seizing Amalie by the arms and spinning her around. She was looking spectacular in a gray black-belted Dior suit with a pleated skirt.

"There's nothing in heaven or on earth you could do, dear Carlo," she said. "Haven't you read your St. Augustine? We can't merit God's grace."

"I'm a Pelagian by trade," he said. "In other times I would have been burned at the stake before the age of thirty."

"Not merely for your beliefs," Amalie said, letting him kiss her on the cheek.

"And the money, Stone. This time it's been carefully counted by our Swiss literalists?"

"Yes," Stone said, never sure when the Prince—or Amalie for that matter—was taunting him.

"The commander of the Nigerian Army is in town. He would love to meet the uncrowned queen of the American White House," the Prince said.

"Tell him I'm vacationing—and Stone here is my CIA escort—with orders to kill anyone who so much as looks at me."

"That could lead to Stone's disappearance, Amalie dear. Is that what you're trying to arrange?"

"Why should I even think of such a thing?"

The Prince shrugged and opened the inevitable bottle of Moet et Chandon. "Perhaps then you plan to poison me and decamp with the money?"

Amalie laughed. "I can make twice that in the next year."

In spite of the air-conditioning, which was at Arctic level,
Dick discovered he was bathed in sweat. Amalie had not
come here for a vacation, he was sure of that much. The
Prince was equally sure of it. He was as alert, as coiled, as
a duelist with a rapier in his hand.

They drank champagne and the Prince discussed Africa.
He said it was not much different from Calabria, where his
family had owned vast estates until Mussolini confiscated
them. He predicted a hundred years of anarchy and chaos in
the wake of the departing Europeans. Planes were the only
hope of binding the continent together. The totally corrupt
governments would never manage to build roads or rail lines.

"And for binding the world together, how goes the supersonic transport?" Pontecorvo asked.

"Slowly. We're still fighting over the supersonic bomber,"
Dick said.

"The potential for commercial profits, Stone, is astound-
ing. I don't understand this hesitation. The British and the
French are discussing a consortium to build one."

"The Democrats are in power. They like to spend money
on public housing, education, civil rights programs."

"But this plane will create thousands of jobs."

"I know. But the Democrats don't think that way."

"I thought steps were being taken to persuade them?"

He smiled at Amalie, his tufted eyebrows raised.

"You don't understand these Kennedys," Amalie said.
"You're deceived by the photographs, the TV footage, where
Prince Hal seems incarnate. Off-camera, they're crude, foul-
mouthed gangsters."

Much later, after a dinner marked by several similar ex-
changes between Amalie and the Prince, Dick sat in his room
staring across the tilted shacks and littered streets of Brazzaville at the jungle. He had knocked on Amalie's door an
hour ago—she was in the room across the hall—and gotten
no answer. That could only mean she was with the Prince—
unless she was with the Nigerian general.

A knock. Amalie stood at the door in a long blue robe.
She stepped into the room and opened her arms to him. The

kiss came from her. She pressed her whole body against him and let her lips wander across his face, his neck. "Oh, Richard, Richard," she whispered, a name she only used when she was amorous. "Do you feel it out there—the jungle, the heart of darkness? I wanted to come to Africa and make love to you in the middle of it. I wanted to streak my face and my breasts and my thighs with Congo mud, I wanted to lure you once and for all from your middle-class fears and follies, I wanted to find a primeval wildness lurking in your bourgeois American heart."

"We'll go now. I'll rent a car. I'll shoot a rhinoceros for you. I'll wear the horn on my forehead."

He was tuned to her mockery, her fantasy, now.

"I didn't let him touch me. We talked business. Nothing but business. But from now on you'll have to be on guard."

"Why?"

"Later, I'll explain later. Coat me with jungle mud, now. Then lick it off. Taste Africa in my body. Create it inside me."

He breathed the perfume in her hair. He accepted her nakedness, so white, so sinuous, as the geography she was demanding. She was a continent not unlike Africa, capricious, incomprehensible, corrupt. But Dick had learned to think as well as feel in his explorations of the many Amalie Bornes he had encountered. When it was over, when she smiled and sighed childishly in his arms, he asked her again for an explanation.

"It's of no consequence. The Prince and I have parted. I grew weary of playing the waitress to his maitre d': I wanted a share of his salary. He indignantly refused. So now, like you and Lockheed, we are competitors."

"What does that mean?"

"It means in some situations, you and Adrian Van Ness may have to decide who is more useful, the Prince or Amalie Borne."

"And in the meantime, we're responsible for your happiness?"

"Of course. Exactly how you arrange that part of it, I leave to your discretion."

Dick did not need a further explanation to grasp Amalie's plan. With him in charge of arrangements, she expected a cascade of cash. Why did she insist on piling burden after burden on their love? Was she still trying to make him hear the warning she had given him the day they met?

In the morning Amalie announced she wanted to see a gorilla colony about forty miles from Brazzaville. The hotel operated a van that took tourists to visit the site. There was only one other person in the van besides the hulking black driver—a short foxy-faced man in a well-pressed business suit who asked them if they would mind if he smoked. Amalie grandly gave him permission and he was soon conversing knowledgeably with them about Africa. His name was Korda and he was a sales representative for the Israeli aircraft industry. He apparently did a brisk business selling helicopters, trainers, and fighters to every country on the continent.

"Mr. Stone is with the American aircraft industry," Amalie said. "A company called Buchanan."

Korda praised the Scorpion fighter extravagantly as they got out and viewed the gorilla colony from a respectful distance. They watched the great apes swinging through the trees, while the females perched on lower branches and nursed and nuzzled their young. Occasionally one of the younger apes would beat his chest and roar defiance at the intruders. Amalie adored the show.

"Now I understand the Americans and the Russians, the French and Germans, the Arabs and the Israelis," she said.

"Unmolested, they're quite peace loving," Korda said.

"Aren't we all," Amalie said.

Korda was silent for the first few minutes of their ride back to Brazzaville. Then he stubbed out a half smoked cigarette and said: "Miss Borne tells me you might be interested in helping Israel to defend herself."

"Oh?" Dick said.

Korda leaned forward in a suavely confidential way, though there was no need to worry about being overheard. "We might find some of the research your designers and engineers invested in your supersonic bomber, the Warrior, quite useful. Compression lift could be invaluable in a new fighter-bomber we're developing."

"No doubt," Dick said.

"You might even persuade your chief designer to give us some personal help. I understand he's quite fond of you."

"I'm quite fond of him too," Dick said. "I'm even fonder of the United States of America. They have first call on Frank Buchanan's mind—and my loyalty."

"We could enable you to be extremely generous to Miss Borne—"

"You must be hard of hearing," Dick said. "Or do I have to translate the word *loyalty* into Hebrew?"

Back at the hotel, Amalie blended innocence and mockery. "I don't understand you, Stone. I thought I was giving you a chance to resolve all your conflicts. You could be a free American primate, beating your chest and cavorting with me in our various bedrooms and a loyal Jew on the side—with a reasonable amount of money in the bargain."

Was it another redefinition of love, the worst imaginable burden she could invent? Or was she testing him in some subterranean way to see if he was worthy of the truth? Dick struggled to control a vortex of emotions: rage, regret, shame. "You don't seem to understand. You don't want to understand—"

The mocking eyes never wavered. "I've always thought my problem was understanding too much."

In New York, Amalie persuaded him to stay overnight to cure his jetlag. He had never seen her so amorous. The next day, Dick flew on to Los Angeles, exhausted and appalled. *She was a whore. She loved him. She was a whore. She loved him.* The sentences rebounded crazily in his head for the entire flight. He tried to tell himself her mockery of love simultaneously affirmed it.

He had barely arrived in his office when his secretary told him Adrian Van Ness wanted to see him. He found Buchanan's president standing by the window watching an anti-submarine version of the Starduster taxiing out for takeoff. There were dark pouches under his eyes. Adrian was starting to look old.

"How was Africa?" Adrian said with forced jauntiness.

"I only saw twenty-four hours of it."

"How many of those were devoted to Amalie Borne?"

"A few," Dick said, deciding it was foolish to lie if Adrian already knew Amalie had spent the night with him. Had the Prince in his pique played tattletale?

"We've got some problems with her," Dick said.

"I'm not surprised, considering the encouragement you've been giving her. Women are unstable creatures, Dick. They're particularly prone to fantasies of power."

Adrian watched the new Starduster climb into the blue sky. "Let's talk about the money first. There seems to be three hundred thousand withdrawn from our Swiss account on your signature without any authorization from me."

"I used the money to buy presents for Amalie," Dick said.

The words dangled in midair in the quiet office for a long moment. What did he feel? Dick wondered. Fearful? Was he looking at a prison sentence for embezzlement? To his surprise—and dismay—he realized his dominant emotion was relief. He had just shed an intolerable burden.

Quizzical wrinkles sprouted on Adrian's brow. "A not entirely objectionable policy—if she can help us get Kennedy to deliver on the Warrior and the supersonic airliner. Is that all there is to it—a desire to keep our princess happy?"

"You obviously know everything. Why don't you just fire me and get it over with?" Dick said. "I'm in love with her. I probably would have stolen twice that if you hadn't caught me."

Adrian seemed to find the criminal language offensive. "The Swiss reported the first fifty thousand. I asked Hanrahan to have you watched," he said.

"I'll clean out my desk and go quietly," Dick said. "I'll sign an agreement to pay it back over the next ten years."

"Don't be ridiculous," Adrian said. "You're not the first man who lost his head over a beautiful woman. I've done it myself. The important thing is to learn a lesson from it. To learn something about yourself—and about women. You can make the money back for us in a year by helping us get a grip on our finances. Those Kennedy bastards in Washington have abolished the cost-plus contract. We're going to have to keep track of every screw, every gallon of paint—and somehow restrain the madmen in the design department, led by their resident maniac, you know who. They think nothing of burning up a million dollars in a mock-up they chop to pieces the next day. You're going to have to do more than project earnings now. You're going to have to create a whole cost-control system."

Dick sat there, numb. "I'm not fired?"

"Dick," Adrian said in his gentlest tone. "Have you gone deaf?"

The similarity to his conversation with the Israeli made Dick shudder. "I—I can't do any of those things. I can't do anything with her on my mind. I'm starting to hate the company, the whole business, because of the way we're using her."

"I think you'll soon find it's the other way around, if the Prince is right. He called me last night from Brazzaville. He says Amalie has quite a lot of his correspondence in a safe deposit box, location unknown. It would embarrass a half-dozen governments if she sent copies to a newspaper."

"She's threatened to do this?"

"She hasn't threatened to do anything yet. She's waiting to see how well you negotiate for her."

"She told the Prince I was going to do that?"

"She saw it as another way to intimidate him."

It made sickening, demoralizing sense. There had to be a purpose beyond or behind the fantasy selves, the mockery of love in the very moment of transcendence. The luminous intelligence that transfixed him had analyzed reality and drawn its own bitter conclusions.

"Is she Jewish?"

Dick knew how absurd the question sounded. But he did not care. It suddenly became the most important fact in the world to him.

"Does it matter?" Adrian said.

In those offhand words, Dick saw the cold hard face of reality as defined by Adrian Van Ness. If he was going to accept the salvation Adrian was offering him, he would have to accept it as the only reality.

Ruefully, bitterly, Dick recounted Amalie's Schweinfurt story. Adrian shook his head in equally rueful admiration. "Women are amazing," he said. "They have the most diabolical imaginations."

He leaned back in his chair and picked up a stainless-steel model of the Scorpion on his desk. "To get practical for a moment," he said. "We have to deal very carefully with Amalie. She may still be useful to us with the Kennedys."

"She doesn't think so."

"There are many ways to be useful beyond the obvious one. We have pictures of her leaving the White House, for instance. Naturally I hope we never have to use them. It would be very dangerous for us—and for her."

A new kind of unreality clouded Dick's brain. Was he sitting here with Adrian Van Ness, talking about Amalie Borne as if she was disposable, loseable, like a copy of a plane in a war?

"For the time being, it's important not to alarm her. Go back to New York in a week or so and assure her that all is well. Spend enough money to convince her. But begin trying to find out where she's stashed the Prince's correspondence. That will no doubt take some doing, but it should be enjoyable."

Adrian was assigning Dick Stone the role he had played with Beryl Suydam. The lover who was not a lover, who was a secret enemy—and still a lover. Dick did not understand why, but he could see that Adrian was enjoying himself.

"Of course I understand it won't be entirely enjoyable," Adrian said. "It will take a lot of self-control. But I think you can do it."

Adrian held out his hand. "Do we understand each other, Dick?"

Dick accepted the hand. Adrian squeezed hard, unusual for him. "Thanks," Dick said.

"Nonsense. It's to our mutual advantage, I assure you."

Gazing into those subtle eyes, the shy yet shrewd smile,

Dick heard that reassurance not once but twice and then three times. Adrian too was an expert at expanding the meaning of words. Mutual advantage encompassed much more than Dick's ability to set up a cost-control system for Buchanan Aircraft. It involved years and years of future arrangements with people like the Prince, in which Dick Stone's acquiescence, his readiness to bury unpleasant costs deep in Buchanan's records, were guaranteed. As he walked out of the office, Dick was no longer a prisoner of love. But he was a prisoner of Adrian Van Ness.

DEATH IN THE DESERT

Cliff Morris sat in the oak-paneled committee room beside Dick Stone and Mike Shannon, watching Adrian Van Ness testify before the Senate Armed Services Committee. Adrian had just finished arguing for the survival of the Warrior bomber. He had laid special stress on its future as a supersonic airliner.

"The plane," Adrian continued, "has won the enthusiastic applause of veteran pilots such as Colonel Billy McCall, one of the first men to break the sound barrier, holder of a half-dozen high-altitude records."

"Excuse me, Mr. Van Ness," said the lean hunched senator from Iowa, shoving his sallow face so close to the microphone he seemed to be swallowing it. "Isn't he your son-in-law? Isn't his correct rank lieutenant colonel?"

"Yes to both questions, Senator," Adrian said, as reporters grinned and several staffers in the seats around them tittered. "Lieutenant colonels are normally referred to in ordinary discourse as colonels—"

"But he is your son-in-law."

"Yes. But Colonel McCall is the sort of man who would

only tell the exact truth about any plane he flew. His reputation as a test pilot is the point here."

"Of course, Mr. Van Ness," the senator sneered.

It was the Creature. He had run for the Senate in 1962 with John F. Kennedy's reluctant endorsement and won. His venal style—in particular his utter indifference to facts—had not changed an iota. Before the hearings began, he had given Mike Shannon a list of things he wanted in return for his support for the bomber. They included an Air Force base within shouting distance of his hometown, an invitation to be the principal speaker at the Air Force Association annual dinner, and a Buchanan factory in Iowa as big as the one they had promised Robert Kerr in Oklahoma. Shannon urged Cliff to say yes. But Cliff said the package was too much for any freshman senator to ask and with Adrian's approval had said no.

Beside Adrian Van Ness, Billy McCall sat very straight and silent in his blue Air Force uniform. In the front row of the spectators' seats, Victoria Van Ness wore a powder blue suit of almost identical color. It was one of her small ways of stating her devotion to Billy. Beside her sat her secret enemy, Sarah Morris.

They pretended to be warm friends. At Sarah's suggestion, Cliff had adopted the same policy toward Billy. It was not that difficult; since the Starduster days, he and Billy had become wary semi-friends. Behind his back, Cliff sabotaged Billy in large and small ways, according to Sarah's plan. He referred to him as "the son-in-law" in conversation with other executives. He wryly predicted Billy would never put up with marriage and hinted he already was straying from Victoria's bed. Cliff had balked in the negotiations with the Creature because he wanted the senator to come into the hearings angry at Buchanan, even if it risked the future of the Warrior.

The bomber was in trouble for far more serious reasons. Defense Secretary Robert McNamara was showing the Kennedys he had learned to play the Byzantine politics of Washington. With the help of the fighter pilots in the Air Force, who resented the influence of General LeMay and his Strategic Air Command bomber jocks, the secretary of defense was promoting another plane, called the TFX or F-111, a smaller, cheaper supersonic bomber that could double as a fighter. General Dynamics and Boeing had been invited to bid on it and their lobbyists and favorite senators and congressmen were pushing it, creating confusion in the ranks of the Warrior backers.

Lieutenant Colonel McCall took Adrian's place in the witness chair. "Why do you think a plane is superior to a missile?" the Creature asked. "Is it because you'd be flying it?"

"They wouldn't let an old man like me fly a serious mission, Senator," Billy said. "We've got young fellows with a lot more stamina and brains than I have."

"The mission this plane would execute would be very dangerous, am I correct?"

"No question."

"The Russians would do everything in their power to stop it?"

"Definitely."

"You seem awfully complacent about letting younger men risk their lives while you sit home giving them orders, Colonel."

"You risk your life every time you fly a plane like the Warrior," Billy snapped.

"Oh?" the Senator said. "I thought this was a breakthrough design, the plane of the twenty-first century, twenty-five years ahead of schedule. Now you're telling us it's radically unsafe?"

"No, sir," Billy said. "But it's a very hot plane. You have to know what you're doing."

"And you—or your father-in-law—nevertheless maintain that this radically unsafe vehicle can become a supersonic airliner? You're asking us to fund a plane that would risk the life of every passenger—every taxpaying passenger?"

"Sir," Billy said. "I wish you'd stop trying to put words in my mouth."

"I wish you would learn a little respect for the civilian arm of this government, Lieutenant Colonel McCall," the senator shouted." I wish the Air Force could find someone with a reasonably objective view of this plane. What can we expect to learn from a special pleader like you?"

Don't answer him, Cliff Morris thought. That was the only way to deal with the Creature. You had to let him dump garbage on your head and hope that you won the sympathy vote.

Cliff was shocked to find himself rooting for Billy. Wasn't that what any man would do, watching another man getting creamed by this piece of political slime? Yet last night he and Sarah had drunk to the possibility that Billy would fall on his face in these hearings.

Cliff watched Billy struggle to control his rage. He had flown 113 missions in two wars to defend the land of the free and the home of the brave. He had seen several hundred friends die in burning or exploding planes to make the world safe for democracy. Now the senator was telling him he did not respect or understand it.

"Senator," Billy said. "Senator—sir—the supersonic airliner would be a different plane. It would be a descendant of the Warrior, which is ready to operate as a bomber. There's a whole range of problems that need to be solved before we can create an airliner. We can learn a lot about them from producing the Warrior."

"Tell me, Lieutenant Colonel McCall, will you be promoted to full colonel if the Warrior gets funded?" the senator sneered.

"I have no idea, sir."

"That's all we need to hear from you."

"Sir—I have a prepared statement. I haven't gotten one word of—"

"Leave it on the table. It will be inserted in the record."

Cliff and Sarah rode back to the Shoreham Hotel with Billy and Victoria and Dick Stone. "That son of a bitch," Billy said. "That son of a bitch."

He did not even look at Victoria. She patted his hand and said: "Daddy thinks you handled him very well."

"So do I," Sarah said, with cool concealed malice. Billy glared at her and for a moment Cliff wondered if he understood the whole game.

Cliff looked out at the massive government buildings along Pennsylvania Avenue, so formidable, so majestic, until you knew what happened inside them. "We thought he was on our side," he lied. "The White House told us he'd protect us from the Republicans on the committee. But he must have made a deal with McNamara. They're going to move Wright Patterson Air Base to Iowa. Maybe throw in the Air Force Academy."

The Warrior, the first plane to cruise above Mach 3, the breakthrough to hypersonic flight, was dead. Cliff told himself it would have happened even without Billy McCall's flagellation. That had simply been the coup de grâce, a gratuitous insult to an already expiring victim. The McNamara ploy of a cheaper alternative, the F-111, was not the only reason. The billions Kennedy was asking for missiles and spaceships to the moon and a bigger army and navy had Congress much too edgy to think seriously about the bomber. The tide had been running against Buchanan for a good year.

At their suite, Billy poured himself a full glass of Inverness and drank it down before the rest of the party arrived. Victoria watched, not saying a word. But her eyes swam with tears. "I'll be in our room," she said.

"Don't wait up," Billy said.

"Let's go shopping," Sarah said cheerfully. "Cheer ourselves up." She and Victoria walked out arm in arm. Sarah's guile was breathtaking. Cliff could hardly believe his dreamy-eyed idealistic little WAAF had turned into this ultimate doubletalker.

The party—or the wake—was going to be an all-male show. Adrian arrived with General Curtis LeMay and the usual squadron of lesser generals. LeMay poured himself a glass of Inverness almost as deep as the one Billy had consumed. "Let's drink to a great plane, ruined by our gutless wonder in the White House."

General LeMay held forth for an hour on the frauds and follies of John F. Kennedy. The Bay of Pigs and then the Berlin Wall, which neither Truman nor Eisenhower would have tolerated for ten seconds. The Cuban missile crisis, which passed up a perfect excuse to get rid of Castro and instead left the bearded blowhard with a guarantee that we would never invade his miserable island. Now Kennedy was committing just enough men to South Vietnam to get us involved in a first-class war—but not enough to end it decisively.

Mike Shannon struggled to defend his fellow Irish-American. But even he found it rough going, after two and a half years of slashing around Washington. He talked about the enormous pressures on a president. All right, JFK was not King Arthur or Lancelot; he did not even approximate a white knight. But he was trying to do the job. He wanted the bomber. But McNamara had stolen the Defense Department from the White House. The ex-automaker and his Harvard Business School doubledomes sat across the Potomac like an arrogant baron and his retainers telling the president to get lost. It was bewildering but probably true.

Adrian Van Ness turned to Curtis LeMay. "General, after two and a half years we've got two supersonic bombers that we can't afford to fly again and pieces of another ten lying around the Mojave desert. We've got McNamara's auditors breathing down our necks every time we turn around to make sure we don't make a personal telephone call on the contract."

"I know, I know," LeMay said. "But you're still on the inside track for the SST."

"Right next to Boeing and Lockheed," Adrian said. "Do you think they're going to let us walk away with it?"

"Fuck 'em all," Billy McCall said and poured himself another glass of Inverness.

"Haven't you had enough of that?" Adrian said.

Billy looked at him for a long moment, then chug-a-lugged it and walked out.

Adrian sighed. "I'd like more than a place at the supersonic starting gate. We deserve some sort of guarantee that we'll receive special consideration. We've already spent fifteen million dollars of our own money on the Warrior. We've supplied our peerless leader with some very charming late-night entertainment. I think you ought to remind him of all that, Mike."

"If I did that, the only thing you'd ever get in the air would be a kite," Shannon said. "Who do you think you are, Brazil or some other semi-independent country? You don't know how to deal with Irish-Americans, Adrian. You never threaten them. You keep reminding them they owe you a very big favor."

They flew back to California, where Adrian laid off ten thousand workers and sold the assorted pieces of the ten follow-on Warriors for scrap. Frank Buchanan tried to be philosophic. He had become convinced since the Russians shot down Lockheed's spy plane, the U-2, at 70,000 feet with an antiaircraft missile that the Warrior was probably obsolete anyway. Those huge engine ducts would leave a signature a foot high on a radar screen.

"From now on," he said, "We have to build stealth into our planes. We have to make them invisible to radar."

Not without relish, he reminded everyone that the Talus never appeared on Air Force radar screens when it was being tested. A flying wing was the ultimate stealth bomber. But he presumed Adrian did not have the guts to revive the plane.

Frank was busy designing the ground-support plane Cliff had urged them to produce. Frank called it the Thunderer, a somewhat blasphemous reference (in his mind) to John the Baptist. "When this fellow drops his payload," he said, "whoever's on the other end will think it's the second coming."

It was unusual for Frank to sound so bloodthirsty. He was worried about the situation in Vietnam, where the Army, deprived of its airplanes since the creation of the Air Force in 1948, was trying to get back in the air with helicopters. Frank thought the helicopter was a lousy way to support troops on the ground. It was too vulnerable to antiaircraft fire and it couldn't drop bombs. He showed Cliff the armor plate he was weaving around the stubby thick-bodied plane on his drawing board. "This thing will bring our kids back alive," he said. "And it can carry more bombs than a World War II B-29."

At home, Cliff discussed something even more important from his point of view: Billy McCall. His career in the Air

Force was finished. If the Warrior had come through, Billy would no doubt have jumped to general in a year and been on his way to command of SAC. But now he was an aging bomberjock who had failed to deliver. Cliff was inclined to think they could stop worrying about Billy. Sarah disagreed. Every day she warned him the danger was greater than ever. Now Billy was certain to retire from the Air Force and join the company.

With the Warrior gone, Adrian became more and more obsessed with the supersonic airliner. He called it their declaration of independence. He quoted figures from Dick Stone that made everyone feel like they were on cocaine. The worldwide market for the plane was worth ten billion dollars. Unfortunately Buchanan was close to the limit of their resources. They needed a massive injection of government money.

Every time Cliff went to Washington, he called the White House to remind Mike Shannon about the Big Favor. He brought along a suitcase full of data on the wind tunnel tests of Frank Buchanan's latest design. The figures demonstrated that their SST could go as fast as the Warrior—at least 2,200 mph. This was some six hundred miles an hour faster than the plane the British and French were building. He naturally omitted some of the more unnerving problems they had not yet solved, such as duct rumble, which would terrify even the hardiest passenger.

Then there was the sonic boom, the noise a jet made when it went through the sound barrier. The Air Force was flying Scorpions over places like Oklahoma City and then sending in teams of researchers to find out how many people were bothered when God seemed to be cracking a giant whip in the sky. The answer seemed to be quite a few—especially when windows shattered and babies woke up screaming and cats and dogs went zooey.

A true patrician, Adrian dismissed these problems as trivialities—like noise complaints near airports. People would get used to booms—or they would find a way to eliminate them. Cliff was not so sure. He could see someone like the Creature using the boom to beat their brains out. Of course, even the scummiest senator could be persuaded by a determined president. But Jack Kennedy did not seem very determined.

As 1963 ran down, the promise of the Big Favor dwindled with it. From the White House came only silence. On June 4, 1963, Juan Trippe, president of Pan American, announced he was taking an option on six Concordes—the name the British and French had given their SST to conceal the immense amount of wrangling behind the scenes. The news drove Adrian Van Ness slightly crazy. He urged Cliff to read all about the Profumo scandal in England. A call girl named Christine Keeler was wrecking political careers and threatening to bring down the government. Once more Adrian talked about menacing the Kennedys with Amalie Borne. Once more Cliff talked him out of it.

At midnight on June 5, 1963, Cliff's phone rang. His daughter Elizabeth walked into the study where Cliff was plowing through more SST reports and said in a dazed voice: "It's President Kennedy." At eighteen, Liz was in search of idols and had found one.

"Hello, Cliff," said the rich Boston baritone. "You've been a very patient fellow. I think I've got some good news for you. Can you come to Colorado Springs tomorrow? I'm speaking at the Air Force Academy graduation. I think you'll be interested in part of the speech."

"I'll be there, Mr. President."

"Good. Good. How's that beautiful doll—what's her name?"

"Amalie?"

"Yeah. Can you bring her along?"

"Sure."

"I think she'll be an improvement on anything we could pick up in Colorado Springs, wouldn't you say?"

Cliff called Amalie Borne in New York. She was very difficult. She wanted a special fee beyond the money Buchanan was paying her. She demanded a private plane. Cliff conceded the fee but balked at the private plane. She finally agreed to meet Cliff in Denver the following morning at 10 A.M. From there they would fly in a Buchanan company plane to Colorado Springs. Dick Stone and his accountants could worry about how much it cost them later.

The next day, Cliff sat beside Amalie and Mike Shannon in the fifth row of the presidential party, looking out at forty thousand people packing Falcon Stadium. In the near distance loomed the snowcapped Rockies. Directly in front of them sat 493 young men, the fifth graduating class of the Air Force Academy. At the microphone, after some preliminary jokes and a somber review of the perilous world in which the graduates would serve, John F. Kennedy said: "Neither the economics nor the politics of international air competition permit us to stand still. Today the challenging new frontier in commercial aviation is supersonic flight. In my judgment the government should immediately commence a new program in partnership with private industry to develop a supersonic transport superior to that being built in any country in the world."

The majestic setting matched Cliff's soaring hopes. Ten billion dollars in sales, here we come! He was making triumphant love to Sarah. He was getting drunk with Frank Buchanan and Billy McCall, telling them, especially Billy, that he was in charge of the company's future now. He could junk Sarah's dirty campaign to ruin Billy. He did not have to be afraid of him anymore.

That was the way it went for that magical summer of 1963. Everyone and everything seemed to coalesce. Adrian Van Ness cheerfully ate his words and raised Cliff's salary. The Navy issued a request for bids on a new attack plane and were dazzled by Frank's Thunderer. Sarah grew passionate in bed with a man who was going to leave Billy McCall so far behind in the race for Buchanan's presidency the famous pilot shrank to toy soldier size.

Cliff did not even worry when Victoria talked Billy into quitting the Air Force to become Buchanan's chief test pilot. Adrian Van Ness said he was delighted. Billy's reputation inside the aircraft world would add momentum to their head start on the SST.

Unreeling, like a terrific technicolor movie that went on and on with resounding background music mingling with the roar of jet engines, that was the way Cliff Morris saw his life in the summer and fall of 1963. Even Amalie Borne seemed pleased by another flurry of visits to the White House. Only Dick Stone seemed unhappy about that—he was apparently still hung up on the dame.

Cliff took Dick to lunch and told him to marry Cassie Trainor. She was the answer to Amalie. It would give her exactly what she deserved—the brush-off—and straighten out Dick's muddled love life. For the first time in their lives, Dick admitted Cliff might be right.

Cliff even managed to continue to sell Stardusters overseas—a nice round eighty to Japan, Thailand, Australia, and India. Sarah gave a dinner party to celebrate and invited Billy and Victoria. Mike Shannon did his imitation of the Creature. It was the hit of the evening. By now Mike was practically working full time for Buchanan, talking up their SST as the only one that made sense.

Congress grumbled and yammered about putting up the money for the new plane but there was not much doubt that they would acquiesce, once they shook a few goodies from the White House tree. Adrian committed two million dollars to building a full size mockup, even though Frank Buchanan was still fussing with a lot of details, such as a new double delta wing that would make the plane much safer to land.

On November 22, 1963, Cliff whistled his way up the Hollywood Freeway to the Mojave to take a first look at a test model of the Thunderer. He was standing on the runway in the brilliant desert sunshine, admiring the barrel-shaped plane, when Frank Buchanan walked toward him with a peculiar look on his face.

"Someone just shot Kennedy," Frank said.

"He's dead?"

"They think so."

That was where Cliff heard it, with another set of mountains in the distance, reminding him of the golden figure facing the snowy crests of the Rockies, urging Americans to accept the challenge of another dawn of flight. It seemed simultaneously horrible—and just right—that he heard it here from Frank Buchanan.

"I've had a feeling from things Dick Stone told me that he was vulnerable to evil," Frank said. "No one can get away with treating women like disposable spare parts indefinitely. The good spirits turn their backs on that kind of a man."

Billy McCall came roaring onto the runway in his wife's red Triumph. He hurtled toward them at sixty miles an hour and skidded to a stop in front of the Thunderer. "I just heard it on the radio. Someone shot Kennedy's head off in Dallas. Isn't that the best goddamn news you've heard in a year?"

It was 11:30 A.M. and Billy was drunk. Standing in the violent desert sun, Cliff suddenly felt engulfed by an alien darkness. It did not come from California. It seemed to be spilling over those guardian mountains from the invisible heart of America. It made a mess of the triumphant technicolor movie of his life.

Cliff tried to tell himself Billy was elated because he shared Curtis LeMay's opinion of Kennedy as a fraud. But Cliff could not escape the feeling that Billy's smile also said he knew his half brother's climb to the executive stratosphere had just aborted. His career was in a vertical dive.

Frank Buchanan seemed to sense the old hatred crackling between them. He tried to defuse it. "Let's have a cup of coffee, Billy," he said. "I want you sober before you fly this plane. Join us, Cliff?"

"No thanks," Cliff said.

MINDS AND HEARTS

"What is it, Stone, what's wrong? Why did you stop loving me?" Amalie Borne said.

"I didn't stop," Dick Stone said, his leaden voice betraying the lie.

They were lying on the bed in her Waldorf Towers apartment, after making love for the last time. Dick had come to

New York determined to demand a final yes or no. Before he could speak, Amalie had told him she did not want to see him again.

"What is wrong with your whole country?" she said, clicking on the TV set from the switch on the night table. "I begin to think you are more hysterical than the Italians, more corrupt than the English, more grandiose than the French, more militarist than the Germans, bigger liars than the Russians."

On the television screen a sheriff's posse and state troopers in Selma, Alabama, were attacking Negro marchers with whips and clubs and tear gas. It was the spring of 1965. John F. Kennedy had been dead eighteen months. Lyndon Johnson had been elected president in his own right by the biggest majority in American history and proclaimed the Great Society—a swarm of federal programs that would give citizens of all ages and colors and creeds equal opportunity, equal housing, equal education, equal health care. He was discovering some serious unk-unks in this grand design.

"I still love you," Dick insisted. It was true. He was just redefining the word again, as they had defined and redefined it from the beginning. Love had become virtually identifiable with lust, with the compulsion to have this woman whenever he was near her. Only regret differentiated it from whorehouse fucking.

"But there's no joy in it, no daring anymore. Nothing forbidden. We're like a married couple, Stone. It's too disgusting to tolerate any longer."

She switched channels. Helicopters whirred over a green jungle to disgorge helmeted South Vietnamese troops beside a rice paddy. Johnson was determined to prove he was just as tough on communism as Jack Kennedy. He was putting more and more men and planes into this confusing war. He had another thirty thousand troops suppressing a Communist uprising in the Dominican Republic.

"Your ridiculous ideas about love were driving me crazy, Stone. You should have done what Adrian Van Ness suggested, fucked me with lies on your lips. I would have adored that, when you finally told me."

"I couldn't do it. I'm not one of Nietzsche's *Über-*

menschen. Sometimes I think you really want to be fucked by a Nazi. Nothing else really excites you."

"What a fascinating idea. You're not as unoriginal as I thought, Stone."

The insults, the diatribes about America, about his personal shortcomings, had become more and more violent since Kennedy's assassination. Gone was the aura of the woman who slept with the most powerful man in the world. Adrian, sensing Amalie's isolation, or perhaps acting on revengeful advice from the Prince, had demanded she surrender all the incriminating papers she had stolen or face immediate cancellation of their agreement. A tearful Amalie had handed the documents over to Dick—after Xeroxing them and mailing them to Madame George. The Prince called a week later and told her that Madame George had turned the copies over to him. Henceforth, Amalie was simply another Buchanan employee.

"Richard, Richard," she said, rolling over on top of him. "Can't you believe me when I say that the only way I can prove my love is by saying good-bye?"

"I don't believe you. I don't accept it," he said, redefining both words. He believed she was both proving her love and punishing him for failing to protect her from Adrian. He accepted it as the price he was paying for his freedom but in a deeper part of his soul he rejected it as unbearable.

"You're as incomprehensible as the rest of your country. I wish I never left Europe. I understood Europe. Here nothing makes sense except money and a sort of blind desire. You all want to fuck but none of you care."

Dick was seized for the thousandth time with a yearning to know if she was Jewish, if the first story was the true one. But now he was afraid of the truth. He wanted to escape this woman. She was destroying him.

"Shannon says I must come to your magnificent capital tomorrow. There's a senator who yearns to meet me. I told him it was out of the question."

Mike Shannon had become Buchanan's field commander in the struggle for the supersonic airliner. He disliked Amalie. She transcended his Irish-American imagination in too many ways.

"Why can't you go?" Dick asked.

"I have nothing to wear. My clothes are falling apart from endless dry cleaning. Either you double my allowance or I'm going back to Paris. Even if I starve, at least it will be in a city I love."

"You're getting fifty thousand dollars a year for clothes now."

"Jackie Kennedy spends that in a month."

"I'll talk to Adrian. Meanwhile, go see the senator. He's very important at the moment. If he votes the right way, you too will be able to fly supersonically."

"And you'll make ten billion dollars."

She rolled off him and lay on her back, staring at the blue ceiling. "I don't need you any more, Stone. I need a man who doesn't care about me. Who doesn't care about himself. Who doesn't care about anything. A man who does reckless acts because they're always preferable to cautious ones. Because he's compelled to risk himself again and again. Is Cliff Morris such a man?"

"No," Dick said.

He put on his clothes, shoved one of her silver-backed white brushes through his hair and walked to the door. Amalie did not look at him. She continued to stare at the empty ceiling. Dick closed the door until he could no longer see her.

"Good-bye, Amalie."

"Good-bye Stone."

Six months later, Dick sat in his car beneath Chimney Rock, a great steep-sided pinnacle of weathered stone in the coastal mountains north of Los Angeles. There was not another car, another human being, in sight. He put his arms around Cassie Trainor and kissed her gently, firmly.

"How about it? Are you ready to get married?" he said.

He had flown up to the Oxnard School the week after he said good-bye to Amalie and began trying to regain his all-American girl. It had not been easy. Cassie was as beautiful as ever. Her auburn hair still seemed to emanate sunlight. She stood as straight, her figure was as slim and firm as a twenty-year-old, thanks to a fierce program of jogging, swimming, and tennis. But some of the spontaneity, the vivacity had been replaced by thoughtfulness. She was a reader and a thinker now.

Nevertheless she responded to his invitation to try to turn back the clock. She too wanted to regain some of that mocking stewardess who had cut loose in Manhattan Beach a decade ago. But it was mostly the other Cassie who emerged as the woman he was marrying. Now she talked back to him, not about whoriness and the Honeycomb Club but about his literary taste and political opinions.

Cassie persuaded him to reread Faulkner and Hemingway and admit her fellow southerner was superior. She read aloud from her favorite southern poet, the long-forgotten James Bannister Tabb, who blended some of Poe's music with a priestly tenderness. Cassie knew who she was in relation to the rest of the country: a southern woman who could live anywhere in America. Dick found himself attracted in an unexpectedly intense way.

For six months they had spent their weekends exploring what Cassie called "lost California," particularly in the mountains that look down on State 1 as it twists along the rugged coast below Oxnard. It reminded her of the empty landscape around Noglichucky Hollow in Tennessee.

They drove east along Route 58 to a hundred-year-old saloon at Pozo, with tractor seats for bar stools. Through fields of barley ablaze with fireweed, the farmer's enemy, they searched for the ruins of Adelaida, a town that no longer existed. Past stands of oaks and meadows sprinkled with wildflowers they roamed the Los Padres National Forest. Dick found Cassie's desire to share this scenery profoundly touching. It was a kind of statement of the loneliness she had felt when he had more or less abandoned her in Oxnard.

Now he was asking her the question that he had been unable to ask because Amalie Borne's shadow loomed between them. He told himself these six months had banished

Amalie's presence. He was in love with this thoughtful American woman he had helped to create.

Cassie kissed him in a sad gentle way and gazed up at Chimney Rock for a moment as if she was remembering shadows in her own life. "I wish we'd done it four years ago," he said. "Why did it take us so long?"

"Emotional retardation," Stone said. "I hadn't quite finished growing from a boy to a man."

He had debated whether to tell her about Amalie Borne and decided it would be a mistake. It was more than a little ironic. He had created an educated woman but he could not bring himself to trust her to be mature about the most important relationship in her life. But Amalie had left Dick too bruised, too wounded, for irony.

The wedding was a small, almost private affair in a white-steepled Baptist church near Oxnard. Most of the guests were from Buchanan Aircraft. Cliff Morris was Dick's best man. One of Cassie's favorite students was her maid of honor. Frank Buchanan gave the bride away. Billy McCall and Victoria, Adrian Van Ness and Amanda completed the party.

Adrian's toast was both a wish and a warning: "May the bride realize she's marrying a man—and an aircraft company."

"God help her!" Amanda said.

Everyone laughed. "I'm not joking!" Amanda said.

"That's what makes it so amusing," Adrian said.

"I would love to be married to an aircraft company. I can't think of anything more exciting," Victoria Van Ness McCall said.

"When you're married to the right man, everything is exciting," Sarah Morris said.

Even though he was well lit on champagne, Dick sensed an undercurrent of malice in Sarah's remark. His years of penetrating the mockery in Amalie's conversation had sharpened his ear for nuances. Sarah's eyes had a feverish glow. She seemed much too excited for a wedding that was decidedly unromantic. Was she needling Victoria—implying that Billy was the wrong man? Or comparing him to Cliff?

Whatever was implied, Victoria ignored it. "I found that out long ago," she said.

She smiled at Billy. A word from Dick's struggle with Amalie lurched into his mind: *voracity*. There were times when he wondered if she had wanted to annihilate him with her relentless reports of her assignations. This was another kind of voracity. For a moment Dick felt sorry for Billy McCall.

The newlyweds departed for a two-week honeymoon on Maui. They rented a plane and flew to other islands. They drank rum swizzles and swam and played tennis, at which Cassie usually beat her out-of-shape husband. By night they made tender love and discussed their future. Cassie wanted to have children and then think about going back to graduate school to get a Ph.D. in American Studies. She had read the recent best-seller, *The Feminine Mystique*, but she still thought a family was more important than a career. "You can take the girl out of the South but you can't take the South out of the girl," she said.

The telephone rang. It was Adrian Van Ness. "Dick," he said. "I hate to interrupt your honeymoon. But I'm afraid you'll have to consider cutting it short. We just heard from Mike Shannon that Johnson's going into Vietnam with both feet. He's committing a hundred and twenty-five thousand men next week and he'll have four hundred thousand there by the end of the year. The Air Force and the Navy and the Marines are letting bids for a dozen different planes. We need you to help us cost out these proposals—"

"I'll call you in the morning," Dick said, slamming down the phone.

"Your leader?" Cassie said.

"If I die and go to heaven or hell, I'm sure Adrian Van Ness will have my telephone number," he said.

He was remembering the night the Korean War began. Making love to Cassie with Adrian Van Ness watching in a corner of his mind. Wondering if he could ever deserve happiness while working for Buchanan Aircraft. Amalie Borne's voice began whispering mockery in that same invisible place.

"Will you love me even if I'm unfaithful with an aircraft company?" he said, putting his arms around Cassie.

"I believe that was in the contract," she said.

She was still his all-American girl.

BOOK EIGHT

BOOK ONE

HATRED AT WORK

"We're out of it."

Cliff Morris was calling from Washington, where the Federal Aviation Authority was selecting the winner in the design competition for the supersonic airliner. With the usual help from Mike Shannon, who had numerous friends in Lyndon Johnson's White House, Cliff had gotten the bad news a month in advance of the announcement.

"Who won?" Adrian said.

"Boeing."

The one company in the business who did not need the contract. Boeing's new jumbo jet, the 747, was on its way to dominating the intercontinental commercial market. Its medium-range 727 was equally triumphant in the short and middle distances in the United States. Worse, Boeing's supersonic design was the one most people in the aircraft business had dismissed. But the Seattle plane maker had Senator Henry (Scoop) Jackson, better known as the senator from Boeing, on their side. Buchanan and Lockheed, the other two supersonic finalists, were among a half dozen California aircraft companies, all busily cutting each other's throats in Washington. They had no such blunt instrument to get the attention of the bureaucrats.

"Adrian, that thing is never going to fly," Cliff said. "Frank says their swing wing won't work. The environmentalists are already screaming it's going to pollute the upper atmosphere. The sonic boom means it can only fly over water. Guys like the Creature are going to eat Boeing for dinner, with Scoop Jackson for dessert. They'll never vote the money for it."

"I hope you're right," Adrian said, hearing the desperation in Cliff's voice. He had spent most of 1966 in Washington in this losing struggle to rescue their plane. Adrian knew how Cliff would translate the comment. If you are wrong you can say good-bye to your hopes of becoming Buchanan's president.

"We've got the Thunderer. The Navy's nuts about it and McNamara wants the Air Force to buy it. We're first in line on this new monster transport. It's a two-billion-dollar contract, Adrian. They're ready to go for a new high-performance fighter to replace the Scorpion. We're near the head of the line for that too. The Air Force loves Frank's design."

"What else is cooking?"

"Vietnam is going from bad to worse. We'll have 600,000 men in there by the end of the year."

Ruined stopped howling in Adrian's head. He had chosen well when he put Cliff Morris in charge of Buchanan's sales. He had become an adept pupil of the Oakes Ames school of political management. Buchanan now operated a virtual hotel on the Chesapeake where Pentagon civilian and military brass mingled with senators and congressmen for weekends of golfing, shooting, and luxury drinking and dining while Cliff and Mike Shannon and a staff of thirty sold Buchanan planes. At crucial moments Cliff injected Amalie Borne into the game with a sense of climax that Adrian himself would find it hard to match.

But the supersonic airliner. None of the other planes Cliff was talking about meant anything to Adrian compared to the SST. He strode out of his office and took the elevator to the ground floor. Walking swiftly down the maze of corridors, greeted by startled security guards at checkpoints, he reached the hangar where Buchanan's two-million-dollar SST mockup sat, bathed in overhead fluorescent lights.

Gleaming white, three hundred feet long, it was a hollow plane, with no wiring, no hydraulics, no engines inside the huge ducts. But it had a full complement of seats, galleys, lavatories, carpets, and other accessories to give visitors the feel of a finished product. They had used the mockup for a thousand publicity pictures. Now Adrian saw it with different eyes.

It was the Warrior bomber with windows. After some early experimentation with a modified wing, Frank Buchanan had developed a strange indifference to doing more design work on it. Adrian, still in the grip of the illusion of favoritism the Kennedys had created, had not protested. After all, the plane had actually flown at Mach 3, something none of their competitors could claim.

Much too late, Adrian remembered Billy McCall's candid admission to the Senate committee that the SST had a whole range of problems that the builder of a bomber did not have to worry about. Fuel economy, landing speed, the complete elimination of duct rumble, or surge, as the British called it. Frank Buchanan had dismissed Adrian's pleas to tackle these problems. He insisted they could be dealt with in the testing and production phase when they would not be spending their own money. Besides, he was too busy with the military planes Cliff had just mentioned.

Behind Frank's smiling refusal, Adrian now saw another motive: hatred. Frank did not want Buchanan Aircraft to win the competition. He did not want Adrian Van Ness to be able to go to the next meeting of the Conquistadores del Cielo and sit down with Don Douglas and Bill Allen of Boeing and Roger Lewis of General Dynamics as the man who was making the most famous plane in the world, the man whose company's name was on everyone's lips.

Frank Buchanan did not want Adrian Van Ness to go to sleep at night thinking that all around the world, tens of thousands of people were whizzing over oceans and continents in Buchanan Aircraft's SST. With uncanny malice, Frank was depriving Adrian of his deepest wish, his hungriest hope.

Hatred. Adrian felt it beating on him, with the glaring intensity of those overhead lights. There was no place he could escape it. At home it confronted him in Amanda's malevolent eyes, in her relentlessly hostile remarks. It stared at him from his son-in-law's cold gray eyes. Even Victoria, the one person in the world from whom he expected an exemption, seemed to reflect it in her moody alienation. Was this his only reward for his years of struggle and anguish?

"Mr. Van Ness? Any news from Washington?"

It was Terry Pakenham, the foreman who had supervised the work on the mockup. A big thick-necked man with the flushed face of a drinker, he had been with Buchanan since 1946.

"We lost. Chop it up," Adrian said.

"Chop it up?" Pakenham said. "Jesus—can't we give it to a museum or something?" Pakenham had tears in his eyes. Adrian kept forgetting how the men who worked on a plane fell in love with it.

Although he felt nothing but rage, Adrian put his hand on Pakenham's arm. "I'm sorry," he said. "Boeing's won it."

"With that goddamn swing wing? Christ, who did they pay off?" Pakenham roared.

Back in his office, Adrian found the company's attorney, Winthrop Standish, and a lawyer from one of Los Angeles's major law firms waiting impatiently for him. The appointment was on his calendar. He apologized and braced himself for more bad news. Last year Lyndon Johnson had passed a civil rights act designed to banish racial discrimination from American life. Since there were virtually no blacks or Mexicans in the aircraft industry, Adrian had paid little attention to it. Almost as an afterthought, a congressman had suggested adding women to the list of those against whom it would be a crime to discriminate. There were quite a lot of women in the aircraft business—all working at lowly jobs.

Adrian squirmed in his chair. The doleful expressions on the legal faces said everything in advance. "Ed here doesn't agree with your inclination to fight these discrimination suits, Adrian," Standish said.

"Why not?" Adrian said testily. Sixteen women in the design department were suing Buchanan, claiming they had been denied meaningful promotion.

"For one thing, Frank Buchanan says he'll testify in their favor. He says he would have been happy to promote them if the company's policy permitted it."

"If a jury hears that, it'll be treble damages," Ed intoned.

"What about the sex-harassment case from Audrey Sinclair?" Adrian said. "That bitch used to work at the Honey-comb Club!"

"Frank—and Buzz McCall—both admit to having sexual relations with her," Standish said, wiping his brow. "Frank says he never approved of the Honeycomb Club."

"Never approved of it?" Adrian shouted. "He donated the land for it!"

"Adrian," Standish said. "That's irrelevant. The point is what he's saying now. What he might say to a jury. Can you imagine what the papers would do with that story? They'd dig up a half-dozen other women who worked there. We'd be smeared as the company who used government money to pay for sex orgies."

"If it makes you feel any better," Ed intoned, "All the aircraft companies are getting hit with these suits."

But how many of them have a chief designer ready to testify against them? Adrian wondered, almost strangling on his rage. The lawyers departed to negotiate away his money. Adrian stared at his reflection in the window. A rumble. The prototype of the Thunderer, their new ground support plane, was coming in for a landing, his son-in-law Billy McCall at the controls.

Crash, you son of a bitch, Adrian prayed. Crash. He wanted to take something away from Frank Buchanan. Something precious and irreplaceable.

He would do the next best thing. He would deprive Frank of someone else who had been tolerated long enough. Once more Adrian lunged out of his office to stride down corridors to the remote cubicle where Buzz McCall sat plastered for most of each day.

Voices. Billy McCall was in the office, having a drink with Buzz, talking about the air war in Vietnam. "It's the god-damndest mess I've ever seen," Billy said. "The fucking president picks out the targets. Or one of McNamara's Pentagon assholes does it for him. Then everybody says it proves air power can't do the job."

Adrian charged into the office. "Hello, Billy," he said. "Buzz. I've got some bad news. We've lost the SST contract.

Under the circumstances we've got to cut costs. You're off the payroll at the end of the week."

"Adrian—Chrissake—gimme somethin' to do. Still make a contribution," Buzz mumbled.

Adrian glanced at Billy. Loathing was all he saw in his eyes. "This is a business, not a goddamn rest home," Adrian snarled.

Other words leaped to his lips. *He killed the only woman I ever loved. I've been waiting twenty-five years to do this.* But he did not speak them.

Back in his office, Adrian struggled for self-control. He could fire Frank Buchanan too. But that would be a mistake. Only time, his ally in the past, time and forethought, could bring him revenge on the scale he sought. In the meantime he had to remember who he was, he had to cope with the hatred in other ways.

His first target, now that Buzz was gone for good, was Billy McCall. He had to get that defiant bastard under control. He wanted to break him, not only because it would wound Frank Buchanan. He wanted to deliver the empty shell to Victoria so she could see for herself what a hoax she had married.

A month later, Cliff Morris came booming into Los Angeles with the proposal for the new transport. There would be a pro forma competition with Douglas and Convair but Buchanan was the guaranteed winner. It was going to be the biggest plane in the world, able to carry an entire battalion of troops into combat. The contract was now worth three billion dollars—a nice consolation for the loss of the SST and the Warrior.

There were several flies in this soothing ointment. The plane would have to be built in Louisiana to keep the new head of the House Armed Services Committee happy—and it would be a fixed-cost contract, a TPP, they were now calling it—a Total Performance Package. The potential overruns—no one had ever built a plane of this size before—were scary.

"Who do you think should be the project manager?" Adrian said.

"Billy McCall," Cliff said.

"What does he know about running something this big?" Adrian snorted.

"Not a damn thing," Cliff said. "But we've got Mike Shannon to cover our asses in Washington. He says half the senators and two-thirds of the congressmen on the armed services committees think this TPP idea is idiotic. We can get back most of an overrun on appeal."

"So?"

"So it's a good chance to see what kind of a manager Billy is. If he can't hack it now's the time to find out."

Adrian suddenly read all the meanings in Cliff's matter-of-fact voice. Here was the ally he was looking for, someone who hated Billy McCall even more than he did.

"I think you're right," Adrian said. "Now's the time."

TICKET TO PARADISE

After calling the ground controller three times on the wrong frequencies, I find the right one. Billy's eyes roll. We taxi onto the tarmac. I set the altimeter wrong. Billy is yelling at me not to use brakes and power at the same time. When I search his face, trying to understand the source of his rage, he tells me to get my eyes back on the taxiway where they belong.

At run-up I get the tower frequency wrong. Finally we are set for takeoff, with a plane just behind us, which rattles me even more than usual. The wheels lift off before I realize it and I am pulling the nose up into a stall. Billy yells at me to get into a lower nose position, to pick up speed as lift increases. Why can't I remember any of these things?

Suddenly we are airborne in a bell jar full of haze. Water droplets make the air glossy, like taffy, iridescent in places. The airport, the runway, the ground disappear. I think it's marvelous and ask Billy if he thinks so too. "When are you going to make your turn?" Billy yells.

A quick look for oncoming traffic in the haze, then I bank left, still climbing toward 2,000 feet. I shoot through the ceiling because I haven't changed the plane's attitude and reduced the power at the right time. Worse, I am supposed to be flying a rectangle around the airport and already I'm arcing far out to sea.

"Why are we out here? Where are we going?" Billy yells. "Why are we still climbing?"

"I don't know!" I scream back.

"Do something. Don't just sit there. Do something!"

I cut the throttle back and bank sharply toward the airport again. It's a terrible bank. The turn indicator ball tumbles far left. Billy points to it and yells "Jesus Christ!"

"We're supposed to be flying a base leg at right angles!" Billy shouts. "Are we too high or too low to make the runway?"

"I don't know," I say, beginning to sob.

"Do something!" Billy shouts.

I throttle back and we drop dead toward the telephone wires on the west side of the airport. Too low. I gun the throttle and now we are too high. I see the aim point but need flaps to steepen our descent.

I look at the ground, trying to estimate my airspeed. We seem to be going like mad. "How many times do I have to tell you to look at the instruments, not the ground?" Billy says.

I come in too hard and too fast and worst of all not on the center line but at an angle. "Fix it!" Billy says.

I try pedaling: right rudder, left rudder. Nothing happens.

"Don't just jiggle the rudder. Use it. Get us back on that center line with our nose straight! Now! Fast! Fast!"

The runway looms under us at ten feet. I try to level out the nose. He yanks the yoke back hard and settles us in. "Victoria," he says. "This plane is not designed to land on its nose. You were diving at five feet off the ground!"

Sarah Chapman Morris sat on the sunny deck of Victoria Van Ness McCall's futuristic house on a ridge in Topanga

Canyon, reading the story of Billy McCall's attempts to teach
Victoria how to fly. It was a disaster from the first lesson to
the last one. Victoria had a poetic mind. Flight to her was
an experience in beauty. The plane was a creature as mysterious as an animal or a bird. She simply could not grasp
the hard technical details of conquering the sky. She either
ignored the dials or chased them obsessively when Billy
yelled at her to watch them. She made major changes in pitch
at low altitudes, where life or death required delicacy. She
admired clouds when she should have been looking for other
planes in her approach pattern.

She had written it all down with unsparing accuracy, portraying herself as a hopeless pilot. She wanted Billy to read
it and laugh and say something cheerful and kind. She was
showing it to Sarah because she needed a confidante and
Sarah was always there, smiling sadly, eager to listen to
every awful thing Billy was doing to destroy his marriage.

A doe bounded out of the trees and dashed across the
clearing. A moment later she was followed by a buck. Somewhere in the nearby woods the buck caught up to his quarry.
Sarah and Victoria listened to the thrashing and panting.
Sarah saw the whole thing in the theater of her mind, the
rutting, the submission.

Did Victoria see it too? Of course. She was Sarah. Sarah
was Victoria. She got up and took one of the tranquilizers
Dr. Kirk Willoughby had prescribed for her. "I hate my
mind!" she said to Sarah. "Do you ever feel that way?"

"Of course. All women do," Sarah said.

Victoria told Sarah she did not know where her husband
was. He might be flying over China Lake, the Navy testing
center, in the Thunderer or lying on the sand at Malibu with
some acid-dropping teenager. She did not know and she did
not want to know.

She could call Frank Buchanan and ask him if Billy was
at China Lake, turning over the Thunderer to the Navy for
testing. If Frank said no, she would burst into tears. If he
said yes she would burst into tears anyway.

Victoria showed Sarah a list of the things she hated Billy
to do. She had written them down yesterday. She was think-

ing of showing it to him. She was even thinking of having it printed in headline-size type and posting it on the wall of their bedroom.

1. Fly without me.
2. Go to Malibu without me.
3. Go to Laguna Beach without me.
4. Insult Cliff Morris.
5. Criticize Sarah Morris.
6. Talk to any woman under thirty.
7. Read the newspapers aloud.
8. Look at the news on TV.
9. Say what the fuck.
10. Say why the fuck.
11. Say how the fuck.
12. Drink in front of me.
13. Drink without me.
14. Talk about World War II or Korea.
15. Talk about Vietnam.
16. Ask me if I believe in God.
17. Ask me why I don't really like to fuck.
18. Tell me I don't really like to fuck.
19. Tell me why some women are better fuckers.

Sarah Morris said it was a very good list. She told Victoria a better way to handle Billy. She had to find something to do outside the house, something that made her look independent without being independent. Because Billy would not tolerate real independence. Sarah urged Victoria to become cochairperson of one of her committees. There was scarcely a volunteer activity in Los Angeles Sarah did not either run from behind the scenes or chair or both. She was always raising money for starving Chicano artists or scholarships for ghetto blacks or a new campaign to eliminate smog. Sarah told Victoria being a committeeperson was very good preparation for becoming an executive's wife. After all, Billy was bound to become a Buchanan Aircraft executive. He might even become president.

Victoria frowned. Lately she had begun to dislike the way

Sarah pronounced Billy's name. Sarah knew she disliked it but she could not stop pronouncing it that way, with a throb, a thud of hatred in it. "I heard Billy made some wonderful suggestions to improve the Thunderer," Sarah said.

Billy, Victoria thought. "Oh? Who told you that?"

"I think it was Frank Buchanan. I was talking to him at the benefit for the Downtown Arts. He's such a sweet man. He adores Billy."

Billy. Victoria thought.

"But then we all do. We're so lucky to have gotten him away from the Air Force. It's such a shame about the SST, though. Cliff is just crushed by it. He so looked forward to working with Billy on it. They would have made a perfect team."

Billy, Victoria thought.

Sarah urged Victoria to join the Committee to Rebuild Watts. A mob had burned down most of this black Los Angeles slum earlier in the year. She said Cliff was going to chair a subcommittee to get more blacks into the aircraft industry workforce. Maybe Billy could join him. That would give him and Victoria something to share, outside the house.

Billy, Victoria thought.

"Your father's going to be honorary chairman. I was talking to him the other day and he complained he never sees you. This would be a good excuse. He wishes he saw more of you—and Billy."

Billy, Victoria thought.

Sarah could see Victoria trying to understand what she disliked in the way Sarah said *Billy*. Victoria shook her head. "I don't want that sort of help. Especially not from *him*."

"That's not being realistic, Victoria," Sarah said. "He wants to help you—and Billy in every way he can."

Victoria sat there, trying to understand why she was suddenly unable to stand Sarah. Was it because of the way she said *Billy* or was it because she was English? That lovely vanilla accent carried Victoria back to Oxford, to days when she sat around talking about ways to save the world. Now all she thought about was how to save her marriage.

The telephone rang. It was Frank Buchanan. "I have some

more books for your mother," he said. "Can I drop them off some time today?"

"I don't think she reads them, Frank," Victoria said.

"It doesn't matter. Just having them in the house, in her room, could make a difference. A book releases emanations. Not as much as a mind but—"

Frank's mysticism was lost on Victoria. She had her father's cold objectivity toward life on matters that did not involve Billy McCall.

"I know it sounds foolish. But it means a great deal to me. I'm very fond of your mother," Frank said.

Sarah had told Victoria that Amanda and Frank had been lovers. She had revealed almost all Buchanan's secrets, carefully portraying Adrian as a much-misunderstood man, hoping it would eventually reach his ears.

"How's Billy?" Frank asked.

"Fine. He's up at China Lake today, isn't he? Delivering the Thunderer?"

"I don't know. I'm spending my days and nights on another plane. A monster transport. I hope it won't look like a monster, of course."

"It won't, I'm sure of that," Victoria said.

"I'll drop off the books on the way home."

Sarah was in the kitchen fixing lunch. Victoria was about to help her when the phone rang again. "Is Billy there?" her father said.

Billy, Victoria thought. He pronounced it the same way. "No," she said.

"Do you know where he is?"

"I thought he was at China Lake. Delivering the Thunderer."

"He did that last week."

Victoria struggled to stifle an impulse to weep. This was the third time Adrian had called in search of Billy. Was he trying to tell her something? Or find out something?

"I just thought you and he might want to hear some good news," Adrian said. "We've gotten a three-billion-dollar contract to build the world's biggest transport for the Air Force. I'm going to make Billy the project manager. He'll be perfect for the job. He'll be able to handle the usual maddening interference from the Pentagon. Cliff Morris will keep Congress at bay. He and Billy will work together beautifully. Do you think he'll do it?"

Sarah, listening on the extension in the kitchen, heard her weeks of patient persuasion pay off. Victoria's resistance dissolved. "I hope so. It's exactly what he needs. More responsibility."

"Ah. I've finally done something right?"

"What do you mean?"

"Ever since you married, I've felt you regarded me as the scum of the earth."

"That's not true!"

"Maybe it's just neurosis at work."

"I'm grateful, Daddy. I really am."

"I'm not doing it for that reason. But it's nice to hear."

"How's mother?"

"About the same. Wondering aloud why you don't give her a grandchild."

"Maybe now we will. If Billy isn't flying any more, there goes his last excuse."

"That thought occurred to me."

"You Machievelli."

"Disraeli. I think of myself as Disraeli. His Victoria was difficult too, at times."

Victoria hung up and sat there, suffused by wistful nostalgic love. Sarah brought a tray of chicken salad and iced tea out on the deck. As Victoria started to tell her the good news, the buck and the doe emerged from the woods. He was nuzzling her. Out of the trees whizzed an arrow that struck the buck squarely in the chest. He bounded high in the air and came down on crumpling legs. The doe vanished into the woods in three huge leaps. Two men emerged from the woods with longbows and quivers of arrows on their shoulders. There were broad grins on their brutal faces.

"You sons of bitches!" Victoria screamed.

She ran into the house and seized Billy's shotgun off the wall. From a drawer she scooped a handful of shells and shoved them into the chamber. Outside the men were standing beside the deer, glaring at the house. Victoria aimed the gun in their general direction and fired. The men fled into the trees.

Victoria reloaded the gun and ran down to the buck, who lay on his side, barely breathing. One eye rolled up toward her; it seemed to ask a question she could not answer. Victoria put the muzzle of the shotgun behind his ear and pulled the trigger. She turned to a trembling Sarah and said: "Sometimes I think the world would be a better place without men, don't you?"

Sarah was enormously tempted to agree with her. But her hateful heart whispered: *it's too soon.*

HOUSE ON FIRE

"Where's Liz?" Cliff Morris asked as the family assembled in the living room to drive to Buchanan's 1967 Christmas party.

"She's not coming," Sarah said.

"Why not?"

"She says she refuses to toast the war machine."

Cliff's face darkened. Seventeen-year-old Charlie grinned in anticipation. He loved these brawls between Liz and her father. He was 100 percent on Cliff's side. Their quiet middle child, Margaret, looked stricken. She tried to stay neutral but she secretly sided with her older sister.

"Liz!" Cliff roared.

Liz slouched downstairs. She was a brunette beauty with her father's chiseled features. Her silken hair streamed to her waist. She wore blue jeans and a work shirt, the uniform of her generation. She had graduated from Stanford last year and was getting a master's in art history at UCLA. Her boyfriend, a political scientist, was the leading antiwar activist on the campus.

"Either you come to this party or you move out of this house," Cliff said.

"I'll be gone when you come back," Liz said.

"You better get ready to pay your own tuition from now on," Cliff said.

"I'll get a job. Maybe on your assembly line. What will you do when they catch me sabotaging one of your murder machines?"

"I'll personally escort you to jail!" Cliff roared.

"Commie freako," Charlie said.

"Junior fascist pig," Liz replied.

"Shut up, all of you!" Margaret wailed.

"Second the motion," Sarah said. As usual, she remained perfectly calm, in total control of her feelings. She had become the family arbiter, the semi-outsider who was able to adjudicate among these overwrought Americans. "We'll discuss this tomorrow. You can postpone your evacuation for a day, Liz."

The Christmas party was bigger, louder, more crowded than ever. It spread over three hangars, with a dance band in each one. New planes were on display, the sturdy ground-support craft, the Thunderer, already in production, a mock-up of a needle-nosed high-performance fighter, the SkyDemon, and a gigantic painting of the projected new transport, the Colossus. Buchanan was booming. The workforce was over fifty thousand. The champagne flowed. But Sarah Morris sensed an undercurrent of malaise.

For one thing, everyone, even Cliff, had to pass through a metal detector to get in. There were uniformed security guards at the doors; dozens more roamed the hangar floors. These days every company in the aircraft industry was the target of a continuous stream of bomb threats and vows to sabotage the production line. In California particularly, the rising protest against the war in Vietnam had focused on the American bombing offensive, Operation Rolling Thunder.

What multiplied the malaise was the failure of the offensive. The Communists seemed as potent as ever and they were shooting down an appalling number of American planes. For the disciples of air power this was a very disturbing development that they tried desperately to explain away. One part of Sarah's mind secretly exulted in this spectacle. Another part—her public self—deplored and regretted it and even sympathized with Cliff as he struggled to explain it to Charlie and his sisters.

Cliff went off to work the crowd in the next hangar. They always separated at big parties to achieve maximum contact. Susan Hardy cruised toward Sarah, a dark brown Scotch in her stubby hand. She was virtually spherical now, with a balloon body supporting a smaller balloon face. She never wore anything but immense flapping muumuus, which covered everything including her feet. But her eyes retained their fierce intelligence and there was nothing spherical about her tongue. She had become a virulent critic of the war.

"I saw a top-secret report on our actual plane losses over 'Nam," she said. "The numbers are unbelievable."

Susan always started her conversations in the middle these days. She was full of energy; an hour or two with her left Sarah feeling exhausted. Susan's divorce from Sam Hardy was a spectacular success. She had taken half of everything he owned—in cash. Sam had been forced to sell almost every piece of real property in his name except his car. Susan proceeded to compound the torment by getting a job in Buchanan's public relations department, which enabled her to keep tabs on her ex-husband's anemic love life and self-destructive drinking.

Lately Susan had become interested in attacking the American war machine—a target more worthy of her mammoth animosity. She had been trying to enlist Sarah in the campaign but she was much too busy fighting her private war against Billy McCall to be helpful.

"You must hear things from Cliff, Sarah. Just pass them along to me. I know what to do with them," Susan said sotto voce, while Margaret and Charlie gazed at the swirling crowd and the planes.

"I never know what's important and what isn't," Sarah lied. She was using Susan to rehearse her role as the sweet, slightly bewildered wife. She was not about to risk Cliff's career to feed Susan's insatiable appetite for revenge on the whole male sex. She only wanted revenge on one particular male.

"Sarah, you're looking so lovely," Adrian Van Ness said, as Susan Hardy ballooned conspiratorially off toward the bar. "It must have something to do with growing up in England. All that rain on your skin."

Beside Adrian stood Victoria Van Ness McCall and her husband. Billy gave Sarah his usual mocking smile. She returned it with maximum malice. *You won't be smiling at this time next year, hero*, she thought. *You'll be the laughingstock of the aircraft business.*

Sarah knew all about the plan to put Billy in charge of the giant transport and watch him fall on his face. She had given Cliff the idea one night after they had cavorted on that dark current that electrified their bedroom. *Get Adrian to give him some big job. Something he can't handle*, she had whispered.

Sarah introduced Charlie and Margaret. "We thought it was time they started enjoying the fun," she said.

"Have you finished testing the Thunderer, Colonel?" Charlie asked Billy.

"The first ones'll be over 'Nam in a couple of months."

"Could you give me a look at the cockpit?"

"Sure," Billy said.

For a moment, watching them stroll away, Sarah almost cried "Stop!" or something equally absurd. Charlie was as tall as Billy now. He was still mesmerized by planes. The physical resemblance remained oblique. No one but her would ever know the possible, even the probable secret.

"You can cross me off your benefit list," Victoria said. "We'll be leaving for Louisiana soon. Billy can hardly wait to get to work on the Colossus."

A pulse throbbed in Sarah's throat. Adrian had been almost too amenable to making Billy the project manager of the Colossus. Sarah had grown alarmed. She did not trust Adrian. Those hooded eyes were too cold. What if Billy pulled it off—built the biggest plane in the world?

Victoria talked about her determination to have a child. Billy had finally agreed to it. She hoped it would be a girl. Her father would adore a granddaughter. "Isn't it strange the way most men favor boys, but Daddy doesn't? I can't imagine how he would have treated me if I'd been a boy."

It was a kind of fugue in two themes, Daddy's fondness and Billy's readiness to have a child. The ideas, the images, wound strands of wire around Sarah's throat until she found it more and more difficult to breathe.

"Fascinating," Sarah said, watching Charlie and Billy climb up on the Thunderer's wing and lean into the cockpit. In profile the faces were virtually identical.

"I've been thinking of putting most of my money into Buchanan stock. Daddy said if I did he'd give me a seat on the board. I think he's teasing but it's a good idea, don't you think? A statement of confidence in the company's future?"

Sarah gazed into Victoria's wide heavy face and confronted Adrian's cold analytical eyes. Was it possible she knew Sarah was her secret enemy? This babble was all part of a carefully calculated plan to unnerve her? For the twentieth time Sarah discounted the idea. She possessed this woman. She *was* her. Every touch, every kiss, Victoria experienced in Billy's arms belonged to Sarah.

"How does Billy feel about that fellow who set a new speed record out at Edwards the other day?" Sarah asked.

An Air Force major had flown another experimental plane, the X-15, made by North American, at an astonishing 4,138 miles an hour.

"He hasn't said a word to me about it," Victoria said.

Frank Buchanan limped toward them, his lined face exuding Christmas cheer. He kissed Sarah and Margaret, then Victoria. "I just saw your mother," he said to Victoria. "She's improved a great deal. We had a very pleasant conversation. It's remarkable how much of her memory has returned."

"I almost wish it hadn't. She remembers every bad thing I ever did or said," Victoria replied.

"It's just her old determination to speak the truth no matter how much it upsets people," Frank said. "She told me I was getting uglier by the minute."

"We adore you anyway," Sarah said.

"That's what an old lecher likes to hear," Frank said, giving her a hug.

Charlie and Billy rejoined their circle. Frank shook hands with them. Sarah could see Charlie was practically exploding with some sort of good news. "You look like you've just seen all your Christmas presents in advance," she said.

"Colonel McCall says before he goes to Louisiana he'd like to teach me to fly," Charlie said. "If it's okay with you and Dad."

"He knows more about the inside of a cockpit than I did when I was his age," Billy said.

"Say yes, Mom. I'll handle Dad," Charlie said.

Billy's smile radiated mockery. Did he know? Sarah wondered. Was he showing her what he could do in retaliation? Take away the son she loved more than both her daughters?

Was that true? Did she love anything or anyone any more? Was it all possession, greed, desire? Sarah relived the vow she had made that day in the desert when she heard Billy inviting Victoria to Catalina. That oath of eternal hatred and revenge spoken to the sun and wind and emptiness. Was that the only thing she loved?

"How can we refuse an offer like that from the best pilot in the country?" Sarah said.

She was in perfect control of her feelings as usual. "Do you wish you'd been flying that new rocket plane out in the desert?" she asked Billy. "It wiped out your old speed record rather completely."

"Only kids go for records," Billy said. His smile was as bright—and meaningless—as ever. He was in perfect control of his feelings too.

"I can't wait to get up there," Charlie said.

"I think we've got a born pilot here," Frank Buchanan said.

ASSASSIN TIME

"Cassie? Listen—I'm afraid it's another late night."

"It's okay. I understand. I married an aircraft company."

The joke was starting to wear thin. Dick could hear the weariness in Cassie's voice. "It's this goddamn TPP contract—you've never seen anything like it," he said.

"I know, I know."

"Kiss Jake for me."

"The last time I did that, he said, 'Daddy? Who's he?' "

Dick slammed down the phone and cursed Adrian Van Ness, Secretary of Defense Robert McNamara, and the aircraft business, in that order. For the past six months he had barely seen his wife and son. The design and engineering departments had been working with him on the Total Performance Package for the giant transport, the C-116—known as the Colossus. It was turning into the most elaborate document ever contrived by the mind of man. Every possible contingency in the development of the plane, every imaginable expense, had to be analyzed, described, and costed in quintuplicate. As Buchanan's money man, Dick was intricately involved in this process, which Frank Buchanan repeatedly called idiotic.

No matter how hard they tried, they were never going to be able to anticipate the problems that might arise in developing a plane this big. Rolls-Royce was still trying to design an engine strong enough to lift it. The Air Force was still debating crucial factors such as the takeoff and landing speed.

Billy McCall, the plane's project manager, agreed with Frank Buchanan about the idiocy of it all. Like everyone else, Dick assumed Billy had gotten this job because he was Adrian Van Ness's son-in-law. He did not have the executive experience to handle something this complex. He was simultaneously supposed to supervise the construction of a new plant in Louisiana and keep track of the paperwork in Santa Monica. It was impossible and Billy did not even try. He let Dick handle the Santa Monica end of it.

A week later—a week in which he spent exactly eight hours at home, most of them asleep—Dick stood with his hands on his hips, watching forklifters trundle tons of paper into the yawning interior of an Excalibur-derived transport. The TPP was taking up the entire cargo space of a plane that ten short years ago was the biggest set of wings in the air.

Billy McCall frowned beside him. "Do you really expect us to pay attention to all that wastepaper, Stone?" he said.

"Somebody does. The Secretary of Defense, for openers."

"It's like marriage, Stone. You can't let the bastards grind you down."

By this time everyone in the company knew that Victoria had failed to tame Billy. The old-timers, for whom Billy was a sexual as well as an aerobatic hero, had rooted against her all the way. They called Victoria "the Queen B" (for bitch) and eagerly retold Billy's acts of defiance, such as failing to show up for Adrian's sixty-fifth birthday party. There was a drumfire of names of women Billy was supposedly fucking at ten thousand feet.

Dick had declined Billy's random invitations to join him in continuing bachelorhood. He was worried about the unhappiness in Cassie's eyes. Practically from the day they married, the whole company had gone into a wartime production mode. The workforce doubled and so did Dick's responsibilities.

"Still flying?" Billy asked.

"I don't have time."

"That's what worries me about this fucking job," Billy said.

Dick watched the Excalibur's cargo doors grind shut on the tons of Total Performance Package paper. He shared Billy's contempt for this harebrained attempt to control costs. They were fighting a war in Vietnam for which the Colossus was desperately needed. They had wasted six months writing the contract for it.

"Let's celebrate a little, Stone. You can't be an old married man all your life."

They headed for a nearby bar. Billy wanted to talk about Vietnam. He was appalled by the way the air war was being fought. Thousands of planes and pilots were being lost while the key targets in North Vietnam, the port of Haiphong, and the Red River dams, were off-limits.

"We could starve them to death in three months if we took out those two items," Billy said.

Dick was not sure he was right. He tried not to think about the war. But he knew it was sapping the morale of the company. Alcoholism and absenteeism among the workforce had soared as parents quarreled with sons and daughters. The old élan, the sense of being on the leading edge of Jack Kennedy's defense of freedom anywhere in the world, was gone. They had developed a siege mentality.

Billy began talking about how much he hated being grounded. He berated himself for giving up the chief test pilot's job to become "a fucking bean counter." Dick was surprised. He thought Billy was as ambitious as the next man. Becoming project manager for the Colossus was a very big promotion.

"Why did you take it?" Dick asked.

Billy was pretty drunk by now. He stared at his image in the mirror. He was still wearing his flight jacket and fifty missions hat, defying his elevation to the executive ranks. "Believe it or not, Stone, I did it to keep my wife happy. Does that make any sense to you?"

"Hell, yes. If you don't keep them happy they can make you damn miserable."

Billy finished his scotch and shook his head. "It doesn't make a damn bit of sense to me."

Dick should have seen trouble plummeting out of the sky toward them like a Starduster shattered by whirl mode. But so many other things seemed on the verge of spinning out of control in the year 1967, he found it hard to focus on a single problem. It was especially hard to worry about Billy, who had repeatedly established his ability to live dangerously and somehow survive. It never occurred to him that on the ground Billy was as vulnerable as the rest of them.

Billy and Victoria departed for Louisiana. For nine months Dick did not give them or the giant plane more than a passing thought. Other planes, the endless war, the seething unrest in American cities and on college campuses, the birth of a daughter, absorbed his attention. A new chief engineer, a brilliant, cheerful Californian named Edwards, collaborated with him on a study that revealed Buchanan's assembly line workers only spent 26 percent of their time actually making planes. The rest was spent looking for tools, schmoozing with friends, and betting on horses and football pools. Edwards hired more supervisors, decentralized tool storage, and raised production rates 40 percent—with fewer workers. Adrian was enormously impressed.

Then came a summons from Buchanan's president. "We're getting very bad vibes on the Colossus program," Adrian said. "I want you to fly to Louisiana tonight and find out what's happening."

Dick flew to New Orleans and drove north a hundred miles to Knowlesville, in the heart of Louisiana redneck country. The Buchanan factory was by far the largest structure in the landscape. It loomed above the tree line ten miles away. Dick introduced himself to the plant security manager, got a badge and went for a walk along the assembly line. The fuselage of the Colossus prototype was taking shape—a whale-shaped creature as high as a four-story building. The wings were so large, they were being fabricated on another line and would be lowered through the sliding roof for final assembly.

"Hey, Clint," one welder said to the man working next to him as he adjusted his mask, "you think this big sumbitch is evuh gonna fly?"

"Hell no," Clint said.

Beyond the prototype fuselage, Dick did not like what he saw. Workers were standing around shooting the breeze. On the line where they were fabricating the tails, a half-dozen were rolling dice.

"Where's your foreman?" Dick said, as a wiry little man

with a mean mouth and shifty eyes won the pile of bills in the pot.

Embarrassed shrugs all around. "Maybe upstairs lookin' for someone to play some acey-deucey," the little man drawled. Everyone laughed and threw more money into the pot.

In the plant manager's office, Dick found balding, bearded Joe Timberlake, a Buchanan old hand, who had run their Mojave plant with admirable efficiency. Joe looked harassed and wan. Everything was wrong. Louisiana's unions were corrupt on a scale unknown in California. Everyone wanted payoffs or daily walkouts and slowdowns would begin to occur. The education level of the workforce was low and they did not train well or, for that matter, particularly like factory work. The supervisors and foremen they had brought with them from California hated the place and were going home in droves. The engineers kept getting wind-tunnel data from California that required expensive design changes.

By the time Dick got to Project Manager Billy McCall's office, he was braced for bad news. He expected a gaunt grim-eyed ghost of the relaxed test pilot he had seen in California. Instead, Billy was tipped back in his chair, his feet on the desk, exchanging hangar talk about his Korean War days with the colonel who was the Air Force's plant representative.

The colonel departed and Dick asked Billy how things were going. "Couldn't be better," he said. "We're a little behind schedule but we'll catch up with some overtime next week. We'll have the monster ready to roll on graduation day."

"How's Victoria?"

"Haven't seen her in about a week. She's in New York tryin' to find out why she can't get pregnant."

"Adrian's worried about costs. We've got to stay inside that bid, you know."

"Ah, hell Dick, that contract's a lot of boilerplate. We've had generals down here and I told them we were probably over budget but they said not to sweat about it, we'd figure something out up the line. The important thing is to get the big bitch rolled out. They really need her in 'Nam."

"I hope you're right. How much are we over budget right now?"

"I haven't got any idea," Billy said.

More than a little stunned, Dick managed to mutter: "Adrian wants some facts. Can I see the books?"

"Sure. You gonna be here long?"

"It depends on how long it takes me to get the facts."

"We're not far from New Orleans. Lot of action down there. Some great light-chocolate stuff. I can fly us down there before you can say pussy galore. The old Lustra's parked out on the runway."

"Sorry. I'm married to a girl who wouldn't appreciate a husband with the clap."

"Christ," Billy said, with a disgusted chuckle. He was the only man Dick ever met who smiled when he was disappointed. "Is there a bachelor left in the goddamn company?"

"Sam Hardy. But I hear he's about to get married again."

"Buzz always said designers weren't in touch with reality. That proves it."

"Where are you cooking the books?"

Billy grinned and led him down a corridor to an office presided over by dapper, energetic Paul Casey, one of Buchanan's best accountants. He had two assistants hired locally and four or five clerical workers. The sight of Dick made all three accountants extremely nervous. Dick retired to Casey's office and told him he was here to examine the books.

Casey began talking very fast to explain why the books were not up to date. The engineers were so busy revising the plans they were always weeks behind with their cost estimates. They were hiring and firing over two hundred workers a week and it was impossible to do more than estimate the obligations to state unemployment insurance, medical plans and the like. They kept getting bills from trucking companies they never heard of—about three months late.

Around midnight, as exhaustion bleared his eyes, Dick began to get some idea of the Colossus's finances. He wiped his glasses and set them firmly on his head again, as if he needed to achieve maximum clarity. "Based on these figures," he said, "estimating all the overtime costs in the past two months, you could be two hundred million dollars over budget."

Casey sighed like a defeated philosopher.

"That's half the fucking net worth of the company!"

Casey groaned like a man undergoing surgery without an anesthetic.

"If the pattern continues, by the time we build a hundred and twenty-four of those things, we'll be two billion dollars over. Two billion!"

Casey gurgled like a drowning man.

"You could buy the whole fucking state of Louisiana for two billion dollars."

"I wish we could—and then sink it," Casey said.

"These are just estimates. I'm going to stay here until we get exact figures, if I have to start reading labels on packing cases and calling up suppliers personally."

"Billy kept telling me not worry about it," Casey moaned.

Dick called Cassie from his motel the next morning to tell her he would not be home for at least a week. She said it was perfectly all right, even though she was starting to wonder what would happen if she tried to stay married to him and divorced the aircraft company.

The joke was no longer thin. "I'm sorry Babe. I really am," Dick said.

Dick called Adrian next. When he gave him the figures there was a long silence, which Dick presumed was astonishment. "I'll call Mike Shannon in Washington and tell him to go to work on damage control," Adrian said. "If this stuff gets out, McNamara will crucify us. He's never forgiven us for the brawl over the Warrior. Can we bury the costs in our budget for the time being?"

Adrian was asking him to cook the books. Dick reluctantly agreed to do it. "Eventually we've got to get the money back or find someone richer than Rockefeller to finance us for the rest of the century," he warned.

"I'm betting on Shannon to get the money. But it may take time. What's Billy got to say for himself?"

"Not a hell of a lot. He doesn't think there's anything to

worry about. I suggest you give him an assistant who can get tough with the unions, the suppliers, the whole goddamn Mafioso circus that runs this state."

There was a long pause. Then Adrian said: "I'm inclined to do something much more drastic."

"Wait a minute, Adrian. You've got some responsibility for this mess. You sent Billy down here without an iota of advice, as far as I can see."

"I thought he was a mature, responsible executive," Adrian said. "Are you defending someone who's in danger of costing us two billion dollars?"

"I see no point in crucifying him. Why the hell didn't you let him go on testing planes? Flying's the only thing he likes to do."

"Dick—may I remind you that I make the decisions on who should—and should not—be crucified? That's part of my job. Maybe the most important part."

Dick found the choice of words—*remind you*—and the metaphor—singularly repugnant. He began to realize something was going on here more important—to Adrian, at least—than the two-billion-dollar overrun.

"I'm sending someone absolutely trustworthy down to help you straighten out this mess," Adrian said. "Cliff Morris will be on a plane in two hours."

Dick drove to the plant in Knowlesville, wondering if he should talk to Billy before Adrian started setting up the cross and handing out the nails. As he went past the project manager's door on the way to the accounting department, he heard Billy call: "Hey, Dick."

Billy had the usual smile on his face. Dick felt a spear of guilt. "Dick," Billy said, still smiling. "I thought we were friends."

"We are."

"Does a friend call the biggest prick in California and tell him his buddy's fucked up?" Billy said. "I just got off the phone with God, otherwise known as Daddy, and more widely as Adrian Van Ness. He dumped about a ton of shit on my head, most of which came from you."

"Billy—I was sent down here with the responsibility for

finding out where we are on this job. You're putting the whole fucking company at risk, do you realize that?"

"Oh, ain't that awful. Puttin' you and Adrian and all the other fuckin' front office paper shufflers at risk. Now they're sendin' the number one asskisser in the aircraft business, Mr. Supersalesman Cliff Morris himself down here to straighten things out. You gonna stay around to help him shove the shaft up my butt?"

"I've got work to do," Dick said. "I hope you and Adrian discussed how to get these costs under control."

"As a matter of fact, I told him it was impossible, if he was gonna have this goddamn thing ready for Lyndon Johnson to inspect on October nineteenth. That's rollout day. I'll bet you a hundred dollars Big Cliff, so well-known for his courage, decides I'm right—after he fires me."

"He isn't going to fire you. Nobody can fire you."

"I can quit. That's what I'll do before I take a single order from that shitheel. Jesus Christ, Dick, couldn't you have come to me first and talked this over? Don't you know Adrian and Cliff and his English bitch of a wife have been tryin' to hang my scalp out to dry since the day I married Victoria? Where've you been?"

Score another one for Amalie Bourne, Dick thought. He had lost touch with what was happening all around him in Buchanan Aircraft. "Maybe you're right, but two billion dollars is still a hell of a lot of money."

"Shit. The missile division blew three billion on that Crusader rocket for the Navy and no one got the firing squad. That fucking thing never even flew. At least we'll have a plane—a great plane—to show for the money."

"But we'll be in hock for a hundred years to pay it off."

"Dick—you should've kept flyin'. You're only two degrees away from turning into Adrian Van Ness."

For a man who seemed indifferent to office politics, Billy had an uncanny ability to deliver a kick to the solar plexus. More kicks were coming. By the time Cliff Morris arrived in Knowlesville that night, Dick had received a call from Frank Buchanan, defending Billy and blaming most of the cost overrun on the Air Force, which kept changing its mind about the plane.

Cliff could not have looked more grim as he stalked into Dick's temporary office. But the moment he closed the door, a gloating smile appeared. "It looks like the son-in-law has finally fucked up," he said.

Again Dick had the unpleasant sense of discovering he was not on the inside of what was happening. He was a passenger, an employee, performing a function.

"What are you going to do?" he asked.

"I don't know. Maybe get the son of a bitch indicted—if you can get us the evidence. Gross malfeasance, that sort of thing."

"You're not getting any help from me."

"Dick—Adrian told me your cooperation was *guaranteed*," Cliff said.

Ignoring that ugly threat, Dick told Cliff why impaling Billy McCall would not work. Frank Buchanan was backing Billy 150 percent. He asked Cliff to imagine Frank testifying at a congressional hearing. Buchanan would never get another government contract.

"If you're trying to knock Billy out of the race for the top job, you've already done it. The board of directors will have to be told about this eventually and they'll blame him. Push him too far and we'll all be looking for new jobs—and maybe indicted in the bargain."

Cliff denied trying to knock Billy out of the race for anything. He was down here to straighten out a mess, that was all he had on his mind. But there was no more talk about indicting Billy—or firing him. After touring the plant and talking to Billy for an hour, Cliff flew black to Los Angeles. Dick spent the next ten days in Knowlesville, grappling with financial chaos. Grimly applying a cost-per-pound analysis to the plane based on the current production pace, he verified the probability of a two-billion-dollar overrun. Each night he called Cassie, who told him it was still perfectly all right. Throughout the ten days, Billy McCall never said another word to him. He stalked past Dick as if he were invisible.

Back in California, Dick went to work on revising the

budget for the current fiscal year to hide the overrun. Adrian's smile was almost beatific as he surveyed the result. "A beautiful job," he murmured. "What would we do without you, Dick?"

He paused and shuffled papers on his desk, always a signal for an announcement. "The next thing I want is a report clearly stating in layman's language—in fact, in language a woman can understand—Billy's gross incompetence on this job."

"Why?"

"There's a particular woman I want to read it. Eventually, I'll want the board of directors to read it too. It's an odd combination of personal and company business. But you understand how those things happen, Dick."

So much for Dick's noble defense of his friend Billy in Knowlesville. Adrian was applying the screws in person now, while Amalie Borne stood in the distance, smiling. The report was as impersonal as a tombstone in a veteran's cemetery. It simply stated the facts, the dates, the figures, comparing what the costs had been predicted to be in the TPP contract and what they turned out to be under Billy McCall's supervision.

"Another beautiful job," Adrian said, the day after Dick handed in the report. He sat Dick next to him at lunch and began telling him his plans for the future. "We're going back into the commercial airliner market. Between the Thunderer and the Colossus, if we can recover those cost overruns, we can finance a new jet to fill a hole in the market—a medium-sized wide body that will make Boeing's humpbacked 747s look like aborted whales who forgot to die. I'd like you to talk it up to Frank Buchanan."

Again, Dick sensed Adrian was reaching out to him, trying to enlist him as a loyal follower. But Dick was not ready to forgive Adrian for forcing him to betray Amalie Borne and Billy McCall. "Do we need another billion-dollar loss leader right now?" he said.

Hubris faded from Adrian's eyes. "Maybe you're right," he said. They did not exchange another word for days.

Planning for the rollout of the Colossus soon gathered

manic intensity. Rumors about the cost overrun were loose in the Pentagon. A civilian employee had turned whistle-blower and was testifying in secret to the subcommittee on government operations, run by penny-pinching Senator William Proxmire with their old senatorial enemy, the Creature, as his right-hand impaler.

Mike Shannon flew in for a conference with Adrian, Cliff Morris, and Dick. "I want Amalie Borne down there for Johnson," Shannon said. "He's looking for consolation these days."

In the face of massive protests against the war in Vietnam, Lyndon Johnson had abandoned another run for the presidency. Cassie, a passionate admirer of Tennessee's James K. Polk, who won the Mexican War in spite of similar criticism, called LBJ the greatest coward in American history.

"Amalie's getting harder and harder to handle," Cliff said.

Amalie had turned into a cost overrun in her own right. She was supposed to work with Shannon in Washington or with the Prince in Europe. She frequently balked at doing either. When she showed up, she often coolly said good night to her escort at the door of her room without even making a decent excuse.

"We'll send Billy to New York to fly her down in style," Adrian said.

His cold eyes asked Dick what he was going to say about that idea. It was a perfect way to make it clear to everyone how low Billy had fallen—from project manager to company pilot. Dick said nothing. It was none of his business, he told himself for the twentieth time. He was just a spectator at this crucifixion.

Knowlesville had never seen anything like the Colossus rollout. All day, Air Force jets roared in with VIPs, climaxed by Air Force One itself, with the President. The Secret Service alone filled every local motel room and most of the high and mighty were booked into New Orleans hotels, which they undoubtedly preferred.

Cassie did not make the trip. She was still nursing their nine-month-old daughter. Frank Buchanan sat next to Dick on the plane, denouncing the way Adrian was abusing Billy, hoping to recruit Dick as an ally. Cliff Morris sat across the aisle reading a magazine, avoiding all Frank's attempts to draw him into the discussion. Next to him sat Sarah of the wide smile. When she lost the smile she looked haggard.

And you, of course, are deliriously happy? sneered a savage voice in Dick's head. It unmistakably belonged to Amalie Borne. She was among the last to arrive, sauntering from Billy's green Lustra in a green suit precisely the same color as the plane. Billy, defiantly wearing his flight jacket and fifty-missions hat, escorted her to the VIP grandstand where she was greeted by Mike Shannon and led to a seat in one of the rear rows.

Dick noticed how Lyndon Johnson followed Amalie's progress. He could almost hear Shannon—or Adrian—selling her to Johnson as Jack Kennedy's favorite. That would make her irresistible to a man who had ruined his presidency by compulsively competing with the ghost of JFK.

An Air Force band struck up "Off We Go Into the Wild Blue Yonder" and the doors of Factory One slowly opened. Out came the snout of the monster, looming over the two tractors that were towing her. A murmur ran through the crowd as the entire plane emerged. The tail was as high as an eight-story building. The four jet engines each looked big enough to swallow a Volkswagen. The whole thing was painted a deep black, which somehow added to the awesome bulk.

Adrian rose to thank everyone for coming and introduced the President of the United States. Johnson stooped over the bank of microphones and recited some of the Colossus's statistics. It could carry 750,000 pounds at close to the speed of sound. The Colossus fleet, when it was finished next year, could airlift an entire armored division any place in the world. If an enemy thought they could attack American soldiers defending freedom in distant lands, they would have to deal with this "new presence" which made us able to strike back anywhere, anytime.

"Now I know how we're going to win in Vietnam," Cliff Morris whispered in Dick's ear. "We're going to drown them in bullshit."

The President was followed by two or three Air Force generals, whose voices choked with emotion when they talked about the wonders of the plane. Finally came the chairman of the House Armed Services Committee, who congratulated the Air Force and Buchanan for building such a marvelous plane and a wonderful factory in Knowlesville, creating twenty thousand new jobs and an "economic renaissance" in Knowles County.

As Adrian stepped to the microphone to thank everyone for coming to the ceremony and urged them to go through the plane and join them on the factory floor for champagne and refreshments, a yellow Jaguar streaked around the corner of Hangar One and tore across the concrete runways to a gate at the far end of the field. Dick's eyes were not good enough to see who was driving. But Cliff Morris's twenty-twenty pilot's eyes were still in excellent shape.

"Holy Christ," Cliff gasped. "That's Billy—and Amalie Borne."

The reception was a melee in which the Secret Service struggled to keep most people at a distance from the lame-duck President, who stood forlornly in a corner. An agitated Adrian Van Ness told Dick to get Johnson some champagne. As he returned with the bottle he heard Adrian trying to explain Amalie's departure.

"She must have been taken ill. That was my son-in-law driving her. Probably to a hospital. You remember him? Billy McCall? The test pilot?"

"It's all right, Adrian," Johnson said. "The way my luck's been runnin' she'd probably've given me the syph."

As Dick poured champagne for the president and a half dozen aides, he saw Victoria McCall in the middle distance, sobbing hysterically. Sarah Morris was trying to calm her.

Much later, as their plane zoomed into the sky toward California, Victoria was still sobbing on Sarah's shoulder in a rear seat. Adrian glared across the aisle at Frank Buchanan. Dick had never seen him so angry.

"Is there anything you want to say in defense of your protégé before I fire him?" Adrian snarled.

"Not really," Frank said, with a sigh. "He's his mother's son."

A confusing mixture of sadness and happiness suffused Frank's face. He was wrestling with memories of Sammy that neither Adrian nor Dick could possibly understand.

"If I have anything to say about it, he won't be my son-in-law much longer," Adrian said.

Dick tried not to think about Billy and Amalie. He tried not to imagine what they were doing in New Orleans as he flew back to California and Cassie. He realized Billy was the man Amalie wanted, the hero who dared without caring whether he survived. She was the perfect answer to Billy's rage, a woman who did not care what he did to her.

Dick told himself he no longer cared what happened to either of them. But he could not prevent images from forming and reforming behind his eyes, an obscene kaleidoscope of lips and thighs and breasts. In spite of his desperate good intentions, Dick joined Adrian and Cliff in hoping Billy McCall would run out of luck on the ground and in the sky.

THE LADY OF DEATH

Wagner's "Ride of the Valkyries" poured from the stereo while Victoria Van Ness McCall sat on the deck of her Topanga Canyon home and made another list for Billy. Beside her sat her only friend, Sarah Chapman Morris.

Victoria had gotten out the earlier lists and had them printed up and hung them all around the house. There were lists of things she did not want Billy to do and lists of things she wanted him to do and lists of books she wanted him to read and lists of movies she wanted him to see and lists of songs she wanted him to hear, above all Wagner's "Ring Cycle." She wanted him to understand through music, not words, how completely their souls were joined. She was

Brunhilde, his Valkyrian beloved, born to be a warrior's bride.

She was now compiling a list of all the lists and their locations so Billy could consult them quickly, efficiently, when he decided to love her again. Her father called six times a day, begging her to come home, telling her he had fired Billy and she should divorce him. He had a lawyer sitting in his office with the papers drawn. All she had to do was sign them. He sent her a copy of a report full of incomprehensible numbers, proving Billy was stupid and possibly a crook.

Victoria told Sarah she was now convinced her mother was right, her father only cared about his power. He hated Billy because he had destroyed Adrian's power over her. Now he was trying to regain her without caring, without even thinking of what that would mean. She would have to leave Topanga and go back to Hancock Park. Back to childhood. She would have to abandon her lists, her hopes, her absolute faith that Billy would come back to her.

With intensity that approached delirium, Victoria told Sarah her father did not understand how a woman conquered a warrior like Billy. He refused to surrender to power, to money, to threats, to promises. Only one thing could break his will—submission. Patient, absolute, total submission. The women who were reading and praising this book, *The Feminine Mystique* were as foolish as Adrian. The feminists were really disguised men, with men's sterile imaginations. They had no ability to envision the power, the drama, the peace, of submission.

Submission annihilated hatred and fear and regret and anger. It left a woman with a feeling of ultimate power because nothing could destroy submission. Nothing Billy or any other man could possibly do—not the vilest betrayal in the history of love—could touch the pure white peace submission created in a woman's soul. Submission was not easy to achieve. But when it happened—oh, that inpouring of pure whiteness, of lightness, the burning essence of the sun and stars. She had found a name for it in Ezra Pound's Cantos: *the Immaculata*.

Only one thing worried Victoria—her dreams. Last night and for several previous nights she had dreamt she was two women. One wore the beautiful white robe of submission. The other wore a breastplate of black armor and a girdle of gleaming brass, with a cup of stainless steel over her pubic hair. She kept menacing the smiling white-robed women with a sword. But the white-robed woman only smiled and ignored the ugly steel tip the Amazon kept holding against her throat.

Her lists of lists completed, Victoria resumed work on a poem in praise of Billy McCall, the warrior pilot. In a low sibilant voice she recited it for Sarah.

Only once has a woman matched his cruel altitude
She took flight and soared beyond his stratosphere
And it changed her life forever.
She saw the world as a bright teacup
And dreaded the idea of breaking it.
So she coasted over seas and stars
Until her exhausted heart wore wings
That scorn horizons. Yet the pilot's eyes
Remained as blind as Oedipus
In his dotage. Why, why? The questions
Linger in the golden twilight
Like deer on a Chinese mountain.

Victoria shook her head and tore the poem to shreds. She told Sarah those words were too self-indulgent, egotistic. They were about her, not about Billy, the warrior who had been betrayed by his country, by his friends, by his gods. She understood so much. She understood the source of Billy's rage. America the good the true the beautiful, the country a warrior would rejoice to defend had become America the foul, the false, the farcical. That was why she was his only hope of salvation. Billy, the ultimate warrior, had to accept the supreme value of submission, which he would transmute into acceptance of history's blunders and deformities. She who could not conceive a child would give birth to the perfect warrior, shorn of his rage but not of his courage.

Crash, bam, slam. A car lunged up the almost vertical road and screamed to a stop in the yard below the deck. It was the yellow Jaguar she had bought Billy for their fifth wedding anniversary. Billy got out. Victoria's joy was beyond words. She turned up "The Ride of the Valkyries" so there was no need to speak.

He stood there, his hands on his hips for a moment, smiling at Victoria and Sarah. The smile meant nothing, Victoria had learned that by this time. "What the hell are you doing here?" Billy said to Victoria. Sarah might as well have been invisible.

"Waiting for you," Victoria said. "Sarah's keeping me company."

"You're too much," Billy said, still smiling.

Amalie Borne was wearing the green suit she had worn in Louisiana. She blended into the trees for a moment, as if she were an animal, a deer. Sarah saw Victoria was glad Billy had brought her. Victoria thought Billy wanted her to see how beautiful Amalie was, how impossible it had been for him to resist her.

"What are you going to do?" Victoria said.

"I don't know. We were gonna stay here for a while. But we can't do that now. I guess we'll go to Catalina."

SarahVictoria knew what Billy was trying to do. He was trying to erase all their memories. He was using Amalie Borne to erase her. It was ridiculously easy to stop him. She even knew the next question he was going to ask. He thought it was supremely brutal. He did not realize he was dealing with supreme submission.

"You want to come?" Billy asked.

"I'd love to come," Victoria said.

Billy shook his head, still smiling. "You *are* too much," he said.

Amalie Borne followed Billy up the steps to the deck. Victoria turned the volume knob of the record player to full. "You like Wagner?" Amalie said, above the booming "Ride of the Valkyries." The effort disfigured her perfect face.

"Yes. I've been urging him on Billy. I think he's the perfect musician for pilots!" Victoria shouted. "So much soaring. Don't you agree?"

"I hate him," Amalie cried. "He's sick, like the rest of Germany."

"I don't agree!" Victoria shouted. "I heard him for the first time at the Hollywood Bowl when I was ten. It made me sense the mountains all around us, even when you couldn't see them in the darkness. Grandeur. That's what I want Billy to feel."

"He feels it already. It's his essence," Amalie shouted. She was beginning to lose her composure.

Billy came out carrying an old battered suitcase. It had contained all his possessions when they moved in. "Still travelin' light," he said, smiling at Victoria and Sarah.

With no warning whatsoever he smashed Sarah in the face with his open hand. She flew across the deck and landed on her back in a perfect replay of her previous punishment from Cliff. Except here there was no rug. Her head struck the wooden deck with stunning force.

From a great distance Sarah heard Victoria cry: "Why did you do that?"

"She's been askin' for it for a long time," Billy said.

Victoria listened to the "Ride of the Valkyries" fade as they descended the mountain. Jammed in the Jaguar's narrow backseat, she suddenly understood why she disliked the way Sarah and her father pronounced Billy's name. She saw the entire scheme, from Billy's appointment as project manager to his brutal removal. She saw Sarah's part in it and for a moment could not believe her vileness. She had told her everything, even about the Immaculata. Somehow the purity of her hope became soiled, ruined.

"Do you know what you're doing?" Amalie said.

"Do you?" Billy said, rocketing up the narrow road toward Burbank Airport, where he parked his Lustra. It would be Victoria's first ride in the plane in two—or was it three?—years. She thought of their happy first year, when they flew all over California in it. Above all she remembered the precious day they had made love at ten thousand feet. Billy had told her she was the forty-ninth woman who had done it with him at that altitude.

Was I the best? Why had she asked that stupid question?

She knew it was a mistake the moment she had said the words. Maybe that was the beginning of Billy trying to tell her the truth about himself and her refusing to listen. But she would listen now with the perfect attention, the exquisite silence of submission.

The Lustra was sitting on the flight line, gassed and gleaming. Billy said he and Amalie had been using it to fly all over California. She had seen everything now, even Baja. Only Catalina remained. Only Santa Catalina. Shangri-la. He had erased Victoria from everything else.

"You'll love it," Victoria said. "We spent our honeymoon there. We loved it, didn't we, Billy?"

"Yeah," Billy said. He was giving the Lustra a walka-round. He kicked the tires, hauled on the wing struts.

"Let's go," Amalie said. She was impatient. A hopeful sign. Billy disliked impatient women.

"You want to get there in one piece?" Billy said. "This plane's almost as old as I am."

"I don't care, really," Amalie said.

A thrill ran through Victoria's soul. She was as daring as Billy, as indifferent to death. That was undoubtedly why he chose her. But Victoria could match her with the perfect acceptance of submission.

"She's sore because your Daddy fired both of us," Billy said, as he taxied out on the runway. "Cut off our salaries. Ain't that awful?"

"I have plenty of money," Victoria said.

"She does," Billy said. "She's worth four or five million."

"Disgusting," Amalie said.

"Yeah," Billy said. "Someone with no fuckin' brains worth mentioning and no figure to match. But I guess there's gotta be some compensation for everyone. You think that way? The big Air Traffic Controller in the sky evens things out?"

"No," Amalie said.

"Me neither," Billy said.

"Frank Buchanan believes in God," Victoria said. "He told me to trust Him. He said you'd come back to me and you have."

"With me," Amalie said.

Billy rammed the throttle forward and the Lustra hurtled down the runway, its big engine thundering. Up, up, they climbed, until California lay beneath them, unfortunately obscured by a thick layer of smog.

"What a disgusting country," Amalie said, looking down at the gray mass of gases. "You can't even breathe freely. Yet you talk of defending the world against tyranny."

"Hey, I told you I didn't go for that kind of crapflak," Billy said.

"Are you responsible for his patriotism?" Amalie said.

"No," Victoria said.

"I haven't been a patriot for a long time," Billy said.

"But you won't let anyone else be unpatriotic," Amalie said.

"Shut up," Billy said. "Take off your clothes."

"Why?" Amalie said, not moving.

"We're going to fuck at ten thousand feet," Billy said.

He turned to Victoria and said: "Can you handle it?"

"Yes," Victoria said.

Billy had failed to teach her how to fly. Now he was teaching her—he was daring her to learn—something else. The robotic submission of the autopilot. Click. He shoved Victoria into the pilot's seat and she was flying the plane while he methodically stripped Amalie Borne.

Victoria did not see any of it. She refused to turn her head. She could not hear any of it either. The sighs, the growls, the groans, were swallowed by the roar of the motor. Click. She was in a state of perfect submission, like the autopilot's slave. Below them gleamed the dark blue Pacific. Up ahead loomed Catalina, with its rim of white beaches, its miniature mountains and valleys. Their continent. Shangri-la.

Suddenly the other Victoria was in the copilot's seat. The amazon. Blood streamed from her maddened eyes. Her pupils were drenched with it. The veins had burst from too much weeping. She had both hands on the yoke and she shoved it forward, tearing it out of Victoria's robotic grip. Submission, the Immaculata—what had happened to them?

The Lustra plunged down down down. Billy and Amalie

were flung in a sickening tangle against the back of Victoria's seat. Somehow Billy struggled to his knees and reached over Victoria's shoulder and pulled on the yoke with all his strength.

"Let go, let go!" Billy roared. "I love you. Let go!"

But Victoria could not let go. She had become the other woman, Califia's daughter, the Lady of Death. Her hands were fastened to the yoke with an eternal persistence, an absolute, relentless refusal. All she could offer Billy was her final submission. She kissed him on the mouth as the Lustra struck the water and exploded into a thousand burning fragments.

AN EMPTY SKY

For a week after the crash, Sarah Morris lay in her bed with the electric blanket turned up full, shaking and shivering with violent chills. Death had suddenly declared her life random, superfluous, vacant.

Again and again she saw Amalie Borne walk from the green Lustra in the harsh Louisiana sunlight. A line from a poem seemed to swirl around her. *All in green went my love riding.*

Occasionally Sarah's husband stood in the doorway watching her, disgust on his handsome face. She was proving what he had suspected for a long time. She had never stopped loving Billy McCall. Sarah did not care what he saw. She could not conceal her pain, her terror.

"Adrian's resigning," Cliff said, on the seventh day. "I'm the new president."

I was wrong, Sarah thought. To whom should she send her confession? Her older American daughter, Elizabeth, stoned on LSD and other drugs most of the time in San Francisco? Her straight younger daughter Margaret, studying

Chinese history at Stanford? Or her son Charlie, everyone's favorite halfback at University High?

Would any of them understand her babble? *I want to warn you against the way love can turn to hatred. The more violent the love the more violent the hatred. I did not believe anything so bizarre could happen to me until I killed him. I killed him and his innocent wife.*

"Get out of that goddamn bed," Cliff said. "We've got work to do. Whatever happened in that plane, it wasn't our fault."

Not your fault, of course not your fault, Sarah thought. You wouldn't have had the patience or the guile to weave the web of hatred around them until the moment of helplessness, of vulnerability, arrived.

I was wrong. She wanted to send it to Billy. He was the only one who would understand it.

"Did you hear me?" Cliff said, looming over her. "Get up. Let's get to work. I've got the job of a lifetime and you're acting like someone in a fucking Greek tragedy. They weren't the first people killed in a plane crash and they won't be the last."

He was using his war, his male indifference to everything but victory, success, to ignore the impossibility of the crash being an accident. His big hand seized her arm and literally dragged her out of bed.

"We're in this together, right?" he said.

Sarah nodded, fascinated by the way he used the argot of the criminal, the murderer, to confirm their partnership. It was thoroughly accurate, even if it betrayed his previous denial. It also underscored who was chiefly responsible for the crime. Sarah Chapman Morris was the real perpetrator. She had borrowed Cliff's adolescent hatred and welded it to her thwarted love to create a death mechanism.

Innocently, of course. Oh, so innocently hoping for the worst. Oh. Oh. Oh. How could she deny it? How could she ever purify her lost vicious heart?

Sarah saw the future, exactly as it unreeled for the next four years. She would become a woman named Mrs. Clifford Morris. She would write invitations, serve on committees, chair benefits, court senators and congressmen, awe hotel clerks and banquet managers, travel to England, France, Japan, China, with her husband while he bribed people to buy Buchanan's planes.

She would go to endless Los Angeles dinner parties where the women left the table after dessert and had coffee upstairs, isolated in a splendid bedroom or dressing room with demitasse cups and rock sugar ordered from London and cinnamon sticks in lieu of demitasse spoons. On the hostesses' elaborate dressing table there would be enormous bottles of Fracas and Gardenia and Tuberose. The dessert that preceded the retreat would invariably be served on Flora Danica plates and would be infallibly preceded by finger bowls on doilies. Wearing Pucci silks to the floor, she would spend these dinners trying not to suffocate while talking through spectacular table arrangements of flowers from their premier florist, David Jones.

Some larger parties would be held in tents with pink lights and chili from Chasen's. In fact, Mrs. Sarah Morris would become moderately famous for the size and style of her tent parties. Once, instead of chili from Chasen's she served burgers from Jimmy Murphy's. Between the dinner parties there would be lunches at places like the Bistro Garden and afternoons of committees, committees, committees.

I was wrong. Maybe the only person who could understand it was the late Sarah Chapman Morris. Maybe she should send the letter to herself and put it in a drawer hoping to find it by accident in five or ten years. Maybe it would have the power to free her from hatred's web.

Once or twice childhood pleas for mercy formed on her grimaced lips. *Immaculate Heart of Mary pray for us* But the words were murmured by a stranger named Sarah Chapman in furtive sleepless hours before dawn. By daylight and lamplight, the other person she had become, Mrs. Clifford Morris, wife of Buchanan Aircraft's president, was much too busy to pray.

For a week after the crash Adrian sat in his office unable to think, barely able to speak. At home Amanda wept and said unbearable things about getting what he deserved. He nodded his assent. He was numb. His only support was a voice that whispered from a vanished England: *It does a man no good to whine*.

At the end of the week, Frank Buchanan burst into the office. He had not come to work since the news of the crash. "Have you learned anything?" he asked, his voice, his hands trembling. He looked like an Old Testament prophet, with his mane of white hair, a five-day beard.

"I don't know. Have you?" Adrian asked.

"The futility, the stupidity of hatred. I was guilty of it, Adrian. But I never dreamt it would lead to anything like this."

Forethought, Adrian numbly told himself. He's here to mock forethought, to ridicule all my gods. "I wished them happiness, Adrian. I truly did," Frank said. "But my hatred of you permeated the whole thing. I'm resigning from the company. I've created enough evil for one lifetime."

For the first time Adrian was able to face the part his hatred had played in the tragedy. For a moment he almost conceded the limitations of forethought, admitted our mortal inability to control fate. He saw himself walking to Frank Buchanan and embracing the man he had hated for so long, asking his forgiveness in turn. Of course he did no such thing. The voice of the man still determined to play the great game remained in control.

"Frank," Adrian said. "The evil was created long before either of us was born. You can't resign from the company. Without you there is no company, there never would have been one. Now it's up to both of us to save it. I'm resigning as president. Cliff Morris will take over. I'm moving to Washington to make sure we don't get massacred by that two-billion-dollar cost overrun."

"Amanda will never be happy in Washington," Frank said.

"Amanda will never be happy anywhere," Adrian said.

"Be kind to her, Adrian. If I hear even a hint of evidence that you're mistreating her—"

"She's all I've got left too!" Adrian cried.

They were enemies again. But Frank Buchanan was still working for the company.

A month later, Frank sat beside Buzz McCall's bed watching him die of congestive heart failure, liver failure, emphysema and a half dozen other complications. Frank tried to console him with the thought that Sammy was waiting for him on the other side.

"I hope not," Buzz said. "That means Tama'll be there too. Between them I'll never get any rest."

He browbeat Frank into giving him a cigarette. "Dames," he said. "We never figured them out, did we? None of us. Even Adrian."

"Especially Adrian," Frank said.

"What the fuck did Tama and Amanda have in common? That still baffles me."

"Womanhood," Frank said.

The word struck Buzz like a bullet. He closed his eyes and pulled on the cigarette. A few minutes later he slipped into delirium. He talked to Sammy, to Tama and other women. "Bitches, fucking bitches," he muttered.

Suddenly he was conscious again. He glared at Frank. "There's only one thing I ever did to a dame I regret," he said. "I helped the goddamn Brits kill that Commie spy Adrian was fucking. I felt bad about that. She was a hell of a pilot."

A moment later he was gone. A terrific tremor of grief and rage ripped through Frank's body and mind. "Mother was right. You're evil. It's a different kind of evil from Adrian's but it's still evil!" he cried.

He was talking to Craig as much as to Buzz. To Billy and all the other pilots who had turned flight into a license to run wild on the ground. Another earthquake-sized tremor shook him. He seized Buzz's dangling hand and kissed it tenderly.

"But I loved you. I loved all of you," he whispered.

No one at Buchanan mourned Buzz. They were all too busy mourning Billy. "How could it happen?" the chief mourner,

Sam Hardy, said over and over again. "Flying to fucking Catalina. How could that happen to Billy?"

Hardy was still Frank's favorite designer, already designated as his heir apparent. Typically, Frank saw only the man's unique gifts and ignored Sam's personal problems. His pursuit of one of the beauties of the Honeycomb Club had wrecked his marriage and turned him into an alcoholic. Kirk Willoughby had stabilized him with psychotherapy and Alcoholics Anonymous. Now he seemed to be coming apart again.

Hardy had fallen off the wagon and had a brawl with his second wife, which had them teetering on divorce. He spent hours talking to Frank about Billy, apparently oblivious to the pain it caused him. There was nothing Billy could not do in a plane. There was no plane—or woman—he could not master. Hardy recalled nights of stupendous drinking with Billy at the Honeycomb Club and stuporous fucking in the dawn. He even remembered a song about a test pilot's woes he had once sung to Billy outside the club at 3 A.M. When he got to the refrain: "Gee I'm glad that I don't fly," Sam wept.

In an odd way the extravagance of Hardy's grief steadied Frank. He began to suspect Sam was weeping as much for himself as for Billy. He was mourning the end of his youth, which Billy's death seemed to confirm and even symbolize. Of course youth had been gradually expiring for a long time, as it always does. But in California it was easier to deny this obvious fact. A man with money could get a tan, put on a tank top and head for the beach in his convertible with a willing twenty-five year old beside him. Frank stopped being a patient listener when Sam Hardy tried to translate Billy's death into an obituary for the aircraft business. "Everyone knows the glory days are over. From now on this is just another big business, like making fucking automobiles," Sam moaned.

"That is absolute bullshit!" Frank roared. "As long as there's a sky up there and men want to fly faster and faster and higher and higher in it they'll be new planes to make. Stop feeling so goddamn sorry for yourself and get to work!"

Was that Buzz talking? His way of saying good-bye? Frank hoped so. Hardy stopped drinking and had a whole new design for their high-performance fighter, the Sky-Demon, on Frank's desk within a week.

Dick Stone also knew the crash could not have been an accident. He responded by becoming a workaholic. He could no longer believe he deserved the happiness Cassie and his son and daughter promised him. In death Amalie Borne's shadow loomed like an impassable barrier between him and any possible promised land. Dick's already heroic hours became a grind of inhuman proportions. Secretaries quit in steady succession until he finally found a Japanese-American who viewed his midnight hours as a challenge to her national reputation for stamina.

Cassie stopped joking about being married to an aircraft company. She *was* married to one. The man she thought she was marrying had become almost transparent. She could not see any other reality in her life except Buchanan Aircraft. Inevitably, she began asking why.

Watching the marriage unravel, Sarah began to wonder if Dick was her only hope of redemption. She did not understand the word or the idea. She only knew it had something to do with forgiveness. She somehow understood she could offer it to him—and he could offer it to her. How or when or where she had no idea. For the time being the skylark was in a cage known as Mrs. Clifford Morris, an entity Dick Stone could only regard with repugnance. She could hardly blame him. She had the same reaction every time she looked in the mirror.

BOOK NINE

LIGHTS! ACTION! CAMERA!

The senator from Iowa's puffy face was a study in righteous frustration. "Do you mean to tell me that you take no responsibility for wasting two billion dollars of the taxpayers' money?" he screamed.

Cliff Morris smiled patiently at the Creature. "*Waste* is hardly an apt word, Senator. We will soon have a fleet of transports that can airlift an entire army overseas. We simply maintain that the responsibility for their unexpectedly high cost should be shared by Buchanan and the Air Force. I only wish our project manager, former Lieutenant Colonel William McCall, were still alive so he could explain to you in detail how Air Force officers assured him again and again that they would share this responsibility. Billy was my half-brother—and one of my closest friends. He told me this repeatedly."

"Who were these officers?" the Creature bellowed. "I want them in this committee room. I want them court-martialed!"

"As I explained to you, Senator, Colonel McCall died in a private plane crash—"

The Creature ranted about corporate greed and military incompetence. The chairman of the subcommittee, the senior senator from Connecticut, home of Pratt & Whitney, who made the engines for the Thunderer and a lot of other Buchanan planes, rapped him into silence and said he agreed with most of what Clifford Morris had said. The country was on its way to having an airlift capacity second to none. Cliff smiled and thanked the senator. In Cliff's head Billy McCall whispered: *nice going, you lying son of a bitch*.

A half hour later, Mike Shannon slapped Cliff on the back as they descended the Capitol steps. "He never laid a glove on you."

Washington broiled in its usual June heat and humidity. They plunged into the air-conditioned white limousine at the bottom of the steps and headed for a reception at the Norwegian embassy. Norway had just bought a half-dozen antisubmarine versions of the Starduster to help guard NATO's northern flank.

Unreeling, it was another technicolor movie of Cliff Morris's life—and this time he was both the director and the star. It was 1970—the second year of his reign. From the moment he became Buchanan's president, he started playing the part.

Gone was Adrian's low-keyed patrician style. Cliff installed himself with a party at the Bel Air Hotel for five hundred people. He hired a personal public relations man and got himself and Sarah a stream of press clippings as they elbowed their way into Los Angeles's upper class. He bought a magnificent new house on a Palos Verdes promontory and another one almost as splendid in the desert outside Palm Springs. He drove around Los Angeles in a white Mercedes licensed *Buchanan 1*.

Gone too was Adrian Van Ness's hesitation about betting the company. Nothing was too splendid or too ambitious for Buchanan Aircraft. The war in Vietnam devoured planes. The assembly lines churned day and night. Cliff announced they were abandoning their tacky Depression-era hangars in Santa Monica for glossy new headquarters in El Segundo, on the edge of Los Angeles airport. He saw a seller's market with Cliff the salesman supreme. He was going to sell, sell, sell everything on Buchanan's menu around the world.

On the commercial airline side of the game, the view was very encouraging to a gambler like Cliff. The jets had created a revolution in air travel. Throughout the sixties, airline revenues climbed month by month as Boeing's 747s and 727s and Douglas's DC8s and DC9s flew crammed with passengers from nose to tail. The airlines were awash in cash and were practically begging the aircraft and engine companies to sell them new planes—especially ones that could fill a hole in the market. Cliff revived Adrian's idea for a medium-sized wide-body. Hoping to stir Frank Buchanan's enthusiasm, Cliff called it the Aurora, in memory of the airliner that was supposed to emerge from the Talus bomber.

Dick Stone, eyeing the two-billion-dollar cost overrun on the Colossus, asked why, if there was a hole in the market, they had to fall into it. But Cliff was determined to succeed where Adrian had failed. The Aurora was given top priority. Hundreds of new designers and engineers were hired to go all-out on a prototype. Millions of dollars were spent on marketing studies and sales brochures.

The days of one or two salesmen pitching a plane in the office of an airline president were over. Each airline now had a committee of engineers and sales and marketing representatives almost as unwieldy as the Pentagon's review boards. All these people had to be wined, dined, persuaded, while Dick Stone muttered about the outflow of cash.

To keep him quiet, Cliff embarked on a world tour to sell the Colossus and the Thunderer to America's allies. The Prince was summoned from his European haunts to join in the quest. The results were disquieting. Other aircraft companies had discovered the secret of Buchanan's overseas success and were imitating them. As often happens, the newcomers did it better. Lockheed, for instance, hired Prince Bernhard of the Netherlands to dispense their bribes. The going rate for persuasion soared with this influx of competition. At home it was matched by a runaway inflation in costs and wages as the country began paying for Lyndon Johnson's cowardly decision not to raise taxes to finance the war in Vietnam.

The Prince seemed to have lost much of his old enthusiasm for commercial combat. He complained endlessly about his liver. One night in Paris he got drunk and lost his savoir faire. "Why did you kill Amalie?" he asked. "Did she threaten to spill the beans, as you call it?"

Cliff spent an hour trying to convince him that the crash was an accident. He did not succeed. The Prince found it hard to believe anyone like Billy McCall ever existed. He was a purely American phenomenon.

The Colossus proved particularly hard to sell overseas because very few of America's allies felt a compelling need to project their power beyond their borders. Italy, for instance, finally agreed to buy four of the giant planes, mostly because the Prince raised Buchanan's under-the-table offer to astronomical heights. It would have been a personal insult to turn down such an inducement, one of the bribed politicians later explained. The huge craft were parked on a military airfield near Milan, waiting for another Mussolini to invade Africa, perhaps. There was no other visible use for them.

Cliff chose to ignore these and other portents. It was easy enough to argue that in the military procurement game, nothing much had changed. The infighting for a head start on new contracts for missiles and planes and radar systems was as ferocious as ever. Congress's arrogance and greed in the politics of procurement were not noticeably different. The new president, Richard Nixon, was an advocate of a strong America. The defense budget remained gigantic.

As the limousine nosed into the rush-hour traffic, Mike Shannon told Cliff that the Senate committee would undoubtedly approve the plan to pay Buchanan three-fourths of the two-billion cost overrun immediately. The remaining $500,000,000 would have to be appealed to several layers of Air Force review boards. But they would get the money eventually. "The White House is with us all the way. Adrian's doing a great job there."

Those last words abruptly cooled Cliff's satisfaction with his performance before the subcommittee. Adrian Van Ness had settled in Charlottesville, Virginia, and made President Richard Nixon his target number one in Washington. He had succeeded so well, Cliff was virtually superfluous in that arena. Cliff did not like being superfluous anywhere.

The Norwegian reception was in the ballroom of the Hay-Adams Hotel, across Lafayette Park from the White House. After shaking the required hands, Cliff looked for more worthwhile targets. Standing in a corner was scowling Colonel Anthony Sirocca, one of Curtis LeMay's deputies in the struggle for the Warrior. Tony was in war plans these days, on his way to his first star.

They exchanged bone-crushing handshakes and Cliff went to work on behalf of Buchanan's close support plane, the Thunderer. McNamara had tried to persuade the Air Force to buy it but they had resisted mightily, in spite of (or because of) the enthusiasm the Navy and Marines had for its performance in Vietnam. They were still resisting the new secretary of defense. Tony listened, his Sicilian eyes glittering with hostility, while Cliff poured on the persuasion.

"I've got a kid in the Marines who may end up flying one of those things. I'm not blowing smoke when I say it's a good plane," Cliff said.

The superstitious side of Cliff's salesman's psyche seized him by the throat. Was he risking Charlie's life, using him to sell the plane? No—he believed in the Thunderer. He had been out to Vietnam. He had talked to the Marine and Navy pilots who were flying it. They called it the Iron Blimp and joked about its speed. But they all swore by its ability to put bombs on a target and take fantastic punishment from ground fire.

Two months ago, Charlie had quit UCLA in his sophomore year and enlisted as a Marine air cadet. Cliff had been moved by the decision. He knew what it meant—Charlie was choosing his father's side in the quarrel that was tearing the country apart.

Sarah, better known to Cliff by an unspoken nickname, the Smiling Zombie, had lost her English self-control and begged Cliff to stop him. But Cliff had already bragged to half the executives in the company the day he got the news. He told Sarah to stiffen her English lip and smile proudly at his side.

Mentioning Charlie softened the resistance in Tony Sirocca's dark eyes. "It may be a good plane, Cliff," he said. "But right now we're more interested in the big one. If that contract doesn't keep you happy for the next ten years, we'll start to think nothing satisfies you guys."

"What the hell are you talking about?" Cliff said.

Tony looked baffled. "The new bomber. Son of the Warrior. We need a production schedule, fast. Like the day before yesterday."

Cliff could only shake his head in bewilderment while a flush of humiliation traveled through his body. "Adrian Van Ness sold the package to Tricky Dick at a private dinner last week," Sirocca said. "Doesn't Adrian bother to tell you little details like a ten-billion-dollar deal?"

"I guess it slipped what's left of his mind," Cliff said.

"Frank Buchanan's got to redesign her for a completely new mission. Instead of flying high she's gotta go low—fifty, twenty-five feet low. With a profile that will go through the other guys' radar like the fucking invisible man."

"How many copies?" Cliff said.

"Two hundred."

"What's the big number?"

"We're figuring fifty million a plane."

That was ten billion dollars, all right. The biggest contract in Buchanan's history. It would require a virtual reorganization of the production lines. The chairman of the board had not bothered to mention a word of this to the company's president.

"Nixon wants a bomber good enough to scare the shit out of the Chinese and the Russians," Sirocca explained. "The B-52s can't handle those SAM missiles."

"How many planes have we lost over Vietnam?"

"Six thousand," Sirocca said. "I wish I could have gotten someone to listen to Frank Buchanan when he told us to go stealth ten years ago."

"I'll talk to Frank this afternoon," Cliff said.

Pretending to be the man in charge. In charge of what? The washroom? Cliff blundered across the ballroom toward the door, avoiding eyes, faces. Who should be arriving but the Creature and an entourage of flunkies, most of them from left-wing think tanks that specialized in trashing the military-industrial complex. The Creature was their darling these days.

"You got away from us this time, Morris," the senator said. "But we put some salt on your tail. The next time you'll tell the truth."

For the Creature, this was almost friendly chitchat. Ordinarily, Cliff would have slapped him on the back and said something about being old friends. But his salesman's personality was submerged by his rage at Adrian Van Ness.

"The next time, Senator, maybe I'll give the committee a

little history of how many lies I've heard you tell since we met at the crash of the Starduster in 1958," he said.

"You can't threaten me!" the Creature snarled. "This only proves how much you've got to hide."

Leaving Mike Shannon at the party, Cliff taxied to Buchanan's Washington office, which now had a staff of fifty working to keep Congress and the Pentagon happy and eager to do business. It cost them fifteen million a year. Dick Stone was appalled but Cliff insisted it was money well spent.

Mike Shannon's busty red-haired secretary, Jeremy Anderson, gave Cliff a sultry look. Shannon had obviously touted him as one of the great lovers of the century. "Adrian Van Ness has been trying to get in touch with you," Jeremy said.

"I'm about to get in touch with him—in spades," Cliff growled.

"Cliff?" Adrian said. "I've been meaning to call you. I was down in Florida with the president and his friend Rebozo."

"We're going to build another bomber," Cliff said. "I just found it out by accident from an Air Force colonel. He was nice enough to wipe the egg off my face."

"Now Cliff—"

"Now Adrian, listen to me, once and for fucking all. You can be a hell of a big help to us here. But not if you start crossing all my wires without telling me."

"Cliff—I apologize."

"Okay. Let's forget it. Let's figure out how the hell we can take on a ten-billion-dollar bomber program, finish the Colossus without going broke, do another production run on the Thunderer and incidentally get the Aurora in the air."

"How does that look, by the way?"

"Not good. Lockheed is coming up fast on the rail with that goddamn L 1011. Douglas is building a DC-10. The airlines are trying to play us off against each other."

"Can't you work your usual magic overseas?"

"The Prince has run out of gas."

"Then it's up to you. Surely you've learned how to play

the game by now. Take Dick Stone along if you still need a partner."

Cliff cursed silently. The Aurora had become his personal challenge, the plane he needed to show the company and the world that he could do it better than his predecessor. Adrian seemed to know it and take pleasure in his difficulties.

"Adrian," Cliff said, "I think we should let someone else build this bomber. It's more than we can handle."

"Cliff—may I remind you I'm still the chairman of the board? I will personally ask you to explain to the other directors why you turned down a ten-billion-dollar contract."

"Because I don't think we should spread ourselves so thin. Because I can see the same headaches we ran into on the Warrior, times ten. Who says Nixon can get this thing through Congress?"

"That's irrelevant. If you expect me to go back to the president of the United States and tell him we don't want to make a plane that I've convinced him no one else can build—you better look up the telephone number of Lockheed's personnel department."

Cliff had not felt so humiliated since Buzz McCall panicked him in SkyRanger II when he was seventeen. He was not Buchanan's chief executive officer. He was Adrian Van Ness's errand boy. In a corner of his mind Billy whispered: *having fun, Big Shot?*

"Okay. I'll talk to Frank about the bomber."

"Let me know if there's a problem. I have some moves I can make with him, these days. We're almost friends."

That only proves Frank Buchanan is one of the simpletons of all time, Cliff thought.

"Ten billion dollars, Cliff! I thought you'd be crawling down the wire to kiss me. I hope you'll communicate a lot more enthusiasm to the workforce when the contract comes through."

"Don't worry, I'll take care of it," Cliff snarled and slammed down the phone.

Jeremy Anderson still had the phone in her hand as Cliff burst out of the office. She had been listening on her extension. "You've got the makings of a third-rate spy!" he roared. "Get me a seat on an eight A.M. plane."

"I was just trying to see if you were still on the phone," Jeremy said, with a guilty pout. "Mike's on line five."

Jeremy's spying was a symptom of Cliff's weakness. Mike Shannon's political skills extended to playing power games inside Buchanan Aircraft. For the moment he was poised between Adrian, Cliff, and Dick Stone.

"What do you want?" Cliff snapped at Shannon.

"What the hell did you say to the Creature? He spent a half hour tearing my ass off."

Cliff's rage deepened. There was only one thing to do, swallow his humiliation and take most of the credit for reviving the Warrior. Adrian's undercover role in its sale would be known only to a handful of top executives such as Dick Stone. If Cliff handled it right, it might not even be known to them.

"Fuck him," Cliff said. "I just got the word from Tony Sirocca. We've got the contract of everyone's dreams. Ten billion bucks to build the next-generation bomber. Son of the Warrior."

"That's no reason to make an enemy out of the Creature," Shannon said.

"Don't worry about it," Cliff said. "We don't have to worry about anything from now on."

The next morning, Cliff flew to California aboard an American Airlines 707. Seated next to him was an angular, not especially pretty brunette with her hair pulled back in a severe ponytail. She was wearing gogo boots, Levi's, and a denim jacket with a *Peace Now* button on the lapel. It irritated him that someone with enough money to fly first class was wearing this revolutionary outfit.

Cliff pulled a copy of *Aviation News* from his briefcase and snapped it open. On its cover was a picture of Buchanan's new high-performance fighter, the SkyDemon.

His companion got the message. "Are you a pilot?" she said.

"I used to be. Now I make them. I made this one," he

said, pointing to the picture of the SkyDemon climbing at a 90-degree angle.

Silence for a half hour. The story on the SkyDemon was positive. Bruce Simons had done a good job. When Cliff looked again, his seat companion was reading a copy of the *Hollywood Reporter*, the bible of West Coast show business. He remembered Tama reading it in the old days.

"You an actress?" he said.

She nodded. "You've probably never heard of me."

"My mother was one. You've probably never heard of her either. Everyone can't be a star."

"How did you get into the plane business?"

"Come on. Say it. How did you get to be a warmonger? That's what you're thinking."

Her smile was rueful but warm. "You don't look like a warmonger," she said.

"Fly forty-nine missions over Germany with guys throwing bullets and shells at you from all directions. It's an instant cure for warmongering. I hate it as much as you do. My son'll be a Marine flier in six months. I'd give a million bucks to make that button on your chest come true."

"Fascinating," she said. "What are you doing to make it happen?"

"Building this," he said, pointing to the SkyDemon. "And other planes that'll make us strong enough to end the war we're in—and make sure another one doesn't start."

She sighed. "You sound like my father. What about trusting people? Just saying we've had enough killing?"

"Who's your father?"

"Robert Sorrento. A character actor. He died last year."

"Character actor, hell. I remember him coming to our house at Redondo Beach to see my mother on Sunday afternoons. He was the handsomest, suavest guy I ever saw. Everyone was sure he was going to be the next Valentino. I used to wish he was my father."

"Was your father in the movies?"

"I don't know what he was in. My mother divorced him before I was born."

"I never saw much of my father either until I got old enough to loan him money."

Suddenly they were telling each other the hidden parts of their lives. He described Tama and her lovers and his stepfather Buzz. She told him about her screenwriter mother, who had lived with a dozen movie actors and executives after she ditched Robert Sorrento. Their tone was rueful, wry, nostalgic. The more they talked, the more they realized they shared a past.

Cliff revealed his long-defunct ambition to become a director. "I guess I always liked to run things," he said.

"How do you direct something as huge as an aircraft company?"

"You pick a good supporting cast—and make yourself the star."

That blew her away. She seemed ready to forgive him for his warmongering. She seemed ready to do a lot of things. Cliff could almost feel the rising warmth.

"I've never seen an aircraft factory. What's it like?" she asked.

"You'll see one today—unless you've got a movie to make."

"I should be so lucky," she said.

They drove from LAX to the new headquarters at El Segundo in Cliff's white Mercedes. He took off her *Peace Now* button and put it in his pocket as they strolled into the building.

"What's your name?" Cliff asked, as the guard opened the visitor's book.

"My real name's Angela Perry. Use that instead of my screen name."

"Don't want to be seen consorting with the enemy?"

She laughed and Cliff felt twenty years younger. He thought of Sarah the Smiling Zombie waiting for him on Palos Verdes, their occasional perfunctory sex in the big bedroom off the windswept terrace. This woman was adventure, conquest—he had no doubt whatsoever he could change her half-baked opinions about plane makers. This visit was the first step.

In a moment they were walking down the assembly line, with dozens of skeletal Thunderers hoisted on jigs. The scream of metal, the hammer of rivet guns filled the huge hangar, which was as long as two football fields. From the balcony dangled a tremendous American flag.

"The workers bought that flag themselves," Cliff said. "It's their way of saying they believe in what they're doing."

Cliff grabbed a balding pot-bellied supervisor by the arm, reading his name off his security badge. "How's things, Eddie? Any problems?"

"Not with this plane, Mr. Morris," Eddie said.

"This young lady's thinking of making a movie about the business. I'm showing it to her from the inside."

Eddie got the idea. "You couldn't get a better guide," he said. "Except maybe Billy McCall, eh, Mr. Morris? And he's not around any more."

"Yeah," Cliff said, returning Eddie's knowing smile, even if he did not have any enthusiasm for the comparison. He was a star. Performing.

Angela was awed by the immensity, the complexity of the show. Exactly what Cliff wanted to happen. They climbed up on the jigs and she sat in the cockpit of a half-finished Thunderer to look at the bewildering instrument panel.

"Imagine yourself in a 9-g pull-out in one of these," Cliff said. "You fly them in your mind all the time. That's the best part of making a plane."

They went into the next hangar, where they were making a half-dozen prototypes of the SkyDemon. They were like slim, stripped swallows compared to the pigeon-breasted Thunderers. Cliff told her how fast the Demons climbed, how incredibly maneuverable they were at fifty thousand feet. In the next hangar, a Colossus was being checked for final delivery to the Air Force. The plane's stupendous black bulk loomed above them.

"You build that too?" Angela said.

"The biggest in the world," Cliff said.

A scene in the technicolor movie of his life began scripting itself in Cliff's mind. A scene that surpassed anything Billy McCall had ever attempted with a woman at ten thousand feet. Careerwise, Cliff Morris was at thirty, maybe forty thousand feet. Eventually he would get rid of Adrian Van Ness and be up there, cruising at sixty thousand. In the meantime he would do something that would send Adrian a message—and make Cliff Morris a legend in his own right.

Back in the headquarters building, they shot up to the sixteenth floor in the noiseless elevator and strolled into Cliff's corner office. His Mexican secretary's eyes widened as she got a look at Angela.

"Mr. Morris," she said. "We didn't expect you until tomorrow."

"Emergencia," he said.

The oak-paneled office had a painting of the *Rainbow Express* fighting its way home from Germany on one wall. It was a duplicate of the one Sarah had given Cliff for the Palm Springs house when he became president. The wall opposite the door was glass, giving them a magnificent view of the airport and the city beyond it, unfortunately almost obscured by smog. They watched a Boeing 727 charge down the runway and head for the sky. Cliff put his arm around Angela's waist and gave her his supersalesman's smile.

She knew exactly what he wanted to do. She wanted to do it too. She wanted to do it here, with the *Rainbow Express* declaring Cliff's miraculous ability to challenge fate and survive. Compounding their desire was the sense of being linked in some mystic way. Destiny, a wild inevitability throbbed between them.

Cliff lifted her against him and kissed her—gently at first, then harder and harder, his hands roving her body. He picked her up and carried her across the room to his executive-sized desk. With a sweep of his arm, he knocked pens, memos, clock onto the carpeted floor. She lay on one elbow while he sat down in his swivel chair and buzzed his secretary.

"No calls, no nothing, for the next two hours. I'm not here."

Cliff began undressing her. He liked what he saw as the Levi's and the jacket and the work shirt came off. The black lace panties and bra suggested she had not let the counterculture obliterate her identity as a child of Hollywood. He flipped the underwear away and ran his hands across coned breasts, a flat muscular stomach, and a dark tangled pussy above remarkably fine legs.

"Now that's a design I like," he said as he undressed.

In a moment he was naked. She boldly took his penis in her hand and slid it into her mouth. An enormous throb of pleasure surged through Cliff's body. He sensed a wish to demonstrate she could be leader as well as led, but for Cliff that was erotic. He liked semi-defiant women. His fingers roved her pussy until they found the zone of desire and vulnerability, the symbolic opening that signified her ultimate surrender. In and out his finger moved while more jets thundered into the sky beyond the windows.

In his head Cliff heard Billy McCall whisper admiringly: *you crazy son of a bitch.* He saw the realization dawn on his secretary's face, saw her whispering the story to friends in the ladies' room and the cafeteria tomorrow, saw the whispers traveling like electricity from secretaries to bosses to the workers on the line to the security guards.

I'll be goddamned, they would think and probably say to their friends. *Billy McCall isn't dead after all. Would you ever think Big Cliff had that much balls?*

Security Chief Dan Hanrahan would come to him in a day or two and tell him Angela was tied up with every left-wing cause in Hollywood. He would solemnly inform Cliff that unless he desisted immediately he would have to tell Adrian Van Ness.

That's exactly what I want you to do, Cliff would say. *While you're at it ask him what the fuck is he going to do about it?*

Be a man, Tama had said. He was working at it. He spread Angela against the window overlooking the airport and slid the joystick into her. The glass was hot against his palms. He imagined the heat on her breasts and belly. "How do you like that?" Cliff asked.

"I like it. I love it. I love you," she said as the jets thundered skyward. She untied her ponytail and her dark hair fell over her shoulders in a silky shower.

It was a fantastic scene in the script Cliff was writing for the technicolor movie of his life. There was only one thing wrong. He had no control over how the movie was going to end.

A FRIEND IN NEED

It was close to midnight on December 23, 1972. Dick Stone sat in the White House's Oval Office beside Cliff Morris, Mike Shannon, Adrian Van Ness, President Richard Nixon, and several aides as the opening credits of *Lusty Lady* unrolled. Dick had brought the film from California. Adrian had introduced it as a "little treat" he thought the president would enjoy.

"Whoa!" the president chuckled, when he saw who Angela Perry was. "This *is* a treat."

In the past two years, Angela had made three movies that zoomed her from semi-obscurity to stardom. Cliff Morris was largely responsible. He had introduced her to a half dozen studio executives with whom he had become chummy since his ascent to Buchanan's presidency.

"She made it years ago, before she changed her name," Adrian said. "One of our security people tracked it down."

The plot involved an anemic scoutmaster and his sexy wife, who take a troop of Boy Scouts camping. The Scouts all look like leftover members of the Waffen SS—blond muscular hunks who eye the wife lecherously from the first frame. In the third frame the scoutmaster falls off a cliff and disappears beneath a foaming waterfall. The Scouts proceed to enjoy Angela in every position and through every available orifice—leaving them all exhausted, while she pants for more.

The president thought it was wonderful. He laughed and laughed. When it finally ended—with a naked Angela in-

specting the exhausted members of each gasping Scout—
Nixon insisted on Adrian getting him a print for private
showings to members of Congress.

The president knew nothing about Cliff's connection to
Angela, of course. He had no idea Adrian was showing the
film not only for his delectation but to embarrass Cliff into
ending his fling with this Jane Fonda clone before she
messed up his career—and Buchanan Aircraft.

Neither gratitude nor Cliff's arguments had altered Angela's politics. She had joined Hanoi Jane and other Hollywood luminaries in raising millions to defeat Nixon for
reelection. To their chagrin he had won in a landslide, thanks
largely to a last-minute announcement that "peace" had been
signed with the North Vietnamese.

The announcement would never have been made without
a massive application of American air power. For the first
time, targets that Curtis LeMay and other air-war experts had
wanted to bomb for seven years were taken off the prohibited
list. Navy planes—Buchanan Thunderers—had mined Haiphong harbor and Boeing's B-52s had pounded Hanoi. For
the heavies it had been anything but a joyride. The fifteen-
year-old B-52s had taken horrendous losses from Soviet
SAM missiles and the enormous concentration of radar-
guided antiaircraft guns around the Communist capital. Morale among the B-52 crews had plummeted alarmingly and
there was even a rumor of a mutiny. But the Communists,
knowing nothing of this development, saw a future of even
more devastating raids and began serious peace negotiations.

Along with a print of *Lusty Lady*, Dick had brought Buchanan's 13,000 page condensation of the thirteen-million
page-Total Performance Package contract bid for the new
bomber, which was going to be simply called the BX to
make it sound as futuristic as possible. Cliff had wanted to
call it Warrior II but Adrian—and Nixon—thought that
would unnecessarily arouse congressmen who had voted
against the previous bomber. Besides, the BX was an essentially new plane, smaller, slimmer. It was not as fast as the
Warrior because it was designed to fly at fifty feet, where
Mach 3 speed would be suicidal. But the plane had some-

thing the Warrior mortally lacked—stealth. Its carbon epoxy fuselage, its virtually invisible engine ducts, left no trace of its path on a radar screen.

After the movie, Adrian signaled Dick Stone to begin his presentation of the BX. Dick struggled to his feet, feeling as if his flesh were sludge and his brain were full of L.A. smog. The TPP contract had consumed him and his staff eighteen hours a day for the past four months. He had finished working on this presentation aboard his flight from LAX. Taking a deep breath to clear his head, Dick set up a rack for his charts and did the job in five smooth minutes. He stressed that the price they were bidding was fifty million dollars a plane. But Dick made it clear that the ultimate cost would be closer to a hundred million dollars. The electronic equipment—especially the ground-hugging radar—they were putting into the plane was fantastically expensive.

"It's all right to surprise Congress, but we don't want to surprise you, Mr. President," Adrian said.

Nixon nodded contentedly. "As long as you know something in advance, damage control is never a problem."

"I trust that goes for the unpleasant noises our Democratic sore losers are making over that break-in at the Watergate apartments," Adrian said.

"Of course," Nixon said. "It never should have happened in the first place. The boys got carried away by our momentum."

A final flip and Dick displayed the mock-up of the BX, flying directly into the camera, its needle nose emanating menace. "Beautiful," Nixon said. "With two hundred of those in the barn, Hanoi won't say boo for the next twenty years—and Peking will be nicer than ever."

"What's the matter with Morris?" one of Nixon's aides asked. "Doesn't he like the plane? He hasn't said a word for a half hour."

"Like it?" Cliff said. "That's the greatest plane, pound for pound, we've ever built. That anyone's ever built. You don't like something that fantastic. You love it."

"I hope Cliff and Mike'll be in the trenches when we send

it up to the Hill," Nixon said. "In spite of the landslide, we're going to need all the help we can get."

"You can depend on Cliff and Mike, Mr. President. Right?" Adrian said.

"You're damn right," Cliff said.

They trudged into the cold Washington night, Dick lugging the film and his presentation kit. "You fucking son of a bitch," Cliff said to Adrian.

"Give him the film," Adrian said. "Hanrahan spent a lot of time and money looking for it."

Dick handed Cliff the film. He flung the hexagonal can into the middle of Lafayette Park. "I wouldn't leave it there if I were you. It can't do your beloved any good," Adrian said.

"Go get it," Cliff said to Mike Shannon.

Cursing, Shannon waded through the muddy grass to retrieve the can. "I recommend a nightly viewing," Adrian said. "I'll even pay for renting a projector."

Adrian hailed a taxi and disappeared into the chilly darkness. Cliff shouted defiant curses after him.

"You're out of your goddamn mind," Dick Stone said.

"Second the motion," Mike Shannon said.

"Fuck you both," Cliff raged. He glared at Dick. "Did you know about this stunt?"

"All I did was carry the can from California," Dick said. "No one told me what was in it."

Shannon hailed a cab and they rode to the Buchanan company apartment in the Watergate complex. Even before Cliff took off his overcoat, he poured a full glass of Inverness and drank half of it in one gulp. "Fuck you and your bomber, Dick," he bellowed. "I'm staying till we get the Aurora straightened out. Then I'm through."

"What are you going to do?"

"First get a divorce from the Smiling Zombie, also known as Lady Sarah. Then become a movie producer. It'll be a snap compared to the fucking aircraft business."

"You'll be a sensation," Dick said. "You're as ruthless as Harry Cohn, as egocentric as Louis B. Mayer, as mean as Jack Warner."

"Second that motion too," Shannon said.

"I'm serious. Angela wants me to produce her next film."

"You'll be working for her. It's insanity," Dick said.

"It's love. Nobody believes it but it really is love, Dick."

There was a desperate appeal in Cliff's voice. He was asking Dick to understand—and simultaneously reminding him why he expected some sympathy from him. But the memory of his obsession with Amalie Borne was still too painful for sympathy. In his mind, Dick evaded the word *love* as if it were a SAM missile. He had not heard the word from Cassie for a long time. Only the children were holding them together. They were a pair of actors pretending affection whenever they performed in front of their special audience. There had been one too many quarrels about his heroic working hours, one too many pleas that Cliff was spending 50 percent of his time thinking about Angela and someone had to hold Buchanan Aircraft together.

"Cliff—the Aurora program is almost out of control. No one else but you can straighten it out. Lockheed and Douglas are mopping up the domestic market. If you can't make at least a hundred overseas sales, we're going to do a Convair."

Dick was talking about the record loss Convair had taken trying to break into the commercial jet market several years ago—440 million dollars. At the time it was the largest corporate loss in the history of American business.

"I've got a tour all lined up. Starting in Japan. If I don't sell fifty copies in Japan I'll buy you a fucking DC-10."

"Cliff—you should be on call for this BX thing," Shannon said.

"You're gonna have to fly solo, Tailgunner."

"In that case, I think I'll get a decent night's sleep."

"Kiss Jeremy for me," Cliff said.

"I will," Shannon said. "Just make goddamn sure you don't try for any on your own."

He departed with a defiant slam of the door. The telephone rang as Cliff poured himself another triple Inverness. "Answer that, will you, Dick?" Cliff said. "If it's Angela tell her I'm asleep. I can't talk to her after seeing that fucking film."

"This is Tony Sirocca," said a gravelly voice. "Is Cliff there?"

There was death in General Sirocca's voice. Dick did not understand why or how he knew it. Maybe he simply felt the Lady's icy fingers on his flesh. Maybe he deduced at IBM-compatible speed that death was the general's principal business and he did not call people late at night for any other reason.

"It's for you. The Pentagon," Dick said.

Cliff grabbed the telephone, feet spread wide in a fighting stance, ready to tell someone else off. Within ten seconds he was bending, crumpling as if Tony Sirocca had kicked him in the groin. "Oh Jesus," he gasped.

He spun on his heel and fell onto the couch, the phone still clutched to his cheek. "There's no hope?" he whispered. "He couldn't have gotten back out to sea? I mean—it's one tough plane, Tony."

Cliff was aging like someone in a science fiction film as he talked. His checks caved in, his chest collapsed, his legs curled up. "Sure, Tony, sure. I appreciate your calling," he said. "I'll call his mother. She couldn't have handled the usual routine. I'm not sure I could."

Cliff did not hang up. He did not have the strength. "Charlie's gone," he said. He slumped there, arms akimbo, one hand still clutching the white telephone. "He flew flak suppression over Hanoi for the B-52s. A direct hit tore the wing off the plane."

"Jesus. I thought he was on his way home," Dick said.

Charlie had been aboard a carrier off Vietnam for almost a year, flying Buchanan Thunderers. "They canceled his orders—they were trying everything to protect the B-52s," Cliff said.

Dick thought of his nine-year-old son in California, the love he felt when he watched him playing or sleeping. It was so acute, it was almost pain. He poured Cliff another full glass of Inverness. "Anesthesia," he said.

"No," Cliff said. "I've got to call Sarah."

"I'll call her."

He went into the bedroom and dialed Sarah's number in

California. The phone rang and rang. Finally a sleepy voice answered. "Sarah?" Stone said. "This is Dick. Dick Stone. I'm calling for Cliff. He just got some terrible news."

"Charlie's dead," she said. "I've been expecting it."

Dick was so staggered he could only gasp: "Why?"

"The sins of the fathers," Sarah said. "And mothers."

"Sarah—I know this is a hell of a shock. But that doesn't make sense."

"Yes it does. You're the one who doesn't make sense, Dick. Trying to rationalize, organize, a business that was shot through with evil from the start."

Suddenly her empty voice was vibrating with rage. "Why are you telling me this?" she hissed. "Doesn't he have the guts to talk to me?"

"Sarah—"

"Get him on the phone. Get the chief executive murderer on the phone. I insist!"

Dick felt his flesh shriveling in the ferocity of the hatred that was coming over the line. "No, Sarah. It would be better if you talked in a few days."

"I'm on the line, Sarah," Cliff said. "Say it to me, not to Dick. I know you've been wanting to say it for a long time. Maybe it'll make you feel better."

"Don't try to soothe me with California pop psychology," Sarah raged. "This isn't an encounter group. It's a marriage. A word, a reality, you've never even tried to understand. A marriage you've betrayed and betrayed until you turned me into a betrayer in my own cowardly way and I helped you betray our son, the best, the finest, the dearest son two parents as worthless as us could ever hope to have—betrayed him to your friends the generals—"

"Betray—betray?" Cliff snarled. "You're the world-class expert in that department, sweetheart. How many goddamn years did you pretend to love me while you were secretly yearning for Billy McCall's cock? Tell me the truth for once. Did you imagine you were doing it with him every time we did it? Was there ever anyone else there behind those saintly closed eyes when you came?"

"I stopped loving him a long time ago. He was more loathsome than you—but I'll say this for him. He wasn't a hypocrite. He didn't lie to his women. He didn't play smarmy husband. If I had to choose between you and him—I'd take him for his honesty—his mad loathsome honesty."

"Why don't you get in a fucking plane and imitate him?" Cliff shouted. "You can be honest together at the bottom of the Pacific. Then I can marry a woman who loves me."

"You don't know the meaning of the word *love*. You never did. It was all slavering appetite. Beach blanket bingo. California fucking. Marriage American style."

"How about English style? Twenty years of playing let's pretend. Appetite had nothing to do with it? You didn't like what you were getting? You were just doing your duty? Is that why you crawled in bed with me in dear old England?"

"All England proved was you can take the boy out of America but you can't take America out of the boy. You're loathsome people. I can't believe you were ever English, that we share one drop of your vile blood. My deepest regret— my only regret—is that my son died in the service of your vicious amoral country."

Hatred, hatred, it was like a million cages of hissing snakes writhing across the landscape, Dick thought. Slithering, biting, thrashing across America over Vietnam, the rise and fall of Negro hopes, the virulent political divisions Nixon seemed to encourage. Women like Sarah concentrated it in their tormented hearts. Why did he find himself almost paralyzed by dread?

Dick slammed down the phone. He did not want to hear another word. He sat in the bedroom while Cliff and Sarah reviled each other for another twenty minutes. Dick stared out the window at the curving ultramodern architecture of the Watergate complex, struggling against a sense of disorientation, disintegration. Were there any certainties in this hate-racked America? Was Adrian Van Ness's smooth assurance that Richard Nixon was the president who would solve all Buchanan's problems worth anything?

As Cliff Morris whirled around the globe selling planes and pursuing Angela Perry, most of the day-to-day decision making had gravitated into Dick's hands. More than ever he felt the weight of being responsible for the survival of Buchanan and the thousands of designers, engineers, salesmen, and assembly-line workers who had put years of their lives into the company.

Thunk. Cliff had hung up. He was draining his glass of Inverness as Dick returned to the living room. "Does that happen often?" Dick said.

Cliff shook his head. "I knew it was there, waiting to come out. The way you know some things in a marriage. You know them but you don't think about them."

Dick nodded, thinking about his own tense marriage. Maybe it was time for some emergency repairs. Exactly what these should or could be, he had no idea.

Dick drank and listened to Cliff talk about Tama and Buzz and Adrian and Billy and the dirty game Cliff and Sarah had played to destroy him. Cliff did not feel guilty about it because Billy was going to destroy him if he got the big job. That was the game they were playing—kill or be killed—the game that had started when Billy had moved into Cliff's house at the age of eleven. It was all so stunningly inevitable, Dick was reduced to speechlessness again.

They went from Billy to Charlie and the mess the United States of America had made of the war in Vietnam. They did not have an answer much less an explanation. They talked as men, as friends, as survivors of an earlier war—and could only agree that America had failed to use its air power in a decisive way. Whether this was the whole truth or only part of it, whether it was even true, was beyond their competence that night. They were dealing with pain, loss, grief, not strategy.

By the time dawn began tinting the Washington sky, they had both drunk so much Inverness they no were longer making sense. Dick hoisted Cliff to his feet and towed him into the bedroom and sprawled him on the king-size bed.

"Dick," Cliff said. "Never forget this. Y'real friend."

"Just promise me one thing. You won't become a movie producer."

Cliff shook his head. "Gonna build that bomber. For Charlie. Gonna make it so fucking good no president has to send kids eyeball to eyeball with flak batteries."

For Charlie and for Billy McCall. Dick was still struggling with his own memories of the part he had played in Billy's destruction.

In the living room, Dick called Cassie in California. "I know you won't like this—but I'm not going to make it home for Christmas." He explained what had happened— why he felt Cliff needed a friend to stay with him for a few days.

"Doesn't he have a wife?" Cassie said.

"They're through. Between this and Angela—she's ditching him."

"Sarah?" Cassie said. She had been on several of Sarah's benefit committees. They had not become friends. Sarah, performing as that empty vessel, Mrs. Clifford Morris, had no friends.

Dick gave Cassie a brief summary of the dialogue between Sarah and Cliff. "I didn't think she could be that impolite," Cassie said.

Dread sucked at Dick's nerves again. He could think of nothing to say. "When can we look forward to celebrating Christmas?" Cassie asked. "Anytime before New Year's?"

"I hope so. I'll call you."

"We'll be so grateful."

Dick collapsed on the couch and slept until noon. He awoke with an even more acute sense of dread. It seemed to ooze from the walls of the Watergate complex. Wrong, wrong, whispered a warning voice in his head. Everything was going wrong. Politically, personally. He heard the bitterness in Cassie's voice and suddenly wanted to be on a plane to California as soon as possible.

Cliff was still snoring. Dick called Adrian and told him about Charlie. "Good God. How did Sarah take it?" Adrian asked.

Dick gave him a succinct summary. "This will make Cliff inseparable from that left-wing Hollywood slut," Adrian said. "She'll rush to console him. For an artist of her minor talents, real-life drama like this is irresistible. It supplies the emotion her imagination lacks."

Adrian sighed. "Are you ready to be the next president of Buchanan Aircraft, Dick?"

"I don't think this is the time or place to bring that up," Dick said.

"I suppose not," Adrian said. "But I'm not withdrawing the question."

Dick went out in search of breakfast. There was no food in the apartment. When he returned Cliff was on the phone. "Wear a fur coat. It's cold as hell," he said. "I'll be waiting at the gate."

Cliff hung up and smiled almost cheerfully at Dick. "I called Angela. She's flying in. You don't have to hang around. Don't you want to get home for Christmas?"

"I missed my plane."

"I'll get you on an Air Force plane."

A call to the Pentagon located a Colossus that was flying replacement crews to Thailand to maintain the B-52 bombing threat until the Communists signed a peace treaty. Dick sat with the young pilots and bombardiers and gunners, listening to them discuss the tactics that were being used over Vietnam. They all thought the generals were idiotic.

"It's World War II stuff," one freckled-faced redhead said to Dick, as if this was synonymous with prehistoric. "We should be coming in low, under the radar."

Dick thought of the BX, the invisible plane they should be flying—that they would be flying if the U.S. Congress was not a collection of pinheads. It had taken a full year to negotiate the TPP contract and write up its thirteen million pieces of paper. Buchanan's enemies in the Senate, people like Proxmire and the Creature, were already threatening to block funding for the program. That meant its supporters and the Air Force would keep it alive by turning it into a stealth item in the budget. This accumulated stupidity and hatred left these kids flying bombers that were almost as old as they were into skies full of radar-guided missiles and antiaircraft shells.

They landed at Vandenberg Air Base in California to refuel and Dick hitched a ride to Los Angeles with a civilian employee. He did not call Cassie. He decided it would be fun to surprise her and the kids. He bailed his car out of LAX and roared up the Ventura Freeway to their house in Nichols Canyon. It was about six o'clock when he unlocked the front door. He found nine-year-old Jake (for John) and şeven-year-old Catherine watching television.

"Daddy!" they yelled and danced around him.

"Where's Mommy?"

"She's visiting up street," Jake said. "At Dennisons."

The Dennisons were real estate brokers. Dick had bought the house through them. Lately they had hired a publicity man and became known as "brokers to the stars." They sold houses for fabulous prices in Malibu, Westwood.

An hour later, there was still no sign of Cassie. "Did Mom say when she'd be home?" Dick asked.

"No," Catherine said. "Sometime she stays up there a long time."

"What do you do for dinner?"

"We heat up TV trays in the microwave. Mom showed me how to turn it on," Jake said.

"I think I'll go tell Mom I'm here."

Dick walked up the steep winding road, his mind racing ahead to what he might find at Dennisons, then denying it as absurd. When he reached the sprawling two-story house, clinging, like his own, to the steep slope of the canyon, he thought it looked deserted. There was only one car in the open garage—a 1960 Dodge. Usually there were three or four, including some flashy sports cars. The Dennisons raced them as a hobby.

Dick rang the bell. Silence. He rang it again and again. Silence. He pounded on the door. Carl Dennison jerked it open. He was a big freckle-faced man with a handlebar mustache and slightly protruding teeth.

"Dick!" he said. "What can I do for you?"

"I'm looking for Cassie."

"Cassie? I haven't seen her."

He was a very inept liar.

"The kids told me she was visiting you. Where's your wife?"

"She—she's away."

"Cassie!" Dick shouted. "Guess who's home for Christmas."

Silence. Dennison stood there, anxiety exuding from every pore. "Listen," he said. "This was a onetime thing. She didn't know Doris had split. We started talking and got carried away—"

"Cassie!" Dick roared.

He shoved Dennison aside and strode into the house. The place was all but stripped of furniture. Doris had apparently split in a moving van. He found Cassie sitting on the edge of an unmade bed off the living room, pulling on a pair of blue jeans. On top she was still naked. She looked ashamed—and defiant. With great deliberation she put on an old denim shirt and buttoned it.

"Merry Christmas," Cassie said.

Dick realized she was drunk. "Let's go home," he said.

They walked stiff-legged downhill to their house. "Reminds me of my stewardess days," Cassie said. "Walking down the aisle while the plane was climbing. Gave all the ginks a good look at the equipment."

"How long has this been going on?" Dick said.

"Not long. Let's have dinner and argue later, when the kids are in bed."

They struggled through dinner with the kids doing all the talking—mostly about school. Dick gave them a laundered version of visiting the White House, which impressed Jake. They watched a dramatization of Dickens's *A Christmas Carol* until nine o'clock. Unreality clawed at Dick's brain. In Washington Cliff Morris grieved for his son, blasted out of the sky by Russian missiles over Hanoi. He sat in California watching sentiments that moved nineteenth-century Londoners to tears, trying to think of what to say to his adulterous wife.

Cassie put the kids to bed. Dick waited in the living room. She finally appeared, a half glass of bourbon in her hand. He grabbed it away from her and threw it into the fireplace.

Seeing her on the booze upset him more than her infidelity.

"Why?" he said. "That's what I want to know. Do you love him?"

She shook her head.

"Then—why?"

"He talked me into it. He made me feel sorry for him. It was better than feeling nothing—the way I feel with you."

"You need help," Dick said. "I'll talk to our medical director. He'll suggest a therapist."

"Great," Cassie said. "It'll be nice to have an intelligent adult to talk to for a change."

"We can work this out. It won't be easy but I'll try to understand."

"I don't want your lousy understanding," Cassie said. "I don't want your goddamn condescending forgiveness either."

She strode defiantly to the bar and filled another glass with bourbon. "You want to know the real reason for this mess?" she said, her voice thickening with tears. "I could put up with your impossible hours. I want to see us win this damn war as much as you do. I could even put up with your stupid guilt about killin' Billy McCall. What I can't stand is knowin' you don't love me. You never have. I don't know what the hell you love besides your miserable airplane company."

Are you ready to be the next president of Buchanan Aircraft, Dick? whispered Adrian Van Ness.

Was this the price he was paying? Was that his secret motive from the start? A sly ambition, nurtured in the small hours of the morning, watching Cliff Morris flounder? No. Dick denied the accusation. He was working for those kids on their way to fly obsolete planes into a vortex of radar-guided antiaircraft fire over Hanoi. Maybe he was no longer working for the greater glory of the United States of America. He was still working for the fliers, for the brotherhood of the air against the greedy ignorant groundlings.

True enough, true enough. But that commitment did not explain why he had lost his all-American girl.

Dick saw Cliff Morris in that king-size bed in the Watergate apartment, entangled with Angela, emptying his grief, his pain, into her. Breaking through loss and bitterness to clutch at joy. *Freedom*—that was what the image said. In some incomprehensible way, the word, the image, belonged to California, even though it was being enacted in Washington. It was not just the freedom to fuck. It was an inward thing, a kind of space between a man's mind and heart where a person lived. Why had Dick Stone lost his space? What was wrong with him?

At first I thought I could not bear
The depths of my despair

Amalie. She was still there, barring his way to happiness.

ECHO CHAMBER

"That was beautiful," Susan Hardy said when Sarah Morris finished telling her husband how much she hated him. Susan helped Sarah weep for Charlie through the rest of that long night. They wept as women and drank like men. Susan let Sarah read aloud the letters Charlie had written her from Vietnam, telling her how much he loved to fly, how unafraid he was of dying. *If I have to die in order to fly I'll take it. I've been dying to fly all my life. It's logical.*

Sarah could see him laughing as he wrote it. He could make a joke out of anything, even death. Courage was as natural to him as breathing.

"Burn them," Susan said.

"Burn them?"

"They're dangerous. Your husband would try to publish them. He'd try to make Charlie a martyr of the air. He'd inspire thousands, millions, of others to think that way. We'd never eliminate the war love from their souls."

Burn them? Sarah could not strike the match. She let Susan do it. She piled the letters in the fireplace and burned them with her zippo. "Zip and they're zapped," Susan said. A bad joke.

Susan had not abandoned their friendship when Cliff became president of Buchanan. She sent Sarah notices of meetings of Women Concerned About the War and similar groups with capital letters. Sarah sent her money. After Billy and Victoria died and she became Mrs. Clifford Morris, the hollow woman, going through the motions of celebrity, Sarah sent Susan even more money.

In return Susan kept Sarah informed about the latest gossip at Buchanan, which she obtained through her "network." Sarah was confused by the term at first. She thought a network was something that broadcast television and radio shows. Susan explained this network broadcast the kind of information women needed to survive in a male-dominated world. She told her Cliff had seduced an actress named Angela-something in his office and was now seeing her almost nightly in her house above Mulholland Drive.

Of course Susan had no idea Mrs. Clifford Morris did not care whom her husband was seeing or what he was doing with her. She was actually relieved that she was not required to be Sarah, to play that part in the bedroom where she had shivered and shaken with horror and terror for the deaths her hatred, her inverted love, had caused. Sarah understood why Cliff was equally reluctant to visit her there, even if he did not understand why, even if he was simply trying to avoid the dead weight of her despair, a potentially fatal drag on his salesman's buoyancy.

If Sarah did not care, what explained that explosion of hatred? Was it simply a performance to please Susan, her only friend? Or was Mrs. Clifford Morris in touch with Sarah on some subterranean level? Perhaps that was it. Lately Mrs. Clifford Morris had been giving Susan Hardy more and more money and going to some of her capital-letter groups with her. She listened to angry women telling each other how their husbands and lovers had abused and exploited them. Many were from the aircraft business but not all. The aircraft business did not have a monopoly on macho males who only wanted one thing from a woman. At these meetings for some peculiar reason Mrs. Clifford Morris found herself able to get in touch with her previous incarnation, Sarah.

Now she sat and watched Charlie's letters burn. Having just resigned as Mrs. Clifford Morris, she had to let Sarah do her thinking. She thought it was a shame. She wept uncontrollably and remembered things that Mrs. Clifford Morris had successfully forgotten. Charlie zooming around the house with a model plane in his hand, smashing lamps and vases. Cliff beside her in the bed upstairs, sharing his fears and hopes about the Talus and other planes.

"You can't stay here any longer," Susan decreed. "You need a different site to launch your new consciousness."

Oh, good, thought the ghost of Mrs. Clifford Morris. I will be neither Mrs. nor Miss. I will be Ms. A nice foreshortening of the self—an alphabetical lobotomy.

They would move to the desert and convert Mrs. Clifford Morris's vacation house into a center for Women for Peace and Freedom. That was Susan's latest capital letter group. After thinking about it carefully, Susan decided it would be better if Ms. Sarah Morris did not divorce Clifford Morris for the time being. Divorce was an ultimate weapon, which should be used when a man was least able to cope with it. For the time being Cliff Morris was riding high on money from the war machine. Better to wait until he was dumped by his Hollywood dream girl or by Buchanan or both and then stick it to him.

A marvelous phrase that summed up msdom, Sarah thought. In the new age that would unfold in their desert encounter sessions, they would acquire the ability to stick it to all of them.

"All the murderers and their war machine," Susan said. She was one of the leaders of the antiwar movement in California. Major politicians conferred with her before making statements. She was in touch with gays and lesbians in San Francisco who were organizing their own political movement. Excitement, energy, surrounded Susan, turning her into a pillar of fire. Out of the flames would emerge a new kind of beast, a woman who could stick it to them.

Once upon a time there was a war machine you loved.

That was Miss Sarah Chapman talking, that difficult, crotchety ghost. Eventually she would dwindle into pale voiceless insignificance, along with Mrs. Clifford Morris, who was totally insignificant from the start to finish of her brief but expensive existence.

"We're going to discover a new declaration of independence, a new pursuit of happiness," Susan said as they piled clothes and shoes in the back of the car.

"A new declaration of independence," Ms. Sarah Morris said. "A new pursuit of happiness."

Miss Sarah Chapman tried to point out that her English ancestors had recoiled from these grandiose phrases. Ms. Sarah Morris merely smiled tolerantly. For the time being she was an echo chamber in which the words resounded defiantly. But that would change. Eventually they could become part of her bones and blood, her new American self.

Want to bet? whispered Miss Sarah Chapman, that persistent English ghost.

In the desert, visitors other than Susan Hardy's cohorts in Women for Peace and Freedom (WFPF) kept the ghost alive. First Sarah's daughter Elizabeth, precariously balanced between drug-free hope and drug-drenched despair. Elizabeth could not deal with a mother who hated her father, who denied her brother was a hero and burned his letters, who told her the man she loved, the doctor who had rescued her from the needles and nightmares of San Francisco's Haight-Asbury because she was so beautiful and now wanted to marry her was a male fraud and tyrant who only wanted to own a toy woman he had created. For one thing Sarah was not sure if that was true, just because Susan Hardy said it was. Even then she saw msdom was not always synonymous with wisdom.

Next came daughter Margaret on the long-distance telephone from England, where she was continuing to become the world's leading expert on China. She had been closer to Charlie than anyone else in the family and she required special comforting. You cannot be a comforter when your soul is consumed by hatred. So Ms. Sarah Morris had to call on the ghost of Miss Sarah Chapman to remember how deep, how pervasive, the love of planes and flight ran in Charlie's blood. She talked about her father and about Cliff. She urged Margaret to go out to Bedlington Royal Air Force base and imagine the *Rainbow Express* landing with one engine while Miss Sarah Chapman stood in front of the Watch Office praying her in. She had to make Margaret, who valued thought above feeling (or told herself she did), accept the awful inevitability of Charlie's death.

Finally, unexpectedly, the most important visitor: Frank Buchanan. He came with tears on his face, hobbling on a cane since arthritis had invaded his bad leg. He brought with him a letter of sympathy, signed by every single worker in Buchanan's El Segundo factory, where the Thunderer was built. Five thousand signatures, five thousand members of the fraternity of the air saying they were sorry and proud and sad for one of their own. Frank put the hundreds of sheets of soiled paper on Sarah's coffee table and she saw them being passed from jig to jig, signed while metal shrieked and rivet guns clattered and the gigantic American flag fluttered feebly on the wall.

Oblivious to her hatred, Frank talked of Billy and Cliff as boys, when he taught them to fly. He told her of his mother's faith—of a world soul that connected everyone, the living and the dead, in which evil fought an eternal war with good. How he had dreamt in his youth that his planes would be weapons of inspiration on the side of the good—but now he had begun to think of them as creatures of evil. They had destroyed too many people he loved, beginning with Amanda.

That was when Sarah learned Califia's fate—what had happened to Amanda Van Ness. Bewildered, appalled, Ms. Sarah Morris realized this lonely old man too needed to be comforted, consoled, forgiven. The ghost of Miss Sarah Chapman was still real enough to feel the ancient tug of daughterhood, the almost extinct wish her own lost father had never fulfilled. It was the first of many visits Frank would pay, in spite of Susan Hardy's growls of hostility.

But the ghost of Miss Sarah Chapman was still only a

ghost. Most of the time Ms. Sarah Morris and her hatred
prevailed. It was not entirely her fault. America seethed with
hatred during those last years of Nixon's reign, with the lying
president's face on the television screens night after night.
Ms. Sarah even welcomed into their vituperative fraternity
Cassie Trainor Stone, who became a contributor to WFPF
and a member of their encounter sessions.

Listening to Cassie pour out her loathing for her absentee
husband and the other Buchanan males she had known in
her Honeycomb Club days, Ms. Sarah shuddered at the
thought of earnest Dick Stone trying to survive this firestorm
of female hatred. When Cassie announced she was divorcing
Dick and returning to her Tennessee birthplace, the house
resounded with mscheers. But Ms. Sarah Morris found herself feeling sorry for the failed husband.

It was the ghost of Miss Sarah Chapman again, trickily
refusing to fade away, remembering the earnest navigator
who hated to bomb civilians, who in turn remembered her
as a daregale skylark scanted in a cage. Was she still one?
Ms. Sarah Morris wondered. Had she only changed cages?

A week or so later, Dick Stone was on the telephone with
a voice leaden enough to send whole flocks of skylarks spinning to earth in 13g dives. The Marines had awarded Charlie
a Distinguished Flying Cross. They wanted to present it at a
ceremony at Buchanan's headquarters. Cliff was in Morocco
trying to sell Auroras to Arabs and Africans and could not
make it. Would she come?

Once more evading Susan Hardy's doubts, Ms. Sarah
Morris said yes. It was wonderful publicity for the company,
of course. She rationalized it to herself and Susan by arguing
that by helping to keep Buchanan airborne she was helping
herself. She was making sure the pie would be big and juicy
when she stuck it to Cliff with the Big Divorce that divided
his assets in half.

It was a heartrending ceremony, which Ms. Sarah Morris
survived only by letting the ghost of Miss Sarah Chapman
take complete charge until it was over. The patriotic
speeches, the pictures of Charlie, the whirring TV cameras
and kleig lights would have been unendurable for the

msshapened soul of Sarah Morris. She would have erupted into obscenities and denunciations of the war machine in the middle of it. Miss Sarah Chapman, who believed in heroes and dying for God and Country, even read one of Charlie's favorite poems, William Butler Yeats's "An Irish Airman Foresees His Death," in which a boy in another war tried to explain why "a lonely tumult of delight" lured him into the sky's murderous embrace.

Afterward, in Dick Stone's office, Ms. Sarah had dazedly returned to her body as Frank Buchanan and others told her how much they had loved the poem. Finally she was alone with Dick, who was looking almost as ravaged as she felt. Insomnia had gouged ridges in his face. He looked like he was barely holding on.

"I'm sorry about Cassie," Ms. Sarah said. "I'm afraid you didn't get much support from our little group of *ms*creants."

He smiled gamely at the joke. "Maybe I didn't deserve any," he said. "Are you going to divorce Cliff?"

"Eventually," Ms. Sarah said and teetered on the brink of revealing the whole program. Why not let Big Cliff know— Dick would of course tell him—all about their plan to stick it to him? Instead, Miss Sarah Chapman took control again. An echoing voice whispered: *like a daregale skylark scanted in a cage*. She realized this mournful man confronting her was her only hope of happiness. He understood everything about her life, even the sad secret of never loving Cliff, of the wizzo WAAF drunk on bourbon and glory who had thrown herself into the big pilot's arms.

In the same terrible moment Ms. Sarah Morris realized she could be this man's hope as well. She saw the knowledge in his haunted eyes—heard his oblique wish in the question about divorce. They valued the same things—honor and honesty and authentic feeling—things that Cliff could never care about if he lived to be a thousand. In a way they were both victims of that voracious all-American hero-pilot-salesman-playboy-pseudo-CEO. Victims of this devouring America with its manic pursuit of money and power and weaponry unto death.

But Ms. Sarah Morris's bitter lips were sealed against testaments of possible love. Dick Stone's lips, hands, heart, were equally encased in that unwritten law scorched on the male brain stem—thou shalt not seduce your best friend's wife. Trapped, sealed, condemned to pirouetting in separate space capsules through the long gray years unto eternity. So there was nothing else to do but murmur meaningless words about how grateful she was to be asked to Charlie's enshrinement and slink back to her desert abode, her Gaza where she waited, eyeless, for the chance to bring down the temple in the name of her mserable revenge.

THE MEANING OF MEANING

Cliff Morris stood at the window of his corner office in Buchanan Aircraft's El Segundo headquarters watching thousands of protestors massed on the company's airfield at twilight, each carrying a lighted candle of peace. Inside the main factory building sat a gleaming white prototype of the BX bomber.

"I still think we should call out the National Guard," Cliff said. "These assholes could attack the plane—destroy it."

"That's exactly what I'm hoping they'll do," Dick Stone said. "But we won't get that lucky."

"Is it worth it, Dick? All this strife, this hatred?" Frank Buchanan said.

"Yes," Dick said.

"Do you agree, Cliff?" Frank asked.

"Yeah," Cliff said with minimal enthusiasm.

He did not like the way Dick Stone had taken charge of this crisis. He did not like the way Dick had taken charge of almost everything in the day-to-day operations of Buchanan. But there was not much he could do about it. Adrian Van Ness had made Dick executive vice president.

"We can't back down now. Among other things, we can't afford it," Dick said.

It was the brutal truth. In Washington, for the third year in a row Adrian Van Ness had won a billion dollars from Congress to keep the BX alive. That was not enough to build more than the prototype but it had provided Buchanan with desperately needed cash. Unfortunately, Adrian had been unable to talk the Air Force into swallowing the five-hundred-million-dollar cost overrun on the Colossus. That cloud of red ink still loomed over the company. Last year their high-performance fighter, the SkyDemon, had lost the fly-off with General Dynamics, F-16, leaving behind it another pool of red ink deep enough to drown them.

Meanwhile, Cliff flailed around the globe frantically searching for orders for his baby, the widebody commercial jet, the Aurora. He had been able to sell 30 to the Japanese with bribes even the Prince would have considered excessive. He was now working on the Egyptians and other national airlines in the Middle East. There the bribes were certain to be even more stupendous. Almost everywhere else, Lockheed was making him look silly with their own highly developed grease machine. So far Cliff had orders for a paltry 120 copies—leaving him and the company up to their ears in another deluge of red ink.

There were times when Cliff wondered if some kind of curse, some evil spirit, began pursuing the company the day he became CEO. Any hope of selling the Aurora domestically vanished when the Arabs created OPEC and raised oil prices into the stratosphere in 1973. The airlines' profits vanished in a swirl of hydrocarbons. Then a careless pilot flew an Aurora into a Florida swamp, killing everyone aboard and triggering a swarm of multimillion-dollar lawsuits.

Nixon, the president who had revived the BX bomber, was gone along with his landslide. Gone too was Vietnam—in Communist hands, abandoned by a Congress who had ignored President Gerald Ford's pathetic cry, "Our friends are dying!" But the BX had survived, thanks to heroic lobbying by Adrian, Mike Shannon, and Buchanan's Washington staff. They had beaten back the onslaughts of the Creature and the other critics of the military industrial complex in and out of Congress.

This year, the nation's 200th anniversary, the critics had changed their tactics. One of the Creature's staffers, a Quaker named Jacob Woolman, decided the BX was the perfect issue to revive the noble emotions of the antiwar movement. He had organized a national crusade against the plane, which was cresting tonight beneath their windows.

A Buchanan helicopter rose from the roof of the main building and hovered over the crowd. From its open doors fluttered thousands of pieces of paper. The demonstrators picked them up and read them by candlelight. It was a statement signed by Cliff, welcoming them to Buchanan Field and assuring them that there were no police or National Guard troops anywhere near the premises.

We respect your right to protest. In return, we are confident you will respect our property and the millions of dollars worth of tools and equipment used to build planes that defend this country and give thousands of skilled workers jobs.

Dick Stone had written the statement. Dick had assessed the mood of the country and decided conciliation, not confrontation, was the way to go. "Instead of them making us look bad, we'll make them look bad," Dick said. Adrian Van Ness liked the idea; hardly surprising—it showed how much Dick had learned from the master of forethought.

The statement was part of the game plan. So was banning the police. Whenever pickets appeared outside their headquarters building, Dick sent them coffee and sandwiches. He had Cliff's picture taken talking to them.

"Don't pay any attention to those lying words," Jacob Woolman screamed from the platform. Behind him a rock band struck up "We Shall Overcome." Woolman, still bedecked in sixties love beads, led the crowd through the hymn. A Catholic priest who had become famous during the same tormented decade read one of his poems about a Vietnamese child killed by American bombs. Woolman gave a ranting hysterical speech in which he attacked the military industrial complex of the United States and Israel. He linked the Palestinians in their refugee camps with the blacks in the ghettos and the villagers in Vietnam.

"Did you hear that, Stone? He's attacking Israel. Why don't you go down there and punch him in the mouth?" Cliff said.

"If it gets the Israeli lobby on our side, I'll hug him instead," Dick said.

Bruce Simons, their public relations director, returned from a tour of the crowd. He grabbed Cliff by the arm. "I found Sarah. She's not going to make a statement, thank God."

Cliff nodded glumly. Sarah was another reason why he was keeping a low profile tonight. She was down there with the demonstrators, using their son Charlie as her justification. Charlie—and Billy McCall. She said she was doing penance for her sins against them both—whatever that meant. Sin was not an idea Cliff understood. It smelled musty, absurd, a word from another century.

She had made no attempt to divorce him after their explosion of mutual loathing the night Charlie died. Somehow that made Cliff feel safe. She was still part of his luck, no matter how badly it seemed to be running. She was still the figure on the runway as he fought to bring the shattered *Rainbow Express* home from Schweinfurt.

Sarah spent most of her time at their Palm Springs house, which Cliff ceded as her turf. They kept in touch on family matters, especially their problems with their older daughter, Elizabeth, who spent a year in a drug rehab center and another year with her mother putting her mind back together. Sarah had done a good job with her. Elizabeth was now happily married to the doctor who had rescued her.

Dick Stone told Bruce Simons to make Woolman's attack on Israel the lead in his statement to the press. "Stress how pained we all were because the heroic Israelis fly so many of our planes," he said.

The roar of airliners landing at LAX kept drowning out the music and the speakers. In about an hour the crowd began to dissolve. By eleven o'clock the protest was over. Everyone agreed by the standards of the sixties it was a flop. Dick

Stone telephoned Adrian Van Ness with the good news. He was not very responsive. His voice crackled over the speakerphone on Cliff's desk, sounding like someone from outer space.

"One more trip over Niagara Falls survived," he said, "Any good news on the Aurora?"

Cliff went into overdrive about the prospects for Mideast sales. The Egyptians, the Moroccans, the Tunisians were in love with the plane. It was a lie, of course. What they loved were the James Madisons in Cliff's briefcase.

"Let me know when love translates into cash," Adrian said. Panic roiled Cliff's flesh but he concealed it with his usual skill.

Downstairs Dick Stone thanked Dan Hanrahan and his security men for playing the game his way. Trying to minimize his surly performance during the demonstration, Cliff shifted gears. "Good flight plan, Navigator. Feel like relaxing over a drink?"

Dick shook his head. "I've got a date with a couple of union leaders at eight o'clock tomorrow morning."

Watching Dick trudge back to his office, Cliff thought he saw signs of strain. Several sources had told him Dr. Willoughby had barred booze from Dick's diet and was holding him together with a careful mix of tranquilizers and antidepressants. It had been a year since Cassie divorced him and went back to Tennessee.

Up the freeways Cliff roared to Angela Perry's house in Holmby Hills, his home away from home in Los Angeles these days. A party was in progress as he arrived. There always seemed to be a party in progress. There were the usual nubile starlets in miniskirts and pretty boys in Gucci jeans, dancing to rock music that blasted from the most expensive stereo system in California.

Cliff found Angela in bed, watching the evening news with one of the ex-sixties activists sitting on the floor beside her. His name was Sam something but Cliff always called him Lenin Jr. He had been tear-gassed in Chicago in 1968 and had showed up at all the other right places from Woodstock to Altamont to Kent State to acquire a niche in the movement's hall of fame. He looked like Pinocchio, except that his nose was not quite as long. He had the same cock-eyed eyes and smarmy smile. He also (in Cliff's opinion) thought like someone with a brain made of wood.

Cliff kissed Angela and rubbed her swollen stomach. She was nine months pregnant. "How is he?"

"Restless," she said.

The child was her idea. She had declared she would have it during that unforgettable Christmas weekend they spent in Washington after Charlie's death. Conception had turned out to be much more difficult than either of them imagined. Angela was in her early forties and Cliff was fifty-two. They had wound up consulting fertility experts and counting sperm and ova.

She had finally conceived—and Cliff asked her to marry him. Her producer, her publicity man, her agent, were horrified. Marrying a right-wing warmonger would destroy her image. After listening to everyone, including several tirades from Cliff, Angela decided it would be better to have a love child without benefit of a marriage license. It was the in thing to do in seventies Hollywood—it would enhance her image as a free spirit.

On television a reporter was asking Jacob Woolman why he had attacked Israel in his assault on the BX. "Because Israel is part of the American war machine!" he shrilled.

Cliff grinned. Bruce Simons had done his job. The reporter was an old Buchanan friend, whom they had taken on junkets to the Paris Air Show and other plush ports of call. By the time Woolman stopped denouncing Israel, his movement would be yesterday's news.

"How could he be so stupid!" Lenin Jr. groaned.

"How come you weren't there tonight, hero?" Cliff said.

"I saw no point in playing into your Machiavellian hands," Lenin Jr. said.

Cliff had made no secret of their strategy. He enjoyed outraging Angela's friends by bragging about the way Buchanan outwitted protestors and congressmen to build warplanes.

"You *are* awful," Angela said in an unusually weary voice.

Cliff kicked Lenin Jr. in the shins. "Beat it, Vladimir," he said.

Lenin Jr. slouched out of the bedroom and Cliff lay down beside her. "You'll feel a lot better in a week," he said.

"Irv said this kid has cost us fifty million dollars." Irv was her producer.

"Sid's turned down *seven* firm offers for major films." Sid was her agent.

"Arnie says people are screaming for new stills. It's amazing how fast an image gets used up."

Arnie was her publicity man.

"You'll be back at work in a month, I'm sure of it."

"I better be."

"I've got to go to New York tomorrow."

"You promised you'd stay for the week! So you'd be here—"

"Honey, there's a guy flying in from Saudi Arabia who swears he can sell a hundred Auroras for us in the Middle East."

"For the usual five million a plane?"

Angela was fascinated by the gritty side of the plane business. She collected stories of corporate corruption to convince herself that her left-wing friends had it right, America was hopeless.

"Maybe six million," Cliff said. For a while he had bragged about the bribes he paid overseas. But Angela's reaction started to remind him of Sarah. Lately he had kept his mouth shut.

"I want you here all week. You promised me!" Angela said, combining moral disapproval and sheer willfulness.

"I'll fly out the minute I hear you've gone into labor."

"I've begun to wonder exactly where this relationship is going," Angela said, her mouth in a Bette Davis pout.

"Honey, you're feeling lousy. Let's talk about it next month. When we've got something to celebrate."

"You'll have something to celebrate. I'll have stitches. You won't be able to touch me for another two months."

"Hey, it's not that bad. Women have been doing this for a long time."

"I'm not women."

"You seem to be forgetting what this means to us."

"What does it mean? You've gone right on making your dirty deals, building your rotten planes. What kind of a future will this baby have with someone like you running the country?"

Cliff was very tired. He had flown in from London two days ago and spent most of the next two days and nights conferring with Dick Stone and Dan Hanrahan on preparations for the protest. The CEO thought he deserved a few words of sympathy, maybe even praise from someone, especially Angela. He liked the rueful way she admired his executive skills and simultaneously damned them. It corresponded to the way he often felt about himself. Instead of sympathy, he was getting left-wing drivel.

"I wish I was running the fucking country! I'm mostly trying to keep our heads above the goddamn mess people like you and Lenin Jr. have created over the last ten years."

"You bastard," she said. "You're standing there in your Hong Kong tailored suit pulling down three hundred thousand a year and he doesn't have a cent. He gave up his career, his life, to try to change this country and people like you have made him a laughingstock. I'm proud I tried to help him. I'm going to go on trying to help him. We're not going to quit because you can outwit a simpleton like Jacob Woolman."

"I'm not going to quit either. I'm not going to quit loving you."

That had always worked in the past. Angela's anger had invariably evaporated into tears. But tonight the words thudded against the wall behind her like wet wads of paper. She barely noticed them. Alarm shivered Cliff's nerves. Was another woman going to turn on him?

"I'm serious!" she said. "I'm beginning to think—"

Her face went from rage to terror in a blink. "Oh my God!" she screamed as the first labor pain struck.

"Call the doctor!" Cliff roared to the rockers in the living room. "Get my car!" he shouted to Lenin Jr.

The baby arrived three hours later. It was a boy, making

Cliff wonder if his luck was turning. Within the hour he was dancing him around the room in his arms, crooning to him while Lenin Jr. watched from the doorway, his smile not quite so smarmy. Angela watched too, barely smiling.

"Isn't this worth it?" Cliff said. "Even worth putting up with me? What are we going to name him?"

"*Not* Charlie. I don't want him to know anything about him. How he died, why we—"

"I didn't expect Charlie. How about something nice and neutral like Frank?"

"After Frank Buchanan, the designer of the BX?" Lenin Jr. said. "I hope not."

Cliff stifled an impulse to kick him in the stomach. "Honey, I've got to get back to New York. Do you understand?"

Angela said she understood but she seemed to be looking at Lenin Jr. when she said it. In New York, the Saudi sheik turned out to be an Iranian with an unpronounceable name who wanted ten million up front to "reassure his contacts." Cliff told him to get lost and headed for Washington, where a lot of things were happening that dropped Angela and their nameless child to the bottom of his list of worries. The 1976 presidential campaign was gathering steam and it was time to collect endorsements from the candidates on the BX bomber. Gerald Ford was no problem. The Republicans had revived the plane and it had virtually become part of their platform.

The Democrats were another matter. Remnants of George McGovern's routed peace-now unilateral disarmers were all over the place, pretending that 1972 never happened and the war in Vietnam was Nixon's fault. The Democratic frontrunner, Jimmy Carter, was an Annapolis man with no built-in fondness for the Air Force. On the contrary, he had undoubtedly heard endless diatribes at the Naval Academy about how the blue suiters had tried to take the Navy's planes away from them.

Nevertheless, after immense wheedling and all-out pressure from key members of the House and Senate Armed Services Committees, Carter endorsed the BX before he got the nomination. That temporarily stifled rumblings from the Creature, Proxmire, and their ilk who were hungry for another attack on the plane.

Cliff called Angela every night. He begged her to bring the baby to Washington. She refused. Her stitches were agony as she had predicted and the baby screamed all night, every night. After the Republican convention, there was a political hiatus and Cliff flew to California determined to settle a few things. He had decided to insist on marrying Angela to give his son a father. He was not going to put up with any more advice from Irv or Arnie or Sid or Lenin Jr. about anything.

He arrived to find the Holmby Hills house swarming with photographers. *People* magazine was doing a story on Angela's defiance of conventional morals. She was posing with the love child in her arms, looking more desirable than Cliff had ever seen her.

"What the hell are you doing here?" hissed a voice in Cliff's ear.

It was Lenin Jr. and he was not wearing his smarmy smile.

"Did I hear you right?" Cliff said.

"The last thing she wants is your over-age face in this story," he said in the same stage whisper. "Get out. Come back in two hours."

Cliff drove to the office and conferred with Frank Buchanan on some ECPs (engineering change proposals) for a new run of the Colossus. Adrian had persuaded the Air Force to buy another fifty-four copies of the monster. Cliff had lunch with Dick Stone and predicted Carter would win the election and immediately order up the BX, solving all their financial problems with an influx of ten billion dollars.

"I don't like Carter's looks," Dick said. "That shit-eating smile reminds me of the Creature."

"It's as good as in the barn," Cliff insisted. "Incidentally, I'm going to marry Angela. Do you think it will upset Adrian?"

"Not any more than you would if you married Jane Fonda."

"Angela's not political in that obvious way," Cliff said.

"The hell she isn't," Dick said.

Back at the office, Cliff, never inclined to temporizing, put through a call to Adrian and asked him bluntly if he was opposed to him marrying Angela Perry. "I wouldn't dream of objecting personally. But I shudder to think of the board's reaction," Adrian said.

The board of directors was a bunch of retired aerospace executives who never had a thought Adrian did not put in their heads. Adrian was much too smooth to let Cliff go to them and decry his interference in his private life.

On Cliff's telephone, the red lights and the green lights began blinking simultaneously. His secretary was pressing all the buttons. What the hell was happening? He got rid of Adrian. A second later the door swung open and he found himself face-to-face with Angela, Irv the producer, Arnie the publicity man, Sid the agent—and Lenin Jr. "What's this?" he said.

"This," Angela said, sweeping past him, "is the conference we were supposed to have an hour ago at my place. Didn't Lee (Lenin Jr.'s real name) tell you to come back in two hours?"

"I've got other things to do," Cliff said.

"Maybe this is a better place to talk," Angela said.

Cliff knew exactly what she meant. He could not tell from their expressions whether Irv or Arnie or Sid knew. But the sneer on Lenin Jr.'s face suggested he knew what Cliff and Angela had done in this office to launch their romance.

"I flew out here to talk to you—alone," Cliff said. He asked Sid and Arnie and Irv if they would like a tour of the plant. "It might give you some ideas for special effects," he said. He suggested Lenin Jr. go with them and pretend he was visiting Disneyland.

"They're here because I asked them to be here," Angela said. She positioned herself by the window, looking spectacular in a cream-colored blouse and long blue gaucho skirt. "I agree with you that our son needs a father. I'm prepared to marry you. I think, in spite of many profound disagreements, we could be reasonably happy. But I have to consider

my career, my public image, the expectations I've raised
among millions of moviegoers."

It's a script, Cliff thought. She's reciting lines.

"This is especially true in the light of Buchanan's recent
defiance of popular protests against your new nuclear
bomber. You'd have to give everyone in the movie colony
very convincing evidence that you've changed your mind
about this and other weapon systems that strike at the hopes
and yearnings of millions of Americans still living in poverty. Arnie here has prepared a statement which I'd like you
to make at our wedding."

Arnie, who was about five-feet-nothing, with a completely
bald head that rumor had it he shaved daily, fished a piece
of paper out of his briefcase and handed it to Cliff with a
somewhat nervous grin.

Irv the producer, who was about six-feet-two and vaguely
resembled a whooping crane, cleared his throat and said:
"There's nothing personal in this, Cliff, please understand
that."

Sid the agent, who had the eyes of a starving piranha in
a face that was mostly suet, reiterated this sentiment.

The statement began with Cliff's apology for having devoted twenty-five years of his life to serving the military
industrial complex. It confessed to the American people that
Buchanan had devoured millions of dollars to build planes
that the country did not need, planes that did nothing but kill
people. It specifically repudiated the BX bomber as a "monstrosity" that would only increase the probability of a nuclear
war. It ended with a glowing tribute to the way Angela had
helped him to confess these atrocious sins and led him to the
"altar of love and peace."

Cliff read the whole thing twice. "Arnie," he said, walking
toward the tiny publicity man. "This is wonderful stuff. It's
good enough to eat."

Arnie responded with a vaguely alarmed smile. He rubbed
his shiny pink head, perhaps hoping for luck as Cliff's six-
foot-four frame loomed over him.

"That's exactly what you're going to do. Eat it." Cliff
grabbed Arnie by the shirt and jammed the sheet of paper

into his mouth, pinched his nose and said: "Chew."

Arnie started turning blue. "You're killing him!" Angela screamed.

"Down on the floor—everyone!" Lenin Jr. yelled.

He fell to the rug and curled into a ball. Angela imitated him. Irv and Sid followed, with considerably more difficulty. Sid weighed about three hundred pounds and elongated Irv found folding up difficult.

"You are now confronted with a sit-in to protest the BX bomber!" Lenin Jr. shouted. "We have press releases prepared and our chauffeur is waiting for a prearranged signal to distribute them to TV and newspapers."

Arnie was chewing frantically but was still turning blue. Cliff let go of his nose and he spluttered pieces of the statement all over the rug. Cliff grabbed him by his collar and the seat of his pants and threw him out of the office headfirst. He did the same thing with Irv, Sid, and Lenin Jr.

Cliff slammed the door and stood with his back to it. "Get up," he said to Angela.

"Lee predicted you'd be violent," Angela said. She was starring in her own protest movie, loving every minute of it.

Cliff dragged her to her feet and pressed her against the window. "You can do this here? You can do this to me here?" he said.

"I'm trying to stop you from doing something worse to me. Something you've been trying to do since we started. Ruin my career. Reduce me to your obedient servant."

Outside an Aurora came whining down in its final glide. Angela was like that plane, an expensive fantasy that proved once more he was a man among men. But Cliff was not going to let Angela humiliate him. His luck might be running all wrong but he was still the pilot who had brought the *Rainbow Express* back from Schweinfurt. He had ridden the Starduster out to the Sierra Wave.

"Admit you still love me," Cliff said, standing over her.

"I don't. I've stopped," she said.

"Bullshit. I told you I'd never stop loving you and I never will. Can you turn your back on that? Can you trade that for the left-wing rubbish you just spouted?"

"It isn't rubbish. It gives my life meaning. You can't give it meaning!"

"I can give it the only meaning that matters!" he shouted.

Meaning. Cliff stepped back, stunned by the impact of those words on himself. They rebounded from the sun-filled glass like twenty-millimeter shells exploding against his body with the memory of so many other meanings that mattered. Suddenly he was talking to Sarah. He was remembering the year before and the year after Charlie was born. What was he doing, trying to make this woman part of that kind of meaning?

"At least—I thought I could—until you came here and ruined it," Cliff said.

Flabby fists pounded on the office door. "Angela! Are you all right?" Lenin Jr. cried.

Cliff yanked the door open and yelled "Boo!" Irv, Arnie, and Sid practically jumped out of their double knits. "She's all yours, boys," he said.

Angela stood there, trying to figure out how to rescue the scene. None of her four directors had a clue. She started to sob. That was definitely not in the script. She was admitting Cliff was right. She had ruined the reckless mixture of defiance and communion they had created in this unlikely place.

For a moment Cliff wanted to take her in his arms and tell her he was sorry too. But someone or something inside him whispered *no*. A hard, cold, bitter *no*. Without saying a word, he watched the entourage escort their meal ticket to the elevator.

Some people think it was Cliff Morris's finest hour in the plane business. Would he have done it, would he have clung to that resolute no, if he had known what a mess it was going to make of the technicolor movie of his life? Some people— the handful who know the whole story of Cliff's life—say yes. More worldly-wise types point out that Cliff's movie was already way over budget and desperately in need of some sort of resolution—even if it turned out to be one he loathed.

AMORALITY PLAY

Beyond the porch of Adrian Van Ness's Virginia mansion, autumn colors glittered in the brilliant sunshine. In the distance, Jefferson's Monticello shimmered on its hilltop, a symbol of classic purity and purpose. Dick Stone sat beside Adrian in this quintessential American setting, discussing how to rescue the Buchanan Corporation from imminent extinction.

Cliff Morris's finest hour in the plane business was about to become everyone's worst nightmare. His beloved, Angela, and her left-wing lover, Lenin Jr., had revenged themselves by sending Buchanan's inveterate enemy in the Senate, the Creature from the cornfields of Iowa, a succinct summary of Cliff's boasts about bribing politicians around the world to sell Buchanan's planes. The Creature was trying to line up his fellow solons to hold hearings on this suddenly nefarious practice.

The Creature had friends inside Carter's White House who were backing him for reasons of their own. Washington was aswirl with rumors that the president was about to renege on his campaign promise and cancel the BX bomber. The hearings would smear Buchanan with enough mud to make a counterattack by their backers in Congress impossible.

Carter was turning into the unreliable president Dick had predicted the first time he saw him. His administration was an unstable congeries of ex–sixties activists and moderate Democrats like Carter himself, incapable of dealing with the pressure tactics of the left. The liberals were demanding a pound of flesh from the military industrial complex and the BX bomber was the most tempting slice.

The Van Ness housekeeper emerged to report that Cliff

was on the telephone. "Put him on," Adrian said. He gestured to Dick to pick up another extension.

" 'Lo, Adrian? Lissen. News isn't good on the Aurora. Only thing to do is end production run. Can't sell another fuckin' copy."

Dick had already told Adrian their wide-body jet was on its way to becoming the white whale of the business. "When are you going to stop drinking?" Adrian said.

"Hey—jus' had a couple for lunch."

"It sounds like a couple of dozen."

"Yeah, yeah. Lissen. I'll be in California for next few days."

"The action is in Washington, Cliff. That's why Dick Stone is here. Where the hell have you been? Mike Shannon has spent the last two days calling you all over the world."

"Adrian—man has a right to a personal life."

"Pussy," Adrian said. "That's all she is, Cliff. You can get the same thing in your own office. There's no reason to get drunk over her."

"Adrian I loved the goddamn woman. She's got my kid!"

Adrian hung up and stared coldly at Dick Stone. "We've got to do something about him—fast."

Dick Stone nodded mournfully. For a year now, Cliff Morris had spent half his time trying to revive his affair with Angela and the other half vainly trying to sell the Aurora while red ink gushed through the Buchanan Corporation.

For months Dick had been conferring with Adrian by telephone about how to service Buchanan's terrifying debts, which were now close to a billion dollars. He was growing more and more weary of shouldering the burden. The loss of the BX could easily shove them into bankruptcy. As the corporation's money man, he saw that as a personal defeat. He was not sure how well he could handle it. Without Cassie and his children, he was vulnerable to crushing bouts of depression.

Dick had come east expecting an aging Adrian Van Ness to let him suggest a drastic answer to their problems—perhaps selling the missile division or some other part of the company to raise cash. Instead, he had found Adrian full of determination to rely on the same combination of guile and grease that had kept them aloft so far. He seemed to be thriving on Washington's rampant intrigue and devious power plays. He had no intention of letting Buchanan get shoved out of any part of what he liked to call the great game.

"Are they canceling the whole BX program?" Dick said.

"That remains to be seen. We might be able to salvage something," Adrian said. "Much will depend on whether we can survive these hearings. Do you have our Geneva, Tokyo, and Casablanca files up to date?"

These were the cities through which overseas bribes were funneled. Dick nodded, not trying to conceal his distaste. "Dick, Dick," Adrian said. "The persistence of your Jewish conscience is the only thing about you that distresses me."

Adrian was shocked by the figures Dick spread before him. "My God," he said. "Cliff Morris is a bigger spender than I thought."

In Japan, Cliff had paid five million dollars a plane to sell the Aurora. Prices had been slightly lower in the Mideast and Europe but Africa and South America were worse—no less than seven million dollars per plane in some countries. It came to an appalling $190 million dollars in the last three years for the Aurora program alone. Cliff had been equally reckless in pushing the business jet that Adrian had christened the Argusair. The supersalesman turned CEO had paid roughly twenty million dollars to peddle 200 of them.

"How much are we likely to lose on the Aurora?"

"Two hundred million," Dick said.

"Mea culpa, mea culpa," Adrian said, scanning the figures.

Amanda Van Ness came out on the porch wearing a high-necked black silk dress and pearls. She looked ten, perhaps twenty years younger than Adrian. Everyone marveled at her smooth skin, her gleaming russet hair.

"The guests are arriving," Amanda said. "You aren't even dressed. How are you, Mr. Stone?"

"Fine. How are you, Mrs. Van Ness?"

"As well as can be expected in exile. What was the temperature in California when you left?"

"Eighty-one."

"Now you know why I hate my husband," Amanda said.

Not knowing what else to do, Dick pretended to be amused. Adrian's smile was strained.

"Have you seen Frank Buchanan lately?" Amanda asked.

"I speak to him on the phone every few days," Dick said.

"Give him my love," Amanda said.

Frank had retreated to a mountain overlooking the Mojave Desert in search of wisdom, leaving Sam Hardy as Buchanan's chief designer. But there was so much knowledge in Frank's ancient head, Dick was constantly begging him for advice in their continuing struggle to perfect the BX.

Adrian's smile vanished with the mention of Frank Buchanan's name. The word *love* made him twitch as if his wife had just struck him with a dart. He shook a pill from a dark brown plastic bottle and gulped it. Dick suddenly recalled Kirk Willoughby muttering about Adrian's heart.

Dick retreated upstairs, put on a fresh suit and joined Adrian as he greeted a swirl of Pentagon undersecretaries and congressmen and senators. Vietnamese servants disposed of their luggage. The VIPs had cocktails on the lawn under ancient oaks, supposedly planted in Jefferson's era. Most of the guests were moderate Democrats like Buchanan's old friend and supporter, the senior senator from Connecticut. Adrian did not waste his time or money on the Creature and his pals. The moderates fretted over the way the Russians were extending their influence in Africa and the Mideast. Adrian suggested the BX and another production run of the Colossus might give the United States the muscle to stop them.

Adrian concentrated on one of Carter's Georgians who was part of the White House inner circle. He plied him with several glasses of twenty-year-old bourbon and then asked, with an air of weary casualness: "Has the president made up his mind on the BX?"

"I'm afraid so," was the drawled reply. "He walked the floor for three nights and finally decided it was the one major weapons system we could cut without endangerin' our strategic posture."

"In a way I'm relieved," Adrian said. "No one likes to

hang by the thumbs indefinitely. We've got other things on
our plate we can get to now."

A gong summoned them to dinner. Adrian fell in step
beside Dick. "Isn't that fellow from *Jawgia* a wonder?" he
murmured. "A year ago he never thought of anything more
strategic than how to write a press release. Now he's picked
up the jargon that spells life and death for the country—and
thinks he understands it."

Adrian produced one of his more enigmatic smiles. "I'm
glad he came, for your sake. One of the purposes of this
soiree is to display the pinheads with whom we're doomed
to deal."

In the paneled dining room, Adrian began the meal by
introducing the entire Vietnamese weekend staff to the
guests. Each told what he had done in his former life. One
had been a cabinet minister with an economics degree from
the Sorbonne, another was a surgeon who had directed Saigon's main hospital, a third had been a professor of history.

The professor was writing a book on the war. "He thinks
if we had the BX in time South Vietnam might be independent today," Adrian said.

The Carter aide squirmed. So did most of the other Democrats. At the end of the evening they conferred with the
senator from Connecticut about the progress of the Creature's
hearings. They learned he had persuaded Frank Church, a
fellow superliberal, to investigate Buchanan with his subcommittee on multinational corporations.

"What if I gave you an unsigned memorandum, telling in
considerable detail how all the other aircraft companies have
been committing the same overseas sins for a long time?"
Adrian asked. "You could slip it to the Creature to prove
your heart is in the right place on this issue."

"What the hell would that accomplish?" the senator said.
He was a little slow when it came to Machiavellian tactics.

Dick saw instantly what Adrian had in mind. The Creature
would find the added targets irresistible. Spreading the blame
would take a lot of the heat off Buchanan. But Dick could
not figure out why Adrian regarded the hearings with such
equanimity from a personal point of view. He had been in-

volved in these overseas payments for two decades.

The rest of the weekend slid by. There was a private visit to Monticello, golf for those who played it, horseback riding for others, led by Amanda, who still rode like a teenager, bounding over ditches and fences. Adrian and Dick Stone followed at a more sedate pace. Dick was not at home on a horse and Adrian was not much better.

"Still enduring divorce?" Adrian said.

"More or less."

"You could be worse off. Try living with a woman who hates you."

"Why does she?" Dick said, surprised by Adrian's confessional impulse.

"Everyone pays a price for trying to reach beyond the rainbow," Adrian said. "Amanda's mine." He pointed toward Monticello. "Read a biography of him sometime. You'll see how many prices he paid."

They ambled on through the autumn sunshine. "Once I told Frank Buchanan it was the pots of gold I was reaching for. Now I know it's something far less tangible. I think we're all pursuing an image of ourselves, a personal apotheosis."

"What was—is—yours?" Dick asked.

"To be a man of substance." Adrian smiled wryly. "So substantial I'd be forever beyond the reach of ruin. What better place to do that than the aircraft business? It says wonders for my judgment, don't you think?"

"You could have done worse. Trying to beat the horses. Or the tables in Las Vegas."

Adrian chuckled. He was enjoying himself. Dick had seldom seen him so genial. "I haven't figured out the gold beyond your rainbow, Dick. What is it?"

"Maybe I haven't either," Dick said warily.

"You should. It's the final step to maturity."

For an uneasy moment Dick felt he had failed a question in an examination where a perfect score was expected.

As soon as their guests departed, Adrian announced they were flying to California. "We've got to put Cliff back together for those hearings," he said. "Find out where Angela is living these days."

That was no challenge for their security men. All they had to do was read the gossip columns about the spectacular new house Angela had built in the Malibu colony. Leaving Amanda in Virginia with the housekeeper, Adrian and Dick flew to LAX and drove up the coast to Malibu. Dick telephoned Angela from a nearby restaurant and asked if they could see her.

Angela met them in white slacks, blue boating jacket, a white beret. With her was Lenin Jr. in his inevitable blue jeans. "I'll get right to the point," Adrian said. "How much will it take to persuade you to kick Cliff out once and for all?"

Angela laughed. "What an outrageous idea," she said. But Dick could see it appealed to her. She gave her revolutionary friend a conspiratorial smile.

"Two million dollars," he said. "Off the books, of course."

"Done," Adrian said. "Give them a check, Dick."

Dick wrote a check on Buchanan's Swiss account and handed it to Angela. "Don't deposit it anyplace but in Switzerland," Adrian said.

They drove to Buchanan's headquarters. "Be sure to include in the explanation for that check something about services rendered," Adrian said.

This time Adrian was much too far ahead of Dick. "I don't get it," he said.

"We're buying silence," Adrian said. "They might have done us a lot of damage at the Creature's hearings. Now Cliff can go down with dignity."

Security Chief Hanrahan informed them Cliff was at the Beverly Wilshire. They drove to the grand old lady of Los Angeles hotels and found the chief executive officer in his underwear, halfway through a bottle of Inverness. A two-day stubble sprouted on his chin.

"What the hell do you want?" Cliff growled.

"Is that what I get for flying three thousand miles to see you?" Adrian said.

"For what? To fire me? Go ahead. I don't give a god-damn."

"What happened? Did Angela throw you out once and for all?"

"Yeah. Yesterday."

Adrian pretended to be amused. "She is clever."

"Clever?"

"She just accepted my offer of two million dollars to throw you out—after she'd done it."

"You're a fucking liar!" Cliff roared.

Dick showed him the carbon of the check he had just written. "I'll get it back," Cliff said, jamming his feet into his pants.

"Sit down," Adrian said, shoving Cliff backward onto the bed. "I'm seventy-eight years old. I had hoped before I died I'd see this company sound, secure, ready to fly into the next century. Instead I've got a self-pitying pussy-chasing play-boy in charge and a conscience-stricken ex-student of the Torah as second in command. Do you think I might be en-titled to feel just a little sorry for myself?"

"Most people—including me—will say you're getting pretty much what you deserve," Cliff said.

"I know that," Adrian said. "That's why I just spent two million dollars to prove something to you—instead of plead-ing for sympathy."

"What else is happening?" Cliff said. He was not stupid. He knew Adrian always had another motive.

"Carter's canceling the BX the day after tomorrow. There may be hearings. I want you sober for them. I want you to cut out the booze and Angela absolutely and totally. Will you promise me abstinence on both counts?"

Dick held up the carbon of the check again. He still did not completely understand the game Adrian was playing. But he wanted to straighten Cliff out for personal as well as cor-porate reasons. They were still friends.

Back in Adrian's car, Dick got another surprise. "I want you to come out to the desert with me and tell the workforce the BX is canceled."

"Isn't that Cliff's job?"

"I want them to hear it from you."

"Why?" Dick said.

"Because such matters may soon become part of your job."

What was Adrian saying? Dick Stone was the next Buchanan president? Then why sober up Cliff? Why not just fire him and let Angela and Sarah worry about the consequences?

The next day, Adrian and Dick flew to the Mojave. The sweep of the desert beyond the factory brought back a surge of memories. The White Lightning, the Talus, the Scorpion, the Warrior. Billy McCall swaggering from the cockpit, Cassie waiting in the bedroom at the Villa Hermosa. Amalie whispering her mocking conundrums. So many betrayals, so many failures, so much heartbreak.

Yet the planes flew. Was that the only thing that mattered? The Colossus filled the sky with thunder. The Aurora was a majestic flow of cursives and thrust in a thousand takeoffs. The new fighter, the SkyDemon, defied gravity, flying straight up as fast as it flew horizontally, even if the goddamn Air Force had rejected it.

Dick rode with Adrian to the fourth floor balcony of the huge plant, the length of four football fields and the width of two. A dozen fuselages of the BX rested on jigs while workers swarmed around them, riveting, wiring, welding. The usual big American flag dangled from the balcony.

"Ladies and gentlemen," Dick said over the public address system. "Could I have your attention? You know me, Dick Stone. You know how proud I am of the work you've done on this plane and other planes. But in this business we've learned a long time ago that hard work, dedication, isn't always appreciated. We just got some bad news from Washington. Tomorrow President Carter is canceling the BX. That means a lot of you may lose your jobs. I thought you ought to know that as soon as possible. But I also want you to know I'm going to do everything I can to keep this plane alive. We're going to try everything to keep you with us. That's a promise!"

The words, especially the promise, were spontaneous. Adrian Van Ness had simply ordered Dick to deliver the news of the cancelation. How he did it was up to him. The sight of that gigantic flag, the unfinished planes on the jigs, had demolished the rational side of Dick's nature—and banished the depression that wrapped his emotions in a leaden overcoat most of the time.

Dick went down on the plant floor to deal with angry questions and furious threats. Some people wanted to trash the BX skeletons on the spot. Others offered to work on half pay to finish them. Most were resigned but very bitter. They had been hired and fired and rehired by Buchanan and other companies too often.

When Dick returned to the plant manager's office where Adrian was waiting for him, he was bathed in sweat. But he had learned something about himself. "We're going to keep that goddamn plane alive, somehow," he said.

"I was hoping I'd hear that," Adrian said.

For the next six months Dick struggled to make good on that vow. He picked up subcontracting programs from Boeing and General Dynamics and Tony Sirocca scraped together thirty million dollars from the Air Force's Independent Research and Development Fund to do some work on a Mach 3 stealth fighter. He grew so absorbed in the struggle, he almost forgot about the Creature and his friends in Washington.

But Adrian, deep in his end of the great game, had not forgotten this threat to their existence. One afternoon in April of 1978, he jangled Dick's nerves with an updated version of Paul Revere's cry. "To arms, to arms, the dimwits are coming."

"Dimwits?" Dick said.

"Congressmen," Adrian said. "The hearings are about to begin."

A few days later Church subcommittee staffers arrived with subpoenas for Buchanan's overseas records. Dick naturally warned Cliff. He brushed it off with a shrug. "It's not against the law. How come it's any of their business in the first place?"

"If they feel like it, they can make anything their business," Dick said. "If I were you I'd start talking to our lawyers."

The lawyers did not have much to offer. Since no one was being accused of a crime, they could not advise Cliff or Adrian to take the fifth amendment. Cliff was reassured to learn Adrian was going to be the first witness.

"I'll just follow his lead," Cliff said.

Dick flew to Washington with Cliff a month later. The hearings were held in one of the Senate's cavernous paneled chambers, with batteries of microphones on the witness table and TV cameras whirring on the sidelines. Adrian sat down in the central chair at the table opposite the senators and they went to work.

"Mr. Van Ness," Senator Church said in his best Eagle Scout manner. "Would you tell us about Buchanan's overseas payments?"

"We never made any while I was chief executive officer," Adrian said. "If we've made any in recent years, they've been without my knowledge."

"You have had no connection with the company since you retired as president?" the Creature sneered.

"Only as a stockholder—and board member."

"Aren't you chairman of the board?" Senator Church asked.

"At the moment, yes. But the title gives me no executive authority. I've been living in Virginia since I retired. Which would make it rather difficult to run a billion dollar corporation in California, even if I wanted to."

"Your innocence is much too studied for my taste, Mr. Van Ness," growled the Creature, who had, if possible, grown uglier with age.

"That is your problem, Senator, not mine," Adrian said. "I am proud to say that except for a few parking tickets, I have never been convicted—or even investigated—for any crime. My reputation—and the reputation of the Buchanan Corporation as far as I know it—is spotless."

"We have evidence to the contrary before this committee!" the Creature roared. "Millions of dollars in what you call overseas payments were nothing but bribes. Bribes to foreigners!"

"I know nothing about it," Adrian said.

There was a lot more sparring, in which Adrian steadfastly denied everything. Mockingly, he wondered if the Creature knew that it was not a crime for an American businessman to persuade foreigners to buy his products by sweetening the deal with some extra dollars. He recounted memories of his days as a merchant banker in London, when douceurs were regularly used to guarantee or enhance overseas investments. He discussed the foreign policy of the Roman empire, which for three hundred years included the fine art of buying friendship with hostile tribes on its borders.

Again and again, when it came to specific details he referred the senators to the next witness, Buchanan's current president, Clifford Morris. The hearings adjourned for lunch with the solons in an exasperated mood.

Adrian, Cliff, Dick Stone, and Mike Shannon taxied to the exclusive Cosmos Club, which Adrian had joined when he came to Washington. He had reserved a private dining room so they could confer without eavesdroppers.

The waiter had barely poured their drinks and departed when Cliff snarled: "Do you think you can get away with this act?"

"I hope so," Adrian said.

"Don't we have records of how you and the Prince operated in the fifties and sixties?"

"The IRS only requires you to keep records for three years," Adrian said. "When Dick computerized everything in 1976, all that material was obliterated."

"Is that true?" Cliff asked Dick.

Dick nodded. "Why wasn't I told?" Cliff roared.

"You've never had the slightest interest in anything that mundane," Dick said.

"I've still got news for you, Adrian. I'm not going to be anyone's fall guy," Cliff said. "If I go, you're going with me."

"I don't think you mean that, Cliff," Adrian said. "I think you care more about this company—even about me—than that threat implies. If you reveal we've been doing these naughty things for decades, it would destroy our image. Newspapers would print vicious cartoons of planes soaring over rainbows with bags of money in them. No bank in the world would loan us a nickel. We'd be out of business."

"Why the hell should I let you put me out of business?" Cliff raged.

"I'm not at all sure that's going to happen," Adrian said. "For one thing, I've supplied the committee with a lot of information that makes it clear we're not alone in making off-the-books overseas payments. If there's one executive who can survive this scandal, it's you. Who else can match your war record? Forty-nine missions over Germany. I'm sure our board of directors will back you without reservations."

Cliff gulped his drink, unconvinced. "It's a gamble, I admit," Adrian said. "But I don't see any other sensible way to deal with it. Do you really want to put the whole company at risk for the sake of petty revenge? Especially when your big mouth got us into this mess?"

He told Cliff where the Creature had obtained the original evidence to start the investigation. Cliff cursed and poured himself another drink.

"There's one more thing I might mention," Adrian continued. "Another more personal reason why you might want to protect me. All these years, I've protected you from a scandal that could have destroyed you any time it was leaked to the press."

"What the fuck are you talking about?" Cliff said.

"During World War II I got a call from a general I did several favors for—Newton Slade. He told me the Red Cross in Geneva had reported a complaint from the German government about a B-17 with a rainbow on its nose that faked a midair surrender over Schweinfurt, then shot down the German pilots who were escorting it to a nearby airfield."

There was total silence in the dining room for a full minute. "General Slade quashed the matter as a personal favor for me," Adrian said. "He sent me the papers. I've saved them all these years. I had a feeling they might be useful someday."

Adrian smiled at Dick Stone and Mike Shannon. "A little example of forethought."

Loathing, that was the only emotion Dick felt for Adrian Van Ness, sitting opposite him in that elegant dining room with the memories of Schweinfurt and other raids clotting the air until it was almost impossible to breathe. Dick wanted to snarl a curse in Adrian's face, urge Cliff to tell the whole truth and damn the consequences. But everything Adrian had said about the consequences of the truth was true. They would be out of business. His vow to those workers in Palmdale would be aborted. But the worst pain would be inflicted on Sarah Chapman Morris. Why did he know that? Why did he still remember the adulation in her blue eyes that day beside the smoking ruin of the *Rainbow Express*?

Dick said nothing. He let Cliff think he agreed with Adrian Van Ness. In a certain sickening sense he did agree with him. Cliff accepted his silence as a final verdict. He poured himself a full water glass of scotch.

"Okay," he said. "I'll play your lousy game."

The hearings resumed that afternoon with Cliff in the witness chair. The Creature began with a right cross. "Mr. Morris," he said. "According to our records, you paid two hundred and twenty million dollars in bribes to interested parties overseas in the past three years, all carried on your books as extraordinary expenses. Could you explain what that term means?"

"Senator," Cliff said. "I resent you calling those payments bribes. I see them under a variety of headings—gifts, payments for special services, agents' fees."

The senators began going through the transactions, one by one, asking Cliff wryly, when he denied the bribe, exactly what he thought the word's *special services* or *agent* meant. The Japanese example was particularly ripe. He had paid millions to a front man for the ruling party, a minor right-wing political zealot, who had a record of virulent anti-Americanism—the last man that an American company would hire as an agent.

The solons wanted to know all about the special services for which Cliff had paid millions in the Mideast. "Were they the world's most expensive hoochy-koochy dancers?" one senator asked.

Cliff was soon begging for mercy. "I'm not an authority on linguistics," he pleaded.

"But you're a walking encyclopedia on how to bribe people," the Creature chortled. "You ought to write a book on it."

The audience roared with glee. Another senator asked Cliff about the various code words used to conceal payments. The word for consultant was *haywire*. "Why did you choose that word?" the Creature asked.

"We let the computer pick it out at random," Cliff said.

"I'm glad to hear at least your computers have a conscience," another senator said. He outscored the Creature on the laugh meter with that one.

Cliff laboriously tried to explain that Buchanan only did what other plane makers, oil companies, ITT, did overseas. He blamed it all on the foreigners who expected the payments. A senator from Delaware asked him if he would condone stealing the designs of a competitor's plane because an opponent did it.

"That's against the law of the United States," Cliff said. "As I've tried to tell you, there is no law prohibiting overseas payments—"

"Do you or don't you steal competitors' designs?" the Creature howled.

"No, sir," Cliff said, as the galleries exploded with laughter again.

Cliff soon became a target of opportunity. "You've cheated people who trust you!" another senator thundered. "It reminds me of the crook who was asked why he did such a thing and he replied: who else can you cheat?"

Boffo. The audience laughed a full five minutes.

So it went for three gruesome days, while Mike Shannon and Dick Stone occasionally bowed their heads to avoid contemplating the butchery. Each night Cliff retreated to his hotel room and got drunk, rejecting their attempts to talk to him.

Frank Buchanan called Dick to offer his sympathy and support for Cliff. "Can't you stop it?" he said. "Why are you letting Adrian make him the fall guy? If it keeps up I'll fly in and volunteer to tell the whole truth."

"Tell Frank it's for the good of the company," Adrian said, when Dick reported the call.

With complete indifference to the careers they were destroying, the senators began reading into the record Cliff's correspondence with prominent politicians in Holland, Japan, Germany, Italy. Adrian decided this was going too far and told Buchanan's Washington attorneys, one of whom was a former secretary of state, to extract an intervention from the State Department that brought Cliff's ordeal to an abrupt halt. No less a personage than the incumbent secretary of state wrote a letter to the attorney general stating that any further disclosure of names would have "grave consequences for the United States."

The infuriated senators turned on the other aircraft companies. They roasted Lockheed's executives over a slow fire. The treasurer of the company could not handle it and committed suicide rather than face the tormentors. As the other companies went on the coals, an embittered Cliff Morris flew back to California. Adrian invited Dick Stone to Charlottesville for the weekend. They sat on the porch in the twilight, gazing at Monticello in the distance.

"If all goes well, in about three months we'll persuade Cliff to resign," Adrian said. "He'll go quietly, I hope—and the purification rite will be complete. We can go to the banks here and in London and get the money we need to keep us going until Ronald Reagan is elected. He's given me his solemn promise that he'll build the BX."

Loathing was all Dick felt for Adrian. He could not disguise it. He did not even try. Adrian's face became florid, his eyes bulged with the intensity of the emotion that seemed to seize him from nowhere.

"You have to see the situation historically, Dick," he said. "My great-grandfather, Oakes Ames, was denounced by

Congress in 1869—denounced by the same people who took his bribes to build the Union Pacific Railroad—which had a lot to do with winning the Civil War by keeping the West in the Union. Our situation is virtually identical. The same hypocrites who took our campaign contributions and our hospitality are trying to wreck us for five minutes' worth of publicity, without so much as a passing thought for the planes we're building to defend the country."

It was the final performance of the student of history who had discovered Oakes Ames's fate on a night of anguish in London. But Dick Stone was too disgusted to understand, much less sympathize with Adrian Van Ness. Instead he heard it as one more betrayal of his shining expectations of the American world he had longed to join after World War II.

Dick realized Adrian had revealed more of himself to him than to anyone else in his life. Dick still refused to give him his approval. He did not care if it cost him the CEO's job. Adrian was unquestionably offering it to him. But Dick could not abrogate thirty years of friendship with Cliff, the memories of the *Rainbow Express*. He still sat in judgment on Adrian. He refused to forgive him for anything—selling out Frank and the Talus, destroying Billy McCall—and now, Cliff Morris.

"Cliff's not the greatest human being in the world but he deserves something better than this for a payoff. He evened things for that moment of panic over Schweinfurt with another twenty-four missions. I don't want the CEO's job on these terms, Adrian."

An almost hysterical trill crept into Adrian's voice. "Cliff'll be well paid in retirement. Isn't that better than letting him wind up in some flophouse in downtown Los Angeles?"

"What if it doesn't work?" Dick said. "What if Reagan—presuming he gets elected—double-crosses us like every other president since Kennedy?"

"He might. But it's still the best gamble in town."

They were betting the company again. Dick heard Buzz

McCall telling Adrian you had to be a man to do that. He felt the lure, the excitement of risk beating in his blood. But he resisted surrendering on Adrian's terms.

"I think we've got to offer the banks, the stockholders, something more than a presidential promise, Adrian," Dick said. "We've got to offer a vision—the plane of tomorrow. We're the ones who can build it. A hypersonic plane that can fly the Pacific in a couple of hours. That's the kind of plane company I want to run. If you make me CEO, that's what you're going to get."

"Vision?" Adrian said, shaking his head in bewilderment. "We're playing for time."

Dick ignored the pleading note in Adrian's voice. "I want seed money for the hypersonic plane as soon as possible. Our best bet is England. You've still got clout there. We can promise Rolls-Royce the engine contract as a quid pro quo."

"England," Adrian muttered. "I haven't been to England for a long time."

"Why not?" Dick said in the same brutal uncaring voice.

"Memories," Adrian said. "Memories I've never shared with anyone."

"You'll have to face them for a week or two," Dick said, utterly indifferent to what these memories might be.

"Could you come with me?" Adrian said. "I'll need a good numbers man."

Dick Stone ignored the plea to share the English memories. He was in control now. Adrian had lost all his leverage—moral, psychological, financial. "I'll give you the numbers on paper," Dick said. "I don't intend to let Cliff run the company without me around even for five minutes."

Loathing. Dick knew Adrian saw it on his face, heard it in his voice. He would have to live with it. He was living with Amanda's hatred. Dick was surprised when a plea for sympathy shredded Adrian's vaunted self-control.

"Why do I have to do all the dirty work?" he cried.

"I seem to recall you telling me it does a man no good to whine," Dick Stone said.

FALL OF A CONQUEROR

Exhausted from a week of nonstop partying and negotiating in London, Adrian Van Ness dozed in the comfortable seat of his Argusair business jet. Instead of dreaming of executive power and glory, he was back on Shakespeare's cliff at Dover, watching Bleriot fly the English channel. His mother and Goeffrey Tillotson were there, exclaiming in awe and admiration as the fragile plane clattered over their heads. Geoffrey Tillotson pointed at Dover Castle and began predicting that the plane would make forts and every other weapon of war obsolete.

He was interrupted in mid-sentence by a passionate kiss from Clarissa Ames Van Ness. She was announcing there was something more important than forts, armies, ships—and planes. They sank to the green grass, wrapped in each other's arms.

"Stop it!" Adrian cried. "Stop it or I'll jump!"

He teetered on the brink of the white chalk bluff. Below him tiny figures ran along the brown sand. Clarissa and Geoffrey paid no attention to him. They also ignored the stares and titters of the people around them.

"Stop *iiiiiiiit!*" Adrian cried and leaped into space, arms spread wide in a pathetic imitation of flight.

"Wake *up*."

A hand shook Adrian Van Ness's shoulder. The chairman of the board of the Buchanan Corporation confronted his preternaturally youthful wife. "You were having a bad dream," Amanda said. Her smile was pleased, even gloating.

The skin was still taut on Amanda's fine-boned high-cheeked face. Her auburn hair still retained its youthful color. No one could explain the phenomenon to Adrian. Dr. Kirk Willoughby wondered if it had something to do with reduced brain activity. "Maybe it's thinking too much that wears us out," Buchanan's medical director had said.

As usual Amanda was wearing a dress with a ruffled collar that concealed the scars she had inflicted on herself long ago. The collar combined with her heavy-lidded eyes, her sullen mouth, her slightly pointed chin, to justify the nickname Mike Shannon, the Buchanan Corporation's Washington manager, had given her: the Queen of Spades.

Adrian turned his head to escape his wife's nasty smile. Outside the small octagonal window beside his seat was a blue sky shot through with glaring light. The dulled roar of two Pratt & Whitney jet engines surrounded him. They were cruising at 547 miles an hour nine miles above the Atlantic Ocean. In front of them dozed two of the most powerful politicians in Washington. Adrian had taken them to London to support his plea for British cash to keep Buchanan airborne.

The stratosphere's blue dome arced upward in a slowly deepening hue until it became the velvety black of space. Adrian thought about the men Buchanan had sent up that arc in rocket planes and in jets, probing the boundaries of flight. In memory's glaring light, Billy McCall swaggered out to the needle-nosed rocket plane, White Lightning, his smile disguising his fear—and his rage. Billy had assumed this feat assured him mastery of the other vehicle on which he loved to soar—the American woman. But there he collided with unknowns—and unknown unknowns—he had never encountered in the sky.

Up here in the stratosphere, the upper air that pilots call light country, Adrian found it easy to contemplate the ironies of four and a half decades in the aircraft business. Irony seemed normal in the stratosphere. Below, in the troposphere, where humans lived their daily lives, detachment was not so simple.

Unfortunately, men and women had to live in the troposphere. Outside the Argusair's tilted windows, the stratosphere's temperature was 210 degrees below zero. Winds were tearing along the jet's wings and fuselage with the force of seven hurricanes. A man or woman could survive for only a few convulsive seconds in that icy oxygenless world. Inside the Argusair, thanks to the wizardry of late-twentieth-century technology, Adrian and Amanda and the two politicians sat in seventy-two-degree comfort and safety.

For a moment this physical security was unbearable to Adrian. What if he spun the aluminum wheel that locked the Argusair's pressurized cabin door and sent Amanda and the politicians and himself spewing into the stratosphere? The pilots, sealed in their cockpit, would survive to tell the story. Would Dick Stone—and one or two others—read about it with guilty eyes?

What nonsense.

The ironist at the center of Adrian's soul regained control of his vehicle. He smiled at his antagonistic wife. "I was dreaming we were back in California," he said. "On the porch of Casa Felicidad. You were kissing me."

"Why were you saying 'stop it'?" Amanda asked.

"Frank Buchanan was there, shaking his fist at me."

"You're lying, as usual," Amanda said.

Needles of pain shot through Adrian's chest. For another moment the ironist's hands trembled on the controls. In recent years Adrian found it more and more difficult to laugh at the unrelenting hatred underlying Amanda's gibes. Last year he had developed angina pectoris, a convulsive knotting of the heart muscle, not unusual in men his age. Adrian wondered if it was a reaction to Amanda's malevolence. Kirk Willoughby, not a believer in psychosomatic illness, dismissed the idea.

Adrian gulped two pills, nitrogen and some exotic new anticoagulant his heart specialist had prescribed as an alternative to surgery. Lighting a small black Havana cigar, against the doctor's orders, he checked to make sure the politicians were asleep and began dictating a letter to Dick Stone:

I saw the Chancellor of the Exchequer and half the bankers in London over the past seven days. At first none of them was inclined to lend us a cent in the aftermath of the bribery hearings. I told them we were about to purge ourselves by offering a public sacrifice for our sins. They instantly understood the charade—which they perform regularly for the electorate—and grew attentive. The senator and the congressman virtually guaranteed some kind of government loan to prevent our demise. With the chancellor, I put on my boldest face and told him if he wanted to get aboard a hypersonic plane, His Majesty's Government had better be prepared to commit a hundred million pounds a year to engine development at their sacred entity, Rolls-Royce. Let me state here my grave doubts about this terrifyingly risky improvisation you've added to my psychodrama. Nonetheless I hope we can raise a glass a year from now and say we're still glad we make planes for a living.

"Have you ever been truly glad about anything?" Amanda said.

The question returned Adrian to the troposphere at sea level, to the real world of gains and losses, fears and compulsions, love and hate. In his weary mind Amanda again became a being with mysterious powers. Angina gouged his chest. He gulped more pills.

Did he deserve this legacy of stifled rage and morbid bitterness? For the thousandth time Adrian pondered the choices he had made and said no. He regretted many things but he refused to wear sackcloth and ashes for the past. At seventy-nine, he resolutely turned his face to the future and insisted that the past was another country, another time, another life, in which he had done nothing that his household gods disapproved.

Turbulence. Adrian buckled his seat belt. They were descending from light country through gumbo-thick clouds above Washington, D.C. He plugged the dictating machine into the radio telephone on the cabin wall and pressed a button. The letter whizzed to a satellite launched with a Buchanan rocket and down to Buchanan's private communications system. In five minutes typists at Buchanan's headquarters in El Segundo, California, would be transcribing it for Dick Stone's eyes.

The Argusair shivered and shook as she encountered the

heavy lower air. In the seat in front of him, the senator from Connecticut awoke with a groan. He had gotten very drunk on their last night in London, after the final meeting with the Chancellor of the Exchequer. The exquisite Eurasian Adrian had imported from Singapore for his delectation had demanded double her usual fee.

Across the aisle from the senator, his counterpart on the House of Representatives Armed Services Committee, a lean, intense Texan who could hold his liquor and his women, laughed and said: "Don't you throw up on me, you son of a bitch."

Lately, the senator was drunk most of the time. Only two weeks ago, Adrian had visited him in his office at 9 A.M. and found him incoherent. The senator's wife had recently died and he was miserable without her. Adrian was still amazed by the unpredictable ways the goddess of fate threatened the survival of the Buchanan Corporation—and the United States of America.

Fortuna was the only deity forty years of making and selling planes had taught Adrian to worship. Fortuna and her tormented opposite, Prometheus, whose name meant forethought. From Prometheus had come the gift of fire that had enabled men and women to achieve dominion over the other creatures of the earth—and ultimately to soar above the world and look down on it with exalted or exultant or ironic eyes. In the Argusair's jet engines were raging flames, kindled, caged, controlled, and directed by man's transcendent mind.

Greek, he had become Greek, Adrian told himself, trying to twist his mind away from memories this visit to England had evoked. His British friends had dragged him to the Imperial War Museum, where they had put together a special exhibit to celebrate the fortieth anniversary of World War II. A good part of it was devoted to airpower, naturally. There was an entire room about the Nelson bomber and its accomplishments, with ample credit given to their American friends at Buchanan Aircraft. In one of the final photographs, Beryl Suydam stood beside the bomber she had flown to her doom. Her smile had turned Adrian's chest into an excruciating knot. He had gulped pills for the rest of the day.

From the Argusair's cockpit came blond, hazel-eyed Elizabeth Hardy, their copilot. "We'll be landing in about five minutes. How is everyone back here?"

"Fine," Adrian said.

Buchanan had gotten some good publicity (for a change) when they made Ms. Hardy (designer Sam Hardy's daughter) copilot of their number one business jet. But tonight, the sight of this beautiful young woman in her trim blue uniform stirred an enormous echoing regret in Adrian's soul. For a moment he felt hollow, a cave of winds through which meaningless words blew eternally.

Hardy returned to the cockpit. Adrian could hear the pilot, Jerry Quinn, talking to the air traffic controllers at National Airport, reporting altitude, airspeed, confirming their approach pattern. Visibility was low as usual in Washington, D.C. in December. The senator stirred restlessly. He was a nervous flier. Adrian remained calm. The Argusair had the best instrument landing system in the world, made by Buchanan's avionics division. It could land at midnight in a Heathrow or Gatwick fog—and find the center of the runway every time.

With no warning the plane rolled forty degrees to the left and dove straight for the ground. The senator emitted a belch of terror and the congressman, who had flown bombers over Italy during World War II, yelled "Jesus Christ!" Outside the window Adrian glimpsed the silver bulk of a commercial airliner hurtling past them in the murk.

Jerry Quinn pulled the Argusair out of its dive and gasped over the intercom: "That idiot should have been a thousand feet above us."

Amanda'a smile mocked forethought; it derided his plane's infallible instrument landing system, its computers that made it almost impossible to stall, its aerodynamic grace. Again angina pierced Adrian's chest. He gulped pills and the pain subsided.

The Argusair's landing gear came down with a reassuring whir. They were in their final approach, the engines shrill as the fire scream became more audible at this lower speed.

Thud. They were on the ground, the engines howling a final protest at their return to this alien element.

The senator and the congressman departed, thanking Adrian for their free ride across the Atlantic and the several thousand dollars' worth of hospitality the Buchanan Corporation had bestowed on them during their week in London. Adrian said he hoped to see them soon in Charlottesville.

Onto the plane bounded Mike Shannon, Buchanan's man in Washington. He kissed Amanda's hand and called her "Your Majesty"—unaware that there was a grisly irony in the title.

"Any *good* news?" Adrian said.

Shannon shook his head. "They're not going to let up on us. I think it's time to drop the guillotine on Cliff."

Shannon was in on the purification ritual. But he did not like it. He and Dick Stone did not like it—or Adrian Van Ness. They had made that very clear. Adrian was indifferent to Shannon's opinion. But Dick Stone's judgment on him was like a hair shirt. Why couldn't he see how necessity and history exculpated everything?

With a final mock obeisance to Amanda, the Irishman vanished into the dusk. In ten minutes the Argusair was over Charlottesville for another landing, this time without heroics. While Elizabeth Hardy taxied to the terminal, Jerry Quinn emerged from the cabin, apologizing again for the near-miss over Washington, vowing to file a report with the FAA. He was an angular Californian, so brimming with vitality he made Adrian flinch.

"This is one terrific plane," Quinn said. "She handles better than an F-16."

Just out of the Air Force, Jerry did not realize he was reminding his employer of a plane that was making one of Buchanan's rivals, General Dynamics, three billion dollars.

Quinn unloaded the Van Ness luggage and they found a porter who wheeled it ahead of them to Adrian's gray Bentley in the airport's long-term parking lot. The chairman of Rolls-Royce had given Adrian the car when he chose their engines for the Colossus. Adrian thought of what that monster had cost him. His ironist's hands trembled on the controls in his mind—and his physical hands clutched the icy wheel convulsively. Memory! It was pursuing him like a wolf pack tonight.

The engine purred at a flip of the ignition key. Amanda ostentatiously buckled herself into the seat beside Adrian. For several years she had been urging him to hire a chauffeur. She insisted he was getting too old to drive a high-powered car. Adrian ignored her, as usual. He did not like chauffeurs or butlers or any other kind of servant. They tended to learn too much about a man—knowledge that could turn out to be inconvenient in certain situations. A housekeeper was the only servant he permitted—and he replaced her frequently.

A mixture of sleet and snow began falling from the twilit sky. "It's below zero!" Amanda said, turning up the collar of her mink coat. Each day at breakfast she told Adrian the temperature in Los Angeles.

Amanda fretted about their latest housekeeper, Mrs. Welch, who was a tippler. Amanda was sure the refrigerator would be empty, they would have to drive back to Charlottesville for dinner. Adrian let her complain. Mrs. Welch was a dunce, but Adrian liked stupid housekeepers. They were unlikely to notice much.

Adrian swung up the drive of their estate past a line of bare ancient oaks. "Not a light," Amanda said, as they drove beneath the portico of the big red-brick mansion. "I wouldn't be surprised if she's passed out upstairs."

Adrian steered the Bentley into the garage on the left of the house and unloaded the bags. Amanda preceded him up the steps into the kitchen. "Oh, where is that switch," she said, as Adrian balanced two heavy suitcases on the top step.

Click. The fluorescent light illuminated the gleaming stainless-steel stove and oven, the walk-in refrigerator, the food processor, and other amenities Adrian had installed, mostly to mock Amanda's refusal to cook anything more complicated than an egg. He heaved a sigh and let the suitcases thud to the floor. Jet lag seemed to be draining life itself from his thick body. Seventy-nine-year-old men should not fly the Atlantic twice in a week.

"Mrs. Welch? Mrs. Welch?" Amanda called up the back-stairs. Her voice echoed through the silent house. Annoying. Adrian did not like Amanda to be right about anything. She gloated over small triumphs for days.

He lugged the suitcases upstairs and dropped Amanda's unceremoniously at the door of her bedroom. There were limits to his readiness to play servant. In his bedroom, he flung his bag on a luggage rack and strode into his study. There were no lights flashing on the eight-line telephone on his desk. Good. He did not want to do any thinking without a night's sleep.

Adrian poured himself an ounce of forty-year-old port. It was like swallowing silk—or memory. English memories. For a moment he recalled the dream of watching Louis Bleriot fly the channel and the lie he had told Amanda about it. The port turned rancid on his tongue. Both scenarios were metaphors loaded with threats. He was assailed by a terrific wish to somehow outwit time and memory, to shed the burdens of the past. But the ironist at the center of his mind knew time and memory were as inescapable as the thing they eventually became, history.

Adrian looked around the study, trying to savor the mementos of a long life. There he was, accepting a medal for maximum production of B-17s from FDR. There was Ike, conferring another medal in a private ceremony for developing the first supersonic jet fighter. There was John F. Kennedy, only a few weeks before Dallas, haunted Lyndon Johnson, tormented Richard Nixon, each grasping Adrian Van Ness's hand, each implicitly admitting how much they needed him and his planes.

The planes were everywhere, beautiful handmade models dangling from wires, full-color photos of fighters in 9 g dives and vertical climbs, bombers roaring over Berlin, Pyong-yang, Hanoi, airliners soaring aloft from Bali, Los Angeles, London.

Beside the telephone on his desk lay a small yellow book-let, with a title in scrolled letters on its cover, *Conquistadores del Cielo*. It contained the member- ship list of this exclusive club. When Adrian had invented it in 1935 they had been a long way from being conquerors of the sky. He picked up the booklet and flipped through the pages, recalling names that were no longer there. He had outlasted so many of the hotheads, the macho swaggerers, the dictatorial spouters.

But the title—was it still ironic? Was the Buchanan Corporation—and Adrian Van Ness—about to become victims of the sky's eternal indifference to life and death? In a flash Adrian was back in the Argusair remembering how often planes had broken his heart, robbed him of love, left him with nothing but irony's exhausting consolation.

Conquistadores del Cielo. The title was pure mockery now. He had conquered nothing, his life had been a series of desperate maneuvers, of hairbreadth escapes and humiliating betrayals.

It does a man no good to whine, whispered that fathering voice, dim now with years and distance. He was still playing the Great Game, Adrian told himself with growing desperation. Why was that no longer a consolation?

Knock. Knock. Knock. Knuckles resounded on the door. It was an unusual rhythm, imperious, demanding. *Knock. Knock. Knock.* Adrian strode to the heavy oak door and flung it open. What he saw in the shadowy hall sent him stumbling, spinning back into the room with a cry of terror on his lips. Queen Califia was standing there, her russet hair streaming, a knife in her upraised hand!

A bolt of pain tore through Adrian's chest. The ironist's hands were ripped from the controls. The room whirled; the vehicle was in a catastrophic spin. Another slash of pain. The anticoagulants—where were they? Adrian clutched the vial in his pocket. He had taken the last one on the plane. The rest were in his suitcase.

"Help!" he cried.

His eyes were entangled with the dangling planes, he was on his back trying to focus on the study door. "Help. Please!" he cried.

Above the house a prop plane began landing at the Charlottesville airport. The motors thundered in the night sky, blending with a voice in Adrian's head roaring *ruined.* Both sounds were swallowed by a tremendous whine, as if all the model planes had somehow acquired life-sized jet engines and were diving on him.

Then silence, the sensation of sinking into a dark pool rimmed with light. Finally a woman's silken voice whispering: *it wasn't your fault, it wasn't anyone's fault.*

Amanda remained frozen in the doorway, her hand raised to deliver another angry knock on the door. She had no idea what she could do to help her husband. When she found the courage to venture into the room it was much too late.

"I wasn't going to hurt you, Adrian," Amanda said. "I only wanted to tell you I found Mrs. Welch upstairs, passed out—and there's not a scrap of food in the house."

BOOK TEN

MESSAGES

Dozing on the couch in his office after his return from his visit to the BX bomber, Dick Stone could have sworn he heard a voice whispering: *apotheosis*. He awoke with a violent start and lay there, slowly absorbing the fact, the reality, the event.

Adrian Van Ness was dead. The telephone call he and Cliff Morris had received last night in the board room was not imagination, not wish or nightmare or conjecture. The Buchanan Aircraft Corporation was swirling around him like a huge ungainly space vehicle with no one at the controls.

Apotheosis, the voice whispered again. It was time for him to find the gold beyond his rainbow, maybe to begin paying the price Adrian and others had paid to make the flight. With the help of his tireless Japanese secretary, Jill Kioso, who had apparently slept on the couch in her office, Dick had called every member of the board of directors by noon and told them Cliff Morris was going to resign and asked them to support him as the next Buchanan president. He read them portions of Adrian's last letter to bolster his case. Most of them agreed without much enthusiasm. Several said they wanted to hear from Cliff too.

Next Dick called the heads of Buchanan's divisions, aerospace, missiles, electronics, assuring them there was no cause for panic, he was in charge and was not going to let Adrian's death alter the company's course in any way. Here the reaction was much more positive. He worked more closely with these men than Cliff; they trusted him. Dick spent another hour telling the same story to chief designer Sam Hardy. Without him, there would be no hypersonic plane in Buchanan's future.

Hardy almost applauded when he heard Cliff was leaving.

Sam still resented Cliff's cracks about his negative sex appeal from the Honeycomb Club days. There was no loyalty crisis in the Black Hole—although Hardy's moodiness could eventually become a problem.

Around five P.M. Dick's secretary laid a sheaf of incoming telephone calls on his desk. Most were from Buchanan supporters in Congress and friends in the aircraft industry. On top was a memo from Dr. Kirk Willoughby, reporting his inconclusive meeting with Frank Buchanan. That was bad news. Dick was going to need Frank's support, especially if Cliff found a backer who wanted to keep him as president. Such a man would only be interested in one thing—dismantling Buchanan for a quick profit, an idea that might also appeal to some members of the board.

"Dan Hanrahan's on the phone from Virginia," Jill Kioso said.

That was the call Dick was waiting for. "Everything's under control. I'm here in the house. I've got the contents of Adrian's safe. It's not that much—barely fills his attaché case. They're shipping the body from the hospital to a crematorium in Los Angeles. I'll bring Mrs. Van Ness back on the plane with me."

"How is she?"

"Fine. All she talks about is Frank Buchanan. I'm glad I came here for that reason alone. You can't let a reporter anywhere near her."

"We'll handle that."

"We're catching a ten A.M. plane. In case Frank's interested."

"I'll tell him if he calls. We can't call him. He's disconnected his phone."

"There's one problem I can't handle without a truck. Mrs. Van Ness showed me a secret room off Adrian's study. The bookcase revolves and you're in this little alcove. There's a trunk in there, full of gold. I guess it was Adrian's way of steadying his nerves when he bet the company on a big one."

Dick heard Adrian saying: *I wanted to be a man of substance, forever beyond the reach of ruin.* "Can anybody else find the room?"

"Not likely."

"Leave the trunk there for the time being. We'll get Shannon to move it out when things calm down."

Six hours later, Hanrahan strode into Dick's office with the attaché case in his hand. "Here's the goods. Mrs. Van Ness is at the Bel Air with my wife. They're old friends."

Dick opened the attaché case, not knowing what he would find. On top were a dozen photographs of Victoria at all ages, from babyhood to her wedding day. Why did Adrian keep them in his safe? Probably because he could not bear to look at them after her death.

Next was correspondence with various presidents, none of it especially startling. Then a folder of poems about the beauty and majesty of flight. Dick was astonished to discover Adrian's name at the bottom of each one. Adrian a poet! That cold-eyed bastard? It was astonishing.

Then came a series of letters from an Englishman named Tillotson, written in the 1930s, full of encouragement and general business advice. Each began with the words: "My dear son." There were copies of Adrian's replies, obviously typed himself, which began: "Dear Father." Mysteries within mysteries. One of these Dear Father letters was particularly revealing. It was written just after Victoria was born. Adrian told Tillotson how much the child meant to him, how badly he wanted to be a "complete father" even though fate and circumstances had prevented him from knowing one in his boyhood.

Next came a sheaf of papers from a primitive forties or early fifties copier. It was mostly in German, which Dick had no trouble reading—although many of the words had faded. It was the protest the Germans had filed with the Red Cross in Geneva in 1943, accusing the *Rainbow Express* of violating the rules of war over Schweinfurt. On top of the first page was a handwritten scrawl from General Newton Slade, telling Adrian he could consider the matter closed.

Finally there was an envelope with a letter in French thanking Adrian for rescuing her from the "bureaucratic Apaches." The rest was an apostrophe to the beauty of California. Only southern France could compete with it. The letter was signed "Madame George." It was dated 1971.

Apotheosis. This time Dick could have sworn he heard Adrian whispering the word. His mouth dry, his pulse skittering, Dick called Hanrahan and asked him if he knew anything about Madame George. "She's living in San Juan Capistrano," he said. "I flew to France and brought her here in 1970. The French cops busted up her operation when she refused to pay them off at double the usual rates. Adrian brought her over to make sure she didn't decide to write her memoirs. He paid for it out of his own pocket and ordered me never to mention it to you under any circumstances."

"Why not?"

There was a long pause. "It seemed to have something to do with your Jewish conscience."

Apotheosis. This time Dick was sure he heard it.

Dick called in Bruce Simons, their director of public relations, and discussed plans for a memorial service for Adrian. He sketched a speech he wanted to make to the board and told him to get a writer working on it. He called Shannon in Washington to find out what was being said and done in the rumor capital of the world.

"It's pretty quiet," Shannon said. "Carter's looking worse and worse. The Democrats are starting to pull in their left-wing horns. I think they'll let us alone—if you can get Cliff to resign. Nothing else is gonna keep the Creature happy. What's the word on the Big Shot?"

"I don't know where he is."

"Wurra wurra," Shannon said.

Dick ate supper at his desk, talking to chief designer Sam Hardy and the project manager for a new Mach 3 high-performance fighter. They showed him slides of incredible vortices on the wings at a high angle of attack and told him how much they were learning about wing loading from the pictures. The research might be very useful in designing the hypersonic airliner.

He spent the next several hours devouring reports from the missile and avionics divisions. When he looked at the clock on his desk, it was eleven P.M. The telephone rang. Cliff, ready to be reasonable? Dick grabbed the phone with hope uppermost.

"Stone here," he said.

"Guilford—Tom," said a shaky voice. "We just lost it. The big one. The BX. It went down about eighty miles from here, on a low-level practice run."

"I'll be there in an hour."

Dick summoned Sam Hardy from the Black Hole and Public Relations Director Bruce Simons from his bed. Their Hydra pilot got his instructions from the tower at Dreamland and in exactly one hour they descended from the starry sky at the crash site. The desert floor was eerily illuminated by huge searchlights the Air Force had flown in to begin the inevitable investigation. Pieces of the plane were scattered across a mile of desert. Most of them were blackened and twisted into junkyard objects. Only the needle nose, ripped off on impact, had escaped the fire and was relatively intact. It lay on its side like a decapitated head, reinforcing the desolation.

"What happened?" Dick asked, as General Anthony Sirocca shook his hand.

"All we know right now is they hit something big. It might have been a bird."

A bird big enough to disable a seventy-ton hundred-million-dollar bomber? Dick could almost hear the anti-defense lobbyists chortling.

A haggard Tom Guilford joined them along with the boyish colonel in charge of the investigation. "We've found all four motors. There's parts of a very large bird in one of them," the colonel said. "It might have been a Canada snow goose. We've got a guy who was stationed in Alaska for a while. He says he'd bet on it from the feathers and the size of the feet. Those birds weigh twenty-five or thirty pounds."

"Why wasn't that designed in?" Dick asked Sam Hardy.

"Snow geese and other birds that size fly at much higher altitudes," Hardy said. "We designed in resistance to birds of up to nine pounds."

"The fucking plane is supposed to go up to seventy thousand feet!"

"But its mission is low-altitude attack. At high altitudes, if a big bird disabled an engine, there'd be plenty of time to handle the problem."

Dick sighed. It was always the same story. Trying to anticipate chance, outwit fate, and save money. For some reason, at least once in every plane, fate—or was it Billy McCall's Lady of Luck?—wanted to let you know who was running things.

"We can't tell the real story," Bruce Simons pleaded. "They'll crucify us. A plane with a history like this being knocked down by a goddamn bird."

Dick stared stonily at Sam Hardy. He was looking more and more miserable. Leave it to Frank Buchanan to pick a bleeder for his successor. The guy was brilliant but he had Frank's soft heart.

"We'll tell the real story," Dick said. "Call it a one-in-a-million accident. Let them laugh for a day. Then design in fifty-pound birds. Fucking eagles and vultures wearing armor plate!"

"It'll add a hundred pounds to each engine," Hardy said. "We'll have to redesign the whole wing."

"So redesign it! Call up your wife and tell her she's not going to see you for the next six months."

He turned to Sirocca. "Who was flying her?"

"That kid who took you back the other night in your Rube Goldberg plane."

"I was afraid you were going to say that."

They flew back to El Segundo in a miasma of gloom. It reminded Dick of the time the Talus crashed. Were they heading for another chop session?

"Has Cliff resigned?" Bruce Simons asked.

"Not yet," Dick said.

Dick could see what Bruce was thinking. If Cliff has any brains left, he can wrap this crash around Dick Stone's neck and let him try to dance with it. After all, Dick was the guy who proclaimed from the balcony of the Mojave factory two years ago that he was not going to let the BX die. Bruce— or Dick—could see Cliff declaiming to the board that he had always been opposed to the plane, he had tried to talk Adrian out of building it, the thing had gotten them a billion dollars' worth of bad publicity. It was the reason why the senators had attacked him so viciously.

It was so simple it was almost irresistible. There was only one person who could stop Cliff: Sarah. Again, Dick felt the wrench of inevitability tearing at his fragile hopes. It was becoming more and more impossible to ask her anything else.

Back in the office, there was a memo from his tireless Japanese secretary on his desk: *Sarah Morris called. She would like to see you at 9 A.M. tomorrow morning.*

Hope or ruination? Dick wondered. There was only one thing to do: gamble everything on telling the truth.

Apotheosis, Adrian Van Ness whispered.

EXILE'S RETURN

Leaving the desert behind her in the rosy dawn, Sarah Chapman Morris drove along Interstate 10 past the stupendous rock formations of Joshua Tree National Monument. At times she had the road to herself, making her feel she was the last human being alive on the planet. She turned on the car radio and listened to a woman announcer with a honey-smooth voice.

"At the top of the hour, the top of the news. President Carter's budget for fiscal 1980 will include money for an additional six wings in the Tactical Air Force. That's good news for Southland's aerospace companies, especially General Dynamics, which produces the F-16 jet fighter.

"The Buchanan Corporation announced it will hold a memorial service for Adrian Van Ness, former chief executive officer and chairman of the board, early next week. Van Ness died in Virginia two days ago. A Buchanan spokesman said he had not been active in the firm for some years."

Sarah smiled wanly to herself, remembering how it felt to be an insider, aware of the superficiality of the news. She had spent yesterday disentangling herself from Susan Hardy. It had not been easy. Susan had accused her of desertion, abandoning all their good causes. With Cliff on the brink at Buchanan, now was the time to stick it to him.

"It's almost nineteen eighty," Sarah had said. "A new decade. Time for a change."

She angled west on state roads until she reached the San Diego Freeway and joined the river of cars roaring north toward Los Angeles. Trucks lumbered past on the right; red, blue, and yellow sedans and sports cars whizzed past on the left. After thirty-five years, she still found driving in southern California a terrifying experience.

She zoomed past L.A.'s downtown with its glossy new skyline, remembering the way it looked in 1945—less prepossessing than a medium-sized British city such as Bristol. In another twenty minutes of survival driving, she was on Santa Monica Boulevard, heading for Dick Stone's house in Nichols Canyon. He had suggested they meet there rather than at company headquarters.

Dick's hair had grown completely gray—almost white. But he still had a lot of vitality in his burly body and wide square-jawed face. His features would have driven a woman to despair but they made him look ruggedly masculine. He smiled and kissed her on the cheek.

"Thanks for coming—and a second thanks for coming early."

"Things must be frantic."

"You've heard the old saying, 'If you can keep your head while those about you—.' So far mine's on my shoulders, I think."

He led her into the kitchen and served scrambled eggs and bacon, hot from the stove. They were delicious. "Some career woman would love to marry a man who can cook like this," Sarah said.

Dick's smile was feeble. "How's Cassie and the kids?" Sarah asked.

"Tennessee agrees with Cassie. She's almost cheerful on the telephone. The kids are okay."

"Has she married again?"

Dick shook his head. "Thank God for small favors."

"What are we here to talk about?"

"Cliff. He's got to resign. If he tries to hang on, we'll go under. If he goes gracefully, we'll complete Adrian's purification rite and borrow enough money to keep us airborne until the next president, Ronald Reagan, gives us ten billion to build the BX bomber."

He smiled tentatively. "I was going to use paper plates in case you started to throw things. But I decided to take a chance on being civilized, no matter how barbarous we may sound to your peace-loving ears."

"I'm not a protester by nature," Sarah said. "Where do I come into this sordid picture?"

Dick avoided her eyes. The words came out in chunks, as if each took a special effort. "I'm hoping you can talk to Cliff—as a wife. Convince him—it's what has to be done. Those hearings—finished him—as an executive."

"That's all he ever wanted to be. You might as well say they've finished him as a human being."

Dick buttered some toast, then seemed to change his mind about eating it. He moved his plate aside. "I hope that isn't true. I like to think there's life after aerospace. I was hoping you felt the same way, after backing away from it for a few years."

"I've caught a glimpse of it. But has Cliff?"

Dick took a deep breath. "We've been friends a long time. But we've never talked on this level. Here goes. Did Cliff ever tell you about certain things that happened—one in particular—aboard the *Rainbow Express*?"

Sarah shook her head. Twenty minutes later, she was sitting at the table, the rest of her eggs and bacon cold, the fork grasped in a hand that had lost most of its feeling, attached to a body that was in a similar condition.

"That's why you volunteered for the extra twenty-five missions?" she cried.

She flung the fork across the bare dining room. A bach-

elor's room, with nothing on the walls, just essential furniture, a table, chairs, a sideboard. They were all bachelors at
heart, essentially indifferent to women, except as commodi-
ties, as bodies to screw, as minds to manipulate.

"Why are you telling me this? Cliff said he did it for me!
For England! I'm supposed to love a liar! Why did you volunteer? Why didn't you let him get court-martialed?"

"Because I felt guilty about it too. The extra missions were
my idea."

It was almost a snarl. There was ferocity in his voice. She
remembered he had flown those missions too. "I begin to
think you're all in need of a purification rite," she said.

"Maybe. But you're not completely exempt, Sarah. Cliff's
never been the same since the night he got the news about
Charlie and you unloaded on him. After that he was a setup
for the movie star."

"He'd been a setup for a long time before that," Sarah
said, her eyes swimming with angry tears. She had been very
successful at not thinking about that night for a long time.

"Not the way he was after that night. We were working
on him—kidding him out of it. After that Angela wrote the
script. It led straight to the hearings, in case you're interested.
She and her friends supplied the information that started the
senators sniffing around."

"What else should I know?"

"Cliff was going to take Adrian, the whole company down
with him—until Adrian told him he knew about the *Rainbow
Express*. After that, he was a willing victim."

"Some victim!"

"I know. We high-minded types want our victims refined
of the dross. Archetypes. Most victims are like Cliff. They
deserve quite a lot of what they get. But not all of it."

"Now you expect me to follow through with the charade—
for the good of Adrian Van Ness's company?"

"Maybe there's a better reason. I'm convinced Cliff went
through with those hearings mainly because he couldn't bear
the thought of you finding out what happened over Schweinfurt. That's a clue—no more than that, I'll admit—to what
he still feels about you."

"You want me to love him!"

The word shimmered and whirled between them like an explosion, showering them both with regret. Sarah was sure this man felt the same wish, the same hope—and he was thrusting it aside. For what? A corporation? A plane? He was asking her to do the impossible.

Dick fussed with his eggs. "I'm the last guy in the world with the right to use that word."

"Why, Dick?"

"Things have happened to me too."

He began talking about Amalie Borne. Dazedly, Sarah heard the anguish at the heart of the story—and what else he was telling her, perhaps inadvertently. Sarah was not the woman of his secret dreams. She was something else, not to be mocked or derided, no; perhaps even worthy of desire. But not an ultimate desire, eliciting reckless adoration, total commitment.

"Did you ever tell Cassie about Amalie?" she asked.

He shook his head.

"Sounds to me like you can't take your own advice about the truth, Navigator. Telling it—accepting it—forgiving it."

"It's myself I can't forgive!"

He almost roared the words. Again she saw his ferocity, saw how formidable he could be when necessary. Adrian had chosen well. Cliff never had this inner anger, this readiness for ruthless combat.

Dick went back to talking about the company. He made her understand their peril. Buchanan was drowning in red ink. She was their improbable savior. The irony was almost too rich. Why didn't she simply laugh in his face and tell him how glad she would be to see the BX, all the planes, spin down into that red flood?

Before she could answer that question Dick Stone was talking about another plane, more daring, more innovative than anyone had ever built. He called it the Orient Express. It would be a hypersonic transport carrying passengers across the Pacific and around the world at 3,500 miles an hour, flying at 120,000 feet. Sarah listened, mesmerized by the fire in his gray eyes.

He was one of the creatures of the sky. Billy McCall's blood brother. She was eighteen again, walking down a country lane with swaggering Cliff Morris, in love with pilots.

God, God, God, he had her, he had her believing again in the beauty, the magic, the mystery of flight.

"I've discussed it with our new chief designer, Sam Hardy. He thinks it may not be as expensive as it sounds. For some crazy reason, the problems with shock waves and vortexes are mostly just below and just beyond the sound barrier. The faster you go the cleaner the whole thing gets. Imagine giving average people a chance to see how the world looks from 120,000 feet?"

"When will it fly?"

"I'm not sure. It'll take all the money we get for the BX and everything we can borrow."

"Betting the company again."

"That's what it takes to sell planes for a living."

"Where's Cliff?"

"I don't know. In your house in Palos Verdes, probably."

"I'm not sure I can do it."

Dick looked at his watch. He had a six-billion-dollar corporation in El Segundo waiting to devour him. "There's something else you should know. The BX prototype crashed last night. We're going to announce it this afternoon. If you get a chance, remind Cliff that the night Charlie died, we talked about building it together as a sort of memorial to him—and Billy McCall."

Somehow she managed to remain calm. The man's daring was beyond belief. "You might give this to him too. It was in Adrian's safe."

He handed her a worn brown envelope stuffed with papers. "It's the protest the Germans filed about what we did over Schweinfurt."

The thing scorched her hand. Somehow she was hoping Dick had made it up, that Cliff would deny it. Without another word Dick drew her to him for a quick, fierce kiss. "No matter what happens—thank you. Thanks—for everything."

For another moment Sarah gazed into those angry gray eyes and saw what she had seen a dozen times before—a wish that somehow fate, life, God, had arranged things differently and he was the man she was going to see in Palos Verdes. Or there was no man in Palos Verdes and he could finally say to her: *Skylark—I'm going to get you out of that cage once and for all.*

And she would reply: *I've been waiting thirty years to hear that.*

Maybe it was enough to know—without ever speaking it—how much love had been possible between them. Maybe, in a certain sense, the love already existed, even though they had barely touched each other beyond the polite kisses of hello and good-bye. At least this last kiss had gone beyond politeness.

QUESTING

The Hydra descended from the cloudless blue sky, its tilt rotors whirling. Cliff Morris climbed out and toiled up the slope to Frank Buchanan's shack. Sweat streamed down his face after ten steps. He had spent the previous thirty-six hours trying to see Angela Perry. His nemesis, Lenin Jr., had stonily insisted she could not come to the phone. Cliff had finally landed on her lawn at four A.M. and stalked into the house, ignoring a pistol Vladimir brandished.

The meeting had been a disaster. Angela not only denied for the tenth time Lenin Jr. had leaked anything to the Creature's committee, she announced she was going to marry the left-wing ferret and elect him governor of California. She said he would be a better father to their son, now a wispy, scared-looking three-year-old.

Cliff was devastated by the thought that the boy was going to grow up as he did, with a succession of indifferent or hostile fathers. Angela was certain to change husbands as often as she changed dress styles. He gave Lenin Jr. two years at best—the only consolation he could find in the fiasco.

That defeat made this visit to Frank Buchanan all the more important. This morning he had called a half dozen members of the board of directors to line up their support. Most of them had been wary, when they were not explicitly negative. But all of them had hesitated when Cliff told them he had Frank's backing.

Frank was on the porch, waving, a smile on his wide, weathered face. It was going to be a breeze. Frank loved him. He had always loved him. He had been a father to him and Billy McCall. Their skyfather.

Cliff had stopped in Palm Springs for a couple of scotches at the airport bar. Just enough to project confidence in the product. The first law of successful sales. With a product like Clifford Morris, how could he fail?

"Cliff," Frank Buchanan said. "What a welcome sight for a lonely old man."

Inside the house, Frank gestured Cliff to the cracked, creased leather chair he had taken with him when he left Buchanan for the definitive last time.

"I've got some idea why you're here. I've already heard the news."

"I came here to ask your help, Frank."

"I can't imagine what I can do," Frank said.

"The board of directors will meet in a few days to discuss the future of the company. Right now it doesn't look like we'll have a future. We're up to our ears in red ink. A lot of the money has gone into funding the goddamn BX bomber. I know you designed it and maybe you don't like to hear me call it that. It's a great plane, Frank. But it's going to ruin us unless we do something drastic. I've got an idea that can save the plane—and get us out of the bomber business."

"I've wanted to do that all my life," Frank said.

Cliff leaped out of his chair, propelled by the sheer intensity of his desire. He was back thirty years, selling planes to

Eddie Rickenbacker and other vanished titans of the airline business, to Arab sheiks and Bolivian tin mine tycoons. This was the climax of all the sales pitches he had ever made.

"It's time someone told the American people the defense industry isn't a free enterprise. We're a branch of the U.S. government. Let's sell the military stuff to Washington and give Congress and the Pentagon direct control of making warplanes. Let them fuck it up. They'll have no one to blame but themselves."

Frank Buchanan dolefully shook his shaggy head. "I talked about doing something like that when they were protesting the BX a few years ago. But Adrian convinced me it was wrong. The French tried it in the thirties. It was a disaster. They practically destroyed their aircraft industry. They didn't have a single decent plane to fight Hitler."

"We can do better," Cliff said. "NASA put a man on the moon."

"NASA buys everything it flies from private companies like us. What would we do with the money, presuming Congress deigns to pay us anything?"

"We'll use it to build planes that will make the country and the world a better place. Inexpensive, fuel-efficient commuter planes and cargo planes. Airliners with fly-by-wire avionics that make it practically impossible for them to crash. All the things you talked about doing but never did because you were always designing a new fighter or bomber or transport."

But they were beautiful. They were all beautiful planes.

For a moment Cliff's antennae glimpsed this response on Frank Buchanan's face. He was eluding the sales pitch, sliding away into that world of aerodynamic ambition Cliff had never reached.

Cliff redoubled his intensity, seizing Frank's arm, deepening, darkening his voice. "I can sell those planes, Frank. That's what I'm good at. With your name on the designs, we can give Boeing and Douglas a run for the money."

"Cliff," Frank said. "I'm touched—and flattered—that you think my ancient reputation could have any influence on the

current boards of directors or the forty-year-old airline executives who buy planes these days."

"I'd handle all the details," Cliff said. "There wouldn't be
any pressure. Not a bit of strain."

Not a bit of power, either.

Again, Cliff caught the edge of the negative response.

"What does Dick Stone think of all this?"

"I haven't discussed it with him. I suspect he mostly thinks
getting rid of Adrian is a wonderful opportunity to grab my
job."

"The last time I talked to Dick, he wasn't this pessimistic.
He told me the boys in the Black Hole were working on a
hypersonic plane. He seemed to think it was feasible."

"Maybe it was, before those Senate hearings. Now no
banker in the world will loan us money. We've got to think
in terms of survival, Frank. This is a public relations ploy
that could save the company."

Up and down the cabin Cliff paced, distancing himself
now, so Frank would have the feeling that he made the decision on his own, without being overwhelmed. He was putting every twist and turn, every shred and scrap of his
experience into this pitch. It had to fly!

"There are people on the board who've been waiting for
a chance to disagree with Adrian's habit of putting us in hock
to the goddamn Pentagon. They didn't have the guts to do
it while he was alive. They'll do it now if you back me up.
It isn't too late. We can change the whole nature of this
industry. You know as well as I do that it doesn't make sense
anymore. If it ever did."

Cliff stopped. Frank did not seem to be listening. His eyes
were not registering any of these ideas. He was somewhere
else, listening, speaking to another person.

"Have you seen—or spoken to—Amanda?" he asked.

"No," Cliff said, bewildered, amazed, dismayed by the
persistence of love in a man of eighty-three. Who, what
would he love when he was eighty-three, if the booze let him
get that far? Angela? The idea was ridiculous.

"Cliff," Frank said. "Forgive me. But I can't do it. The
Buchanan Corporation is Adrian Van Ness's company. It was

mine for a little while but Adrian made it his creation. I'd feel like a liar—a fraud—if I walked into the boardroom and pretended I wanted to change the way Adrian did things out of some superior wisdom. Much as I loathed some of the things he did, I have to admit that without him, Buchanan wouldn't exist today."

Life drained from Cliff's face and body. He slumped into the leather chair. Frank barely noticed his collapse. He was thinking about something more important.

"Dick Stone's instinct is sound, Cliff. Build for the future. A hypersonic plane! I'd bet the company on that anytime. Buchanan has the know-how, the guts to reach into the next century. I've got a few ideas I'll send down to the Black Hole in a week or two, free of charge."

"Where the hell are we going to get the *money*?" Cliff said.

"I don't know. We've always gotten the money somewhere, somehow. I know you don't agree with me, Cliff. But I think we're all under guidance in this thing. We never would have survived this long without some kind of higher protection."

Cliff's exasperation made it clear that he had no faith in Frank's spiritual universe. "You're telling me I should I should watch the company destruct to build the plane of Dick Stone's dreams?"

"It's the plane of all our dreams, Cliff. The next plane always becomes the plane of everyone's dreams. You've seen it happen. You know what I mean."

"I know what you mean but I'm sick of it. I'm sick of living on the goddamn edge of failure year after year."

Frank Buchanan let those words drift up to the dark ceiling. "Maybe you should resign, Cliff, if you really feel that way."

Cliff said nothing. Did Frank sense how close he was to despair? There was concern on his face, affection. "You love it, Cliff. In spite of all the disappointments, the heartbreak. You love the planes."

Cliff could not respond to this exhortation. His body seemed to be turning into some heavy mushy substance that his bones could not support. His voice sounded like a microphone in an echo chamber.

"Maybe I do. But they've cost me so goddamn much—"

"They've cost us all too much. But if you're a man you learn to take it."

A man. The words evoked so many things Cliff wanted to forget. Buzz using that word as a taunt. Tama telling him that was all she wanted him to be. A man. What did it mean? They did not think you had the stuff that goes into the word, into the gut.

"Would you say that to me—would you throw me out this way—if Billy was sitting here asking you for help?" Cliff said.

He imagined the words echoing across the desert, all the way to the house where Sarah lived with her feminist friends. She did not care either. Cliff had failed her test of manhood too.

"Yes," Frank said. "I would have said it with far less hesitation. Billy was born to fly. Much as I hate to say it, that seemed to incapacitate him for the rest of life."

"Frank—it still stinks. I don't deserve to go out this way! I've sold a hundred and fifty million dollars' worth of planes for this company! I lost—"

He could not say the name. He could not invoke Charlie for any deal, however sweet. Frank Buchanan seized his arm. Tears streamed down his lined face.

"I know what you've lost, Cliff. We've all had our losses. Even Adrian. But the planes are flying. That's the important thing."

Cliff struggled to raise his head, his heart to match that apotheosis. But he still wanted the sweet deal, more swaggering years as a man of importance in Los Angeles. If he could not have them, there was Tama's choice, the disappearance. Maybe it was the way to go. The way to tell all of them what they had done. To leave them choking with remorse and guilt. Dick Stone, Sarah, Angela. Even this man.

Cliff stared down at the desert, remembering the darkness that had spilled over the mountains with the news of Jack Kennedy's death. Maybe now it was time to swallow it, to let it swallow him the way it had swallowed Tama and so many others.

"Don't," Frank Buchanan said. "I know what you're thinking. Don't do it. For all our sakes."

That only made the choice more tempting.

IS THERE LIFE AFTER AEROSPACE?

Sarah Morris spent most of the morning driving around Los Angeles. She parked in front of their ranch house in their old development, remembering the pudgy English war bride gorging on sweets until Tama launched her redesign program. She strolled through the faded lobby of the Beverly Wilshire, where the trim American wife had met Billy McCall. She wandered past the opulent shops on Rodeo Drive where she had shopped and charged as Mrs. Clifford Morris. So many lost or discarded selves. Who was she, anyway?

She called her daughters to tell them what she might do. Elizabeth, no longer in revolt against the establishment—she now had two sons by her San Francisco doctor—encouraged her. Margaret, on her way to being one of the country's leading Chinese scholars at Stanford, was scathingly negative. She wondered how Sarah could go back to a man who was still a glorified adolescent.

That afternoon Sarah drove to Palos Verdes, full of doubt and hesitation. She tried to regain the night of mutual surrender with the big playboy who had wept and vowed never to hit her again. But she could not stop remembering the night in Lima when he had fucked her with triumphant indifference to her feelings.

The house looked deserted, even abandoned. Blinds drooped at odd angles, curtains dangled. Cliff's white Mercedes in the driveway was the only sign of life, and that might have been left behind by the fugitive she was seeking. Inside, the living room made her wince. Newspapers and magazines littered the couches. Ashtrays were full of butts. An empty scotch bottle stood on an end table. The smell of liquor hung in the stale air.

She flung open some windows and the terrace door. The sea wind swirled through the place, blowing papers every which way. Footsteps thudded in the study. Cliff stood there in his shorts, running his hand through his uncombed hair.

"Hello," Sarah said.

He was not as gray as Dick Stone. Probably because he was getting touch-ups regularly. That was what a man did when he pursued a younger woman. But there were fault lines in his face that revealed age and loss—he was too much of a man's man to ask a plastic surgeon to remove them.

"I'm on the telephone," he said.

Sarah picked up the extension in the living room and listened to him talking to a man with a Texas drawl. He was telling Cliff he was not interested in a takeover of the Buchanan Corporation.

"It'd be like rustlin' a herd of starved longhorns, Cliff. I'd lose my shirt keepin' you alive before I could get you to market."

Cliff started telling him about a new missile the rocket division was developing. He suggested Buchanan might merge with Northrop and the raider could take over both companies. He read him a glowing report on Northrop's finances in a recent issue of *Aviation Week*.

"Sorry, Cliff boy," drawled the prospect. "I'm on the prowl for a drug company with a cure for arthritis. That sort of thing. You hear 'bout one, let me know. There'll be a finder's fee."

The line went dead. Cliff emerged from the study again, pulling on a pair of chinos. "What brings you here?" he said.

"I'd like to come home," Sarah said. "Is it possible?"

"It's still your house as much as it's mine," Cliff said. "That's the law in California."

"Am I welcome?"

"Give me one reason why you should be."

"I spent the last year in the desert looking at a Joshua tree. Eventually it started talking to me. It said go home and ask your husband to forgive you."

Cliff padded to the bar and poured himself a drink. Was he trying to blot her out in advance? Sarah looked past him at the windows opening on the Pacific and kept talking.

"In order to do that I had to ask myself if I forgave him. The answer was maybe. There was another reason. The longer I looked at that tree raising those stubby arms to the sky, the more I began to realize how much I wanted to try to love you again as my husband—someone who tried to achieve certain things in his life and succeeded sometimes—and failed sometimes. The way I tried to love you and failed and tried again and succeeded. Then failed because of so many things. Peru, the Prince, Vietnam, Charlie—Billy. Things we didn't expect. So we weren't very good at coping with them."

"Who sent you here?" Cliff said.

"Dick Stone called me. He told me about Adrian. Before he died, Adrian sent me a copy of the letter he wrote you, urging you to resign."

"That's why Dick called you! Can't you see that? He wants you to help him get rid of me. How the hell can you play Dick's game and tell me you love me?"

For a moment the whole room blurred. Sarah felt the wind blowing through her flesh into her bones, shattering them one by one. Was it finally ultimately impossible?

"I'm playing my own game," she said, her voice sounding as if she was shouting into a gale. "I'm trying to convince you there's life after aerospace. There's a life we can have together we never had except in fits and starts and failures."

"I don't want your goddamn pity!" Cliff roared. "I want a woman who loves a man, not a has-been!"

For a moment Sarah almost gave up. The wind tugged at more than her bones and flesh. It was blowing away everything, memory, hope, understanding. The word *has-been* seemed to abrogate both their lives. All Cliff could see was his corporate title. He did not exist outside it.

She tried one more time, clutching the back of a chair for

stability. "I don't see a has-been. I see the man who brought the *Rainbow Express* back from Schweinfurt with more holes in it than anyone could count. I see a man who volunteered for another twenty-five missions because he was ashamed of something he'd done on that raid. A man who had the courage to do that—in spite of his fear—is a man I want to spend the rest of my life trying to love."

Cliff clutched his glass as if it were the only thing keeping him erect. "Who told you about Schweinfurt? Adrian? That son of a bitch—"

"Dick Stone told me. He said he had enough confidence in my judgment—to believe I could share it with you—in the right way. He gave me this—for you. He found it in Adrian's papers."

Cliff grabbed the envelope stuffed with the German protest. He flipped through the sheets of paper and slowly crumpled them into a moist mass in his big hands. He began breathing in deep gulps. Tears gushed from his eyes.

"I should have told you. But I never thought you'd forgive me—I never had that much confidence. I was—"

"Afraid. Not of me. But of your idea of me. Little Miss England, the hero-worshipping cockteaser. Afraid of that stupid idiotic girl who only knew what she could see and touch and kiss. You were so handsome—and I was so young. You were almost as young."

The wind was roaring through the room now, a gale, a cyclone. "Cliff—let's say good-bye to both those sad wonderful people. Good-bye forever—without regrets. With affection."

He hunched over his drink, refusing to abandon his misery. "I lied to you."

"That was part of being in love. I lied to you too. Telling you I was in love with you when I was really in love with an idea, with the drama, with the heroic anguish of watching you take off and praying you back again."

Neither of them had moved an inch. They were like a pair of talking stanchions. Sarah felt the wind shoving her toward him but she was afraid he would flee.

"You had a hero—now you've got a has-been," he said,

regret, ambition still gouging him. "Do you expect me to believe you love both guys? Why don't you tell me to go down fighting? Why are we going to let that bastard Adrian Van Ness have the final say?"

"You did go down fighting. In those hearings. That's when I started to love you again. I saw you really didn't believe you'd done anything wrong. I watched the rest of those hearings and saw why you played the game that way. Everyone else was doing it. In a sense—a very special sense—you didn't do anything wrong."

She walked to the bar and put her hand on his arm. "But in another sense you did. It was wrong. All those men you bribed—in Japan—Holland—Germany—they've gone to jail. They were breaking their laws, if you weren't. We were both right—and both wrong that night in Lima. I didn't—I couldn't love you enough to explain it."

"Because of Billy?" he snarled.

The wind almost flung her across the room and out the door. She had to cling to something and it turned out to be his arm. "You could say that. It wouldn't be completely untrue. But he was only part of it. The other part was the way we'd failed—we hadn't loved each other before he arrived on the scene."

He was facing her on the bar stool, listening, seeming to agree. He abruptly turned away. "Yeah," he said, in the same bitter voice.

A wildness swelled in Sarah's throat. It reminded her of the night with Billy McCall in the desert. She had gone too far. She was not going to let this man escape her.

"You know what I see us doing?" she said.

"What?"

"Learning to fly. Buying a plane and flying it together, all over the country, the world. I'd feel so close to Charlie. Closer than we could ever get on the ground—"

A different man confronted her. Defeated and full of an emotion darker than anger. An ominous compound of bitterness and violence. "You really want to fly with me? After what happened to Billy? That wasn't an accident, you know. Somebody put that plane into that dive. I've thought about doing the same thing. I don't know when the impulse will suddenly get too strong to resist. You ready to fly with that kind of pilot?"

"Yes," Sarah said. "I'm ready to fly with that kind of pilot."

"I mean it," Cliff said. "I sat here half the day thinking about how to do it. Thinking about Tama—"

Sarah walked past him into the master bedroom. In the back of a drawer full of old lingerie, she found Tama's letter. *I was wrong.* The words glared up at her again, full of even more meanings now. She walked back to the living room and handed it to Cliff.

"Your mother sent this to me the night she died. I saved it for some reason. Maybe so I could give it to you now."

"What does it mean?" Cliff said dazedly, clutching the blue-bordered page.

"Whatever you want it to mean."

"Jesus," Cliff said. "Jesus."

He ran his fingers over the words. "Sarah," he said. "It means so many goddamn things. Wrong about marrying Buzz. Wrong about putting that son of a bitch in charge of my life. Wrong about trusting Adrian. Wrong about—"

"Yes," Sarah said, putting her hand on the paper too, letting all the wrongs she had committed and had been committed against her mingle in the words. "Maybe she's saying she was wrong about what she did that night too. It would be so wrong for you to do it now and leave me without the only man I ever tried to love."

Tears streamed down her face. Cliff's arms were around her. His lips were in her hair, on her throat. "Sarah, Sarah. It's okay. It's not going to happen now. You're right. Everything you've been saying is right. Dick Stone can have the goddamn company and welcome to it. I've got you. That's enough for me."

He was still the salesman, selling himself on the idea. She knew it would not be that simple. She knew there would be times when he would see an Aurora soaring into the sky or a Colossus rumbling toward a runway and he would hunger for the glory days. But she promised the good angels who had brought her here and given her the words of consolation and hope that she would not falter, she would not fail again.

The telephone rang. They both gazed at it, recognizing it as an enemy, the world beyond these walls, intruding with a demand or a question. "Answer it, will you?" Cliff said. "If it's Dick, tell him he'll have my letter of resignation on his desk tomorrow morning."

"This is Mark Casey of the *Los Angeles Times*," said the smooth voice in Sarah's ear. "Is Cliff Morris there? We just got word of the crash of Buchanan's experimental bomber. I was hoping he might have a comment on it."

It was an ultimate test. Why not find out now? For a moment Sarah wondered if she should remind Cliff of the night he had promised to build the plane as a memorial to Charlie. She decided not to take Dick Stone's advice. She wanted this to be a test of what they had just said to each other, nothing else.

She told Cliff who it was and why he was calling. All the implications flashed across his face. Here was his chance to destroy Dick Stone, to create a vacuum that the board of directors might ask him to fill, for want of a better candidate.

"Hello, Mark," Cliff said. "It's a shame about the plane. I know. I agree. There are times when some planes seem jinxed. They break your heart along with your pocketbook. This is one of them—"

Cliff was looking at Sarah as he said the next words. But she sensed he was also seeing something or someone else she could not share.

"But these things happen in the aircraft business. One of the fathers of flight, the German, Otto Lilienthal, summed it up on his deathbed with a famous phrase—sacrifices must be expected. That's our motto—it's every planemaker's motto. We'll find out what went wrong and fix it so it won't happen again. We'll have another prototype of the BX ready to fly in a month or so."

They went out on the terrace, arm in arm. A mile or two at sea, a green plane was doing stunts. Loops, barrel rolls, immelmans. Writing his artistry on the blue dome of the sky. Sarah's heart almost stopped beating.

"That guy can fly," Cliff said.

"We'll be doing the same thing soon."

"I'm not that good," Cliff said.

"Yes you are," Sarah said, and almost believed it.

DESTINIES

Throughout the day, while the uproar over the crash of the BX swirled around him, part of Dick Stone's mind was elsewhere—with Sarah in the house at Palos Verdes, trying to imagine what was happening between her and Cliff, realizing ruefully that he could not do it. No matter how well you knew a couple, there was a zone of intimacy they alone had experienced.

At other times he traveled to San Juan de Capistrano to ask an old woman a crucial question. For some reason he postponed it, although disappearing for a couple of hours might have been the best way to handle the maddening mixture of condescension and scorn that descended on the company from the media and Washington.

The Creature and his cohorts in Congress churned out a sickening mixture of jokes and sneers about the crash of the BX. Editorial writers and TV anchors rushed to wonder if anyone in the American aircraft industry knew what they were doing, citing a dozen other failed programs.

Apotheosis, Adrian Van Ness whispered. It was perfect on-the-job training for a man who might soon become chief executive officer of an aircraft company. The media and the politicians were proving once more that Adrian was right in his cold-eyed assessment of them. Still Dick delayed his trip to San Juan de Capistrano. He found himself wondering if he really wanted to be CEO of this shot-up machine. Buchanan was an updated version of the *Rainbow Express*, staggering home on one and a half engines—with no one praying them in.

That night, pacing his lonely house in Nichols Canyon, Dick told himself if Sarah failed with Cliff, he would step aside and let the Big Shot and the wreck go down in flames together. *Apotheosis*, Adrian whispered. Somehow it had a mocking sound. As if he was telling him to stop kidding himself.

At 8 A.M. the next morning when Dick arrived bleary-eyed for work, his secretary handed him Cliff Morris's letter of resignation. With it was a note from Sarah. "It's your turn, Navigator."

It was time for his trip to San Juan de Capistrano. Following Hanrahan's directions, Dick found Madame George in a comfortable cottage a block from the semi-restored mission. She was a withered chip of a woman but her mind was clear. Of course she remembered Adrian Van Ness. And Richard Stone. And Amalie Borne.

"Dear Amalie. She was both the best and the worst of my girls," she whispered in her husky baritone.

"She told me a story—the night I met her," Dick said. "She said she was Jewish—raised in Schweinfurt." He choked out the rest of it, feeling like he was in a plane coming out of a 13 g dive that was turning his body and brain to mush.

"I know the whole story. She told it to me in 1945."

"Was it true?"

"Absolutely. I was in Schweinfurt myself for most of the war. A forced laborer imported from France. When the Reich collapsed, I met Amalie there, roaming like a wolf girl in the ruins. I went to her so-called protector and forced him to give me all the cash he had—or I would tell the Americans what he had done to her."

Madame George lit a cigarette. "I told the Americans anyway. The money got us to Paris. But Amalie. Dear Amalie— I tried so hard to help her forget the past, to live in the present, surrounded by beauty and love—"

Tears streamed down Dick's face, turning the room, the husky-voiced old woman, into a blur. "I loved her," he said.

"You were not alone," Madame George said. "Prince Carlo—so many others loved her. She could not love anyone in return. It was as if those nights in the attic, the furnaces in the crematoriums had annihilated her heart. All anyone can do—all you should do—is forgive her."

"I do. I do," Dick said, wiping his streaming eyes.

Suddenly Jewishness was no longer an unwanted burden, it was part of his history because it was part of his love and that love justified everything, the bombs on German cities and the treachery over Schweinfurt and the embezzled money and the bombers and fighters and attack planes Buchanan built to defend America. His history was part of the pain of all history, pain that only love and courage could confront.

Was this his apotheosis? To be both American and Jewish without regret or shame or hesitation? To be both so passionately they were one thing?

Dick drove back to his house in Nichols Canyon. He walked through the empty rooms thinking of Cassie and the children. A huge corporation was crouched a few miles away, waiting to leap on his back. But he felt incomprehensibly free for the first time in a decade. He was ready to fly to Tennessee and tell Cassie the truth at last. Maybe she would laugh in his face. Maybe not. Whatever happened at tomorrow's board meeting, it seemed almost unimportant now.

Twenty-four hours later, Dick stood in the darkened boardroom of the Buchanan Corporation, finishing his first speech as president. "The hypersonic transport—the Orient Express—will fly people farther and faster than they've ever flown before. It will create the kind of revolution in air travel to the Far East that the subsonic jets have created in Europe. Imagine Japan and China only two hours away!

"But this is not the final installment of my dreams for this company, gentlemen. I have one more to share with you, based on a plane we built—and mistakenly destroyed—thirty years ago."

He punched a switch on the slide projector and onto the

screen glided a gigantic flying wing. "This is the transport of the future, the airlifter to end them all. It will be five hundred feet from wingtip to wingtip and it will carry as much cargo as a ten-thousand-ton freighter. We're calling it the Buchanan."

The screen went dark. The lights came up. Frank Buchanan was sitting next to Dick. "You should have given me some warning, at least," he said with a sad smile.

Dick squeezed his shoulder and turned to the board. "There's one more thing I want to say. Something that may surprise some of you and even make you reconsider the support most of you have promised me when you vote in a few minutes.

"We've done some things wrong in this company. You know what some of them are. I'm not going to list our sins. I could explain why we made some of these mistakes. The explanation would satisfy most of you. But an explanation is not an excuse—or a license to go on making the same mistakes. I want you to know I think they were wrong and we're not going to do them anymore."

Dick stepped away from the lectern. "That's it, gentlemen. Those are my dreams and my principles. If you disagree with them, now is the time to stop me."

The board endorsed Richard Schiller Stone and his program unanimously, while Frank Buchanan smiled his approval. The directors had already accepted Cliff Morris's letter of resignation and voted him the generous pension suggested by the new CEO. Dick thanked them and invited everyone outside for Adrian Van Ness's memorial service.

On the sunny terrace of the headquarters building was an urn containing Adrian's ashes. The clerical and middle-management employees formed a wide semicircle. Beyond them, several thousand members of the day shift stood in their coveralls. A clergyman recited the Twenty-third Psalm. Dick turned to Frank Buchanan and asked him if he would say a few words. It was a calculated risk. Dick had debated it with Bruce Simons and Kirk Willoughby only a few hours ago. Simons had been jittery about it. Willoughby thought Frank would not say anything too outrageous.

Frank limped to the microphone. "Adrian Van Ness's contribution to flight was a special awareness that no matter how high we soared or how fast we flew, we were still flying through history. He tried to help us cope with the tangled tormented past that creates so much of the turbulence in our lives. Sometimes he succeeded, sometimes he failed. But ultimately there was courage in his struggle—courage we designers and engineers and pilots did not always appreciate. May his courage—and all the other varieties of courage in our sky—help us to continue the struggle to solve flight's mysteries and endure its failures and heartbreaks in the years to come."

Overhead, while Frank was speaking, a prop plane began circling. Down, down it spiraled until everyone recognized it as a SkyRanger, Buchanan's first airliner. From its open door showered a rainbow of rose petals.

Dick watched Frank pick up one of the red petals and press it into Amanda Van Ness's hand. Earlier in the day, he had witnessed their reunion in his office. Kirk Willoughby had examined Amanda and said she was capable of living happily with Frank. Dan Hanrahan had snorted and said he did not need a doctor to tell him that.

A few feet away, Sarah Morris scooped up a handful of petals and flung them back into the sky. She stood on tiptoes and kissed Cliff Morris on the cheek. Dick picked up a yellow petal and imagined pressing it into Cassie's hand. Had they crossed another boundary? Were some of them, at least, beyond the rainbow?

Apotheosis, Adrian whispered one last time. *You'll make your compromises like I did. If the Orient Express and the Flying Wing turn out to be paper airplanes you'll go to work on the next-generation bomber, fighter, helicopter, dirigible if the Air Force wants it. You'll double the plant capacity and try to do everything simultaneously if you get the orders. You'll probably kill yourself from overwork in the process.*

Maybe, Dick Stone whispered to his American father. *Maybe.*

.   .   .

BEYOND THE RAINBOW

The icy desert wind hissed out of the night through the open
door of Frank Buchanan's cabin on the slope above Tahquitz
Canyon. He sat there, ignoring the cold, pen in hand on the
open page of his loose-leaf folder.

A Buchanan helicopter had flown him out to the cabin to
clean it out. He was moving to a house in Topanga Canyon
with Amanda. On impulse, he had told the pilot he wanted
to spend one more night here. The helicopter would return
in the morning.

Frank had held Amanda in his arms and the last vestige
of his hatred for Adrian Van Ness had been cleansed from
his soul. From Amanda had also come a suggestion that had
given him new hope for Billy. Previously he had only tried
to reach him. Frank had no fears for someone as innocent as
Victoria. But Amanda had convinced him that he should try
to reach both of them.

"Wherever he is, she's there too," she said.

Still only silence, except for the wind. "I'm waiting,"
Frank whispered.

From the shelf above his head, a book catapulted across
the room and struck the opposite wall. It lay on the floor, its
pages fluttering in the wind like the wings of a spent bird.

Frank picked it up and spread it open in the lamplight.
His fingers were on the last page of Ezra Pound's Cantos.
His eyes found the final lines.

Immaculata. Introibo
For those who drink of the bitterness.

The Immaculata! The light beyond the rainbow, beyond
Eden, beyond the suns and stars. Billy had reached it with

Victoria's help. Soon he and Amanda would be there too, embracing them.

But first there was the Orient Express. One last wing to design. Shakily, Frank's ancient fingers began sketching the ultimate plane.